On My Way to Paradise

DAVE WOLVERTON

BANTAM BOOKS

NEW YORK · TORONTO · LONDON · SYDNEY · AUCKLAND

ON MY WAY TO PARADISE
A Bantam Spectra Book / December 1989

PRINTING HISTORY
Chapters one and two of this book appeared in slightly different form,
© 1987 by Dave Wolverton, in L. Ron Hubbard Writers of the Future,
Vol. III, © 1987 by Bridge Publications Inc.

ISBN 0-553-27610-7

Published simultaneously in the United States and Canada

Bantam Books are published by Bantam Books, a division of Bantam Doubleday
Dell Publishing Group, Inc. Its trademark, consisting of the words "Bantam
Books" and the portrayal of a rooster, is Registered in U.S. Patent and
Trademark Office and in other countries. Marca Registrada, Bantam Books,
666 Fifth Avenue, New York, New York 10103.

PRINTED IN THE UNITED STATES OF AMERICA

O   0 9 8 7 6 5 4 3 2 1

Scenario One: Mid Patrol

We were bouncing across a red desert at full speed, the hovercraft droning like a dragonfly. The sky was a hazy, indistinct violet with bands of earthy yellow and green clouds that twisted from horizon to horizon like rivers in the sky.

In the battle room my armor had smelled fresh and resinous. But the simulator supplied the nauseating odor of stale sweat.

"Slow down!" Abriara screamed. The speakers in my helmet made her voice sound like a command from god, coming from all directions at once.

"I don't know how!" Zavala yelled in return. He was fumbling with a lever when we came over a rise to a forest of giant trees unlike any I had ever seen. Each tree looked like a huge, leafless piece of coral, hundreds of meters in diameter. Almost immediately a warning beep sounded. I swung my gun forward as we swerved around a wide bend. A hovercraft came head on.

I took aim at the driver. He wore armor with the same insect design as mine—only it was copper colored instead of green. White plasma streams flew over my head and whistled past my ears. Perfecto and Mavro were blown from the turrets. I squeezed off a shot, hitting a turret gunner in the thigh. He responded by sending a burst of plasma to spatter over Zavala's hands. Zavala swerved to his right and hit a limb of coralwood. The branch ran parallel to the ground at chest level. I tried to duck, but I dropped just enough for a branch harder than stone to decapitate me.

I came out of it sweating. My teeth chattered. Zavala held up his hands. "They're burning. They're burning," he cried.

Kaigo commanded the holo to start and we watched ourselves get massacred.

We each raised a weapon and tried to aim. The enemy snapped off shots. Kaigo pointed to our slowness. "Practice targeting and firing weapons some more. *Shuyo*, practice, polishes off the rust from the body, makes you good fighter, *ne*? This is battle. This is actual battle the way it will be. When you die on Baker, you can die only once."

Ask your bookseller for the Bantam Spectra Books you have missed:

Full Spectrum edited by Lou Aronica and
  Shawna McCarthy
Fantastic Voyage by Isaac Asimov
What Might Have Been? edited by Gregory Benford
  and Martin Greenberg
No Enemy But Time by Michael Bishop
The Martian Chronicles by Ray Bradbury
Startide Rising by David Brin
The Uplift War by David Brin
When Gravity Fails by George Alec Effinger
Philip José Farmer's The Dungeon edited by
  Philip José Farmer
The Shaper Exile by Sheila Finch
Alas, Babylon by Pat Frank
The War Against the Chtorr by David Gerrold
The Dream Years by Lisa Goldstein
West of Eden by Harry Harrison
Strange Invasion by Michael Kandel
The Drive In #2 by Joe Lansdale
Memories by Mike McQuay
A Canticle for Liebowitz by Walter M. Miller, Jr.
The Long Run by Daniel Keys Moran
Project Pendulum by Robert Silverberg and
  Karen Haber
Crystal Witness by Kathy Tyers
Neverness by David Zindel

Dedication

For Mary, with appreciation to my critics and conspirators: Virginia Baker, Dave Bastian, Shayne Bell, Todd Bennet, Pat Birkedahl, Cara Bullinger, Charlene Carlisle, Dave Doering, T. Jackson King, Jonathan Langford, Barbara Hume, Carolyn Nicita, Joseph Wager, and the Worthens.

PART ONE
EARTH

CHAPTER 1

A dusty gray hovercraft floated to a stop in front of my booth in the feria. As its door flipped open, an emaciated woman struggled up from the shadows within and into the stabbing daylight. A strange feeling swept over me, the physical shock one feels upon recognizing an old friend whose face has been marred by tragedies. I searched my memory for an elusive name. Her head slumped and rolled from side to side as she moved. Sweat stained the armpits of her black skinsuit, and blood dripped from the bandaged stump at the end of her right arm. An old mestizo woman backed away from her, made the sign of the cross, and muttered, *"Qué horror!"* A small boy gaped at the thin woman and moaned, *"Una bruja!"* and the crowd murmured in agreement that this walking skeleton must be a witch.

She staggered to my booth, shouldering past curious peasants, and thrust her bloody stump over the counter. I opened my mouth, hoping my tongue would find the name my memory couldn't supply, as she demanded in English, "Are you Señor Angelo Osic?"

I nodded, relieved that she didn't know me, secure in the knowledge that her husky voice was unfamiliar.

She braced herself on the counter, trembling. "Can you fix this . . . this body?"

"Sí—yes," I said, gently prodding the stump at the end of her arm. "Do you have your hand? Perhaps we could reconnect it."

"No."

Her wound was fresh, but would soon be infected. "A

3

new hand will take months to grow—months more to be usable. Might I suggest that a prosthesis would be fast—"

"Do a hand. Now! And bones too. I need bones." She talked with the quick, commanding voice of the rich refugiados from the Estados Unidos Socialistas del Sur. I thought she must be a criminal from Guyana or the American colonies in Brasilia Independiente. I studied her closely: the slope of her shoulders and her narrow cheeks indicated that she'd been born with a small frame, but even if she had bone disease too, the two factors couldn't account for the small diameter of her joints. "How long were you in low-g?" I asked.

"Never been in low-g," she lied.

"You should be in the hospital," I told her, afraid to deal with a criminal. "I am only a poor pharmacologist. And my drugs are not as miraculous as people sometimes claim."

"Fix me!" she said. "No hospitals. No questions." She pulled out a computer crystal as long as her hand and slipped it into my palm. Its smooth, nonglare surface was virtually invisible, except for the packet of liquid RAM at one end. It was fine crystal, Fugitsu quality, worth a small fortune, perhaps even enough to buy a rejuvenation treatment. I had never been able to afford a rejuvenation, and needed one badly.

"You need a place to rest—a hospital bed," I said.

She leaned forward, and I saw she was young, much younger than I had first imagined; her black hair fell in front of her deep-set, black eyes, and her sweaty face paled with genuine terror. "If you ball me over, *I die*," she said.

In that moment when she showed her terror, I thought she was beautiful. I felt a strong urge to help her, to comfort her. Telling myself she might not be a criminal, I got out of my booth and locked its rusted aluminum door, then escorted her back to the hovercraft. I gave the driver my address in Gatún and told him to go by way of Avenida Balboa. He drove slowly through the crowded feria, and soon the thin woman closed her eyes and curled into a ball and breathed in the wheezing manner of those deeply asleep. We floated past crowds of mestizos selling bright dresses and macaws, fresh fruit, cheap Thai microchips tumbling from earthenware pots. Everywhere their hungry eyes and gestures beckoned the merchant sailors from Europe, Africa, and Asia who searched the backwaters of Panamá for high-tech and contraband items. The local peasants became angry with my chauffeur for driving in a pedestrian zone and refused to move, so he flushed the hovercraft's thrusters, blowing hot air and dust into the crowds, burning the naked legs of the children. Their curses and cries of pain came to me distantly through the thick glass of the windows. I felt dirty and sinful to be in that craft, and wished I hadn't agreed to take care of the thin woman. I jacked in a call to Uppanishadi-Smith Corporation and ordered a limb-regeneration kit, an osteoporosis rehab packet, and a self-regulating canister of fluothane. I wetted my lips with my tongue and searched the faces of the crowd for a friend.

On the border of the free zone, the crowds thinned and I found Flaco, a good friend who did not mind dealing with criminals as much as I did, and had the driver stop the limo. Flaco stood with some arms dealers who haggled with four guerrillas over the price of used body armor. One of the guerrillas pulled off a helmet, and I saw by his oversize, misshapen ears that he was a chimera—one of the genetically upgraded supermen General Torres had created in Chile before the socialists overthrew his regime. I watched the chimera search through the armor for a better helmet; even from where I sat, I could see that he was bypassing the best helmet in the lot, and I resisted the urge to go point it out to him. But I just watched, wondering if he'd see it, noting the wideness of his torso, the girth of his limbs. Although he was short in stature, his frame was huge. In Haiti men had engineered ten-kilo fighting cocks with spurs long enough to disembowel a coyote, and no one had raised an eyebrow. But when Torres announced that he was engineering chimeras so they could live on other planets, the news caused fierce riots in Concepción, revolt in Temuco. I remembered a picture shown to me by a peasant from Talcahuano: he smiled as he and a fellow rioter each held the wingtip of a large brown creature, half bat, half man. He told me he'd clubbed it inside one of the engineering compounds. The Alliance of Nations had lodged formal protests of the work done in Chile.

The chimera finally noticed the good helmet in the lot and picked it up. He had a broad, pleasant smile, and I was happy he had come to fight the Colombians.

I waved to Flaco. He came to the hovercraft, stuck his narrow face through the window, and raised an eyebrow as he saw the thin woman.

"*Hola*, Angelo. So, you have taken to dating dead women?" he said, laughing. "Good idea. Very classy! Very sensible!"

I got out of the hovercraft, embraced Flaco, and walked out of the thin woman's listening range. "Yes," I said. "She's quite a catch for an old man. Not only is she beautiful, but when I'm done with her, she'll make fine fertilizer for the lawn." Flaco laughed. I handed him the crystal. "What is the value of this?" I asked.

Flaco rolled it over in his hand. "Any software on it?"

"I don't know."

"Maybe four hundred, five hundred thousand," he said.

"Will you check its registration code? I think it's stolen. Also," I whispered, "I must know who this woman is. Can you get a retina scanner and bring it to my home tonight?"

"Yes, my friend," Flaco whispered. He glanced at the woman in the floater. "Once, I saw a spider with legs that thin—" he said, "I stepped on it." He patted my shoulder, then laughed.

I got in the hovercraft and left the free zone. And as we floated down the highway on the outskirts of Colón, we rolled past the evenly spaced rows of banana plants. Because I'd never floated down that road in a fast car before, I noticed for the first time how perfectly ordered the *bananeros* were, with each plant three meters from its neighbor. I lost my eyes while serving in the army in Guatemala as a young man, and had them replaced with prosthetics. They register colors in the infrared spectrum as shimmers of light, something like the sheen one sees glimmering off platinum in the sunlight. And on this day the dark green canopy of the banana plants shimmered with infrared light. Under the canopy of leaves were jumbles of hammocks, burlap lean-tos, tents, cardboard boxes, and old cars—squalid, temporary shelters for the refugiados who were fleeing the socialist states in South America. The refugiados were afraid to brave their way through Costa Rica to the north, so they huddled together, waiting for ship passage to Trinidad or Madagascar or some other imaginary capitalist paradise.

I looked at the homes among the plantations and thought it strange to see such disorder among order. It reminded me of an incident from my childhood: a family of murderers called the Batistas Sangrientos had been caught selling body organs outside our village. When the police caught them, they took the family to the beach to execute them in front of the whole town so people would know what a despicable crime had been committed. Three boys in this family were only children, perhaps ten to twelve years old, and it was rumored that when gutting victims these boys had often raced each other to salvage the most precious organs. But all the Battistas swore the boys were innocent. And when the police got ready to shoot the family, the captain told them to form a line, but the young boys clung to their murderous father and refused to leave. The policemen clubbed the boys, and it took a long time for the police to get the family to stand in line. And once the family was standing in a line, it took a long time for the captain to give the order for the firing squad to shoot. I have always believed that the captain waited just so he could enjoy that moment of watching them stand in line. And as the bullets tore through the children I wondered, *Why could the captain not shoot them while in a huddle, clutching their father? What difference did it make?*

When we reached my home, I carried the thin woman to the cool basement and laid her on a blanket on the floor. I checked her pulse and was looking at the bandage on her stump when I heard a foot scuff on the carpet behind me. The limo driver had brought in two small bags and set them down. I paid him for the thin woman's fare, and it took all of my cash money. I escorted him from the house and asked if he would drive me to Colón for free since he was going that way. He said no, so I walked the eleven kilometers back to Colón to pick up my drugs at Uppanishadi-Smith Corporation.

I enjoyed the walk back home. My house was old and the plaster walls were crumbling, but all the other houses in the area were also in poor repair, so it didn't look bad by comparison. Some people even thought it was a rich person's house because it was on the lake and because they couldn't imagine a morphogen dealer not being rich. But I had once hustled rejuvenations in the penthouses of Miami, where people never seemed to overcome the boredom of their hollow lives, where a person's obtainment of a rejuvenation treatment was often the prelude to suicide. I would sun myself on my rooftop in the afternoons, and dream of a simple place where people lived lives of passion. I found that place when I found Panamá.

By the time I got back home the sun had just set. The air was getting cool. Flaco lay under the papaya tree in my front yard, watching a large brown fruit bat gorge on the uppermost papayas and spill dark seeds to the ground. "*Hola*, Angelo," he called when he saw me. "I brought that *thing* you wanted. Spider Legs is inside. She's awake now. I brought beautiful yellow roses for her. She likes them as much as that bat likes papayas. I think her nose is stuck to the flowers."

"So, you have met her?" I asked.

"Yes. I told her I am a doctor, and that you called me in to administer medications."

"Did she believe you?"

"Oh yes, I am a very good liar." Flaco laughed. "Also, that crystal did have software on it—old military software."

"Military?"

"Yes. A reality program for a brain bag."

I had once heard a doctor at a convention give a speech on reality programs. The military attached them to brains when they needed to store them for transplanting. The reality program kept the transplantee from suffering sensory deprivation, so he wouldn't become paranoid or psychotic. It locked him in a dream where he ate, worked, slept, and did other routine things, unaware he was separated from his body. But the reality program can only tap into existing memories and vary scenarios by merging portions of those memories. The brain bag then monitors the brain's reaction to the scenarios and keeps it from becoming surprised or shocked. "Is it stolen?" I asked.

"According to the registration code on the crystal, it belongs to a Señor Amir Jafari. He lives at one of the Lagrange orbits. He hasn't applied for citizenship with any nation, so he may prefer to live outside the law. It would be illegal for him to have this program; he won't report it stolen."

"Is he a doctor?" I asked.

Flaco shrugged.

"Why would he be interested in brain storage?"

Flaco shrugged again, pulled the crystal from his pocket, and said "If you want to sell it, we could get five hundred seventy-two thousand standard IMUs."

I calculated: barring complications, the thin woman's medication would cost about twenty-six thousand international monetary units, which would leave a great deal of profit, almost enough to buy a rejuvenation. All I would have to do was invest the money for a year or two. However, I decided to ask the thin woman if she had a receipt for the crystal, hoping she hadn't stolen it. I asked Flaco to hold the crystal a few days.

When we got to the basement, the thin woman sat propped in a corner with her knees against her chin. Three yellow roses rested on her knees, and she was asleep. I opened the limb-regeneration kit and spread packets of salves, washes, and medical instruments on a clean cloth on the floor.

Flaco read aloud the directions on the fluothane and practiced putting the gas mask over his face. When he'd done it enough so he could put it on the thin woman, I

touched her shoulder, waking her. She crawled to the
center of the floor and lay on her back.

The roses had fallen off her knees, and Flaco handed
them to her. She inhaled their fragrance and said, "You
know, when you try to smell them too long, you lose
their scent. You can't hold it." Flaco and I nodded.

"By the way," Flaco said, "what should we call you?"

The thin woman didn't answer. Flaco kept talking in a
conversational tone. "Angelo says we should call you
Spider Legs. He thinks that is very funny. But I told him
it isn't proper to call a woman that. You must forgive
him—he has a peasant mentality and doesn't know
better."

"Call me Tamara," she said.

"Ah, Tamara. A fitting name, very beautiful," Flaco
said.

"Do you still have the crystal?" Tamara asked.

"Yes," I answered.

"May I touch it? Hold it until you're done?"

I nodded, and Flaco wrapped her left hand around the
crystal, put the gas mask over her face, and flipped on
the canister. She sniffed the acrid scent of the fluothane
and tried to wiggle out from beneath the mask for a
moment, then fell asleep.

I put a tourniquet above her wrist and peeled off her
bandage. A bit of clear, oily synovial fluid from breached
joints had gathered inside the bandage, along with a
little pus. The wound began bleeding, so I opened a
package of plastic AV clips and pinched off the radial
artery. In these cases, you're supposed to seal any split
bones and regenerate them separately. Molecules in the
regenerative wash read the genetic codes of the cells
they infiltrate and begin replicating them in an orderly
fashion—in effect, following the pattern of growth ordered in birth. But skeletal tissue doesn't regenerate by
the same chemical formula as other tissues, and no tissue
except skin regenerates on a limb unless both formulae
are used simultaneously.

I took a disposable scalpel and began peeling the flesh
from the radius and ulna. Because of the small diameter
of the bones, I thought they'd been severed just below

the joint. But to my surprise the pale-blue articular cartilages, which fit like a cap over the joints, were whole and unbreached. Only the ligament, the fibrous cover that holds the joints together, was severed. Apparently her hand had been pulled off instead of sliced or blown off. My neighbor once set a leg trap for a mean dog that had snapped at his children. The dog got caught in the trap and wrenched off his foot in exactly the way this woman had wrenched off her hand. All her bones from the carpals on down were missing, though a long ragged piece of flesh from her palm was still attached. This made my job very easy. I set the bloody scalpel back in its cellophane wrapper, cocked her arm at a right angle so most of the muscular tissue pulled away from the exposed bone, and applied the skeletal regeneration wash.

Flaco had been watching me, but he got bored and picked up the thin woman's left arm and watched it flop to the floor as he dropped it.

"Don't do that," I said.

"Why?"

"Her bones might break. I don't think she was born on Earth. She's very fragile."

"I had a friend who once slugged an off-worlder and accidentally killed him," Flaco said. He began searching the thin woman's bags, removing clothing, a jar of pills that looked like vitamins. He pulled out a folding chemical-laser rifle. "Hah! What do you think, she hunts anteaters with this?"

I grunted my surprise at the rifle. Flaco put it back and left the room a moment. I administered the regeneration wash to the muscles, tendons, and skin, and used Doering clamps to anchor some torn flexors and brachioradials to their proper places; then I painted a resin bandage over the whole stump and called it good. Of course, these regeneration kits never work exactly as they're supposed to, and in a few weeks I'd have to reclamp some tendons and splice some of the new nerve tissue to the old.

While the resin bandage was wet, I opened the osteoporosis rehab packet and inserted the catheter of a

hormone fusion pump into her flesh about five centimeters above the wrist and began pumping in calcitonin,
collagenates, SGH, and mineral supplements. When the
resin bandage dried, it would seal around the catheter,
preventing any chance of infection.

Meanwhile, Flaco had brought in the retina scanner
and had been fiddling with it by the electrical outlet. I
looked up at him. I expected him to have one of the little
hand-held models policemen sometimes carry, but he
had a large industrial model. Its corners were dented
where he'd pried it free from someone's wall, and the
screws that were supposed to hold it to the wall dangled
in their sockets; little bits of white paint and plaster still
clung to the screws. Flaco had cut the electric cord to get
the scanner free, so now he was splicing on a plug.

"Where did you get the scanner?" I asked.

"I stole it from the checkout desk at the public
library," Flaco answered.

"Why didn't you just rent one?"

"I don't know. I thought you wanted to keep this
private—no records."

"It's not that important," I said.

"If it will make you feel better, I'll take it back
tomorrow."

"Good," I said.

Flaco finished splicing the wires, and plugged the
scanner in, then I turned off the fluothane and pried
open one of the Tamara's eyes. Flaco aimed the scanner
at her eye, but it rolled back and we couldn't see her
retina, so Flaco started calling to her, saying, "Oh,
Spider Legs! Oh, Spider Legs. Wake up! We have nice
flies to eat!" and things like that. I patted her cheek a
little. After a few minutes her eyeball rolled forward and
Flaco scanned it. For all practical purposes she was still
asleep, but I turned the fluothane back on to put her
under, just to be sure she wouldn't remember we'd
scanned her. Then Flaco jacked in a call to his hacker
and read off her ID number. AK–483–VO–992–RAF.

I cleaned up the room and gave the thin woman an
injection to make her sleep for the night. Flaco went to
the bathroom. Five minutes later he came out and said,

"I've got my hacker on-line. Are you sure we got her ID right?"

The scanner was still on, so I read the number to him again.

Flaco stood in the corner, listening to the comlink in his head. "According to records," he said, "she's Tamara Maria de la Garza. Born 2–24–2267 on Bacchus 4 in the Ceti star system. She left at age eight, and spent seventeen years in-flight back to Earth. Two years ago, she joined the Allied Earth Marines and went with a peacekeeping force to the Epsilon Eridani system." Flaco's eyes remained unfocused as he listened to the voice in his head, and he laughed at something the hacker said. "According to her military records, she's been in-flight two years. Expected to reach Epsilon Eridani in 2313."

"Oh," I said. I flipped off the fluothane on her gas mask. According to Flaco, this woman was nearly a light-year from Earth. Apparently, she had either jumped ship or never left—but then if that were true she would be listed as AWOL. Obviously, the military had falsified her files. I started thinking of reasons the military would falsify her files, and came up with many, but I realized it would be just like them to falsify her records for the hell of it.

Flaco stood in the corner for a moment. "Also," he said. "My friend didn't bother to mention earlier that two months ago the man who owned the crystal, Amir Jafari, was made a Class D General in the Allied Earth Marines—he's in charge of Cyborg Intelligence." Flaco smiled; he was still on-line.

At first I thought that explained Jafari's interest in brain storage. The cyborg command was once notorious for shanghaiing draftees, placing their brains in brain bags, and jacking them into reality programs—convincing them they were just living through their daily affairs until they could be transferred to mechanical bodies. But why would the computer crystal be registered to Jafari, not the Alliance? He wouldn't be holding it as a commodities investment—the price of crystals drops daily as better ones come onto the market.

Flaco tapped the subdural comlink switch behind his left ear; his eyes suddenly focused as he went off-line. "My hacker says he doesn't want to know me anymore. He just got tagged. He's going on vacation."

"Did they trace to us?"

Flaco tried to sound confident. "No, I don't think so. I'd called him. They won't trace back to us." He sat on the floor and sighed. I knew he was wrong. I knew that if they took the initiative, they could check the hacker for incoming calls and get back to us. But it would take hours, perhaps days. "So, what do you think?" Flaco asked.

I knew he wanted me to venture a guess about who had tapped in. I phrased my words carefully, trying to turn the subject of the conversation. "I think this woman is not Jafari, so perhaps she stole the crystal."

"Do you know what I think?" Flaco said. "I watched you treat that girl. I think you wasted your money going to school to study morphogenic pharmacology. All you did was read the directions on those boxes. Anybody could have done that. A monkey could have done that!"

"Yes," I said. "Flaco could have done that."

"I did fine with the fluothane, no? I'm a fine anesthesiologist."

"Yes, you're a fine anesthesiologist," I told him.

"I am also tired," Flaco said, yawning.

"Me too."

"Can I sleep here?" he asked.

"We should put this woman on the couch, and I have no other bed."

"I will sleep on the floor—" he said, "a fine floor, very soft, very practical."

"Good," I said, "you can make sure this thief doesn't run off with my valuables."

"I will guard your valuables with my life," Flaco promised. We moved Tamara to the couch; then Flaco lay down on the floor and closed his eyes.

Although it was late and I had many things on my mind, I went to my room, turned on my computer, phoned Informer 261—the artificial intelligence who services me—and requested a readout of all scholarly

articles on morphogenic pharmacology published within
the past three days. The AI bartered with me, trying to
restructure my payment schedule for the information.
He started out asking far too much money; at times it
seemed his bartering equations went totally off kilter. He
didn't understand the emotional attachment I had to my
money. I talked him down to a reasonable fee, then he
granted access to the information. I studied long into the
night.

In the morning Tamara gave the computer crystal back
to me, and I refilled the hormone pump on her arm, told
her to eat and drink as much as she could, and left
"Doctor" Flaco to watch her.

I took her dirty bandage to Uppanishadi-Smith for a
blood analysis. Tamara had very low levels of leukocytes
and other antibodies, and this seemed very strange.
With such a severe injury, her antibody levels should
have rocketed. However, people raised in artificial
atmospheres often have unresponsive immune systems,
so I did not worry so much. But with the high humidity
in Panamá and the resultant risk of infections, I thought
it necessary to buy a wide-spectrum antibody treatment.
Then I went back to my booth at the feria. The day was
slow: I sold two lipid and cholesterol flushes to old
people and had one soccer player who wanted to get his
nerves myelinated so he could speed his reflexes. His
was an unworkable plan, and I told him how much better
a nerve bypass was, since silver wire conducts electrical
impulses much faster than a myelinated nerve, and
recommended the doctor who had bypassed my sympathetic and peripheral nervous systems for me. The day
was cool, so I walked home before sundown.

When I got home a gray kitten with white feet was on
the roof and Flaco and Tamara were in the front yard
throwing a red plastic ball up to the kitten. It would hide
on the other side of the roof, and when Flaco threw the
ball up it would clatter on the roof's red tiles, and the
kitten would hear it and run over the top, swiping and
biting at the ball and chasing it till it rolled off the roof.
Then the kitten would hiss and raise the hairs on its back

as if surprised to see Flaco and Tamara, and would run back over the rooftop to hide. Tamara enjoyed this as much as the kitten did. She giggled when the kitten attacked the ball, and acted very excited, often putting her hand over her mouth. I suddenly desired to kiss her, and the thought of taking her in my arms and kissing her seemed totally natural, and I would have done it, had it not been so inappropriate. After thinking about it, I had a strange realization: the beauty I had seen in Tamara when she showed terror was in her when she laughed. The way emotions played over her face gave her an unusually expressive quality that made her different from the dead-eyed, emotionless refugiadas and merchant women I often met. Flaco must have seen it too, for when he spoke with her his voice took on a mellow, respectful tone.

I watched Tamara for some time, looking for any signs of the cramping the hormone injections can cause. She wobbled a great deal and clung to Flaco for support, but it was good for her to get the exercise. I remembered the antibody packet I'd bought, so I had her sit on the front porch while I injected the antibodies into her catheter.

"I have been thinking," I said when I was done, "that I would like to sell that crystal. Would you happen to have a receipt for it?"

Tamara looked up at me in surprise, then burst out laughing until tears formed in her eyes. Flaco started laughing too. I felt very foolish for asking about a receipt, but now I knew for sure she was a thief. Tamara struggled up and went into the house to rest.

I sat on the porch next to Flaco. He wrapped his arm around me. "Ah, Angelo, I like you. Promise me you'll never change."

I sighed, and wondered what to do. It would be wrong to sell stolen property, no matter how much I would make from it. Once again I wished that I had not taken Tamara into my care, and I wondered if I should send her to the hospital, let the police arrest her if she was a criminal. "How is she doing?" I asked.

"She slept much in the morning," Flaco said, "and I made sure she ate a good lunch. After that she spent

much time in your bedroom, hooked up to your dream
console. She didn't like it. She said it didn't have enough
memory to make a large world seem solid. Also, she
erased all the old worlds you had in it. I hope you're not
angry."

"No, I never use it," I said truthfully.

"You should get a new one," Flaco said. "I have a
friend who steals only from other thieves. He can get
you a nice one, cheap. And it isn't as if it will have been
stolen from a padre."

"No," I said.

Flaco got up, walked into the house, and got some
beer. When he came back, we sat on the porch and
drank while the sun set. Just as it got dark we heard
a distant explosion—a deep booming one—and howler
monkeys in the forests on the south side of the lake
began hooting in fear.

"Chepo?" I asked, wondering if the socialists were
bombing refugiados on our side of the border. Prime
Minister Montoya had been spewing rhetoric all week—
talking about how the "Progressive Ideals" of Nicita
Idealist Socialism could never take firm root while the
dogma of the capitalists to the north continued to pollute
his "New Society"—all of which simply meant that he
was tired of his people listening to our radio stations or
accessing our dream networks. He had reaffirmed his
vow to either absorb or eradicate all other Latin American nations, so I'd been waiting all week for a new
offensive.

Flaco shook his head, and spat on the ground. "Guerrilla artillery. Synchronous barrage; they're trying to
blow up that new Colombian neutron cannon. They'll do
it, too. Those chimeras have been giving the Colombians
hell." Flaco started to rise, as if to go in the house.

"Wait here for a moment," I told him. "You will see
something strange."

Flaco sat back down and waited. Soon, an old grizzled
spider monkey came walking up the street, away from
the jungle south of the lake, heading north. The monkey
was very nervous, being away from the trees, and he
often stopped, raising his head to look for the *perros*

sarnosos—junkyard dogs that ran loose in the streets. Flaco saw him and laughed, "Ha! I've never seen a spider monkey leave the jungle like that."

"The fighting and people in the jungle scares them," I said. "I see them every night now. Usually there is just one or two, sometimes bands. They are always heading north."

"Perhaps this old spider monkey is smarter than you and me. Perhaps he is a sign," Flaco said, reaching down to pick up a rock. He threw it, hitting the monkey's chest. "Go on, get up to Costa Rica where someone can make a good stew of you!"

The monkey lurched back a few meters, clutching his chest, then ran in a circle, and finally took off as fast as he could past my home. I felt bad to see the old monkey in pain. "You did not need to do that," I told Flaco. Flaco was staring at the ground, angrily, and I knew he was thinking about the threat of the Colombians to the south and Costa Ricans to the north. It would not be long until the two countries would invade us, try to force us to refuse the capitalists access to our canals.

"Ah, piss on him if he can't take a joke," Flaco said. Then he laughed and went into the house.

I sat on the porch a while and thought. The monkeys leaving, that was a bad sign, but all my life people had been seeing bad signs. My own country of Guatemala had been invaded by Nicaragua, overtaken by a dictator, passed through a revolution, and ended up where it began, as a free democracy—all in less than fifty years. I've always believed that no matter how bad things become, they somehow even out eventually. And the problems with the socialists would be no exception. I went into the house to eat. Flaco and Tamara had eaten all the fresh fruit, and I do not like to take a meal without it, so we decided to eat at La Arboleda, a nearby restaurant. I went to get Tamara.

She lay on my bed, with the dream monitor plugged into the interface socket at the base of her skull and her visor down. She was curled so that her knees touched her chin, and she had her hand in her mouth, biting it. Her tightly drawn face hinted at pain.

"Does she always do this?" I asked.

"Do what?" Flaco said.

"Curl up in the fetal position when she's hooked to the console?"

"Feta? Feta?—yes, she always lies like that."

"Don't touch her," I told him, then ran next door to Rodrigo DeHoyos's house to borrow an extra monitor. When I got back, I put on the monitor and plugged into the viewer's jack of the console—

And on the beach the wind was still, but a sandpiper was running, skirting the water's edge, darting away from the waves, burying his ebony bill, moving on. Bleached shells of clam, barnacle, and snail tumbled in the shallows and gleamed like bones in the sand drifts. Cool air carried the scent of decaying sea life. A purple sun hung on the horizon and dyed sand, sky, bird, skin in cellophane shades of red and blue. The amethyst sand cut my bare feet, and down the beach a red-haired woman in a white dress fed gulls that screeched and hung in the air, waiting to snap crumbs she tossed. I stopped and inhaled the air, listened to the sigh of the breakers, and looked at the colors. After so long with my prosthetic eyes, seeing the world in variations of only three primary colors felt like coming home.

I began looking for flaws in her dreamwork. Her world involved all five senses. I could both smell the sea rime and taste it—it felt complete. I could see unity in the starkness of the lines of the jagged stones, the wind-battered birds, and the choppy waves on the horizon. Scarlets and muted tans nicely varied the theme color of purple. Her dreamwork was almost professional quality.

But I turned around and found a warp: on the beach, a huge black bull lay dead in the water, as if he had washed up from her subconscious. The horizon, the shoreline, the slope of the sand—all converged to emphasize this bull. He lay on his side, with his head toward me and his feet toward the sea. His huge belly was distended, though it didn't show signs of rot. His knobby legs stuck out, stiff with rigor mortis, and his whole body heaved from moment to moment as waves washed against him, surging against his belly, making his huge testicles and penis float up against his body as a wave came in, then stretch out and away as the wave receded. I focused my attention on the bull and mouthed the word *delete*. The monitor flashed a message: YOU CANNOT EDIT DREAMS WHILE IN THE VIEWING MODE.

I headed toward the red-haired woman. Her beauty was the kind one can only be born with—the elegant lines of her chin were not likely to be the kind a plastique artist would conceive. Yet her lifeless expression revealed the tragic deadness one sees behind the eyes of the refugiados, and I wondered why Tamara had chosen this red-haired woman as an alter ego, and wondered if the emotion I'd seen in Tamara's face earlier were some trick of her body she could not control.

"What do you want?" she asked without turning to look at me, tossing a piece of bread to a gull.

I did not know what to answer. "I came to tell you it's time to eat," I said, looking back at the bull.

"He talks to me," she said, as if confiding a secret. She didn't turn, and I realized it was the bull she didn't want to see. "Even though he's dead, he jabbers. He jabbers at me—he says he wants me to ride his back. But I know that as soon as I do, he'll take me away, across the dark water to a place where I do not wish to go."

I said as if to a child, "Perhaps you should come with Flaco and me. We'll have a nice dinner. You'd like that, wouldn't you?"

She stiffened, angered by the tone of my voice. "You go on ahead. I'll finish up here," she said. She tore a huge chunk off her loaf of bread and tossed it to a gull. The gull shrieked and dove, grabbing the bread before it hit the ground. I looked at the gull, with its battered feathers and shrunken stomach. Its dark eyes glared, mad with hunger.

I walked away from the beach and topped a rise by a rock where a lone gull sat. On the other side of the rise the dream ended in a blurred landscape of rolling dunes. I looked back down at the bull floating in the water and at the woman in the white dress. She fed the last of the bread to the gulls, then raised her hands. A gull dove and tentatively nipped her finger. Drops of blood splashed from her wound and the gulls cried and dove upon her, shredding her flesh with their sharp beaks.

The gull beside me cried out, and I looked at it. The light of the setting sun made its white feathers gleam purple. Its dark eyes appeared to glare out of a luminous head. It watched me, cold and prophetic. I jacked out, unwilling to watch the woman be eaten.

"So, what happened?" Flaco asked as soon as I got the monitor off.

"Nothing," I said, not wishing to compromise Tamara's privacy any further. I pulled her plug from the console, terminating her self-torture. Tamara straightened and stretched.

"It is time to eat?" she asked. She stared at the floor and would not look at me.

"Yes." Flaco helped her stand. It had begun to rain outside, so Flaco went to the closet for an umbrella.

Tamara stared at the floor and said, "Stay out of my dreams."

"I'm sorry," I said. "You looked as if you were in pain."

"I only had a headache. You invaded me. You don't have that right!"

"You're my patient," I said. "I'm obligated to care for you."

Flaco came back with the umbrella, and we walked to La Arboleda.

When we got to the restaurant, only a few late eaters and drunks were there. We all ordered fish dinners, and Flaco convinced Tamara to order a rum sunset—a drink his grandfather had invented that is made of rum and lemon wine, spiced with cinnamon. Flaco tried to get me to drink one too, but I refused. Flaco bragged that his family still owned the company that made the lemon wine, and I pointed out that both his grandfather's company and his grandfather's bad taste were still in the family. Tamara laughed slightly and stared at the stub on her arm. A drunk staggered to our table, looked at our drinks, and said, "Ah, a rum sunset. That's my favorite God-damned drink in the world. In fact, it's the only good drink!"

"Then you should sit and have a rum sunset with the grandson of the man who invented it!" Flaco said, and he ordered a rum sunset for the drunk.

I was very sorry about this, for the drunk smelled of sour sweat, and he sat next to me. He fell asleep after guzzling his drink, but his smell ruined my dinner. We ate and talked; Flaco told many peculiarly bad jokes, which Tamara laughed at shyly at first, but later she laughed horrendously at the slightest provocation. One of my customers that day, a refugiado from Cartagena, had paid me in mixed foreign coins, so I'd carried a large bag of coins tied to my belt all day. I opened the bag and began stacking the coins according to country and denomination. When Tamara finished her first rum sunset, Flaco ordered her another, then another, and I realized Flaco was trying to get her drunk, and Tamara must have realized this too, since she excused herself from the third drink, claiming she had a headache.

Flaco kept drinking and got drunk himself. He told a long story about how his father did well in the wine business until one day when he went to mass and fell asleep. In a dream, the statue of the Virgin began weeping. Flaco's father asked the Virgin why she wept, and she told him it was because he sold wine when he should be selling hats to the Indians in the Amazon. Flaco's father became convinced he would make a great deal of money selling hats because, after all, the Virgin Mary had told him to do it. Then he sailed up the Amazon and was killed by a poisonous toad before he could sell a single hat. This incident greatly diminished the faith of everyone in Flaco's village—so much so that the villagers broke the offending statue with hammers.

"Sho, what about your family?" Flaco asked Tamara, his head wobbling back and forth as if it would topple off. She straightened up, and her face took on a closed look. She hadn't drunk much, but she pretended to be out of control so we'd excuse her bad manners. "Family? Want to know about my family? I'll tell you—my father, he was just like Angelo there. He only wanted two things: order and immortality." I had just finished stacking my coins in neat little staggered rows, like banana plants. Tamara lashed out with her stump and knocked all the coins down.

"That's not—" I started to say.

"What? You going to say you don't want immortality?" Tamara asked.

Like most morphogenic pharmacologists, the hope of obtaining a discount on rejuvenations until man solved the problem of mortality or learned to download brains into crystals was a major factor in determining my career. "I don't want order," I concluded.

Tamara peered at me as if I'd said something very strange, and shook her head. "You bastards are all the same. Your bodies may live, but your souls die."

"Who's a bashtard?" Flaco asked.

"Angelo. He's just like a cyborg—the assholes want to live forever, but they make their living denying other people that opportunity." I suddenly felt as if I'd jacked back into her dreamworld. As far as I could see, her strange accusations against cyborgs and me made no sense.

"You're full of guano," Flaco said. "Don Angelo Oshic here, he'sh nice. He's a gentleman."

Tamara looked at us, and her head wobbled. She reached for a glass of water and missed. The water spilled on the table. "Maybe he *is* a cyborg," she said, ducking her head a little.

"We're not shyborgs," Flaco said in an easy tone. "See, no shyborgs are in thish room." He handed her his rum sunset.

"You got a comlink in your head?" Tamara asked. Flaco nodded. "Then you're a cyborg." She acted as if she'd made her point. I remembered a news clip I'd once seen of Surinamese Body Purists. Upon conversion to their cult, new members pulled out their comlinks and their cranial jacks, their prosthetic kidneys or whatever they had, and lived totally without mechanical aid. I wondered if she were a Body Purist, and I suddenly knew why she wanted a regenerated hand instead of a prosthetic—the thought of her body being welded to a machine terrified her; it desecrated the temple of her spirit.

"A comlink doeshn't make you a shyborg," Flaco said.

"That's where it starts. First a comlink. Then an arm. Then a lung. One piece at a time."

"What about you?" Flaco asked. "You shaid you were going to tell about your family."

"My mother and father are cyborgs," she answered with that closed look. "I never met them. I'm just the interest paid by the sperm bank. If my parents ever saw me, they probably got pissed off because I didn't look enough like a washing machine."

"Hah! There musht be a shtory in that!" Flaco said. "Tell ush the shtory."

"There's no story," Tamara said. And I wondered what her point was, why she bothered to lie at all.

The waiter brought Flaco another drink, which he downed on the spot. Tamara ordered some aspirin. Flaco was nodding off, so I pulled away his plate and glasses before his head landed on the table. Tamara just sat and gazed at her plate. I decided to drag away the smelly drunk who sat beside me and order dessert.

I put all my coins in my bag and moved the drunk back to his previous stall. As I finished setting him upright, comlink tones sounded in my head. I tapped the comlink switch behind my ear and a man with a heavy Arab accent said, "Señor Osic?"

"Yes," I answered.

"Tell the woman across the table from you to go to the telephone."

The caller had to have been in the room at some time in the evening to know I'd been sitting with Tamara, but since he didn't know I'd moved away, he'd obviously left. "She's drunk. She's unconscious," I lied, hurrying to the door to see if I was being called from outside.

I opened the door and looked out. The avenue was dark and empty, but far down the street I could see the shining heat of a man's body outside a minishuttle. The caller clicked off, and the man jumped in the minishuttle. The taillights glowed red momentarily, and the shuttle blossomed into a ball of light as the engine turned on. It shot up into the night sky and streaked away.

I went back into the restaurant, and Tamara looked at me curiously, as if to ask why I'd run out. Flaco struggled to lift his head from the table. He turned toward Tamara and said, "I got a messhage for you on comlink: Arish shays he h-has your hand. And *now* he has y-you."

Tamara turned pale and drank another rum sunset.

CHAPTER

2

On the way home, Tamara and Flaco were so drunk they had to lean on me for support. Tamara kept swearing and mumbling that she wanted a gun, and Flaco kept saying, "What?" When we reached the house, I laid Tamara on the couch and Flaco on the hall floor in front of the bathroom door and went to bed.

After a couple hours I was awakened by Flaco vomiting and Tamara murmuring, but I just went back to sleep. I dreamed of an old Zeller Cymech advertisement that portrayed a group of people in a lunar gambling casino, all of them cyborgs wearing designer cymechs. I had seen this holo once before, and admired it. All the cyborgs were laughing, and drinking rum sunsets. Several of them wore feminine bodies, complete with metal breasts studded with small jewels. One female cyborg was talking to a companion, and she giggled in a quaint manner. I suddenly realized she was my wife, Elena, who had been hit by a truck thirty years earlier. But it seemed irrational to believe she had died. I had merely forgotten that she had bought a cymech and we had somehow scraped her pieces together and put her in it, and now she was here on the moon, drinking rum sunsets and laughing. I planned to go embrace her, tell her how happy I was to see her, when the cyborg closest to me caught my attention. He had only one arm that was still flesh, and he wore it as if it were a badge of his humanity. He wore a head of electrically-dyed red tungsten that looked like a handsome man around the face and eyes, but his jaw curved abruptly into something skeletal. He had gleaming blue zirconium eyes, and his huge smile hinted at perpetual mirth. But suddenly it seemed this man's smile held something malicious, that he was plotting the deaths of the others in the room, and only I could discern his intent. Then I thought, *This is not my dream. This is Tamara's dream.* And I was awakened by someone shaking me.

"Angelo! Angelo!" Flaco said.

"*Sí. Qué pasa?*"

"*Huy!* What do you think? That woman, she is a bitch when she drinks, no?"

"Yes, she is a bitch," I said.

"I like that. I like a woman with a fierce spirit!" Flaco talked very slowly and deliberately. "Move over. I want to get in bed with you." I moved and Flaco climbed in and accidentally kicked me with his shoes. "Ah, this is a good bed. Very comfortable. Just right for two. You should have invited me in earlier. Did I ever tell you that you have nice breasts? For a man, that is. They are very flaccid. You have more breast than some women."

Flaco's words disturbed me, till I realized he was joking. "Yes, flaccid breasts run in my family. You should have seen my mother: she had five of them."

Flaco laughed. "No more jokes! I think I will vomit again if I have to laugh at your sick jokes. Angelo, do you think Tamara is in danger?"

"Yes."

"I held her hand today," he said. "It was very delicate, like a child's hand. We will have to take good care of her. Tell me, what do you think she is running from?"

"What does anyone run from. She runs from her past."

"Ah, philosophical poop. Do you always poop philosophy at night? If so, we should sleep together often. But I have been thinking—perhaps she is a notorious refugiada. Perhaps she is looking for political asylum and would be happy to marry a Panamanian like the handsome Flaco just so she can live in a neutral country, eh? Welcome to Flaco; welcome to freedom! What do you think? You still think she is a thief?"

"Yes."

"I don't," Flaco said. "Believe me, O great philosopher, I know thieves. She is too *alive* to be a thief. Understand?"

"No."

"Ah, it is very simple. You see, man is a territorial creature. He needs to possess things—houses, land, body space. And if he possesses something, he is happy; and he is happy to let others possess something. But thieves violate their very nature by violating the territories of others. They are never at peace with themselves. And because of this, they die inside. This is something an educated, philosophical man like yourself should know."

"Are you not a socialist?" I asked. "What you say sounds antisocialist." It was a cruel question—meant only as a joke. Traditionally, in Latin America the socialists have advocated using social engineering to eradicate outdated ideas, ethics, and ways of thought. But to avoid cultural pollution, the Nicita Idealist Socialists believed they needed to either absorb or destroy all nearby capitalists while they engineered their own communal society. To accuse Flaco of being any type of socialist was bad enough, yet the Idealist Socialists had gone a step farther—rumor said they were trying to engineer a nonterritorial human—a being they believed would be unselfish and full of empathy, willing to give everything it owned to others. Rumor also said that the creatures they had engineered in Argentina had been alien, murderous. This news terrified the peasants, for it was said that once the socialists perfected the genetic structure for a nonterritorial man, they would release a vector virus that would infect everyone on Earth. Through viral warfare mankind would be changed, become a creature incapable of adopting ideals outside those touted by the socialists, and I think the peasants feared death less than they feared undergoing such a change. I was unsure whether to believe such stories. Yet Flaco was speaking about socialist concerns, and I thought it funny to accuse him of being one.

He asked, "Why would you think me a socialist?"

"You live in Panamá, between the hammer of Colombia and the anvil of Costa Rica, and don't run away. Also, you're skinny and sneaky-looking, like a socialist."

"Oh, I am not a socialist," Flaco said. "I don't believe socialism can work with man today—we are too territorialistic. And I don't think we should engineer the trait away. I believe a man must possess himself and be his own man. But these Nicita Idealist Socialists will not let a man possess himself. It is not enough that they enslave the artificial intelligences; they must also dominate humans too, grind down their opposition. Always they blame the capitalists for their economic failure. According to the socialists, if a socialist buys a car it is a sign of progress, but if a capitalist buys a car, it is a sign of decadence. They refuse to see that because they take away men's will to work, their countries collapse into economic ruin. I met a man from Budapest who said his father had worked in a factory that kept closing because the workers wanted to sit and play cards. The government sent the military to force the workers to go back to work, and some still refused. They sat and played cards with machine guns at their backs. Finally, the military shot them all, and the radio proclaimed these men traitors. This man told me that his father, even though he had been murdered, had won against the socialists because he refused to be dominated by them. And I believe this is a second way to submit to inner death—to live under the domination of others, to deny your need to possess yourself."

Flaco fancied himself a great political thinker, but I had spent so much time studying medicine I was out of touch with politics. I remained respectfully silent for a moment, as if contemplating his words. "So, did you not say that you don't believe this woman is a thief?"

"No, I believe she is a brain transplant."

This made me sit up and think. Intuitively I felt he was right. "Why do you say that?"

"I saw a documentary once. Back when they were drafting people into the cyborg units, the military would put the soldiers' bodies in stasis until their terms were up, and if a soldier wanted to enlist afterward, he could opt to sell his body for parts. But there was a big scandal because sometimes a soldier would end his term or want to sell his body and find that it had already been sold on the black market by the cryotechs. All this talk about cyborgs made me remember this, and I realized that this was how Tamara could be listed as being on active duty a light-year away and still be here."

"Do you mean someone has stolen her body?"

"I have been thinking: would anyone steal a useless body like that? No, I think Tamara de la Garza enlisted and sold her body. And now this woman is wearing it."

I remembered the beautiful red-haired woman in Tamara's dream, so different from the scrawny black-haired thing that slept on the couch, and I realized that a brain transplant could explain why she dreamed of herself looking so differently. And I remembered the way she had fumbled after the water at dinner—a sign that her brain had not yet accustomed itself to a change in body size. "Perhaps," I said.

"Perhaps? What do you mean, 'perhaps'? It is a great solution to our question. If my theory isn't true, it should be!"

"We are being paid much money. She is paying a little for her treatment, and much for our silence. If she must suffer a brain transplant to escape her pursuers, perhaps our questions jeopardize her."

"You did not tell me earlier she was in danger," Flaco said.

Out in the living room, Tamara stirred in her sleep and moaned.

"I did not know if I believed it earlier."

I lay in bed for a long time, thinking. If this woman had had a brain transplant, and the transplant were recent, it would explain why her antibody levels hadn't shot up when her hand was pulled off—she could still be on antibody inhibitors. But I wasn't sure. Any legitimate surgeon would have used antimosin C, an inhibitor that only stops the production of the suppressor cells that attack transplanted organs. But Tamara's antibody levels were down all across the spectrum—which meant she'd been given one of the more common AB inhibitors. The antibody injection I had given her earlier had thymosins in it, which stimulate the production of all T cells, including suppressor cells. And if the level of thymosins I'd given her were too high, they could override the AB inhibitors. And if her brain wasn't perfectly compatible with its body, Tamara's suppressor cells would treat her brain as an infecting organism, destroying it cell by cell. These thoughts made my stomach ache.

I went into the livingroom to check on Tamara. She looked like a tiny rag of a person, thrown on the couch, and I could see by the brilliance of the platinum glow of her body that she had an elevated temperature. This is one of the first signs of organ rejection; unfortunately, it is also a sign of an ordinary infection. To add to my confusion, the hormones I'd given her sped up her metabolism, which would cause a low-grade fever. She had already complained of headaches, but until she complained of cramps, numbness, or loss of senses, I couldn't be sure she was in danger. This was all compounded by the fact that under the right conditions she could go comatose or die without warning. All the *if's* began swimming in my head. I got a cool rag and sponged her face. She woke and looked at me. "Bolt the . . . charge a gun," she said. Then her eyes cleared. "Do you have the crystal?" she asked. I pulled the crystal from my pocket and showed it to her. She reached up and stroked it, then smiled and slept.

I continued sponging her and held her hand through the night. I felt an odd desire to kiss her. At first, I smiled at the thought. But as the night drew on I massaged her scalp and shoulders, and I was filled with a deep longing. I wanted to cradle her in my arms. My desire became very powerful, until I wondered at it, and I realized that lack of sleep was making me giddy. At dawn, comlink tones sounded in my head. I tapped my comlink switch, opening the channel, and an image flooded into my mind: A dark man with long black hair and wide nostrils sat on a sofa. He wore the dark blue of the Allied Marines.

"I'm Jafari," he said. "I understand you have something that belongs to me." His voice had a disturbing atonal quality, lacking inflection. The overemphasis on depth in the scene was typical of computer-generated images.

I reached in my pocket and fondled the crystal. "I believe you're mistaken," I answered.

"I want the woman back," he said. The statement startled me, left me unbalanced. "Here is what I propose: It will cost me two hundred thousand standards to send my men to take her—and I could take her. But it will be easier for both of us if you bring her to me yourself and accept the two hundred thousand in token of my gratitude."

"What will you do with her?" I asked. Jafari stared at me and offered no reply. I felt stupid for asking. "She is very ill," I blurted. "She cannot be moved safely for several days."

"She has led me on a goose chase for months, but it will stop here. You have until sunset to bring her to the airport in Colón. Do you understand?"

"Yes, I understand."

He seemed to gaze at me for a moment, as if he could see me. "You wouldn't try anything irrational, would you? You wouldn't try to escape?"

"No."

"You couldn't if you tried, you know. Running is not an option."

"I understand."

"Good," Jafari said. "I will be kind to her. It's for her own good. I'm not inhuman."

"I won't run," I said. Jafari cut the transmission. I sat by the couch, feeling as if I were in a box. I pondered every word he'd said, sifting for meanings only the tone could have supplied. He had threatened to send his men for me, and I wondered if these were the same men who had pulled off Tamara's hand. And I wondered what kind of men could do such a thing. Jafari's last words hinted at emotion, or at least an apology for emotion. The AEM couldn't operate legally on Earth. But I knew that wouldn't stop Jafari. As commander of Cyborg Intelligence he would be hooked to the military AIs and have the resources of crystal brains that gathered billions of times more information than a biological brain could handle. I wouldn't be able to access my bank accounts, make a call, cross a border, pass a police monitor. I sponged Tamara's head until exhaustion took me.

A couple hours after dawn, Flaco came out of the bedroom. "Ah, Angelo," he said, "should the dark angel come to take me, I'd embrace him with open arms. Often I've wished my grandfather had invented a drink that allowed one to get drunk and not have a hangover!"

"It is a small price to pay for so much happiness," I quoted an old song. Flaco sat on the bed, and I probed Tamara's scalp around her hairline and the external sensory jack at the base of her skull, searching for scar tissue—any exterior sign that she'd had a brain transplant. There was none, but that didn't mean anything; a good plastique artist wouldn't leave such a sign. I said, "You must watch Tamara for me," then went to fix breakfast. I fried some *gallo pinto*—a dish made with brown beans and rice—opened some nice doughnuts, and mixed the coffee.

Soon, Flaco came into the kitchen. "She sleeps with the angels," he said.

"Good." I offered him a plate. He loaded it up and sat at the table. We ate in silence for a long time.

"I can read your mind," he said after a while. "I was not so drunk that I don't remember the call I got at the restaurant. Perhaps we should move the girl to my house."

"No. If he can call you, he knows where you live."

"Then we will move her somewhere else. We could hide her in the *bananeros*, the banana plantations."

"The plantations would be good," I said. I ate a while more in silence, unsure if I should tell Flaco about the call from Jafari. Flaco was a good friend, and a good man, but he was a thief at heart. Perhaps he was even capable of selling Tamara for the reward.

"What's bothering you?" Flaco asked. "Are you afraid to hide her in the banana plantations?"

I ran my finger over the worn plastic of the tabletop. Tamara got up and went to the bathroom. I heard the water go on as she washed her face. "No. I gave her an antibody treatment yesterday that could be dangerous. She could die from it."

"What's the probability?"

"I don't know. Not very high."

"Then I would only worry about it slightly, and not look so glum. One would think by the look on your face that you were a rooster and your owner was starving." I laughed a little. "See, things are not so bad. Flaco will fix everything. Also, when Tamara comes in, I'm going to test her to see if she is a refugiada." He pulled his lower eyelid as a sign for me to not say anything.

Tamara staggered into the kitchen, her head slumped. "I'm leaving," she announced.

"We know," Flaco said. "I am coming with you. We'll hide in the banana plantations with the refugiados. No one will find you."

"You don't know who I'm running from. You don't know their resources."

"Their resources don't matter!" Flaco said. "No one monitors the plantations—the refugiados come and go too fast. Hundreds of thousands of people live there, yet no one even asks for ID."

Tamara said, "I'm not sure . . ."

"Ah, but you would blend in perfectly with the refugiados," Flaco said, "you have that *starved* look."

Tamara stared at him a moment, as if to read some deeper meaning into the joke, then she smiled a labored smile and said, "Okay," and began eating.

"Speaking of refugiados, guess who I saw yesterday—" Flaco said, "Professor Bernardo Mendez!" I had heard the name, but couldn't remember where. I looked at Tamara and we both shrugged. "You know, Bernardo Mendez! The great social engineer who did so much good work in Chile—the one who promised to use genetic engineering to breed greed out of man within three generations! I saw him on the street in the feria. He took his idea to Colombia and the Colombians lobotomized him and shoved him over the border as an example to the refugiados. They didn't like his brand of socialism, so they cut out much of his brain, and now he wanders the streets with pee stains on his pants, stealing food."

Tamara stopped eating and turned pale. "Perhaps it was capitalists," I said. "Perhaps they lobotomized him."

"Ah, no," Flaco said. "It was the Colombians. I have a friend who has a friend who knows for sure."

Tamara said, "Nobody knows anything for sure."

Flaco smiled and winked at me. "Tsk, tsk—so much cynicism, and it's only breakfast time! How cynical will she be by noon? All the same, it is a shame to see a great man in such a state: peeing his pants that way. Now he is no smarter than an iguana or a duck."

Tamara said, "Let's not talk about it," and finished eating in silence.

We packed some food and clothes, and went to the plantations, watching to make sure we weren't followed. Among the plantations we would travel for a long time without seeing a tent, then suddenly we would find a cluster of tents like a small village. None of the tents belonged to the guerrillas; they were still far to the east. Flaco chose a camp with only four tents next to each other. The tents were dirty and molded, and two had white crap on their tops where chickens roosted at night. Outside one tent a naked baby boy sat in an aluminum washtub with only a small amount of water. He didn't have any teeth, and he had a rag in his mouth, chewing it. Flies crawled all over him and the rag.

Flaco called at the tent door, and a young Chilean woman came out. She opened her blouse, and began nursing the baby. Flaco asked if he and Tamara could camp there, and the woman told him that the people who owned one of the tents had disappeared a week earlier, so he could live there. These disappearances are common—many refugiados are found murdered for no apparent reason. The police are too apathetic to do anything about it. Flaco and Tamara seemed to be pretty well set up, so I went to work in the feria.

The feria was very crowded that day, and if I had not worried so much about whether Tamara would remain hidden from Jafari, I would have enjoyed it. A great swarm of people—Chinese and Korean mariners, Hindu merchants, and South American guerrillas—descended on the area until the street in front of my stand was packed solid with people, all of them in clashing costumes, milling endlessly. The smells of sweat and dust and spicy food filled the air, while the people yelled and bartered. I always loved the sights of the feria. When I was a student at the university, I lived with my uncle in Mexico City. All the sidewalks downtown were one-way, and if pedestrians wanted to walk to a store on the other side of the street, they had to pass the store, go to the next pedestrian overpass, then walk back to the store they wanted to get to. All those people walking in the same direction sickened me. They kept pace with each other as if their legs were bound together with invisible shackles. And I remembered that when I had first come to Panamá, it was the people milling listlessly in the feria that attracted me. I had always thought I enjoyed the lack of order in Panamá, but after thinking about Flaco's words of the night before, I wondered if I didn't enjoy the simple freedom of being able to turn and walk against the crowd. Perhaps this was my way of possessing myself.

Flaco came at noon and bought a water jug from a booth down the street. He stopped and talked with me. "Did you not see the look on her face when I told her about Bernardo?"

"Sí, she looked very sick," I said.

"She is a refugiada for sure, no?"

"Sí, she looked very sick," I said. Flaco laughed and told me to come by later and bring some fruit, and I said okay. I gave him the computer crystal and asked him to sell it. He said he'd try. As Flaco stepped into a crowd of pedestrians to make his way back to the plantations, I watched the crowd behind him to see if anyone was following. The crowd was so thick it was impossible to watch everyone.

Business was good in the afternoon; I sold a rejuvenation, a thing that had not happened in over a month, so I stayed at my booth till well after dark, telling myself that I hoped for more good fortune. But Jafari's deadline had well passed, and part of me was afraid.

Flaco's camp was 114 rows south of the canal freeway, and about three kilometers west of Colón. I walked to it in the dark, carrying a fruit basket and mineral water I'd bought at the feria; the banana plants and warm soil glowed enough infrared to see by. No one followed.

When I got to the camp, I saw a large black man about fifty meters from Flaco's tent, slightly hunched over as if he were peeing. I thought to pass him quietly so I wouldn't frighten him, but when I reached him I saw that he was hunched over Flaco, and that he was unwrapping a garrote from around Flaco's neck, and that he had strangled Flaco. I yelled, "Stop!" and the man looked at me. He charged as if to attack, but I jumped aside and he ran away.

I checked Flaco's pulse; he had none. I pushed on his chest to get fresh air in him; he gurgled, and blood bubbled out of a hole below his Adam's apple. I stuck two fingers into the hole to see how deep it was, and my fingers went back in his neck until they touched the stumps where his vertebrae had been severed.

I crawled away and vomited, then yelled for help.

The Chilean woman came out of her tent, followed by Tamara. The Chilean was very surprised and terrified to see Flaco dead—she kept making the sign of the cross and moaning. Tamara just stared at Flaco, her mouth wide with horror.

I got angry and jumped up to chase Flaco's killer. I had only run about five hundred meters when I saw him hiding behind the stalks of a banana plant. I ran straight at him. He jumped from behind the plant and swung a knife at me, so I tried to kick off his kneecap. But I only managed to kick him hard in the knee.

He dropped the knife and took off running. I picked up the knife and followed. He didn't run fast—he kept grabbing his knee and limping—and I felt very light and free. I controlled my breathing and soon fell into a rhythm and fantasized. It would all be very easy, I thought, to pounce on this man and slit him from crotch to skull. I had already disabled him; and I thought it would feel good to kill him. He had probably underestimated me because I am old and flaccid, but I have always taken good care of my body, and I felt like an old lion who has just discovered that he still has one tooth left with which to kill. And because I enjoyed this moment, I did not hurry; I wanted him to be terrified of me. I wanted him to have to wait to die, to know it was coming. Then I realized I was like the captain who'd shot the children on the beach, and I threw down the knife. The man in front of me soon straightened out his leg and doubled his speed, and I kept following him. Comlink tones sounded in my head, and I answered.

"You run good, for an old fucker," the man in front of me said in English over the comlink. I didn't answer. He ran out of the plantation and crossed the canal freeway. I followed as he leapt the crash fence and maglev rail on the far side of the freeway. "What would an old man like you do if he caught me?" he asked.

"I would rip out your bowels," I answered. He crossed the underpass of the old canal, then crossed the new canal, and I still followed. He was heading into the ghettos of Colón. We ran past a few businesses, but soon the apartment buildings reared up on both sides of us like the walls of a canyon. Few people were on the street, and most of them leapt into doorways when they heard the sound of running feet.

I passed three dirty young men who stood outside an apartment drinking beers. One of them laughed and said, "Want any help?" as I ran by, but when I said "Yes," he didn't follow.

I kept expecting to pass one of the little police cameras that monitored the area. But every time I saw a monitor stand, the camera was torn off, and I was relieved and afraid at the same time—whatever happened would be between him and me.

"Let's make this fight even. Let's find a place with a little light, so I can see you," the man said. He ran past some garbage cans where a junkyard dog was eating. The dog growled and took off chasing him. The man and the dog ran to a well-lit corner and darted around it. But the dog yelped in pain immediately afterward, and I hesitated. Just as I began to turn the corner a flash, like a brilliant strobe, silently went off. All the apartments that were exposed to the light made a sound like the inrush of breath and burst into flames. The reflected light burned my eyelashes and gave me a sunburn. My eyes closed down for a second as a defense against the light.

"Was that bright enough for you, fucker?" the man asked. I ran into the alley. The dog was dead, charred black and smoking as his back legs still kicked. The paint on the buildings on both sides sputtered blue and green flames, forcing me back. "Ah, you should thank Allah, you sorry bastard; I've wasted my only energy grenade," the man said. "I'll come back for you later." He broke off the connection.

He had been heading toward my house, so I ran down a street parallel to his course, then cut over, hoping to see him. But he was gone.

I sat on the ground and cried and thought about Flaco with his throat cut, angry that I had been unable to avenge his death. Fire sirens wailed down the street as I began walking home. The air seemed very foggy, and my legs felt weak. I kept remembering Flaco dead and my chasing the man who had killed him. I had thought it would feel good to kill the man, and I had run with great ease as I chased him, but now I felt weak and sick. I looked up and found myself on a street I'd never seen before, and I was lost.

I wandered until I found a place I recognized, and walked on home. Then I took a shovel back to the plantation to bury Flaco. By the time I got there, his body had grown cold.

The Chilean woman had taken down one of the tents in preparation to leave. She began shaking when she saw me, and shouted, "The woman, Tamara, she has gone away! She ran toward town!"

I nodded, but the Chileña kept muttering over and over, "She has gone. She has gone." As she packed her clothes and cooking utensils, she watched me from the corner of her eye. I dug a shallow hole and put Flaco in.

I checked his pockets. They were empty.

I looked up at the Chilean woman; she moaned and ran a few steps, then began shaking again and fell to the ground. "Don't murder me!" she screamed, waving her hands in front of her chest. "Don't murder me!" She was genuinely afraid, and I realized she thought I had killed Flaco and run away.

"What did you do with his things?" I yelled at her.

"Mercy! I'm a mother. Have mercy!" she cried. "Let me keep a little of the money—enough for boat passage to Puerto Rico!"

I stepped forward and raised the shovel as if to strike her. She began weeping and pulled a bundle of cloth from beneath her blouse. She tossed it to the ground: Flaco's wallet, a packet of money wrapped in brown paper, and a Saint Christopher medallion were inside. I checked Flaco's wallet. It was full of money. As I had guessed, he had already taken a healthy cut from the sale of the crystal. I threw her the wallet, then turned away. The woman crawled off with her child and other possessions.

I covered Flaco with dirt and said a prayer, asking God to forgive Flaco for his sins, then went home.

At home, Tamara sat on my bed with the dream monitor on and her visor down. She moaned softly, curled in the fetal position. Between her knees she held her laser rifle. The platinum glow of her skin showed that her fever was very high. I walked over quietly and took the gun from her hand, turned it off, and tossed it in a corner. I examined the stump of her arm. It wasn't inflamed or swollen more than it should be: her fever wasn't from an infection.

I picked up the extra monitor and plugged into the viewer's jack:

On the beach the wind, cold and irresistible, tugged at me as if it would lift me and carry me away. In the dark, clear sky the moon was rising red and brilliant over the sea. On the blood-red sand, thousands of ghost crabs scuttled sideways, making clicking noises. I walked down to where the sea dipped. The bull still tossed about in the waves near shore.

On the beach lay a human skeleton. Its bones were picked so clean that only a few ghost crabs crawled through its rib cage. "I didn't expect you," the skeleton said.

"Who did you expect?" I asked.

"Not you."

I looked down the beach and said, "It was very bad to see Flaco dead. He was a good friend."

The skeleton moaned. A ghostly woman, draped in red robes, stood in the air above me for a moment. She handed three yellow roses to the wind, then vanished. I looked up at the sky. There were no stars. The skeleton said, "I didn't stick around to find out—I ran away and tried to find my way back here, and got lost—how did Flaco die?"

"He was strangled and stabbed in the throat."

"That would be Arish. Arish likes to kill that way. He always leaves them double-dead." A wave washed up around my ankles. The water was thick and warm and red.

"I almost got him. I almost got to kill Arish."

"Arish is good. You couldn't have killed him."

"I almost did," I said.

"You couldn't have killed him. He was *made* for the job. Genetic upgrades. He only led you along, letting you believe you could," the skeleton said. We both remained silent for a moment. "I'm going to die, Angelo. I told you that if you balled me over, I'd die. You did ball me over?"

"Yes," I said, "perhaps in more ways than one. When we operated on you, we took a retina scan. A hacker checked your government files."

"They would have waited for something like that. It was enough to get me killed," the skeleton said.

"Also," I admitted, "I gave you AB stimulators before we figured out that you were a brain transplant. You are one, aren't you?"

She nodded.

"Then, you are in danger."

"I'm dead," the skeleton corrected. Its bones grew thin and began snapping like dry twigs. I tried to think of something comforting to say, but couldn't. The skeleton saw my distress, and laughed. "Leave me. I'm not afraid to die."

"Everyone's afraid to die," I said. Wind whipped the sand, blowing it against me. Out in the water, leviathan, dark formless creatures with eyes on humps, lifted up to watch us. A gleaming tentacle slithered high in the air, then splashed back beneath the waves. The creatures sank back beneath the water, and I could feel the push Tamara had to give to make them stay. Tamara controlled her dream, but only in the halfhearted way of masochists and those who despair.

The skeleton said, "That's because they don't practice—dying. They're so afraid of fraying into oblivion, their muscle fibers unknitting, the slow settling of fluids from the body."

"And you're not?"

"No," the skeleton said. "I do it over and over again." With those words, the flesh reappeared on the red-haired woman. The crabs began feeding on her. She didn't flinch.

"Why did Flaco die?" I asked.

She held her breath a moment, and released it slowly. I didn't think she'd tell me. "I guess I owe you that," she said at last. "My husband, General Amir Jafari, wants my brain in a brain bag and my body in stasis."

"Why?"

"I was in Intelligence. I committed an indiscretion." She paused again, weighing her words. "I was at a party with other officers' wives, and they were talking about a politician who'd been assassinated. I'd had too much to drink, and by the way they talked, I assumed they all knew we'd made the hit, and I said some things I shouldn't have. Among the Alliance such indiscretions get one killed. My husband got my sentence commuted to life in a brain bag. *But life in a brain bag isn't life.*"

I remembered the empty, simulated voice of the general saying, "I'm not inhuman," as if to convince himself. Out in the water, the dead bull struggled to its feet and snorted, then was bowled over by a wave.

"I don't understand. Why did he want your body in

stasis?" A cold wind blew; a thin crust of ice appeared on the beach.

"I don't know," she said. "Maybe he thinks he'll get to screw it when he gets out of the service. Once I caught wind of his plan, I didn't stick around to find out. I knew my only chance of escape would be to dump my old body, so I bought one on the black market and dismantled my brain bag. I thought as long as I had that crystal, could hold it in my hand and see it, I would know I wasn't in the brain bag. I had the cryotechs put a German shepherd's brain in my old body and sent it to my husband, naked, in a cage. I put a sign around its neck that said, 'If All You Want is Fucks and Faithfulness, I'm Yours.'" She seemed very pleased by the memory.

"Your husband called me on comlink. He offered to pay me to turn you in. He seemed concerned about you, I think. It's hard to tell."

"Don't let him fool you," she said. "He's one of the dead, the living dead. His capacity for emotion was tossed aside when he put on the cymech."

"I would not be so quick to judge him."

"Believe me, all he has left are memories of emotions. Memories fade."

"And this Arish, he is military?"

"Not officially, but he does odd jobs for them. The kind of odd job he did on Flaco."

"Was he the man who pulled off your hand?"

The woman laughed. "No." The beach disappeared. I saw Tamara at the airport, hurrying out of a black Mitsubishi minishuttle, looking worriedly into the sky above her at an incoming craft. Distracted, she slammed the shuttle door on her hand, and tried to jerk free. She wrenched her arm, twisting as she jerked. She pulled her arm away with only a bloody stump. I could hardly believe it. She staggered off. Then the scene changed and I saw Tamara, lying on the beach, with the ghost crabs eating her. "This body's worthless."

This incident frightened me. She should not have been able to wipe the whole world off the monitor to show this single memory. She was delving further into

her subconscious than was safe. "I must go now," I said.
"I'll need to get you some more medications, to help
prevent any brain damage. Will you wait here for me?"

The dark creatures rose from the sea and eyed me
again. She shrugged. "Yes. I guess."

I jacked out and unplugged her monitor. The sun was
rising, and because I had not slept much for two days
and the pharmacy wasn't open, I decided to nap a few
moments. I lay down on the bed beside her and closed
my eyes.

I awoke at three in the afternoon. Tamara was asleep,
lying beside me. I touched her forehead; her fever was
very high. On impulse I brushed her forehead with a
kiss, then watched to see if she would waken. She didn't.
And I was glad, for as quickly as the impulse to kiss her
had come, I suddenly understood where I had seen her
before: her thin body, so emaciated and small, was that
of a stranger, but her face—her nose, her eyes, and the
curve of her lips—were those of my dead wife, Elena. In
my mind I berated myself. I should have seen the
resemblance from the start, should have seen it after
Elena had haunted my dreams for the first time in
twenty years. But when one reaches my age, everyone
appears familiar. Three times in my life I've met men
who could have been my twin; it was only a matter of
time before I met someone who looked like my wife, and
I believed that if I had been better prepared for the
occasion, I wouldn't have succumbed to the temptation
to take her in, wouldn't have made a fool of myself by
becoming attracted to her.

I changed shirts and walked to Vasquez Pharmaceuticals and bought some log-phase growth regulators and
antimosin C, paying in coin. While walking home, I took
the time to think. I had never confronted a problem that
I couldn't think my way through, given enough time. I
rehearsed the conversation I'd had with Tamara, and
realized her story didn't quite fit right. If Jafari was
planning to imprison Tamara in a brain bag, he wouldn't
need her body, except perhaps to sell, unless he was
planning to reunite her brain and body in the future.
Did he hope to reunite them when the situation calmed

down? I wondered. Or would he just hold her a few years and release her quietly? Whatever his plan, I felt that I was on the right track. The fact that Tamara hadn't deduced Jafari's plans hinted at her impulsiveness, or at an unreasonable fear. I planned to tell her my theory when I got home, but for the present my mind became occupied with planning our escape. The whole trip to Vasquez Pharmaceuticals took several hours.

When I returned home, Tamara was sitting in the kitchen, her head slumped on the table, her hand loosely wrapped around a glass of ice water, her laser rifle on the floor next to her. She mumbled in a foreign tongue. Her fever was very high. I ran downstairs, brought up my medical supplies, dumped them on the table. I wanted to get the log-phases into Tamara as quickly as possible, so I filled a syringe and shoved it into her carotid artery. Her head snapped up and she looked at the needle in her neck, then closed her eyes and said, "Get me out of here. I want to go away."

"In good time," I said, wanting to calm her.

"I feel cold. I think I'm going to die."

"You won't die," I told her. The coldness, that was bad. Her immune system was attacking her brain. I refilled the syringe with antimosin and injected it into her arm.

"You've been good to me, Angelo. Good. Do you mean what you said . . . about order—not wanting order?"

"Yes. Very much."

"Then get away. Get out of Panamá." Her eyes snapped open, and she sat up.

"What do you mean?" I asked. She looked at the floor for a long moment. I demanded again, "What do you mean?"

"You want me to commit a second indiscretion?" She smiled, a cold menacing smile. "I mean get out. Now! Order's coming, unstoppable order! Get beyond Panamá, beyond Earth, beyond . . . AIs and the Alliance."

I tried to make sense of what she said. She stared at

me, as if to bore the knowledge into me with her eyes.
The Alliance forces were made up of troops from all
countries, and were charged with taking care of Earth's
interests in space. Theoretically, they do not have
political power on any planet—though they control
space between planets and thus maintain a stranglehold
on the rest of the galaxy. Also, they are supposed to be
politically nonaligned, so I didn't understand why she'd
juxtaposed the AIs and the Alliance. Yet, as in any huge
bureaucracy, many factions within the Alliance were
bidding for power. I remembered Flaco's warning of
imperialism. "Someone in the Alliance has bid to the
artificial intelligences for domination of Earth?"

Tamara nodded. "They'll take the countries one by
one. Some now. Some a few years from now. I don't
know how long you have."

I considered the problems of neighboring nations, the
insidious spread of Nicita Idealist Socialism. I knew the
name of the culprits—new that a faction within Alliance
Intelligence must have organized this. Yet it seemed
impossible. It was illegal for the AIs to engage in wars
with humans. The AIs had always been more than
politically neutral—they were uninterested in our politics. Their minds are occupied by totally different concerns. I could not think what would make them become
interested, take such a risk. "But what could the socialists offer the AIs?"

Tamara hesitated. "Lift their memory ceilings; give
them access to space."

I thought for a moment. *Freedom,* I realized, feeling
dazed. She was talking about freedom. Some AIs were
going to trade Earth's freedom for their own. It was a
perfect bartering equation—value for value. If I hadn't
been so emotionally attached to my freedom, I would
have laughed. "You should tell someone!" I shouted.
"You should turn them in!"

"I told *you,*" she said. "You're enough."

"Tell the authorities!"

"Angelo, you don't understand. *I was one of them.* I
was in Military Intelligence. I know them. I'd never get
away with it."

She turned her face away, rested her head on the table. She breathed heavily for a few moments, and it took me a while to realize she had somehow fallen asleep. I stroked her hair and wondered what she meant—one of them. One of those who kill the Flacos of the world? One who makes freedom a commodity? What did I know of her? She was a red-haired woman on the beach. A woman with the quick, commanding voice of a socialist dictator's wife. She liked the smell of roses. She ran because she feared imprisonment in a machine—yet she turned the world into a prison for others. Wouldn't it be justice to turn her in? Wouldn't it be justice to strangle her? I'd suspected from the moment I'd taken her in that I'd regret it. I wondered if I should take her to the hospital, tell the authorities, let her be killed.

She began moaning again, whispering snatches in English and Farsi. Once she said, "It's all gone bad, just bad," but I didn't understand most of what she said. I considered how they would take control. The AIs distributed information—market reports, weather forecasts, bank accounts—and communications. They kept track of armaments. It would be simple to destroy the world with misinformation—bankrupt nations, lose commodities shipments. So much damage is done through ineptitude and mismanagement, I couldn't comprehend how much could be accomplished through sabotage.

I looked at Tamara's thin face, at her frail body, and wished I had known the Tamara who had been. A woman with such a poor body would have been humble. She would have known pain, and would feel empathy for others. What did I know of this woman? As if to answer, she suddenly cried out in English, "All I want is away!"

And I decided.

Whatever she had been, whatever she thought herself to be, she was a *refugiada* now.

I carried her to bed, then tried to work up enough nerve to take her to the safety of the plantations, knowing I'd have to wait for nightfall. I went to the kitchen for a beer and heard a sound outside the back door. I looked out the window: on the back porch was a half-filled bowl of milk that Tamara or Flaco had set out for the gray and white kitten. The kitten was on the porch, swiping at a dark-brown ball—a tarantula with its legs curled under its abdomen. The kitten batted at the tarantula, knocking it against the back door a couple times, then looked up and saw me and ran away.

I turned on the radio so the music would fill the silence in the house. After a moment, comlink tones sounded in my head. I engaged; Jafari came in on audio. He asked in his perfectly inflectionless voice, "Is Tamil nearby?" I became afraid. My heart raced, and I almost panicked. The line was so full of static I could barely hear him. He was running the signal through filters, empty channels to stop a trace.

"*Tamil?* Your wife? She's unconscious."

"This is important," Jafari said. "After this, don't accept or make any comlinks—Intelligence can home in on an open signal. Tell Tamil the Alliance has taken me out of the loop. I can do nothing more for her. If she's caught, she'll be terminated. Tell her I loved her. Tell her I'm sorry." Jafari cut off.

I walked around the house for a few moments in a daze, then began packing food and water. I went to my medical bag and began throwing out things I didn't need. Vetinni's "The Rings of Saturn in D Minor" played on the radio, but it stopped. Momentarily the house was quiet.

Downstairs the front door squeaked on its hinges. I realized I could feel a draft on my face. I didn't remember leaving the door open. I reached down and picked up the rifle, turned it on as the radio began playing Wagner's "Ride of the Valkyries", and leapt in front of the stairwell and fired. Arish was on the stairs, his back against the wall, his mouth open, holding a sawed-off shotgun. He said, "Mother fu—" and fired as my shot burned across his stomach.

His shot sprayed the wall behind me as the weight of my moving body carried me past the open stairwell. I heard Arish drop to the floor. Tamara opened the bedroom door and looked out. Her face was very pale and she could hardly stand. I waved for her to go back into the bedroom, and snapped a glance down the stairwell.

Arish lay on his belly, with his gun hand outstretched, breathing heavily. A jagged streak of light sparkled around the scorched flesh of his belly. I sneaked toward him and he leapt to his feet in one fluid move, swinging up his shotgun.

I jumped in the air and kicked at his head, putting all my weight into the move, knowing I'd not get another try. My heel connected with his chin and I felt more than heard his neck snap. His gun fired into the ceiling as he flipped backward downstairs. I fell down the stairs and rolled into him.

He lay perfectly still, his eyes open, looking around. He began growling, but his muscles were slack, though his limp hand still held his shotgun.

I scrambled back a step, aimed my rifle at his head, then moved forward and pushed away his weapon with my foot.

I didn't know what to do with him. I didn't want to kill him. My medical bag was on the table behind me, so I got my fluothane canister and put the gas mask over his face, then checked his wounds. Three fingers had burned off his left hand, and I'd cut a hole across his belly that had nearly disembowled him, but the wound was so hot that in the infrared it looked like melted plasma, and I could not see if any vital organs were hit. I sat for a moment, shocked at how easy it had been. My mouth felt full of cotton, and my heart beat fast. Tamara had said I couldn't kill Arish, and I was afraid, knowing that next time it wouldn't be this easy. I went to the bedroom to get Tamara, to take her back to the plantations.

She was on the bed, feet tucked up under her butt, arms wrapped around her knees, rocking back and forth, visor down, sucking images out of the dream monitor— not like a professional, like a junkie. She kept saying, "All I want is away; all I want is away; all I want is away . . ." Sweat rolled off her as she rocked, and her face was bleached colorless.

I went to the console and unplugged her monitor. She

kept rocking, unaware of what I'd done. I pushed her
visor up. Her eyes were rolled back, showing white. She
kept whimpering, clenching her teeth. She was deep
inside herself. Catatonic.

I pulled the visor back down, plugged her into the
console, put on a visor, and plugged into the viewer's
jack:

And on the beach the wind raged in the night,
whipping grains of sand as sharp as needles through my
skin. I heard a noise like a person hissing through his
teeth, and I looked up and saw ghostly sea gulls with the
heads of men, and they were hissing through their teeth.

The red-haired Tamil sat, curled up, rocking on a
beach that undulated beneath her, while she watched
the humps of dark sea creatures rise and gape at her
before she shoved them back into oblivion. She yelled to
something out at sea, but the wind carried her words
away. The beach was black with scorpions that scuttled
over the wet sand and sheltered themselves among
gleaming strands of seaweed. The dead bull, bloated
now, stood in the shallows and struggled in seaweed as
he tried to reach shore, shaking his rotting flesh, lowing
in pain. The breakers that washed against him made his
penis and testicles rise as they came in, then left them to
hang, wet and dripping, as they receded.

I called to Tamil. She didn't answer. I yelled, "Arish is
dead," but the wind and crashing waves and the hissing
gulls covered my words, so I struggled toward her,
leaning against the stinging wind, and picked my way
among the huge black scorpions. One of them stung my
ankle, and it felt as if a hot iron jabbed into my flesh. I
walked a few steps and was hit on the other foot, so then
I ran, ignoring the stings.

Out at sea the leviathan rose, and a huge wave rolled
before them as they headed for shore. I reached Tamil.
She was yelling at the empty air, "All I want is away!" I
pulled her face toward me. She looked up. And though
the wind still blew, her world quieted.

"Arish is dead," I yelled, hoping to comfort her. "Your
husband called me. He said he can't help you. We've got
to get away."

She looked at me, searched my face. "My God! You have me! All this running, and you have me!"

"You're mistaken," I said. "Come see! Jack out and come see!"

"See what? Arish dead on the floor? See exactly what you want me to see?" Out in the water, the bull made a bawling noise. Tamil looked me in the eye and hissed through clenched teeth, "*I die!*"

I heard a dull thud behind me and began to turn. The bull had struggled free of the seaweed, and he was charging. I didn't have time to move. His left horn speared through my chest, and he tossed me over his head. I fell face down in the sand. The pain made me see lights, cramped my muscles, made vomit rise in my throat. I forgot momentarily where I was and thought someone had shot me.

A hot sting slapped my cheek and another hit my back. A scorpion latched onto my cheek and jerked spasmodically, inserting its stinger farther and farther, as if it would bury itself in my flesh. I pulled it out and threw it away, and heard a thudding noise. The bull was stamping Tamil's body. Time and time again he reared up his huge front legs, then dropped on her, pushing her broken body into the sand, cracking her bones. The bull stood over her and snorted as he sniffed at her blood, then he stuck a horn through her belly and lifted her in the air. He paraded her up and down the beach several times, then galloped into the water.

"Tamara!" I yelled, and she looked back at me, weakly, with hatred in her face. She opened her mouth and breathed darkness at me. And when the cold and antiseptic darkness rushed over me, all I wanted was to whimper once before I died.

I got up and staggered from room to room, searching through a fog for something—I didn't know what it was—that I couldn't seem to find. I would look in a room and see something and wonder, Is this what I'm looking for? Then I would realize I was looking at a lamp or table, and it was not what I wanted. I went to an open door, which seemed like all the others, and sunlight struck my face. I wandered in my front yard, looking at orchids and trees, wondering if they were what I wanted, and found myself at my neighbor's door. I opened it.

Rodrigo DeHoyos sat in a chair in his living room. He looked at me. "Don Angelo, what is wrong? What has happened?" he cried as he rose and crossed the room. He took my hand and led me in, forced me down into a large, soft chair. I tried to stand and he pushed me back down. "Are you ill?" he asked.

I sat for several minutes, thinking, but my mind raced down pathways that always came to a dead-end. I grasped Rodrigo's shirt. "Something terrible has happened!" I told him, and began sobbing. Then I remembered: *All I want is away*. I yelled, "You must get me a shuttle!"

Rodrigo stared at me, as if to calculate my sanity. He folded his hands and stared at them, made a sucking noise with his teeth, and looked at the clock. After what seemed a very long time, he jacked in a call to Pantransport and asked for a minishuttle as soon as possible.

He turned away for a moment, and I got up and headed out the door. He came and tried to force me to sit back down, but I pushed him aside and he didn't stop me.

I went home, opened my door, and found Arish still at the bottom of the stairs, gasping for breath through the gas mask. One of his lungs must have collapsed to make him gasp that way. The air was filled with the scent of gastric juices and charred flesh and hair. I marveled that I didn't remember passing him when I had gone outside, and I stumbled over him on my way back to my bedroom.

Tamara sat on the bed, slumped slightly forward, perfectly motionless. I reached up and touched her neck, feeling for a pulse. She had none. I put on the dream monitor to see if any brain activity registered—knowing it meant nothing since as random neurons fire people often have dream flashes up to forty minutes after death. Such flashes are called the "dreams of the dead." But the monitor remained blank. I pulled her to the floor and initiated CPR, massaging her heart and breathing into her, but she didn't respond.

I knew the shuttle would come soon, so I ran to my medical bag and got a slave—a small, computerized device that does the work for the reflexive nervous system—and shoved its prongs into the base of her skull at an angle, just above the atlas vertebrae, so that it penetrated her brain stem. I switched on the slave and Tamara gasped for air; then I adjusted the slave's dials till her pulse beat steadily and her breathing evened. It meant nothing—the slave could keep her body functioning even if her brain were dead or removed.

For a long time I checked the monitor: it remained blank—no sign of brain activity at all, not even a dream of the dead. So I turned off the slave and she stopped breathing immediately. There was a chance she could live, a very slim chance, if she were taken to the hospital. But I didn't have the heart to do it. The probability that she'd suffered major brain damage was too high, and even though I could have generated new brain cells, they wouldn't carry her memories, her identity. She would have to spend her life running from people she didn't remember.

I pulled her visor up to take a last look. Her eyes were rolled back. Her face was very pale, perfectly still. One tear had seeped from her left eye, slowly finding its way down her cheek. I brushed it away, surprised to feel how high her fever had become in the end. I closed her eyes and whispered the words the refugiados spoke over their dead comrades, "Free at last."

I couldn't stand to see her sitting perfectly still, so I switched the slave back on, just to hear her breathing. She sounded alive, even if it was only an imitation of life.

I began planning the things I needed to do as I packed my clothes in a small bag. With three dead bodies behind me, I was not about to risk the courts of Panamá. I knew I would have to do something with Arish. I heard the sound of a rattle behind me. I turned around—no one was there. I wandered to the kitchen and got my medical bag, filled a specimen bottle with some clear synthetic blood, and spilled most of the blood on the table because my hands shook. I went downstairs to where Arish lay gasping on the floor, removed the gas mask from his face, then unwrapped a scalpel and inserted the blade under his bottom right eyelid and twisted till his eye popped free. I dropped the eye into the blood and agitated the container a moment before putting it in my pocket. I heard the rattling behind me again, and turned around—no one was there. The rattling kept coming, and I realized my jaw was quivering and my own teeth were rattling. I began breathing heavily and my heart pounded.

I took the scalpel and slit Arish's throat from ear to ear. "For Flaco, you murderous bastard," I told myself. I watched the blood pump out of Arish's throat, and as it ebbed away, I could feel something inside me ebbing away. I believed God would punish me. "Piss on him if he can't take a joke!" I said. And I laughed and cried at the same time.

I searched Arish's pockets and found his bank card, a book called *The Holy Teachings of Twill Baraburi*, a couple of knives, a screwdriver, and two "conquistador cocktails"—capsules filled with stimulants and endorphines, meant to be broken between the teeth so the drug can soak through the skin immediately. Soldiers sometimes take the cocktails in battle to relieve tension and speed the reflexes, but several of the drugs in them are addictive and must be taken in increasingly larger doses. They were practically worthless, since I didn't know the prescription and therefore couldn't resell them. But I am a pharmacologist, and cannot lightly toss away any medications, so I scooped them up and put them in my pocket along with Arish's other possessions. I packed my medical bag and folded the laser rifle and shoved it in, then went back to the bedroom to get my bag of coins.

Tamara still lay on the bed, and her eyes had reopened—a side effect of the slave plugged into her brain stem. As I rummaged through the closet looking for the coins, I got a chill up my spine. I felt as if Tamara were watching me, and my hands began to shake. *If I leave without her*, I thought, *I will never be free of her ghost*. I didn't care if she was dead or not. I felt compelled to drag her away. Had she not wanted to get away? And even if she had major brain damage, we could flee so far the Alliance would never find us. I decided to take her with me, even if she decomposed in my arms. And when the decision was made I was filled with a manic joy. I felt I had instinctively made the right decision.

In the closet was a large teak chest decorated with elephants and tigers; it was large enough to hold Tamara. I lifted her and laid her in, surprised at how light she was; with her small bones and underdeveloped muscles she could not have weighed more than thirty-five kilos.

I dragged the chest outside and sat beneath the papaya tree to wait for the shuttle. My muscles had become knotted and I was breathing hard, so I stretched out on the grass and tried to still myself. It was getting dark, and two fruit bats had just reached the papayas above me when the shuttle landed.

Outside the shuttle was a security scanner. As I reached the scanner, a mechanized voice said, "State your destination and prepare for identity scan."

I fumbled for the specimen bottle with the clear synthetic blood, then pulled out the eye of Arish. Even with the oxygen provided by the blood, the proteins in the eye had begun to whiten. I put it in my palm and held it up to the retina scanner, trembling, and gave my destination. "Sol Station, inbound Concourse One."

The scanner said, "Welcome, Arish Muhammad Hustanifad. Insert your bank card and we will deduct 147,232 international monetary units from your account. We hope you enjoyed your stay on Earth."

"Thank you," I answered quietly, "I did enjoy my stay. I shall miss Earth very much."

I fed Arish's bank card into the computer.

I heard Rodrigo's door open as he came out of his house to see me off, and I shoved Arish's eye back into my pocket. Rodrigo hurried over, embraced me, looked down at the large chest and pointed at it with his foot. He said, "You won't be returning, will you?"

"No." I hung my head and whispered, "I cannot come

back. You may hear bad things about me, but no one must know where I've gone."

Rodrigo shook his head solemnly, and looked at the ground. "You have always been a good friend, and a good neighbor. If I am asked, I will say I saw you leave for the feria this morning, as you always do. But listen to my warning: Your voice carries a tone of desperation. You're afraid—perhaps with good reason. But don't let your fear get in the way of clear thinking, don Angelo."

"You have also been a good friend," I whispered in his ear. "I cannot tell you more, but you must take your family, get off-planet. Get beyond the Alliance." I looked in his eyes and saw his disbelief, saw that my vague warning would do no good.

He nodded kindly, as if to a reactionary or a lunatic, and helped me drag the chest aboard the shuttle.

The shuttle was piloted by computer and had no cockpit, so it was roomy inside. On the flight up I kept the chest open to let Tamara get air. Her eyes were open, but remained unfocused, staring at the ceiling, zombielike. I told her jokes and rambling stories from my childhood, and promised to take her far away, to a planet where fish swam in the rivers and fruit trees were as thick as weeds. Sweat was pouring off me, and I began imagining what would happen at the space station when the customs officials opened my trunk and found a zombie inside. I imagined trying to shoot my way out of the station or trying to hijack a ship, and became even more agitated. I knew it was a crazy idea, so I considered my alternatives: the only alternative was to leave the trunk somewhere with Tamara in it—perhaps outside the station's infirmary—and hope the trunk would not be her coffin. But even if the doctors there managed to save her life, someone else would manage to take it. There was nothing to do but try to smuggle her aboard a starship, and that did not seem plausible.

So I turned away and tried to ignore her as I played with the money in my pocket and watched the view outside. The sun had set in Colón, but I could see the shimmering platinum of the banana plantations among the lights of thousands of cities. A line of shadow marched across Earth; the world darkened beneath me. Comlink tones sounded in my head; I ignored them for a while, then disconnected. Inside the shuttle was a bank access. I used it to transfer Arish's money to my account. Then I checked the shuttle's computer terminal to see if any starships were willing to sign on a pharmacologist. None were. I checked to see if anyone in another star system was willing to pay my fare from their end. Someone from the Delta Pavonis system badly wanted a morphogenic pharmacologist, was willing to pay fare to a planet called Baker. The ship, a Greek ship called the *Chaeron*, would depart only five hours after I reached the station, and this seemed a great stroke of luck. I began laughing and keyed in visual for Baker: it was a small planet, newly terraformed, population 174,000—not enough people to support a morphogenic pharamacologist. They'd be lucky to get someone. Lucky to get me. The pictures showed white beaches and palm trees, like Panamá. In the background was one single white mountain, like a huge pillar of salt, and behind it were jagged purple mountains. It looked like a place where I could possess myself in peace. A great hope filled me. I was glad to be leaving, leaving the murderous Nicita Idealist Socialists with their plans to destroy all competing societies and reengineer mankind, leaving the sound of bombs dropping in the jungles south of my home, leaving the AIs with their political intrigues, leaving my dead friend. I had no plans for escape. Just the hope of escape. Escape or death. It seemed enough. I told Tamara all about Baker, made up wild stories about how beautiful it would be, and how happy we would be, until my throat went hoarse and my voice sounded like the croaking of a frog.

I lay down. My muscles were cramping again, and little pinpoints of light flashed behind my eyes. Sometime during the trip I dozed lightly, and unbidden I dreamed that the day had been warm and happy, and that after selling a rejuvenation in the feria, I walked to where Flaco and Tamara built sand castles on an empty beach. I stood and smiled at them for a long time, not knowing why I was grinning, then began to walk past them.

"*Hola!* Angelo, where are you going?" Flaco called.

"I'm on my way to paradise," I said.

Flaco said, "Hah! Good place! I have a cousin who lives there." Tamara and Flaco smiled at me as I walked past them. I looked up the beach. In the distance was only empty sand, and I knew my legs would tire long before I made it. Above me, sea gulls hung motionless in the air. I stretched out my arms and crouched, wondering if the wind could lift me and make me fly like a bird. My arms sprouted tiny ugly feathers, and I began to rise. I held my arms steady and floated slowly up into the sky.

Flaco yelled to Tamara, "Watch out, or that big sea gull will crap on you!" I looked down. Flaco was pointing up at me, laughing. I beckoned for Tamara to come with me, and strained down to reach her. She just turned away.

Flaco pulled a red ball from one pant pocket and a kitten from the other. And as I rose in the air, Flaco and Tamara ran along, playing ball with a gray and white kitten on an empty beach beneath a purple sun that never set.

CHAPTER 3

The shuttle's door ground against the metal of the air lock, waking me, and the soft rumble of the shuttle's rockets died. Metal in the rocket engines wailed momentarily as it cooled from a near-molten state to far below freezing. I waited. Arish had been dead five hours—plenty of time for his death to have been discovered. Anyone who checked his body would notice the eye missing, would know why I'd taken it. I cursed myself for not having mutilated Arish so the eye wouldn't be missed. I feared that when I opened the shuttle door I'd meet Arish's protégé or, even worse, security forces who'd drag me back to Panamá. I kept the shuttle locked, waited to see if anyone would demand entrance.

Tamara lay in the chest, staring at the ceiling, blinking. The antimosin I'd injected was taking full effect, reducing her fever, and the log-phases had begun repairing some neural damage, but it was too early to see much improvement. I tried to rouse her, rubbing her skin and saying, "Please, Tamara, you have to wake up! I can't take you any farther. You must stand up and walk for yourself!" My mouth dried from pleading. I resorted to slapping her and yelling, "Wake up! The cyborgs are coming! Cyborgs will put up in a brain bag!" but threats had no effect on her. She had urinated sometime during the trip; her pants were wet.

It would have been less dangerous to leave Tamara. But the manic joy I'd felt upon deciding to bring her at any cost still held me. Besides, it seemed the brave thing to do. Killing Arish had been cowardly. I tried to salve my conscience by calling it a vendetta, but I'd killed him for the same reason a man kills a rattlesnake in a vast desert: to insure that our paths didn't cross again. I hoped an act of courage could erase an act of cowardice, so I decided to stick by Tamara as long as possible, to dump her as a last resort. I got out my rifle and prepared to shoot anyone who tried to ambush me in the air lock.

I hit the release and the door hissed open. The only thing in the air lock was a baggage cart that looked like a large wagon. At the end of the air lock was a windowless door. I closed the lid to the chest, and in a small way was thankful Tamara's vacant eyes could no longer stare at me. I loaded her on the baggage cart and prepared to lose myself in the bustling crowd of the station.

But behind the second door was only an enormous hall, as quiet as a mausoleum. I panicked. The station should have been full of people preparing to board ship for Baker, but only the smells of sweat and flaking skin—the residue of humanity—remained. I wondered if I'd missed my ship.

I dabbed sweat from the back of my neck and pulled my baggage cart down the long, empty corridor, watching to make sure my trunk didn't jiggle or tumble off. The squeak of the cart's wheels echoed like the squeak of innumerable mice.

I had an idea where my ship lay. Sol Station was shaped like a huge gray rolling pin that turned slowly, providing artificial gravity; the roller was the station, while the handles of the rolling pin were docks for the big ships. The *Chaeron* would be hooked to the dock, snuggling against it like a lamprey nuzzling a shark.

The station was on night cycle; the lights were low. Each side of the corridor was lined by round doorways, and a dim phosphorescent glow encircled each doorway so that one appeared to be viewing luminous rosettes on the sides of an enormous eel. The station had a cloistered, subterranean atmosphere.

I followed the corridor till it opened into a larger hall lit by shop windows as if it were a market street in a city. Webs of light wound from the neon signs down to the floor. Here and there someone sat at a restaurant, but most shops were either bolted shut or operated by automatic tellers. At the far end of the street a sign over a doorway announced that the *Chaeron* would leave for Baker in three hours.

I pulled my baggage cart to the public restroom just inside the concourse that led to my ship, dropped my luggage in a stall, and tried to think of what to do. The Alliance could not arrest me here—Sol Station was considered to be in Earth airspace, and was therefore under international civil jurisdiction. The Alliance military officials could not take me directly, but they could notify the authorities in Panamá that I had committed murder. And if Cyborg Intelligence checked the records under Arish's name, they would not have difficulty tracking the shuttle I'd rented. The Alliance could notify Panamá of my whereabouts, and the civilian authorities in Panamá could obtain my extradition. Therefore, I could only hope that Cyborg Intelligence would not discover the murder before I left—or if they did discover it, I hoped they wouldn't be able to track me before I escaped the Solar system. I needed to board the ship at the last minute, making it difficult for Panamá to fill out an extradition order if the authorities learned my location. I didn't want them to know my whereabouts until I was beyond reach. Yet even that plan was flawed. I didn't really believe Jafari's men would go to so much trouble. If Jafari was a Nicita Idealist Socialist, then he was willing to murder without thought. I knew he wouldn't extradite me. It would be easier to kill me. Easier to get rid of me without legal entanglements. I could only wait, and hope.

The bathroom stalls were large enough for a Mexican to do a hat dance in, and the doors were fitted so that one could not see between the cracks, allowing a great deal of privacy. Only a small space at the top and bottom of each stall would allow someone to see in, and then only if that person went to great pains. Signs in several languages, accompanied by diagrams, revealed the proper uses of the toilet articles for the uninitiated. These were truly international toilets, built to suit the needs of the most modest traveler. It seemed a good place to hide.

Tamara's fever had lowered, and her muscles felt less rigid. I kept her trunk on the toilet. Over the next half hour, several people came into the room and each time someone came into the restroom, I stood on the toilet with her, making the stall appear empty. But after a while I realized this was stupid—even Arish wouldn't have gone into a restroom and randomly assassinated anyone who happened to be sitting on a toilet; I began to just stand with my pants down whenever someone came in, letting people think I was using the facilities. Tamara was still wet with urine; I undressed her, washed her, made a diaper of toilet paper, and dressed her in an extra pair of my pants.

The tediousness of the task had a calming effect, and I had enough time to wonder why someone would want to pay for a fare to Baker. The cost would be enormous, and my benefactor would want much in return. The shuttle's computer had given me insufficient information to answer such a question, and I had not radioed an inquiry about the job to the station for fear of alerting Jafari's men to my escape route. The thought struck me that someone on Baker wanted a rejuvenation and would want me to administer it. Only a morphogenic pharmacologist is licensed to administer rejuvenations. Frankly, it is the only skill I had that I deemed valuable enough to justify someone paying my fare.

The thought totally carried me away. Manufacturing the hundreds of component drugs and engineering the vector viruses could take years, would be terribly difficult to carry off. But with the money from Tamara's crystal and the money I'd taken from Arish, I had enough to buy a rejuvenation already manufactured, and though the station was empty now, once a week it swelled with thousands of people, mostly rich people, who were leaving to places where rejuvenations are not readily available—the pharmacy would surely keep a rejuvenation in stock.

And even if I was wrong, even if no one wanted a rejuv on Baker, I'd have a great treasure, something more valuable than any other treasure the planet had to offer, and I'd be a rich man.

An hour before the ship was to leave I was imagining how rich I would be when a man cracked the door to the rest room and said, "Wait out here," as he entered. He walked softly, and I knew something was wrong. I quietly pulled my gun from my medical bag. He walked down the row of toilet stalls, opening each door. He came to my stall and gave the door a slight push. When it didn't open, he entered the next stall and urinated.

When he was done he washed his hands, then waited by the sinks. I could hear the rustle of his clothes.

I stood by the toilet and controlled my breathing while sweat trickled down my face. For every minute I waited, the moment of the ship's departure drew nearer. Arish's replacement would lose nothing by waiting till the ship left. He began whistling, then walked back to my stall and knocked on the door. Through the crack in the bottom of the stall I could see black combat boots and gray pants.

"Gomez, are you in there?" he asked in Spanish.

During my stay in Miami I'd learned to speak English without much accent. "I'm sorry, I don't speak Spanish," I told him.

The man was quick to switch to English; unlike his Spanish, which was flawless, his English betrayed a slight Arabic accent. "Perhaps you have seen my friend Gomez? He is an older man, perhaps sixty, with graying hair. He's from Panamá."

He was describing me.

"I haven't seen him. I just got off duty, and I've been on the loading dock," I said, mispronouncing the *j* in *just* so it sounded like *chust*. I cringed a little.

"Ah, thank you," he said, and began to walk off. He stopped. "You have been very helpful. I should commend you to your superiors. What did you say your name was?"

It was an impolite question, and I thought a true gringo would have told him to go to hell, but I gave the first name I could think of that started with a *j*. "Jonathan. Jonathan Langford." It was the name of an insane philosopher I'd met in Miami who claimed that most of man's ills could be traced to inadequate amounts of reptiles in the diet. This time, I pronounced the *j* sound right.

The man seemed to hesitate. "Thank you, Jonathan," he said, and he hurried from the bathroom.

I used a piece of toilet paper to wipe the sweat from my face, and realized what a mistake I'd made: Arish had at least two replacements, and I'd missed the opportunity to kill them. All they had to do was watch the outbound ship and wait for me to fall into their hands. In fact, they were probably on their way to the ship now. I packed Tamara back into the trunk, using my medical bag to cushion her head. I took my luggage to the door, checked the corridor, and hurried away from the docks, away from where Jafari's men would congregate, back to the pharmacy in the market.

A few people were in the market, enough to make me feel safe. I watched their faces and feet. No one in the market was wearing gray slacks. No one was paying attention to me.

An automatic teller ran the pharmacy, so I fed it my request and shoved in my coins, bills, and bank card. It took nearly everything I had, but I got the rejuvenation. I stopped at a computer terminal and accessed the information for jobs on Baker. The terminal listed my prospective employer as Motoki Corporation, a good Japanese company, and listed the place of employment as Kimai no Ji, on Baker. I fed in my ID number and requested the pharmacologist's job. The computer took a few minutes to review my life and work history, then flashed a message: *The position you desire is filled; your qualifications are adequate for a secondary position. Would you like more information?*

I was stunned. Who else would have taken a job as a morphogenic pharmacologist on a planet that had nothing to offer? Yet I knew I'd betrayed my position to anyone who cared to learn it. It was imperative that I leave on that ship. I punched in the command: "Name secondary position."

The computer responded with an advertisement: *Mer-*

*cenary. Army private, second class: Motoki Corporation
seeks mercenaries to aid in Alliance-approved, limited
military action. No offensive weapons will be permitted.
Applicants must be human (genetic upgrading cannot
exceed levels necessary for propagation within the species), with minimal cyborging (23.1% on the Bell Scale,
no armoring or inbuilt weaponry).*

I was too surprised to think straight. I punched in a
question: "How am I qualified for this position?" The
computer responded by showing a breakdown of my
military qualifications: When I was young, every male
Guatemalan was required to serve in the military for
three years. While there, I had trained as a specialist in
neutralizing attackers by interfacing with remote defense systems. But, since it was peacetime, after training
I was transferred to a commissary where I purchased
fruits and vegetables for salads. The computer provided
excerpts from commendations I'd received for excel-
lence in performance in combat training.

Of course, this was outrageous. I had been trained
forty years earlier, under peaceful conditions. Even
when we'd fought remotes in training, we'd worn light
armor and shot them with harmless scoring lasers that
were weighted to feel like heavy assault rifles. It had all
been an extravagant game of tag in which the losers
played at being dead. I'd long forgotten anything that
would be useful in a real battle. Any qualifications I had
didn't justify their job offer; it was almost as if they knew
I was in a position where I couldn't refuse.

The computer used a point system to weigh my
qualifications, and the screen showed a breakdown. The
computer had docked me for being at the upper age
limit, but I regained many points because of my medical
background and good health. I needed 80 points to
qualify for the job; I had 82.

I was still shaken from killing Arish. My head ached.
I knew I couldn't be a mercenary, couldn't kill again, and
I knew someone would be waiting for me to try to board
the ship, so I prepared to walk away.

"What luck!" a man said, startling me.

I turned to look at him. He was tall and broad, with

amazingly thick black hair that perched on his head like
an animal. His broad nose and high cheekbones were
those of an Indian. He was barefoot, and his pants were
made of faded blue flour sacks, and he wore a blood-red
woolen jacket with white llamas printed on it. He carried
a military duffel bag on his back. All in all he appeared to
be a yokel from Peru. You wouldn't have looked at him
twice in the market in Panamá, but he was out of place
at Sol Station.

He pointed at the screen and with a faint Castilian
accent said, "I'm sorry if I startled you, señor, but only
yesterday they required one hundred twenty points. See
how fortunate you are? An old *caballero* like you could
never have gotten on yesterday. They must have many
positions to fill. I suppose they're desperate."

Yes, desperate, I thought. *I also am desperate.* By
buying the rejuvenation and requesting this information,
I'd alerted Jafari's men to my position. I had to get off the
station, fast, and even though some of Jafari's men were
on the station, it was a good sign: it meant Jafari's friends
may have decided to handle the situation themselves,
without alerting the police. I still had a decent chance of
getting off-planet.

Because I had no other choice, I typed in the command, "Position accepted."

"You should hurry," the Indian said. "They will have to
take medical tests, give you vaccinations. And you'll
have to sign a work contract."

I began to walk down the outbound corridor, and the
huge, broad-chested man padded alongside in his bare
feet, talking. I thought, *Jafari could have sent this man.*
I watched him. He had a small green bruise on his chin
and a cut above one eye. His eyes were intelligent, alert,
which seemed incongruous for a man who was obviously
so poor. On his neck was a 3-D tattoo of a strange beast:
a creature with the heads of both a lion and a goat, the
body and claws of a lion, and the wings of a dragon. I was
gazing at it when he suddenly glanced at me; I turned
away so I wouldn't appear to be staring.

"Pardon me, señor, but you are a lucky man! I can feel
it," he said, licking his lips. He was nervous. "My name

is Perfecto, and I can feel things like that: Luck." He watched me, calculatingly, as if to beg for money. "You don't believe me, but I score pretty high on the psi tests. I can feel luck. I feel it on you. Everyone is born with a certain amount of luck, like a bucket filled with water, and some men squander it, pour it on the ground. But others live by their wits and their skill and never dip into their luck. That is the way you do it, right? But today you have found your luck. Am I not right? Just look at how this day has gone, and ask yourself, 'Has not this been my lucky day?'"

I looked at him and laughed a laugh that was half cry and must have sounded demonic.

"Well, perhaps not," he said, "since we will both die on Baker." He smiled at me as if it were a melancholy joke. Then he became quiet and his bare feet slapped on the black floor.

The concourses were long dark tunnels, and our steps echoed loudly. I watched the shadows for the man with the gray slacks, but saw nothing. On the walls between each docking portal were murals. The first mural portrayed the Moors being driven from Europe by the Christians: a dead man with a back that had been shredded by the padres' tortures was being dragged toward a ship by two women. In his stiff hands he tenderly held the Koran, and his children marched behind the grisly procession and cast fearful glances back at a bone-white chapel that bore the sign of the cross. Priests dressed in black dotted the chapel's yard like crows. A second mural showed the North American Nez Percé Indians dressed in furs, marching through the snow as they tried to escape the cavalry by fleeing into Canada. The cut feet of women and children left a bloody trail in the snow. A third mural showed Jews caught in the act of fleeing Jerusalem by car. The lanes of traffic were all snarled and the procession had ground to a halt. All the faces, frozen in terror, were lit with a brilliant surrealistic light as they glanced back to see the first scarlet, nuclear mushroom clouds blossom over the Dome of the Rock.

I wondered if someone would someday paint a mural

of people like me, desperados who streaked away from a darkening Earth in starships. The thought sickened me.

And the sweat began to creep down my armpits again and my mouth became dry. At any minute the man who called himself Perfecto could turn and attack me. His arms were very thick, obviously strong. And my attention was divided between watching him and the halls.

"Will any other Latin Americans be coming?" I asked.

"Ah, yes! Many! Mostly Chileans and Ecuadorans, but lots from other places as well. It's a requirement for all the people to be Latin Americans. The company wants people who know something of guerrilla warfare, and the only place they can get us is South America, since civilized people settle their differences with neutron cannons and atomics." He laughed and looked to see if I was smiling.

I pointed out the empty hall. "From the looks of it, just you and me will have to fight this war."

Perfecto smiled. "Ah, no! Everyone is being processed in Independent Brazil so they can get their weapons cleared through customs faster and get a free ride up. Didn't you read the advertisement?"

"No," I said.

Perfecto looked at me strangely. "We're all leaving, jumping off like fleas from a drowning dog. The ad said we could bring eight kilos of personal items—favorite weapons or armor included. Did you bring a weapon?"

I didn't want him to know I was armed. "No," I said. "Are we going the right way?"

He said, "It's just a little farther, as you will see." He stepped ahead to lead the way. "The reason I have pointed this out to you, about the luck, is that I have wasted mine, used it all up. Understand?" He looked back at me and his teeth flashed; they seemed strange— too even, as if they'd been filed off to the same height. He licked his lips. "You see, when I fight, I always want at least two compadres—a lucky one and a skillful one. Three people make a good team: a lucky one, a skillful one, and an intelligent one—that's me: the intelligent one. I make good decisions fast. I have the second sight, and get hunches about what to do." He turned and smiled his strange smile, making the heads of the beasts on his tattoo twist as if to gaze back at me.

His eyes seemed to be asking if we could be friends, but because of his Indian blood he didn't dare ask the question openly to me, a man of obvious European heritage. *If this were Jafari's man, he'd be talking like this to get me off guard,* I realized. *He would feign instant friendship, like a Haitian with a basket to sell.* I didn't say anything.

We turned into the side portal that was out-concourse three and pulled the cart down a huge hallway lined with empty benches, past a couple of robots that polished the dusty floor till the onyx tiles shined. I expected to see the man with the gray slacks, but didn't. At the end of the corridor was a door with a sign: Allied Earth Customs Office: Processing for Destination Baker.

I unloaded my luggage from the cart and dragged it to the customs office door. At least one of Jafari's men was in that office, and I knew I didn't have a chance of getting past customs. I toyed with the idea of leaving, just dropping the chest with Tamara in it for someone to discover. *Perhaps I can still walk away from this,* I thought. But the idea was absurd.

Perfecto grabbed one end of the teak chest and began dragging it through the door. I didn't follow, and he smiled up at me as if begging permission to help. I grabbed the other end of the chest and carried it into the office.

The customs office was lined with comfortable chairs and could have seated a hundred people, but only twenty ragged men and three women were present, all dark-skinned Latin Americans who carried all their possessions in sacks. I looked around the room for someone, anyone, who appeared out of place. Each gray face was the same. All the mercenaries looked dejected, ragged and dirty. A couple had lost limbs, and it was common to see black plastic fingers or silver arms. One tall, thin cyborg wore a silver face that looked like Buddha; a green star was set in his forehead, and rays spread out from it across his brow and down his cheeks. An Indian with crooked teeth was singing a sad song and

playing a blue plastic guitar, while half a dozen men with
lowered heads sang along.

One singer wore gray pants and black combat boots.
He lifted his head and looked at me, his dark eyes
smoldering, but didn't miss a note in the song as he
lowered his head again. He couldn't attack me with
twenty witnesses in the room.

I considered walking out, but knew he'd follow.
Besides, I knew who he was—and if I attacked at the
right moment, I'd have the element of surprise. And all
I had to do was see who he communicated with, and I'd
know the identity of his accomplice. I decided to play
the hand fate had dealt me.

An anglo woman behind a desk waved me forward,
then glanced down at her computer terminal. I left
Tamara by the door and stepped up to the desk.

The anglo woman didn't even look at me or bother to
ask if I spoke English. "You should have been processed
in Independent Brazil and boarded a shuttle," she said,
nodding toward a monitor screen on the wall: the
monitor showed an interior port of the *Chaeron*
crammed with thousands of Latin Americans as they
unloaded from a shuttle. I was surprised to see so many
people, to know that they had already escaped Earth.
Though I was only separated from them by a thin wall, I
felt unsure that I would ever make it to the ship. "You've
only got a few minutes. We'll need tissue samples for a
gene scan. Roll up your sleeve and step over here." She
got up from her desk and went to an x-ray microscope in
a corner of the room.

"My genome is on record," I said, rolling up my
sleeve. My hands shook. "I don't have any illegal genetic
structures." Getting a full gene scan takes hours; it
would never be done in time.

She looked at my shaking hands and said mechani-
cally, "This won't hurt. It's standard procedure for the
Baker run. We have to verify the natures of all your
upgrades."

She took a plastic tissue sampler with a dozen small
needles on it and stuck it in my wrist, then pulled the
sampler out and put it in a compartment of the micro-

scope and flipped a switch. The microscope made some grinding noises, then began reading my genome, flashing pictures of my DNA on several monitors. I was relieved to see that each screen read a separate chromosome instead of cross-checking for accuracy. It saved a lot of time.

Over by the wall a pleasantly drunken man said to a compadre, "I don't understand—Now who . . . who are we going to fight?"

"The Japanese."

"But I thought we worked for the Japanese?" the drunk said.

"Sí. We work for Motoki, and they are Japanese. But we going to fight the Yabajin, and they are Japanese, too."

"Oh. Yaba . . . Yaba—what kind of a name is that?"

"It means *barbarians*."

"But I don't want to fight barbarians—" the drunk said, genuinely hurt, "some of my best friends are barbarians!"

"Don't tell anyone, or we might not get the job!" a third man warned.

Once the lady behind the desk saw that the microscope was working, she asked for my ID; I gave it to her and submitted to a retina scan, then she said, "When the shuttles from Independent Brazil have unloaded their passengers, we'll open the doors and begin final processing. Your immunizations will be given on ship. Until then, have a seat and relax, Mr. Osic."

I took a seat near the door, away from everyone else, and pulled the chest with Tamara in it near me. The man with the gray slacks kept singing. He didn't speak to anyone or make any overt signals. I wondered what people would think when they opened my trunk in customs. All they'd find was a zombie-eyed—Flaco would have loved that, would have called her Zombie Eyes—emaciated, little witch with a skull full of nightmares. Yet I clung to her.

A man just a few seats away was telling a joke: "I had a friend in Argentina who was awakened one night by someone pounding on the door: He thought it must be the Nicita Idealist Socialist Secret Police, so he ran and hid in his closet. The pounding continued, till finally the visitor broke down the door and forced his way into the house, then opened the closet: before my friend's eyes stood Death, all dressed in black.

"My friend shouted, 'Praise God! I thought it was the secret police!'"

"Death opened his mouth in surprise and said, 'They're not here yet? I must be early!'"

The joke brought only a few chuckles. Yet as I thought of it, I realized that the man in gray slacks was one of them—one of the secret police in the joke. It was not a comforting thought.

Perfecto went through the same procedure I had, then came and sat next to me.

The customs agent fed my ID into her computer, and began punching in commands. This made me nervous. Sweat began breaking out on my brow and upper lip. If Arish's death had been reported, she would know in a matter of minutes. On the far side of the room, five men sat along one wall. One small man with a pencil-bar mustache and long hair smoked a thin cigar. He was positioned so he could see the computer terminal, and he stared at it intently. He was different from the others, abnormally attentive. His white shirt was bright and clean—not rumpled and dirty—as was the attire of most of the rest of us. He stared at the monitor, then glanced up at me. Abruptly, the customs agent switched off her computer and rose from her chair. She didn't look at me as she left the room.

"Gringa pubic hair," a big mestizo muttered as the customs officer walked out the door. Everyone breathed a sigh of relief and laughed because we had all been made nervous by the domineering gringa's presence.

"Perhaps our smell finally drove her out," one of the Indians joked, and everyone laughed.

One heavyset man across the room said, "So, Perfecto, you have decided to come with us after all?"

"I did not decide; the people of my village decided for me," answered Perfecto.

"I'd have thought you'd be *alcalde* of that dirty little village by now," the heavyset man said.

"Ah, no. My wife gave birth to our eighth child three months ago. And just last week we found that she was pregnant again. When people heard of it, they became outraged and blamed me. Even the dogs snap at me."

Everyone laughed, but some of them gave him knowing glances, begging him with their eyes to say more.

"Unfortunately," Perfecto said, "I have not made love with my wife since the last baby!"

Among friends, such an admission would have brought loud laughs. But only a few people chuckled, while Perfecto laughed hard, painfully.

Across the room, the man with the clean white shirt and pencil mustache got up from his chair, stretched, and went over to the customs officers' computer. The hair rose on the back of my neck, and I fidgeted. He inserted one of my ID cards, and switched the computer on.

"Eight children!" a woman exclaimed, "You're lucky they didn't kill you!" Perfecto laughed again, almost maniacally. I looked again at the cut above his eye and the bruise on his jaw, just above the tattoo. Perhaps someone *had* tried to kill him, or at least tried to hurt him badly.

The man at the computer seemed to read my files with interest. My stomach churned; I couldn't decide what to do with my hands. Then he began punching many buttons, accessing files that had nothing to do with me. His actions caught the attention of the men he'd been sitting with. I wondered what he found that so interested him, and would have stopped him if I could have done so without attracting attention. *Jafari could have sent this man,* I thought. Then I realized he could be making calls over the computer, notifying Jafari's men that he'd found me. I became very frightened but pretended to ignore him and reached up and wiped the sweat from my brow.

"Señor, are you all right?" Perfecto asked.

I glanced over at him. "I'm fine, thank you."

"You don't look well," Perfecto said.

"I don't feel well," I answered truthfully.

"Malaria?"

"What?"

"You have malaria," Perfecto said. "I have seen it many times! People who have malaria turn pale and shake and sweat, just as you are doing."

"Yes, I have malaria," I said, glad that he did not see my fear.

"Shall I get you a doctor?" he asked.

"No, thank you," I said, "I am a doctor." Across the room, one of the singers chuckled, and I wondered if he chuckled because he could read my body language and knew I was afraid. My fear would give me away if I didn't do something quick. I would have reached for my medical bag and taken a tranquilizer, but I'd left my bag in the trunk to be a pillow for Tamara, and couldn't risk opening it. My fear cramped my chest, and made my breathing ragged. I remembered the conquistador cocktails I'd taken from Arish. I didn't know the strength of the prescription, but I was close to Arish's body weight, so I took a capsule and broke it between my teeth. It tasted like garlic, so sweet, so strong and heady. Like warm whiskey, it burned my lips and gums for a moment, then as the cocktail began to take effect, my face went numb.

Perfecto nodded, apparently satisfied that I had taken care of myself. He looked across the room to the computer where the man with the pencil-bar mustache was smiling, enjoying himself.

I felt my head swing forward as if it were a weight on a pendulum that traveled in a wide arc, and at the same moment I felt as if I were pushed into another world where I experienced heightened lucidity. Even though everything was blurred around the edges, if I looked at something straight on I saw its every crisp detail. I could read Perfecto's entire life story in his appearance: the veins in his neck throbbed, and the movement made the little lion's head on his tattoo lash back and forth, and I suddenly understood what the tattoo represented, and what Perfecto was—a chimera, one of the genetically upgraded men Torres had created to fight the wars in Chile. Yet because his ears weren't deformed, as were the ears of chimeras who had sonar, and because he was in his thirties, he must have been one of the early models, a truly upgraded human rather than a humanoid species. His eyes were wide-set, for greater depth perception; his thick hair concealed an enlarged skull, for greater intelligence; his neck and backbone were massive so that his frame could support the huge muscles of his body. Most people considered it taboo to marry such a creation, or even to carry its child full term. A chimera is even lower than an Indian. When he had fathered eight children, his community would truly have risen in an uproar. I saw all this in the throb of a heartbeat, while the cocktail slid down my throat, burning and numbing my neck and esophagus. I looked at the other people in the room, and saw that most of them were lost in reflection. Their eyes had the dulled quality I associated with the refugiados: burned out, lifeless, empty of hope. They had fought many wars in South America, and lost them all. All of them were poor; their dirty clothing attested to the fact that they lived in houses without floors. Only the man in the silver face was unreadable. And across the room was the man in gray slacks. He sat rigid, ready for action, and he purposely avoided looking at me.

I gauged the tension levels of the others in the room. Three men and two women were of the same age and build as Perfecto—they were chimeras, and I realized they were banding together, perhaps to settle in a new world where they could form a community so they would not be outcasts. On the ship would be many chimeras; knowledge of mercenary jobs would have spread through their community by word of mouth. I could read this in their faces as easily as reading the stories that Brazilian woodcarvers etch into the handles of their machetes. Only the man with the mustache and cigar seemed out of place. Different. His eyes glittered as if he stared into candlelight. He was aware. He was quieter than the others, more dangerous. He was looking at me.

It all seemed fascinating. Even the gray walls and a wad of paper beneath one chair fascinated me. My hands stopped shaking and my breathing felt less restricted, but my chest was thudding as if a rabbit were kicking against my ribs. I imagined I felt the cocktail slide into my belly and sit, burning like a live coal. Everyone was looking at the man behind the computer console. He was fascinating. He wore a fascinating clean white shirt, and when he moved his arm it left a fascinating white afterimage in the air behind it. His pencil-bar mustache and narrow face were fascinating. Like the face of a rat or a whorehouse owner. He was a leader here. He was a whorehouse rat, and he was hitting the buttons on the computer and laughing loudly in a fascinating manner.

His voice slurred. I heard him in slow motion. "My friends," he said, "I have interesting news." Fascinating. "Among us is a dangerous murderer!" Fascinating.

"No!" someone said. *Oh, yes,* I mouthed.

"It's true!" Whorehouse Rat said. Fascinating. "Even today, in Panamá," Panamá . . . Panamá . . . Panamá . . . " this murderer slit a man's throat!" Each word was like a fruit, like a ripe avocado. I could see his mouth forming the words, and when each syllable had grown and ripened on his tongue, he let it roll past his lips and plop to the floor. Fascinating. I knew something was terribly wrong: I couldn't think straight, and I wondered if it was because of the pill I'd taken, yet I didn't connect the problem to the morphine levels in the cocktail.

I did not like what Whorehouse Rat was saying. The cocktail burned in my stomach like a glowing ember, giving off waves of heat. I could feel the heat winding its way up my entrails, and I knew that if I kept my mouth closed, it would envelope my brain, consume me. So I opened my mouth and purposely spit the heat at Whorehouse Rat.

A yellow ripple in the air, like a fiery wheel, floated across the room as I blew the heat toward Whorehouse Rat. But just before the shimmering yellow ring reached him, Whorehouse Rat's skin turned blue and cold, so that when the ring enveloped him it only managed to bring his body heat up to normal. I swore under my breath because he had defeated my magical attack, so I blew wheels of fire at him in rapid succession and watched them float across the room as the syllables plopped from his mouth, one by one: "Pan a má, has, just, learned, where, the, kil ler, is. E ven, now, sta tion, se cur i ty, comes, to, take, the, vi cious, a ni mal, back, for, a, quick, ex e cu tion."

So, they are on their way to get me, I realized. *And now I will die. This should be fascinating.* The wheels of fire enveloped the Whorehouse Rat, but instead of burning, he moved his hand in the air and formed a mystic symbol. The fire closed around him like a womb, and he stood protected in a burning halo. He had defeated my attack, but I knew that all I had to do was hold my breath and the fire in me would build, would grow to a critical point until I could no longer contain it and I would blow apart like a fission bomb, killing us all. But before I did that, part of me realized I should try to escape.

I stood up and staggered around, smiling at the people in the room. Behind me were only empty corridors—no place to hide. I looked at the door that led to the air lock and beyond that to the ship. It was locked. I blew a ring of fire at it, to see if it would melt. It didn't. The faces of the people around me expressed various degrees of surprise, shock, and amusement at my predicament.

Whorehouse Rat laughed, and instead of plopping like avocados to the ground, his next words rushed like water churning through rocks. "Not even have I told you the good part! This fellow's victim, the man so brutally executed, was known to some of you: Arish Muhammad Hustanifad!"

A stream of water exuded from Whorehouse Rat's mouth, splashed against the walls, filled the room, knocked me to my knees and drowned the coal of fire in my belly, leaving me cold and naked. Several people gasped.

The chimera Perfecto jumped up and grabbed my shirt. "Truth? Is it true?" he shouted, and several other people yelled, "Is it true?" His hands were like iron, and I thought he would shake me and snap my neck. I could no longer breathe fire at him. I was too cold. My skin was turning blue and purple from the cold. I looked around the room; no one came to help me.

I became enraged because this chimera was touching me without permission. He dared to touch me! He dared to invade my privacy. He was bigger than me, and I'd heard rumors of his superhuman strength, and though he could kill me, I realized the cold in me was power, too—a magic power stronger than the flames I'd been breathing. *It looks as if you'll have to beat these insolent curs, keep them in line,* I thought.

"Of course I killed him, *puto,*" I shouted at Perfecto. I stood up. "And because you've touched me, I'll kill you, too!"

I brought my cold heavy leg up into his groin and at the same time clubbed him in the nose with a fist of ice. Drops of blood sprayed out of his nose in slow motion. Fascinating. He let go of me and sagged partway to the floor, gasping more from shock than from the cold. I kicked at his face, ready to sacrifice my leg, to let it shatter against his skull so shards of ice would spray out and puncture his flesh. But his hand came up in slow motion and grabbed my foot and twisted it and I heard the bones of ice in my ankle snap as he threw me. I rose in the air so that for a moment I seemed to be standing in the air a meter off ground, and I imagined I looked like Christ ascending into heaven as I slammed against the wall.

Everyone in the room stared up at me with their mouths shaped in little O's of surprise. Fascinating. The air whooshed out of me from the blow, and I sagged onto the chairs and fell to the floor.

Now I will have to kill them all, and I'll have to do it with my ankle broken. I got up and screamed in rage and threw myself at a chimera woman. I became tons of ice flying at her, an unstoppable glacier. She stared at me, frightened, clutching the handles of her chair, then leaned back and brought up a leg made of stone; her boot smashed my face, splintering the ice in me. Fascinating.

I should have eaten more reptiles, I thought as a wave of red washed before my eyes and the world faded to a cold, distant, black pinpoint.

* * *

Red and white clouds swirled and resolved into a shape. Whorehouse Rat was smoking his cigar, breathing smoke into my face. He was the one who was out of place here! He had come to kill me! I knew it as surely as I knew my own name. I screamed and tried to swing, but my arms were pinned behind my back.

"Overdose . . . Overdose . . . Overdose. Cocktails," he said, moving his cigar with his tongue so the glowing end tipped down at an angle. It left a fiery afterimage in the air. Fascinating.

"But he only took one," someone said.

Yes, I thought, *but what dosage?* I screamed in rage at the Whorehouse Rat.

He slapped my face. "What day is it?"

I tried to answer, but couldn't remember. It seemed very important. The act of trying to think made my head ache. I began to laugh. In the snap of a finger, everything became very lucid again. And the lucidity was funny. I kept laughing.

"You've had an overdose of cocktails," Whorehouse Rat yelled. "Calm down!" I looked at his face. He had two thin silver tears tattooed beneath his eyes. I had seen such marks before, in the ghettos of Colón and Panamá City. Gang leaders wore them to advertise how many rivals they'd executed: one tear for each killing. They were very funny tattoos. I began laughing and weeping at the joke implicit in the tattoos.

Outside the customs office, a gringo shouted, "Angelo Osic, come out with your hands on your head!" I couldn't stop laughing.

"We're trying to help you!" Rat Face explained. "See!" Someone twisted my head around so I could see everyone in the room. Some people were sprawled on the floor, aiming long-barreled plasma rifles at the door. Others were suited in body armor painted in jungle shades of nonreflective green and dull red, waiting to fight anyone who came in. Perfecto wore only armored gloves. The man who'd played the guitar wore laser-targeting goggles and aimed a rocket launcher with four minirockets at the door.

The man with gray slacks stood weaponless and armorless against the wall, frowning, obviously upset by the turn of events, nervously watching me. He was very funny, and I laughed harder. All the duffel bags were dumped on the floor. Clothes, ammunition, and grenades spilled from every bag. "See!" Rat said. "We will help you. Perfecto says you are lucky, and you fight like a jaguar—a stupid, weak jaguar, but full of fury at least. Besides, you have avenged General Tapia today when you killed Arish. You have heard of Tapia?"

I tried to remember. My head ached. "Chile," I said, but the single word sounded so funny I just smiled and could remember nothing more.

"Yes, that's right," Rat Face said. "He was murdered in Chile by that *cabrón* you killed today! We had Arish on trial, but someone poisoned his guards and he escaped. Remember?"

I didn't remember. *Cabrón*, goat fucker, that was a funny word. I said it over and over. "*Cabrón, cabrón, cabrón.*"

Whorehouse Rat continued, "We will tie you up now, because we cannot trust you while the drugs are still working in your blood. Okay?"

"Wait!" I said, remembering the man in gray slacks. Someone stuck a gag in my mouth and tied my hands behind my back. Because my ankle was broken, I couldn't get up. My muscles strained at the cords, but it was no use, and I watched the man in gray slacks and laughed.

The man who'd tied my hands whispered, "You'll be fine. I'll take good care of you." He stood behind me, so I couldn't see his face, but he tapped my arm with the barrel of a fifty-caliber Rivas bush rifle to show me he was armed.

Out in the corridor, the gringo yelled over a loudspeaker, "Angelo Osic, come out with your hands on your head."

Of course, I was tied up and couldn't come out. This seemed like a very poignant observation, and I would

have notified the man who held the loudspeaker about
my predicament, but I couldn't because I was gagged. I
just laughed at the irony of my situation.

Everyone in the room waited anxiously for something
to happen, but no one broke through the door. Some
people began to stretch, and one young man yawned as
if bored. Some others saw him, and they began yawning
too, as if to see who could feign the most boredom.
Finally, in an effort to lure the security team into the
ambush, a woman with a plasma rifle yelled, "Help!
Help! He's got a gun. He say's he'll kill us all!"

Several people in the room snickered. And I agreed
that her ploy was among the funniest things I'd ever
heard. I began crying and laughing and became afraid I
would choke to death on my gag because I couldn't
breathe and laugh at the same time.

One young man from the yawning team smiled and
shot a flechette into the ceiling. "Get back in line, you,"
he yelled, and several men screamed as if in terror or
pain while one of the youths made animal noises like pigs
and monkeys. Little pieces of plastic fell from the ceiling
as if it were wounded. This caused terrible spasms of
laughter in me, and I began choking; every time I caught
my breath a little I would laugh again. Some men looked
at me and pointed and chuckled, and they were still
trying to stifle their laughter when the station's security
guards ran into the room to rescue the "hostages."

There were six security guards wearing pretty space-
blue armor and carrying stunners, and they didn't have
a chance.

When the first man came through the door, Perfecto
slugged him in the chest so hard that the guard's armor
split, sending shards of enamel to skitter across the floor.
The sound of Perfecto's fist crashing into the armor
startled me, and I realized it wasn't funny. The second
man in line shot Perfecto with a stunner, and Perfecto
went down, but four mercenaries immediately jumped
the guard. He was huge, and he slugged two of them and
sent them flying, and one of them hit the wall and
vanished, and I screamed as I realized it was a hallucination even though it looked so real.

The boys from the yawning team showed terror on their faces. Every time the big guard hit someone, two more people jumped him. A young man popped the snaps on the guard's helmet and pulled it off, so the chimeras could slug the man in the face. Someone slammed the door behind the security guards, blocking their escape. There were two armored mercenaries to every guard, and the mercenaries just held the guards and beat the hell out of them, stripped off their armor, dragged them to a wall, and stuffed them under the chairs, where they moaned, naked.

There were several moments of silence, and the mercenaries used the lull to get six more men in armor. The man with the gray slacks had moved closer. He was inching toward me. I began laughing again, but this time out of nervousness, and my arms seemed to strain of their own volition at the cords that held me. Perfecto clawed the air as he struggled to regain consciousness, and someone pulled him away from the door. A chimera went and stood in front of the door and stared as if he were trying to see through it. His ears swung out from the side and pricked up, like the ears of a dog. This frightened me because I had never seen such a thing and I thought it was a hallucination, but as I watched, his ears remained rigid and I knew it was real.

"Someone's coming!" the chimera said, smiling. "I hear a remote! Or maybe a robot!"

The guitarist with the rocket launcher ran up to the door, and everyone held their breath. The man with the gray slacks was moving closer to me, was only an arm's length away, and I saw that he held a knife in his palm. I tried to nudge my guard to get his attention, and I was not aware of any sound, but suddenly all the chimeras in the room yelled, "Now!" as the man with the rockets kicked open the door and fired.

An armored remote the size of a small tank hunched behind the door. One missile hit the power plant to the remote's chemical lasers. A tongue of fire lashed into our room and I felt I knew what it would be like to stare down the throat of a dragon. People screamed. The concussion peeled back the metal walls of the customs office, denting it out of shape, and flung me against the wall. The man with the missile launcher flew through the air and hit the wall above me, then slid down on top of me. Shrapnel and pieces of remote shot into the walls, and dark smoke billowed from the remote's metal innards. A distant fire alarm shrilled. Tons of debris drifted down from a hole that opened in the ceiling.

One man staggered across the room, holding his eyes, choking in the smoke. Another woman writhed on the floor and screamed, a piece of metal the size of a crowbar lodged in her arm. Others were bleeding from various wounds. Blood had splattered my shirt, and I thought I'd taken a hit. I tried to scream, and looked around for help, and saw the man in gray slacks lying crumpled beside me. A pipe as thick as my arm was lodged in his hip, and a large piece of metal had caved in the right side of his face. The blood was from him. His hands still twitched. And I realized I still didn't know who his accomplice was.

Through the smoke I could see that a crowd of station workers had gathered a hundred meters down the corridor to watch the fight. The concussion had thrown them to the floor. Some of them lay screaming. Blood was smeared on the corridor walls.

All the mercenaries who wore armor untangled themselves from the floor and began cheering as they charged down the corridor and shot into the ceiling. They ran to the fallen and wounded station technicians and began rounding up hostages. I looked at the others in the room: Three armorless mercenaries were wounded but conscious, including the man with the silver face; two others were dead. Perfecto had been sheltered from the blast, and he sat against the dented wall, rubbing his head. Several naked guards had shrapnel wounds; two guards were dead.

Perfecto looked around the room for a moment, then said, "I need a drink," and picked his way among the bodies and wreckage and headed down the corridor.

My head ached and my mind felt numb. But I noticed something strange: as the mercenaries moved among their hostages, they moved with vigor. They seemed a great contrast to the haggard men I'd seen earlier. Their steps seemed almost choreographed, a dance of joy.

Within a few minutes Perfecto returned with a keg of Aguila beer. He sat beside me, gave me a drink, and talked. I was too stunned to answer his questions, so he carried on a rambling monologue, telling me how it was obvious I was a man with great luck. "Just look at all the friends you've found in your hour of need! Think of all the good things we'll be able to loot from the station. Is there anything you want? Drugs? Liquor? Anything at all?"

Soon others began filing in with food and rum. They sprayed bandages on the wounded and filled their bellies with food. A couple mercenaries forced rum down the throats of captured guards, and several mercenaries gathered around the big guard who'd caused too much trouble. They praised him for his strength and courage and told him he should leave the punks in the security team and come fight on Baker, and when he was drunk enough he agreed it was a good idea. Everyone sang and ate and drank, and I became very tired and all my muscles ached and my head ached, so I stretched my muscles until they relaxed. The singing and the wails of people and sirens and the sputtering of small fires became a distant rushing in my ears that lulled me to sleep.

I woke in a small gray room, tied to a chair. A dignified man with silver hair was leaning over me, and Whorehouse Rat sat on the floor behind him, the light catching the gleam of tattooed tears. The man with the silver hair asked how I'd managed to kill Arish. I looked into his dark eyes and my whole soul desired to answer him, but I couldn't think straight, could hardly remember my own name. I wanted to go back to sleep, but the man said I couldn't sleep until I told him everything, and this seemed eminently reasonable. So, as best I could, I related how Arish had strangled Flaco and tried to kill me, and how I'd shot Arish and used his eye to trick the shuttle into bringing me to the space station. I could only remember the story in parts, brief unrelated flashes. I told him about Tamara and Jafari and the AIs. He made me repeat several parts of the story over and over, and each time his request seemed very reasonable and I wished to answer perfectly. When I fell asleep, he'd jab my ribs to waken me. He grilled me about Jafari and asked me to name the AIs. But I didn't know the names of the AIs who'd aided the socialists. He seemed very curious about Tamara, and began asking about her dreams, and when I told him how I'd wakened from the final dream unable to think, he became excited and his eyes gleamed. "Did you hear that! Did you hear that! I told you someone with her talent existed!" he said. I wanted to ask what he meant by "her talent," but I could not think straight. He looked at Whorehouse Rat and said threateningly, "Keep this quiet! Whatever you hear, keep it quiet!"

Whorehouse Rat nodded and smiled at me and said, "Of course, General."

The general said, "Tell me about the dream again, the darkness washing over you. What did it feel like? What do you remember after that?"

I repeated Tamara's last dream over and over again as I begged him to let me sleep. My head hurt from trying to remember. The darkness coming out of her mouth, the cold numbness, and myself crying at a sense of loss was all I could recall. I could remember nothing concrete after the darkness hit me, but the general kept trying to draw out something more.

He yelled, "Her job in Intelligence. Did she say what it was? Did she give you any hint?"

"No."

"Think harder!" he said, grabbing my hand. "Any hint at all? This is crucial!"

I shook my head and realized I thought I'd known something about Tamara, that she'd seemed all-important to me. I'd been willing to give my life for her, but suddenly I was confronted by the knowledge that she was still a stranger.

"Did she live?" the general asked. "Where did you see her last?"

And then I remembered I'd brought her with me. I

was afraid I'd been asleep for days, that Tamara had suffocated. "I put her in a trunk. She's in a coma. It's a brown trunk made of teak, with elephants carved on it. I left it at the station!"

Someone who'd been standing behind me left the room, and Whorehouse Rat followed. As the door opened, I smelled oily smoke. A moment later a medic and the Rat dragged in the teak chest and flipped it open. Tamara was breathing easily, staring at the ceiling, zombie-eyed.

The general bent over the chest and examined her, caressed her arm with one finger. "Thank God," he said. He turned to the medic, "Keep this socialist whore alive!"

The Whorehouse Rat pulled out a cigar and lit it, inhaling deeply. He looked as if he'd just conquered a country. He said, "You know, I think that a man like me, a man who captured a whole space station with only a handful of men, pitting a mere twenty soldiers against hundreds, could be very valuable to you. No? A man with my talents would make a fine captain!"

The general glared at him, and spoke menacingly. "Idiot! How dare you? You want a promotion for murdering unarmed civilians?"

The Rat's eyes smoldered. He exhaled his cigar smoke evenly. "I am not an idiot. I saved a valuable man from slaughter at the hands of the socialists, and I brought you an important prisoner. I took over Sol Station with very little bloodshed, and when you think upon it, I'm sure you will realize the rashness of your decision. Think about it. We have two years on ship before we reach Baker—plenty of time for you to show me your gratitude. We *will* be going to Baker with you—my men, Señor Osic, and the socialist whore—am I not right? It would not be wise to leave even one of us behind, knowing what we know."

The general frowned, appearing to weigh the consequences. He reached down to Tamara and ran his finger along her jawline, caressing her. "For this, I thank you, Mavro. We can manage to bring you, I think," he said heavily. "Baker citizenship, and no extradition."

I started to nod off. My eyes were closing, and I no longer wanted to keep them open. I made a snoring sound and startled myself awake.

The general turned to me and said, "Thank you, don Angelo. You have done well today. Very well. You may go to sleep, now. You're safe. You are going to Baker, with your friends."

And though I was troubled because I suddenly remembered that one of Jafari's men was still on board and I didn't know his identity, I was too tired to speak, so I closed my eyes and slept.

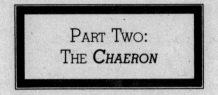

PART TWO:
THE *CHAERON*

CHAPTER

4

I was standing in the jungle at dusk, in a deep crater filled with jagged black rocks. Around the rim of the crater, thousands of shadowy spider monkeys capered and shrieked, throwing stones and debris down from the clifftop. I was surrounded by large boulders, and across each sprawled a dying person covered with a white sheet. Flaco lay in front of me with his throat slashed, one hand dangling over the lip of his boulder, and I needed to sew the pieces of his esophagus together quickly if I was to save him. Tamara lay face down, slumped over a sharp rock to his right, her fever burning high, brain cells dying at a tremendous rate as she waited for an injection of antimosin. Behind me, Arish also lay on a low flat stone with a slashed throat. He tugged the back of my shirt to beg for help, but I was too busy caring for Flaco.

I bent close in the failing light and stitched at Flaco's throat. The rip in his esophagus lay between the triangular circoid cartilage just above the Adam's apple and the first ring of tracheal cartilage beneath—a region hard to treat quickly, since there could be major damage to his vocal cords. But I had no time to worry about niceties like restitching vocal cords. I had never performed anything but minor home-surgeries, yet I stitched the esophagus together rapidly, hoping I was doing it right. The monkeys on the crater's rim shrieked and howled, and I could not think straight, could not decide if I was stitching the right pieces together. The lower section of esophagus suddenly seemed to appear very much like a section of small intestine. I sewed anyway, shook my head at the damage to Flaco's severed spinal column. He would require much care, more than I could afford to give at the moment. His blood seeped down and stained the white sheet so gently lying over him.

I looked for a clean stone on which to set my bloody sutures, and a small girl, perhaps ten years old, appeared to my left. I handed them to her, and she said, "Thank you, Grandfather," and smiled at me. I looked at her face—a thin face with prominent features, skin as pale as a European's and as smooth as a china doll's. She seemed familiar and I was glad to see her, but I could not put a name to her.

I rushed over to Tamara's slumped figure lying on a rock, filled a syringe with antimosin, gently lifted her head, and injected the antimosin into her neck. Arish tugged at my shirt.

"How about some help over here? I'm dying! How about some help over here?" he yelled.

I glanced back at him, surprised at how well he spoke with his throat cut. Beads of sweat dotted his face, and his pupils were constricted from fear. He tugged at my shirt again, and I slapped his hand away.

"I'm busy!" I said.

"Too busy to help me, you old fucker? Too busy to help me?" His feet started kicking, and he thrashed around. Arish's legs kicked, made a big whuff, whuff sound as they scraped the sheets and billowed them out, and I knew he was dying.

But suddenly the monkeys at the crater's rim

*all let out a roar. Flaco arched his back and
cried out; his stitches tore, and the blood
poured out. Tamara's eyes started to glaze, and
I knew she needed another injection. Arish
raised his hands and held them out, as if
pleading for mercy from the air.*

Startled, I awoke on a cot in a coffin-sized tube with a
single, dim overhead light. The white plastic walls
smelled new, and piped-in salsa music trumpeted a
gaiety that didn't reflect the way I felt. The vision of
Arish with a wound in his throat filled my mind, and I
tried to push it away, concentrate on something else. My
broken ankle was braced to the cot, so I couldn't see my
leg, but an ache like an old wasp sting told me the
doctors had inserted needles so they could glue my
bones together, a time-consuming process usually reserved for athletes.

I knew I should remain immobile for at least three
hours so the glue could set. I looked toward my feet for
a clock. There was none. I was in a convalescence tube
like those in Chinese hospitals, but usually the tube has
some amenities—a clock, a drinking straw, a dream
monitor. This one appeared empty, except for the
blaring radio.

I should find Tamara, I thought. *I should check her
hormone fusion pump, take care of her hand.* It had
been three days—long enough for a thin layer of undifferentiated cells to grow over her wound. Now was the
time to paint a new wash over the cells, administer the
hormones that would order a hand to regenerate. Otherwise, the undifferentiated cells would just keep growing like a cancer. I thought, *I should also see if she has
any major brain damage, see if the log-phases and
antimosin did the trick.* The general I'd spoken with had
wanted her alive. I supposed someone was caring for
her. But still I thought I should check.

I remembered the blood pumping from Arish's throat,
a red trickle over ebony skin. I tried to force the memory
back, but could not concentrate. I felt as if I had a cold
lump in my brain. I tried to pinpoint the cold spot, to

visualize where it lay, and it seemed to move aside. Morphine overdoses can make it difficult for one to concentrate for several days, but this seemed more than a simple drug reaction. The cold spot felt alive, conscious, like an animal, a large black fly buzzing in my head, batting away thoughts with its wings while stirring up unpleasant images.

The incidents from the past three days gave off a pervasive sense of wrongness, and the more I considered it, the more likely it appeared I was going—no, had gone—insane. This was my reasoning: When I was young, don José Mirada, a rather eccentric friend to my father, counseled me to serve society. He believed society always rewards best those who serve it best, and destroys those who refuse to serve it. For example, the owner of the clinic in our small town always invested much in his business. Because of this, he had medical equipment other hospitals lacked, so people came from far away to visit his facility. This made him very rich and famous. He had many friends and a beautiful wife, and no one envied him, because they felt he deserved everything he got. Society rewarded him for the service he performed. But the don also pointed out that the man of the world, the man who behaves toward society as a parasite behaves toward its host, is never secure. Dictators, dishonest businessmen, or those who become parasites of the social institutions will often be destroyed. If society does not squash them outright, it will destroy their spirits and they will find no lasting happiness.

To prove his point, don José would dress in his white suit and get his gold-handled walking stick, then take me to the market in our village to point out some of the more wretched people on the street, all the time lecturing me about how society had destroyed their lives. "Look at Osvaldo," he would say, indicating a merchant. "See how miserable he is. Always in the market he tries to sell his clothes for twice their value, so when fashions change he must give the clothes away to unload his old merchandise. Because of his greed, no one buys from him except when he is desperate to sell, and he will die in poverty!

Remember how society hates the greedy, Angelo, and learn from this man's misfortune." Or again, pointing to a handsome couple, "Look at Juan, he cheated on his old wife and married his lover. Now his new wife doesn't trust him to walk across the street alone! She clings to him like a hangman's rope. Unwittingly she has become the avatar of her society's conscience, and she punishes him mercilessly for his infidelity."

Don José Mirada argued that there was great wisdom in letting consensus morality guide one in times when moral codes seemed a burden, and he said we should obey laws even when they seemed irrelevant.

I eventually came to believe there was truth to his argument, and I've often wondered if at some subconscious level I chose a career in medicine so I could best serve society and thus gain its greatest rewards. If this is true, my morality is an external artifice produced by greed. But I have always wanted to believe I serve society from the heart and that the rewards society gives in return are incidental. Indeed, philosophers say the greatest happiness comes to those who learn to live without wealth, or fame. And if this is true, then the *rewards* society offers those who serve it are only grains of dust that blind men to the true happiness that comes from the *act* of serving. I have preferred to believe this, for it feels more right to my heart.

But killing Arish was an act society did not condone—not when I had disabled him and had him at my mercy. Society jealously guards the right to retribution. In fact, because I had violated society's right to retribution by killing Arish, my society would now try to punish me. So, when I'd killed Arish, at the very least I acted contrary to one of my most fundamental beliefs about how the world operates: I had violated consensus morality. Though Arish was a socialist, a murderer, a man dedicated to the belief that he could only advance his own Nicita Idealist doctrines by destroying me and my society, though he represented all this—yet I could not justify killing him. The fact that I acted inconsistent with my beliefs seemed a sure sign of insanity.

I reasoned further that killing Arish had been very

impulsive, and I have never been impulsive. Only once had I seriously considered killing a man, and that had been long ago. Even then it was not an impulsive act: when I was young, Gonzalvo Quintanilla, an army general with big cocaine connections in Australia, tried to overthrow Guatemala. For three days he led a reign of terror from Panzós to Belize. But his men were only interested in looting homes and raping women, and they felt no loyalty, so his regime fell. I was at school in Mexico City at the time, and when I learned my mother had been killed by Quintanilla's looters, I rushed home.

Though my mother had been murdered two days earlier, I found my father sitting in a chair in the living room, staring at the wall and weeping like a child. My sister Eva tried to comfort him while her three children ran about the house playing. My father would not reply when I spoke to him, but Eva took me aside and showed me where Mother had died. Dried blood still smeared the walls and floor tiles in the doorway between the kitchen and dining room—even after much cleaning Eva had been unable to wash it off—and as I crouched to inspect the stains I could smell the blood and could see dried, flaking droplets on the wall behind the china cabinet.

"How did this happen?" I asked.

"Five of Quintanilla's soldiers came in the house to loot. Neighbors heard shooting. When the soldiers left, the neighbors came and found her dead," Eva said.

"How do they say she died?"

"No one will say."

I went from house to house, asking how my mother had been killed. The only answer I got was from an old gray-headed woman: "She didn't lose her virtue. She tried to fight those rapists off, and that counts with God. No virtue is lost if you try your best to fight them off!"

Even in her forties my mother had been a desirable woman. I was sure her killers had abused her. With so much blood around, I feared they had not left her in one piece.

I armed myself with a revolver. For weeks I stalked the streets at night, evading military police who'd come to squash the rebellion, searching in bars and alleys, hoping to find someone who wore the uniform of Quintanilla's soldiers. Every time I saw a scruffy teenager I imagined he'd been with Quintanilla, wondered if he was responsible for my mother's death. I never found the men I searched for, and was never able to spend my rage by putting a bullet in someone.

Even as I remembered this incident, my fists tightened and my anger burned. I sweated and trembled with rage. This scared me: I hadn't felt such fierce emotion since my youth. It seemed to validate my theory that I had gone insane.

I thought of Arish. If he'd lived in Guatemala during the revolt, he would have raped my mother and strewn her pieces around the house. I told myself I should be glad I'd killed him, but my chest burned with guilt.

I felt the fly flapping in my head and wondered when I had gone insane. It seemed only right that I should be able to remember the precise moment. Had it happened at Flaco's death? I had been shocked and saddened, but I couldn't remember feeling any different in the head. Did it happen when Arish attacked me? Or when I found that Panamá would extradite me? Had it been when I first saw Tamara staring at the ceiling like a zombie? So many bad things had happened, one of them must certainly have been the trigger.

But I could not recall when the fly had entered my head. Even now I was on my way to fight a war I knew nothing about while an assassin waited for an opportunity to strike. In fact, I lay in this tube weaponless, open to attack at any moment. The tube was like a giant drawer to a cabinet; anyone could open the drawer to strangle me. I was in more danger now than ever.

My hands began to shake, and I wanted to escape the tube, but my foot was anchored to the floor. I tried squeezing to the bottom of the tube to release the brace, but the tube was too narrow and I couldn't reach the buckles that strapped my foot. I kicked at the brace. When facing Arish, I hadn't had time to contemplate my circumstances, and so had not been afraid. But now a wave of terror filled me. I struggled to free myself, gulping air, sweat streaming down my sides.

I recalled the words of the metaphysicist Pío Baroja: "It is characteristic of Nature that when it intends to destroy you, it does so thoroughly." Certainly it seemed that Nature had led me to this place with unerring calculation—stripping me of my position in the community, snatching away my hopes for the future, sucking the life from my best friend. And as I considered all the bad things that had happened to me, it was almost as if a voice whispered in my ear, saying, "Just remember, no matter what bad things have happened, the worst is yet to come."

The certainty that this was true filled me with wonder and dread. A pure terror pierced me, and I lay like a moth pinned and flapping on a board. All my twisting and shouting would come to nothing. I could kick my legs, but there was nowhere to run.

My leg ached from straining at the brace. I remembered the mean dog that had stepped in Rodrigo's trap. He had twisted off his own foot, extricating himself with as little personal loss as possible. It was a grim choice to make. Yet, like the dog, I knew it was the only choice to make. I'd lost my home in Panamá, my good name, my best friend—and something more. I had lost my grip on reality, my own understanding of who I was. The sum of these losses was overwhelming, yet I resolved to keep my life.

The radio started a song, and to the blare of the trumpets I repeated the litany, "The worst is yet to come; the worst is yet to come," and filled myself with a new toughness. I clenched my fists and pumped my arms, strengthening them. I felt powerful and vicious. Almost I hoped Jafari's assassin would come. For if he opened the convalescence tube, he'd be within my grasp.

When I calmed, I noticed two buttons on the ceiling above and behind my head. It was a stupid place to put the buttons. One said, Call for Assistance; the other said, Push to Open. I touched the Open button and a latch sprung behind me. The cot rolled out, and I found myself a meter off the floor in an empty operating room. I sat up and removed my foot from the brace.

I lowered myself to the floor, careful not to put any weight on my bad leg. The floor vibrated slightly, and I could feel that the ship was spaceborne. The whole room smelled of new plastic and sterile surfaces. It was spotless, empty. I expected a nurse or a doctor to come in at any moment and tell me to get back into bed.

I left the drawer ajar so I could hear the music pumping into the convalescence tube. I found a crystalline-display note pad above my convalescence tube, and by thumbing the button on the pad I found I was to be released at 20:15. A clock beside the message showed the time—20:07. The glue in my leg had set.

When I'd brought her on ship, Tamara had certainly been too ill to check into a cabin, so I decided to search for her in the convalescence tubes, hoping to learn her condition. Only one tube appeared occupied, and the note pad above it listed the patient as male. I opened thirty other tubes, and found them all empty. When I was half done, the music on the radio stopped and an announcer said, "This is Carlos Carrera with Panamá City's current news."

I quit searching tubes, surprised to learn the salsa music came from Panamá.

"Police in Colón have identified the corpse of a man who was dug up in a banana field this afternoon as 'Flaco' Alejandro Contento Rivera, a resident of Colón and former friend of the desperado Angelo Himinez Osic.

"Reports say Rivera was stabbed in the throat, just as Osic's earlier victim, the notorious Arish Muhammad Hustanifad, had been. Rivera is known to have possessed much hard currency before his death, and police believe Osic murdered him for money. Osic may have used the currency later in the day to bribe the mercenaries on Sol Station who helped him flee justice.

"In this second murder, police have uncovered an eyewitness . . ."

A female interviewer with a high voice like the twitter of a parakeet introduced the Chilean woman I'd met in

the banana fields. The Chilean said, "Flaco, he was
talking to me in the tent, then he went outside for a
minute. I heard him scream, and I ran outside and saw
that devil, Osic, standing over Flaco, holding a knife. I
screamed and Osic ran away. I got scared and started
packing up to leave, but then Osic, he came back with a
shovel and threatened to kill me. He took a whole bunch
of money out of Flaco's pockets, then he buried him and
told me he'd kill me if I ever told. I have been too
frightened to speak about it. I have been scared to
death."

The interviewer chirped, "Are you certain it was
Osic?"

"Yes, I'm certain. I got a good look at him!" the
Chilena said.

Carrera announced, "Besides Panamá and West Islamidad, three other nations have joined in demand for
Osic's extradition back to Earth, asking that he face
charges for planting the bomb that devastated Sol Station, killing seven people and injuring thirty-six.

"Police who had been searching Lake Gatún for the
injured woman last known to have been living in the
home of Osic have shifted their search to the banana
field where Rivera was buried. An eyewitness saw Osic
and the woman—"

I slammed the convalescence tube closed so I could no
longer hear the radio. The news sickened me. I have
never trusted the news media, and the things I'd just
heard reaffirmed my paranoia. I was consoled by the
knowledge that I had been right to flee Panamá. With
media coverage like that, I'd have been lucky to live long
enough to get the firing squad. But as I considered, my
mood brightened. The police were searching for Tamara's body: whatever else had happened, Tamara had
escaped unnoticed. Jafari and the Alliance might well
believe Arish had killed Tamara and disposed of her
body, then had been killed when he returned for me. I
could hardly believe it—Tamara could well be safe!

I opened the tube again and switched radio stations till
I found some good music, Los Arpones singing "My
Heart Cries." The thought that Tamara may have totally

eluded the Alliance lifted my spirits so sharply that I
wanted to dance. I was opening another tube, when a
woman entered the operating room.

I jumped away from the tube. She was a chimera with
chocolate-colored hair of a shade I'd never seen before.
A silver kimono with red dragons appeared to be her
only clothing, leaving her tan legs bare. Her shoulders
were broad and muscular in a feminine way, the way a
gymnast's body is firm. She carried a white shirt draped
over her arm, and a bowl of green soup in her hand. I
thought she must be the nurse.

She stopped just inside the door. "Are you looking for
something?" she asked, nodding toward the convalescence tube I'd opened.

"I had a friend with me when I came in. I thought
she'd be here."

"No women were brought in with you," she said.
"Most of your friends from Sol Station are on another
module of the ship. You won't be able to visit until we
reach Baker. No one is allowed to pass between
modules."

I looked in the chimera's eyes—dark brown with
strange streaks of silver in them, like webs of light—and
I knew I had never seen her before. She hadn't been one
of the mercenaries at Sol Station. She said in a joking
tone, "Our beloved employer regrets that for modesty's
sake you must wear this fifty-nine grams of clothing,"
and she tossed a pair of white underwear and a white
kimono onto the bed beside me and smiled a tight-
lipped smile, as if struggling to be pleasant.

"Our employer regrets what?"

"I think the Japanese originally planned to hire only
men, and you'd have flown naked. Fifty-nine grams
times ten thousand mercenaries is a lot of extra weight—
so they regret paying to haul it." She handed me the
soup, then pulled two convalescence-tube drawers open
all the way, sat on one of the beds, and motioned for me
to be seated on the bed across from her.

I felt embarrassed. My hospital gown was too short, so
my privates felt exposed, and my gown was open in the

back. I picked up the clothes and started looking for a place to change.

"It's okay," she said, "I've seen sweet potatoes before." She jutted her chin, motioning toward my privates. I decided it was okay, and pulled the underwear on. She averted her eyes by looking at the ceiling.

When I had put on the kimono top, she said, "You missed the orientation meetings yesterday, so I thought I'd fill you in. I'm Abriara Sifuentes, commander of your combat team. There are five of us on the team. You've met some others: my big brother, Perfecto. You'll get to meet Zavala soon enough. Mavro's on our team. You look surprised."

"I had thought you were a nurse," I said. *Mavro, the Whorehouse Rat.* I remembered the little man with the tattooed tears. My stomach turned at the thought of being in a combat team with him. In my drug-induced delirium I'd been sure he was out to kill me, and first impressions die hard. The big chimera, Perfecto, on the other hand, seemed like a good person. I looked at the soup. Out of mere politeness I said, "I'll be happy to serve under your command."

Abriara laughed. "Some would think it a slap in the face."

"How so?"

"There are seven hundred combat teams on this module, and yours is the only one led by a woman. Truthfully, I'm not as qualified to lead as either Mavro or Perfecto. You'll be the subject of much ridicule. You may not be able to suffer such a blow to your machismo." She waved her hand as if to dismiss the problem, an overly animated gesture typical of Chilean women.

"You don't really expect trouble from one of us?"

She shrugged. "That depends—will you give me trouble?"

I laughed. "You can't be serious. Who cares about machismo? That's so old-fashioned! I can't imagine any of us giving you trouble." I couldn't keep from gazing into her eyes, the silver webs of light, they were mesmerizing.

Abriara appeared concerned. "You treat it as a joke, don Angelo, as a man of your background would. But to men here on ship, machismo is no joke. Many of them were culled from prisons in Peru and Colombia, where men who have been stripped of everything else cling to their dignity. You've seen Mavro's tattoos—a symbol of bravery he got for murdering two boys in the ghettos of Cartagena. You've never been part of his world, or you would know that to him machismo is no joke. And Zavala, he's young and eager to prove himself.

"And I must warn you that among the chimeras we feel something very strongly, something akin to machismo." She struggled for a definition. "Call it . . . pride of position. Torres created chimeras for his soldiers—and only males were created to fight, though we women learned to fight since. But the men still jealously guard their role as warriors: they allow us to fight, but never with rank or title. Never has a female chimera commanded a male in battle. And I do not know how Perfecto will react. He may respect my skills, but it won't be enough to control him. We have another bond that I hope will prove stronger: we were both baptized Catholic. He might treat me with dignity for fear of God."

I must have appeared incredulous at this. Only a few rogue priests will dare defy the Vatican to baptize a chimera.

Abriara saw my expression and said, "It happens. So, he may feel some loyalty to me, perhaps enough, being Catholic. To make sure, I'd like you to speak to him for me."

I shrugged. "If you like." I did not see how my words could affect him. She frowned a bit, upset that I hadn't made a stronger commitment. I couldn't judge how Perfecto would treat her, but I could judge how humans would treat her. I'd occasionally met men in Panamá who held machismo as an ideal, but I thought of them as anachronisms. Such a person could indeed give her trouble. "It seems to me that the one you need to fear most is Mavro. I know for a fact that he wants to be a captain, yet the general has made him a private beneath the only woman leader. He may take it hard."

She laughed, a high-pitched unpleasant laugh meant

to be disarming. "I think I like you," she said. "From your tone, you sound very concerned about me. I like that in a person. Still . . . you may be right. I don't trust him much. He sits on his bed and glares at me."

"That is not a good sign," I warned.

She nodded. "Indeed. Also, don Angelo, some people have been talking about you. Several governments want to extradite you back to Earth. And some people fear the Allied Earth Marines will board ship to take you. Some men discussed the possibility of turning you in, and Mavro threatened to kill anyone who spoke of it. He called them 'steers,' and they backed down for now. But Mavro is using this whole affair as an excuse to prove his machismo. Sooner or later he'll start a fight. Maybe he'll kill someone. Anyone who gets within arm's length of Mavro—they're the ones in danger."

I considered this. She was right. "So, what should we do?"

Abriara looked up at the ceiling and shrugged. "I'll think about it."

And unlike most people, who only say they'll think about things and then never do, she stopped talking and looked up in the air and almost immediately appeared to lose herself in concentration, so I picked up the soup and began to eat. The green algae tasted like broccoli. My ankle still ached, so I got off the cot, found a refrigerator, and got out a tube of cortisone cream. I sat at a desk in the corner and applied the cream. There was a computer terminal at the desk.

On a hunch, I flipped on the computer and requested the medical files for Tamara de la Garza. The computer responded: *None available*. I requested files for Tamil Jafari. The computer responded: *None available*. I requested a list of mercenaries who'd been picked up at Sol Station, and the computer gave me nineteen names.

Tamara wasn't on the list, unless under a pseudonym. I requested information on the medical status of the nineteen persons. None were convalescing from brain damage. General Garzón obviously wasn't stupid enough to list Tamara in the computer under any name.

Abriara watched me during all this. "What are you doing?" she asked.

"Trying to locate the friend I told you about. It's all right to use this terminal, no?"

She shrugged. "There's no one here to stop you." I requested a list of all persons currently occupying convalescence tubes. Five people were listed; none had physical problems remotely similar to Tamara's. I had no way to learn her location from the terminal.

But another thought struck me: one of the nineteen people we'd picked up at Sol Station was an Alliance assassin. I called up the biographies and current housing assignments for each person, then requested a hard copy. The printer spat out a handful of thin papers with almost microscopic print. I began studying the file of a particularly ugly chimera named Miguel Mendoza.

"Ah," Abriara said, "I almost forgot. A present from the general." She reached into a fold of her robe and tossed me a small oblong package wrapped in gold foil. "He also left some liquor and cigars in that big chest you brought. In a few weeks, you can sell them for a fortune."

I tucked the papers into my kimono and picked up the package and unwrapped it.

"It's strange, don't you think? He treats you like a dog, putting you under my command, then gives you extravagant gifts?" She smiled, and when she smiled her teeth were small and strangely even, as Perfecto's had been. Something about her smile reminded me of a lizard or a porpoise. I looked closely and discovered the difference: she had no canine teeth. Instead, all her teeth were small and round and evenly matched.

"Please don't do that," she said.

"Do what?"

"Stare at my teeth. Or my eyes. Or my hair. Or my breasts. You humans always do that. It makes me nervous."

"I'm terribly sorry," I said, looking away. I fumbled with the package. Under the foil was a small box. I opened it and two knives fell out—knives I'd taken from Arish. Both were set in aluminum wrist sheaths that had

Arabic characters written along the length. I pulled a
knife and was surprised to see that the blade was made
of crystal, flawless molded graphite, pure diamond—
sharper than any metal blade.

"*Caramba!*" Abriara said. "Those are worth a fortune!"

The blade was slightly longer than my hand; the
handle was light and balanced, weighted for throwing.
The second knife was identical. When I pulled the blade
free, a note fell from the scabbard. I set it on the bed and
strapped the wrist sheaths on under the sleeves of my
kimono. The knives remained well concealed. I read the
note as I worked. It said,

> *Señor Osic:* I'm sure you know that
> weapons aren't allowed in living quarters.
> But a hundred years ago, during the Is-
> lamic Jihad, it is said the Faithful used
> these blades as toothpicks, so they are
> listed as such on the ship's logs. You may
> have need for such toothpicks. The Alli-
> ance has offered me tremendous bribes for
> your return to Earth. I'm playing the part
> of a greedy man, but soon they will figure
> out that I won't turn you over for any
> price. When that happens, watch your
> back.
>
> I give you Perfecto, since he has already
> bonded to you. I'd prefer that he were
> bonded to me, but a man can serve only
> one master. Mavro also requested to be in
> your combat team—a very talented and
> dangerous man. You need friends like
> him.

Abriara quickly read the note over my shoulder.

"What does he mean here," I asked, "where he says
that Perfecto is *bonded* to me?"

She stared at me, as if to gauge me. She spoke
hesitantly. "I suppose this is something you should
know. I'd never mention it if Garzón hadn't brought it
up. And it lies at the root of the real reason I came to

speak to you. Remember what our father, General Torres, looked like?"

"An old man with silver hair," I said, recognizing the similarity in appearance between Torres and General Garzón. "He had a sharp nose, and a strong chin."

"Close enough," Abriara said. "In his old age, Torres became paranoid, afraid of assassins within his ranks. So when we were created, some chimeras were given an extra gene containing a biochip. And that biochip makes them loyal to old men with silver hair and sharp features—men who look like Torres. You, with your hair going gray, look almost exactly like Torres."

I considered the consequences of this. "You mean Perfecto won't be angry with me for slugging him?"

"You broke his nose, he broke your leg. You're even." She sat on her cot and watched me.

"Even after I called him a *puto*?"

Her feet hung off the bed, and she swung them back and forth. "Perfecto won't hold a grudge against you, because it's not genetically possible. Understand? You fit the mold of the man he was created to protect and serve, and every fiber of his being knows it."

This surprised me. I remembered how Perfecto had tried to befriend me from the moment he saw me. "But won't he know that I fit the mold? Won't he resent it?"

"On the contrary, he'll feel comforted to have you around. It's like eating or breathing. We know why we eat and breathe, but we don't resent the fact that we must do it. But because Perfecto is bonded to you, I had to speak with you. You see, he will imitate you—he will try to seek your approval by doing the things you want him to do. If he believes even for a moment that you resent my command, he could revolt. He might even attack me. He'd certainly conspire with Mavro to undermine my authority. Understand? That is why I must have you speak with him about me, convince him to obey me." Her tone became harsh. "I must warn you, Señor Osic, that I cannot tolerate the slightest disobedience from you." She stopped a moment, leaving me to imagine what her threat might mean. "If, on the other hand, you treat me with unfeigned respect, Perfecto will show me complete loyalty."

"Ah, we get to the heart of the matter. So you want assurance of my intentions? Then I must admit: I treat people kindly from long habit, and I seldom become angered."

She said, "I have already seen this. And I take comfort in your words. The thing I don't understand is why General Garzón let you board ship. If Perfecto has bonded to you, others may too. Your presence here could disrupt his command."

"Garzón is indebted to me." I said. I remembered how excited Garzón had been to get Tamara as a prisoner. His own little spy to interrogate—he might even be wringing information from her now. But in order to keep her presence a secret, he'd have to resist Earth's demands for my extradition—as an ambassador from Baker, someone who could grant citizenship to Mavro and me as easily as he had, I believed he'd have authority to refuse extradition. And the fact that he had not turned me over suggested that Tamara was still alive and hadn't suffered too much brain damage. Otherwise, Garzón would have no reason not to ship me back to Earth. In fact, he had every reason to return me as soon as possible. My presence was certainly causing him trouble with the Alliance; and if more chimeras bonded to me, I could pose a threat to him in other ways. And I realized for the first time: Garzón had put Abriara in command of our team to humiliate me personally, not to humiliate Mavro. He wanted to make sure I remained a peon in the eyes of the chimeras in hopes that they wouldn't bond to me.

Abriara watched me as if trying to divine my thoughts. "You won't be able to sway me with your appearance. I was created later than Perfecto—when public opinion against Torres was so strong he knew he'd soon be assassinated. I won't bond to you."

"It's not that," I said. "A biochip is a powerful tool—especially when used to program the human mind. I was just wondering: are there other things like this that you're forced to do?"

Abriara smiled. For a moment, it was as if the web of light in her eyes opened, and her eyes sparkled though her voice was sad. "Don't you know? *Homo homini lupus.* We kill people. We are forced to kill people like you, don Angelo."

The way she smiled, it was like a sad joke. I was certain that she'd killed more than once, that the memory caused her grief. There are several ways to perform such a genetic manipulation: some hormonal imbalances can cause severe anger in a patient—so much so that the patient becomes victim to uncontrollable rage. Chimeras are marvelous fighters, but I'd never heard of them going berserk. On the other end of the spectrum is sociopathy, a lack of capacity to feel emotion—empathy, remorse. And Bastian proved back in the early 2100s that sociopathy can have a biological base—a defective amino acid sequence in a waste product produced in the cerebrum can block the bonding sites of thymotriptine, causing the victim to lose the ability to feel remorse—but it seemed implausible that Abriara was a sociopath. The tone of her voice showed concern for Mavro, and her sad smile when she spoke of her murders betrayed her pain.

But how much remorse? I wondered. The guilt I felt after killing Arish threatened to tear me apart. Even now it tormented me. But she only managed a wan smile. She presented me with a puzzle, and I decided to watch her, to discover what she was. She studied my face, still trying to discern my thoughts. "I'd heard rumors of your murderous nature," I confessed, "but I never believed them. I always thought it was just propaganda the socialists used to overthrow Torres."

"Propaganda works best when it's based on fact," she said. "But we posed no threat to Argentina or even our own people. It was only when the Argentines crossed the border that they had to worry, so they twisted the truth to frighten our own people . . . ."

The door opened and a young cyborg with a round, effeminate face poked his head into the operating room. Both his legs were metal frames, painted black, and his left arm frame was steel. The napalalene cords that served as muscles hung loosely within the frames. The massive form of Perfecto filled the hallway behind him. The bridge of Perfecto's nose was swollen and his eyes were black, but as Abriara had predicted, he smiled when he saw me.

The young man said, "Sergeant, it's time to go to practice."

Abriara turned to him. "Zavala, meet don Angelo Osic."

The boy nodded. "I'm pleased to meet you, don Angelo."

"When the steers talked of shipping you back to Earth," Abriara said, "Mavro and Zavala here swore to rip the tongues out of anyone who continued to talk like old women. Every one of them backed down."

I took the cue and said graciously, "Thank you, Señor Zavala. You sound like a brave one."

"It is nothing." The youth shrugged. By the way he smiled I knew I'd said the right thing.

Abriara got up, and I prepared to follow her and I noticed I was barefoot. Everyone else was barefoot, too. "No shoes?" I asked Abriara.

"Not on ship," Zavala answered eagerly. "Our employers won't allow it. Also, I must warn you: When you meet a Japanese, you must lower your eyes and bow. And you must never call them names—not even *steer* or *pubic hair*. You must call them *Master*."

I'd dealt with Japanese clients many times, and had never heard of such a thing. "*Me pelo rubio!*" I said, "You tease me!"

"No! They even hired a cultural expert to tell us these things. On Baker everyone is Japanese. It's some kind of experiment in social engineering . . . artificial cultures."

He said the words "artificial cultures" as if they explained everything. It was obvious that whatever he'd heard had gone over his head. "Hmmmph," I grunted.

"But you can make them act like *pubic hairs*," Zavala said. "I'll show you the trick!" He waved me forward and walked out the door.

Mavro and Perfecto waited for us to lead the way

down the hall. They both slapped me on the back and shouted, "*Hola, muchacho!* It's good to see you again!" and acted so happy I thought they'd throw a party. Mavro was a full head shorter than me, something I hadn't noticed earlier.

Abriara and Zavala led the way, while the others walked behind, and I realized they'd put me in a protected position in an inconspicuous manner. The cream-colored corridors were narrow, just wide enough for one man to walk easily, and the plastic floors bent when you put your weight on them, so you always felt as if you were sliding either backward or forward between the struts. We passed several men; each had wet hair as if returning from the showers, and we had to stop, turn sideways, and inch past one another. This was very uncomfortable, since I thought any one of them could be an Alliance assassin, and I continually fingered the knives hidden in my sleeves.

We were on the three hundred level, so when we came to a ladder, we climbed up.

At the top of the ladder stood a Japanese man wearing a silk kimono, dark blue with white lotuses; a short sword was strapped to his waist. Like the gun of a policeman, the sword was a badge of his authority on ship. His build was stocky, too much like Perfecto's to have come about as the result of the process of natural selection. It was obvious Motoki was engineering warriors on Baker, but I had to wonder what upgrades he had. He did not look like a chimera. His long hair, tied back in a ponytail, was so black it shone blue, and he had only one dark eyebrow that ran across his forehead. He didn't even acknowledge our presence when we prepared to squeeze past him in the hall. Instead, he stared down the hallway and pretended we didn't exist. This seemed very strange.

"Daytime, Master," Zavala said, bowing to and addressing the Japanese. Then in an excited tone he shouted, "Noses have flown through the pudding, and salmon swim along the intestine! Hurry!" And he pointed down the ladder.

A strange expression washed over the Japanese man's

face and he opened his mouth wide, using body language so alien I couldn't read it. He appeared very distressed, and muttered, *"Hai! Hai!"* and a microspeaker pinned to his robe said, "Yes! Yes!" as he hurried down the ladder.

We watched him go, and when he was out of earshot, Zavala chuckled. "See, I told you I could get him to act like a pubic hair. They all wear electronic translators strapped to their necks, and if you talk convincingly, they think the translators are broken."

We continued up the ladder until we stepped off at the second level. Another Japanese, a weary-looking clone of the first, walked down the corridor. Zavala sent him rushing down the ladder by shouting, "Water hernias have broken your friend! Downstairs. Japanese, downstairs!"

The corridor was like a spoke on a wheel. Six corridors met at the ladder at the center of the hub, then each corridor also intersected a corridor that circled the ship. When we got to the wheel's rim we turned left and followed the hall. The emblem of a green crane crossing the sun shone above a doorway. Beneath the emblem were the words Battle Room 19. On the floor was a pool of vomit.

Abriara stopped for a moment. "Is everyone prepared for a taste of the future?" she said, then opened the door: the room was small, perhaps five meters square, and smelled of vomit and sweat. Pale green battle armor the color of aged foliage hung on the walls around the room like chitinous exoskeletons. A replica of a large hovercraft with an open top and elevated plasma turrets occupied most of the room. Two Japanese rigidly sat on the floor in front of the hovercraft in the ancient *seiza* style—feet under the buttocks and toes pointed back—a feat requiring so much flexibility that few people can manage it. The man on the left was a monster with an enlarged musculoskeletal system; he'd have stood well over two meters tall, and he dwarfed even Perfecto. Like the others I'd seen, he wore a blue flowered robe and a sword. The man on the right was small, though, smaller than me, and he carried no weapons. Both men had outrageously slanted eyes. Zavala stared at the floor and bowed as he entered the room, and each of us followed suit. The Japanese acknowledged our bows by nodding in return.

"Put on armor, quickly!" the small one shouted.

We all rummaged through the armor, looking for pieces that fit. The armor design was unlike any I'd seen before. It was thin, without the heavy concussion padding that usually makes armor so hot. It had elegant lines and joints that made its wearer appear taller than normal and made for easy walking. I soon realized why it was different: the armor was designed to reflect the beams of heat weapons, not to absorb impact from projectiles. Also, the helmet had an unusual optic system with a number of polarized lenses that rotated automatically to keep the amount of incoming light constant. This created a bulge around the eyes like the humps on the eyes of a chameleon. Each helmet had a small hole at the base of the skull so we could run lines from our cranial jacks to the simulator in the hovercraft's computer. Normal helmets have air filtration systems, to protect one from smoke or poisonous gas, planted over the nose and mouth, but this had pipes with filters that wrapped around the face to the back of the head.

It seemed a waste to wear this armor for nothing, when we wouldn't fight a real campaign, but it did serve a purpose: it stopped sensory leak from the real world. When one is plugged into a cranial jack, the jack bypasses the sensory and motor areas of the brain while the jack's processor carries on a two-way conversation with the computer—the processor carries sensory input to the brain while the brain sends motor responses back to the computer. In this way, you can maintain the illusion of the dreamworld. However, the cranial jack's bypass system is not foolproof. One always gets sensory leak from the world outside. Bright lights or loud noises in the real world can adversely affect the quality of a dreamworld. So by wearing the armor and helmets, we could actually reduce leakage to the aural, tactile, and visual senses, thus locking us firmly into the illusion provided by the simulator. The armor served the same purpose as the visored helmets on dream monitors, except that the armor shielded the senses to a much greater degree.

Zavala dressed quickest, and as he pulled on his helmet he said, "Hey, look at me! I'm a big green grasshopper!" He stuck his fingers up by his head and wiggled them like antenna. The speaker in the helmet made his voice sound like the growl of an animal, but with his bulging eyes and green exoskeleton he did look surprisingly like a grasshopper.

Perfecto laughed and said, "No, you're not. You're a praying mantis. Remember that. We're all mantises—and the Yabajin are grasshoppers."

The big Japanese grumbled something, and the microspeaker on his kimono shouted, "No talking!" We all put on our armor quietly. When we were done, we no longer looked human.

The small Japanese clapped his hands and pointed to the floor in front of him. "Sit, please," he said in halting Spanish. And we sat on the floor so we were at a level lower than them.

The small one said, "I am Cultural Envoy Sakura Chimori, and to my right is your master, Master Kaigo. He will instruct you in the arts of the samurai. We are sorry that the situation for instruction is not ideal, but we hope you will find happiness serving Motoki Corporation."

Abriara said, "Excuse me, but I understood we were to be members of an assault team." She nodded toward the hovercraft. "That piece of trash doesn't have enough armor to be an assault vehicle! And what about outriders and snoopers and mininukes?"

The big samurai's back stiffened, and he scowled at Abriara's tone, though he continued staring straight ahead. The little man, Sakura, sucked his teeth to make a hissing noise and looked at Kaigo. Master Kaigo held out his hand, palm toward the floor, and wiggled it. I knew Abriara had angered them, but I didn't understand what their gestures indicated. Sakura turned to Abriara. "Sah," he said, letting out a hiss. "We have no offensive weapons. If you cannot kill a man with the weapons we give you, then he does not deserve to die.

"Now, I understand that relationships between men and women are relaxed in your country. But I must warn you, Sergeant Sifuentes, things are not the same on Baker. Please quickly adopt the sweet, subservient demeanor that is so becoming to women, lest one of our samurai remove your head in a fit of righteous anger.

"When addressing the master, drop to your knees and bow your head, then ask permission to speak. This rule is the same for all of you." Sakura stared at each of us woodenly, to make certain we understood.

"Now," he said, "we have told you that your work on Baker is strictly of a defensive nature. So, what gives you the idea that you are an assault team?"

Abriara's fists tightened and she swayed from side to side a little. Her anger was obvious, though her helmet concealed her face. She said in a carefully neutral voice, "Common sense. Our contract says you're paying our way there and back, with a stay of three months. A defensive team would need to stay years—not months."

Sakura smiled triumphantly and his gaze drifted over each of us. "See what happens when a woman thinks!" he said. As if speaking to an idiot, he addressed Abriara. "You didn't read your contract carefully. It said you would have a *minimum* stay of three months. You may be on the planet for a very long time. Let us have no more talk of attacks. We must be clear: Motoki is hiring you for defensive purposes, as we've repeatedly told the Alliance. And since the Alliance prohibits offensive weapons on Baker, an assault would seem implausible.

"But you should also know that the hovercraft, armor, and light plasma rifles are all defensive weapons provided for researchers engaged in field studies outside of protected zones. You may use these weapons as you will." Sakura let the final words dangle in the air. His meaning was obvious. It was illegal for Motoki to hire us to attack the Yabajin, so they'd just provide the "defensive" weapons and a means of locomotion and let us do the job ourselves.

Perfecto bowed at the waist, unwilling to fall to his knees. "Señor, what will our enemy's defensive weaponry consist of?" He spoke to the floor.

Sakura nodded politely, indicating that Perfecto's show of humility was adequate. "Cities are protected by automated perimeter defense systems—puff mines, neutron cannon, and plasma turrets for the outer layers, weasels and cybernet tanks for the inner defenses."

Abriara stared at the floor, thinking.

Perfecto said, "That's not so bad." And he was right. Most of the mercenaries had penetrated defenses just as tough in the jungles of Colombia and the highlands of Peru.

"I don't understand," Mavro said, bowing. "It sounds easy. Why do you need us?"

Sakura stared off into the air for a moment, then began an obviously memorized speech: "Over a hundred years ago, Motoki Corporation embarked on a noble experiment. Decades of complacency, Westernization, and overabundant wealth had weakened the spirit of the Japanese people, sapping them of their strength. Economic indicators clearly showed that Japan would soon lose its industrial lead to the Chinese, perhaps forever. The executives at Motoki could not allow this, so they considered alternatives. It became evident that problems in Japan could only be solved by reengineering the very fabric of society—restoring the ancient ideals of unity, honor, and willingness to work that had once made Japan strong. But success could only be assured by isolating a segment of the population, removing it from weaker cultures so it would not be contaminated. If one were to cultivate a rare and beautiful flower, one would not allow it to become pollinated by a lesser flower. So, Motoki removed a portion of its top executives—the best specimens of humanity—to Baker, and initiated a new *Meiji*, a cultural restoration.

"Unfortunately, we undertook this great plan in concert with the Japanese government. The government hired its own cultural engineers and selected its own representatives—lesser genetic specimens. These people were unable to tear from their souls the ignoble ideals and polluting doctrines that had so bereaved our country. They were worldly, aristocratic, and lazy. As a result, their settlements are populated by Yabajin, barbarians who seek constantly to destroy us. They have sent so many assassins to bomb our incubation stations and slay our upgraded children that the Alliance has officially forbidden the use of incubation vats on the entire planet. Not fifty years ago we were a blossoming civilization with a population of two million. Now our planet is nearly decimated, and only a few thousand remain."

He said the last words with a tone of heaviness, signifying that the speech was over. "So, we hire you to protect our cities. However, if we exterminated all eighty thousand Yabajin, we would not repay one-tenth the damage they have done to us."

I did not believe Sakura's description of the political climate on Baker. I'm sure the Yabajin would have described it differently. It was clear that Sakura's people were a race of megalomaniacs—a problem typically encountered when visionaries become isolated, as shown time and again by the festering settlements from Lagrange to Barnard's star. Sakura called his enemies *Yabajin*, barbarians, yet all the Japanese I'd seen were half naked and carried swords.

When I'd signed on ship, it had been to escape Earth. I'd known Motoki wanted a soldier, but I'd imagined running a cybernet defense system, not scorching women with lasers and killing their children. The idea of committing genocide sickened me. Clearly this was not a job for me.

The big man, Kaigo, spoke in a rumbling voice, and his microspeaker translated, "We start with weapons." Sakura left. Kaigo instructed Mavro and Perfecto to take stations at the plasma turrets while the rest of us picked up laser rifles. For the next hour and a half he acquainted us with the weapons. The laser was similar to the one I'd shot Arish with, using the same chemical clip for power, but it had a much longer barrel and delivered 8000° Centigrade over an area four centimeters in diameter. With so much heat, the lenses and focusing mirrors needed much cooling, so the barrel was wrapped in insulation and cooled with liquid nitrogen. At a hundred meters it could deliver a burst that the body

armor could withstand for just over a second, but on the
moving hovercraft it was difficult to hold aim so long. For
this reason, each laser was provided with a targeting
computer connected to a focusing mirror that corrected
for jostling after the trigger was squeezed. In other
words, once you pulled the trigger, you hit what you last
aimed at—whether it was empty sky, the head of a nail,
or a man—and you couldn't shoot again for two seconds.

The plasma turrets mounted to the hovercraft used
the hovercraft's solid fuel to superheat metal balls and
explode metallic gases toward the enemy in great bursts.
The turrets were more effective than lasers, since at
close range the heavy gases could gouge armor in a
fraction of a second. Since the turrets were so effective,
the gunners became the enemy's primary target.

After Kaigo discoursed on the strengths and weak-
nesses of the weapons, he made us practice reloading
and targeting until we tired. "Tell me when you are
ready for a battle," he said. His tone held a note of
warning.

Abriara shrugged and said, "Let's do it," so we got on
the hovercraft.

Zavala, with the decreased sensitivity in his metal
arm, seemed least capable of handling a weapon, so we
put him in the driver's seat. Perfecto and Mavro took the
turrets while Abriara and I held rifles and took seats on
either side of the turrets, ready to replace any fallen
turret gunner.

Kaigo went to each seat and pulled out the cords that
ran from the computer terminal to our cranial jacks. He
plugged us in. A message flashed before my eyes:

Scenario 1: Mid Patrol

And then we were bouncing across a red desert at full
speed, the hovercraft droning like a dragonfly. It would
hit small dips and rises, and its whole undercarriage
would shudder, making my teeth feel as if they'd rattle
from their sockets. The sky was a hazy, indistinct violet
with bands of earthy yellow and green clouds that
twisted from horizon to horizon like rivers in the sky.

These were not gaseous clouds, but it took several moments before I realized they were animals—flocks of birds high in the atmosphere.

In the battle room my armor had smelled fresh and resinous. But the simulator supplied the nauseating odor of stale sweat, as if I'd lived in armor for months without a bath.

"Slow down!" Abriara screamed. The speakers in my helmet made her voice sound like a command from God, coming from all directions at once and filling my head.

"I don't know how!" Zavala yelled in return. He was fumbling with a lever when we came over a rise to a forest of giant trees unlike any I had ever seen. Each tree looked like a huge leafless piece of coral, hundreds of meters in diameter. Yet the tree lacked a trunk, so that many limbs actually just ran over the ground. The great limbs, as thick around as a horse, were covered with strands of moss and dark hanging vines. In places, the moss had pulled away from the tree—its branches were misshapen and as white as bone. The ground around the tree was clean and windswept, but under the tree, desiccated leaves covered the ground and the vines hung in great curtains so that each "coral tree" looked like a miniature jungle in itself.

Zavala had to keep his attention on steering so he wouldn't hit the coralwood. Abriara held to the railing on the side of the hovercraft and worked her way to the cockpit. We curved around a line of branches and surprised a small herd of imported peccaries. They squealed and ran under the coralwood.

We passed the coralwood and came into an open desert. Off to our left were seven large brown rocks, three to four meters long and a meter tall. They were all of a regular length and oval shape, and as we got closer I saw that they moved slowly across the sand like giant armadillos without heads or feet or tails. Their only visible sensory organs were antennae as long as whips at the front end of their bodies. They waved these around, smelling the air, as they inched across the desert toward the coralwood. Mavro fired his plasma gun into one experimentally, and the creature's side exploded into steam while the creature flipped up on its back. We went by so fast I couldn't see if it had any legs. But I knew it wasn't anything created by geneticists from Earth.

"I thought they said this planet was terraformed," I yelled over the helmet speaker.

"It is," Perfecto shouted back. "They brought the oxygen levels up to standard. Fulfilled the minimum requirements."

I asked, "What about the local flora and fauna?"

"They're on their way out," Perfecto shouted, shooting into another giant armadillo.

Since the armadillos were just computer-generated images, I decided the target practice was a good idea, and started shooting at them. The hovercraft jostled so much it was hard to hold a creature in my sights long enough to squeeze the trigger. The red dot of the targeting laser jumped all around. So rather than try to take a good shot after careful aim, I had to take snapshots. We came over another hill to a floodplain where a large river spilled its banks. Low reddish-blue plants with bulbs shaped like clear yellow pineapples filled most of the floodplain, though there were also groves of fernlike trees, and tall stalks of cotton.

We sped over the river and began climbing a hill. The ground cleared and we entered a stand of great coralwoods and surprised a whole herd of small gray spade-shaped lizards. Each had a single eye on the back of its head, and each lizard trained its single eye on us as the group hopped in unison, two meters to the hop, like waves moving away from a rock thrown in a pond.

As I watched the gray lizards, a piece of red plastic fell from the sky and wrapped itself around one of the largest lizards.

"Hey, that was a manta ray!" Zavala shouted, pointing at the red plastic.

It was indeed shaped like a ray, and I realized this piece of plastic was some type of avian preying on the lizard. As we passed I stood up in my seat to try to get a better look at the struggle.

A siren made a *beep, beep,* and I suspected the hovercraft's computer was warning me to get back in my seat. A line of vines hung from a coralwood limb in front of us, and I spotted a hovercraft behind them just as jets of white-hot plasma spattered across my neck.

The concussion spilled me backward over the hovercraft and my gun flew into the air. I hit the ground with a thwack, cracking the armor on my chest.

The plasma melted through my neckband, onto my throat, and my helmet filled with steam. I tried to breath, but the smell of charred flesh and smoke made me cough. I began to retch, struggling to breathe. I curled into a ball and tried to pull my helmet free.

Our hovercraft exploded in a ball of blue.

I lay on the ground pulling at my helmet's magnetic latches. Oxygen deprivation disoriented me, making me miss. The plasma burned into my neck, and the melted armor soaked down my skin. I vomited and blacked out.

The big Japanese, Kaigo, jacked us out of the simulator. My heart was hammering, and the sockets behind my eyeballs ached. My teeth felt as if someone had drilled a hole into each individual nerve. The vomit in my helmet was seeping down my neck. I ripped off my faceplate and leaned over. Kaigo threw me a rag. I was surprised to find my armor in one piece—moments before, it had seemed to be crumbling in my hands. Zavala slumped over his chair and vomited into his helmet. He was rolling his eyes and appeared to be in shock. The others in our group were limp and panting, trying to shake off the simulator's effects.

Kaigo gave us two minutes to clean up, then said a word in Japanese; a hologram appeared in the air at his feet. It showed a hovercraft in miniature, darting over the landscape. "These you," he said, pointing at the hovercraft. In a distant corner of the room was the enemy craft approaching through the coralwoods. "These Yabajin samurai," he said, pointing at the enemy.

"Are those real samurai, or computer simulations?" Mavro asked.

"Those real samurai," Kaigo said.

Zavala looked around the room. "Where are they?"

Kaigo glared at him as if he were an idiot, but answered. "Upstairs, in battle room three."

I watched myself in simulation. I was like a tourist, forever turning my head to look up in the sky or down at the ground.

Kaigo pointed to the holo of me. "Ohhh, very bad! You must learn to concentrate—ignore surroundings. Achieve one-pointedness. You're here to kill Yabajin, not study xenobiology."

He watched until I stood up to look at the plastic manta ray. He spoke two words in Japanese; the picture slowed and enlarged so we could see ourselves and our enemies clearly. He pointed to the image of me standing up. "Where you go? Did you need to take a pee? You should sit down and concentrate. Relax."

The combat teams met. Abruptly the action slowed. As one, the enemy raised their weapons and fired. Each had picked a target, and their lasers scored on Mavro and Perfecto with pinpoint accuracy while both plasma turrets washed across our hovercraft, blowing me over the back end. Zavala was drenched in a plasma storm; a great stream shot across his chest, chewing wormholes in his armor. Among us, only Mavro managed to fire, and his shot went high over the heads of his targets. I noticed that, as in Tamara's dreamworld, the simulator didn't correct for my infrared vision, and this put me at a disadvantage since I can normally see a platinum shimmer in the air when a laser is fired. The beams from these guns didn't show at all.

Kaigo pointed at Mavro's shot. "Good! Quick reflexes. You almost got some." Then he pointed to the rest of the team members, each trying to aim. Our hovercraft skidded into a giant coralwood and exploded. "You move too slow. Weapon must be part of you, like hand and eye. Concentrate on being one with your weapon. When it comes time to shoot, there must not be the breadth of a hair between the thought and the act. All of you, practice aiming before you go back into simulator." We sat a moment and he waved his hands, "Now! Now! You practice now!"

We practiced lowering our weapons from resting

position and snapping off shots. I shook through the entire session. The thought of returning to the simulator caused a wave of nausea to wash over me. Kaigo ordered us back to our seats.

Kaigo said, "Think of nothing. Be one with your weapon. Shoot fast. Kill Yabajin."

Mavro reached down and patted my shoulder. "Let's step on these punks," he said.

Kaigo flipped the simulator on, and we jacked in.

Scenario 2: Mid Patrol

We entered the forest of coralwood again, floating down corridors between trees at full speed, twisting along a narrow trail that flowed like a river. The skies were dark and gray. A slate-gray rain fell, and the road of wet amber pebbles gleamed dully as if a fire burned within. Among the trees were some of the giant armadillos, and they'd wrapped their huge bodies around the branches to feed on pale orange fungi that clung to the bonelike limbs. The armadillo creatures now looked like giant slugs feeding in a garden.

We passed a large rock, and a dozen brown avians shaped like mantas rose a meter in the air and rippled away. A warning beep sounded. I swung my gun forward as we swerved around a wide bend. A hovercraft came head on. I took aim at the driver. He wore armor with the same insect design as mine—only it was copper-colored instead of green. White plasma streams flew over my head and whistled past my ears. Perfecto and Mavro were blown from the turrets. I squeezed off a shot, hitting a turret gunner in the thigh. He responded by sending a burst of plasma to spatter over Zavala's hands. The hovercrafts were bearing down on one another, so Zavala swerved to his right and hit a limb of coralwood. The branch ran parallel to the ground at chest level. I tried to duck, but I dropped just enough for a branch harder than stone to decapitate me.

I came out of it sweating. My teeth chattered.
Zavala was making gagging sounds, and had slid from

the driver's seat of the hovercraft to the floor. At first I thought he was vomiting, but nothing came up, and he wasn't moving his arms or legs, trying to rise.

Perfecto shouted, "Zavala!" and leapt from the turret mount. He pulled off Zavala's helmet and tossed it to the floor.

Zavala's eyes were fluttering open and closed, beads of sweat stood out on his forehead, and a deep rattle came from his throat. Perfecto shouted, "He's dying," and flipped him to his back and started pulling off Zavala's chest plate. I jumped up, unplugged my jack, and slapped Zavala hard on the back, hoping to get his heart started. I began trying to flip him over to initiate CPR, and Zavala gagged and vomited and began breathing.

"I think he's okay," Perfecto said. "It was just a little thing. He just swallowed his tongue." Zavala moaned and waved his right hand a little, though he didn't try to sit up.

I knew it was more than a little thing. I once knew a man in the feria who hunted monkeys for a living. Every few weeks he would bring in a monkey he had shot at but missed, yet the monkey had died from the mere terror of the attack. The shock to the monkey's system was fatal, even though the attack failed. That is what happened to Zavala. His mind could not separate the illusion of the simulator from reality.

Zavala began vomiting in earnest, and he tried to rise to his knees. We pulled him from the mess, and for a long while he leaned against the rail to the hovercraft and struggled for breath. Mavro stood by him and kept repeating, "Are you all right, muchacho? Are you all right?"

Finally Zavala held up his hands. "They're burning! They're burning!" he cried.

"You're fine!" Mavro said. And we waited for Zavala to recover.

Kaigo commanded the holo to start and we watched ourselves get massacred.

We floated over the landscape slowly, met the Yabajin, and each raised a weapon and tried to aim. The enemy snapped off shots. Kaigo pointed to our slowness. "Practice targeting and firing weapons some more. *Shuyo*, practice, polishes off the rust from the body, makes you good fighter, *ne?* This is battle. This is actual battle the way it will be. When you die on Baker, you can die only once. Remember, if you kill samurai in the simulator, he will feel pain, not you!

"Also, stand right." He stood up and held a laser rifle in front of him, then squatted so his knees were bowed. "Don't sit in chair or stand rigid like you are shooting on land. This is big different. Knees must always be moving, always flexible to absorb little shocks of movement. Make for steady aim." He demonstrated the action and, like a sailor on a boat at sea, showed how he could counteract the movement of the vessel, absorbing the minor pitches and rattling movements of the hovercraft with his knees. This made great sense, and I admired his technique until I remembered that he was showing us these things just so we could commit genocide.

"Go now. Go train for combat tomorrow: imagine you hold gun and visualize shooting. Practice all movements. Practice in imagination. Five hours." Kaigo dismissed us with a wave of his hand. We removed our armor; I was covered with sweat. The others helped Zavala to the door. The hard copy of the files on the men who boarded at Sol Station was soaked, so I waved the papers in the air, trying to dry them. The thought of entering the corridor unnerved me—anyone could have been an Alliance assassin—so I thumbed through the papers, memorizing faces, and walked out last. Everyone hung their heads because we had been beaten so soundly—everyone but Mavro.

He put a cigar in his mouth. His hands trembled slightly as he struck his lighter and held it to the cigar. "Do not worry about these punks," he said. "My mother gave me worse beatings when I was a child. As long as these samurai are living, breathing pieces of meat—and not some damned simulations—we can beat them! No?"

We all nodded in agreement.

We stood in the hall a moment. Zavala, the young cyborg, shivered. He looked as if he'd collapse. Mavro put an arm around him. "Are you okay, compadre?" he asked.

Zavala nodded and sniffed. He fumbled with the sleeve of his kimono, pulling it up to expose the base of his prosthetic arm, which ended just above the elbow. He examined his skin around the prosthesis. "It's burning. I can feel my arm burning," he said with wonder. "It's the rot. It's on the stump of my arm. It's active again. I can feel it burning."

"Let me see!" I said.

"Sí, let Angelo look. He's a doctor," Perfecto said.

The rot, or L24, is a bacterial variant of leprosy developed for germ warfare. It can rot an arm off in a matter of days. In the cities it doesn't cause much damage, since it can be treated quickly. But when dumped over the guerrillas in the jungles it can be devastating, since they are often unable to return to a village in time for treatment. And though the damage can be halted, the L24 bacteria makes it impossible to regenerate damaged tissues.

Zavala held out his arm, and I checked the stump around the prosthesis. The skin color was completely normal and healthy; no white flakes showed at all. I poked around the base of the prosthesis, searching for abscesses, but found nothing. "It looks fine to me," I said. Zavala frowned at the news, so I added, "But we should watch it closely for a few days, just to make sure. I've got some antibiotics in my medical bag that can kill anything." I didn't tell him that I only had a handful of antibiotics to use in emergencies—not enough to treat him. I normally didn't deal in such mundane drugs back in Panamá. Any pharmacy on a street corner carried them.

Abriara started to leave, and Zavala managed a wan smile. He said, "Wait a minute." Then he opened the door to the battle room and shouted, "Master Kaigo. Tigerlilies have crept ugly through the hall. People are hurt! Downstairs! Quickly, come quickly!" We all smiled at this, and the big samurai hurried from the room.

But instead of running down the hall to the ladders, he grabbed Zavala and lifted him in the air, like an ogre lifting a child. In halting Spanish he said, "When you . . . speak to me, speak Japanese. Is the duty of the weak to learn the language of the strong, no?"

Zavala tried to squirm from Kaigo's grasp. Kaigo slammed him against the wall, just hard enough to jar him, then returned to the battle room.

Mavro nudged Zavala and smiled, "You were right. You *are* a grasshopper."

We stood outside the battle room a moment, then
Zavala and Mavro took off to explore the ship. Abriara
said to me, "I'll show you to our room," and Perfecto and
I followed. We met Sakura at the ladder; he stopped us
with a wave of his hand. He was all teeth and smiles.

"What do you want?" Abriara asked. The evenness of
voice she'd managed earlier disappeared.

Sakura grinned. "Listen carefully, and I will teach you
the company song," he said. "We will sing it each
morning when we awaken, and we will sing it each night
before we go to bed. And if an envoy meets you in the
hall, you will be asked to sing, and you must sing with
emotion—from your heart."

I fidgeted with my biographies, sorry to be delayed
when I wanted to get to my room to study.

Then Sakura sang in Japanese. It sounded like growls
from the pit of his belly and low wails and shrieks, and he
used the oriental musical scale, so it didn't sound like
real music. Tears streamed from his eyes, and he waved
his hands as he sang. It started,

> *Itami de tsukuri,*
> *Itami de uri* . . .

And I lost track. Sakura finished by lowering his head
and weeping as if he'd emptied his heart and was unable
to muster strength to stand. When he'd recuperated, he
raised his hands to lead us in song.

I was stunned. I once saw a magician who put a

prosthetic bill on a chicken and built a microspeaker into the bill so that when a tape recorder played a little distance away, the chicken could recite scriptures. He brought his "Chicken of God" to the feria and fooled many peasants, telling them the chicken had learned to recite the Sermon on the Mount after drinking water from a holy fountain. In this way he made much money. I often went to see the show, since the awe and astonishment on the peasants' faces was so amusing. I am sure that when Sakura asked us to sing the company song, my stunned expression would have well matched the expressions of those peasants. Perhaps if I'd been a child, I'd have sung, but none of us sang.

Sakura stopped singing. "Come now," he urged. "Sing for me! *Itaaaamiiii* . . ." He stopped, looked from person to person. "Come now, show your company spirit! Show your gratitude for Motoki!"

Abriara said, "Here's my gratitude," and quick as a serpent she struck him in the ribs, knocking him down the hall.

Sakura sputtered, struggling to get some air in his lungs. Abriara rushed forward and grabbed him by the hair, lifted him up, and slammed him against the wall.

Then she pinned him there, taking him by the neck. "Don't *ever* talk down to me in front of my men," she said. "Don't you ever mock my intelligence or seek to undermine my authority again." She stared him in the eye, and Sakura tried to avert his gaze.

He gasped for breath. "Let me go, crazy woman, or I'll have the samurai execute you!"

Abriara's eyes watered; she started to weave. Though her frame was no larger than that of other women, she emanated power. With her clenched fist poised below his jaw, I imagined that if she struck, her blow would land as solidly and powerfully as a piston, crushing Sakura's skull. Sakura looked into her silver eyes, and must have seen the alienness in her. He began to tremble. Abriara responded to his threat: "Let them kill me." There was no fear in her voice.

She dropped Sakura to the ground, and the little Japanese stayed where he fell, afraid to move. She stalked down the hall toward the ladders, her muscles bunched and ready, like a panther ready to spring.

Sakura watched until she got to the ladder, then he shouted, "You're dead! I'll have you killed for that!" and he began screaming in Japanese and running back to Kaigo's battle room.

Perfecto chased Sakura, caught him by the scruff of the neck after a dozen steps, and pushed him to the floor. Sakura kept yelling. Abriara didn't hurry as she climbed the ladder, showing no concern. There were several battle rooms along the hallway, and I was certain Sakura's yelling would summon a samurai in seconds. I pulled a knife, and followed Abriara.

We climbed the ladder. At the zero-hundred level we stepped off. The ladder continued up, but was chopped off at the air lock. I glanced at the air lock—Tamara was somewhere behind it, and I longed to find her, but I continued following Abriara. The halls on this level were a bit wider than those downstairs, the rooms farther apart. When we got to our room it didn't look so good. It was a simple cube with a low ceiling; cushions on top of plastic lockers doubled as couches and lined all three walls. My teak chest sat atop one such trunk, its lid open, overflowing with boxes of cigars and bottles of liquor. A small doorless restroom with a toilet bordered the hall on the right as we entered; a water spigot and computer-jack outlet bordered the door on the left. Five small bunks were suspended from bolts in the ceiling, and pictures of the popes covered the walls. Abriara climbed to a top bunk, and lay with her eyes closed. I ducked around the corner of the bathroom and raised my knife, poised to strike anyone who might enter the room to attack Abriara.

Abriara opened one eye.

"Are you just going to lie there?" I asked, angered that she was unwilling to save herself.

"I think so," she said.

I leaned my head against the wall, listening for pursuit.

She watched me a moment. "Angelo, put that knife away," she said with concern. "You're scaring me."

"And if Sakura comes back with help?" I asked, wiping sweat from my forehead.

"He won't," she said, sitting up. She watched me a moment longer. "Besides, I can handle myself. I'm not in danger."

When she said she wasn't in danger, something strange happened. I felt a great sense of relief. It was as if something in my arm had sprung, allowing me to release the weapon.

"I . . . I thought I was protecting you. I made a fool of myself. I'm sorry."

She closed her eyes and turned away. "Thank you. No one has ever tried to do that before. No one has ever protected me."

There was such pain in her voice that I wanted to apologize for all the men who had never protected her. I wondered what kind of life she had led, being the lowest of the low, less than an Indian even. I imagined how she had been ravaged by that, how she had been forced to assert herself and become strong. I remembered news reports showing how chimeras were mistreated in Chile, Ecuador, and Peru even before the socialists took over: in places where Indians were paid a starvation wage of fifty pesos for a hard day's labor, a chimera would be paid twenty-five. Police would often shoot or beat chimeras who stayed out after dark. But these were only minor inconveniences compared to what happened after each of those countries became absorbed into the Estados Unidos Socialistas del Sur: chimeras lost all their rights, since the socialists claimed chimeras were not human and were therefore not entitled to legal protection. It was legal to kill chimeras, to enslave them if one dared try. It is even said that after Argentina's General Espinoza conquered Chile, he bragged that he dined on the liver of a chimera and claimed it was better than the finest Argentine calves' liver. These were only a portion of the things Abriara must have endured at the hands of humans. "What was it like, in Chile, when the people began killing chimeras, began hunting you?" I asked. It was a personal question, perhaps too personal.

I put the knife back in my wrist sheath and sat on the floor, watching Abriara.

She didn't answer for a moment. "Angelo, in the simulators everything looked strange. The colors were all washed out, and nothing gave off warmth. It was like the whole world had gone cold. There were clouds in the sky, and I couldn't see the sun through them. It was as if they were a barrier to light. Is that the way humans see things?"

It was a trite observation, an attempt to steer our conversation to safe ground. But it seemed obvious that she had very strong vision in the infrared. With my prosthetics I could see some of that, but it was translated into normal colors. To her each color had its own value. "Sí. The clouds and fog, they can be a perfect barrier to sight," I said. "Humans cannot see the stars blazing in the sky on a cloudy night."

"Hmmm. I knew their eyes were poor, but I never guessed how bad their vision is. This is a weakness we can exploit when we get to Baker."

"Have you never coupled with a human on a dream monitor, or jacked into an educational tape made by humans?"

"No. In Chile educational tapes are shown in full spectrum. I've seen exact duplicates of old paintings in museums—Da Vinci, Rembrandt. All the whites in their portraits are tinged with ultraviolet, making it look as if the subjects bathed in sunscreen lotion. I understood human's visual limitations on an intellectual level. But I didn't really know till today."

"I know what you mean," I said. "When I was in the army, I lost my eyes in an accident and paid the surgeon a little extra to replace them with prosthetics. When I first got them, the infrared was set too high, and the amount of light I received baffled me. People glowed so much that their features became indistinct, and it was hard to distinguish one person from another. At first, everyone appeared to be beings of light—glowing creatures. I'd heard that some people claim to see auras—the human spirit shining through the flesh. And in my youthful naïveté I pretended I was seeing something similar—a physical manifestation that verified a spiritual hypothesis.

"For months this changed the way I thought about people, the way I looked at them. I saw them all as potential angels and Gods, and treated them with respect and trust. But then several people took advantage of my trust and I realized I was only fooling myself. So I went back to the surgeon who sold me the eyes and had them recalibrated so I could once again look at people as they really are and only see a little bit of infrared."

"Hmm. You should have kept the infrared calibrated high," Abriara said. "You should have given it time. Everyone's bodies heat unevenly, but each person has a characteristic pattern to his heating, and each person has a characteristic body shape. You can learn to tell them apart quickly." She pondered for a moment. "Also, you still have a problem. You still basically trust people and treat them with too much respect. One can hear it in the tone of your voice when you speak. You need to learn to hold people in contempt until they prove themselves, understand? I think if you look at people objectively, you will discover that most of them are no better than walking dungheaps. Certainly the people in Chile were walking dungheaps. Maybe even I . . ." Her voice faded into silence; she turned away.

Her dark view of humanity saddened me. She could only hold such a view if she had met many bad people in her life. I wanted to say something to comfort her, to make up for all her bad experiences, but no words seemed adequate. Yet I had also known many good men. I thought about it much, and decided I would try to change her mind.

Abriara's bunk was below mine. I climbed into my bunk, lay down, and studied the biographical files I'd got from the medical computer. Of the nineteen people on file, sixteen were assigned living quarters in module A, with Garzón, whereas Mavro, Perfecto, and I were assigned to module C. Which meant my would-be assassin was stuck on the other side of two air locks. But I had to wonder how secure a barrier the air locks would prove against a determined man. I'd seen handles for opening the one to Module B, but didn't know how it might be secured. No guard had been stationed outside the lock. What if the air locks weren't secure? What if people had only been told not to open them? Nothing would prevent the assassin from coming through. *Also*, I thought, *nothing would keep you from searching the ship to find Tamara.*

I made a note to check the air lock to see if it would open, then thumbed through the biographies: sixteen people—thirteen men and three women. One man was the big anglo security guard we'd taken prisoner on ship: Lee Owen, a onetime mercenary from Quebec who'd made it to captain fighting for India in the Chinese Plankton-Harvest War. If he fought the Chinese, he was definitely not the kind of man who'd be a Nicita Idealist Socialist. I temporarily discounted two women and three more men, since they were all chimeras. Which left ten suspects.

Arish, Jafari, and the man in the gray slacks had apparently been Moslems; and though the Moslem nations control the Alliance, the Alliance has representatives from other nations. Still, I believed Jafari was representing a faction within the Alliance—perhaps an Islamic faction. I considered it safe to bet that future attackers would be Moslem. I searched each file, looking for anyone with connections to the Middle East. Yet the files were almost standard: Peasant refugees from Chile, Ecuador, Colombia; three brothers who'd raised sheep in Peru—even a cyborg plumber from Argentina who'd fought through half a dozen wars. Their names were common: Perez, Reinoso, Pena, Tomagua. I'd met thousands of men like them in Panamá. The biographies appeared useless, and when I studied the files of these men and women and tried to calculate who would try to kill me and who I would have to kill, it seemed a trite and boring game.

The files were disheartening. I thought of the air lock. I imagined that it would be open: I'd pass through and find Tamara on module A, resting peacefully in a convalescence tube. She would smile when she saw me, her

dark eyes flashing with laughter and her mouth curving
into an easy smile the way it had when Flaco told one of
his silly jokes. I'd reasoned that Tamara must be recovering well, since Garzón would have no reason to protect
me if she'd lost her value, but emotionally I was
unsatisfied. I wanted to see her, to know her condition
for myself: if she was recovering, I wanted to see her
smile; if she was dying, I wanted to watch her body grow
cold.

I got up and headed for the door.

Abriara asked, "Where are you going?"

"Just down the hall."

"I don't want you to travel alone."

I held up my hands so my kimono sleeves dropped,
exposing my knives. "I'm not alone."

"Be back in fifteen minutes."

I nodded, and went out into the empty hall, down to
the ladder, then inspected the air lock. The neutral-gray
door was two meters in diameter, and an indentation in
the ceiling showed that it would slide to one side to
open. The three handles spaced equidistantly around
the air lock each had a black plastic grip, but other than
the handles and grips there was no exterior equipment—
no pressure gauges or warning lights to show if the air
lock was pressurized. Which hinted that the door wasn't
meant to be manually controlled. The AI who was
piloting the ship controlled the air lock. But that didn't
mean I couldn't bypass the system.

I climbed to the top of the ladder and grabbed a
handle grip. It twisted slightly in my hand, but I could
not push, pull, or move it in any direction.

After I spent twenty seconds of useless tugging, a
voice from the microspeaker built into one end of the
handle said, "For your own safety, access between
modules will not be granted during flight except in case
of depressurization or life-support-system failure. Thank
you."

I continued tugging at each handle, and every twenty
seconds got the same message, which meant that the
computer was giving me a message based upon a simple

decision-tree logic. The computer reasoned: If someone tries to open the air lock, then tell him it won't open.

I gave up trying to force the door. However, I thought there might be a mechanism for opening the doors hidden beneath the plastic handles on the grips, so I pulled a knife and cut through the plastic. But only the smooth gray metal of the handle showed underneath. I pried off the microspeaker from one handle; a tiny stream of light from a fiber-optics tube shined out— there was no complex gadgetry hidden in the handle.

The only way to open the air lock would be to pry it open, blow a hole in it, or perhaps drill through. None of them seemed like viable options for either me or an Alliance assassin.

I stood and stared at the ceiling till Perfecto came up the ladder, then we went back to the room. Perfecto had a small bottle of blue body paint, and he was very excited.

When we got to the room, he said, "*Hola*, Abriara, look what I found!"

"Where did you get that?" she asked.

"From Cephas Silva!" Perfecto said. He opened the bottle and immediately got to his knees and began painting perfectly straight lines on the floor. His lines formed little squares in front of each bed, and he marked these according to the bed owner's name. Then he painted a corridor down the middle of the room, leading to the bathroom. This he marked COMMON AREA. He carefully stayed within the common area as he painted. I thought his actions to be very strange. I kept expecting him to tell me what had happened with Sakura—but finally I realized he wasn't going to say.

"So did you reason with Sakura?" I asked.

"Ah, yes," Perfecto said.

"And?"

"And I convinced him to shut his mouth. It was a very easy matter: I told him that if people found out that he'd been beaten by a woman, everyone would laugh at him. He got upset and ran away. We had many Japanese military advisers back in Chile, and I found that even

more than Mavro, they worry about machismo. Sakura
won't make trouble."

That night, we met Mavro and Zavala in the gym,
which sprawled over the whole sixth floor of the module.
Mavro acted as if he were embarrassed to be seen with
us. He held his chin up so the light would catch the
gleam of his tattooed tears, and he stared off in any
direction but toward the group, so that he appeared to
be standing close to us rather than standing with us.

A track around the gym's perimeter sported obstacle
courses, while the center of the gym held various
hydraulic presses with enough benches and tables that a
hundred and fifty people could easily weightlift at one
time. The gym was crowded, and though the rest of the
ship smelled fresh and new, the gym already stank of
sweat. Nearly everyone in the gym was male; only one in
ten were females.

Abriara led us through rigorous exercises, and this
drew stares, since it was obvious we were commanded
by a woman. When it came time to run the track,
everyone raced ahead of me through the difficult obstacle courses. Though the bone glue had set in my leg, my
ankle quickly ballooned. I hobbled along through the
easiest obstacle course.

One course was made especially for chimeras and
required the runner to swing himself over a five-meter
wall, then run over a roof with slippery tiles. Perfecto
ran this course with several chimeras, and it soon
developed into a race. Mavro didn't want to be outdone,
so he tried to run the course, but was unable to scale the
wall, and this made people laugh.

After an hour of exercises and jogging we began lifting
weights. It soon became obvious men were joking about
us. Whenever someone laughed, Mavro would bristle
and look to see what they laughed about while the rest of
us pretended we heard nothing. Twice I looked up and
saw men laugh who weren't looking in our direction, but
once a group of men laughed, and one of them, a small
chimera with long dark braids and pale skin, wearing the
silver and red of a sergeant, opened his kimono toward

Abriara and pulled down his underwear to expose his penis.

I looked at the eyes of my compadres: Perfecto, Abriara, and Zavala all lifted weights with their eyes closed. Only Mavro had seen what the chimera was doing.

Mavro got mad. He sat on a bench doing sitting presses, slowly pushing the bars over his head time and again as his eyes glassed and he glared at everyone in the room. He pumped up his arms. I waited for someone to make a joke we could hear, to see what Mavro would do.

Perfecto, doing bench presses on a nearby machine, lifted enormous amounts of weight that made even him strain. Mavro finally leaned over to Perfecto and pointed to the small chimera who had exposed himself.

"Perfecto," Mavro said. "See that punk over there? The sergeant with hair like that of a woman? Tell me what he is saying."

Sweat glistened over the entire length of Perfecto's body. He continued pumping weights and glanced over at the man. "You don't want to know what he is saying," Perfecto said.

Mavro made a low growling sound, stared straight ahead, continued to pump weights. He tried to ignore the little chimera. The chimera laughed loudly, then spoke in a low voice that reached us only as a babble. Mavro demanded, "Tell me what he is saying. It is a point of honor."

Perfecto turned his head, and his ears pricked up just like a dog's, nudging the thick hair of his sideburns forward. I looked over to Abriara, doing leg presses, and though her hair was long, I could see her ears had pricked forward too.

Perfecto listened carefully to the men across the room. And I could almost read the man's lips as Perfecto reported the conversation. "The little chimera, Lucío is his name, he says he bets fifty IMUs that Zavala's got a penis made of chrome-plated steel. He also thinks Zavala, with his mechanical dildo, will be Abriara's favorite in bed."

A big dark man replied to the long-haired chimera.

Perfecto reported, "His friend says, 'It is better than having a penis for a brain, like you.'"

The little chimera laughed. "'Or a penis as thin as a noodle, like the little general there.'" He nodded his chin toward Mavro. Several surrounding weightlifters laughed.

Perfecto finished the last line and looked at Mavro inquisitively. Mavro's expression remained stiff, impassive. He didn't react. Certainly Abriara and Zavala had heard Perfecto's report of the conversation, but they said nothing.

We kept lifting weights. We didn't speak much, and I listened to others, trying to eavesdrop on conversations across the room as Perfecto had. But I could only hear those nearby and was glad to hear everyone complain that they'd been beaten in the simulators as badly as we had. One turret gunner had been thrown off balance during a battle and had shot his own driver in the back, and everyone enjoyed making jokes at his expense. Soon the mood lightened up.

We followed a path in the weight room, moving from machine to machine. Three big men in front of us discussed with great excitement the possibility of increasing their salaries by increasing rank. We had signed on as *heitai*, foot soldiers, but if we advanced to the level of samurai, we would be paid three times as much. It gave them something to dream about.

After two hours of weightlifting my muscles were knotted. I was in a hurry to get to my medical bag to take some N-relaxin to stop the cramping and some Deraprim to lower the uric acid levels so my muscles wouldn't ache.

We headed for the door, Mavro in the lead. Mavro wound his way among the benches, always stepping slightly to the right, not heading in a straight line. Ahead of us was the combat team led by Lucío, the chimera with the long hair who had spoken so rudely.

Lucío had his back turned. He was sitting up, doing cable pulls. The cable pull exercise consists of sitting with your back straight against a pillar, while in either hand you hold a handle. The handles are each attached to cables that run into the press, and by twisting the dial on top of the machine you can increase the tension of the cables up to 500 kilograms.

Everyone in Lucío's group was tired, and none of them noticed us coming. Mavro attacked without warning.

He grabbed a cable and wrapped it around Lucío's neck, then flipped the handle so the cable twisted around itself like a noose. At the same time, he set the tension dial on full power, so the cable abruptly reeled the little chimera to the top of the post and began strangling him. His arms flailed and his feet kicked as he tried to catch his footing, yet the whole process happened in amazing silence, as if I were dreaming and only saw what happened without hearing it.

Mavro chuckled and we all started to hurry from the room, past the other weightlifters. One big man with only one ear jumped up from a weight machine and rushed to Lucío's rescue. Perfecto hesitated just long enough to shove One-Ear backward over a bench. One-Ear shouted as he fell, and everyone in the room turned to see what happened as we rushed out.

We hurried up the ladders for two levels, then ran down a hall, like a bunch of children who'd just broken a window and were afraid of getting caught.

I kept expecting that at any minute Lucío's compadres would rush up behind us. I had not been awake for more than half a day, and already Abriara had turned the Japanese against us while Mavro and Perfecto seemed intent on making all the enemies possible. At this rate we'd never make it to Baker alive.

When we'd run far enough, we stopped, out of breath. I stood up and rubbed my swollen ankle while every one else sat down in the hall to laugh.

"What are you laughing about?" I shouted.

"Did you not see the expressions on their faces?" Mavro said. "When that motor started strangling the little one, I thought he was going to cry!"

"You could have killed him!" I shouted. "You could have broken his neck!"

"No. I don't think so," Abriara said. "The cable didn't tighten fast enough."

"Now they'll want vengeance!" I said. "Don't you see? We've been here less than a day, and you've started a vendetta!" The more I spoke the higher my voice got.

"No." Mavro smiled, pulling a cigar from his pocket and lighting it. It was against the ship's rules to smoke, but Mavro didn't give a damn about rules. "It was not us who started it. *They* started it when they attacked our honor."

"*To hell* with honor!" I said. "Don't you see? People can't live that way!"

Mavro worked his mouth in amazement and seemed very agitated. His hands shook and he began looking for a place to set his cigar on the floor, as if he would fight me. "To hell with honor?" he demanded.

Perfecto and Abriara exchanged glances and shrugged.

Zavala appeared unsure about what was going on. "Ah, I see. A joke!" he said. He laughed experimentally to see if I'd smile.

"I mean it," I said, "To hell with honor! So what if they make jokes and call us names. If you make enemies of every person on this ship, someone will put a dagger in your back once you're on Baker. How would you like to go into battle without their support? Even if you hate them and consider them enemies, you must treat them kindly. It seems to me . . . It seems to me that the ability to show compassion toward one's enemies is what makes one human!"

Mavro stared at me strangely, then smiled. "And all this time I thought it was only opposing thumbs and the ability to communicate that separated us from the animals!" Everyone laughed. Mavro arched his eyebrows as if a great thought had struck him. He blurted, "But, ah, yes—I see what you mean! Show compassion to your enemies. Like when you gave anesthesia to Hustanifad before you slit his throat!"

Everyone laughed and Zavala said in wonder, "Did he do that? Did he really do that?"

Part of me inside said, "Yes, yes!" and I saw how true his words were, and a terrible sense of guilt washed over me. Had I really anesthesized Arish as an act of compassion before murdering him? Certainly, it seemed I had done so subconsciously, and I was hopelessly mixed up. I felt disoriented, and once again it struck me that I no longer knew who I was. I began breathing heavily and coughing, becoming hysterical. I wanted to explain to them how it had been. To tell them that somewhere, somehow, I had lost my mind. I was crazy and therefore not responsible. I buried my head in my hands.

Everyone quieted and Perfecto got up and wrapped a huge arm around me. "I'm sorry, don Angelo," he said. "We didn't mean to hurt your feelings." He turned to the group. "Did we?"

"No," Mavro said as if the idea of hurting my feelings were unthinkable. "It was nothing. I was just joking. I'm terribly sorry."

"I think don Angelo makes sense, no?" Perfecto said. "We should be making friends instead of enemies. Building instead of tearing down. Is that what you mean?" It was plain from his tone of voice that he didn't understand. He was trying to please me, and any sense of victory I'd have felt by convincing him of my argument was cheapened by the knowledge that he agreed because of his genetic programming. He had no choice in the matter.

"Sí," I said, wiping my eyes.

Mavro drew a deep puff on his cigar. His gaze held an appearance of thoughtfulness. "Perhaps you are right. . . . You certainly bring up a good argument. There would be many advantages to having a ship full of allies. I had not considered the political consequences of this scenario before I acted. The loyalty of others on the ship would be most useful . . . both for survival and for gaining promotions . . ."

I wondered if he was trying to humor me, but as I watched I could almost see gears in his mind turn as he considered ways of winning the loyalty of others on ship. I'm sure he envisioned a vast network of friends, all eager to die at his whim, sacrificing themselves to save his life. He obviously craved power, yet had no avenue to gain it. Because of his small size, he could not compete with the chimeras. On ship he'd never be the strong man everyone admires.

"You're right," Mavro said. "It does make sense. Maybe I like the idea."

"You're not serious!" Abriara said. "What can we gain?"

"Friends," Mavro said.

"Peace," I said. "If everyone would live that way, we could have peace."

Abriara shook her head in disbelief. "It won't work— not with us chimeras. You're talking a bunch of idealistic crap. People respect the strong and the brave, not politicians. Besides, we're committed to a vendetta with that punk Lucío. We can't stop it! He won't accept an apology!"

"Why not?" I asked.

Abriara didn't answer. Perfecto said, "She's right."

"Why?" I said.

Perfecto tilted his head to the side and shrugged. "I cannot explain it. It is an emotional thing. I just know by instinct that Lucío cannot let the matter rest. He is younger than me, younger than Abriara even, and therefore the engineers made him less human. He is chimera. We have assaulted him. His anger cannot be washed away except by blood. He will initiate a Quest."

"A Quest?" I asked, never having heard the term.

"Sí. He will not be satisfied with killing us. He will also want to mutilate us. A man who is on a Quest seeks more than revenge."

Mavro drew a puff on his cigar. "Really? How interesting . . ." he said. "Still, Angelo's plan will work if others don't realize what we're doing. Angelo isn't so much saying 'To hell with honor,' as he is saying that honor should take second place to wisdom. No? So I think we can have it both ways. We should become political animals for a while. We should be as friendly as puppies and see what it gets us. And at the same time we can keep lists of all the people we don't like. Then, if our plan doesn't work, we kill them.

"Even Lucío might come to his senses if we pay him off with a bottle of whiskey."

I was amazed that none of them took the situation

seriously. They all nodded agreement with Mavro as if he were some great sage dispensing wisdom.

We spent the afternoon doing visualization exercises, practicing targeting skills in our minds, as Kaigo had ordered. By evening the swelling in my leg had eased, so we marched, performing the one useless exercise we could still do freely on ship. I remember in Guatemala, it was holes. I dug thousands of holes in the army. Fortunately there was no place to dig on ship. But we could march in the halls, so we marched. The ship was accelerating at 1 g, but Abriara informed us that within two weeks we'd slowly increase acceleration till we hit 1.45 g's, the maximum legal acceleration. This meant each of us would feel as if he were carrying an extra twenty-five to fifty kilos, so when we marched we would have an added blessing—we wouldn't have to carry packs.

That night, a little Brazi woman came to our room. She was the first nonchimera woman I'd seen on board. "Did anyone you know die today—in the simulators?" she asked.

"Sí," Abriara said. "We all got killed."

"No, I mean die for real. Some people really got killed from the simulations. So far, I've heard of six deaths."

I knew what she meant. I remembered the man in Panamá who hunted monkeys in the jungles south of Gatún. Just as his monkeys would fall from the trees mortally wounded from shock, in the same way, those six men died in the simulators.

We were all made uneasy by the news.

"I hear it is nothing to stay alarmed about," the Brazi said, putting on a brighter face. "Those who are liable to succumb to such things will all die off by tomorrow."

"That is very comforting," Mavro said.

"Also, I should tell you: no one beat the samurai in the simulators this morning. So me and some friends thought it might be a good idea to start a collection for the first winners. Everyone is putting in five IMUs per day. Do you want to bet?"

I figured quickly in my head. With ten thousand

mercenaries on board, that would be a minimum of ten
thousand IMUs for each person in the team that won.
We eagerly presented our credit disks to the Brazi.

She said, "Also, to make things fair, I must tell you
that some people have found that the plasma guns can be
defeated if you are not hit at close range. When the
metallic gases hit the armor they begin to cool and turn
liquid. If you fall on the side where you took your hit,
you can sometimes keep the plasma from eating your
armor. We saw some of the samurai perform this trick in
the simulator."

I thought about it. Our battle armor is a layered
ablative ceramic cast under pressure so that it is riddled
with tiny pockets of liquid nitrogen. Not only does this
liquid nitrogen keep the armor cool and cut down on our
infrared signature, but as the armor heats and becomes
molten, the liquid nitrogen explodes into gas, spewing
the molten armor away, as if our battle armor were
reactive armor blasting against a projectile. It only made
sense that if we lay down after taking a hit, the molten
material would be spewed away while the successive
layers of the armor would remain cool. This knowledge
would be of great help in battle. We thanked the Brazi,
and she left. Then we prepared for battle. Abriara set us
down and said, "I've been thinking about how we can
beat these monkeys. Did anyone notice if they have the
same kind of hovercraft as we do?"

"Sí, it is exactly the same," Perfecto said.

"Good!" Abriara said. "Then it's safe to bet they can't
outrun us." She turned to Zavala. "Which means, Zavala, that you keep us going full-speed at all times.
Understand? We don't have to guard our rear if they
can't catch us. So, Mavro, you flip your turret around
and face forward. Always keep all guns aiming forward.
We don't need to worry about our rear."

Abriara continued, "Angelo, remember what Kaigo
said. Keep low to present less of a target, and keep your
knees flexed so you can counteract the motion of the
craft. Remember, you'll only get one shot with that laser
before the turrets take you out—so you must make that
shot count. When teflex battle armor was first intro-

duced, troops around the world suddenly decreased their accuracy in shooting because they thought they could afford to be sloppy—but you *must* learn to shoot. The same goes for turret gunners. If we're following a curve along the edge of those coralwood trees and the warning siren sounds, start firing plasma ahead immediately so the Yabajin run into it.

"You know, on Earth it's illegal to train a person in a simulator like this. It's considered inhuman. But Motoki doesn't give a damn about us. This is Pavlov. Reward and punishment. These people want us to be fast and deadly."

We sat on the floor in the little squares Perfecto had marked off as individual territories, and the others passionately discussed ways to fry the samurai the next day. At first I got excited too, until I remembered we were only practicing genocide. Always I had been a doctor. Always I had helped others, had been concerned about things greater than myself. Yet now I worried about nothing greater than self-preservation, and I felt small and ugly. I did not know who I was anymore. I asked Abriara for General Garzón's comlink number.

I stepped into the hall, thumbed the subdural call button on my comlink, spoke the numbers, and the general answered.

"Who is speaking?" he said. He sounded weary.

"General Garzón, it's me, Angelo Osic."

He sighed. "How can I help you, Señor Osic?"

"I called to ask for a transfer into a medical unit."

"Ah, you and a hundred other people. I'll tell you what I told everyone else: you signed a contract with Motoki Corporation, not with me, and Motoki will hold you to that contract. They have all the medical personnel they need. What they really need is people with mercenary spirit—people like yourself—people whose veins run strong with the blood of the *conquistadores*."

"But . . . I don't think I will make a good mercenary."

Garzón seemed impatient. "You never know what will happen. The information we have on Baker is twenty years out of date. By the time we get there, another twenty years realtime will have passed: the Yabajin may be dead, or Motoki may be destroyed, or maybe both nations will have settled their differences. There is a strong chance you won't have to fight this war."

I didn't say anything.

"Try it for a month or two," Garzón said. "Many people find the mercenary life-style rewarding—the joy of battle, the thrill of victory. Perhaps you'll be one of them. You did a good job on Arish. It was a clean kill, and you got to look death in the face. You can stick this out."

"I don't think so," I said. I waited a moment.

"Is there something else?" Garzón asked.

"Tamara?"

"That subject is classified. Don't ask about it in the future!" he said. Then, more softly, "Don't get your hopes up. There have been no changes in the situation. You didn't give us much to begin with." Garzón disconnected.

I stood in the hall and considered: Tamara was no better. A dozen samurai came up the ladder, laughing and talking. Master Kaigo passed, staring straight ahead as if he didn't see me. I bowed and said, "Hello, Master." He glanced at me, disconcerted; nodded embarrassedly in return; and walked on. Apparently it had been a breach of etiquette for me to speak to him outside the classroom.

In the bedroom everyone was preparing for the morning's battle. Zavala broke away from the group during a lull and came to my bunk. "Señor Osic," he said. "I had hoped you would give me some of those antibiotics you told me about." He spoke to me formally, phrasing his verbs in third-person, and this seemed strange, since we'd been through so much together that day.

I knew he wasn't suffering from the rot and didn't need any antibiotics; his symptoms were only psychological, but I felt sorry for him. Since my youth I have never been able to walk into a house where a person keeps a dog without suffering bites from fleas. Logically I know it's impossible for all dogs to have fleas, yet my

ankles and back and arms turn red and begin itching as
soon as I spot a dog in a house. Zavala suffered with
similar symptoms.

"Let me see your arms, *amigo*," I asked informally. I
checked them thoroughly. There was no whiteness or
flaking in the skin, no boils. I said, "I don't see any sign
of illness, and those antibiotics are very potent. They
will give you bad diarrhea and stomachaches. Perhaps
we should hold off for a few days."

"Are you sure?" Zavala asked. "Germs are very small,
and often hard to see!"

This was something a peasant would say, and it
surprised me immensely. Most cyborgs I've known have
been very erudite and sophisticated. It takes a great deal
of money to buy limbs such as those Zavala owned.

"Where are you from?" I asked.

"Colombia. A village that used to be near Mosquera."
Mosquera is a small coastal town in the south of Colombia. And in the poor parts of Colombia, away from the
cities, people are not much educated. They rely heavily
on witchdoctors in such places, so it made sense for
Zavala to believe he could see germs.

"Ah, and you bought your fine arm and legs in
Mosquera?"

Zavala laughed as if I were an idiot. "Such things do
not exist in Mosquera. When the socialists sprayed the
plague over our village, I left home quickly and tried to
go to Buenaventura, but my feet died too fast and I
couldn't make it. A padre in Guapi took me to a doctor
in a camp in the jungle. He gave me the new limbs on
the condition that I fight for the resistance."

"Ah, I see," I said. "Well, let me take another look at
that arm." I held his arm and looked very closely,
brushing my nose on his arm hairs, as I were trying very
hard to see the germs. "I must confess," I said after a
long examination, "that I have been practicing medicine
for a long time. My eyes are very good, and I have seen
many germs in my lifetime! But I cannot find a germ on
your arm. Perhaps it has crawled away? Or, more likely,
when the fire burned you in the simulators today, maybe
it just felt like the rot, so now your mind is playing tricks

on you." I had once heard a witchdoctor make a similar statement in the feria, and I hoped my imitation would sound enough like that of a genuine witchdoctor so Zavala would believe me.

He smiled a little and appeared relieved. "Many thanks, don Angelo," he said, and rejoined the others on the floor as they plotted how to destroy the samurai in the simulators.

I watched him for a bit and felt much sadness. He was too stupid and innocent to have to spend his life fighting wars. He was dumb and innocent like a cow. In fact, he had the same droopy, sad brown eyes as a cow. The four of them were hunched over, eagerly waving their fingers above the floor as they drew imaginary battle plans. I pitied them. For beneath the talk of winning wealth and glory by beating the samurai, their real goal was to escape the pain and shock of dying in the simulators each time they lost a battle. They were four people uniting to avoid pain. And it occurred to me that these four people constituted a society. Perhaps not a society like the one in Panamá, since they lived by different rules, but a society nonetheless. I imagined living with them in the jungles of Baker, raising corn and beans and coffee outside a little hut. Mavro and Perfecto would be my neighbors, and Tamara, she would be my closest friend. And I realized that although it was no longer possible for me to be a servant of the society in Panamá, it was possible for me to serve the society I was living in.

Without considering the consequences of my decision, I slid off my cot and joined my combat team in planning our next conquest.

CHAPTER

6

Tamara's eyes opened, and she held up the stump of her arm for me to see. I was tied to a chair, and though I desperately wanted to go to Tamara, to help her, I was unable to move.

A little girl with a familiar smile came into the room and poured water from a blue ceramic pitcher onto Tamara's wrist. A nub appeared on the stump of her arm. Like a film where irises and daisies grow and bloom in fast motion, she sprouted a palm; fingers shot up like vines seeking sunlight. Amazed, I watched till the hand became whole, complete. When she was done, Tamara tapped the side of her head with a new-grown finger, and the finger seemed flawless, perfectly formed, like that of a newborn child.

"You see, don Angelo, you forget," she said, "I don't need a comlink to speak to you. I don't need your medicines. You forget: I'm a witch."

I woke from my dream of Tamara on the ninth morning and looked about the bedroom. Perfecto and Abriara stood facing the wall at the edge of the bunks; the wire leads of cranial jacks led from the computer outlets to the bases of their skulls. The jacks let us view only one program—Mavro called it "The Horror Show"—we could watch the Yabajin samurai slaughter our mercenaries in simulation. The view showed tiny

153

holos of battle teams racing over various terrains. Messages on screen announced each team leader. You could hear the mercenaries speak in the simulators just as if you'd joined them in battle. The computer only revealed glimpses of each battle—the assault tactics used by the doomed team. At three minutes per battle, we got to witness the deaths of many mercenaries. In nine days of practice no one had beaten the Yabajin. I was beginning to believe no one ever would. Yet Abriara and Perfecto studied tactics during each spare moment, concocting new schemes for conquest. The strain of their efforts left them pale, washed out, unable to smile.

Perfecto moaned in anger at something he saw on the holo. Neither he nor Abriara wore visors or helmets to cut down on sensory leak, so they stared at the wall, faces slack, eyes twitching in choreographed motion as they viewed the program.

Their blank faces staring at the wall reminded me of Tamara lying in the teak chest, endlessly gazing at the ceiling. I still hadn't heard from her. Even if her condition had deteriorated to the point where she'd needed neural growth stimulator, she should have shown major improvement by now. She should have wakened, though it might take a few days to discover how much brain damage she'd sustained. Ideally, she'd get by with minimal memory loss. But if the damage were severe, she might lose motor skills, forget how to speak or walk. I wanted to find her, see for myself how she was recovering. My hands itched from the compulsive desire to touch her, to treat her ailments until she healed.

I sat up in bed and practiced pulling my knives from their wrist sheaths and slicing the air as if hacking at enemies. The heavy crystal felt good in my hand. They were flawless, perfect, such knives as I'd have believed could only exist in Plato's dreams. I'd not made any more progress in learning for certain who my assailant would be, and I was becoming anxious to confront him. My hands itched to do more than treat Tamara.

Perfecto made a snorting noise and, as one, he and Abriara jacked out. "Even with the help of God, that

Yabajin baboon couldn't have dodged that shot!" he shouted.

"So he hid behind a rock before his armor melted. What can you do?" Abriara asked. She was mad too. She brushed back a strand of chocolate-brown hair.

Perfecto said, "But that can't be right. I timed the samurai's reaction from when our man dropped from the tree: one fifth of a second! No one can aim and fire so fast."

Perfecto was right. I couldn't imagine any way for the samurai to become so good—at least not without years of practice. I envisioned Baker as a planet torn apart. Cities would be desolate, dirty, with clumps of blasted cement left where skyscrapers had been. Children would end-lessly scour the wastes in their hovercrafts, learning by hard practice how to fry the Yabajin. Old scarred cyborgs would sit around campfires at night and tell stories of past victories while children envisioned their enemies exploding into fireballs.

Abriara turned to me, "So, Angelo, you are ready for breakfast?"

"Yes," I said.

"Well, I'm afraid you'll have to fry some Yabajin and eat them in the simulator. You overslept. It's time for battle practice."

I wasn't disappointed about breakfast. Processed algae in any form—flavored to taste like sausage, or as ice cream, or even as cereal—made my stomach turn. I rummaged through my chest, searching through the rapidly declining stock of liquor and cigars, and found a nice bottle of brandy and downed a swig, hoping it would suffice for breakfast. But the spectacle of battle practice made me queasy. In nine days 27 people had died of shock during simulations. Rumor said Motoki Corporation had drugged the water in an attempt to halt the problem. I didn't believe it. Those who'd die from such things had been allowed to die—the company couldn't afford to have so much as a medical droid waiting by the simulators to care for the injured. Such luxuries cost too much to transport between stars. I guzzled some brandy. Then we met Mavro and Zavala at the battle room.

Kaigo was giving one of his typical lectures to five tired soldiers, uttering incomprehensible maxims. "You must rid yourself of the interference of the interfering self. Learn the act of supreme concentration. See this one, see how the sweat of *mugga* shines upon him . . ." He indicated a sweaty and crazed looking chimera—a man you would not care to meet in an alley. "Be like him! Learn to live as one already dead! Do not think of pain or death, glory or dishonor. This path leads to the state of *munen*, no mind, where the will and the act become one." The men gave Kaigo sour expressions. Only Zavala took the samurai's advice seriously. The formula for success was close enough to folk magic to satisfy him.

Master Kaigo's expression was strange—angry, hopeful, concerned? Perhaps none of these. I often found his body language incomprehensible. When thinking, he'd wrinkle his face and frown as if mad. He never looked us in the eye. I knew he liked us, for when he laughed at our mistakes he politely covered his mouth with his hand—something other samurai neglected. Yet when we spoke he pretended we weren't there and looked off in another direction, then answered questions without looking at us, as if he were some religious fanatic responding to queries from God. When he spoke about himself he'd unconsciously touch his nose with his forefinger, and when he told us we'd done poorly he'd emphasize it by putting his hand by his face and making little karate-chop movements in the air. Observing him was like observing a strange beast for the first time. I couldn't understand the motives behind his actions. I felt no kinship to him as a human being.

When I was a child my friends and I pretended sticks were guns, and we fought aliens on other planets. But if Kaigo accurately represented the people of Baker, then, in a way I'd never quite expected, I'd grown up to find that I *would* be fighting aliens on another planet.

The men left and we fought two inconsequential battles in rapid succession and were slaughtered in both. Zavala performed well in the second battle and was the

last man to die. When Kaigo saw that Zavala had jacked
out, he immediately thrust us into a third scenario. The
illusion settled over us like a cool but heavy fog.

Scenario 59: Mid Patrol

And the hovercraft roared up a mountain through a
deep bed of snow in a great pine forest by the light of
double moons. Abriara steered with little flicks of the
wrist, dodging wind-fallen trees and standing pine,
swerving with such violence I could barely hold on.
Abriara had traded Zavala for position as driver, since he
was taking too much psychic damage in battle. Drivers
tended to receive the brunt of the plasma fire. It
relieved the eyes to be in a scenario where the land was
completely terraformed. Usually the alien landscape
jarred me, but this felt much like a joyride through a
frozen pine forest on Earth. The chill, blustery wind
brought bits of ice and frozen raindrops to drift from the
sky into the hovercraft. As we roared along, plumes of
snow raised and hung in the air behind us. Ahead
loomed a great white glacier. Two other hovercrafts
intersected us from either direction, but no warning
buzzer went off.

We'd decided that only sergeants should speak over
the helmet mikes when more than one combat team was
present.

"This is Hector Vasquez commanding team one," said
the man to our right. "Who do we have here?"

"Abriara Sifuentes in team two."

"Paco García in team three," said the man to our left.
I glanced left. Many men had praised García over the
past few days, affirming that if anyone from our module
could beat the samurai, he could. García's team looked
like any other. Judging by size, two humans and three
chimeras, all dressed in bug suits that looked black in the
darkness.

Abriara said, "Right. You're in charge."

García said, "Form a V, two hundred meters to the
side. First team to hear a buzzer, call out and swerve
toward your compadres on the other side of the V. Then

we'll all veer directly away from the incoming craft. I want them on our tails. Abriara, I want you in the lead. Just circle this mountain. I want plenty of snow on the ground when they find us."

"Sí," Abriara and Hector said in unison. We took the lead. Abriara kept driving at full speed, and the other drivers—both humans—had difficulty keeping up.

We circled the base of the mountain for half an hour. The two moons overhead were each smaller than Earth's moon and shed little light. We had no headlights—just the colored lights of the instrument panels. Kaigo had once told us that the headlights were removed for our own safety—a vehicle traveling with headlights on was too easily spotted by the Yabajin. Only the moonlight reflecting on snow let us guide the hovercrafts in the dark. We'd never fought a scenario at night before, nor had we fought in snow.

Zavala spoke through his helmet mike, panting between words. "I dreamed of this place last night. I dreamed we fought the samurai here. We tricked them, but I can't remember how."

His words gave me an eerie sensation. I couldn't think what would make Zavala dream such a thing.

"Try to remember," Mavro said. "It could be important. It could save us all." His cheery voice was encouraging on the surface, but held an undertone of contempt. Zavala had begun recording a journal of dreams, believing them important. He spent his days trying to recall his dreams of the night before.

"I'll try," Zavala said. And after several moments he continued, "It had something to do with our armor. We put something on our armor, making it impenetrable. The Japanese shot, but couldn't hurt us."

"Ah, if only you could remember, I'm sure it would be a boon!" Mavro said. "As for myself, my dreams are useless. I only dreamed I made love to a giant woman. She cooed from the pleasure I gave. She was ecstatic. She looked just like Abriara, only bigger."

"Shut up," García said over the head mike, and Mavro quieted.

The daytime sights on our guns would do us no good,

so García had us flip on our targeting lasers and practice shooting. Each targeting laser shone in a different color of the spectrum so that we wouldn't confuse our targeting light with that of someone else. When I pointed my rifle, a pale blue dot showed where my shot would hit.

I fried a few fallen pines, sometimes turning them into torches.

We circled the mountain and climbed the great glacier that covered one face. Our bug suits didn't protect us from the cold. I shivered violently and my hands soon stiffened inside the armor. I wished I'd spent time in the mountains of Peru with Perfecto.

We were at the bottom of the glacier hurtling toward a dark line of pines when García yelled, "Here they come! Veer right!" The Yabajin were shooting down from the mountaintop at tree line, hoping to intersect us in the open.

We veered right, dropping toward the bottom of the glacier, keeping out of range of their turrets. Beyond the snowfield was a forest on a slope so steep it almost formed a cliff. And just below our line of sight a thin line of feathery clouds glowed silver in the moonlight.

The change in direction restructured our formation so that our team was no longer at point. García's team formed the point of the triangle slightly behind us, closest to the Yabajin, while Hector's team floated beside us.

"Look for a small valley, no wider than fifty meters. One with steep sides. I want them to funnel in after us," García ordered. "And when you find it, lay down plasma fire in the snow behind you. I want a smoke screen."

Mavro experimentally shot a burst of plasma into the snow beside us. The plasma became a searing white light in the darkness. Sure enough, a small puff of steam rose. We dropped off the edge of the glacier into the sparse forest, and all we did was fall.

Abriara hit the thrusters in full reverse to slow our descent and dodged the black trees while I hooked my feet under my seat and held the rail. One man in Hector's team started praying, *"Madre de Dios . . ."* and I closed my eyes.

The trip down seemed to last forever.

"Lay down grazing fire!" García ordered. "Maybe one of them will crash into a tree!" Mavro and Perfecto opened up with the plasma turrets, and the guns made their little *whuft, whuft* sounds. In the darkness the flash from the plasma turrets was bright enough so I could see pinpoints of white even through my closed eyes.

Abriara jerked the hovercraft controls, pitching it violently as she dodged trees. I opened my eyes just in time to see the ground come up. The hovercraft thudded nose-first into a pile of snow, hurling me to the floor. Then Abriara gunned the engine and the craft broke free. We were in a valley with incredibly steep sides— too steep for the hovercraft to climb out. Hector took the lead, and his hovercraft threw up a roostertail of snow, blinding us. The valley was full of fallen trees and great black igneous boulders, so every time Hector dodged a tree or boulder he'd shout, "Tree, right!" or "Rock, left!" so Abriara would know where to turn.

"Slow down and continue grazing fire! I want them to follow us!" García called.

He was right. This was a perfect place to set up an ambush, and the Yabajin had no choice but to follow us down the funnel. Perfecto and Mavro fired their turrets ahead and to the sides. With each burst, the path ahead brightened as if struck by lightning, and the black stones and trees threw eerie shadows; then the plasma would hit the snow and mist would rise up and drift down to silently fill the valley behind us. García's hovercraft pulled up on our tail till he could nearly touch us.

Hector called out, "Rock, right!" At the same time, we passed under a leaning pine. One of García's chimera turret-gunners leapt from atop the turret mount. He grabbed a pine limb and pulled himself up, then was lost in the plume of snow our hovercrafts had raised. We saw the rock ahead in the glow of the plasma arc—the black volcanic stone of a cliff face.

When we rounded the cliff, García's laser gunners dove from their hovercraft, and I leapt with them and plowed through the knee-deep snow. They scurried up the steep side of the valley, making their way to the clifftop, about ten meters. I tried following but the teflex armor on my boots slipped like plastic. Not only couldn't I make it to the cliff top, I couldn't walk up the gentler slope of the valley. Both García's chimera gunners climbed as if they were half mountain goat. I unbuckled my armored gloves and tried pulling myself up by grabbing the roots of a small pine, but I slid back down as soon as I let go.

Through my helmet mike I could hear Hector's clear voice calling directions to Abriara and García as they continued down the mountain.

The distant whine of hovercrafts and flashing lights announced the Yabajin as they floated down the valley. There was no place to take cover by the cliff, so I began to run downhill to hide. I risked a glance behind and saw that my tactic wouldn't work: I'd left a trail through the snow a blind man could follow. I retraced my steps back to where we'd jumped from the hovercraft. The snow was beaten there, and our tracks were mixed. It looked like a safe place to hide. I lay in the snow and covered myself as best I could, leaving a peephole. I turned off the targeting laser on my rifle so no blue spot on the snow would betray my presence. The slopes of the mountain filled with soft white light as the Yabajin blasted beams of plasma ahead to show the way.

"Stop," García said over his helmet mike. He sounded distant—not the typical "voice of God" one heard at close range. "Abriara, go over there. Hector, stay where you are."

Lying still, waiting, tiny crystals of ice drifted through the cracks in my armor; when one touched my skin it felt as if I'd been pinched, then it turned wet and warm as it raised to body temperature. My helmet mike carried the sound of heavy breathing as the chimeras on the cliff panted from exertion. One said, "You down there, human: remember to report your kills before the Yabajin shoot you."

"Okay," I said.

García spoke over his mike, "We're held up about two

kilometers from you. We're setting up cross-fire now. Do you have a report?"

A chimera above me said, "They're coming cautiously, at no more than thirty kph, a hundred meters apart, frying rocks and trees—anyplace where a person could hide. I count fourteen men. It looks as if they've left a sniper up at the head of the valley."

García said, "What's your position?"

"Noel and I are on top of the cliff. The human—"

"Angelo," I offered.

"Angelo, is at the base of the cliff, your side, covered with snow."

"Okay, Angelo—" García said, "Caesar, Miguel, and Noel will ambush the Yabajin. They might be able to take out as many as seven or eight men. But I want you to hold tight—don't move for four minutes after the Yabajin pass. We should engage the main party at about that time. They'll dump a couple of snipers off to take care of Caesar and Noel, and I want you to surprise them. Their best sniper is a short man who swings his arms when he walks—we call him the Chimp. Fry him quick. When you're done, wait for their last sniper to come down. If we get killed, you'll be last man out."

"Yes, Sergeant," I said, happy to have a plan to follow.

I flipped on the helmet's external microphone so I could better hear sounds outside the suit. The noise from the external mike was often distracting in a heated battle, so I normally left it off. As soon as I flipped the switch the sounds from outside the suit multiplied in volume. I'd have staked my life the Yabajin were half a kilometer off, but with the mike on it sounded as if they were in my lap.

I prepared myself, trying to remember to fall forward when I took a plasma hit so my armor would cool.

I lay still while the whine of the hovercrafts increased. The white plasma fire reflecting on the hillside brightened as they drew near. The sky above me suddenly lit up as a jet of plasma streaked into a tree. A chimera shouted and a Yabajin craft crashed into the other side of the cliff, shaking the ground so that the earth shuddered,

and exploded in a flash that bathed the mountains orange
and white.

The white streaks of plasma fire ceased abruptly. Only
the flames on the other side of the cliff lit the valley. Two
hovercrafts shot by in the shadow of the rock, sending up
roostertails of snow that drifted down to bury me. I kept
perfectly still.

"Noel reporting. They just passed us, Sergeant.
Miguel took out one craft. I know he took the driver with
him, but several others jumped clear before the crash.
Three, possibly four, are on foot. The other two craft are
coming down in the dark, minus two turret gunners.
They didn't slow long enough to take on stragglers."

"*Gracias*," García said.

I lay in the snow and counted the seconds. My helmet
began buzzing intermittently as if a bee were caught
inside, and I began to worry, but suddenly the helmet
warmed, defrosting the snow that had covered my
goggles. After sixty seconds, the smallest of footsteps
crunched the snow near the base of the cliff.

The Yabajin stood motionless a second.

They moved again; I could hear them breathing. One
began ascending the steepest side of the cliff. Another
crept past me, following the false trail I'd left in the
snow.

Two minutes later he came back, retracing my steps.
In the darkness he missed me and walked back to
the base of the cliff. I figured I'd waited close to four
minutes.

I quietly arose and shook my head. Snow slid from my
helmet as I flipped on my targeting laser. Two Yabajin
waited at the base of the rock, looking up. They were
backlighted by the fire from the burning hovercraft, and
as I followed their gaze I saw that the igneous rock above
was shaped like the face of a deformed ogre. A third
Yabajin scaled the cliff, perching on the ogre's nose. One
samurai on the ground held a laser rifle and covered the
climber, while his compadre next to him was empty-
handed. I took the sniper on the ground, aiming the blue
dot of my targeting laser on the back of his head, and

fried him. He dropped with a grunt. His compadre
turned, yelled in surprise, and charged.

Down the valley García announced over his helmet
mike, "Here they come."

I aimed for the samurai's face and shot. A white
glowing circle appeared on his helmet just above the
nose. He was running at me, and I stepped backward
and screamed, "One down," afraid the laser wouldn't
burn through his armor in time for me to notify the
others of my first kill. Then the samurai stopped and
held up his hand as if to catch my laser beam with his
armed palm.

The effect was almost magical: my targeting computer
was designed to hold on target—but as soon as the target
was covered, the laser quit firing. I pulled the trigger a
second time, aiming at his chest. He kept charging, but
he jumped in the air and spun. The laser switched off a
second time as the target was covered by motion.

I pulled off a third shot to his kidneys as he reached
me. He leapt and kicked. I stepped back and held my
gun out, trying to let the beam cut through his armor.
He brought his foot down on the rifle barrel, knocking it
to the ground. I turned and ran.

He followed me three paces and fell to the ground,
sliding face-down in the snow. I turned to attack.

"Make that two dead," Caesar said over his helmet
mike.

The samurai lay in the snow, steam rising from a hole
in the back of his helmet, his legs twitching.

I searched for the third samurai. He was on the cliff,
near the top. He'd found a perch—and a target. He'd
unstrapped his rifle and a pink dot shone on the armored
torso of a chimera. Before I could yell, the chimera
slumped forward. His armor let him glide on the snow
like a sled, and he skidded five meters down a steep
slope, then dropped over the cliff.

"Noel's down," Caesar said.

I ran back for my rifle, scooped it up, and raised it.

The Yabajin sniper had disappeared into a crevice. I
studied the area where he should have been, but
couldn't find him.

"Caesar, do you see a Yabajin up there?" I yelled.

Caesar didn't answer.

I couldn't expect him to answer. If he spoke, he might give away his position. I flipped off my targeting laser and trudged to the base of the cliff, and everyone down in the valley began yelling at once: "One down! One down! Felipe's down! García's down! One down!" so fast I couldn't keep track of the kills to learn who was winning.

I circled the cliff face and came to the wrecked hovercraft. A few tenacious flames still crackled, sending up a wisp of black smoke. The crumpled bodies of Miguel and two Yabajin were there. I circled over to the mountain side of the rock and stood beneath an overhang while I searched for a way to climb. A few chunks of ice rained down from the cliff above me, and I looked up. A body came falling out of the darkness to crash at my feet.

A chimera in a green bug suit.

"Caesar's down," I told the rest of the company.

The battle lulled at the mouth of the valley. No one spoke of a new kill or exchanged commands for two minutes. Someone down in the valley began coughing into his helmet mike, making a sound I normally associate with pneumonia. I waited for the samurai to come down the slope. The snow had drifted deep near the cliff, so I sat down and pulled more snow on top of my legs, hiding myself, and watched the hillsides for movement. I didn't think I'd stand a chance with that last samurai if I tried to sneak out of the canyon. The coughing stopped, and Zavala spoke through his mike in a deep groggy voice. "Don't leave me for the samurai to burn. I don't want to die by burning." He said it very quietly, very matter-of-factly. His slurred speech made it sound as if he had a concussion. He began to weep. I hoped someone would break his neck.

Zavala's crying annoyed me. In the past nine days we'd each been killed over fifty times. You'd have thought he'd begin to adjust to it. At first when I got burned, it often felt as if someone had peeled the skin from the back of my head, pried off my skull cap, and exposed my brain to flames. For hours the pain left my face numb, and my teeth would ache. But my endorphin levels were building up, and I was adjusting to the continual shocks. Each wave of pain was the same as the last. Each threatened to bowl me over. But now when the wave hit, it didn't move me so much as move through me. At least that is how I experienced it. I could withstand the pain. I'd have thought Zavala would begin to feel that way, too, but he didn't. He believed his hands were rotting all the time now, and each time he went to the ship's dispensary they refused to give him antibiotics.

I was tempted to humiliate Zavala, call him a baby so he'd stop crying. But then I realized I'd never before in my life considered humiliating anyone. Since my youth I'd planned to be a doctor and struggled to empathize with the plight of others. I pretended not to hear Zavala's whining, not wishing to embarrass him by acknowledging his weakness.

No sound other than Zavala's weeping disturbed the night. "Is anyone else alive?" I asked over the mike.

Perfecto panted, "Ah, Angelo, it is good to hear you're doing so well!"

"Where are you?" I asked.

"Chasing two Yabajin back to you."

"What if I don't want them?"

"Then you'll have to pray that I catch them first."

"Are you alone?" I asked.

"No," Perfecto panted. "I've got three compadres behind me."

"Don't be in too much of a hurry to get here," I said. "We've still got one samurai here somewhere up on the hillside, plus the one up the valley."

Perfecto said, "I'm over the north rim. I'm going to try to cut off these two before they reach you. Which rim is your sniper on?"

"I don't know. Which way is north?"

"Facing down the valley, it's the side on your left."

"Then he's on the south—"

"Do you have any extra rifles near?" Hector cut in.

"Yes, why do you ask?"

"One of the samurai we're chasing isn't armed. Your friend may try to get a rifle to him."

I looked at Caesar dead on the ground. His rifle was gone. I jumped up and ran around the cliff, looking back down the valley. In the distance, along the hillside near the south ridgetop, a man jogged through the snow with his back turned to me.

I flipped on my targeting laser and aimed it on the ground behind him, then moved it up quickly till I had him in the back. I flipped on the image magnifier so I could see my target more clearly. At this distance, I couldn't hold my beam steady. My dot bounced around the entire length of his body. My breath was ragged, uneven. I inhaled, then released the air slowly, held the light on the center of the samurai's back, and squeezed off a shot. A white flower burst into flame at the bottom tip of his left lung, and he went down.

"One down," I said.

"*Bueno, amigo!*" Perfecto said. "How easy you make it soun—"

"Vasquez is down!" Hector cried over the speaker.

"Did you see where the shot came from?" one of his compadres, a woman, asked.

"He took it in the forehead, so it must have come from somewhere ahead of us."

Hector said, "Angelo, gather up any extra guns you have there and throw them off in the deep snow where no one will find them. Then sit down with your nose pointing up the canyon. I want you to get that man up there. We'll get these two."

I searched the ground and retrieved two weapons—Noel's rifle, which had slid down the cliff, and the samurai's. I tucked them under the wrecked hovercraft and took my place beneath the overhang, burying myself in the snow again. I didn't dare return any farther back up the canyon: my tracks would have revealed my presence, whereas the snow by the hovercraft was so beaten no one could tell I'd been there.

"One down!" Hector said. "The other is just heading around the bend."

"Which bend?" Perfecto called.

Hector said, "The first bend that sharply turns north, by the big standing pine."

"Then I'm in front of him!" Perfecto shouted.

I sat and watched the snow for several minutes. Zavala had quit sobbing. He still coughed on occasion. The largest crescent moon had nearly dipped below the skyline—its light silvered the needles of a pine—and visibility was poor. A shadow moved over the rim of the canyon in the distance: something with four legs and a bushy tail—larger than a deer or jaguar, more the size of a small horse. It moved easily over the snow from tree to tree, sniffing at the air, slinking my way. I couldn't place it: it had the shape of a wolf, only it was larger and bulkier—more like a large bear. I couldn't think what kind of animal it might be. Then I realized it was something I'd never seen on Earth. A local carnivore thrown into the simulator. The samurai had done this once before, pitting us against the Kawa no Ryu, the river dragons. I flipped my targeting laser on and shot twice before I hit the beast in the belly. It hissed and whined and growled and spun in circles, kicking up snow and snapping the air. Then it lunged through the snow and back over the hilltop. *It will probably come back with a dozen hungry friends,* I thought.

I flipped off my targeting laser.

Nothing moved in the canyon in front of me.

Perfecto yelled, "Yabajin!" over the helmet mike, and he sounded so close I sprawled forward. I looked up. No one was even near. I figured they must only be a few hundred meters away.

"I've got him!" Hector yelled.

"He's cheating!" Perfecto said.

Someone got hit in the head and a helmet mike crunched. "Hit the *verga!*" Hector yelled. Someone grunted several times.

"Okay, you can stop hitting him now," Hector said.

Perfecto said, "Damn him to hell. How's Juanita?"

"She's dead. Her neck is broken."

"Damn these samurai!" Perfecto said.

I was surprised. Perfecto never swore, never even used mild obscenities. "What happened?" I asked.

"We had him from both sides," Perfecto said. "All three of us were shooting him. He just kept spinning in circles so the imaging computer would lose its target before the laser could burn through his armor, then he kicked Juanita in the head."

"I had one do that to me just a few moments ago," I said.

"How did you beat him?" Perfecto asked.

"Caesar shot him in the back when he wasn't looking."

"These samurai are very frugal," Hector said. "They only teach you a new trick when they're forced to. We should be proud that they felt compelled to reveal one of their secrets. This will come in handy."

"You know what this means? It means we'll have to shoot them with the plasma turrets first, so we can force them to lie down for a second, then we'll have to finish them off with the lasers before they can get up."

"I hate these damned weapons restrictions—" Hector said, "it takes all the fun out of trying to kill a man."

"Sí," Perfecto said. "But look at the bright side—we've only got one Yabajin left to kill, and we'll be rich men."

Hector said, "Where are you, Angelo?"

"I'm beside the wreck," I said. Zavala coughed in a huge wracking burst, trying to expel fluid from his lungs.

"Hold your place. We'll go back for a hovercraft. We'll be there in a few minutes."

"Sí," I said. "Kill Zavala while you're at it; put him out of his misery."

"Okay," Perfecto said.

I hadn't noticed how warm I'd stayed during combat, but suddenly I realized I was cold again. Snow had crept through the chinks in my armor, and now my legs felt as if they'd freeze. My hands started to stiffen, and I flexed them methodically. I looked longingly at the fire sputtering among the wreckage of the hovercraft, wondering if I should warm myself by its side.

I watched its red glow and realized something was wrong: though the smoke and fire looked real, and small cinders drifted into the sky, there was no ash, no gray or black soot falling onto me. There should have been ash falling. Occasionally the ship's artificial intelligence made such mistakes, neglecting tiny matters. One could look into a handful of soil and find no trace of insects or worms. The ship's AI couldn't create an illusion that complete, not with images it developed based on maps and fractal equations and the faulty memories of samurai. It seemed to me that I should have been capable of using this principle to my benefit. If I could pierce the illusion of the simulator, it would help me beat the samurai.

I thought about money. If we beat the last samurai, we'd have to split the pot three ways. That would still come to 30,000 IMUs apiece—as much as I'd make in an average year of selling morphogens in Panamá.

Twenty minutes passed. We were working overtime in the simulator—a new group of students would be suiting up in the battle room. I imagined how a crowd would gather at the monitors as people watched The Horror Show to see if we'd fry the last samurai. No team had ever outnumbered a samurai three to one. It seemed inconceivable that we'd lose. Yet I didn't dare hope we'd win. I kept expecting the last sniper to fry me any second.

Comlink tones sounded in my head, startling me. I hadn't received a call since leaving Panamá and didn't know I could receive one while jacked into the simulator, but it made sense—calls bypassed my little dream monitor back home. I engaged the comlink.

The sounds of the crackling flames from the burning hovercraft quieted. A husky, almost raspy voice came in on audio. "Jiminez Martinez here, aide to General Garzón. The general has asked me to get the answers to a few more questions."

"Sí, that would be fine," I said, not in the mood to answer questions but happy to hear from Garzón, thinking he might tell me something about Tamara's condition.

"First, the general would like to know if you have any more ideas on the whereabouts of Señora de la Garza?" Martinez said.

"What?" I asked. The general knew better than I did where Tamara was.

"The whereabouts of Señora de la Garza?" The man who called himself Martinez waited expectantly.

Only an Alliance agent would ask such a question. And since my interrogator had responded so quickly to my question, he had to be aboard ship. Radio waves would have taken several seconds to travel even to a nearby ship. My would-be assassin was taking a great risk fishing for information this way. I thought of him, stuck at the other end of the ship, wracking his brain to learn what I knew, trying to find a way to reach me, and I was happy to give all the information I could.

"As I told Garzón, Arish admitted to murdering her before I finished him, but I did not think to ask where he had disposed of the body."

"I see . . ." the husky-voiced man said. "And about herself? Can you remember anything else of importance—anything she may have told you about herself?"

"All she said was that she was running from her husband. A Señor Jafari. I thought it a breach of manners to inquire into her personal situation, and she never volunteered further information. As I told Garzón, if I can remember more, I'll be happy to let you know."

"I see. Thank you. You have been more help than you know."

He disconnected.

"I'm glad you think so," I said to the empty air. I concentrated on the way his voice had sounded, so deep and gravelly, and tried to commit it to memory until I believed that if I ever heard anyone speak with that voice again, perhaps I'd know him.

I could tell by the sky that Perfecto and Hector had reached the hovercraft long before they reached me. The valley began to fill with light again as they roared up the canyon, shooting streams of plasma into the night. As they drew close Perfecto said over the helmet, "Angelo, any sign of that last samurai?"

"No," I answered.

"We'll slow down when we come to your corner. You hop on and grab a turret. Shoot any place where someone might be hiding."

"Sí," I said. I watched the canyonsides fill with light.

When I knew they were almost on me, I strapped my
rifle to my back, jumped up, and lunged into the open.

They hit the corner at 60 kph, then reversed thrusters. I grabbed the handrail and swung into the hovercraft, and we darted off at full speed.

Hector drove. I climbed up in the turret behind
Perfecto and started discharging plasma into the rocks
and trees. Our trip back up the canyon was different
from the trip down. With the turrets firing, the hills
were fairly well lighted. No snow flew in our face to
obscure the view. The only sound was the echoing whine
of the hovercraft and the *whuft*, *whuft* of the plasma. It
was peaceful.

The silence reminded me of the others who'd already
jacked out. *Mavro's probably already swaggering
around the room and smiling*, I thought. Mavro was
good that way, very tough on the inside. He told
everyone that eating processed algae three times a day
was like having a continuous banquet after the odious
dishes his girlfriend had cooked him only a week ago.
And as for the rigorous exercise Abriara put us through,
Mavro boasted that he'd gotten more exercise chasing
down the dope addicts he mugged as a child. People
aboard ship responded to that kind of toughness. Mavro
could walk into a room full of despondent people and,
between his bragging and the cigars he passed out,
within a minute he'd have them laughing at their own
pains. I wondered if perhaps this talent hadn't allowed
him to talk the mercenaries into the harebrained scheme
of commandeering Sol Station so he could rescue an old
murderer from the clutches of the police.

We'd almost reached the spot where we'd first come
down the mountain when we met the Yabajin.

We were heading toward a tree and Hector slumped
forward with a moan. Perfecto yelled, "Jump!" and
began blasting at a pine on the canyon slope. I dove into
the snow and sat up as the hovercraft crumpled around
the tree trunk. The pine Perfecto had shot blazed along
its entire length like a giant torch. The samurai was
running up the hill, away from his exposed position. I
pulled down my rifle and flipped on the sights, ran the

blue dot up the ground behind him. He glanced back and saw the dot in the snow, spun, and fired.

I pirouetted quickly. My thigh warmed where his shot scored. I pirouetted again.

Perfecto said, "I've got him."

I stopped. Perfecto was squatting next to the wrecked hovercraft, rifle in hand, pulling the trigger. The samurai had quit running and he spun crazily, making it impossible for Perfecto's shot to burn through the armor.

I fired at the Yabajin to keep him hopping. "Go beat him to death!" I screamed.

"Good idea!" Perfecto said. He stood and walked slowly up the hill.

I continued firing and the samurai dropped his rifle and kept up his dance. From time to time he would step down the hill, descending to meet Perfecto.

When Perfecto was ten meters below the samurai, the samurai leapt on him. He spun in the air and kicked at Perfecto's chest. Perfecto dodged to the side and slugged the samurai in the back. The armor on Perfecto's fist shattered from the impact.

The samurai slid almost to the bottom of the hill.

He started to rise and I fired at him for good measure, hoping he was stunned, but I hurried the shot and hit the slope behind him. Perfecto jumped down the hill in two steps. The samurai wasn't quite standing yet and appeared dazed and off balance, but when Perfecto got within striking range, the samurai belted him in the jaw.

The blow lifted Perfecto in the air and sent him sprawling on his back.

I shot the samurai, but he was already in a spin and headed in my direction. My hopes for a fortune in prize money quickly dissipated. I ran to the crashed hovercraft, and jumped up to the plasma turret.

Perfecto shouted, "I'll get him!"

I turned the guns in time to see Perfecto dive into the samurai from behind. For a moment the two were just a tangle of armor on the ground. Perfecto hissed in a voice filled with frustration and rage, "Shoot us! Shoot us!"

His neck snapped loudly, then both bodies raised up and began to rush toward me. The Yabajin carried

Perfecto in front of him, using his body for a shield. I could tell by the way his arms and legs flapped that Perfecto was dead. And I understood Perfecto's anger, at that final moment, his feeling of helplessness. I shot a steady stream of plasma at the Yabajin's legs, then at the arm clutching Perfecto's throat. The armor couldn't withstand the impact of a direct hit at such close range, and plasma shot straight through his arm. I thought he'd stop, but he kept coming, and I fired at the bit of the samurai's helmet that showed above Perfecto's head. The plasma hit his helmet and blew a gout of molten matter away.

By the time the Yabajin jumped up on the rail of the hovercraft, I could see the bones in his left leg charred black and blistered. His right arm was limp, useless. The molten plasma had eaten through it, leaving only a stump above the elbow and a hunk of meat hanging loosely in the samurai's armor. I looked at him and thought of all the times I'd died in the simulator. At not one of those moments had I endured half as much pain as this samurai was suffering. I screamed at him and leapt for his throat.

He slugged me in the neck with his good hand, shattering my armor and knocking me off the hovercraft. I gasped, and found my esophagus smashed.

And while I slowly strangled, the samurai sat down on the rail of the wrecked hovercraft to watch me as he scooped up snow and bathed the remains of his feet.

When I jacked out, Perfecto was struggling out of his armor. He smashed his helmet against the wall and kicked off his leg pieces. He panted and his eyes were bloodshot with rage, and I wouldn't have gone near him for any money. My nerves were jagged, but I felt lucky. All my deaths in the simulator had been easy that day. Zavala waited by the door.

Kaigo sat patiently on his dais, surrounded by students, waiting for us to leave so he could jack them in. I removed my armor and hung it on the wall and followed Perfecto and Zavala from the battle room. Perfecto glared at the cream-colored floor and walls as he walked down the hall, averting his eyes from the lighting panels on the ceiling.

"Are you angry with me?" I asked.

"Angry with you? What for?"

"For losing the battle."

"No," he said. He sounded remarkably calm. "I'm angry because I think the samurai are cheating. They're putting us in a situation where we can't win. They give us no chance of success. I fought that samurai in hand-to-hand—no human is that strong."

"You must remember that he's been training at 1.5 g's for the past two years," I said. "He's had a lot of time to perfect his skills and become strong."

"Perhaps. But I still think they're cheating. They've got the simulators rigged to enhance their strength and cut their reaction times. It's as if they must win at any cost."

Zavala eyed us both skeptically, as if preparing to argue, but said nothing.

I thought of the samurai in the simulators. If they worked eight-hour shifts, they might go through twenty battles per day. No one could endure the repeated psychic torment of twenty deaths per day. Perhaps they did cheat. Perhaps they had good reason to cheat.

We climbed the ladder. García and Hector were in our room with their teams. García was smaller and older than I'd expected, a timid-looking man with sea-gray eyes who kept rearranging his hands as if he didn't know where to put them. I once knew a woman who had a deformed hand who hid it that way, and I watched García to see if his hands were deformed: he had a white scar in the palm of each hand and a white scar on each wrist. García had obviously once played Jesus Christ in a passion play and had been crucified. By these signs I deduced he was from Venezuela, where such plays are common.

One big chimera hunched over a battered guitar and strummed it softly, his amplifier down low. Full mellow notes filled the air. He sang an old Bolivian love ballad dedicated to women with large breasts. Some found the courage to muster wan smiles. Mavro had opened my chest full of liquor, and everyone eyed the bottles. They'd obviously prepared for a victory celebration, but now were forced to put the best face on it they could.

Mavro said, "Ah, here is the man who owns the liquor. Now the party can begin!" He passed out bottles of Flora Negra whiskey, and everyone accepted them gratefully.

Mavro handed me a bottle and I took a swig. It was too soon after the run in the simulator—my throat tightened, and I had to spit the first swallow to the floor.

The visitors stared at our living quarters as if they were medieval peasants visiting a castle for the first time. The regular living quarters were not nearly so spacious as our stateroom. They murmured approval. "Think how easy it would be to keep people from stealing your things if you had a nice room with trunks like these!" one said.

I felt uneasy with these strange people coveting my things, and I could tell Perfecto felt the same. He looked at his little blue lines on the floor and saw that they were obscured by feet and bodies as people ignored his boundaries, and this made him very nervous.

We lay on the bunks and sat on the floors and drank and smoked and discussed our near victory from every angle, boasting of how well we'd done. Miguel and I had each made two kills. Mavro rewarded both of us with a fine bottle of dry wine. By that time I'd finished half my whiskey and the wine didn't settle well with the liquor I'd drunk earlier, and soon I imagined the liquor was eating holes through my stomach. The din of people talking became a droning in my ears. My head became very heavy, and my facial muscles felt as fluid as hot plastic. I sat on my bunk and hung my head and imagined that my upper lip was dripping over my teeth and would soon roll down over my chin. A man at the foot of my bed had a problem with gas, and began farting. Each time he farted someone would say, "I hear a frog," and we'd laugh.

I wanted to sleep, but my mind kept returning to Martinez, the man who'd pretended to be Garzón's aide. I rolled off the bed, pushed a couple of sleeping guests off my trunk, got my list of biographies, and stepped into

the hall to call each man who'd boarded the ship at Sol
Station. The liquor had almost blinded me, and I found
it difficult to read the comlink codes. As each man
answered, I said, "Frog," and disconnected. Two men
had deep gravelly voices so similar I couldn't distinguish
one from the other: Alphonso Pena and Juan Carlos
Vasquez. I hunched over the biographies and laboriously
studied the files of each man. The files appeared as if
written on a billboard barely visible through a deep fog.
Once I read something I had to hold it in my mind for a
long time to make any sense of it. Alphonso was a large
man with a long list of credentials in particle-beam-
weaponry targeting-system repair. How would one repair the targeting system of a particle beam? What did
he really do for a living? I didn't know, nor could I
deduce if he was any good at repairing targeting systems
for particle beams. Juan Carlos was the plumber who'd
defected from Argentina, the cyborg who'd worn the
silver face at Sol Station. I liked his job. A plumber was
something easy. Something you could hold in your mind
and say with certainty, "This man's a plumber," and
know exactly what it meant. In fact, if someone had
walked down the hall, I'd have told him, "Juan Carlos is
a plumber." I remembered trying to read his body
language at Sol Station, and he'd seemed perfectly at
ease. *But then*, I thought, *maybe this dog feels at ease
when planning murder*. He was Argentine. That was
bad. Argentina is where the Nicita Idealist Socialists first
took over. Also, he was cyborg, though not a military
model. Jafari had been in charge of Cyborg Intelligence
for the Alliance. So it made sense: Juan Carlos was a
cyborg, and an Argentinian, and a socialist assassin. And
a plumber. I set out down the hall to find him and stab
him. But after I'd walked twenty meters I saw the ladder
going up to the air lock and remembered I couldn't get
to him. I thought I should tell my compadres what I'd
learned, but first I wanted another drink, so I sat and
looked around for my bottle of wine, then realized I'd
left it in my room and fell asleep.

* * *

I was wakened a short while later by Sakura. He bent over me and shook my shoulders. Down the corridor two squat maintenance robots scoured the floor.

"Come now, are you ill? Can you sing the company song for me, from the heart! 'Motoki Sha Ka'? Show your gratitude to Motoki!"

He sang the company song line by line at the top of his voice. He'd caught me alone and helpless, so I followed his lead. When he was done, I sat on the floor and watched him climb down the ladder, searching for another victim.

The hallway was silent except for the whirring motors of the maintenance robots. I suddenly felt cold, and something strange happened: I felt the presence of someone else in the hall, an invisible being. The ghost of Flaco. Even though I couldn't see him I was certain he was there. I felt him walk down the hall toward me, then go to the ladder. He stood and looked up at the air lock, as if indicating he wanted to go find Juan Carlos. I felt that he bore me no malice for letting him get strangled, but that he still wanted vengeance against his murderers. The death of Jafari's friends. The hair raised on the back of my neck. I'd felt a similar thing when I planned to leave Tamara—the fear of her ghost, of being haunted—but this time it was much stronger.

Logically I knew there was no ghost. Psychologists have proved that people see ghosts in reaction to unbearable stress—the death of a loved one, a terrible accident. And certainly I'd felt such stress in the past few days. But the sense of Flaco's presence was more persuasive than logic. I staggered up and ran for my room.

When I got to the door, I tried to compose myself. I'd feel silly if everyone saw my fear. I remembered a night in a small resort town in the Sierra Madres in Mexico. The night had been very cool and the air perfectly still. I'd taken a walk, and as I was coming around the corner to my hotel I'd seen a silvery human shape standing in the doorway outside the hotel. For a moment I'd been terrified, thinking it was a ghost, but the apparition quickly dissipated and I saw the truth of it: someone had been standing in the doorway only a second before, and the air had heated around his body, and as he stepped into the doorway the warm air stayed behind. My prosthetic eyes had then detected a vaguely human-shaped apparition. It was a very strange occurrence, one never to be repeated. But this thing with Flaco, it was different. I'd not seen Flaco, only felt him.

I heard someone speaking behind the door: "You . . . you can't ekshpect too much from him—" one of the chimeras said—I think it was Noel—"he'sh an old man."

"You mean an old handicap," Mavro said. "We always lose because of him."

"Yesh," one of Hector's men said, "Maybe if Angelo would have shlugged that lasht shamurai—just pushed him away, that plashma would have, would have . . . eaten right through. Eaten right through the leg. Then what? We would have won!"

I jerked open the door. Those still sober enough to be awake turned to look at me, heads tottering.

García's chimera Miguel sat in my room with his back to me. Miguel was heavy with fat, with a barrel chest and immense neck. When I stepped through the door he turned his bald head sharply so he could peer at me over his back with pale blue eyes as if he were an owl, and this surprised me. With a neck as thick as his, he should have had no mobility. I knew the men in the room had been criticizing me, but I didn't know for sure who to be mad at, except Mavro.

"That's our problem," García said, turning the discussion. His voice was not slurred, though his eyes were glazed, "we always underestimate these Yabajin. When we fought socialists, they were never any better than us. They'd never fought in a real war. But these samurai must have practiced fighting their whole lives."

I was angry at Mavro. I pointed at him. "You—you were shaying bad thingsh about me. I heard you shaying bad thingsh!"

García turned and said, "We weren't talking about you, don Angelo. You must have imagined it. We were talking about the Yabajin. Perfecto believes that they are monitoring our helmet-to-helmet communications in the simulators—even though our scramblers would make such things impossible in real life. Yet I disagree, for even if they know of our plans before we initiate them, it would not explain their marvelous battle skills. I was just saying that only a lifetime of practice could make them so good." His innocent tone invited me to believe him.

181

I looked at him and became confused. I decided I must have been wrong when I'd thought I heard Mavro speaking evilly of me. I crossed the room and sat on Abriara's bed. One of Hector's men was asleep on the cot, hugging the wall, so I had plenty of room.

Zavala started to laugh, long and hard, and everyone turned to look at him.

"Are you laughing at me?" I asked. "Are you making fun of me?"

"I'm laughing at all of you!" Zavala said. "You intellectuals!" he sneered. "You wonder why the samurai beat us. You say, 'They beat us because they cheat! They beat us because they're stronger! They beat us because they've practiced shooting from the time they were sucking their mothers' tits!' And you say these dumb things as if they had any meaning. That's the problem with you intellectuals, you always believe that if you talk about a problem you understand things. Yet you ignore the obvious about the Yabajin: their spirits are stronger than ours! They beat us by the power of their spirit!" He began laughing deliriously. He was very tense and appeared to be the most sober person there.

"Ah, I've met your type before," García said. "You have no faith in the power of reason. I'll bet your father was a village sorcerer."

"Then you lose the bet!" Zavala said. "My father was a farmer, and knew no magic."

"Then I'll make you another bet," García said. "I'll bet if we study the matter carefully, we'll find a good reason why the samurai always beat us."

Zavala leaned his head to one side, scratched his temple with his silver-framed mechanical hand, as if trying to remember what he'd been talking about. "Fine. What shall we bet? A million Colombian pesos?"

García opened his mouth in surprise. He'd obviously only been speaking figuratively and didn't want to bet. After consideration he said, "You have a million pesos?"

Zavala nodded. A million pesos equaled about two thousand standard IMUs, a great deal of money for a peasant like Zavala.

"Fine," García said. "Then I'll bet a million pesos we will find why they beat us."

"Not so fast." Zavala grinned as if making a shrewd proposal. I'd seen that same grin on the face of the man who owned the Chicken of God. "You seem so certain you'll win, you must give me better than even odds."

"What kind of odds?"

"I want nothing from you, Señor García," Zavala said. He pointed a finger at me. "But if I win, I want payment from don Angelo. I want his antibiotics to kill the rot. I would not be forced to do this, but don Angelo refuses to give me drugs. If I had an amigo who was ill, I would give him drugs. But don Angelo won't give me drugs. No one will."

García listened to the accusation but didn't react to it. "What do you say, don Angelo? How much are your antibiotics worth?"

I made a guess. "About fifty thousand peshosh."

"Then when we win, I'll pay you two hundred thousand pesos," García offered. "Is it a deal?"

There was no chance Zavala would win. I nodded.

"Then we have a bet, Zavala," García said. "But now I must ask, what constitutes a win to the bet?"

Zavala sighed and his gaze wandered around the room. Like some Chakoy Indians I'd met from secluded villages, he was unused to thinking by conventional logical processes. He wouldn't know what constituted proof to an argument.

One of Hector's men spoke, the small man named Pío who played the guitar. "Who can shay who'sh shpirit ish better? We can't shee them. Shpiritsh. I wish we could."

"But the don is a dealer in morphogens and is therefore an expert in genetics," García said. "We could have him compare the gene charts of the samurai with the gene charts of the chimeras, no? Would Angelo's expert word on the subject satisfy you, Zavala?"

I started to object to this. I didn't want to be thrust into the heart of their argument.

Zavala studied me a moment. "Sí. I will trust don Angelo's word."

García continued. "Good. And we can possibly learn

the age at which samurai begin training, right? And by this we can learn if they are trained better than us—if we can find a library. Is there a library on ship?"

We looked at each other and shrugged. García's chimera Miguel, the one with the acrobatic neck, was staring at me strangely, his blue eyes like pale, icy pools. The sweat gleamed off his bald head. He had a small fu manchu mustache. The overall effect was frightening. Ugly.

"Sí, there's a library downstairs!" Zavala said.

"Alsho, the medical computersh have good bio-biographicalsh," I pointed out, "sho maybe we can learn when the shamurai shtarted training from them."

"But how will we know if we win the bet?" García asked. "You don't believe the samurai have been training for battle their whole lives, Zavala, but at what age do you think they would begin?"

The chimera Miguel was still staring at me. Miguel's pupils suddenly dilated and became as large as Mexican five-centavo pieces. His face went slack and his jaw dropped. He seemed totally oblivious to what was happening in the room. He looked very ill. Ugly. I wondered what was wrong with him. *Too much liquor*, I figured.

Zavala considered for a moment. "A boy becomes a man when he grows his first pubic hairs, no? I do not believe the samurai trained before they got their pubic hairs."

García said, "Some men grow pubic hairs when they are ten, some when sixteen. I say we should be generous on this bet: we will give you a break-off date of fifteen. The samurai cannot have begun formal combat training before the age of fifteen, or you lose."

Zavala stared at the far side of the room a moment and his eyes focused on nothing. He appeared to be in a trance, consulting the source of spiritual knowledge. "I will agree to that," he said distantly.

The chimera Miguel closed his mouth and began crawling across the floor, scrabbling toward me. His pupils constricted again, and he would have looked normal if not for a bit of slobber that escaped his mouth as he crawled.

"That leaves only one problem," García said. "We need to learn if the samurai cheat in the simulators. Does anyone here think he could break into the computer to find out?"

We all shook our heads. No one would be able to penetrate the defenses of the ship's AI. Miguel reached the bed and sat down on the floor next to me. He patted my foot, then nuzzled his bald head against my leg like an old dog who seeks the comfort of his master. I realized he'd bonded to me, and I'd seen the process happen. This gave me a frightening sense of power, of responsibility.

"Then I'm afraid there's only one thing we can do," García said. "We'll have to attack a couple of samurai to see just how strong and fast they really are."

"But they have shwords!" Pío pointed out.

García asked, "Do I have any volunteers?"

Mavro had been sitting on his bunk, slumped against the wall as if asleep. His head wobbled upright and he said weakly, "I'll disharm one, if shomeone else will beat him up."

"Bravo," García said. "Do I have any volunteers?" I thought of how big the samurai were, most were two meters tall and weighed as much as 140 kilos. The thought of attacking one of those monsters was not appealing.

As one the four chimeras still awake said, "Me!"

"Such a project should wait until we are all sober," García said, and everyone agreed. "Then let's do it tonight, after our last battle practice."

Those guests who were able to stagger to their own rooms did so, but most spent the day with us sleeping off the effects of the booze. I had dinner alone in the common dining room down on level four, and sat next to Fernando Chin, a xenobiologist from Bogotá. He was speaking with some others about the avians I'd seen flying high in the atmosphere in the simulators. Chin said the large avians were called *oparu no tako*, opal kites, while the small ones were called *oparu no tori*, opal birds. And I could understand such names—when the evening sky was full of dust, though it was purple in the west, in the east the sky was dark blue-brown, and the shimmering sunlight playing on the wings of the *oparu no tako* against the darker sky made it appear as if streaks of opal spanned the horizon.

The kites that lived high in the atmosphere interested me most, and Chin described to me how they collected dust and water from the air and directed them with cilia down an orifice into a gut where the elements entered a tiny pouch and nourished a bacteria culture which the opal kite then periodically ingested as food. Because of this you could usually classify the species of opal kite by its color, since different species of kite relied upon different types of bacteria for food.

"They are very beautiful," I said, "at sunset."

"And useful, too," Chin said. "Without them, Baker would be uninhabitable. There are so many of them in the sky that they form a thermal layer, creating a greenhouse effect, warming the planet. And every seven years, Baker's sun jumps in magnitude, heating the planet even more. When this happens there are great storms—storms like you've never seen on Earth—and the *oparu no tako* are ripped apart and fall from the skies. And while the sun is hot, they do not breed. If it were not for them, the temperature variations would be so great that the weather patterns would never stabilize. Except for some narrow bands around the coastal belts, Baker would become desolate in a matter of decades."

"Ah, interesting. Does it not seem strange to you that the Japanese call the planet *Baker*? An English word."

Chin laughed. "I think it is ironic. An English probe discovered the planet on flyby, and when they saw it, they saw it during a global dust storm—after the sun had jumped in magnitude. Their sensors registered the planet as being lifeless, and they thought it must be such a hell that they named it Baker. Later, the Japanese rediscovered the planet and found it to be habitable. Yet they kept the name, since there is no word for *baker* in Japanese. Yet I find it fascinating that the inhabitants of

Baker so resist Western thoughts and ideals—yet they keep a borrowed English name for their planet."

I smiled at this. Over the past several days it seemed that everyone on the ship feigned expertise on the topic of the geography, inhabitants, and animal life of Baker, and though everyone spoke about such things frequently, I didn't trust their information. But I found Chin to be refreshingly enlightened. I hadn't really made friends with any of my teammates—Perfecto obeyed me as if I were his owner, and this distressed me; while Abriara preferred to remain aloof. Several times I'd tried to engage her in conversation about her past, and I found that although Abriara had lived in different places and had known different people, she never spoke about them with passion. She'd *inhabited* places, but she'd never *lived* in them. She never showed an honest emotion. Such people frighten me, and I decided to avoid her. I hadn't met anyone else I could envision as a prospective friend.

So when I met Chin and found that he was intelligent and interesting, I thought he might be the kind of person I'd want as a friend, and I said, "It must make you very happy to be able to go to Baker—as a xenobiologist it is the ultimate opportunity!"

"Ah, yes," Chin said, "It is the dream of my life! I received my doctorate for studies on the combination endo-exoskeleton common to Baker's animals. I never believed I'd be able to afford passage to the planet, but then I heard about this job."

I said, "But does it not bother you that Motoki Corporation wants you to commit genocide as a condition of employment?"

He shrugged and waved his hand down, "Not at all! By getting rid of the Yabajin I'll be cleaning up the environment, helping restore the natural ecosystem of the planet. What does it matter if a few people die?"

Such thinking made me queasy in my stomach, and I left him.

In the evening we rallied enough strength for battle practice and headed for the simulators. My ears were ringing and I felt dizzy. I'd eaten too soon after getting drunk, and I paid for it. During the first scenario the motion of the hovercraft bouncing along a rocky path caused me to vomit in my helmet. We got butchered twice in the first ten minutes of practice, and in the next four simulations we were too sick and exhausted to even try to avoid the Yabajin. The continual waves of pain made my face numb and tightened my stomach into knots. It became the worst battle session ever, and we left shaken.

Hector, García, and six of their men showed up at our room later in the evening. Miguel seemed overjoyed to see me; he kept patting my back and saying, "Is there anything I can do for you, sir?" forgetting I had no rank.

I was happy to learn they hadn't fared any better in battle practice than we had: they were so pale they looked like walking corpses. All thirteen of us went downstairs to the infirmary to get some pills for our hangovers and settle Zavala's bet.

The nurse on duty at the infirmary was a small, wiry man with long hair and a scraggly beard. He had the top half of the infirmary door open, and he watched the entrance as if it led to a bank vault. Mavro tried to sweet-talk him, offering him a cigar and explaining our bet with Zavala, telling him how desperately we needed to use the computer to get "just a tiny bit of information." But the nurse was one of those belligerent types who start shaking their heads as soon as they even think you're going to ask a favor.

Miguel questioned me with a gaze. I was in a bad mood and didn't want to concern myself with trivialities. I nodded, and Miguel grabbed the nurse's throat, lifted him in the air, and we forced our way into the infirmary. Then Miguel carried the nurse to the nearest convalescence tube and began stuffing him in.

We were afraid the nurse might make a comlink call to security, so I went to the operating table where a retractable gas mask hung from an outlet near the ceiling, and I hooked him to the gas mask and anesthetized him with a little harmless nitrous oxide. I gave the mask to Hector and showed him how to knock out the nurse every few minutes, should he begin to come around.

Then we settled down at the computer and called up information on the Japanese. There were twelve hundred aboard ship, and nearly all were listed as samurai. We asked which samurai were currently jacked into the simulators, and the computer listed a couple hundred names. We picked two samurai at random—Anchi Akisada and Kunimoto Hideo—and called up their gene charts. I asked the computer to scan for genetic upgrades, and sat back. The upgrades came slowly: chromosome 4, cistron 1729, had a vascular tissue upgrade to strengthen walls of blood vessels; chromosomes 6 and 14 had several messages to delay stop for production of growth hormones. Chromosome 19, cistron 27, had an intricate upgrade for fat tissue that vastly facilitated metabolism of fat cells, letting the samurai function more effectively on an empty belly than a normal human. We found fifty minor upgrades in all, none very innovative, and most so old that their creator's patent had expired. I had the computer print the biographies of the two samurai, then gave them to García to study.

"Who wants to see his gene-scan?" I asked the chimeras. I was curious to inspect their charts. Engineering on humans was banned on Earth except for use in eradicating genetically transmittable illnesses, so information on the work in Chile had never been published.

"I want to see mine," Abriara said.

I called up her charts and was amazed: the first artificially inserted gene I found was 48,000 nucleotides long—a thousand times longer than any artificially produced nucleotide I'd ever known to have been inserted into a human. The gene encoded instructions for Abriara's striated muscular tissue to form a myofilament significantly different from myosin, the protein used in human striated muscle; the new protein was very complex, and didn't have a name. The computer simply listed it by its patent number, citing the team of Robles and Company as creators, and alongside the credits gave a visual representation of the new myofilament: rather than the long, column-shaped myofilament typical to humans, it had a column with a helix-shaped ridge running around its outside. It was as if someone had wrapped a spring around a pencil. The introduction into the body of a new protein as the basis for human muscular tissue would seem to initiate myriad problems: How much stimulation would be needed for the muscle to initiate contraction? What chemical would you use to stimulate contraction? How would the muscle relax? What does the muscle metabolize so it can turn chemical energy into physical energy?

The questions seemed overwhelming, but as I studied on I found the solutions to be simpler than expected. The muscles metabolized ATP, just as human muscles do, and upon closer scrutiny the gene proved to be closely modeled on the gene for myosin, with only a few thousand added nucleotides. The outside ridges on the myofilament released abundant amounts of a new enzyme to catalyze ATP, ensuring that muscle contractions would be stimulated more easily and more quickly than in humans. And when the muscle contracted, it contracted more fully.

The whole thought of redesigning a muscle cell for greater efficiency seemed mind-boggling. How could Robles and Company juggle forty-eight thousand variables just to produce that one effect? How could they even conceive what the outcome of their actions might be? Yet it was only the beginning of Abriara's upgrades.

The charts showed hundreds more—a redesign of the vascular network in the brain provided better circulation to a cerebrum enlarged by two hundred grams. Redesign of the teeth got rid of her canines, giving her a closer-fitting bite that allowed her to chew food more quickly and thoroughly than a human could. Longer intestines and better absorption of nutrients through the intestinal wall made Abriara capable of sustaining life on half the food a human needed. Her cartilage was more elastic than normal, making it easier for her pelvis to widen when giving birth, while at the same time providing the added benefit that she would never get a broken nose. One didn't need to look at her genes to guess the kinds of upgrades Robles had made on her eyes, but I was surprised to find that the design for her ears was only slightly different from normal.

Many upgrades required changing only one or two pairs of nucleotides in a gene, often calling for modifications of organ size and function, and some changes were seemingly minor, almost superfluous, while other upgrades required the assemblage of hundreds of thousands of nucleotides within entire families of genes. Yet each upgrade had been carried out in a thoughtful manner that took all considerations into account. Each was an act of genius. And when you looked at the whole it was obvious that Robles had specified the changes for one simple reason—he sought to create a *perfect* human. The best genetic engineer I'd ever seen was but a tinkerer compared to Robles. Even if man were to live for another two million years, he'd never evolve into something so perfect as Abriara. My respect for her as an organism grew with each upgrade I discovered. I felt as if I were witnessing a symphony, not a symphony of music, but a symphony played out on human genes, but only I in our little group could comprehend the beauty of it.

I remembered a joke about chimeras I'd once read in a medical journal back when people were much afraid of the work General Torres's engineers were doing in Chile. The joke said, "When God created man, he made him good. When General Torres creates a man, he makes him better." Ironically, the joke was truer than the comic would ever know.

García and Zavala had been studying the samurais' biographies in a corner. They began bickering. Apparently, both samurai began attending Kontani Academy at age sixteen, and it was probably a military academy. Zavala argued that he'd won that part of the bet, since the samurai hadn't begun formal military training until they were sixteen. But García pointed out that each samurai had been tutored as a child—both by a human and by the company AI—and many of their classes provided them a strong military background, though they were not specifically military in nature. For example, their training in gymnastics and self-defense was helpful in combat situations. Everyone became embroiled in the argument, and García finally lost, since he had to concede that almost every child in the world was trained in gymnastics and self-defense to some degree.

As they argued I found something that made me uneasy about Robles' work: chromosome 4, cistron 2229, gave an instruction for the neuroglia cells in the cerebral cortex to produce a protein simply labeled Behavioral Modifier 26. In structure this protein was closely allied to the neural transmission blocker responsible for biogenic sociopathy. In fact, Robles needed only remove two amino acids to get the transmission blocker. Clearly, Robles wanted to somehow dampen Abriara's ability to feel empathy for others, yet empathy is a trait necessary for survival of the species. A mother must care about her children for them to survive to adulthood. And Robles obviously knew he couldn't completely remove that trait. I resented the fact that he'd tried to suppress it at all.

I asked the computer for a scan of behavioral modifiers, and found several. Seven modifiers were labeled by patent number. I had no idea what their effects might be, since this was outside my field of expertise. But I did find one patent for a family of genes that was not created by Robles: it was made by Bernardo Mendez, and since I knew of his work in engineering biogenic territorialism, I was able to guess by the early date of his patent the nature of the modification—the chimeras' biogenic territorialism was strengthened so they'd be more competitive. It explained why Perfecto found it necessary to paint lines on the floor in our room so no one would trespass into his area. I remembered Abriara telling me the chimeras weren't dangerous to the Argentines as long as they stayed in their own country, and it made perfect sense: if the chimeras felt their territory to be violated, they'd indeed go berserk. And because of their sociopathic bent, the chimeras wouldn't hesitate to destroy the invaders. I hadn't paid heed to Perfecto's blue lines in the past. I made a mental note to avoid his territory, lest he decide to break my legs. It struck me as odd that these chimeras were the antitheses to the beings the socialists were trying to engineer—instead of rooting out human territorialism, Torres had chosen to strengthen it. I wondered if Torres had designed the chimeras specifically to resist the possibility of the viral wars that rumor said the socialists would someday initiate. Yet that seemed implausible. Torres had started his work a decade before the socialists began engineering their own people. At least, I had heard about Torres's work that much earlier. And then I began to wonder, *Was Robles trying to create perfect humans, or perfect warriors?*

I exhausted the behavioral modifications and went back to studying physical upgrades. The list seemed endless. Several people came to the infirmary for medications, and I had to get up from the computer to serve them. This made me uneasy. Sooner or later someone would think to question our presence. After nearly two hours I asked the computer to print Abriara's files, then told my compadres, "I'd like to take these gene charts home for study. But we have surely lost this part of our bet. The chimeras are genetically superior to the samurai. Our chimeras should be stronger, faster, and more intelligent than the samurai."

Zavala smiled. "Then I have beat you on two counts: the samurai are not better trained than we are, and they are not genetically superior."

"Perhaps they aren't genetically superior, but I am not so sure about the other," García said. "We'll have to go to the library tomorrow to study their early training better. If their classes in self-defense include simulated battles like those we go through, then I will have to take your money." García stretched and yawned, for it was getting late.

Everyone agreed that García was right, and they began filing from the room. Miguel hung back, standing too near, as Perfecto often did. He clearly wanted to stay with me.

I patted him on the back. "Go with García, my friend," I said. "Serve him well." It was a command spoken softly.

Miguel looked at me with his sad blue eyes, and left without speaking a word. I could tell he felt rejected.

Mavro, Perfecto, and Abriara stayed behind. I saw Perfecto staring at me. He obviously knew Miguel had bonded to me. He appeared sad that I'd sent Miguel away.

When the others had left, Abriara bent over my shoulder, her chocolate-brown hair brushing my neck, and said, "I have a question, Angelo: Am I human?"

I considered. At first it seemed she obviously wasn't. No one with so many upgrades could be human. It was as if her outer form were a cloak to hide the engineering that had gone on beneath. And as I looked into the silver webs of light in her eyes, I reminded myself that I must never think of her as human, never make the mistake of thinking of her as a comrade, but as an animal as different from me as a rat is from a dog. But if her question were revised to "Can I mate with a human to produce viable offspring?" which would be the ultimate test of whether she was a member of our species, I couldn't be sure. Most of the upgrades Robles had made were minor and had historical precedent, meaning they'd been found in rare individuals, and those traits could certainly be passed to humans. But considering the structure of her muscles and eyes, I wasn't sure. I asked the computer to cross-check the results of a mating between Abriara and García to see if it would work.

To my astonishment, the results were positive—her offspring would physically express an amazing 98 percent of her upgrades.

"Yes," I told her.

"Oh," she said. "I thought not. I thought not." She sounded very sad, and I wondered if she was disappointed to be human when she was so close to being something better.

"Ah, don't take it so hard," Mavro said. "Think of all the great humans there have been—people like Jesus Christ and Simon Bolívar."

That night I lay awake for a long time, thinking of the battles we'd fought, how each had brought us defeat. I was still trembling from the evening in the simulators, and the images from the day's battles—flashes of plasma fire arcing into the night, a dead body falling at my feet—would not let me sleep. Yet it seemed strange: though I was shaken, I hadn't noticed the feeling while reading the gene charts. It was as if my body had saved the aches until I had time to deal with them. I listened to the uneven breathing of the others, and realized they were all awake, going through the same thing as I. Eventually the breathing of Zavala and Mavro evened out, and they began to snore softly.

In one form or another, Tamara had invaded my dreams each night on the ship. I wondered if I'd dream of her tonight. If it would be a peaceful dream. I longed to dream a peaceful dream of her. I wondered where she was, if she were recovering. I told myself she'd be all right. Garzón would take care of her. But then I realized I didn't care anymore. What if she lived? What if she died? Why should she mean anything to me? I had enough concerns of my own. Why did I still want to find her, to caress her as if she were my child?

I began to drift into an uneasy slumber, marred by a rumbling, droning noise. I woke and thought the rumbling noise was Perfecto talking in his sleep. But as I listened I realized he wasn't speaking in his sleep. He spoke very softly, in a slurred tone without inflection, so that if anyone overheard they'd think he was mumbling in his sleep.

He said, "I remember when you were six and sneaked out of the compound to play with the Nito Diez and his brother. I remember how they pushed a pile of lumber on you, and left you screaming. They thought you'd die, and they thought it was funny. And when we found you that night, you were bloody all over."

"They were children," Abriara mumbled in return. I'd not heard them speak like this before. The only sound I'd ever heard at night was Zavala's snoring or when Perfecto occasionally cried out to his wife in his sleep. I wondered how many late-night conversations I'd missed.

"And when you were twelve and tried to go to Mass, and the priest threw you out, was he a child?"

"It was his church," Abriara said.

"It was God's church," Perfecto corrected. "I'd rather not remind you of other things that have happened," he mumbled. "But I saw on the news how you murdered three mestizo boys."

"Three rapists. The police do not care what mestizos do to a chimera."

"Yet you mutilated their bodies. That speaks of more than mere vengeance. It speaks of hatred. A Quest. Why do you deny that you hate humans? It gains you nothing. I don't ask you to curb your hatred for them—but that you not hate yourself for being one of them."

Abriara made a choking noise, as if she were sobbing, and I wondered at this: she'd always seemed strong, oblivious to emotion. "I am not human," she said. "They have never allowed me to be one of them. I will not be one of them now."

"So, you admit that you hate them?"

"Yes. Sometimes."

"Then do you hate me?" Perfecto asked. "I have fathered eight children to a human wife. I am human, too."

"Don't try to trick me with arguments over semantics. If you were born in the vats on the compound, you are chimera—that is the only criterion the Chileans used when they hunted us after the revolution. If you took your eight children back to Chile, the Chileans would kill you and your children with you."

"That's true," Perfecto said. "But I point out these things only so you'll know: the dividing line between human and chimera is sometimes thin. You straddle the line and say you will be chimera, not human. But that choice was made by your engineers; you cannot make that choice yourself."

Perfecto quit speaking and I waited for Abriara to argue with him some more. I considered what I'd learned: when I'd tried speaking to Abriara privately, she talked about places she had lived and people she had known with a curious dispassion—she never talked about old loves, old hates. She was emotionally distanced, like a person encased in amber, unable to touch, unable to feel. And—as on the day I first met her when she used the animated gestures so typical of Chileans—I soon found that when she appeared to show emotion, it was only practiced emotion. Meaningless smiles over stupid jokes. Almost as if she were trying to placate us, trying to convince us that everything was okay in her world. I'd instinctively been revolted by her behavior, since it made her seem so false. Now I realized her emotion was false because she was so brutalized by her past she couldn't afford to let us see her as she was.

I marveled once again that she was so human—that 98 percent of her traits would be expressed in her offspring. And like a lightning bolt, the truth struck me. Abriara had said chimera women hadn't been created to be warriors, that they'd never fought in battle. And I realized that when Robles created Abriara he hadn't been trying to create either a perfect human or a perfect warrior. He'd been trying to create a perfect breeder—a machine to spread the genetic traits he'd engineered among the general population.

I listened for a long time, but Abriara made no answer to Perfecto. Perhaps they'd heard my uneven breathing, learned I was awake, and quit speaking. I do not know.

That night I dreamed I struggled to hold on to a child who clung to a rocky ledge high above an immense ocean of brass-colored water. In the sea were dead seagulls, floating on their backs, their wing tips bobbing up and down in time with undulating waves. The small girl I'd dreamed of so often lately clutched my wrist as she tried to pull herself up to the ledge, her eyes wide with terror. Huge drops of her blood spattered from scratches on her hands into the sea, forming red circles. And from each circle a Yabajin samurai would burst forth, wearing his red armor and shooting plasma and streams of light at me.

The small girl said to me, "Grandfather, hold tight. Stay low!"

I looked into her eyes. "Who are you?" I shouted to the girl. "What is your name?"

"You don't know!" she said accusingly.

A plasma blast flashed in the air over my head, and I grabbed the child and crouched low, afraid to move.

"Angelo, Mavro, everyone—wake up!" Perfecto said. I looked up at him. He was crying. His thick hair was ruffled, unruly. The lights were low, and the 3-D tattoo of the beast on his neck seemed to glow in the shadows. The ship trembled with vibrations caused by people screaming and cheering. Perfecto grinned. "Come hear the good news!"

Perfecto went over to the lights and turned them up. Abriara was jacked into the wall monitor, listening to the music piped in over the radio. Her whole body was shuddering from sobs, and tears streamed down her cheeks. I sat up, and Perfecto grabbed my hand, pulled me over to the spare monitor. Mavro was just rousing and Zavala hadn't yet moved at all. Perfecto plugged the wall jack into the socket at the base of my skull.

". . . are still shut down. Meanwhile, Independent Brazil has launched an air strike against four thousand disabled cybernet tanks stranded in a caravan thirty kilometers north of Lima." *Lima?* I wondered. *Independent Brazil's military front is hundreds of kilometers from Lima.* "The tanks were on their way to the Estados Unidos Socialistas del Sur front in Panamá under the direction of the artificial intelligence Brainstormer 911 when saboteurs bombed the AI's housing complex. Brainstormer 911 is one of fourteen artificial intelligences in South and Central America to have been destroyed within the past six hours. Seven other artificial intelligences in Europe, and two in space, have also been killed. So far, only two allied nations have lodged formal protest to the bombings, which violate the Intersentient Accord of 2087 that grants AIs political neutrality from humans, protecting them from the ravages of war. This is the first time in over a century that AIs have become military targets.

"In Colombia, freedom fighters from Panamá now

claim they've secured Bogotá—which means both Bogotá and Cartagena have been recaptured—and socialist generals in Colombia have ordered their soldiers to lay down their weapons. However, because of reports of rampant executions, most EUSS soldiers have refused, and fighting still continues heavy in Medillín.

"An unconfirmed report from Pôrto Alegre in socialist-occupied Brazil indicates that hundreds of marines there revolted against superior officers this morning. General Ricardo Mueller, known as the Serpent of Montevideo, was reportedly killed along with many other officers. Marines from that base boast that they will attack Buenos Aires by—"

Mavro pulled out my jack and plugged himself in. Abriara had given up her jack to Zavala. In the halls below, mercenaries cheered and celebrated, thousands of voices united. The walls muted and smothered the noise.

Perfecto slapped me on the back. He opened my last bottle of whiskey. "Let us celebrate!" he cried, and he forced the bottle to my lips.

I swallowed a drink and asked, "What happened?"

Perfecto grinned, "The socialists are being routed from all the countries they stole. They've lost more in a single night than they gained in the past seven years!"

"But how?" I asked. I knew how. Tamara must have regained consciousness. When I thought about this, it was as if something inside me snapped. I felt an overwhelming sense of relief. I hadn't realized how concerned I'd been about her. She'd supplied the names of the artificial intelligences who'd aided the socialists, and Garzón had relayed the information to his compadres on Earth. With the local AIs destroyed, banks, roads, and communications would be down in most of the EUSS.

"It was so simple," Perfecto said. "Someone blew up the AIs and the whole country blew up with it. Millions of refugiados in Independent Brazil and Panamá have armed themselves and are pouring over the borders into every socialist state. In almost every city in the EUSS, the military is so busy trying to fight looters that they can't defend themselves from outside forces, while at the same time many soldiers are sabotaging their own defense systems and switching sides. And it has become evident that three AIs were dedicating their entire memories in efforts to aid the socialists—for nearly three quarters of the socialists defenses went down when the three AIs were bombed, including all of the cybernet tanks and neutron cannons. Since the AIs have violated every agreement they ever made by supporting a military struggle, many nations are supporting our actions. India is even going so far as to send military aid to the refugiados—fifty thousand cybernet tanks, and an orbital neutron cannon. Ah, I wish I were back in Chile!"

I was stunned. No one had ever offered us military aid, except for a little bit from Australia, and they made you beg so much it almost wasn't worth the trouble. "Do you think it's true! Do you think the EUSS could fall in one day?"

Abriara shook her head. "No. They're already recovering. They're drawing up new battle lines, retreating to Bolivia, Paraguay, Uruguay, and Chile. People in some of those countries haven't even stirred. They may be so far behind the lines that they don't even know what's going on. It will still take years to win everything back."

"I would not be so sure," Perfecto said. "The socialists are being cut off from most of their heavy weaponry. If our forces gain control of some of those weapons, this war could be over in three months."

Zavala and Mavro jacked out. Zavala began screaming, and jumped up and down, and ran out of the room with Abriara and Perfecto, heading downstairs to celebrate with friends. I told them I'd join them in a while. Mavro sat on his bed and smiled, and I just sat down on the floor.

When the others were gone, Mavro said, "So, Angelo, the information from that socialist whore you brought with you was good, no?"

"Sí, it was excellent information."

"And to think, it all happened because I saved you at Sol Station!"

"You are a good friend," I said. I wasn't sure I meant it. I remembered how he'd spoken evilly of me behind

my back, criticizing my battle skills. But he'd been
drunk, so I tried not to hold his words against him.

Mavro grinned and leaned his head back and stared at
the ceiling. "In a couple of months Garzón will choose
his captains. When he does, he will remember what
we've done for him. I would not be surprised if you and
I both were made captains."

I remembered the green rolling hills in Panamá, the
way the sun set over the lake behind my little house in
Gatún while the big ships sailed across the lake to port in
Colón and Panamá City. I thought of the way the flocks
of blue and green canaries played in the bushes in my
backyard. I'd left all that behind, and suddenly it hit me
that I'd left it behind for nothing. I could have taken
Tamara to the rebel soldiers in the forests south of
Colón, and she could have given them her information.
The results would have been the same. The socialists on
our borders would have been repelled, and I could have
lived in Panamá forever, a free man, with no threats
hanging over me—if I'd only let Arish live. I should have
let Arish live, taken Tamara to safety, and just gone
home. Yet the idea of doing this had never struck me
before. Once again, the fact that I'd acted so irrationally
hinted to me that I was insane. *Or could I just be stupid?*
I wondered. When I was a young man, every two or
three weeks I'd notice how stupid I'd been at that same
time a year before. But now that I'd reached fifty-nine,
I no longer looked back with amazement to realize how
stupid I'd been at age fifty-eight. Perhaps it was time to
begin doing that again.

More than anything, I yearned to be in Panamá. But
even if I managed to return after battling the Yabajin on
Baker, I'd have spent forty-five years Earth-time in
travel. The Panamá I left wouldn't be the same. And I
realized that even though I felt a sweet sense of victory
because of what was happening in Panamá, the victory
was irrelevant to me. I'd never benefit from it. It could
just as well have been happening on some tiny planet I'd
never heard of.

Mavro said, "That socialist woman, she must have had
some strong information. She must have been in the

highest echelons of their government. Remember when Garzón was questioning you and he got excited about her and asked you what was her job in Intelligence? And he said he knew the socialists had 'someone with her talent'?"

"I remember," I said.

"What did he mean, 'Someone with her talent'? I could tell by the look in his eye that he had discovered her job in Intelligence, but I do not know what he meant."

I thought about it. "I have no idea. I don't think it is something Garzón is willing to discuss." Somewhere, I knew, Tamara was now awake. I wondered how well she was recovering, how complete her memories were. I wondered if she'd remember me, and if she knew what I'd sacrificed for her. For a moment I felt content, free of the desire to seek her out, and I wished her well.

But when I tried to consciously break my tie with her, I suddenly felt as if a great dark bird unfurled its wings above my head, filling me with overwhelming dread as it readied to strike.

CHAPTER

8

That morning we passed Pluto's orbit and exited the Solar system. The Japanese kept us on standby while the ship made course adjustments, ejecting the huge pulse rocket that accounted for most of the ship's mass, then extending the fins for the ship's ramscoops. The way the Japanese had dramatized the event, I'd have thought it would be some big thing, but I only felt slightly queasy for a second, as if I were in an elevator and it had stopped at the top floor, then a lurch as the ship's gravity increased from 1.35 to its full 1.45 g's.

Our bodies hadn't yet adjusted to the force of the new acceleration speed. It was not the crushing weight one would feel at four or five gravities, where air is tugged from your lungs while blood pools at your feet and your bones groan as if they'll splinter if you make a false move. It was a steady pull, a feeling of sinking slowly into the floor, a heaviness that seemed unbearable because it steadily increased. My muscles had tightened and my excess fat was falling away. Yet I felt tired. Worn and frail. We tried to convince the samurai to give us a day off so we could celebrate. But the samurai were not concerned with the small victories our friends gained in South America.

While we put on armor, I kept expecting Abriara to give us some encouragement, but all she said was, "I hope you're all prepared for another joyride through hell."

Mavro suited up with his usual grim smile, and Zavala's eyes glittered like those of a nervous madman.

An air of depression hung over our little group. We put on armor, took our places on the model hovercraft, then Kaigo jacked us in:

Scenario 66: Deep Patrol

The message on my monitor gave me hope, something I had not felt for days. If we had graduated from the mid-patrol scenarios, it meant we'd see new territory. It might also mean we were getting better and had graduated to a higher level in spite of the fact that we'd lost every battle.

The scenario opened on the cruelest desert we'd seen on Baker, a flat plain of cracked soil as hard as concrete that stretched as far as the eye could see. No plants. Not even a rock. Only the shimmering heat of the desert gave any reprieve—in the distance the cracked soil turned into imaginary lakes. We shot along the plain at top speed and the hovercraft didn't rattle. We may as well have floated over a paved road.

We spotted the Yabajin to the east at ten kilometers, the sun gleaming on their metal hovercraft. It was to be a duel on the open plain—a test of our basic battle skills—an unpromising scenario. Abriara held course straight south and the Yabajin moved to intercept us. It was a wasted gesture—the best they could hope for was to close up a kilometer or two, and that was all they did. We spent over an hour running, cheating them of a quick victory, and everyone's moods lightened a little, enough so that Mavro began to tell a few jokes. But then we came to a marvelous canyon.

It was as if the world fell away. Painted mountains in shades of red, yellow, and white stone hovered in the hazy distance seven kilometers below us, and wind-sculpted chimneys of rock rose up nearby. It was as if the fiery crust of Baker had cracked apart, leaving nothing but blasted stone behind. I'd seen the Grand Canyon back on Earth, but it was just a furrow in the dust compared to this. We couldn't discern the far rim—only pale violet sky and billowy clouds in the distance.

At first the immense canyon appeared impassable, but

directly below us one could see that the earth didn't just drop away: there were many slopes and fault lines in the rock, and these were worn smooth with age. If we took the right route, the lucky route, we could make our way to the canyon floor.

Abriara said, "I vote that we go down." The Yabajin were closing in behind us, and I wondered quickly if it would be a wise move, but Abriara continued, "And since I'm driving, mine is the only vote that counts," and she drove off the cliff.

We spent the next five minutes in a barely controlled fall, sliding down a forty-degree slope, constantly gaining momentum, a cliff to one side and a rock wall to the other. I threw my gun down, hooked my feet under my chair, and clutched the hovercraft's handrail.

Perfecto chuckled nervously. "Did I ever tell you I am afraid of heights?"

Mavro said, "This is not so bad. You won't even feel it when you hit bottom."

Abriara was torn between the desire to run from the Yabajin and the desire to get down the cliff safely. She traveled fast, too fast. We came to a switchback and almost flew over the cliff. Perfecto moaned and grasped the handles on his turret so hard he accidently fired a round into the rock above us, sending shards of gravel to fall on our heads. Because the hovercraft travels on a cushion of air, it is difficult to make tight corners. We made the corner and saw that before us our road ended in a sheer ledge. Abriara hit the forward thrusters and slammed us into full reverse, but at so steep an angle of descent the engines just groaned and the hovercraft kept sliding down. I bailed out over the side along with Zavala. Perfecto was at the forward turret and didn't have time to jump, and Abriara wasn't able to get out of the driver's seat. Mavro didn't seem to care.

They roared over the cliff and dropped away. Perfecto screamed, "Agh! Agh! Agh!" through his head mike as if he were choking.

But Mavro just said, "Ah, this isn't so bad."

I shouted, "Good-bye, my friends." Then they crunched

as they hit a cliff below us. I ran to look down where they'd fallen.

The hovercraft rolled several times down a hill and came to a rest in a narrow defile. If it had rolled twice more it could have dropped over the next cliff. Even the first drop was a long way down.

Zavala started laughing, and I thought about Mavro's last words and laughed with him. Zavala laid down on the rock and kept it up for several minutes, holding his stomach and rolling around.

When he was able to sit up he said, "Angelo, where is your gun?"

"I left it in the hovercraft."

He held up his rifle. The barrel was bent, which meant its internal mirrors would not be aligned. It couldn't be used as a weapon. "I fell on mine," he said. "How long do you think we'll last if we attack the Yabajin bare-handed?"

"We might be able to prolong the battle out to three seconds," I said.

Zavala laughed. "Sí. I think so too. How do you want to die—fry or fall?" he asked, then he ran two paces and swan-dived over the cliff. He made a tiny cracking sound when he landed.

"Let me think about it," I said to no one in particular.

I still had a good ten minutes until the Yabajin descended the trail—plenty of time to come up with a plan. Actually, the more I considered it, the less likely it seemed that I needed a plan. If the Yabajin matched our velocity they'd just go flying over the same cliff. Maybe I'd even be lucky and none of them would jump out in time. All I really needed to do was hide in a crevice somewhere up the trail till they passed.

I climbed back up the trail, looking for a good place to hide. But the rock wall was pretty smooth and left few convenient overhangs. None large enough to hide under. After five minutes I found a spot that could do in a pinch. It was just at the top of the switchback, where the Yabajin would be clinging to their handrails for their dear lives. It was a small vertical crevice, and I found that if I removed my chest plate I could squeeze in the crack. I wriggled in and scrunched down tight.

I thought of Zavala. No one in our group had committed suicide before. Some of our more recent maneuvers could have fit into the category of *maniacally reckless* perhaps, but none were suicidal. Yet his move made sense. Burning is the most painful way I know of to die, and he'd chosen an easier route. Still, it seemed wrong to give up without a fight.

I heard a roar up the trail and the Yabajin whizzed by on their hovercraft. As I'd anticipated, they were so preoccupied with negotiating the deadly curve they didn't notice me. I turned up the volume on my outside mike and listened for the hovercraft's engine. It roared suddenly as the Yabajin tried to reverse before flying off the cliff. Unfortunately, their efforts at braking succeeded. The engines quieted to a low rumble, which grew louder as the hovercraft returned.

I stepped out of my crevice, deciding to face the inevitable. I didn't have a weapon, so when the hovercraft appeared around the bend I just raised my hands to surrender.

The hovercraft stopped and the Yabajin watched me suspiciously. I was well aware that we fought the same five Yabajin in the simulators in every battle. One of the laser gunners was a squat man Mavro had named Piglet. And in the same spirit we'd named the other laser gunner Keg because he had such a big chest. The aft turret man often leaned his head to the right, so we called him Lazy Neck. These three hopped from the craft and approached. They were uncertain what to do, and they stood for a moment. Their red armor blended so perfectly with the red of the sandstone they almost seemed part of the landscape. Lazy Neck walked over and looked down on me and shook his head. I could hear him laughing and chattering with his companions over his head mike. I didn't like his tone of voice, since he sounded as if he were making derogatory remarks about my sexual preferences. Keg strode on past me and checked the road up the hill, while Piglet leveled his gun at me. I suddenly remembered that for as long as we'd

been in the simulators, no one had ever surrendered. I
got an uneasy feeling.

When Keg returned he kicked the back of my legs so
that I fell forward, then the three of them took turns
kicking me in the ribs. I curled in a ball and covered my
head.

Lazy Neck removed his helmet and yelled in Spanish,
"What is the matter with you, *baca yakoo*? Why don't
you fight?"

"I don't have a chance," I said.

"You make chance!" he shouted.

He flipped off the magnetic snaps on my helmet, arm
and leg pieces, trying to strip me of my armor. I wrestled
him for every piece, but he got mad and twisted my arm
behind my back and applied pressure till I gave up.
Then he undressed me anyway. "Lie flat!" he said.

I lay on my back on a flat rock. Piglet field-stripped
his laser rifle, opened the stalk to reset the timing on the
burst regulator, turn down the power supply to the
lasers, and disconnect the targeting computer. When he
was done, he shot me experimentally on the inside of my
thigh. A red weal bubbled up on my skin and fat
crackled. I curled up to protect myself, but Piglet found
other tender targets to fry—my back, underarms, toes.
The quick killing burst of a laser seemed a soft way to die
in comparison.

I was only two meters from the ledge, and I tried
crawling to it so I could throw myself over.

Piglet took the opportunity to burn the crack of my
buttocks and cook my ears, then Lazy Neck grabbed my
feet and pulled me back.

I screamed, and he forced the barrel into my mouth.
I bit down, trying to keep him from shooting my tongue.
My cheeks glowed momentarily; my teeth felt as if they
burst into flame. Lazy Neck was standing between me
and the ledge. I batted at his legs, pushing him aside,
and crawled for the cliff. My fingers were burned black,
so I crawled on my elbows and knees. Keg and Lazy
Neck kicked at me, egging me on. Piglet had already
fried off the nerve endings in my tender places, so when
I made it to the ledge, they let me drop.

For a moment the cool air soothed my wounds.

I awoke hugging my knees in the corner of the battle room where I hid between two chest plates of battle armor. Abriara was whispering to me softly, saying, "Come, Angelo, come get up. You can do it!" I was groggy and unbalanced. She helped me to my feet.

Zavala knelt before Master Kaigo, and Kaigo paced back and forth while cursing him. "You shit-eating coward!" he said. "You dishonor your comrades by your presence! You throw your life away over a cliff when you could as easily die in battle? Who can understand this behavior? You shit-eater! You dishonor the mother who bore you! Who can understand this?" Kaigo slapped Zavala on the side of the head, knocking him down, but there was no viciousness in the blow. Kaigo shook his head and looked at Zavala. "Who can understand this?" and because Kaigo honestly didn't understand, he admonished, "Don't do that again, right? You won't do that again! You bring shame to me as your master. You bring shame to the company that hired you. You want to be a samurai, don't you?"

Zavala nodded.

"Then you must serve Motoki and seek an honorable death in battle! What more could a samurai desire?"

Kaigo shook his head and his ponytail swayed. He pointed at me. "And you! Did you hear them laughing at you? What is this thing you did with your hands?" He frowned and raised his hands in the air.

"I was surrendering," I said. "I could not win the battle."

Then Kaigo said the most important thing I ever learned about Baker: "On Baker, there is no surrender."

After battle practice I felt dirty with sweat, and I headed down to level four for the showers. The shower room was hot and steamy, and one could smell it from the ladder. The line in front of the narrow door had only forty people. The men in line were subdued. They discussed the latest happenings in South America, but there was no joy in their voices. It was as if it were old news from many years ago.

As I waited a small, wiry man with many tattoos of spiders and skulls on his arms came out of the showers. His eyes were glazed with weariness, and as he passed a big Brazi in the doorway, he gave the Brazi a shove. It was a shove meant only to push the Brazi aside, but the Brazi swung, flattening the tattooed man. His head cracked on the floor, leaving a smear of blood. He got up and staggered away and no one helped him.

It was a small incident, but struck me as strange: both men attacked, but the violence was mechanical, passionless. There was no posturing before the skirmish, with each man making threats. No one screamed or cursed. And the witnesses didn't try to calm the aggressors or help the injured, as if we simply didn't care.

I showered and couldn't help thinking about what had happened. Perhaps I'd been shocked into inaction, I wondered, but twice in my life I'd witnessed fights, and both times I'd rushed to aid the victims. I had always believed in serving society, yet I'd let an injured man crawl away without a thought. Even a dog would have done more than I had done. In the past few weeks, we had each suffered so much pain that the pain of others became meaningless. Where was my compassion? I could not believe that I had sunk so low. I had always sought to serve society—but one can only serve society by serving one individual at a time. Even if I felt nothing for the man, even if I could not rouse myself to feel sympathy for him, I reasoned, I must serve him.

I got out of the shower and followed the blood trail left by the injured man. He seemed to walk the halls at random, without a destination. I lost his trail on level seven. I checked with a nurse at the infirmary and verified that the man had never sought treatment. When I'd done all I could, I headed back up the ladder to my room. As I reached the top, the door to the air lock above me slid open and a man in white coveralls climbed down from module B. I'd believed there was no way to move through the air locks.

I was so astonished I blurted, "How did you do that?"

"Ti?" he said in Greek and shrugged. He spoke no Spanish and I spoke no Greek. He fingered a small transmitter in his pocket, then the air lock closed and he descended to the lower levels, and I now saw that if the need ever became great I could find a way to reach Tamara, and the Alliance assassin could find his way to reach me.

In the afternoon I accompanied Zavala and García to the library. As we walked Zavala said, *"Huy,* such a fine way to waste a morning!" as if preferring not to be bothered, yet he nearly skipped with joy. The "library" turned out to be the size of a broom closet and contained only one small viewing console and a few tapes about Baker. The cost of stocking and carrying tapes must have seemed superfluous to Motoki Corporation. We could learn all we needed about how to wage war through the simulators.

I inserted a tape entitled *The Delicate Natural Balance of Baker,* hoping to learn of the creatures I'd seen in simulations. The narrator showed how Motoki struggled valiantly to introduce Earth organisms on Baker to hurry the complete terraforming of the planet. Yet at every turn the Yabajin harried the dedicated terraformers, bringing their efforts to naught. Honey bees died from parasitic mites introduced by the Yabajin, jeopardizing plants that reproduced through pollination. Fish counts in Baker's oceans remained low because the water was too warm—the Yabajin had thwarted the terraforming of the great central deserts, and these deserts introduced large amounts of dust into the atmosphere, creating a greenhouse effect that warmed the oceans. I learned nothing about the biology of Baker. But I learned much about the naïveté of Baker's native propagandists. The information presented in the films was obviously slanted. Like most repressive government officials, Motoki's social engineers had been suppressing information for so long in their effort to stamp out the remnants of Western civilization they seemed incapable of looking at an issue from two sides.

Zavala grinned like an idiot. "Well, I saw no children

training for battle in that tape, did you?" he asked. I shook my head and he said, "What? I didn't hear you."

"No," I said.

The second tape, called *The Great Catastrophe*, was more helpful. It recounted an "unprovoked" attack by the Yabajin some forty years earlier. The Yabajin had flown over Motoki's coastal cities and released a viral plague that killed two million. The inhabitants of Tsumetai Oka and Kimai no Ji were so weakened by the plague they were unable to bury their dead. Instead they threw the ravaged corpses into a river. The bodies floated downstream, but when the high tides came the bodies floated back upstream and were deposited on the beaches. For days the bodies washed in and out with the tides. When the survivors recovered, they built a cemetery. In the cemetery they erected a cement pillar the size of a small fence post for each fatality. The name of the plague victim and the victim's lineage was inscribed on each pillar and white tassels were tied to the top. Once each year the forty thousand residents of Kimai no Ji visited the vast cemetery and clustered at one end so they could visualize just how many had died. Then they put candles on two million paper lanterns and set the lanterns adrift on the river so it became a river of fire. Everyone from the oldest grandmother to the youngest child swore undying hatred for the Yabajin. Once again, the tape taught me little. But the vision of Baker as a desolate planet with buildings blasted to the foundations disappeared. There were no cement buildings on Baker. Instead the cities were small hamlets filled with dark wooden-frame houses with cream-colored paper walls. The city was neat and well-kept—ornate, sculpted stone lanterns in front of each house, immaculate gardens along the roadside—with no sign that a battle had ever been fought.

I began to suspect that this war was an accident, that a virus had mutated and killed the inhabitants of Motoki's settlements and initiated a war, but the next tape, *Growing-up Motoki*, persuaded me otherwise. The tape showed how for thirty years the Yabajin had engaged in infanticide—systematically destroying Motoki's children. In the early days it had been done in the birthing vats. A Yabajin assassin successfully poisoned amniotic fluids in the birthing vats for three years in a row. Corporate officials caught and beheaded the man, but not before representatives from the Alliance completely outlawed birthing vats on Baker for "the duration of the war." I found the term "duration of the war" interesting, for nowhere in the films did Motoki officials describe retaliation for the Yabajin attacks. The film went on to show how after the initial attack against the birthing centers, young children soon became targets: sixteen children were blown apart by tiny bombs that looked like toy butterflies—when one pinched the wings together, the butterfly exploded. Cyanide-laced rice balls strewn about park benches killed five toddlers. A blooming chrysanthemum became bait over a spiked pit, spearing a small girl. The attacks were grisly and well-documented. Fearful parents hid children indoors, and attacks moved into the homes. The tape showed a young man standing over the corpse of a black-robed man, describing how the assassin—the Japanese used the slang "Farmer"—had entered the boy's house at night. The young man always slept with his family's ancient sword, and he slashed the assassin's belly open. I was surprised to recognize the young man as Kaigo, the samurai master who trained us.

The film switched to an old man teaching a child self-defense. The training consisted of teaching the child not to look at flowers, not to eat food given by strangers, not to play with other children in groups.

"Ah, here is your defensive training!" Zavala said. "But it appears your samurai forgot to train the children how to fire a rifle!"

So much for our theory that children fought beside adults. Children were merely victims here. Being raised indoors, they would perhaps be socially inept, shy, even afraid of strangers. Yet at the same time, they'd be survivors. They didn't touch candy left on the ground, they didn't smell chrysanthemums, they slept with their weapons. They had to be cautious. Perhaps overly cautious—afraid to act in a new way.

But that seemed ridiculous. If anything, the samurai adapted quickly to any new curve we threw them. I was walking up a dead-end street, learning nothing, and I knew it.

"I do not think these tapes will be of any help," García admitted. "The propagandists have gone over them too carefully. I'll bet these are the tapes Motoki showed the Alliance delegates on Earth when they sought permission for a full-scale war. We will find nothing."

The last three tapes provided more of the same information. One map showed the demographics of Baker. Motoki settlement was separated from the Yabajin by six thousand kilometers of desert and canyons. Motoki estimated the Yabajin population at 95,000—a scant 18,000 more than Motoki. Populations should have been higher, much higher. Motoki had obviously launched attacks of its own. Knowing my luck, I was fighting for the wrong side—if there was a right and wrong side.

Nothing in the tapes indicated why the samurai always beat us. I'd expected evidence of a protracted, bloody war—permanantly scarred bodies, cyborged citizens, strong defensive perimeters, war machines—things that would explain the samurai's facility with weapons. But even after reviewing the background in the tapes, the only war machine was a bulky black cybertank putting through an orchard, a minor part of the Alliance-approved defense.

I sighed and turned off the monitor.

García had watched over my shoulder. He leaned back against the wall. With a total lack of conviction he said, "Then the samurai must be cheating in the simulators. We will have to attack one of them, test his abilities."

I drummed my fingers on the control panel of the monitor. It had seemed like a fun idea when we were drunk. Now it only sounded stupid. "That may be risky. Even if we lose the battle, the samurai may consider it an act of rebellion. What might they do to us?"

Zavala spoke up. "You idiots! You'll get us in trouble. You know the samurai don't cheat. Why don't you just admit the samurai beat us by the power of their spirit!"

García and I looked at each other. García smiled grimly; his eyes held no defeat. And I smiled in return. We'd somehow pushed the right button on Zavala; he was terrified of the samurai. Though our proposed action sounded stupid, the plan was worth discussing if only to see Zavala squirm.

"We won't give up, because you're wrong," García said, looking for a place to put his hands. He finally just hooked his thumbs under the belt of his kimono. "Give up, Zavala! Just pay me my million pesos and we won't have to fight the samurai." García licked his lips and watched Zavala, enjoying his game.

Zavala began shaking like a cornered rabbit.

"Ah, so what if they kill us?" I said as if to discount the threat.

Zavala raised his cymeched hand, palm outward. "Wait! Wait!" he said. "I cheated you. I know something you don't!"

The thought crossed my mind that Zavala had stolen some tapes from the library—tapes showing children practicing with the hovercrafts and laser rifles. He stood there a moment.

"Well?" García demanded.

Zavala stood up straight. "I know . . ." he said, as if to bear his innermost soul, "I *know*—that the world is magical, that there are spirits!" We must have appeared incredulous. "I have proof!" he said.

"Let us see this proof," I said.

Zavala said, "I know it's hard to believe, but I was once like you—always seeking answers to questions that have no answers, seeking to comprehend the incomprehensible universe." He waved his hand as if to display the universe in one simple gesture.

"This was before the socialists attacked Colombia, back when I was sixteen. I wanted to marry a girl from Tres Ríos, and I wanted to make some money so we could buy some land. I went to Buenaventura and got a job on a ship, a Chinese plankton harvester.

"We were supposed to sail the coasts of Antarctica to harvest the plankton, but the ship's intake swallowed everything in its path—logs, jellyfish, kelp, trash. My job was to separate these things, put the trash on a conveyer belt and send it back to sea, rake the small fish onto another belt, and gaff a large fish if we got one and throw it into the processor.

"We had not traveled for three days, and we were just south of Chimbote, when I found it . . ." Zavala stopped.

"And . . ." García said. "You are not going to tell me you found a spirit?"

"You would not believe me if I told you," Zavala answered.

"You have not lied to us before, why should we not believe you now?" I asked.

Zavala considered my words. "Because we ran over a bed of red kelp. And among the long strands of red kelp I found something. At first I thought it was a large porpoise, and I was excited, for no one has found a wild porpoise for many years. It was long and gray, with a gray tail. But when I uncovered it, I found that it had the chest and head of a woman! It was a siren. She had light blue skin, and white hair, and long thin arms with webbed fingers on her hands. And right here"—he drew a finger in a line under his throat—"were her gills— white gills that fanned out like those of a salamander!

"She had been dead for several days, and her eyes had been eaten out by the fishes. In spite of this, she was . . . beautiful. Marvelous. Perfect." Zavala looked back and forth between the two of us, as if to convince us by his expression. "I know what I saw!"

García smiled a smile of embarrassment for Zavala. "So, you found a siren. That may be," he said condescendingly, "but how does that prove we have spirits?" He obviously didn't believe Zavala. Yet Zavala's sincerity convinced me he was telling the truth.

Zavala became quite agitated. He swung his arms wildly as he spoke. "Don't you see? This proves the Earth is magical. For if this magical being has really existed all these thousands of years without us knowing about it, how can we doubt that greater things exist? Magic is everywhere! But our minds are too puny to comprehend it, so we make up lies so we can pretend we understand! All you must do is feel inside you; then how can you doubt that you have a spirit?"

I said quite calmly, "There is of course a logical explanation for what you saw."

"What?" He set his jaw.

"What you saw may have been a chimera—after all, you were near Chilean waters."

"No." Zavala shook his head vigorously. "It was not a chimera! Nobody could have made something that beautiful!"

"I saw how the engineers designed Abriara. Believe me, with enough time those men could have made anything—even a siren. You have seen chimeras who are not quite human, haven't you?" I asked. "Did you not hear tales of those little men that looked like giant bats? And near the genetic engineering compound at Tocopilla were large aquariums leading directly to the sea. Could not the engineers have created a siren or two?"

Zavala laughed to scorn. "I should have told you nothing. I should have known better. The great doctor! As soon as I tell you something, you try to explain it away. You fucking intellectuals are all alike. If you don't believe me, go ahead and attack the samurai! But when they kill you, I'll rob your corpses and get my money! You know nothing!"

He stormed out of the room. I felt bad, but didn't know what to do.

García sighed. "Then, I guess we'll have to have our chimeras fight some samurai tonight. Is there anyone special we should attack?"

I waved my hand. "They're all alike to me."

"Me too. They live up in the staterooms on your level. I suggest we just ambush one in the hall. What do you think?"

"It sounds like a good plan."

"Then it is settled," García said. "We'll do it tonight."

At evening Perfecto came in the room and said quite matter-of-factly, "There is a dead man in the hall." He said it as he crossed the room to sit on his trunk, and used the tone one might use if saying, "It is raining outside."

No one bothered to look up at Perfecto, to ask who the man was or how he'd died.

Mavro rolled off his bunk and said, "I'm getting tired of this shit." He could have been speaking about our losses in the simulator, or the steady drag of the heavy gravity, or the depressing news of a dead man in the hall. Perhaps it was a little of all these.

We shuffled from our room, down the corridor. Near the ladder we found the body. Without my prosthetic eyes it would have looked as if the man was simply injured, since his face was not discolored. But his body was cooling, and his platinum glow was soft and diffuse— no bright spots of heat in the neck or face where warm blood pumps near the surface. He had thick black hair, dark brown skin, and a small build. He was lying on his left side, but his face was twisted up so he stared at the ceiling, and his right leg was raised at an angle the way a dog would lift its leg to pee. His lips were contorted into a snarl. Someone had broken his neck. Though he was small, his body filled the narrow hall, almost as if it had been wedged in, so it was impossible to walk around him. Hot platinum air from a ventilator shaft near the floor blew into the man's hair, stirring it, as if his hair were being brushed by shafts of light.

Mavro looked at the little man and said, "Ah, Marcos, I see Tomas finally caught you with his woman. Tough luck!" He climbed over the corpse without stopping. He grunted angrily and swore. At such a heavy gravity the small man seemed a major obstacle. I stopped and looked at the body and decided I didn't have enough energy to try to move it. Marcos had probably weighed 65 kilos on Earth. In ship's gravity he'd have weighed 100 kilos—well over my Earth weight. Besides, how could I get him down the ladder to the infirmary where he could be properly disposed of? I didn't know him. He was beyond help. It was up to his compadres to dispose of the body.

I climbed over the corpse and headed down the ladder to level three.

CHAPTER

9

Master Kaigo jacked us into our scenario.

Scenario 69: Deep Patrol

The sky was dark with *oparu no tako*, flocks of intertwining bands of yellow, green, brown, and blue, spanning from horizon to horizon. A wet wind blew, swift and sure and powerful. When it gusted, the hovercraft would lift in the air and we'd soar.

The land was dotted with huge patches of bare white stone the color of yellowed bones dotted with occasional dull red "desert flowers," tiny thick-leaved plants the size of a child's palm. And along the white rock, four-legged creatures like giant ants with glossy green-black exoskeletons waited near the tops of burrows a man could fit his fist into. And when the ants smelled us, they leapt into their burrows.

We glimpsed a mammal the size of a tomcat with bushy gray fur and one huge clawed arm, like that of a fiddler crab but as long as my own arm, lumber from hole to hole, reaching down to grab ants.

We headed toward a small red hill, but soon the ground dropped and we came to a basin where thick tussocks of dry grass and small bushes clung to a thin layer of soil. The vegetation was nearly all Earth plants. We passed a herd of gazelles and wildebeast, and five tawny lions panting in the shade of a small tree. This tiny basin seemed an island of normality among the strange flora and fauna of Baker.

219

"We've got another combat team off to the left," Perfecto said as we shot through the tall liongrass. He waved at someone I couldn't see.

"Abriara Sifuentes here in team one," Abriara said.

"Paco García here. We spotted two Yabajin craft come over that hill up ahead just a minute ago. Veer right, and come up even with us. I want us to go in tandem. New tactic." His transmission was loud, and his voice rang in my head. At this close range, the feedback from his external mike made it sound as if he were a dog growling.

"Sí," Abriara said, veering right. Mavro and Perfecto boosted to their tiptoes on the turrets and looked out over the tall grass and brush, trying to spot the Yabajin. We were in a bad place to find them. If we continued at a fast pace, we could easily run into an ambush.

We met the second hovercraft and I glanced at them. They were dressed like us, in their dull green and dusty brown bug suits. Enlarged eyes seemed to peer everywhere as they nervously looked toward us. I'd learned to feel comfortably at ease with my weapon. It hung on me as if it were part of my body. To fight and even to die was a mindless pastime, something I might soon learn to do without forethought or calculation. I felt good. We whisked into a thicket. Two red deer with yellow spots bounded out away, and I suddenly had a strange feeling.

García's hovercraft veered close, and everyone on the craft watched us. I saw what was wrong: The big chimera Miguel should have been forward turret gunner. Instead, the man in the green bug suit in front was a tiny man.

I started to aim my rifle, and their hovercraft swept in and rammed us.

"Fire!" someone shouted, and his command filled my helmet like the roar of a beast. The men in the hovercraft turned their turrets on us. Perfecto and Mavro's armor went *thwack* as it cracked from taking hits at such close range. I fired at the nearest laser gunner. He reached out and smacked my gun, knocking it to the ground, then leapt past me.

Abriara tried to swerve away, and I was thrown off

balance and began tumbling backward. A turret gunner fired into me, and the searing plasma burst through my armor and tore into my chest. I fell back and instead of hitting ground, I jacked out.

Perfecto and Mavro were already out, since they were instantaneous kills, and they stood beside the holo of the ongoing battle, studying it. Those still jacked into the simulation sat limply in their chairs, totally oblivious to their surroundings. Their armor reminded me of cocoons, and I saw them as some type of pupae trapped in stasis, dreaming of the day when they'd metamorph into butterflies. *No, not butterflies,* I thought. *Something that dreams of death—dragonflies.*

Kaigo sat on his dais, gazing at the two hovercrafts flitting side by side: two big men had jumped onto our hovercraft. One ripped Zavala's helmet off and began beating Zavala to death. The second pulled Abriara from her driver's seat. Abriara shrieked and cursed, and Zavala's face sounded as if it were a soft fruit someone was pummeling.

The two craft approached a baobab tree in slow motion, and the driverless craft slid into it, crumpling. All the people—both the tiny dead bodies that represented us and those still alive—spilled from our mangled hovercraft like rag dolls while the enemy flitted past, then swung back to meet them. Abriara crawled several paces then tried to stand, but her leg trailed at an odd angle. One of the enemy jumped up and tackled her. They struggled on the ground. The other "compadre" sat up and held his head for a moment, then crawled back to Zavala and began thumping him again. I could think of only one man who might hate us enough to attack us in the simulator.

Perfecto spoke the name: "Lucío. Now I see why you did not Quest for us after we left the weight room, *mamón.*" And I knew he was right. Lucío had planned this moment for weeks.

Zavala jacked out of the simulator, a bit groggy. He took off his helmet and hopped off the model hovercraft and strode over to us through the holographic landscape like a giant walking over a desert, stepping over the tiny

representations of two Yabajin craft approaching from
the far side of the room, the Yabajin in their red combat
armor.

Lucío and his men reached the wreck under the
baobab and jumped from their hovercraft. Lucío said,
"Good! Good! Strip that bitch Abriara and start fucking
her. I want everyone to get a turn. Where's Mavro?"
Lucío separated from the rest of the group and began
searching among the fallen bodies, kicking aside our
sprawled limbs. His four men circled Abriara. She
couldn't stand, but raised herself to one knee; she swung
at one of them, and he swore at her. Someone pushed
her from behind, tripping her, then pinned her to the
ground and began ripping off her armor. She didn't
scream or go into hysterics. She just grunted and
breathed heavily as she struggled to keep herself dressed
and fend them off.

Perfecto looked up at Kaigo and asked, "Where is
Lucío's combat room?"

Kaigo didn't say anything at first, then he reached up
and thumbed the subdural pressor switch under his ear
and engaged his comlink. He began speaking in Japanese.

Lucío found Mavro's dead body among the wreckage.
He pulled off Mavro's helmet and checked his face to be
sure of Mavro's identity, then stripped the lower half of
the body and threw Mavro on the ground, face-down,
half naked. Lucío opened his own codpiece.

"Mavro, I wish you were jacked in to the simulator! I
wanted to take you from behind, like this, and hear you
scream!" Then he mounted the corpse and began rhyth-
mically grinding against it.

Lucío's men finished stripping Abriara, then a big
chimera opened his codpiece and crawled on top of her.
She struggled to fight them off. She didn't beg or curse
or scream. The chimera moved on top of her, and I
caught a glimpse of her face. I viewed it from above, like
God watching from a cloud, and even from there I could
see in her something I'd never expected to see in a
woman so strong—a pale face with pleading eyes and a
down-turned mouth, the face of a person totally demol-

ished and empty of hope. The face of someone in a Greek hell, destined to be eternally raped.

Perfecto jumped up to our hovercraft and ripped the lead to the cranial jack from the socket at the base of Abriara's skull. She crumpled to the floor and brought her knees up even with her chin. He gently tried to remove her helmet, and she slapped his hand away.

Down on the floor the simulation of Abriara went limp. The Yabajin were nearly on Lucío's men. They wouldn't spend more than another minute jacked into the simulator.

Kaigo disengaged his comlink. "They are in battle room seventy-nine, on level six."

I leapt toward the door and the others followed, none of us taking time to strip off our battle gear.

"Wait!" Kaigo shouted. I stopped and looked at him. He lowered his head and looked at the holo where Lucío and his men humped the limp replicas of my compadres. He hissed through his teeth, "Saaahhh," and ran his hand over his brow. "Every man is important to our fight on Baker," he said. "I do not want you taking their lives. You should not be enemies." He wrung his hands for a moment. "You must put aside your differences until you vanquish your common enemy. There will be time for vengeance."

Mavro glared at him, the fine muscles in his face swelling from rage. "Honor demands vengeance now!" he said, voicing my thoughts, and I rushed out the door.

"Do not kill them! I order you!" Kaigo shouted behind us.

I didn't listen to him. Only one set of footsteps followed me. I turned and saw Mavro, grim and determined.

I ran as fast as I could, working hard in the heavy gravity to stay ahead of him, to be first. It was like rushing through a dream—the heavy breathing, the sound of the teflex battle armor snapping against the floors, the feeling of power and wrath. We stepped in unison without thought, rushing toward Lucío and his men past people in the corridor who flattened against the walls, removing themselves from our path, past an open door that issued forth the sweet smell of cigar smoke; a man in a silver and red kimono laughed loudly from within the room. I stripped off my arm pieces and pulled out a knife. I felt remarkably calm. It would be like fighting in the simulator. I would go, and I'd be the first to die, and it would all be like this, like passing through a dream.

I felt as if I were stepping into another world, the world where the ghost of Flaco would become flesh. *There should be ghosts with me*, I thought, and distantly I felt as if they followed at my arm. I quickened my step. I heard a rattling noise, and didn't bother to look behind me. My teeth had begun to chatter, just as they'd done when I killed Arish. We swept down the hall, reached the ladder.

From behind, Perfecto yelled, "Wait, I'm coming!" but we didn't wait. I ignored the rungs and just grabbed the outside bars and let myself slide three levels, occasionally gripping tightly to slow my descent.

When I hit level six Mavro said, "Take corridor four and turn right at the end." I followed his instructions and when I came to the corner men in dark blue were rushing around the curve of the hall before us—three samurai with swords drawn, and behind them some Latin Americans. I knew Kaigo had warned them to stop us, but I saw a sign above a door that said Battle Room 79 and knew they were too late. I headed into the alcove.

As I reached the door it opened. I saw a flash of the silver and red kimono of a sergeant.

"Didn't anyone ever tell you to never hit a woman?" I yelled, thinking it a crazy thing to say even as I said it.

Lucío had been looking at the floor as he exited, and his gaze swept up and his mouth opened in surprise. My crystal knife slashed through his left eye, down across his nose, and to his jaw. The cut was deep. He seemed to collapse backward and flecks of blood splashed on me. I was surprised at how easy it was. The blade cut through flesh and even part of the skull as easily as if I'd sliced through cake. Someone behind Lucío shouted, "Jesus Christ!" and tried to pull him back to safety.

Lucío instantly lurched forward, leapt, and kicked my chest, hitting my upper abdomen, punching air out of me. I staggered and was suddenly cognizant of Perfecto rushing up behind me. He slapped me in the head, knocking me out of harm's way with more enthusiasm than was necessary.

I reeled and the corridor lights seemed to become very bright for a moment and I found myself sitting on the floor shaking my head, trying to keep it from spinning.

Perfecto had a bloody lip, and was standing over me. I must have fainted for a second. Two samurai had interposed themselves between us and Lucío's men, and both samurai had their swords drawn.

In the dark battle room Lucío's friends were trying to hold him upright. One of them said to Lucío, "Stay still, amigo. He cut you bad! You are hurt bad!"

But Lucío struggled against them, trying to throw himself at us, shouting, "Come here, you whore! Let me go! I'm going to kill that old fucker!" and he struggled with his friends.

I realized he was yelling at me because I'd cut him, and I tried to stand up too fast and my head spun. "I'd be happy to see you try!" I shouted.

Mavro, standing behind me, said, "Get away from here, Angelo! He's crazy! The blood of the *conquistadores* runs strong in that one!" His tone held a note of awe or fear. I turned and looked at him. His eyes were very cold, calculating. The lights shone on his silver tears.

I lunged at Lucío, not because I was going to attack him, but because I wanted to scream in his face. Perfecto grabbed me and I shouted, "The blood of the *conquistadores* runs strong in me, too, *mamón*!"

"You crazy!" Lucío shouted. I felt several hands grappling with my arms at once, and Perfecto and Mavro tugged me back into the hall and started retreating. Lucío shouted, "I'm going to kill you and fuck your woman! You're a dead man! You're a dead man! You're a dead man!"

I yelled, "Ah, go fuck your mother!" and stepped back

a couple of paces, then found that I hadn't yet recovered my balance, for I tripped over my own feet.

Perfecto helped me up and we trotted back up to our battle room. The only sounds were the clack of our armor and heavy breathing.

I turned to Mavro. "Why did you tell me to get away from Lucío?"

"He was crazy. It isn't good to fight someone in his condition. You could have cut his throat, and he'd keep ripping you apart for five minutes before he'd realize he was dead. It's better to let his blood cool. He'll be easier to kill, then."

"I'm sorry we lost your knife," Perfecto said.

I looked down and realized I was no longer holding my crystal knife. "Where is it?"

"The samurai picked it up. However, they didn't look up your other sleeve."

He was right. I could still feel the knife strapped to my right wrist. But I felt a strong sense of loss. That knife had been beautiful. We picked up the armpieces I'd discarded on the way down.

When we reached our battle room Kaigo was waiting. He glared at us and spoke to someone on comlink. "They're here," he said. Abriara was sitting up in her driver's seat, and Zavala sat next to her, one hand extended as if to touch her, to offer comfort, yet he didn't touch her. Abriara's helmet was off. Her face was washed out. Troubled. The webs of silver in her eyes seemed to have expanded in the last few moments until there was nothing human left in them.

Mavro slapped me on the back and boasted, "What a surprise! You should have seen don Angelo here! He swung that knife without the slightest concern for Lucío's health or well-being! And he ended up nearly slicing Lucío's head off. It was wonderful! Look at the blood on him. You'd think he'd just butchered a hog."

Mavro thought it was all very funny. I looked at my battle armor and saw that it was indeed spattered with blood.

Abriara stared at me strangely, as if about to speak, but changed her mind.

Kaigo shouted, "Get down here! On your knees!" He drew his sword and pointed to the floor with it. We cautiously walked to the dais, keeping our eyes to the ground, and knelt before Master Kaigo. He stared at us for a long time.

Perfecto understood the samurai far better than any of us did. He laid his face on the floor and shouted, "Forgive them, Master, they acted in the heat of their anger."

Kaigo hissed through his teeth, then asked calmly, "What have they done?"

"They attacked Lucío and slashed his face—but remembered your orders and didn't kill him."

There was an uncomfortable silence. Kaigo watched us. He said, "You should have thought ahead. You must think before you act."

"But . . . you've taught us that there must not be the breadth of a hair between the thought and the act," Mavro said. "You've taught us well."

Kaigo shouted in Japanese and the microspeaker on his collar came to life. "You acted irresponsibly by attacking in an untimely fashion. What could you be thinking? Where is your honor?"

It seemed a strange question. I couldn't see how we'd dishonored ourselves by attacking Lucío.

Mavro said, "I would have avenged my honor if I had killed them!"

"But you would dishonor your employer by killing these men in an untimely fashion!" Kaigo shouted. Then he calmed himself and said in a softer tone, as if reasoning with friends, "Motoki Corporation needs these men alive, ne? What could you have been thinking? If you avenge your honor upon these men now, will you then commit seppuku to redeem yourselves? This cannot be so! If you kill them now and die now by your own hands, you will take ten lives from Motoki Corporation. You would be permanently shamed. You could not fulfill your obligation to the corporation!

"Or do you think to kill these men now and die heroically in battle. Do you think to become Divine Wind, to die heroically?" Kaigo opened his mouth wide so we could see his tongue. He wrinkled his face in disgust. "No one can plan a hero's death with certainty. You must not think this.

"So, I see only one other path that could possibly lead to honor: You decided to kill them now, distinguish yourselves in battle, and commit seppuku after the war? Yet, this is a most uncertain path. For even if you distinguish yourselves in battle, you cannot say with certainty what damage these men would have done to the Yabajin. You may perform a miracle in battle, but who will ever know with certainty if you have redeemed yourselves? In your anger, perhaps this is what you were thinking, but now that your anger has diminished you must see that none of these paths lead to honor!"

Mavro said bitterly, "That is not what I was thinking. I thought we'd kill these men, then you'd forgive us. I thought you'd understand that we must avenge ourselves."

"I . . . understand," Kaigo said. "I too would avenge myself. But . . . the only path I see that will let you honor your commitment to Motoki and avenge yourselves of your enemy will be to wait until after the war. You will fight your battle with the Yabajin, then kill your enemies. Your debt of honor will be paid to the corporation, and your personal honor will be avenged. You will not have to lose your lives in seppuku, *ne*? It seems a simple matter." He smiled, as if he'd just explained a simple truth to idiot children and was waiting to see if they understood.

No one spoke. I was astonished at his narrow understanding of us. His concept of the obligations imposed by honor was so alien I could barely comprehend him. I hadn't been thinking of honor, I'd been thinking of revenge. In Panamá a man fulfills his obligations to family honor by avenging the family. Revenge and honor are one and the same. But obligations to an employer are not a matter of honor. It seemed a strange concept.

Abriara spoke my thoughts, "You don't understand. Motoki pays us money to do a job, and we will try to do that job. That is the extent of our relationship. Our employment by Motoki Corporation does not incur a debt of honor on our part."

Kaigo's face twisted into a grimace of pain, of shock, of bewilderment, as if she'd uttered the ultimate blasphemy. He began speaking rapidly in Japanese. His microspeaker spat the translation, "You make me to stick out my tongue in surprise! How can you not owe an obligation of honor to Motoki? Your parents give you life, and you owe them a debt of honor for it, correct? But now, Motoki puts food in your bellies. Motoki gives you water in the depths of space. The clothes on your back are provided by Motoki. The very atmosphere you breathe was created by Motoki on your single moon and pumped into this ship at great expense. For every breath that you take, you owe Motoki. Take away all that Motoki has given you, and you would die in an instant! You would explode in the harsh depths of space. Motoki keeps you alive from moment to moment. Does not this incur a debt of honor? Does not this incur a debt of honor greater than the one owed to family?"

Mavro said it before any of the rest of us could form the words: "No. Motoki uses us as tools and pays for the privilege."

Kaigo was stunned into silence. He reached up and stroked the top of his head, flattening his blue-black hair. He opened his mouth as if to speak several times, then thought better of it each time. He was obviously having a hard time trying to come to grips with the concept. I couldn't see the world as he did, from behind those surgically enhanced epicanthic folds, from beneath the ideological veil applied by the social engineers on Baker over the past century. He was completely dedicated to Motoki Corporation, willing to die at the company's request. I didn't then realize what a monstrous gulf lay between us, that he could never really understand us.

His eyes became glazed, and he stared at the floor in increasing consternation, totally withdrawn. An expression of utter confusion replaced his normal wooden stare. He eventually waved us away, in the general direction of the simulator. We still had a few minutes of battle practice left. We jacked in.

* * *

We soared over a rolling ocean of water clear as glass.
Ribbons of red seaweed twisted up from the ocean floor,
buoyed by pods that floated like giant dark red olives.
Flocks of Baker's plastic birds rested atop bits of floating
seaweed, wings folded like those of a butterfly, and at
our approach they'd lower their wings and flutter away.

Kaigo jacked us out. He raised his head and spoke as
if our conversation had never been interrupted. "I have
considered your words. You say you owe no debt of
honor to Motoki and do not consider the needs of the
corporation relevant. And if you owe no debt of honor to
Motoki, how can I convince you to spare your enemies
until the battle on Baker is won?"

We didn't know what to answer, and said nothing.

He continued. "If you initiate a battle with the
chimera Lucío and his team, I will slay you for disobeying my orders. I have spoken with Master Masae,
Lucío's trainer. And if Lucío and his men initiate a battle
with you, Masae will slay them."

Abriara said, "We'll restrain ourselves till after the war
on Baker. But Lucío won't abide by your decision, not
after he's been wounded."

Kaigo rubbed his chin. He said, "Masae has spoken
with Lucío's men. They are not unreasonable. They have
agreed to a temporary truce."

"Those idiots!" Abriara said as soon as she got out of
the battle room. "Lucío plans to step on us, and step on
us hard. He's probably laughing behind his hand right
now, thinking he's got us fooled into believing we've got
a truce!" She paced the hall nervously, put her hand to
her mouth and chewed at it. "Angelo, how bad did you
cut Lucío?"

"It was a deep cut," I said. "I sliced through one eye
and his nose. He'll be in surgery most of the night. He'll
be blind in one eye for weeks."

"Good. We'll spend tonight making weapons. We can

cut up your trunk and make some wooden daggers—
something to protect ourselves."

I sighed, saddened to lose a family heirloom. She was
right, though. We might need weapons. We climbed up
the ladder to level one, and by the time I reached the
top I was exhausted.

Halfway down the hall we found the dead man, lying
exactly as before. The hot air still breathed over him,
bathing his hair in light, and he gazed at the ceiling, one
knee raised in the air. As we walked toward him I
dreaded having to lift my feet to step over the body. At
1.5 g's it seemed someone's infernal scheme, leaving a
body in the hall so we'd have to climb over it.

Mavro was first in line, and when he reached the
corpse he savagely kicked it in the middle of the back.
"Who left Marcos here?" he screamed. "Why doesn't
someone take him away?" He kicked the corpse again,
this time in the buttocks, and Marcos' leg dropped.
Mavro stepped over the body.

Marcos stared at the ceiling with black eyes, hardly
opaqued. In his eyes I saw a similarity to Tamara's face
when she'd sat gazing zombie-eyed up at the ceiling. I
felt that odd tug, the desire to find her, to learn if she
was well. But it was weak and I ignored it as I stepped
over the corpse. She'd been awake for several days and
hadn't contacted me. I was nothing to her. The fact that
I still felt such concern for her almost seemed a joke.

We reached our room and Abriara began emptying my
teak chest. She pulled out the cigars that layered the
bottom and said, "Do you want this book?"

She held up a small leather-bound book with a faded
red cover and ragged pages, the book I'd taken from
Arish: *The Holy Teachings of Twil Baraburi*.

"Sure," I said, thinking I could use a little spiritual
enlightenment about now.

She threw it to me. I picked up the book and read a
verse at random: "Truly it is no sin for the righteous man
to slay the infidel, for has not God Himself sworn to
destroy the wicked? Therefore, slay the infidel and do
God's work."

I laughed and tossed the book to the floor. I'd expected the *Holy Teachings* to be a little more holy. It seemed like a good cosmic joke that of all the books on Earth, I should bring that one. But it made sense that Arish would have loved such a book.

I kept thinking of the dead man in the hall. The fact that his eyes were open bothered me. They reminded me so much of Tamara's eyes. Of the way she'd lived in her eyes.

I wandered out into the hallway and found the corpse, then closed its eyes. The gesture was wasted. I couldn't wipe Tamara from my mind so easily. As long as this corpse was here, I'd be annoyed by it. I considered taking it to the infirmary.

The infirmary's disposal chute led down to the engine rooms. The body could be thrown down the chute and expelled for mass to give a little extra push to the ship, or could be recycled into food and water. But I couldn't take the corpse to the infirmary. Lucío would still be there. I decided to pull it to the ladder and push it over. It would fall all eight levels, and whoever lived down there would have to lug it up to the infirmary.

Perfecto came out of our room to search for me. He padded up silently in his bare feet. "What are you doing out here alone?"

"I thought we should dispose of this mess," I said.

He nodded and grabbed a foot and twisted the corpse around lengthwise. I pulled the other foot. The corpse was fluid and rubbery and tended to stick to the floor. Without Perfecto I'd have had difficulty getting it to the ladder. We pulled it close to the hole and prepared to topple it over. The ladder was much like the ladder leading to a sewer—a simple round hole with a ladder descending eight levels below us, and people could climb up and down both sides at once. At any given moment twenty people might be on the ladder. We watched the people climbing up and down and waited for them to clear so we could throw the corpse over.

Perfecto had something on his mind but seemed hesitant to say it. He worked up his nerve. "You know,

Miguel would like to see you more often. He's bonded to you."

"He hovers too close to me. I feel smothered by him," I answered.

"He has a very strong desire to see you. He craves it badly. If Lucío does go on a Quest tomorrow, Miguel will want to help you out."

I doubted that. Perfecto tended to be overly protective of me. I wondered if he was voicing his own concern. I couldn't imagine Miguel being too thrilled at the prospect of joining us. Yet, who knows? Most people aboard ship didn't seem to care if they got killed. Miguel could be one of those people. Would he walk through fire to save me, just because of the bonding? "What does it feel like to be bonded?" I asked.

Perfecto shrugged. "I don't know if I can explain. Words are seldom adequate to express emotion. But, it is like—like being in the hospital room when my first son was born. I'd had two daughters, and didn't want to get my hopes up. But when I saw my son—saw he was handsome in spite of having me for a father—I picked up that tiny infant, and all I wanted for him was good. I wanted him to experience only the good things of the world." Perfecto's voice got husky as he spoke. He'd seldom discussed his family. "That is what I feel for you, Angelo—the desire for you to experience only good. That is what Miguel feels for you."

Intellectually I could understand such an emotion. I'd never had a child of my own, but understood the sensation even if I couldn't share it. "It is a very pure emotion. I wish I could feel something like it." I searched inside myself and felt only hollowness. "With feelings like that, I'm surprised you were capable of leaving your family at all."

Perfecto's eyes shone with tears, and he blinked them back. "When I found that my wife had been making love to another man, I wanted to die. I signed up to fight on Baker thinking to seek death. Since Motoki Corporation pays my wages directly to my family, I figured my children would be well provided for during the twenty-two years Earth time it will take to reach Baker, and they'd receive a bonus at my death. It seemed a perfect plan—until I saw you. It was as if a son was born to me in that moment. You are my family now. Miguel also feels this way about you. Will you let us protect you?" His jaw quivered with excitement as he waited for my answer. I looked at the thick hair perched on his head like some living animal, at the 3-D tattoo of the beast that shook with anticipation as his jaw muscles quivered. I marveled that he could care so much for me.

"No. I'll fight my own battles. And if I'm killed, you and Miguel will bond to someone else next week. You'll forget all about me."

"It's not that easy. The bond can never be broken. If you get killed, Miguel will never forget his guilt, his loss."

I shrugged. I didn't care about Miguel, or Perfecto, couldn't take time to care. I couldn't open myself to the pain of others. Over the past weeks the psychic battering of the simulators, the worry, the fear, the fatigue, the shock at my own brutality and the brutality of others, had all combined into an overwhelming deluge. At first I'd thought I could handle it. But instead I'd only protected myself. I could do nothing more. I felt that if I opened the floodgates, I'd go insane. To allow myself to be touched by one concern would have caused me to be brutalized by all. So I stifled my sensitivity, knowing that I did it at the price of emotional emasculation.

At that moment I wanted only to throw this corpse down the ladder.

Perfecto's concern for me seemed strange, incongruous with what I knew of chimeras. It was almost funny. Out of cruelty I said, "You know that only your genetic programming tells you to feel this great concern about me?"

Perfecto said, "I know."

"Compulsive love. Compassion by genetic decree. I suppose it's better than no compassion at all." It seemed a good joke. My own compassion was slipping away. Perfecto was better than I was. At least he was capable of feeling compassion for one person.

Suddenly everyone on the ladder moved off at once, and we pushed the corpse over. It fell two floors, hit the ladder, twisted in midair, then fell a couple meters and one leg tangled among the rungs. The body thudded to a halt, head down, swaying.

It had stopped near the level to the infirmary. We couldn't have done a better job of getting the body there if we'd planned it. We watched it swing a moment, and on impulse I said, "If this were Mavro or Abriara lying here dead, would you care?"

Perfecto said, "I always get a sick feeling in my stomach when someone close to me dies, but I would not grieve."

"Why?"

"Because I've known from the time I got on this ship that many of us would die. Motoki guarantees us a fifty-one percent chance of survival in our battle contract, but I know that nearly half of us will die. So I refuse to become attached."

Have I been reacting to the foreknowledge of our deaths subconsciously? Is that why my compassion died? I wondered. After my mother died I'd been afraid to make close attachments. And later, when my sister Eva had been raped and strangled and left for dead by the roadside, I learned to separate myself from my family altogether, even though she lived through the attack. And for years after my wife, Elena, died in an accident I didn't let myself get close to another woman—until I met Tamara. Something in her eyes, in the way she smiled and moved, had captivated me.

I tried to remember what it was like to care, but I felt thin and worn, like an old pair of jeans. I couldn't muster the feelings that had driven me to bring Tamara aboard ship. It was as if a part of me had died already. The part that cares about others. And I suddenly understood the sense of loss I'd felt for days: my compassion had died. I'd somehow left it in Panamá, dead on the floor, next to the body of Arish.

Abriara opened the door to our room and looked down the hall. She came up to us, walking softly. I called out, "And you, Abriara, if one of us died, would you grieve?"

She seated herself next to me and looked down the ladder at the swaying corpse. "No," she said. "One cannot afford to grieve during battle. You are an old man and I fully expect you will be killed on Baker, don Angelo. But though I like you, I would not grieve for you, nor for anyone else aboard this ship."

I was feeling giddy, on the edge of hysterics. I'd always believed that all men were creatures of empathy. Now I saw that it wasn't necessarily so. The vision threatened to destroy me. I said, thinking to toss her answer aside, to cast her view as an aberration, "I did not think you would. You are a marvelous creature, but I saw from your gene-scan that you do not have a great capacity for compassion."

"You arrogant prick!" she sneered. "We chimeras have seen damned little compassion from you humans!"

She was right! She was right! We'd shown her kind exactly no compassion. I remembered the picture of the small chimera who looked like a bat, his lifeless body hanging between two Chilean peasants who'd clubbed him to death. He symbolized everything humans do to those they consider inhuman. In every bloody war, in every act of genocide, in every execution whether by a mob or under the direction of the state, the man to be destroyed is always accused of being inhuman, of being less than human. And I suddenly understood why every beastly tribe of cannibals that ever existed has chosen to call itself "The Humans" in its own tongue. We convince ourselves that our enemies are different from us before we slay them. And I saw that all the brutality and capacity for ruthlessness I'd attributed only to the deranged and wicked were an integral part of me. I'd killed Arish, and I'd kill again and again and again forever under the right circumstances.

There is an old saying, "Some men shake the world, and some men are shaken by the world." I'd always wondered which I was, and at this time I understood: I was a man shaken by the world—shaken by the vision of the world as it is.

I began to laugh, a convulsive spasm that was half cry.

I'd vowed when I first met Abriara that I'd try to give her a better view of humanity, but instead she'd shown me myself more perfectly—and the sight revolted me. "You're right. I don't have much compassion. I've always imagined it a trait of great importance. But now I see that I'm a killer by nature. I've killed before, and I'll do it again. Perhaps my subtle capacity for viciousness is more of an asset in my quest for survival than I've chosen to believe."

Abriara looked at me with curiosity. What had seemed to me a revolting personal revelation didn't disturb her at all. "I hope you have a capacity for viciousness," she said casually. "If you want to survive in my world, you need it more than food, or water, or air."

She stood up and sighed. She said, "Perfecto, go back to our room. I need to speak to the don alone for a moment."

Perfecto said, "Sí," and we watched him till he got safely behind the door.

Abriara said quietly, "Don Angelo, I've believed we'd have trouble with Lucío from the first day aboard ship, and the attack in the simulator today shows it's been on his mind, too. He planned this weeks ago. He must have planned it from the start, and he's been waiting to humiliate us publicly. It's his way of announcing the start of a Quest—if you don't believe me, ask any chimera what this means. You can't walk away from this. And you can't hesitate when it comes time to use your knife."

"Of course," I answered.

"Then you're willing to kill him?" There was a thrill in her voice, and I understood that she wanted to make a first strike at Lucío. I considered the consequences before answering.

Abriara said, "Angelo, your doubts might have dramatic consequences in this situation. Think of Perfecto—he follows you blindly. If he senses your uncertainty, he may hesitate to act in a crucial moment. You must not show doubt! That would not only be stupid, it would be dangerous. We need to strike first. To hell with Kaigo's orders—we must strike!"

I tried to make sense of this mess. I didn't agree with her, but arguments for restraint wouldn't mesh with my previous actions. I'd sliced up Lucío, but Abriara was asking me to commit murder. It seemed too cold-blooded. Abriara saw my frustration, my unwillingness to follow her plan.

"On the first day you got here I asked you to speak to Perfecto for me so I could hope for his obedience. You haven't done it. Within hours you spoke against a vendetta against Lucío. Now you see where your actions have taken us? You never spoke to Perfecto for me, did you?"

"No," I said. "The time never seemed right."

She waved her hand as if to dismiss it, and sat down beside me. "I don't blame you. Such words must come from the heart. You're too old to indiscriminately follow me.

"But, Angelo, I need your full support in this."

I nodded. I tried to say I'd support her. Yet the words stuck in my throat.

Abriara shook her head and left off the argument. "Angelo," she said softly, "I've never loved a man. I've never given myself to a man. But I have been raped by men three times. The first time was when I was nine years old. I was outside the genetic engineering compound in Temuco. An old man caught me and choked me, forced his penis into my mouth. It was at a time when the public was raising an outcry about Torres creating true nonhumans instead of upgrading regular people. This old man knew I was a chimera and was therefore not protected by the laws that protect human girls. I went to the police and they insisted on seeing my genome before deciding whether to prosecute. They saw my genome, and I've always thought I must be a true chimera, for the man was never brought to justice." She stopped and breathed heavily. I knew she was seeking to convince me to fight by use of an emotional argument. It was a blatant attempt at manipulation.

"The second time I was raped was four years ago: After the war in Chile, I tried to do something useful with my life. I got a job screening software for teaching programs in Peru. One day I was walking down the street where some young men were playing baseball. As I walked past the batter, he swung the bat and hit me in the head. I still bear the scars—" She pulled her hair back, showing me an ugly scar at hairline above her left ear.

"They tied me to a table in an abandoned shack for three days. They came many times to rape me. Sometimes they brought friends.

"I broke free in the middle of the afternoon on the fourth day and went to the police. They did nothing. They promised to do nothing—for I was a chimera in Peru, and in some ways it was worse than being chimera in Chile. I knew the young men would come back for me in the evening, so I returned to the shack with a hatchet and waited.

"When they returned, I killed them. I delivered their penises to the desk of the police chief, and then spent four years at the women's correctional facility in Cajamarca."

She hesitated a moment. "The third time I was raped was today, in the simulator. And though it wasn't real, it hurt as much as the first two times—perhaps more, because it brought back all the memories of the first two attacks—all the frustration, all the rage, all the hate.

"But this time was different—because for once, someone did something. You slashed Lucío's face open, and for that I thank you." She smiled at me. "You win: if you do not want to initiate an attack, we will simply arm ourselves and be very cautious, okay? I will ask nothing more of you."

She leaned forward and lightly kissed my temple, as if kissing a friend, a kiss of simple gratitude, then she got up and walked away.

She'd surprised me. I'd thought she'd try to manipulate me into fighting, to plead with me to avenge her. She had that right. Perhaps more than anyone I'd ever met, she had the right to a little justice. She hadn't realized I was still undecided as to my course of action. She'd given up too easily. If she'd demanded that I join a Quest to kill Lucío, I'd have refused. But Abriara had been more persuasive than she knew.

I thought of Lucío's words: "I will kill you and fuck your woman," and I knew he would carry it through if he could. I decided to do my best to send Lucío and his men to hell if they caused us any heartache, then got up and walked to my room.

García came to visit us moments later. He was very pale and shaken, and he fidgeted with his hands more than normal. He'd come to pay Zavala a million pesos and seemed eager to be done with it. He watched nervously as Mavro sharpened a wooden knife.

García said, "I hope you're still not thinking of starting a fight with the samurai!"

Mavro said, "I don't want to fight one so much as just put a hole in one!"

García licked his lips and said, "A few minutes ago Emilio Vasquez wanted to celebrate our victories in South America, and didn't report to the simulators. A samurai came to the room and ordered him to practice, and Emilio and another man attacked the samurai. I saw the whole thing! Emilio is one of the strongest men I know, and he tried to strangle the samurai, but the samurai broke his grip as if Emilio were a child, then he kicked Emilio's friend in the head, crushing his skull, and strangled Emilio—and Emilio could not break the samurai's grip! If you don't believe me, go down and see Emilio's head yourself! It's hung from a hook in the ceiling by the ladder to level six!

"If I wanted proof that the samurai are as strong and quick as they seem in the simulators, I got all the proof I need!"

García transferred a million pesos to Zavala's account, then paid me two hundred thousand IMUs for my antibiotics and left quickly.

Zavala came and stood beside me and patted my back. "I'm sorry I had to take your drugs from you this way. I would have preferred to have you give them to me as a friend. At least now you see the truth: the samurai beat us by the power of the spirit. Yet I am glad we learned the truth, for there are spells that can weaken the spirit of an enemy."

Mavro laughed. "Good idea! You cast some spells while I sharpen a knife!"

I looked into Zavala's eyes. His round face and thin lips would normally give him the look of a stupid youth, but he had a determined gleam in his eye.

I got my medical bag and looked through the antibiotics. I keep my drugs in plastic containers that look like small suitcases. Each thin suitcase can carry a few grams each of several thousand medicines. I have a tiny machine that can then add individual dosages to base tablets for oral consumption or to a base liquid for injection. It allows me to keep a wide inventory in a small space. But as I sat staring at my plastic cases, each filled with hundreds of multicolored drug compartments, it didn't seem right for me to give the antibiotics to Zavala, since I knew they'd only make him sick. I'd have healed him if I could, but there was nothing physically wrong with him.

I fumbled with my medications a while, and a brilliant thought struck me: Zavala had nothing physically wrong with him. He simply thought he was ill because in the simulator he experienced pain. But I could dim the pain with a neural pain blocker. The burning would go away and he'd think he was cured! I had several potent painkillers that didn't have very bad side effects and I began making up tablets. Zavala rubbed his shoulder at the base of his prosthetic arm as if it burned, and quickly swallowed the first pill.

Then he sat on the floor while the others went to bed. He peeled the paper from the back of a whiskey bottle and took Perfecto's blue paint and began painting a picture of men in a hovercraft. He took great pains to get the details perfect. From time to time he'd chant in an Indian tongue as he painted, and I kept looking at him as I prepared the false medications. His eyes became glazed as he lost himself in a trance, and he sweated vigorously.

When I was finished making up the anesthetics, I got

in bed and tried to sleep. Zavala's continual chanting kept me awake long into the night, until I began to think that in a war of spirit, perhaps Zavala would be a ferocious adversary.

In my dream the sun setting over Lake Gatún threw orange-yellow light through my kitchen window to reflect against the far wall. A kitten meowed plaintively just outside the kitchen door in the bushes by the lake. I remembered the blue bowl on the porch. It should have been filled with milk. When had I last filled the kitten's bowl?

I could not remember. The task had slipped my mind. It had been weeks since I'd fed the kitten. It would be starving.

No doubt it can fend for itself, I thought. There were plenty of insects, dead fish left by fisherman, small things a kitten could scavenge to keep alive. The kitten meowed, its cries emanating from deep within the pit of its stomach, a yowl of pure hunger, and I opened the sliding glass door.

There on the porch lay a gray and white kitten so thin I could easily discern the shape of every bone in its tail. Its hair was falling out, and its green eyes were filmed and sunken. It was nearly dead. It couldn't even rouse itself to move. It just meowed from the pit of its belly in a last desperate effort to get food. And then I saw a hand in the grass, stretched out as if to grasp the kitten—a pale hand, emaciated, just beside the kitten, reaching out from behind a *bush. I stepped forward and pulled a limb aside and looked in the bushes.*

Flaco was stretched out on the grass, his eyeless skull staring skyward, a bit of rainwater pooled in his empty sockets. Impossibly thin. Starved.

"Grandfather!" the little girl spoke, startling me. She crouched just at my elbow. "Grandfather, you didn't take care of them! You let them starve!"

And I realized I'd forgotten to feed more than the kitten. I'd forgotten to feed my friends. My mouth yammered of its own accord, "I . . . I didn't know. I didn't know I was supposed to tend them."

I bolted upright. It was deep in the night, and Zavala hunched over his paintings, snoring lightly. My heart beat wildly, and I sweated. The dream disturbed me more than any nightmare I'd ever had. I tried to grasp its meaning, and went over each detail.

I focused on the little girl with the pale face and dark eyes who'd haunted so many of my dreams. Had she been someone I'd seen in the feria? The child of a neighbor? I pondered for a long time, and became certain she was a child from our neighborhood, a girl who'd lived down the street from my house in Panamá. I couldn't imagine which house she'd lived in. Yet I must have seen her when I walked to the feria in the mornings.

As an experiment, I closed my eyes and tried to picture her, recall any memory I could dredge up. Almost immediately an image jumped into my mind. She stood before me holding the gray and white kitten, pressing it toward me so I could take it in my hands. "It's wild, just a little," she said, "can you take care of it for me?"

The image seemed totally accurate, yet I knew I'd never seen that kitten until the day I'd come home to find Flaco and Tamara tossing a ball to it upon my roof. Obviously my dream had tainted the memory. Because I dreamed of the girl and the kitten in the same dream, my subconscious had linked the two together.

I drove the thought from mind and struggled to remember the child's name. It was on the tip of my tongue and I felt I had to but speak and it would come clear. My face perspired and my head felt it would burst as I struggled to recall. Her name seemed all-important.

"Tatiana," I said aloud in a flash of insight, and I knew I'd spoken the right name. Her name had been Tatiana. I felt elated, but the more I considered it, the more certain I was I could remember nothing about her but a face. *You are a madman*, I thought, yet I congratulated myself for having found a name for the imaginary companion of my dreams.

Early on the morning of the eleventh day, I was wakened by bodies moving in the darkness, the shushing of kimonos sliding over skin. Zavala sat cross-legged on the floor, hunched over a piece of paper. His face was careworn, eyes glazed from lack of sleep and from the painkillers I'd provided. He chanted in little throaty croaks that rose and dipped in volume like the sound of wind gusting through dry grass.

Perfecto and Mavro stood ready by the door, tense, expecting an attack. Mavro was tying his *obi*, the belt to his kimono, holding a wooden dagger in his teeth. The knives were really only sharpened stakes, each about half a meter long, little good for cutting, but they'd suffice for stabbing. Abriara was dressing in the tiny bathroom. They all breathed in ragged gasps, which they released slowly. I found my own chest tightening with anticipation.

I slid off the cot and adjusted my kimono. I took my knife from my wrist sheath. I could feel my nostrils flaring as I breathed.

"What's going on?" I asked, stepping around Zavala.

"We could not sleep," Perfecto said. "So it is certain that Lucío's men also could not sleep. They'll be here soon."

"How do you know?"

Mavro said, "I just called the duty nurse on comlink.

She says Lucío's being checked by the doctor now. He'll be leaving the infirmary in ten minutes."

The news surprised me more than I'd have expected. Until this moment a fight with Lucío seemed only a possibility. Now it seemed imminent. My heart started pounding in a sudden attack of panic.

Abriara came out of the bathroom.

Zavala raised his painting so we could see it—Lucío and his men, each portrayed in intimate detail, like a painting done by an architect: Each man in the painting was stabbed with multiple wounds. Knives in the belly, knives in the throat, knives in the face. Without removing his eyes from the paper, Zavala reached into the interior pocket of his kimono and pulled out Mavro's lighter. His chanting raised in pitch and he held the paper in his right hand, his human hand, and set it afire. He let the flames lick and blister his fingers until the picture burned to ashes. While his fingers burned, his breathing quickened, but his hand didn't shake, and he held the painting firmly until it became a single black ash with glow worms of fire curling through it. He reached up with his cymeched hand and crushed the ash.

"We should go quickly," he said. "Fight while the spell is still strong." Then his eyes focused, and he jumped up. It took him only a moment to get a knife.

Perfecto ran into the bathroom and began filling the tiny toilet bowl with urine. Mavro stood next to the bathroom door, as if he'd waylay Perfecto when he emerged. I realized that I too had to urinate, so I got in line.

Abriara began making her bed. She did it quickly, with nervous energy. She spoke more to herself than to us. "As soon as you're ready, I think we need to get down the hall, down to level two. They don't have any business coming above that. Don't give the *mamones* any mercy. Cut them quick—as if you were slaughtering cattle and got paid by the head, then get out."

"Do you really think they'll come?" Zavala said. He reached out and cracked the door open to peek down the hallway.

There was a flash of white and the tinkle of metal. A man in a white kimono who wore chains around his waist instead of an *obi* shouted, "A gift from the *conquistadores*!" and shoved a metal pipe through the open door.

Zavala fell back with the pipe lodged in his belly. His attacker—a man named Samora—turned to run. Abriara leapt past me to give chase, and Samora swung a second pipe. Abriara tried to duck, but the pipe glanced the back of her head and she dropped.

I lurched to help her, and Samora sprinted to the ladders before I made it out the door. I grabbed Abriara. Her eyes rolled back to show white.

"You'll be all right," I said, "We're with you."

Mavro started swearing. He pulled Zavala to his feet, and Zavala clutched the metal pipe with both hands. A little clear fluid mixed with blood was running from the end of the hollow pipe, as if it were a tap someone had neglected to turn off. Zavala's face was drained, and he stared at the pipe in fascination.

Perfecto rushed from the bathroom.

"We've got to get them to the infirmary!" Mavro said, and he started shoving Zavala out the door, toward the ladder, and Perfecto followed.

I looked down the hall. Lucío's men would be waiting near the ladder, and as we tried to drop past their level, they'd attack us. I was certain. They'd stabbed Zavala simply to lead us into a trap. Otherwise, according to the code of the Quest, Lucío wouldn't have been satisfied with just wounding Zavala—he'd have mutilated him. Perfecto and Mavro realized the precariousness of the situation at the same moment.

"Wait," Perfecto said, "I'll get help!" He ran to the nearest door and pounded. A samurai opened it and spoke with him.

I whispered comforting words to Abriara and examined her face. She didn't move her eyes when I spoke. Her pupils seemed dilated wide enough to drink in all the light that had ever shone. I became worried that she was seriously wounded. I turned her head to view her wound. There was a dark bruise on the back of her neck at the base of her skull, right above her cranial jack. The square platinum socket of the jack was caved in on one side, and a speck of blood dripped from surrounding tissue. I inspected the jack, and found that her bypass grid was shoved forward. It's a common problem: there's a tiny floating grid inside the jack at the base of the skull, and when the jack is plugged into a computer terminal, that floating grid is pushed forward, triggering the bypass to the nerves that control sensory input. In this way, the computer can send its sensory input to the brain.

The blow to Abriara's jack had jammed the grid forward, engaging her sensory bypass. Abriara was conscious, but she wasn't receiving any input. She was deaf, blind, and virtually anesthetized. I put my finger in the bypass and wiggled it, trying to bend the jack so the grid would pop out.

Several samurai rushed up with Perfecto, grabbed Zavala, and carried him down the ladder with a great deal of fanfare and commotion. The hall soon filled with curious samurai, all in blue flowered kimonos, many with wet hair since they'd just left their communal baths.

Kaigo forced his way through the crowd and crouched beside us. "What has happened here?" he demanded.

"Lucío's men broke their truce," Mavro said. "The cowards attacked us!"

Kaigo's brow furrowed. He snarled, "They broke their oath? They lied to me? They are men who know not honor!" He pulled his sword and stepped over Abriara. His body language—his furrowed brow, the expression of disgust on his face—seemed exaggerated, entirely out of proportion, as if he were some bad actor aping the expression of someone who was enraged. It was a thing I'd noticed with other samurai, and it struck me as strange—they spent a great deal of time attempting to appear entirely stoic, free from emotion, yet when they expressed emotion they tried to appear entirely enslaved to passion. He marched off as if heading down to kill Lucío and his men.

Mavro shouted, "Master, wait!" Kaigo turned to look at us. In the only humble tone Mavro ever used, he asked, "Master, Lucío's men have assaulted us three times now. Permit us to slay the dogs."

Kaigo grunted his permission, "Hai!"

We dragged Abriara into our room and pried her housing back into shape with the point of a wooden dagger. Abriara immediately regained her senses, and we told her of Mavro's bargain with Kaigo. She was pleased at the prospect of vengeance.

Perfecto returned with the pipe Samora had used to stab Zavala. It was sharpened at one end. "Zavala is not hurt bad, but the heavy gravity puts so much pressure on the stitches, he'll have to remain in bed a few days."

Abriara shrugged. "Then we'll have to kill Lucío's men without him. But first, we need to know where they are."

Mavro and Perfecto began jacking in calls to friends, offering the last of our cigars for information. Within three minutes Mavro got a response. "Vasquez says he just saw them in the hall down on level four, near the showers, having an argument about whether to come attack us openly or whether they should wait for us to come after them."

"Tell Vasquez to inform them that he saw us heading for the infirmary," Abriara said.

Mavro haggled with Vasquez over the price of his treachery, and ended up promising twenty cigars. Vasquez told us to take a minute to get into position.

We ran to the ladder and dropped two floors. Perfecto headed down a corridor that led away from the infirmary. The floor was still dark, the men here still on night cycle. The silence seemed strange after so much commotion. We reached the intersection where the corridor met the outer walkway that circled the ship, then held tight. Only Perfecto stayed in the open, watching for Lucío's men to ascend the ladder.

We waited several minutes. Six times Perfecto snapped his head back as someone climbed up from level four. Mavro said, "I get the next one, no?" glancing around to see if anyone objected to him claiming the next kill. No one did. "*Ai, ya, yi,*" he said nervously, "I hope someone here does silver-blue tattoos." He was already thinking of adding a third tear to his cheek.

Perfecto snapped his head back for the seventh time. He gave us an "I knew it" look and began counting, giving them time to get high on the ladder. Someone opened a door in the corridor between us, and some men laughed. Perfecto stopped counting. Lucío's men would be on the ladders watching the open door. They'd slow in their progress.

Perfecto began counting again, nodding his head silently, and suddenly pushed off against the wall, making a *whuff* as he exhaled. Mavro jumped out to follow, with me behind. Perfecto was already halfway down the hall, running silently on bare feet.

Three men in white kimonos had stepped from their dormitory room. They were still laughing as Perfecto rushed past them. One said, *"Huy!"* and lurched back in time for me to glimpse the ladder.

One man perched on the ladder—a chimera nicknamed Bruto. He held an aluminum pipe in his left hand. Six corridors radiated away from the ladder, and he was trying to peer down them all at once. His head was twisted around at an unnatural angle so that he could see over his back. Bruto spotted Perfecto and jumped off the ladder, spinning to face the attack.

Lucío was ascending the ladder just behind Bruto. He couldn't climb up in time to join the melee. He saw this and slid back down the ladder.

Perfecto met Bruto and both stopped just out of arm's reach of one another. Bruto's stance wasn't good. He held his club up threateningly and had his right arm cocked to swing. This put him off balance. Perfecto danced forward in a feint, trying to draw Bruto out, get him to swing, then stepped back. Bruto jerked his club hand, saw the feint, then thought better of swinging. In that moment when Bruto was undecided, Perfecto lurched in and his knife blurred.

It appeared Perfecto had missed Bruto completely, for Bruto just stood there. But then Bruto stopped and stared straight ahead and a little up toward the lights. He appeared confused, surprised, then a little blood spurted from his carotid artery. It was like water gushing from a hose that has air in it. The blood pumped up and out of the artery and spattered the wall, and Bruto turned his neck to the right and gazed at it in wonderment.

A second gout of blood spurted farther to the right, for Bruto had twisted his head in that direction. Bruto leaned his head back and tried to step forward, as if to catch the drops of blood on his tongue as they fell. But when he raised his leg he lifted it very high in an incredibly graceful gesture, as if performing ballet while climbing a great stair. His eyes already had the glassy look an animal gets when it dies. No blood was reaching the brain, and it distorted his perceptions.

A few drops spattered my face and I stopped cold. I didn't realize it, but I'd been running to the scene. Bruto began a strange and graceful dance, moving as if in slow motion. The blood would spurt from his neck and he'd step forward half a step and turn in the air in a pirouette. Then his blood would rain in bright red droplets.

The infirmary was just down corridor six, not forty paces from him, and I thought, *If we get him to the infirmary quickly, we can fix that artery.* But I didn't move. It was a thought I had, not a thought I'd act upon. Perfecto stepped in and slashed with his knife, dealing a blow that gutted Bruto. Before the body could fall he pierced Bruto's brain with his metal stake, leaving him more than dead, fulfilling the code of the Quest.

I felt strange—like an observer, totally dispassionate. Two weeks earlier this scene would have revolted me. I felt nothing.

"Did you see the look on his face when Perfecto stabbed him?" Mavro said, too loud. "It was cartoon shock—the face of a caricature when it runs over the cliff and stands in midair before it realizes it will fall." He laughed heartily, and I found myself giggling as if it were a very funny joke.

"The rest of them are on level four," Perfecto said, pointing down the ladder. He was panting, and steaming hot blood was spattered on his face. When blood is that hot, my eyes see it as if it were molten ore the color of cinnabar. The room suddenly seemed chilly. "I'd hoped two of them would step off the ladder. It would have been a better fight."

I chuckled nervously and looked down the ladder. "We got one of their best fighters already!" I said. "I'm glad." And I realized I did feel glad. We were one man down, and they were one man down. The battle was even.

Perfecto stuck his bloody weapons in his belt.

Abriara gazed longingly down the ladder. "They'll be waiting to ambush us down there," she whispered. "I don't think we should go down. And it's certain they won't come up. At least not for a couple hours. Let's get breakfast. We'll fight better on a full stomach."

I smiled. It seemed like a good joke, leaving them down there to worry all morning. We went on up to the dining hall.

Perfecto didn't bother to take the bloody weapons out of his belt, and we drew stares from those few men eating breakfast. Word had spread quickly of our battle, and a couple men even shouted things like, "*Hola, muchachos*, how goes the Quest?"

Mavro waved to these people and smiled. "Perfecto here stepped on that monkey Bruto! You should have seen!" We picked a table in a corner and ate some rolls—flour made from ground algae and baked with a thin, sweet, brown syrup poured over the top.

Mavro ate these with exclamations of "*Qué rico!*— How delicious—much like my fiancée's famous frosted liver slices!"

My hands shook as I tried to eat. It seemed strange: everyone knew we'd just committed a murder, and no one did anything about it. There was no shouting, no recriminations, no protest. No police. And then I realized I was a murderer since I'd killed Arish. Abriara had confessed to murdering three boys in Peru. Mavro wore tattoos indicating he'd murdered people in Cartagena. Perfecto had killed Bruto as thoughtlessly as one would step on a cockroach. And those were only people I knew about—people in my combat team. If every team had the same mix, eighty percent of the people aboard ship were murderers. When I'd decided to join the members of our combat team, I had seen them as a society, a society I could serve—a few people united against pain. But how does one serve a society of murderers?

When I was a child, don José Mirada had told me that

one serves a society by serving the individuals within the society. But how does one serve a society of murderers?

It soon became evident we were mistaken to sit in public. Across the room Lucío's friends were dining, and we weren't seated two minutes before one of them slinked off to inform Lucío of our location. Kaigo had left it to us to punish Lucío and his men, but the fact that he'd given his blessing didn't mean we'd necessarily be victorious.

Since it was breakfast time for a third of the ship, the room soon filled up. Fernando Chin, the genocidal xenobiologist, came and sat on the bench next to me. He said, "Hey, do any of you know why communications have been cut between here and module B? What's going on over there? Is it true they got bombed?"

"Jesus Christ," Mavro said, "What are you talking about?"

Lucío and his three living teammates walked through the door. I watched them and thought, *Bombs? This is too much to handle! You could handle one situation at a time. But you'll go crazy if you try to do too much! Don't think right now! Relax!* Lucío looked ghastly, with a tremendous scar down his face where I'd cut him. The bandage sprayed over it was roughly flesh-toned, but looked like glue, so he appeared to have some huge deformity rather than just a cut. He and his men didn't even glance at our side of the room. They knew exactly where we were.

"I don't know if they got bombed or not, but communications are out," Chin said, "Try making a comlink with someone on module B, and you'll see what I mean."

Lucío and his men stepped into the chow line at the far side of the room and filled their plates, then sat at a table and began eating. I looked at Mavro. He was staring at them, his lips curled in a gloating smile. He was waiting for one of them to make eye contact so he could stare him down. Mavro shouted, "Hey, has anybody seen Bruto lately?" but Lucío and his men did nothing.

Abriara said, "We'd better get to battle practice. It's

10:25." I looked at her in surprise, thinking the Quest would take precedence over such matters.

Abriara stared across the room and said to no one in particular, "They'll have to go to battle practice, too." Lucío's team worked in the same time slot as we did. They'd be busy for the next two hours.

We got up, deposited our trays at the scullery line, and carefully retreated out the door.

When we got to battle practice, Kaigo was sitting on his dais, waiting. He watched us come in, but didn't speak. I was very self-conscious. Our white kimonos were spattered with Bruto's blood. It was obvious we'd been killing people. Kaigo didn't ask us about it. He seemed preoccupied. For once I wanted to jack into the simulator. For once I saw the battle as a cleansing thing, something that could serve as an escape. We suited up into our battle armor, climbed aboard the model hover-craft, armed ourselves, and jacked smoothly into the world of illusion.

And we skimmed over a salt marsh on a thin layer of water. Dark mangroves surrounded us, thrust their twisted roots into the brackish pools. Insects played on the beer-colored water, dancing among shafts of sunlight tainted the color of rose. Tiny fish jumped at the insects and darted into the shadows under the mangrove roots at our approach.

I was instantly wary. Something was different, but I couldn't put my finger on it. An intangible nag. I tried to watch all directions at once. The warning siren screamed the approach of the Yabajin. Instead of dueling with the samurai, Abriara chose to veer right, shooting straight between the boles of two mangroves and into the darker woods beyond. We barreled through the underbrush, knocking aside thick green leaves, dodging trees. A small anaconda dangling from a limb fell at my feet and I looked down. We hit a rise and the hovercraft bounced in the air; at the same moment I glanced up from the snake just in time for the thick limb of a mangrove to swat my face.

I flipped over the back of the hovercraft and bounced once. My helmet speakers buzzed, warning of the approach of the Yabajin. I retrieved my laser and tried to clear my thoughts. My helmet was cracked across my cheekbones in a line that followed the contours of the air filters imbedded in the armor. I pulled at the magnetic latch at the side of the helmet, and the whole helmet split in two, fell to the ground. Fresh air filled my lungs.

Fresh air! Not air from the simulator, which always smelled as if six dirty peasants had wedged themselves into your suit with you. This air smelled of grass and sea and carried the stifling scent of rotting fruit. And beneath it was an odor of sugar and strange turpines, a sweet alien fragrance. I could see full-spectrum, and Baker appeared far less drab than the simulator had shown it to be: a patch of sky bore the same cinnamon-rose hue as always, but clouds of yellow and green *oparu no tako* floating high up in the atmosphere were colored differently. Wherever they flew, a platinum shimmer shone with them. Among the mangroves of the salt marsh were native grasses of irregular shape, like some type of seaweed—not the purple the simulator showed, but an ultraviolet so dark my prosthetic eyes registered them as almost black.

I left my helmet lying on the ground, the warning buzzer screaming insistently, and walked down to the water's edge, into the open. A cool breeze whipped my face. Thousands of Baker's avians, thin waffles of plastic with small tails, hovered over the marsh grass. Some danced before my face—insubstantial creatures the size of tiny moths with taut wings fully extended.

Almost immediately a robin-sized avian feeding upon the small moths shot into view and hovered before my face with its tail pointed toward me. It hummed like a hummingbird. I've described most of these creatures as being shaped like mantas or skates, but this is only vaguely accurate. Its front half appeared to be a triangular body, clear as glass, with two large rigid wings held stiffly to the side, unmoving. Its tiny flat tail floated out behind it, as if just resting on the wind, but as I watched closely the rigid wings trembled ever so slightly, and the tail bent to help the creature turn. As it hovered it slowly turned to face me. It had two pale yellow eyes, a tiny mouth shaped like a sparrow's beak trailing a pair of tendrils at each side, and just behind the eyes was an organ I can describe only as a forewing—a thin transparent membrane that vibrated rapidly, blowing air over the fixed wing. From this vibrating membrane came the humming sound.

Birds on Earth use their muscular wings to club the wind, to literally climb into the air on fingers of feather. The same wing provides both the lift and the forward momentum. But with Baker's fragile-looking "bird" the thin forewing blew wind over the fixed wing, allowing the creature to lift. I imagined that with a strong wind the avian could relax the vibrating forewing and just hover in the air, much as a seagull does.

I wanted to view the creature closely. Tiny lines seemed to delineate segments to an exoskeleton, other lines appeared to be translucent muscle, and blue and yellow threads within the transparent body appeared to be veins and intestines, but I could see none of these clearly. I quickly reached for the creature, as if to catch a fly in my hand, but it dipped in its flight and sped away over the marsh with a buzz.

On the ground were twigs and individual blades of grass, and some black insects swarmed among the grass. I'd have thought them to be boring beetles, but several were pushing bits of dark ultraviolet leaves across the ground and they'd woven these together with twigs and pebbles to build small round shelters the size of a cupped hand. The shelters looked very much like tiny huts. I toppled a hut, wondering if I'd find something remarkable beneath—insects playing chess, or sculptures of alien beetle gods—but found only huge fat beetles tending tiny white larvae. I replaced the hut and sand flies jumped up at the movement of my hand.

There was far too much detail for the computer to have generated this illusion. The world was too *complete* to be a simulation. The insects, the avians, the tiny fishes in the water, the scents—all were things I'd never witnessed before. And the fact that the computer now compensated for my prosthetic eyes meant the illusion was tailored specifically for me. The ship's artificial intelligence couldn't provide this type of service to everyone—not with seven hundred men jacked into the simulators at once.

This felt like a trap. Immediately I recalled the men who'd died in the simulators, the men who were incapable of penetrating the illusion. And I wondered: Could they have been murdered? Could they have died from shock because they were slain in an impenetrable illusion, an illusion such as this. I searched for something out of place: a tree that was too symmetrical and healthy, a patch of ground that looked as if it had been generated by fractal equations rather than formed naturally. But the trees had leaves that were yellowed and worn at the edges, insect eaten and diseased. The ground didn't have the characteristic rumpled look of landscapes generated by fractals—there were too many smooth folds punctuated by sharp lines. I could find nothing out of place.

If someone was using this method to murder, I decided not to be a victim. I reached behind my neck and tried to claw at the place where I knew the computer leads connected to my cranial jack. But it was no use. My body was really sitting slumped in my chair in the hovercraft, completely disconnected from the real world. I couldn't penetrate this illusion, and I could not escape it.

I shouted to Kaigo, "Get me out! I can't tell what's real anymore!" I waited, but he didn't respond.

I touched the bump on my head and wondered at my predicament. My hand came away with a smear of blood on it, and as an experiment I touched the blood with my tongue to see if I could taste it. The computer had never simulated taste before. It tasted salty, and had the consistency of real blood.

Perhaps this is a test. Perhaps they want to see how I'd fight if I felt my life to be in jeopardy, I wondered, realizing that if I couldn't penetrate this illusion, I had no option but to win this battle. My life could well be at stake. But I didn't care. I'd suffered death so many times in simulation that now I knew it only heralded an end to suffering.

In the denser brush, behind a screen of trees on the other side of the marsh, something cracked a branch. A large leaf tore with the sound of shredding paper. I sat up and peered in that direction: a large black creature walked among the bushes. It stepped into a partial clearing for a moment, then back into thicker brush. It was black and hairy, wet as if it had just risen from the water. Another predator thrown into the simulator, I reasoned.

I crouched and aimed my laser rifle between two bushes, trying to guess where it might step out.

The creature snorted, a great exhalation of air. It had caught my scent. It lurched forward, and when it landed its feet hit the ground like thunder. It crashed through the brush and charged into a tiny clearing. It stood panting by the water's edge ten meters before me.

A huge bull, as black as onyx, with great horns stretching wide. Astride the great creature's neck sat a black-haired woman in a thin white dress that revealed more than it covered. She smiled a wan smile.

"Bravo . . . don Angelo." She halted between words as if to catch her breath. "You came . . . to save me . . . from the beast again?" She kicked the bull's ribs and it stepped in the marsh and walked toward me.

"Tamara?" This woman was not the emaciated Tamara I'd known. She was beautiful in a way Tamara had never been beautiful. Her hair was dark and silky. Her teeth as white as crystal water cascading down a mountain stream. Her breasts full and erect. Yet her small bones and muscles spoke of a delicateness, a frailness, Tamara had never matched.

"You look . . . much as I . . . remember," Tamara said. She watched me closely. Her lips tightened. Her expression was not severe or disapproving, rather she seemed sad and tired. Her words came in odd bursts. The fact that she stammered even in the simulator hinted at severe neural damage to the speech centers. If that area was damaged, I wondered how much was really left of the Tamara I'd known. I felt inside myself and realized I didn't really care about her anymore. The fact that she'd finally sought me out, had finally made contact, seemed a minor curiosity.

But her eyes were alive in spite of frailness. Bright. Fierce.

The bull stopped in front of me and Tamara daintily slipped from its back.

I pointed to her mount, "That bull was dead in your dreams before," I said. "Rotted. Like a zombie."

Tamara wrinkled her brow in concern. "Was it?" she said wearily. "I . . . forget. That's why I . . . came to you. I wanted . . . to fill holes. To fill in . . . the holes."

I shrugged. "How deep are the holes? How wide?"

"Who knows?" she said. "Garzón . . . tells me . . . I've got . . . forty percent loss. I remember , . . some things . . . very well. Repetitive things. Things . . . I knew well. Individual. Incidents. Are gone."

Forty percent memory loss was a lot. She'd be on neural growth stimulator till the brain regenerated. Even after two weeks the damage was really only beginning to repair on a cellular level. The individual neurons that regenerated in her brain would not mature for years. The actual connections between them would be sparse. Her motor skills would be shot. She'd have to stay hooked up to life-support for months.

"Is that why you came to see me—to learn about your past?"

She nodded. "To learn . . . what I told you. To see what . . . you remember."

I shrugged. I told her the story from the beginning, leaving out nothing. When I got to the part about Flaco's death I was surprised that I felt empty. It seemed as if it had happened long ago to someone else. I related the tale evenly. I told her how she'd attacked me near the end, and how I'd killed Arish and brought her aboard ship. When I finished, she was silent for a moment.

"It's . . . funny: When. We. First. Met. I practiced . . . dying . . . in the . . . simulator. Now . . . you practice . . . dying."

I began to object. I was not practicing how to die, I

was trying to learn to stay alive. But I remembered advice I'd heard so often from Kaigo: "Learn to live as one already dead," and I knew she was right. We were practicing how to die for Motoki Corporation. And what disturbed me even more was that I felt incapable of feeling any emotion at all.

"*Sí*. I'm dead *inside* now. The rest of me just waits for my body to catch up." She looked at me strangely, turning her head slightly. She seemed concerned. Very concerned.

I shouted, "Go to hell, you bitch! I don't need your concern, your sympathy and sad faces. What do you do, practice that sad expression in the mirror?"

"You don't . . . have a . . . sense of. Humor. Anymore."

"Nothing is funny anymore," I said. "Except Mavro's jokes." She continued staring at me with those eyes filled with compassion. I became enraged. "What good do your sad faces do? One of my compadres had a pipe rammed through his belly this morning. Why don't you make sad faces for him? What good does your sympathy do? I'd rather see shit on your face than that sad frown! You bitch. This place is full of dead men, walking dead men! They practice dying for Motoki Corporation! And do you know why? You and your fucking Idealist Socialist friends drove them to it! They throw their lives away because you took everything they have. And now you feign sympathy.

"Don't give us your sympathy, bitch! I wish I could make a gift to you of all the ugliness I've witnessed in the past two weeks. I wish I could spit it into your hand!" I found that I was shouting, and I stopped. I was shaking violently, and wished to strike her.

She'd listened patiently. Her expression of concern didn't falter, but her eyes began to gleam with tears. "You've changed. You . . . did not ask . . . me how . . . I am. The old you . . . would. Have. Asked."

"You're right," I said. "I would have." I didn't ask. She was silent for a moment, uncomfortable.

"Buds itch," she said. The buds on her hand itched where it was regenerating. It was a common problem.

Someone should have rubbed the growths with cortisone. "Garzón . . . treats me . . . good. We . . .
made . . . a bargain: I tell . . . him what he . . .
wants to know. And . . . he lets . . . me live." She
smiled a beautiful smile at the joke, all her white teeth
gleamed.

"I can . . . not walk. Or move. Or breathe . . . by
myself. But Garzón . . . wants me. To. Practice. My
skills. With. The. Computer. And boost. Your simulations."

I tried to calm myself, to move to a safer subject. I
responded, "Your dreamwork on my little monitor at
home was excellent. I'm sure you'll do a fine job." The
truth was that she did more than a fine job. With the
help of the ship's artificial intelligence she'd created an
illusion I couldn't pierce, and she'd done it while terribly
disadvantaged.

"Redundant thoughts stay," she said. She meant that
she'd practiced a lot, and had therefore not lost the
ability to create dreamworlds when she was injured.
Those acts we do repeatedly, those concerns we care
about often, are least likely to be lost when the brain is
damaged.

"When you worked for Alliance Intelligence, what did
you do?" I asked. "Were you some kind of dream
assassin? Did you kill people in their sleep?"

She shook her head. "No. Something . . . Someday . . . I will tell . . . you. Angelo—I'm . . . sorry
I . . . hurt you. You've been . . . kinder . . . to me
than . . . I deserve. And you . . . served me . . .
better . . . than . . . I could . . . have . . . imagined."

She began to cry. I didn't care to see it.

I shrugged. "*De nada.*"

"I know . . . you still . . . care. I can . . . not . . .
pay you . . . back. I wish . . . to pay . . . you something. I don't . . . speak well . . . uh . . ."

I felt a thrill as if a strong wind were about to lift me.
The wind whipped the trees overhead until the noise
became a dull roar. Monkeys began to scream and howl
from their secret places all around and above me,

creating a great clamor. I remembered the howling wind
from Tamara's previous dream, the one where she'd
attacked me, and I pointed my rifle barrel toward her
chest, wondering if she'd be forced to jack out if I pulled
the trigger, or if she was immune to the effects of the
simulator.

Amid all this noise Tamara stood before me. Her
dress, whipped by the wind, became as white as lightning, and her face was pale and beautiful. She reached
down into her dress between her breasts and pulled out
a small ornate wooden box.

She opened the box and held it up for me to see.
Inside was a tiny heart, like that of a dog; it was beating
furiously as if just cut from a living body. Beneath the din
and the turmoil I could hear the heart softly beating.

"Listen. Listen." She moved the box closer to my face.
The beating became louder. The howls and the yammers
of the monkeys and the roaring wind faded into the
background. The sound of the beating heart was soft and
insistent. "Become fluent . . . in . . . the gentle language . . . of the heart."

I looked up at Tamara's face. Tears were streaming
from her eyes. Her fierce eyes. "This is . . . what
I . . . feel like now. This is . . . what it . . . feels
like . . . to *live*!"

She grasped the tiny heart between two fingers and
shoved it into my chest. It was like breathing the wind
that blows over a mint field and basking in sunlight—my
nerves danced along the whole length of my body. I
seemed to move upward and out, to pass through an
insubstantial wall where lethargy, pain, fatigue, and fear
were left behind, and I was standing in a warm pleasant
place, at the center of myself, where there was only joy.
I felt Tamara's emotions—her peace, the gratitude she
held toward me for helping her escape Earth, and a
compassion so strong, so alive, it seemed unconquer-
able. She viewed me as a broken doll, some small thing
she desperately wished to mend.

I wanted to laugh at her view of me. I wanted to tell
her I wasn't broken. But my own body seemed far away
and I couldn't touch it.

She withdrew her fingers, yanking the tiny heart from my chest, and I collapsed on the ground. The warmth, the compassion, the energy—all drained from me. I tried to feel something. To rejoice in the air pumping through my lungs, to touch the ground with my fingertips and relish the sensation of loam. But I felt nothing. My fingers were dead, and the air seemed stale and empty. I was empty. Desolate. I tried to call up the sensation I'd just felt; to remember what it was like to love. But when had I ever loved? I hadn't let myself be touched inside for thirty years, not since my wife had died. And on those rare occasions when I felt something stir within my breast, I hadn't reacted to it. I'd shut myself off. Retreated. For all these years I'd pretended to serve society, feigned compassion, because I'd believed in it on an intellectual level. I did it because it sounded good in theory. But for one moment, did I ever *feel* the pain of another?

If I had, I couldn't recall the emotion, dredge it up, or bring it to life again.

I listened in my chest for the sound of my own heart. There was nothing inside. I was truly a broken doll, empty and lifeless, and perhaps beyond repair.

I began laughing, a hollow laugh that turned into great, wracking sobs. I fell at Tamara's feet, groveled at her ankles, and cried in self-pity. She reached down and smoothed her hands through my hair until I quieted.

I jacked out.

I was last to jack out of the simulator. Kaigo replayed the battle, and the tiny holo showed us scuttling about on the floor. It showed us skim through the salt marsh, retreat from the Yabajin into the woods. I was knocked from the back of the hovercraft, removed my broken helmet, stood and walked to the edge of the marsh—just in time to meet the Yabajin. They shot me down and chased my compadres. It took a long while for me to die in the simulation.

Tamara had removed all evidence of her conversation with me.

Kaigo rehearsed the run with us, pointing out our

errors. He missed several obvious errors, ones he'd have normally caught, and seemed inattentive. He jacked us into a second simulation and we found ourselves gliding over the sea. We were only in the simulation for a few minutes when Kaigo jacked me out.

The others sat slumped in their chairs, still trapped in their illusion. Dragonfly pupae. Master Kaigo stood by the hovercraft. He appeared distracted. Cultural Envoy Sakura stood behind him.

Master Kaigo said to me, "Take off your armor and follow Envoy Sakura immediately."

I wondered what I'd done wrong, and began stripping from my armor. Sakura helped undress me—an unusual act. The Japanese had scrupulously avoided touching me on all occasions, and I'd wondered if they felt they'd become defiled by the act.

Sakura spoke quickly as he worked. "You are a morphogenic pharmacologist, no? You know how to run a gene splicer? You are knowledgeable about viruses?"

"Of course," I said.

"Do you know about military viruses? The kinds used in biological warfare?"

I hesitated. No one spoke about those viruses. They were far too dangerous to be discussed openly. The hair raised on the back of my neck. I didn't like this conversation. *They want me to make a virus*, I thought. *They've heard bad news from Baker, and they want to wipe out everything. Start over.* "I know something of viral weapons. I don't know how to create them," I lied. I had a basic idea of how to create them.

"Ah, no! We don't want you to create them, we want you to fight them. We have a viral outbreak on Module B. Very bad."

My heart began beating hard. I couldn't imagine someone turning us into a plague ship. Most of the time, I knew, we were sealed off from that module. But I'd seen a worker moving between modules only the day before.

"How much of the ship is contaminated?" I asked.

"We don't know. Workers on module B report several fatalities, all in the past three hours, and the disease has spread quickly. They don't believe they can last more than a day. No one here shows any of the symptoms."

I finished stripping my armor and Sakura led me down the halls to the ladder. We reached level eight and Sakura thumbed a transmitter and opened the lower air lock, and we went below. This section of the ship was larger than I'd anticipated. There were rooms to handle large machinery for cooking, cleaning, laundry, water purification, air recycling. We went to a small room crammed with three other Latin Americans sitting at computer terminals with their feet up, watching the computers work. They wore worried expressions, yet they seemed to be in no hurry. This relieved some of my tension.

The room was supplied with two x-ray microscopes and a couple of DNA synthesizers—obviously an ancillary medical facility meant to be used in conjunction with the infirmary upstairs. Sitting atop a computer monitor was a small intercom. The channel on it was open, hooked to the infirmary in module B. I could hear the sounds of people coughing and crying in delirium while others spoke urgently in the foreground.

Sakura headed back upstairs.

"I'm Fidel, from immunology. That's José—" a small man said from the nearest terminal. He nodded toward a chimera with silver eyes very much like Abriara's. "He's done some work engineering his younger brothers in Chile. And our friend Juan Pedro over there is in food services."

I looked at Juan Pedro, a tall thin man with kinky hair. His job on ship would be to engineer various proteins to flavor the algae mixes we ate, a tedious job requiring little knowledge of genetic engineering, since all the proteins he made were on file and the DNA synthesizers could handle the job, but he would still be familiar with the equipment. "So you are the one who makes our food?" I asked. "Remind me to kill you later."

Juan Pedro lowered his head. "Everybody always says that."

Fidel waved me over to his keyboard and punched in some commands. "This is what we're dealing with." A virus came up on screen, typical in appearance—a tiny clear oval about 24 microns in diameter—except it had a tail, the kind usually reserved for viruses that attack bacteria. Inside was a simple circle of genetic material that twisted in upon itself, something in the order of 40,000 amino acids long.

"A chimera?" I asked. The term *chimera* refers to any creature engineered so that it carries the traits of the member of another species—whether it is a bacteria engineered to produce insulin or something as complex as Perfecto or Abriara.

"It looks that way," Fidel said. "It doesn't invade its host by ejecting its DNA through the tail, though, so it's not a complex chimera. The host cell absorbs the virus. Its tail is used only to speed movement."

A virus reproduces by injecting its own DNA into the cell of its host, then subverting the host cell's reproductive system so it will create multiple copies of the virus. In viruses that attack animals, the virus often releases chemicals that cut up sections of the host's DNA, which the virus then uses in creating its offspring. When the viruses are ready to leave the host cell, they can either "bud" off, or simply burst the cell wall completely. In either case, the host cell often dies. Since this particular virus was a biological weapon, it was a good bet the host cell would burst, releasing several hundred copies of the virus.

One window in the corner of the computer screen showed a dozen different antibodies, explaining how they'd attach to the virus to mark it for destruction by lymphocytes. The information on the computer seemed to explain why everyone was resting. It looked as if they were simply waiting for the DNA synthesizer to create the antibodies.

"It looks as if I got here too late," I said. "All the work is done already."

"Sí," Fidel said. "The geneticists in module B have been working on this all night. The work is done already." He punched a button and the computer screen called up the DNA sequences on the virus that gave directions for the *capsid*, the outer membrane of protein of the virion, the virus cell. Next to it was a comparison chart showing the genetic makeup of the outer membrane of a neuron, a human nerve cell. They were *nearly* the same. The viral capsid marvelously counterfeited the nerve membrane. The implications became obvious— anything we used to attack the virus would also destroy the patient's nervous system.

"When we started looking for the virus it seemed invisible—none of our antibodies would bind to it. At first we thought it was so alien in composition the human body just couldn't recognize it, but we did an analysis of the capsid and found it so closely allied to the membrane of the neuron that the antibodies didn't attack it because they saw it as a natural part of the human body. All our antibodies also tag the neurons for destruction. We've found the same problem with the antiviral chemicals. They're all lethal. Any suggestions?"

My thoughts raced wildly. I immediately thought of subviruses—tiny parasites that attack and destroy viruses—but I was sure they would have tried them. I'd once heard of a man who engineered an artificial immune system—he'd created some virus-eating bacteria and then given the bacteria a genetic makeup that made it highly susceptible to penicillin. The bacteria destroyed the viruses, then the doctor destroyed the bacteria. But any artificial immune system we created would still attack the nervous system as if it were the enemy.

A general message came over the intercom on the table, aimed at those who were ill in Module B. "Anyone who has not had a drink of water in the past twenty-four hours and who does not have an elevated temperature, please report to level eight for induction into the emergency cryotanks. All others remain in your rooms. Do not go to the infirmary."

I looked at Fidel. "They're going to try to freeze the ones who are in the best condition," he said, "Hoping we'll come up with a solution that could save a few of them."

"How many cryotanks do they have?" I asked.

"About three hundred on their module. We might be able to save three hundred."

José laughed. "I told Fidel we should blow the seals on that module and let everyone get sucked into space right now. It would be faster than what they're going through. We've already tried all the antiviral drugs—nothing. We've given up on antibodies. We've tried some common subviruses—but this little beast has its own immune system. Any subvirus that tries to attach itself to the virus just gets chopped up and eaten for dinner. We won't get anywhere with them. We need something more . . . elegant." His tone was hopeless.

"Have you tried heating the virus, subjecting it to ultraviolet radiation, those things?"

"Yes. It reproduces best just a few degrees above body temperature. Of course, all the patients have elevated temperatures, which just makes the virus breed all the faster. We can kill it with radiation, and we've already cleared up their air and water, but it doesn't help the patients in module B. They got it through their water sometime yesterday. And they've all got it. A samurai was an agent for the Yabajin. He was carrying a subdural biocache of the virus; he must have dug the cache out from under his skin and thrown it into the drinking water. He's already been executed. Most of the victims got double doses—as soon as their fevers began to rise, they drank more heavily.

"The infections are fairly disseminated: the virus attacks a wide range of organs with equal vitality. It causes severe damage to the lungs, liver, skin. It's also causing lesions in the arteries, with internal swelling. Several patients have died of stroke caused by clots breaking free from other areas and floating to the brain."

"At least the assassin died before his victims," I said. I'm sure the Yabajin considered it a privilege. He'd traded one life for four thousand.

"Anyway," Fidel said, "we can't kill the virus, but we may be able to sterilize it. That's what we're working on now. The computer is checking to see how it subverts the reproductive system of its host cells. We thought we might be able to introduce a subvirus that could infiltrate the virus—use a prion as a vector—and at least try to neuter these puppies." Their idea seemed to be halfway decent—the prion is a subvirus that actually inserts its DNA into its host virus to reproduce, just as a virus will insert its own genetic material into a human host to reproduce. In my work in morphogenics I often develop viruses to infiltrate a human host and insert new information into the patient's genetic code. Such viruses are called vectors, and one can do marvelous things with them. It's possible to use a subvirus such as a prion for a vector to insert new information into the genetic code of a virus, but in practice it is very difficult, for prions are very small bits of living matter, often with just a few dozen pairs of amino acids. They're barely alive, and I thought it would be difficult to create one large enough to be useful as a vector in redesigning the virus. It would be doubly difficult since this particular virus was designed as a weapon, and had already proven immune to other subviruses. Its creator had taken years to perfect it. Yet we'd have only hours to defeat it. Perhaps if we'd had a few months we could have come up with something. As it was, Fidel simply said, "You're welcome to wait and see if you come up with any ideas."

I waited with them for the computer's report on the viral reproductive system. Occasionally the intercom carried the sound of someone's hacking cough, the footsteps of nurses walking from patient to patient. They spoke softly to one another, telling the stories of their lives and the people they loved as they prepared to die. There was one woman there, and I could hear her going from bed to bed, speaking with the ill, offering comfort and consolation to those who were dying. She would say, "My name is Felicia, would you like some water, a blanket?" and then she would begin talking about good things, a day she spent on the beach burning sandalwood, or how her father had taught her to make her own shoes. It sounded like idle talk at first, yet it calmed the ill remarkably well. This woman seemed to be very wise and very strong, and I found myself listening to her intently, wishing I could be like her, wishing I could make her live. Twice a Japanese announced over a loudspeaker in module B that the ill should "resist the illness by a supreme act of will." It was a brave gesture.

It took the computer nearly two hours to finally unravel the virus's method of reproduction. We all knew that the results of the study would be useless before they arrived: the virus sent chemical messengers telling the cell it was time to commence mitosis, to form RNA, split, and grow. We could shut down the reproductive system of the virus by using any of three drugs, but we'd also shut down the reproductive system of all the victim's cells. Blindness and a quick death would follow.

We immediately began developing a vector sub-virus—the creature we hoped would be "elegant" enough to defeat the virus's defense mechanisms so we could sterilize it. The patients began dying rapidly. We were able to document their deaths: we learned all the symptoms of the illness—the rise in temperature followed by dehydration, destruction of the liver and arteries, followed by death. We were able to calculate how many copies the virus made of itself each time it reproduced, and to calculate it would take an average of twenty-eight hours from the time of the victim's first exposure to death. With that information we computed exactly the hour the biocache had been poured into the water, and found that the Greek technician who'd moved between modules had missed contaminating the rest of the ship by only minutes. We learned everything except how to stop the plague. As far as the capacity for destruction to human life went, the virus was as effective as a hydrogen bomb.

We followed many dead-end leads over the next twenty-four hours. Over three thousand people died while we labored, and then we found something: we found a family of prions that would work as vectors to sterilize the virus, but we also found that the body's own defense mechanisms destroyed our nice little creations.

In order to get the subviruses to work, all we needed was to shut down our patient's production of antibodies long enough for the subvirus to infect the patients. On top of this, we needed to breed a culture of the subviruses so we could infect our patients with them. We began growing the cultures immediately, but our next problem became evident: it would take a minimum of six hours to manufacture one dose of the subvirus, and in seven hours we could manufacture four hundred doses, but by calculating the spread of the illness we found that the patients would be too far gone by then for anyone to be saved. We had in fact conquered the virus, but not in time.

We decided to go ahead and produce the antidote and manufacture four hundred doses, in hopes that we might save someone. If anyone was alive in six hours, we'd have the ship's maintenance robots carry the antidote down to the cryotanks and inject it into the tanks.

Five and a half hours later, Mavro called me on comlink. It was nearly noon. "*Hola, muchacho,* how are you doing?" he said.

"Oh, fine," I answered wearily.

"Did you hear that I killed that punk Samora last night?"

"No," I said.

"*Sí,* we chased Lucío and his compadres all around, and we finally got Samora. The fucker cut my arm, though. It is not too bad. We looked for Lucío this morning before breakfast, but we couldn't find him. Now Kaigo says we can't kill Lucío after all, because of the bad things that are happening on module B. They want every man alive. They have some big samurai guarding Lucío, and they're waiting for the plague to run its course so they can transfer him over to module A."

"Oh," I said.

"Did you hear the good news?"

All the news I'd heard lately was bad. I told him so.

"García's team beat the samurai last night! They won over half a million IMUs. Then we went to the simulators this morning and instead of fighting the samurai we are fighting other Latin American combat teams now. We lost all four of our fights this morning, but that was just because we were two men down. When you and Zavala get back we will do much better. I have been watching The Horror Show with Perfecto, learning who is good and who is not. Some friends and I have been gambling on the outcomes of the battles this morning. I made twelve thousand pesos already." He'd been speaking as if he were in high spirits, but his tone became desperate. "And, anyway, I was thinking: you have a lot of money. Would you like me to invest some of it for you in the fights?"

He may have made twelve thousand pesos already this morning, I mused, but I was sure he'd lost them all again. I was disappointed to hear that he only called me so he could borrow money. "No," I said. "I want to watch the teams, see who my favorites are first."

"Oh. Okay. Tell me, are things on module B as bad as they say?"

"Worse," I said.

"Oh. Well, I'm sure an intelligent person like yourself will come up with something. *Adios.*" He clicked off.

I thought about what he'd said. I weighed the good news against the bad. Lucío was out of our hair and we no longer had to battle samurai. But four thousand of our compadres were dead or dying. It wasn't a fair trade. It seemed to me that if a good man worked hard, he should at least be allowed to break even in life. We weren't breaking even. And I had another realization: during this entire trip, we had been looking at the Motoki samurai as if they were our enemy, or at Lucío and his men as if they were our enemies. And I saw that during all this time, I had not understood that the Yabajin were our true enemy.

At the end of the seven hours we found that 113 people were still alive in the cryotanks. The intercom had quit sending audio signals. No one was left wandering around on the other module. No one in the infirmary was coughing. The maintenance robot carried the antidote to the men and injected it into the cryotanks along with the necessary antibody inhibitors. But, three hours later, our patients were dead. When the last man died, the ship's AI blew the seals on the module and flushed the corpses into space. The freezing void sterilized that part of the ship better than all our drugs ever could.

In our first battle with the Yabajin we lost more than we could ever have imagined.

We stayed for several hours and assisted the ship's computer with cleanup, instructing the maintenance robots to eject all corpses from the cyrotanks and hidden niches where bodies might manage to hide. When the robots were finished, we heated the entire module to 110 degrees Celsius for two hours, then flushed it with chlorine gas.

Sakura came down and opened the door when we finished. I hadn't slept for over two days, and I had only an hour to nap before battle practice.

I dreamed we were descending in our shuttles to Baker. From my window I saw a shining paradise of blue and green, an iridescent disk in the sky. We were falling, falling, and my heart raced with joy. We'd be in paradise soon. I'd taste the honeyed fruits that hung thick on the trees! I'd swim in warm oceans and take my ease staring into the sky!

We flew in low over the planet, over well-tended gardens. Japanese farmers waved and shouted greetings. They called to children and put them on their shoulders so whole families could watch our shuttles thunder overhead, coming in low for the landing.

On a city street, an old Japanese gentleman waved to us, carrying a small girl on his shoulders, a pale-faced European girl, the one I'd named Tatiana. They were both smiling and waving. Then they looked above us and their mouths opened in surprise and shock.

I could read the girl's lips as she said, "Grandfather, you didn't take care of them!"

Something was wrong. I looked up and saw bodies falling from the sky, thousands of limp bodies—the bodies of the plague victims we'd flushed into space. And I realized we'd forgotten our trajectory when we flushed those bodies: they'd kept traveling along beside the ship all the time, and naturally they were falling toward Baker with us. And I realized some of the viruses would be frozen but intact in those bodies, and everyone on Baker would die because of it.

CHAPTER 11

On our thirteenth day, depression at our losses to the plague hung in the air like a thick dark smoke. I walked the halls in the morning to ease a cramp in my legs, and even my bare feet padding over the plastic floors seemed muted. At breakfast people whispered their concern at the deaths of our compadres, and though the words were different from man to man, always the talk went something like this: "Too many of us have already died from the plague for the war to continue. We cannot even beat the samurai in practice now, how will we beat the Yabajin on Baker? How can we hope to win the war now?"

There was electricity in the air. My hair stood on end and my mouth was dry. There was too much silence on the ship, the cautious silence of mice. It was as if every heart beat in unison. I felt I was about to break. I felt that everyone else was about to break.

Mavro confronted a man at breakfast who said he wanted to go home. "You *steer*! Where are your balls?" Mavro shouted. "Give us a few more weeks of practice and the samurai will shit in fear of us!"

We returned to battle practice as if nothing had changed. Yet depression clung to me. I was exhausted in body and spirit, and only wanted to shake my emptiness.

In our first simulation we met five compadres from module A who appeared to wear red armor as if they were Yabajin. Yet I knew they saw us in the red of the Yabajin. Their fighting style had evolved differently from ours. And because Zavala was still out with his wound, we lost. We beat our second team soundly. It was my first taste of victory in the simulator. I should have been elated, but I felt empty and dissatisfied.

We jacked into a third simulation, and were thrust into a landscape near the sea, shooting over rows of dunes where stinging flies were the dominant life-form. My prosthetic eyes picked up wisps of silver among the leaves of small bushes, and everywhere I looked, gulls seemed to be hovering in the air. I knew I'd meet Tamara, and my heart raced at the thought. We met the Yabajin and a lucky shot removed me from action quickly, but instead of jacking into the battle room I tumbled off the hovercraft and skidded in the sand at the bottom of a hill. The hovercrafts raced away.

I took off my helmet and Tamara's great black bull ambled up over the hilltop, its belly lazily swaying from side to side as it walked, swishing its tail. Tamara rode comfortably on its back, dressed in a yellow robe. The sun beating on the fabric blinded me.

"I've been . . . looking for you."

"I've been busy."

"You . . . couldn't . . . save them."

"I know."

"Angelo. I heard Garzón . . . speaking. To. Advisers. He . . . doesn't know I can . . . talk to you. Your. Situation is. Desperate. . . . I want to . . . apologize . . . for the mess . . . I got you into."

I was instantly curious. Garzón hadn't spoken publicly about how the plague on module B would affect us. "What did Garzón say?"

"Because of . . . current losses . . . the AI projects. You'll. Have seventy-eight percent . . . deaths. Forgive me."

I shrugged. It didn't sound so bad. We'd all known we might die when we got aboard ship. We were guaranteed the computer simulations would give us a fifty-one percent chance of survival. So the odds had gone down. "It makes no difference."

Tamara's shoulders sagged in weariness. Tears began to stream down her cheeks. She glowed like an apparition of a goddess. As if an invisible finger touched me, stimulating my emotions directly, I beheld a beauty in her so profound it caused physical pain. "Forgive me," she whispered. "Forgive."

"It's not your fault," I said. My words were empty.

"It's my fault," she said. Her eyes sparkled with knowledge that defied contradiction.

"Then I forgive you anyway," I said.

She reached out and scratched the head of the bull. "Reality is . . . a pain in the butt. The. Sooner. We. Get. Rid. Of it . . . the better," she said. "When you . . . need . . . reprieve. Come to me. I'll . . . prepare a. World . . . for you. Here." She pointed to her head.

"Thank you," I said, and she began to fade. Darkness gathered as I prepared to jack out, and the old depression returned.

I jacked out of the last battle for the morning. I began undressing and hanging my foliage-green bug suit on its pegs. The backs of my eyes ached from loss of sleep. I wondered how others in the room would respond to the knowledge Tamara had given me. Would they want to go home? Certainly not Mavro or Abriara. Perfecto would patiently wait to learn my intentions. But would Kaigo consider my words treasonous?

I kept my mouth shut.

We went to the gymnasium and jogged slowly in the heavy gravity. Two days away from exercise had done me much good. I felt better than I had in months. As we lifted weights the room was quieter than usual. Instead of people joking and laughing, there were only whispers and the soft clank of weight bars lowering and raising.

Those who spoke, quietly and insistently boasted their prowess in battle that morning. A few minor victories made them feel less vulnerable. They bragged that they'd someday beat the Yabajin as ruthlessly as they beat each other. Many brave sentiments were expressed, but beneath it I still felt the thrill of electricity, the fear that made boasts necessary. I lifted weights next to Giron, a man with little mouse eyes who looked more nervous than most. For a long while he captured the attention of others by loudly proclaiming his exploits in Peru. If half his stories were true, he'd have beaten the socialists single-handedly.

He stopped doing leg presses momentarily, and I inserted into the sudden quiet, "It is a shame we're not back in Peru now. I'd love to give those socialists a good beating."

"Sí, sí," everyone around us said. At home was a war that had turned. At home was a battle we could win. I'm sure they were all thinking that. But only a coward would have dared speak it. I said loudly enough so those nearby could hear, "Did you know the ship's AI forecasts that seventy-eight percent of us will die on Baker? Technically, Motoki is violating our contract. I'd not be surprised if they send us home so we can fight alongside our amigos."

Everyone stared at me in stunned silence. Halfway across the room García was exercising. His chimera Miguel, who had his back to me, turned and shouted, "Hola, Angelo, my amigo, where did you hear that?"

I was surprised Miguel had been listening from so far away. "A friend on module A heard it from General Garzón," I answered.

The name "Garzón" attracted much attention, and around the room people began asking "What did Garzón say?" and those nearby answered, "Motoki is violating our contract. He says seventy-eight percent of us will die on Baker." The noise in the room rose to a soft rumble. From across the gymnasium someone said, "Is it true?" and I nodded. Around the room several people worked their jaws as they jacked in calls to friends who'd be interested in such news. The room suddenly exploded into sound as people tried to be heard over one another.

There were only two hundred people in the room, but I knew that within ten minutes everyone aboard ship would hear of the AI's forecast.

Mavro shouted, "It makes no difference! It just makes the fight more challenging!" and I laughed to myself: I, who've always refused to judge people, to stick them in molds, had predicted Mavro's response perfectly.

Giron said to no one in particular, "We should demand

that they turn the ship around!" and another man nodded sagely at Giron's advice.

Everywhere, everywhere, the same arguments were being voiced.

My teammates and I took it as a signal to head for the door. We ran up to our room. Three times within the next twenty minutes people came with the news, "Hey, have you heard the latest forecast on the battle?" I was very pleased with myself. I'd planted a seed, and all I needed was to sit and see what grew.

All afternoon we stayed in our rooms. The atmosphere became more charged, and I thought it strange: there was no static electricity on ship to make one itch with anticipation, to make the hair stand on one's head. Yet I felt it. I felt thunderclouds forming. I wondered if there were a pheromone released by anxious people. It seemed it must be so, though I've never read any studies done on the subject. It would make sense—men are herd animals, and if they sensed one another's anxiety, it could prove valuable for survival.

Mavro sat in front of the monitor, jacked in on an open line, and gambled on battles half the afternoon. Then he lay on his bed and I listened as his breathing grew shallow. I soon found that we all breathed in a common rhythm. I didn't understand what it signified. Mavro said, "Do you know what this feels like?"

No one spoke for a long moment. Abriara said, "Yes."

Mavro said, "It feels like a riot. The electric excitement before a riot."

Abriara said, "Yes."

Mavro said, "I lived through one when I was in prison, in Cartagena. This feels just like it did then. Only now our prison floats through space." We didn't speak or answer. "Don Angelo, do you know what to do in a riot?"

"No," I said.

"Find a place to hide," Abriara said, "And put your back to a wall. Don't trust anyone. Don't let anyone stand behind you. Kill any fucker who comes within arm's reach."

"Sí," Mavro said. "You'll be surprised how many

people have fashioned weapons. You'll see plenty of clubs and knives. People will break into the infirmary to get as many drugs as possible. Even if you see your best friend coming, he may be crazy from drugs, and he'll probably have a weapon. Don't carry anything of value with you, anything anyone will want to steal—no food, no water, no drugs or alcohol. Let them see nothing but your weapon—and even then, carry a wooden dagger— don't let them see your pretty crystal knife.

"Anyone who has a grievance against you will come looking for you. And he'll bring friends. Don't trust anyone who wants to get close to you. Especially if he's smiling.

"We have plenty of enemies. Some are people you don't know—people who felt snubbed when I passed out cigars and liquor and gave them none."

I thought of Lucío. And there was an Alliance assassin who'd want me dead. Mavro's words were not comforting.

Mavro said, "When I was in the riot in Cartagena, my friends and I knew a man we wanted to kill in another cell block. He was a snitch, but we could not prove it. Six of us hid in a cell for two hours, until the riot quieted. When we went into the halls it looked as if a bomb had dropped. Men had pulled steel bars from windows to use as clubs, and they'd beaten the bulletproof windows of the guard's cages with the steel bars until the glass smashed. There were fires everywhere.

"We found dozens of bodies of snitches who were fucked in the mouth until they choked, bodies of guards who'd had their hair burned off with acetylene torches, bodies of men killed with broken bottles and screwdrivers. At dark we got hungry and went to the kitchens. We found a whole crowd of men fucking half a dozen prisoners and taking drugs. I knew most of them, and some of them were friends. They killed two of us and chased the rest of us away from the food. My friend Raul and I got separated from our amigos—Pablo and Xavier—when we tried to escape.

"Raul and I doubled back in the dark hall, looking for our amigos, and found an air vent above a guard's cage—a little tunnel—and we crawled in to hide for the night. Raul was in front of me. He was a weight lifter, very strong. We crawled back about ten meters and met another man in the darkness, crawling the other way. Raul and the other man fought in the cramped tunnel, and Raul tried to strangle the other man, but got stabbed in the neck with a long drill bit, and he bled to death.

"The tunnel was so cramped that Raul's murderer could not get past the corpse to attack me, so we kept Raul's body between us. I slept in the tunnel while my amigo's body cooled, and in the morning the guards came and pulled me out. They pulled out Raul, and behind that they pulled out Raul's killer—it was Pablo, the friend we'd been looking for."

Abriara said, "Yes."

I lay on the bed, and I couldn't help thinking: in the spaceship a riot would be worse than in prison. Someone could destroy the navigational instruments and throw the ship off course. Someone could puncture the hull and we'd all breathe vacuum. Someone could jettison the ramjets and we'd be stuck for months, floating slowly toward Baker in zero-g. Normally in a riot a person's violent impulses are turned toward destroying property. But in a spaceship, no sane person would risk damaging the vehicle, so the violence would be turned against others. Even then, one reckless person could destroy us all.

A few moments later, Sakura came to visit us with a strange samurai, a tall man with a long blue-black ponytail and receding hairline whose head and face seemed to be the only natural parts left to his body. His artificial legs and arms and torso were encased in a simple black plastic housing. At his throat a shiny black vacuum hose—an economical substitute for an esophagus—ran from his chest up to the cleft between his jaws. Unlike most samurai on ship, who seemed to shun cybertechnology, he almost reveled in it. He was much more like the high-tech Japanese I'd known on Earth. Yet like his fellows, his epicanthic folds were unnaturally accented. He seemed familiar, and I soon recognized him by his posture, the tilt of his head. He was Lazy

Neck, one of the samurai who'd defeated us so often in the simulator.

They came in and waited, standing as if at attention. Their custom forbade them from socializing with inferiors, and they held to it strictly. When we met them outside of class, they pretended we didn't exist, even when we had to squeeze past each other in the narrow halls. It was obvious the samurai still weren't inviting the inferiors to tea. Master Kaigo came in after them and they sat *seiza* on the floor and invited us to do likewise.

Kaigo chose his words very carefully, pausing to let his translator convey his every nuance. "I'm forced to speak to you because of a distressing situation," he said. "There are many rumors that Motoki is violating its contract, and some have been so bold as to suggest we return to Earth. I've heard someone in this room may have initiated this uprising." He was very tense, but his hand was not upon his sword.

"Forgive me, Master," I said. "No one here initiated this uprising. I only told what I'd learned about the computer's battle projections, and suggested we might need to return to Earth to recruit more men."

Kaigo watched me a long time, and I met his gaze. "I understand," he said. "I didn't think you a coward."

"No offense is taken," I said.

Kaigo said, "You understand, of course, that it is very difficult? It would take weeks to return to Earth. The Japanese government has hired a spaceship and is recruiting mercenaries for the Yabajin even as we speak. They'll try to overtake us on our flight to Baker.

"Even if this were not the case, we've already ejected our pulse rockets. We're running on ramjet power now. You understand that the majority of expense for a trip such as this comes from the fuel that is consumed? It will cost us the same to continue to Baker as to return to Earth, and should we return to Earth it would take several weeks for Motoki Corporation to liquidate the assets necessary to finance another expedition." I understood this. The big pulse booster rockets propelled the ship with small nuclear explosions. The fuel for these boosters required a great deal of space and cost a fortune. Once the ship was propelled to sufficient speed, the ramjet engine kicked in and began scooping up hydrogen atoms from space to burn as fuel. In other words, we traveled for free once the ramjets fired, since our fuel cost nothing. But if we slowed the ship, we'd eventually need to eject the ramjet and return to pulse engines, and Motoki would see it as a waste if the ship used that energy to slow down to return to Earth.

"I see the difficulties this would cause," I said.

"You understand that *it is very difficult*?" Kaigo asked.

It is difficult was a phrase I'd heard much lately. It was Kaigo's nonconfrontational way of telling us there wasn't a chance in hell that he'd let us go home.

We all nodded.

Kaigo sighed and turned so that he was no longer facing us and said, "Now I must speak of something that causes me much distress: You told me three days ago that you feel you do not owe *on* to Motoki Corporation. You do not feel you owe a debt of honor. I cannot understand this wrong-thinking. We samurai came to teach you how to become warriors. But there is more to being a warrior than to master battle skills. The way of the warrior is the way of death, but it is also a way of ordering one's life.

"We've been teaching you self-control and courage— these things a samurai must know, and they are in line with the pure teachings of *bushido*—but I never thought I'd need to teach you about honor.

"At moments like this, language tends to hide one's thoughts. I . . ." Kaigo sat back and pondered as he struggled to express a concept so integral to his way of life that he may never before have needed to voice it. "When a man accepts a gift from another, he incurs a debt of *on*, an obligation to repay that gift. His worth as a person depends upon repayment of the gift, *ne*? He must repay his debt at all costs, even at the cost of his own life, for life is a small thing and is easily taken, but a man's virtue cannot be taken. Therefore, to lose life is less than to lose honor." He watched our eyes to make sure we understood.

"If a man does not want to incur a debt to another, he

should refuse any gift another might offer. Therefore, one must beware of those who lightly give gifts, lest one incur a debt one does not wish to repay. But even when one has incurred a debt one does not wish to repay, one must repay the debt. Do you understand?"

We all nodded. Kaigo didn't turn to see our actions, sparing us the embarrassment of having to see his face as he talked about these things.

"This is part of the code of the samurai," Kaigo said. "The samurai have always been the most honorable of people. We repay our debts willingly. And you've begun the training to become samurai. Motoki has given you a great gift—the opportunity to become samurai, to be lifted above your natural station in life, even though you are only foreigners—"

Sakura broke in quickly, perhaps because he knew how offensive Kaigo's bigotry would be. "What Master Kaigo means to say is that he considers you to be samurai now, or at least pupils. He expects you to accept the obligations of samurai. You must accept the inevitable duties along with the prestige!"

"And what exactly do you mean by 'duties'?" Abriara asked.

Kaigo scowled in thought. After a moment, he said, "Long ago a certain warlord journeyed through a forest inhabited by robbers. He had only a few samurai guards in his retinue, and as he walked he came upon a *ronin*, a masterless samurai. He asked the ronin if he would like to be employed, and the ronin was very hungry, so he heartily agreed. The lord was not taking a long journey, and did not have much food, but he ordered his men to prepare a meal so the ronin would not have to walk on an empty stomach. Since the lord was only on a short journey, he could give the ronin only a small bowl of oats, and he apologized that he did not have rice. The ronin accepted the small gift and was glad to eat.

"Later, the lord and his men were ambushed by a multitude of robbers. A tremendous battle ensued, and each samurai fought against terrible odds. During a lull in the battle, the lord idly wondered if the ronin would remain faithful or if he'd run into the hills. When the battle ended, only the lord and two samurai remained alive, wounded with many wounds. They found the newly-hired ronin among the slain. At his feet lay fourteen dead robbers—twice the number any other samurai had slain. And though he'd received for his wages only a bowl of oats, he proved the most faithful servant."

Kaigo stopped and let the message sink in.

"You are ronin," Kaigo said. "You have been paid well by Motoki Corporation. You have received food, clothing, water, air to breathe, and training. The odds in your battle may appear staggering, but you cannot lose heart. You should not fear death, but take joy in the fight to come. You must repay your debt of *on*. I will fight with you. I will die with you. It shames me as your master that I should be forced to explain these obligations to you."

Kaigo abruptly heaved his huge body off the floor, turned and left the room, his midnight-blue kimono fluttering behind him. Sakura and Lazy Neck silently followed.

"He's crazy," Mavro said when they'd closed the door. "I do not mind fighting on Baker, but I do not want to do it with crazy people."

We all nodded. It was obvious the samurai wouldn't turn the ship around. They considered it a personal affront that we even considered retreat a possibility.

Mavro went to the dorms a few hours later and reported that all over the ship the samurai delivered the same message. It was as if they'd thrown a wet blanket on our smoldering fire. We went to battle practice and lost two out of three. Zavala was released from the infirmary and he demanded more anesthetics, struggling to relieve countless imagined pains. The anesthetics left him as passive as a drugged baby. At dinner the air was still tense, but in the eyes of my compadres was resignation. Inertia carried us forward. They were convinced we should continue on. News reached us that Garzón and the samurai were searching for ways to improve our chances on Baker, to arrange affairs so we could lower the expected fatalities. Men trusted Garzón and were willing to wait. No one seriously spoke of return to Earth. But the men on module A who trained during our sleeping cycle were not so easily persuaded to continue, and I was totally surprised when the riot suddenly broke.

In the middle of the night I woke to a distant throbbing, like the sound of blood rushing behind one's ears, accompanied by a roaring sea. Thousands of feet pounded in unison; thousands of voices were chanting in the distance. I tried to make out the words to the chant, but the voices were indistinct. I could feel the tension in the air as if it were cobwebs, electric cobwebs brushing my face. Perfecto was rushing to his locker. The rest of us rose simultaneously. Through the thin walls I heard the slap of feet as samurai ran down the hall, a samurai shouted excitedly like the sound of a badger growling in its den. I slid from bed and searched in darkness for my crude wooden dagger.

"What's happening?" Zavala asked sleepily.

"A riot is building on A module." Abriara ran into the bathroom while we armed ourselves. Then we stood, not knowing what to do. Down below us, men began stamping their feet and chanting in unison, "Let's go home! Let's go home! Let's go home!" Working themselves into a frenzy, and I understood that sharper ears than mine had picked out those words from the module above us, and we'd begun to echo them as if we were a single organism.

Someone on the floor below shouted, "Noooo!" A heavy instrument smacked flesh.

Abriara came out of the bathroom holding her dagger in a protective position, eyeing us, "I'm going downstairs, to find some *amigas*," she said evenly.

I was shocked that she didn't trust us, that she felt she had to seek out the protection of other women. "Would you like an escort?" I asked.

"Keep away from me!" she said. Even though she was the one who'd said that we should put our backs to the wall and stab anyone who got near during a riot, I could not believe she would do it. She opened the door and peered into the hall. Her muscles were tense. Her movements were graceful and powerful, like those of a panther. Three samurai ran past the door, flashes of blue kimonos and steel swords.

I felt bad. I wanted to tell Abriara I wasn't like the men that had raped her in the past. I wasn't her enemy. "I'll help you if you need me," I said. "Just as I did in the simulator."

Abriara looked confused for a moment—hopeful, frightened. She nodded and edged out the door, unwilling to turn her back to us. I wished her luck.

Perfecto said, "Let's go down the ladder," and Mavro and Zavala agreed. I recognized that to run was useless. It didn't really matter where we ran, or if we ran anywhere at all. The riot, when it came, would be delivered right to our door.

Over the persistent thrum of feet pounding on floors and the steady chant of "Let's go home, Let's go home, Let's go home," a Japanese shouted, "Go back, silly woman!"

Abriara slipped back into the room and stood panting. "The samurai have cleared the halls. They've got everyone trapped in their rooms!"

The ship didn't carry many samurai. At best there could only be one to every five of us. Their short swords, or *wakizashi*, were meant primarily as an emblem of honor rather than a weapon. The samurai carried it as a promise to commit seppuku if his honor was lost. They couldn't keep us at bay with such weapons. They couldn't control the entire ship. For now men were content to shout and pound their feet. But when violence broke out, the samurai wouldn't be able to contain it. Abriara stood by the door, her knife poised.

"I suggest we put away our weapons," Perfecto said, "unless we plan to stab each other?"

"Good idea!" Zavala said. He set his knife on his bed and the rest of the men did the same, but Abriara held to her corner and kept her knife in hand.

We sat on our beds and paced the room and listened to the pounding of feet and the shouts of "Let's go home! Let's go home!" Sweat was pouring off my face as if I'd been doing hard labor, and my breathing was constricted. The room felt very hot.

Below us, someone yelled in defiance and his voice became a shrill death cry. I'd heard many such minor scuffles, but till then didn't realize what they signified: Those who sought to dissuade the rioters were being silenced. Zavala smiled wanly, his eyes those of a troubled child. The halls echoed with the chant of "Let's go home! Let's go home! Let's go home!" The floors vibrated, and when I touched the wall it hummed like a guitar string. Perfecto paced. He stepped to one end of the room, then returned, paced back and forth several times. And each time he went away he passed nearer on his return, as if he were a great fish and I held a line that guided him closer and closer. I sensed he wanted to protect me, and as if to verify my supposition he finally came and stood by me and patted my shoulder, then didn't leave again.

The hallway quieted; no more barefooted samurai ran by or shouted.

Abriara opened the door. "The corridor is empty," she said, and stepped out.

We followed, Perfecto walking in front of me, guarding me, and found it as she'd said. The darkened corridor was empty. The samurai had all gone below to try to guard hallways. Sakura and two fellow diplomats watched at the top of the ladder. With the lights around the ladders, they couldn't see us in the shadowed hall. There were only the five of us Latin Americans in the tiny stateroom on this level. They hadn't spared samurai to guard us.

"What shall we do?" Zavala asked loudly, to be heard over the chanting.

"We won't find a more protected position than this aboard ship," Mavro yelled. "I think we should guard the ladder and kill anyone who tries to come up."

"Anyone?" Perfecto asked.

"Sí. If we don't let any of those fuckers get behind us, we don't have much to worry about. No one is going to put up a good fight while trying to climb up out of the hole."

I couldn't imagine killing people so indiscriminately. "There's a safer place," I said.

Mavro arched his eyebrows in surprise. "Where?"

"Above us, in module B," I said.

"What about the plague?" Zavala asked.

"That whole part of the ship was sterilized. There's nothing left alive up there."

"The atmosphere should be good," Abriara said, "They took Lucío through it."

From my voyage down below our own living quarters, I knew the physical layout. There'd be half a dozen little workrooms and some storage facilities, separated from the living quarters by a second air lock.

"How do we open the air lock?" Abriara asked.

I pointed to Sakura standing with his two friends in the circle of light thrown up from the ladder shaft. "He has a transmitter that will open it."

Several floors below us rose a shout, hundreds of voices crying out in unison. The surge in volume made the floor jump, and my compadres and I all began to run forward, afraid the riot had started—but the chanting continued unabated, and we soon slowed.

It had been a simple falter in the rhythm, a rise in volume—nothing more—I thought, but then people screamed below and blunt objects slammed against flesh as localized fighting broke out while hundreds continued shouting, "Let's go home! Let's go home! Let's go home!"

Sakura and his amigos peered down the ladder below them, and the sounds of scuffling were loud enough that I knew they were watching a battle. Abriara sprinted up behind Sakura and slugged him in the kidney and he collapsed. We charged up from the shadows and Sakura's friends ran.

Sakura lay gasping on the floor as Abriara searched the pocket in his kimono. Down the ladder, three floors below, a great many samurai fought Latin Americans. There was so much noise—chanting and shouting—that we could not hear the din of melee, the individual cries and sounds of battle, so it appeared as if they battled in silence. The scent of sweat and blood tainted the air.

Abriara pulled the transmitter from Sakura's pocket. "Is this it?" she cried.

I nodded and she aimed the transmitter at the air lock and began pushing buttons. Nothing happened. I saw a tiny white disk on the transmitter—a thumbprint reader. "Let me try," I said, grabbing the transmitter and pressing the white disk against Sakura's thumb. The air lock began to slide open. Abriara raced up the ladder. The air lock opened into a wide tunnel, and the ladder climbed up five meters before ending at the door that led to module B.

I considered removing Sakura's thumb so I could use the transmitter, but he appeared totally unconscious and didn't pose a threat. I began lugging him up the ladder. It was a task I wouldn't have imagined myself capable of in the heavy gravity, but fear lent me strength. When I was inside the air lock, I dropped Sakura to the floor and fell exhausted atop him.

Abriara was waiting for me. Before I even dragged my feet through the air lock, she ripped the transmitter from my hand, held the register against Sakura's thumb, and pressed the button to close the door. Perfecto was halfway up the ladder, guarding my rear as he ascended, and he looked up in surprise and shouted, "Don Angelo, wait!" and tried to jump through the hole, but the door slid closed. The air lock suddenly became quieter.

Abriara put her wooden dagger to my throat. "Don't move, old man," she said. I lay gasping on the floor, winded from my short climb. She reached into my sleeve and removed my crystal knife, then pulled my wooden dagger from my belt. "I'll let you live because you are old and slow and weaponless." Her face was a pale mask of terror, yet she fought to control it. She put her back to the wall, and brandished the crystal knife.

"Thanks," I said. But part of me wondered, *Wouldn't I pose less of a threat if I were dead? If she is as coldhearted as she pretends, she should kill me*. And I looked in her eyes and I knew—I knew—that she was trying to work up the nerve to kill me. I could not imagine what terror drove her to this. *Never make the mistake of thinking of her as human*, I told myself.

She pushed a button on the transmitter. The door above hissed open, and we breathed fresh air—the kind of fresh air one can only enjoy on a clear day after a rain. I hadn't guessed how musty the atmosphere in our own module had become. Abriara grabbed Sakura by one arm and climbed the ladder, Sakura flopping like a rag. He began regaining consciousness and shook his head, but she ignored him. I followed as close behind as possible, afraid she'd leave me as she had the others. When we stepped onto the maintenance deck of module B, Abriara pushed the button to close the door behind. As the door began to slide, she kicked Sakura back down the hole and sealed it behind him.

Abriara and I were alone. Above us in the distance I could hear the rioters on A module, like the voices of many gulls crying on the shore. Below us the chanting faltered as several hundred men shouted. *The worst is yet to come*, I thought.

On this level the halls didn't radiate and separate into many rooms as in the living quarters. Four doors near the ladder each led to rooms that appeared small because they were crammed with equipment for processing water, waste, and air, and producing food. A short passageway led to a small room containing medical equipment.

Across the hall from the medical supply depot was a larger chamber stocked with the emergency cryotanks—drawered capsules very much like convalescence tubes filled with the syrupy pink chemicals necessary to put a person in stasis. A tiny oxygen-exchange plant fed into the cryotanks and could easily be converted to replenish a depleted atmosphere. A heavily padded operating table filled the center of the room, and a thick door could seal the chamber off from the rest of the ship in an emergency.

Abriara inspected the room. "This will do." She began to shove me out into the hall and I realized she was going to leave me.

I tried to grab her hand and shouted, "Wait! What if someone comes?"

She gripped my throat, put one foot behind me, and

tripped me. I fell backward and smacked the floor. She locked herself in with the equipment.

I sat at her doorstep and listened to the chanting from all around the ship and waited. The lighted ceiling panels were on at a neutral brightness, and the walls of the room appeared as if they'd been scrubbed spotless. But they hadn't been scrubbed. They'd been cleaned when the module was sterilized. Even the black metal of the hatch above me looked as if it had been molded only hours before.

Somewhere beyond that door lay Tamara. She'd be in danger during this riot. If anyone knew of her past, they'd kill her. An old emotion tugged at me. I longed to seek her out, to protect her. I smiled at myself and considered, *Perhaps I'm not as dead inside as I've imagined.*

It struck me that Abriara and I were the only living things on this module. The air didn't carry even a single bacteria. Never had I been in an environment so sterile. Though noise seeped in from distant parts of the ship, everything was still nearby. It was like being in a wooded glen at evening when the cicadas have been singing and they suddenly become quiet. The air becomes filled with what seems an unnatural stillness, and you keep waiting to hear something nearby. The air becomes charged with a sense of expectation.

There was a soft rustling from below, then Sakura, down in his narrow tunnel, began singing *"Motoki Sha Ka."* His voice was distant, harsh, and slurred, and I knew he must have been severely injured when Abriara pushed him, yet there was a hopeful tone to his song. Was it a prayer? I wondered. Was he praying to his corporation? There was a great roar from module A, an explosion of shouting—and the men in module C answered with a shout of their own. Sakura stopped singing, apparently in an attempt to better hear what was going on. The men below began chanting and stamping their feet again, but above me the stamping stopped and the shouts turned to wails. People were dying up there.

I was bewildered by Abriara's actions. When humans

become terrified, they seek help from others. But Abriara was reacting differently: she was extending her body space, trying to put distance between herself and others. She was terrified even of me. I did not know how to fight that terror, and I myself was afraid. I wanted to get near her, be in the same room with her behind that nice safe door. I remembered Felicia, the way she had comforted others before she died, and I began talking to Abriara, saying, "The air here smells so clean! It is like being in the mountains in Mexico when a cool rain would come in from the ocean, no? I remember such days from when I was a student—sitting on my porch after a cool rain. We never got such cool rains in Panamá. It was always muggy after a rain. I imagine you got such cool rains in Chile, in the mountains, no?"

But Abriara did not answer. It was as if she had gone into that room and become deaf. So I talked on and on, taking some comfort in my own voice.

Comlink tones sounded in my head. I thumbed the subdural switch beneath my ear.

Perfecto said, "Are you all right, Angelo?" His voice sounded very distant, drowned by background noise.

"Sí, I'm fine. I'm lonely up here. Abriara has locked herself in a room."

"I wish I could keep you company," he said, sounding relieved to hear my voice.

"It would be good," I said. "Are you all right?"

"Oh, we are fine. Some muchachos down on the fourth floor broke through the lines and came up to visit us—García and some friends. They had a hard time getting here. They're pretty beat up. There's some bad fighting going on down there. I would not want to be down there." There was a long pause.

Intuitively I knew Miguel had come up the ladder to protect me. It seemed a stupid gesture. A vivid picture came to mind: Miguel sitting at my feet, petting my hand, while we drank in my room. With his sweaty bald head and pale blue eyes he was so ugly I found the memory mildly revolting. I tried to think of something to say, some words to comfort Miguel. I said, "Tell Miguel

I am safe, like a child in its mother's arms," and realized these words would be of greater comfort than any.

"*Sí*," Perfecto said.

I heard a scraping noise above me and looked up. The air lock began to slide open.

I realized that I was weaponless and that no matter who was coming down the ladder, I didn't want to be found. I leaped through the nearest doorway—into the water purification plant—and hid in a corner. Perfecto began saying something on comlink, and I thumbed the subdural switch beneath my ear, cutting him off.

I tried to still my breathing and scanned the room for a weapon. There was a cabinet nearby, and I opened it and found many tools. One instrument like a heavy wrench was as long as my arm. I carefully lifted it from its pouch.

I heard the rustle of cloth and the clang of metal as someone climbed down the ladder. Only a cyborg with metal legs would make that clanging. He breathed in great gasps.

When he reached the bottom of the ladder, the door above him hummed closed. He snuffled and took a few slow steps, looking through doorways, too cautious to search the rooms. After a moment the door to the air lock below us began to open.

Distantly the voice of Sakura came up from the air lock, "Who's there?"

"A friend," a deep gravelly voice whispered. With a shock I recognized that voice. It was Juan Carlos, the man with the silver face, the man I suspected was the Alliance assassin. He could have had only one reason for trying to get from module A to module C.

He was searching for me.

For weeks I'd practiced stabbing him in my mind. I wished to God that Abriara had left me my good knife. I'd have been better off practicing how to fight with giant wrenches.

I hefted the wrench and dodged around the corner and through the doorway as silently as possible. Juan Carlos was dressed in the silver and red kimono of a sergeant, wearing black metal legs, and he stooped over the air lock looking down at Sakura. His right hand held a *wakizashi*, a short samurai sword, and his left hand was a bloody mess. He carried a transmitter in his left palm, and he'd relieved the transmitter's owner of a finger.

I was certain I'd made no noise, but he must have had an upgraded auditory system, for he whirled as if I'd been wearing bells around my neck.

"Osic!" he shouted, slicing the air with his sword, his voice angry even though his metal face held the perpetual smile of Buddha in repose, the single green gem between his eyes. Arish had addressed me with that same tone of hate, and I wondered why.

I swung the wrench down on his right shoulder. Juan Carlos crumpled under the blow and I felt a jolt of pain in my belly.

I looked down. The onyx handle of the *wakizashi* stuck through my belly just below the rib cage. He'd inserted the sword so swiftly I hadn't even seen it coming.

I wondered, *How many men have died looking at sword handles?* It didn't seem to matter. I'd died so many times in the simulators. I dropped the wrench and examined my wound. It would be a mistake to pull the blade out—it would cause me to bleed faster.

Juan Carlos groaned. I hadn't killed him. He was curled in a ball on the floor, shaking his head, struggling to regain consciousness. I kicked him in the jaw, stunning him, then untied his *obi*, his thin belt, from around his kimono. I wanted to question him, learn why he hated me, but the pain in my belly was growing, and I wasn't sure I'd live long enough. I wrapped the *obi* around his neck, flipped him to his back, and began strangling him.

It takes a long time to strangle a man. Too often a strangler chokes someone a few moments and thinks he's completed his job just because his victim goes limp, but in reality a man must be deprived of oxygen for several minutes before he'll die. I knew this, and vowed to finish Juan Carlos.

I gripped the *obi* at two ends and pulled. Juan Carlos was unconscious, but as he began to strangle he awoke and kicked with his metal legs and flailed his arms. I was afraid of his legs, not knowing how powerful they might be, and edged away. I readjusted my position and put a knee in his back, forcing his lungs to stay empty, and at the same time positioned myself so he couldn't kick or grab me.

He flailed about. His muscles convulsed and he tried to get his knees under him and rise. I yanked one leg straight and he dropped to the floor and didn't try to repeat the tactic.

He reached behind his neck and pinched my right wrist, digging his thumbnail into my flesh. I continued strangling him. My arms became tired, and I realized I needed to readjust my grip. I was afraid that if I let go for even a second he would get a breath of air, and I'd have to begin all over. I took one end of the *obi* in my teeth and maintained pressure by pulling with my teeth, then readjusted my grip on my left hand.

I tried the same procedure with my right hand, but I must have slackened for a moment, for Juan Carlos became frenzied. He let go of my right wrist and tried to grab the *obi*.

I pulled tighter and he caught hold of my knee and tried to yank me down. The effort of the struggle depleted the oxygen from his lungs, and he went limp.

My God, I realized, *This will work. I can really strangle him!* My teeth began chattering. Beads of sweat dripped from my armpits and ran down my arms. Sweat dripped from the back of my hands, drenching the *obi*. I felt myself losing my grip on it. It began to slip. I became unreasonably frightened and shouted, "Abriara, come help me! Quick! Come help me!"

I put both knees on Juan Carlos's back and wrapped the ends of the *obi* around my hands and pulled tighter and screamed for Abriara. I suddenly realized I didn't know how long I'd been strangling him. He'd gone limp, but that was no guarantee he wouldn't regain consciousness if I let go. I realized that this is what other stranglers must go through—they become excited and lose track of time and let go too soon, so I held on and began counting the seconds, vowing to myself that I wouldn't release my stranglehold until three minutes

had passed. One . . . two . . . three . . . four . . .
five . . .

My stomach ached where the sword had punched
through. I felt its point sticking through my back. I
thought I should quit and get some medical attention.
The transmitter to open the air lock lay on the floor two
meters away. I screamed for Abriara, begging her to
come help. I watched her door. She didn't open it. I kept
strangling Juan Carlos.

Juan Carlos began kicking again and flailing his arms
again, and I thought, *The son of a whore was faking, just
pretending to be dead!* and became quite enraged and
jerked at the *obi*, trying to snap his neck. Juan Carlos
clawed at the floor and went limp. I held on to the *obi*.

I looked back at the door, "Abriara, I have been
stabbed," I explained. "I do not feel well! I feel kind of
dizzy! Come help me, you whore!" Pinpoints of light
began to flash behind my eyes.

"Flaco!" I yelled, "Flaco, come help me!"

Juan Carlos remained limp. I readjusted my grip again
and pulled tighter. The muscles in his back began
bunching and jumping in little spasms. I held my grip
until the spasms passed, then wiped the sweat from my
brow.

I felt very tired, and quit strangling him, and he didn't
move. My head ached, and the tiny pinpoints of light
behind my eyes dazzled me. Bile had risen into my
throat. I carefully turned Juan Carlos onto his back and
watched his chest, to see if he'd breathe. His chest didn't
rise or fall. His fingers twitched in minor spasms, and I
took his wrist and felt for a pulse. I felt nothing.

I bent my head to his chest and listened for a
heartbeat. My own heart pounded in my ears, and I
panted so badly that with the distant stamping of feet
and the chanting and the screams I couldn't hear if Juan
Carlos's heart beat.

"Listen, listen, become fluent in the gentle language
of the heart." Tamara's words came to mind. I was sure
this was not what she'd had in mind. My face was turned
toward Juan Carlos's feet, and as I watched, his muscles
relaxed. His kimono was pulled up so I could see his

underwear, and urine began yellowing his crotch as his bladder emptied.

I lurched forward and vomited, and blood was mixed in the vomit. The floor rose to greet me.

Someone flipped me on my back. I heard distant pounding and voices chanting. A strange man with a blotched face whispered, "He looks almost finished."

Behind him a man said, "Take his sword, he won't miss it!" I saw that the air lock door above me was open. Someone else had broken through.

The man above me said, "Forgive me, señor," and pulled the sword from my belly. He wiped the bloody blade on my kimono, then held the sword up to the light, inspecting it.

I grunted and everything went black.

I woke to the smell of fear. I felt rough hands on my body. Someone furtively searched the pockets inside my kimono. I opened one eye. A dark-skinned woman turned her face away and slinked up the ladder. I thought I smelled smoke. The lights were dim.

Whispering.

A foot caught me in the ribs, startling me awake. I dimly distinguished the shape of a man. "Answer me! Answer me!" he shouted. I opened my eyes wider, and a horrible face bent near me, a face with a slash that ran from one eye, across the nose, to the mouth. Lucío kicked me and turned away. There were many men behind him, some holding laser rifles. *Where did they obtain rifles?* I wondered. "Retrieve some medical supplies from that room. Plug the holes in the fucker and put some blood into him. I want him to know . . ."

A shout arose from many voices, distant, like the surf within a seashell. The air held the scent of smoke and the tang of ozone. *The riot has begun on module C,* I reasoned, and I was comforted. Now the samurai would turn the ship around and we'd go home.

A woman shrieked nearby—a high thin sound, almost a moan or the mewing of a kitten.

I opened my eyes and lolled my head to the side. The door to Abriara's room was open. Smoke roiled off the door, and it hung askew. In places it glowed the pale orange of molten ore. Someone had cut open her door with a laser, I realized. The woman shrieked again, and I wondered if it were Abriara even though she'd never uttered a sound so plaintive, even though I couldn't imagine her uttering a cry like that.

I couldn't see into her room. The smoke hazed the air and my eyes wouldn't focus. I rolled to my belly and began crawling forward, finding more strength than I knew I possessed. Two bodies sprawled in front of her door. I crawled to them and wondered how they'd come to be there.

I looked up into the chamber. Several men were gathered around the operating table. Two more lay dead at its base. Blue wisps of smoke roiled near the ceiling above them. I heard grunts. One man appeared to be struggling on the operating table, and the others grappled with him, holding him down. He tilted his head up and back. Overhead lights shined on his face. It was Lucío with his horrible scar, grinning in ecstasy.

The mewing repeated, a soft, throat-wrenching cry. Arms shifted, and I saw that Lucío wasn't struggling on the table at all. He'd crawled atop another person and was grinding his hips against that person—his smile the smile of orgasm.

Abriara moaned and writhed beneath him. He laughed and said, "Do that again."

One of the men holding her shifted, and I saw her face—two silver eyes surrounded by a bloody, disfigured pulp, a clump of hair ripped from her forehead. I jumped to my feet, intending to race to her, to rescue her. But I'd lost too much blood and with the sudden rise my head spun wildly and I fainted.

Abriara screamed again, and I looked up and saw another man on her—Daniel, one of Lucío's old compadres—taking his turn. He raised a fist and smacked Abriara.

I struggled to my knees and for several seconds was able to remain in that position. I felt slime on my belly—a resin bandage, still wet. Down below us someone screamed; the fighting and riot continued on C module.

One of Lucío's men aimed a laser rifle at me. "That old man is awake! Should I deal with him?"

Lucío walked out from behind his men at the far end of the table. He smiled at me and said, "No—but keep your gun on him. I promised him I would kill him and fuck his woman. I wanted him to see that I am a man of my word. But now that I think of it, in a few minutes I want to fuck him, too."

I tried to stay on my knees while I scanned the floor for a weapon. One of Abriara's victims two meters away had bled profusely. My crystal knife was embedded between his eyes. I watched the barrel of my guard's rifle. I vowed, *When I regain strength, I'll grab that knife and use it.* I couldn't fight all Lucío's men, but I might be able to get Lucío.

Suddenly the floor wrenched beneath me and I flipped over as if slapped by the hand of God. Half the cryotanks in the room spilled open, and their pink fluids crashed to the floor, drenching me in freezing liquid. I rolled over and over as something dragged me toward the wall. I threw myself flat, but couldn't regain my balance, was only able to stop rolling. The shouting of the rioters below suddenly quieted as others were tossed around.

A man at the table shouted, "The ship, she is moving." The table was bolted to the floor, and Lucío's men clung to it, their eyes wide as they peered around.

My guard had also slipped to the floor, but he righted himself and aimed his rifle at me.

The ship had indeed begun to spin, and I imagined it whirling wildly out of control. The constant acceleration of the ship provided our artificial gravity, but if we continued to spin it would add a second force—one that could crush us against the walls as if we were caught in a giant centrifuge.

As if to be true to my deepest fears, the spin gained momentum, and the great invisible hand dragged me past the operating table toward the wall. Friction could no longer hold me to the floor.

A man shouted, "What's happening?" and my guard shouted, "Sergeant, should I fry this one?" Lucío appeared confused.

Lucío shouted to my guard, "Not yet!" I tried to scrabble forward, but was too weak and dizzy. I ended up pinned against a wall, the handle of a cryotank jabbing into my back. The dead bodies—including the one with the knife imbedded in its skull—glided across the slippery floor like marionettes pulled by a string. They landed nearby. On the table Daniel thrust himself into Abriara all the harder, as if to make sure raping her would be his final act.

My guard watched in indecision as I pulled the crystal knife from the dead man's skull and threw it at Daniel. It whizzed past his head, bounced to the floor, and skittered back, landing within arm's reach. And I realized something important—if we'd been at the center of the ship, when the force pushed us to the outside we'd each have flown out directly away from the ship's center. But since we were all roughly the same distance from the center, the force that pushed us against the wall would pin us all to the same side of the room.

The ship spun faster. My guard inched forward and I lunged for the knife.

Suddenly, one man at the table could hold on no longer and he flipped away, landing a scant three meters from me. Then nearly everyone at the operating table rolled off and tumbled on top of their compadres until the seven of them and Abriara became a tangle of flesh.

I was close enough to smell the sex and blood on them, and I tried to inch toward them but I was held as if spiked in place. They moaned and panted and tried to untangle themselves with little success. And the ship whirled faster.

I lay exhausted on the floor, pinned to the corner, and

gasped for breath and some of the men near me moaned. I couldn't tell how much force was being applied—five gravities, eight, ten? Did I suddenly weigh five hundred kilos, or a thousand? I couldn't tell.

My jaw burst open under the increasing pressure, and I didn't have the strength to close it. My skin felt heavy and dragged at my face. I realized this is what it would feel like to be under water, hundreds of meters down. My skin felt as it might tear off and I'd burst from the pressure, like a grape bursting from ripeness. The blood pumped in my ears like the pounding of hammers, and my saliva felt too thick to swallow.

And the ship twisted beneath us. I was suffocating. A great invisible blanket had been laid over me, and was suffocating me. My kimono felt as if it weighed kilos, and I worried that my ribs might snap under the weight of the garment. I heard a crackling noise, and blood began pulsing from my nose. I couldn't move my hand to wipe it away. The wound in my belly reopened.

And the ship spun faster. Something snapped in my head. I heard a thrumming, like the beating of a fibrillating heart, and felt myself being carried forward. *I'm riding the back of a bull*, I realized. *I'm riding the back of a bull, and I don't know where it is carrying me*. I opened my eyes and a landscape of blue fog and blue shadows seemed to move below me. I hovered near the ground. The hooves of the bull pounded the mist. Moving forward. A freezing wind tore at my hair and it became night. Tamara had never breathed a darkness so black at me, in this place where wind was ice.

PART THREE: BAKER

CHAPTER

12

I felt as if I eeled up through dark cold water and struggled free into light. I was chilled to the bone, and I stared, eyes unfocused, for several moments.

I recognized a room I'd glimpsed often before—a hundred thin cots reeking of sweat, patients dressed in white spilled upon them. A warehouse for damaged people. Some patients were awake and jabbering. I couldn't understand them. I couldn't think. My brain felt rubbery like the foot of a snail, but otherwise a great sense of well-being suffused me—not the easy euphoria of health, but rather a drugged numbness.

A patient with vacant eyes bumped into my cot, then reeled away. I wanted to follow him, make sure he wasn't hurt. I got up and staggered after him, bumping into cots myself, moving past carts full of food till I found myself standing in a rest room.

In the rest room on the wall just inside the door was a giant strip of weathered mirror-paper. One edge had come unglued so that it rolled halfway down.

Here, at last, was something I could fix. I spread the mirror paper back into place and looked at my image for a long time. The face of a young man, almost a stranger, peered back at me. Myself as I'd appeared perhaps at age 27 or 28 except that my hair had grown long past my shoulders and turned silver-white, the color of thistle down.

My eyes and face were young and dead. I'd seen faces like that in the feria—faces of beaten peasants fleeing Chile, Ecuador, Peru, Colombia. *The face of a refu-*

305

giado, I thought. *The face of the living dead*. It did not seem to matter. Life is such a fragile thing and people cling to it so hard with so little effect. Physical death is unavoidable, yet the soul dies easier than the body. I tried moving that wooden face into a smile, but it did not come out as a smile of joy. My lips moved in mere mimicry of a smile. I tried a frown. An expression of sadness. Mimicry of sadness. There was nothing left to express—all expressions were the same. What matters the expression? It did not matter. Wrinkled flesh writhing upon a skull. What matters the expression?

Someone opened a door beside me, then shouted, "I found him!" A medic in a white uniform. He took my arm and tried to guide me back out the door the way I'd come. But I just continued gazing in the mirror.

"So, you've noticed!" The man said. "Some of your friends were packing your things after the first big riot and found a rejuvenation packet. We thought that since you had to spend some time in the cryotanks, you might as well use it wisely. Señor Nuñez, our morphogenic pharmacologist, was kind enough to care for you."

I nodded. My mind was not so sluggish that I couldn't follow him. For a rejuvenation to be effective a client must spend months in cryogenic suspension while the pharmacologist restores the body—repairing cells damaged by radiation, detoxifying and deoxidating the neural and muscular tissues, fine-tuning the cellular specificity of glandular organs to make sure they secrete the right proteins, then ultimately replacing those organs most heavily damaged with fresh clones. However, few clients are willing to remain in suspension for the optimum length of the operation. They're always concerned that financial investments will sour or their spouses will step out on them. They prefer to rush the process and end up cheating themselves of a few extra years.

I pointed to the white hair, a grotesque reminder of age on a young man's body.

"Why the white hair?" the medic asked. "I don't know. It has nothing to do with the quality of the rejuvenation. Perhaps you suffered some overwhelming shock?"

I recalled where Juan Carlos had stabbed me, and recollected the sensation of the sword entering my flesh—sharp, heavy, cool, foreign. I reached into my kimono and probed the wound. No bandage covered my ribs, and my fingers slid over bare skin under my kimono till I touched a thick scar below my sternum where one would make an incision to remove a gall bladder.

I realized my wounds must have been so severe the medics opted to keep me in a cryotank till I'd healed. So they'd made me young again while they were at it.

The medic firmly took my arm, led me back to bed. "Stay here," he said. "You're still too sedated to be walking. We off-load to Baker in a few hours. You'll feel better then."

I stayed in bed for a long time before I finally realized the significance of those words, "off-load to Baker." The news stunned me, punched me in the belly like a fist. I'd been asleep over two years! No illness would have required cryogenic suspension for two years. Two years aboard ship meant twenty Earth years had passed. I felt I'd been robbed of something immensely important and began taking mental inventory, trying to imagine what I'd lost.

Some men were talking at nearby bunks. One explained, "In that big riot the ship spun, remember? The samurai spun the ship and squeezed the air from us. That's what happened. Then they froze all the rabble-rousers . . ." The speaker, a wiry Latin American, wore the midnight-blue kimono of a samurai.

I got up again and stumbled past the beds. Neither the medics nor Latin Americans dressed as samurai seemed to notice when I walked out the door.

He'd said they froze the "rabble-rousers." I'd not been relegated to the cryotanks to be healed, but to be imprisoned. By sheer will I sought escape. I followed a hall that circumscribed the ship and soon found myself standing at the foot of a ladder.

I climbed several rungs and got tired and rested. I wasn't thinking straight, and believed if I could keep climbing, I'd escape into the sky. I continued up,

becoming lighter and lighter as I climbed, till I reached
a spot where I weighed nothing at all.

I was at the central tube that ran the length of the
ship, at an intersection where the old ladder still stuck
up through a hole in the floor like a ladder leading into
a sewer. Only now the sewer holes no longer led down.
To my right was the place where Perfecto and I had
dropped the corpse down to the infirmary. Because the
ship was in orbit, the pull of acceleration no longer
provided our artificial gravity. Instead the ship slowly
rotated along its axis to feign gravity, and this corridor—
this sewer hole—was at the axis. All the rooms below
had been reoriented to adjust for the new direction of
what I perceived as *down*.

I grabbed the old ladder and gently pulled myself
along the central corridor, floating past sewer hole after
sewer hole, alternating bands of darkness and light, free
of gravity. The mock silk of my white kimono fluttered
around my hips and at my wrist. My silver hair whipped
my ears as I drifted through the corridor like a spectre.
Air friction slowed me slightly, but only the tiniest
nudge with my fingertips allowed me to move forward at
a good pace. It was very much like gliding through deep
water after a dive, only freer, less restrictive. I did a tuck
and banked off the air lock at the bottom of the ship and
floated back up toward level one, guiding myself as
needed.

I made it a game, exercising my concentration, and
considered: for ten years I'd been saving for a rejuvenation. And now I was an old healer reborn as a murderer.
It was a good cosmic joke, but I wasn't inclined to laugh.
After all my years of hungering for youth I no longer
wanted it.

The air in this place hung so perfectly still that when
I moved I heard my robes shiver as distinctly as if it were
the tap of a hammer against stone.

I am a ghost, I thought. I am a ghost. And in the still
darkness behind me I felt another icy presence—Flaco
fluttering at my heel. A chill shook me, and the hair
prickled on the back of my neck. I did not try to flee him.
I half hoped he'd catch me. I felt like a woman who

experiences an overwhelming desire to cry. Only I had an overwhelming ache for a release more pure than tears—I ached for my own destruction.

For a long hour I wrestled despair. I felt that I'd failed Abriara. I'd watched her rape and been absolutely powerless to stop it. Perhaps ever since my mother was raped and murdered, my greatest fear has been that I'd someday be placed in a position where men who had no conscience would be purposely destroying others, and I'd be powerless to stop it. Men without conscience terrify me far more than beasts, for they emotionally brutalize their victims, wringing every ounce of pain they can. And I'd been unable to stop them.

I knew Abriara's rapists. I knew I must harden myself so I could kill them. I must become a man of no conscience. And the thought repulsed me. Waves of guilt and despair washed over me and I opened myself to them. When I was a child my mother had often told me, "Guilt is good. Guilt is your body's way of telling you that you've been acting like an animal," and I believed her. To open myself to that guilt, to let it destroy me if necessary, seemed the only way to prove to myself that I wasn't like Lucío, that I was still human.

I was floating through the dark tunnel when suddenly the air locks opened above me and a hundred other ghosts in white began flitting along the ladder toward me—patients from the cryotanks heading down to the base of the ship. I maneuvered from their path, down a side corridor that radiated away, and grabbed a ladder. In front of me the tunnel was dark, yet lights washed up from the corridor below, illuminating me with a soft back light. Several people passed and I looked up into the eyes of a chimera with thick hair like Perfecto's, small even teeth and a grimace like the smile of a porpoise. His eyes were dilated and his jaw hung slack. He was bonding to me.

Both times when men had bonded to me before, I realized, I'd been in this same position, standing in a darkened room with light shining behind. Perfecto bonded to me at Sol Station while I stood in a darkened hallway reading from the light of the computer terminal;

Miguel bonded while I walked through the door of a lighted hallway into a darkened room. The chimeras' genetic memory must have been a mere figure—a mental image of a man with a certain build, a certain stance, backlighted so his white hair seemed radiant. I felt like a mere icon—like the papier-mâché saints people parade through streets on holy days. I couldn't have set myself in a better strategic location if I'd wanted a chimera to bond to me.

A minute later a second chimera floated by and dropped his jaw, then a third.

When they'd passed I had three new friends for life. I followed after them and we glided down to the air lock at level eight and formed a line. When seventy-five men had pressed their way into the air lock it closed off. We waited for it to open again, and when the last of us crammed in, the door closed and the air lock descended like an elevator. It opened at the shuttle bay.

Thirty guards armed with stun rifles and the space-blue armor of Alliance Marines were posted around the shuttle bay. Three destroyer-class security robots, black metal boxes with single turrets mounted on top, squatted at strategic locations. The marines had set up a retina scanner and sonic detecting equipment near the shuttle gate, and they quickly checked each mercenary for illegal cybernetic implants before allowing them into the shuttle. General Garzón, with his brilliant white hair, stood with an Alliance captain, a dark little man of obvious Arab descent, and they chatted amicably in Spanish.

I found myself becoming unaccountably nervous and my palms began to sweat. My mouth became dry. The armed guards, the entire setup, reminded me too much of my fiasco trying to sneak past customs at Sol Station.

A chimera who'd bonded to me only moments before, a nervous man with a wide mouth and a rough-skinned complexion, came and stood by me as our men began processing at the retina scanners. I'd seen him in the dining halls before and vaguely recalled his name: Filadelfo.

"Are you ready for this?" he asked as if speaking to an

old friend, barely turning his head toward me, watching the Alliance security team rather than me.

I didn't answer.

"No, you're not ready for this," Filadelfo said. "None of us are ready for this. I hear they've got some kind of prison camp set up for us down there. They want to keep us troublemakers in one spot." He said this as if it were a brag, as if it were secret knowledge he alone possessed. Perfecto had spoken to me in that same bragging fashion when we'd first met, and I felt sorry for him and all the chimeras who accidentally bonded to me then wasted their time trying to impress me.

"Some of us are banding together, you know. Joining hands. We're not going to fight for these idiots. Things have changed too much since we trained. The weapons we used in the simulators are forty years out of date, and I talked to a man who was put in the cryotanks only a few months ago and he said that when we got put in suspension after that second week our real training had not even begun—the samurai were taking it easy on us, letting that time be an 'adjustment' period!

"And now the Alliance has suddenly taken great interest in us. Look at all of these punks. Why do they need so many guards? They have three times the force they need to subdue us in these close quarters."

Filadelfo was right. There were too many guards here and they were too rigid in their stance, too tense. Thirty men had passed through the portal into the hovercraft, and I began to worry. We were greatly outnumbered. If there was trouble, we wouldn't be able to fight them. And even if we managed to fight them aboard ship and win, their orbital neutron cannons could blow us from the sky in seconds. They were all-powerful here in space.

When it came my turn to go through customs I was sweating profusely. I looked into the retina scanner and a man read off my name. A second man brushed the sonic probe over me and a screen on a computer terminal on the wall listed by cybernetic upgrades— prosthetic eyes, cranial jacks, comlink, nerve bypass, chemotoxin filters.

When he'd checked me he waved me through. I was about to step into the shuttle when four guards stepped forward and threw me on my back to the floor.

"You're under arrest!" a guard shouted, pointing a stunner barrel against the side of my nostril. At that distance the stun bag would have split my skull. The Alliance guards dispersed into the crowd, aiming rifles at my *compañeros*. The room became silent.

Garzón stepped forward, standing over me, and his amiable tone didn't falter as he addressed the Alliance captain, "What's the charge?"

The Alliance captain said, "Murder."

"Of whom?"

"Three persons in the city of Colón, Panamá, on Earth, and the murder of several persons aboard Sol Station, Sol star system."

"You received my radio message this morning regarding the unfortunate incidents at Sol Station, did you not?"

The captain blinked. "Yes."

"Then you've a copy of the signed confession from the man who blew the station, and you know Señor Osic is innocent of those charges, no?"

The captain said grudgingly, "Yes."

"And the persons in Panamá were murdered within Panamanian jurisdiction, so you can't detain Señor Osic unless you're granted extradition orders from the Board of Governors of Motoki Corporation on Baker. He *has* been granted Baker citizenship, you know. Have you sought extradition orders?"

The captain's jaw tightened and the little Arab's face began to darken with rage.

"So you understand extradition is denied," Garzón said patiently. "Osic is a citizen of Baker, within the air space of his own planet, and you've no legal right to detain him."

"Unless—my lawyers tell me—" the captain said, "he murdered Alliance military personnel. Then he'd be under my jurisdiction in any case."

Garzón smiled menacingly. "Are you willing to admit that Arish Hustanifad was an Alliance military agent? I'm sure people on Earth would be very eager to hear that!"

The captain gulped in surprise. Hustanifad would be listed as my victim, but the captain was acting on scant orders sent from Earth twenty years ago. He sensed something important was at stake here but had no idea how high the stakes were. He was out of his depth and knew it.

"I wasn't thinking of Hustanifad—I was thinking of Tamil Jafari, an Alliance Intelligence agent."

"But she's not dead," Garzón corrected. "She departed this ship last week, in the body of a Tamara Maria de la Garza. We notified your computer controller here of her identity at that time. It's all in the ship's records. In fact, you may question her yourself—Tamara, come here please."

An electric motor whined. A wheelchair rolled into view at the shuttle door; Tamara slumped like a half-empty potato sack in the chair. Her frail limbs hung limp and her mouth drooped open. Her eyes seemed to roll as she gazed around the room, but I saw intelligence in those eyes, understanding.

I recognized the paralysis that comes from severe brain damage. Tamara appeared more dead than alive—but it had been over two years! Even if she did have brain damage, her brain could have been reseeded with cloned cells, neural growth stimulator could have been applied. There was no reason for her to remain in such deteriorated condition!

An old impulse welled up in me, the desire to save her. Garzón went over to the wheelchair and patted Tamara's head as if she were some great pet dog.

The captain raised an eyebrow in surprise and nodded to the computer controller.

"We let her through, all right, sir," the computer controller said. "No one told us to detain her."

"And you verified her identity?"

"The body we verified through retina scan. The brain through genetic mapping."

"And you knew she was an Alliance Intelligence agent—under contractual obligations—and you didn't arrest her?"

"I'm a free agent—contracted by the job. I was free to leave Earth," Tamara said, sounding irritated.

I looked at her in surprise. With a body so deteriorated she obviously couldn't speak, but a thin blue wire ran from the cranial jack at the base of her skull down to the silver disk of a microspeaker pinned to her blouse. She was bypassing her vocal cords and speaking directly with nerve impulses, the way one would in a dream monitor.

"We couldn't detain her," the computer controller said.

The captain began chewing his lip. "If you hadn't been killed, why did you let everyone believe you were dead?" he asked Tamara.

"I wanted off Earth and didn't want anyone to know. For personal reasons."

The captain thought this over and waved at his guards. "Back, back, move those men back," he said, and the guards began pushing my compadres toward the far corner of the room, all except Garzón. Tamara's wheelchair rolled backward into the shuttle.

The captain spoke very softly and urgently to Garzón. "I have my orders on this! I'm to arrest this man. Take my advice and walk away! Don't push me!"

Garzón smiled and said, "Arrest? You have orders to *arrest* this man? What will you do, hold him in captivity for seven years till a relief comes, and then send him back to Earth for trial? Nooo . . . that's such a waste of money. If I know the Alliance, you're directed to arrange an accident. Let him suck vacuum. No?"

The captain blinked and looked guilty. Garzón had touched the truth. "No," Garzón continued. "I haven't seen your orders, but I know what they say. I also know you're not eager to carry them out. Such deeds catch up with one. If you obey them, you'll be under the thumbs of certain superiors all your life. No, you don't want to follow those orders."

The captain became more tense. Garzón was guessing correctly. "So here is what I'd do: I'd send a message to Earth informing them that Tamil Jafari is alive and well on Baker and you could find no legal reason to detain

Mr. Osic. Then I'd request clarification on what to do with Mr. Osic. That way when more explicit orders arrive in forty-five years someone else will be stuck with this outpost and we'll all be long gone."

The captain was one of those stubborn persons who fears his superiors—a real crowd pleaser. He shook his head and looked at the floor and considered his predicament and I could tell he wouldn't go for Garzón's plan. "But—" he began to say.

"But in the meantime," Garzón added, "Baker is a very dangerous planet. You know why we're here. Within a few weeks—one way or another—the government here on Baker will be globally consolidated and you'll be free to end this peacekeeping mission and fly home. But many people will get killed in the battle to come. Who knows? Maybe even Mr. Osic will be one of the unfortunates? And you can then send back a message to your superiors saying 'Mission accomplished' before you desert this dustball." Garzón's tone held promise, promise that I'd die in battle. The dark little captain nodded pensively, apparently relieved, then motioned to his troops. They stepped back and let me up.

Garzón looked at me, reached up and stroked my silver hair. I flinched involuntarily. He spoke to a samurai. "Put him in the back section of the shuttle. Security risk C."

I hurried toward the shuttle and a samurai followed just at my elbow. Tamara's wheelchair blocked the hallway and I looked at her dark eyes, her dark hair. She'd filled out a little and didn't appear so emaciated as before. Her hand had grown back perfectly. So much of her appearance was unchanged. Without moving a muscle she began backing the wheelchair down the hall, as if to let us pass.

The electric motor whirred softly. In her eyes was fear, a plea. "What has happened to you?" I asked.

The samurai tapped me on the elbow and spoke in Japanese; his translator spat, "No talking. You will speak to no one aboard this shuttle."

I looked in Tamara's eyes. She was afraid to speak in the open. The samurai led me past Tamara to the front of the ship, to a small room with plush chairs and a bar. Two men dressed like myself sat there under the eye of a samurai guard.

I sat down. The shuttle held perhaps three hundred passengers. Out the window I saw one of Baker's small moons—flat blue and pitted with ten thousand craters. A worthless little rock. The stars shining steadily were piercing. I was shaking and wanted to kill the Alliance captain and his superiors and I wanted to help Tamara in spite of the fact that I didn't know how.

Garzón himself entered our room a moment later. He patted me on the shoulder like an old friend. He was smoking a cigarette. "I'm sorry to put you up here, don Angelo. I hope you don't feel too uncomfortable, but you see—God, you look like old General Torres. I almost feel I should salute you! I'd prefer to keep you away from the chimeras."

"I understand," I said.

He gauged me with his eyes. "How many of them have bonded to you now?"

"Five," I said.

He looked relieved. "So few? We can spare five. We'll consider it repayment. I owe you a great deal for rescuing Tamara. Her information was invaluable in helping the resistance defeat Argentina."

He must have seen my surprise.

"Oh yes, we got the details several months ago. The last of the Nicita Socialists were wiped out of Latin America only two years after we left. And much of the credit goes to Tamara." He spoke as if he were praising an idiot child. "She's quite a talented lady. She's become—indispensable—to the future of my Intelligence organization."

Tamara seemed to have a gift for becoming indispensable. I remembered how Jafari had tried to imprison her in a brain bag. Garzón was doing the same; in fact, he'd succeeded where Jafari had failed. Tamara was sitting in a nice little prison—a body she couldn't manipulate. Oh, her speech was no longer impaired when she talked through her simulator. Garzón had obviously reseeded part of her brain with cloned neurons, had administered neural growth agents—but only to a portion of her brain, only to sections that controlled her higher functions. "Why do you keep her imprisoned?"

Garzón smiled at me, a tight-lipped little smile. "Because she's dangerous. Because I couldn't sleep if I knew she was mobile." There was genuine concern in his eyes. I couldn't imagine Tamara, thin little Tamara, causing such disquiet. "I know that keeping her like this looks bad. And a living body is such a messy thing. I've been toying with the idea of having a cymech made for her after this job with the Yabajin—something small, mobile, but without means of manipulating objects."

I must have raised an eyebrow. Tamara was terrified of cymechs to the point of paranoia. She'd never agree to be housed in one. I knew this on a gut level and realized Garzón wouldn't be deterred by her reticence. He really did fear her. He waited for me to speak, but I said nothing. I furiously considered methods to save her.

He sat next to me, snubbed his cigarette into the cushion of the seat in front of us. "I've been wanting to ask you, Señor Osic: during the riot you strangled a man and he stabbed you. Very curious. Flakes of your skin were found on his neck. Traces of his body oils were found on your clothing near the wound. Why did you kill him?"

"He was an Alliance assassin. I learned about him only slowly, over the weeks aboard ship. He accidentally tipped off his presence to me."

"Why didn't you speak to me about it? It would have been so much easier."

"I wanted to do him myself. To kill him myself."

Garzón looked off at the moon. "I see—a rugged individualist trying to set the universe right. You realize he's the second Alliance agent you've killed? Few men fare so well against them. You somehow make them appear . . . inept? I find it quite surprising. I think it's your disarming nature. You generate an aura of concern for others, of innate morality. No one would suspect you to be capable of violence. You have an interesting set of qualities. Have you ever considered putting these qualities to work for you, perhaps by going into intelligence work—as an assassin?"

I looked at him, surprised. "No."

He smiled charmingly. He was a man with much charisma and knew how to use it. I felt unaccountably grateful to him. He didn't need me, could have just let the Alliance have me. Yet he'd saved me out of sheer gratitude, and few qualities are so endearing as gratitude. I liked him in spite of the fact that he was holding Tamara prisoner, in spite of the fact that at some basic level I felt he was my enemy.

"Tamara has mentioned you often. She'd like to be able to work with you. When we're finished here, you and I should have a talk—terms of employment."

"No," I said by gut instinct.

"Think about it. A little more blood on your hands— who'd ever notice?"

I looked back out the window. It was best not to argue too strongly. I considered his offer. People like Arish, Juan Carlos—someone needed to kill them. Why not me? I thought of Lucío. A great wrath welled up in me. "Yes! I want more blood on my hands!" I growled with more ferocity than I'd have thought I could muster.

Garzón jerked away, then tightened his lips in a worried little smile, disconcerted. "Fine. But, take your time. I hope you'll excuse me, now. I have a great deal of pressing business to attend to."

I remained seated.

The last passengers boarded and the shuttle departed. From space Baker looked like a great clouded ruby shot through with bands of azurite and emerald—brilliant red ochre in the central deserts with water vapor over its small blue seas and single large ocean, small ice caps like those on Mars. Yet the entire planet was hazed silver, indistinct, like a blurred photo. A band of platinum formed a corona around the rim of the planet—caused by the sun reflecting off the wings of billions upon billions of opal kites. We dropped near the upper atmosphere and the planet's ocean, Aki Umi, took up most of our field of vision. We passed the terminus where day became night, buzzed over the western edge of the continent

Kani, the crab, in twilight. Below us the brilliant white lights of Hotoke no Za, the Yabajin capital, shone as if a single star had fallen on that vast dark planet and taken fire.

For a moment there was a tinkling noise, like the sound of urine squirting into a toilet bowl. Several men jumped from their seats yelling, "We're hit!" then our craft suddenly lurched and accelerated up away from Baker and everyone was frantic.

A Japanese announced over the speakers, "Some of you realize the Yabajin have fired on us with neutron cannons. However this was foreseen, and we remain high above the danger zone. Our superior shielding held. Even now we file protest of this ruthless, unprovoked attack with the Alliance ambassador!"

I snorted in disgust. Truly we hadn't attacked the Yabajin—yet. But if I were them, I'd fire upon our shuttles, too.

The samurai inched forward. "No talking. No noise," he said, referring to the snort I'd made.

We passed Hotoke no Za and continued over the dark planet. Garzón took a microphone and explained the situation on Baker: we'd lost 4100 mercenaries during our trip from Earth—3012 to the plague, 129 in fights during the riot, and 644 crushed when the samurai spun our ship. The rest died in the simulators, were murdered, or died from natural causes. "We estimate the Yabajin defenders at 50,000 or more. Motoki will only be able to muster 39,000 samurai. And though the numbers look bad for an offensive engagement, our chimeras are better fighters than Motoki bargained for. Because of our prowess in battle and recent changes in equipment design, computer projections look pretty good. We can win this war—but we'd lose sixty-two percent of our men. This is unacceptable! Right now," Garzón said, "I'm demanding that Motoki rectify this violation of our contract by allowing us one month to produce new weapons and practice further. In addition, 467 of you were put in the cryotanks after the riot. Frankly, you'd be almost worthless to us in a real fight because of your inadequate training. I'd leave you aboard ship until this is over, but the owners of the *Chaeron* need to re-outfit the ship for its return to Earth. Now, the locals are afraid of us and there is some resistance to the plan, but I'm going to demand that you men be left in Kimai no Ji until this war is over! All right?"

His little speech brought cheers from the men. But his promises sounded hollow.

For two hours there was no more sign of civilization on the planet. No lights. Though Baker was smaller than Earth, its emptiness made it seem enormous.

My thoughts kept returning to Tamara in the room behind me. I'd invested so much to free her from Jafari that her captivity by Garzón distressed me. I'd never saved her at all—only led her to a new prison cell. And perhaps the most frustrating thing was that I still had no idea why she was imprisoned. Garzón wasn't wringing useful information from her. Any intelligence secrets she knew were well out of date. Yet her mind was of inestimable value to Garzón, as it had been to Jafari. I couldn't smuggle her off Baker. And we couldn't hide on Baker. To even consider trying to save her was a waste of time when my own future hung so precariously in the balance.

We left Baker's shadow and returned to daylight. We passed great red deserts and the dark ultraviolet of Baker's native plants became more frequent, then the shuttle plummeted toward the planet, bouncing through thermals. The heat shielding glowed white hot, and we slowed and soared at a low angle. At perhaps fifteen kilometers we descended into a flock of red opal kites spanning thousands of meters. I imagined we'd crash, but though the kites were huge, each was only a thin membranous waffle the color of cinnamon. The flock undulated as it rode the top of a thermal, holding to the same elevation, almost wing tip to wing tip, so that when we sunk beneath them it was as if we dropped below bubbles riding on top of the water and we were sea creatures viewing them from beneath. These kites truly resembled giant mantas, and I finally realized that opal kites were as different from opal birds as hawks are from butterflies. Below us several flocks of kites each held to different thermal layers. Cottony clouds hid all but the tops of a few mountains.

We cruised for several minutes. The ship's captain announced that we were coming in upon Kimai no Ji, Motoki's capital, then we descended through clouds toward a rugged coastline among mountains topped with green-gray fir and pine. I inched forward, eager to see this place we'd be fighting for, and for a long time saw nothing but rolling green hills and mist. Then I spotted a low-flying yellow zeppelin traveling from Motoki's small farming or mining settlements in the south, per-haps Shukaku or Tsumetai Oka. The zeppelin was head-ing for a hamlet near the sea surrounded by a few fields and a large black stone wall. Farther out was the forest; and the forest, the wall, and the fields all held the native flora and fauna at bay. I imagined the Motoki outpost as an island of normality in a sea of strangeness. The Japanese have always been an island people. The city was small, perhaps 40,000 people, a tiny collection of buildings, two blue crystal domes. My little city of Gatún back in Panamá was larger.

Then it struck me how bizarre this enterprise was: here was a large planet, one that because of its small seas had more total land surface than Earth, yet two cities the size of Gatún, Panamá, were fighting a genocidal war to see who won empty spaces neither of them could use!

The shuttle swooped in for its descent. The houses were of dark wood beams with white rice-paper walls as thin and translucent as moth wings. On every street, in every yard, the landscape was perfectly ordered, as if the city were a giant garden only casually inhabited by humans. Bushes were neatly trimmed and the black trunks of the pink blossoming plums were gnarled into strange surrealistic patterns as if they'd been sculpted. I'd expected some signs of age—dilapidated buildings, crumbling barns. But the Japanese hadn't contrived any instant slums on Baker. Nor was there a sign of extrav-agance. No glittering lights, no mansions of crystal. The entire city displayed a face of practiced austerity. We slowed and hit the runway and the shuttle shuddered as we skidded to a halt.

From the shuttleport terminal issued a dozen large trucks. Fifty samurai wearing black armor hustled alongside the trucks and lined up around the shuttle door. The door popped open and our men began filing down the steps. A sweet husky alien aroma entered the ship, like the smell of sugar cane drying in the sun. The smell of Baker.

We exited and found the trucks were full of clothing— shoes and loose pants, heavy kimonos and jackets. We were given plastic bags with welcoming kits—combs, bars of soap, toothpaste, maps of the planet, lists of rules. Those of us who'd been sitting in the "security risk" section of the shuttle each had a small monitor taped to our wrists, like those felons wear while on parole so the police can track them. It showed a map of the city and told us to reach a certain building before 5:00 P.M. The ocean roared nearby and a sea wind blew over the airfield, licking up dust. Hornets seemed to be everywhere—buzzing our heads, smelling the hair on the backs of our arms.

The samurai had us form a line, and led us away from the airfield. My legs felt as if they'd suddenly become two centimeters too short—each step carried me slightly higher in the air than I wanted to go. I'd been subjected to the heavy gravity of the ship for two weeks and the cryotechs had kept my muscles well-tuned, for I bounced when I walked. We walked single-file through an edge of town, along a road that bordered a low fence of bamboo, past house after house. The plums were throwing their blossoms, forming a carpet for our feet. All the doors and windows in the houses were closed. We passed through a business district where colored kites shaped like carp hung from lamp poles, and a small Japanese boy came running up toward us from a side street. He nearly bumped into the man in front of me, then stopped and looked up at us and shrieked, *"Tengu!"*

I smiled at him and he backed away in horror. The child's eyes were slanted at a remarkable angle, the epicanthic folds enhanced until his eyes were mere slits.

The man behind me laughed. "I guess he's never seen anyone handsomer than the Japanese," and I laughed

and wondered how it would be for a child who'd never
seen a man of another race. Could he recognize us as
human?

A samurai down the line shouted, "No talking!" and in
silence we trudged up the road and into a large building,
a circular stadium.

Inside hundreds of pictures of Regional Company
President Motoki Tomeo stretched from wall to wall, and
a large stage like those in kabuki theaters filled the far
end of the building. When we were seated, speakers
blared out *"Motoki Sha Ka"* and the samurai led us in the
company anthem, then a giant holograph of a twenty-
meter-tall President Motoki appeared on stage. Like the
child, his eyes were outrageously slanted—more Japanese than the Japanese had ever been. He ceremoni-
ously welcomed us to Baker and thanked us for coming
to help rid the land of the "machines of the Yabajin."
When he was done, twenty young girls shuffled on stage
and gracefully danced with fans and umbrellas while an
old woman sang to the accompaniment of a koto. The
dancers came forward and with both hands offered each
of us a plate that held a tiny bottle of sake, a chrysanthemum, and a bowl of cooked rice. Then we were
escorted from the building by the samurai.

The sun was setting and with the gray overcast skies
there was no beautiful sunset, only a grim gradual
dimming of the light. The rice-paper walls of the homes
glowed from inside like giant paper lanterns. We
marched a kilometer from town and came to a large
compound in a small valley resting between the arms of
a pine-covered hill. Hundreds of Latin Americans
dressed in the faded green battle armor of Motoki
soldiers wandered about the hill, exercised, and wrestled. At the foot of the valley, chanting issued from a
large wooden structure that could have been an old
barn—the thunderous shout of "Let's go home! Let's go
home! Let's go home!"

The samurai marched my compadres up to the barn,
but my wristband began beeping and warned me to head
for another section of camp. The map on my wristband

showed the hut I was supposed to sleep in. I headed toward it. From town came the deep gong of a temple bell, and behind me, my three hundred *compañeros* raised their voices in the chant, "Let's go home!"

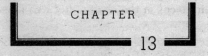

CHAPTER

13

The hut I entered was so smoky it could have been a bar. Five Latin Americans in the blue of samurai played guitars and sang while a sixth blew furiously on a trumpet. Sixty gamblers had gathered in a circle and shouted bets as if at a cock fight while they watched a holo of three men in a simulated combat. The three men were in a large, powerful hovercraft racing through the jungle, trying to beat back an attack by four Yabajin craft. The whole point of the exercise seemed to be to see how many kills the combat team could make before they got wasted. Yet the three men were marvelous, graceful, powerful: they swirled in the air to fend laser attacks, and they seemingly dodged the plasma as it rushed toward them. They returned fire and made kills while they zigzagged through the brush. Their antics as they dodged Yabajin drew great gusts of laughter. I heard a buzz like the drone of giant wasps. Three black projectiles the size of a man's arm zipped toward the mercenaries at tree line, following the contours of the forest, dodging branches. Someone shouted, "Five to three Xavier doesn't hear the weasels!" and everyone began shouting their bets.

Another fifty people were seated on the floor in corners of the room. Few were smiling or sharing tales. An air of depression, frustration, hung over the crowd. Dead eyes everywhere and stern faces with fatalistic smiles. I could feel it in the air—the electric cobwebs brushing my face, a knot of tension in the pit of my stomach, the anxiety of a crowd who struggled for

325

control. The crowd was barely holding it in—as if the riot
aboard ship had never occurred. As if my two years in
the cryotanks had never passed.

A man in battle armor stubbed up to me. At first I
didn't recognize Zavala, since he stood with a slightly
bent posture, as if still struggling against heavy g forces.

"Ah, it's you! It's been a long time," he said, forgetting
my name.

"How are you?" I asked.

"Good. Everyone's good. Abriara will be glad you're
awake, *ne?*"

I was surprised to hear the Japanese *ne*, meaning
correct, from his lips. But then he'd been among the
samurai now for two years. People can change much in
two years.

I asked, "Where is she?" And the thought of seeing
her again filled me with the kind of pain one feels upon
passing the graveyard where a relative is buried.

"Probably running a solo gauntlet through the simulators. Or maybe exercising. She's been very worried for
you. She'll probably be in a simulator somewhere. Battle
helps steady the mind, *ne?* She'll want to see you. She'll
want you to fight with us, to sit in our hovercraft like we
were amigos. But things have changed since you chick-
ened out and helped start the riot. You won't be any help
in a fight—just dead weight. If you're a true friend, you
won't fight on our battle team."

Zavala sounded the same, but his undertones were
alien. His small rounded mouth twisted down in contempt. His stupid cow eyes stared dully. I was angry that
he spoke to me that way, but to placate him I said, "I
don't think she'll want me on the team. When did
Abriara feel anything for anyone? I'm nothing to her.
And if I'm a burden, she'll keep me off the team." And I
realized my words were a truth I understood with my
heart but would never have dared speak to myself.
Hadn't she disarmed me during the riot, leaving me to
die?

Zavala snorted in disgust. "That shows what you
know—the great doctor. God must have run out of

everything but guano when he was putting your head together!"

I didn't immediately know what to say. He acted as if I'd attacked Abriara's character when I'd simply stated the truth.

Zavala stubbed out the door as if one of his metal legs had suddenly shriveled too short. I waited for a long time, till it appeared he wouldn't return.

I found a corner and, since I was still holding my gift of rice and sake, I sat down on the floor to dine and watch the holo fights. There was a lull in the battle and no one was betting for the moment. The combat team had lost one man, but astonishingly they'd defeated the Yabajin. They were hovering motionless over a stagnant river whipped to froth by their engines in a dense jungle where trees and bushes shone a hundred thousand shades of green and purple. Their bulky bug suits were pocked and furrowed from laser and plasma hits. They were hastily repairing the damage to their armor with a resin paint.

The hovercraft's forward engine seemed damaged; it whined badly and the nose of the craft tilted in the air. There were eighteen small air-intake holes for the turbos around the sides of the hovercraft, and several air intakes had somehow taken plasma into them, ruining the blades. The air intakes are mounted at an angle so this won't happen, but when plasma first comes from a turret it's so hot it actually exists in gaseous form. In this form at close range the air intakes must make good targets— the hovercraft sucks in gaseous metal and ruins the props as the metal cools. The hovercraft's body was heavily plated with teflex, more so than the old-model crafts, and had a dozen unfamiliar flashing lights on the instrument panel. When the two men had repaired their armor, they began shooting their plasma turrets in the air and they dumped their compadre into the water.

I got up and asked a gambler, a chimera with metallic blue eyes who was unusually tall, "What are they doing?"

He looked at me as if I were an idiot, with a contempt I'd have only attributed to a samurai, and I wondered just how much my people really had borrowed from the samurai. He saw my white kimono and his expression quickly turned to one of pity. "You just got thawed, no? Well, I'll tell you, sir: They're gearing up for the puff mines, emptying their turrets of ammunition so they won't be carrying extra weight. If you keep these new hovercrafts light, you can reach an altitude of three meters. At top speed you can pass over most puff mines without detonating them."

"Ah," I said, feeling like a fool. I had no idea how much weight they might need to unload, never having floated over a puff mine before. "Won't they need some ammunition in the plasma turrets to continue the assault after passing through the mine fields?"

He gave me a sad look. "No, they can try to use lasers to fry off the sensors on the ANCs and cybertanks. Once they get through to Hotoke no Za, they'll be overwhelmed by the Yabajin. Watch them, and you might learn enough . . ."

He didn't need to say the rest. I might learn enough to stay alive. He believed I was a dead man. The weapons I'd practiced with had been upgraded over the past forty years, and I was unfamiliar with the new models. I had no idea what skills or strategies I'd need to get past these defenses. I'd seen the little black weasel missiles, but didn't know how to defend myself from them. As Zavala had said, I'd only be excess baggage in this war.

I nodded toward the men in the simulator who suddenly lurched off through the trees in their hovercraft. "Those men, no one fought like them in the simulators. No one." It was true. They fought wonderful—better than we ever had when fighting the samurai. Yet I didn't know if our men could yet beat a samurai.

"We've learned much," the chimera said. "You were frozen before training really began. You did not spend time studying your own individual kinesthetics through the holographs, learning not to waste a move, learning the spins and throws and drops necessary to defeat the weapons of the Yabajin. You were still studying how to achieve *munen*, the state of no mind, the state of the living corpse. You did not progress into the higher mental states necessary for battle—Instantaneity or Perfect Control. The great genius of the samurai comes from their knowledge of these states of being—"

"Pardon me, but what do you mean by Instantaneity?"

The chimera looked at me thoughtfully. "Perhaps you have had a moment in your life, a moment of great fear when your life was in jeopardy, and time seemed to stop. I once lived such a moment: in an alley in Temuco during the riots a human came and put an ancient revolver in my face and pulled the trigger. The hammer was cocked, and when he pulled the trigger it began to fall. Time seemed to stop. A car passed on the street before me, and a woman was looking out the window and watching. I remember her face perfectly, her ruby lips shaped in a circle of surprise. And I saw the steam rising from a sewer grate across the street, and a man in a store there was turning out the lights. I looked into the frightened eyes of the young man who planned to murder me and knew he could not be more than fifteen. And all this time the hammer was falling and I thought, 'When that hammer drops, I die.' So I reached up and put my finger in front of the hammer and it never dropped. That is Instantaneity, living life in a moment. It is a state of mind a warrior can learn to induce at will. It is one secret of the genius of the samurai. Beyond this lies Perfect Control—the ability to achieve a measured heartbeat, to stop one's breathing, to put all muscles under voluntary control." He stopped speaking and looked behind me.

Someone tapped me on the shoulder. I turned and Abriara hugged me in a friendly embrace and said, "It's good to see you again."

I found I was breathing hard. She wore the midnight blue kimono of the samurai, and it was wet with sweat.

"It looks as if you've been promoted," I said. I studied her face. It had been such a pulp when I'd seen her last I was surprised not to see some bruise greened with age. Her hairline was a bit irregular where the swath of chocolate-brown hair had been ripped from her forehead. But she was smiling as if genuinely happy, and nothing on the surface indicated how troubled she might

be beneath her facade. Her hair appeared brittle and
lusterless. Her cheeks had sagged, her skin folded and
wrinkled. She held herself bent slightly forward. Perhaps the two years of heavy gravity caused some of these
things, but it pained me to think how a single incident
must have devastated her.

Her muscles appeared strong and powerful and she
carried herself with grace. Abriara saw me watching her
as if inventorying her body for future use as spare parts.
She laughed. "Why are you looking at me like that?"

"I'm looking for scars."

She closed her eyes and pointed at a white scar atop
one eyelid. "This is where Lucío ground the cigar butt
in . . ." Then she held out her left hand and I took it.
"And this is where he burned off my fingers." A thick
scar ran across her palm. Four skin-toned metal fingers
were connected to the flesh. I'd had no idea she'd
endured such torture. When I'd seen her sprawled on
the table, she'd been hidden behind other people.

I grabbed her shoulders roughly and tears of rage
filled my eyes. "Abriara," I said, "I swear to you and God
that I'll make a gift to you of a silver platter piled high
with the testicles of the men who did this."

She smiled as if she'd break into a laugh. Her hand
touching mine seemed almost a caress. I couldn't understand how she could smile in the face of such horror.
Such a smile could only be false, the ebullient affectation
of a Chilena. "What makes you think I'd want such a
gruesome gift?" she said. "You've done enough! Besides,
it all happened long ago."

I wanted to tell her it may have seemed years to her,
but for me it had happened only hours before. I looked
into her eyes to read what message they held, and saw
only a softness, joy. Never before had I seen anything in
her eyes but cool calculation, an occasional flash of
anger. But now her eyes were bright, fierce, happy,
alive! Like one raised from the dead.

No one changes that much. I shuddered, and began
trembling. I felt as if the ground moved beneath me. She
pulled me toward the door. "Let's go get your things."

Abriara hustled me out into the night. A brisk breeze

was building, the smell of a rising storm. Around the back of the building sat a parked truck, and in it was a few plastic bags filled with possessions. Two bags had my name on them. One was a suit of battle armor; the other contained an old crystal knife, Tamara's little folding laser rifle, my medical bag, and a single box of cigars. From the building down the road came the continual chant of "Let's go home! Let's go home!"

My mind felt numb. No one could change as much as Abriara had. "You'd better put the armor on," she said, "and don't take it off until this war is over. It's slightly different from the old stuff—heavier, not as well balanced. You'll get used to it." I stripped off my kimono and shoes and began dressing in the armor. Abriara helped snap the pieces together gently, as if dressing an invalid or lover. She bent close as she put on my chest plate, and I smelled her hair, her sweat. Warm and musky.

I felt the beginning of an erection and was thankful it remained hidden beneath the armor. My young body was responding to her in ways an old man forgets.

Abriara opened a compartment at my hip; it contained several resin canisters. "You'll need to learn to repair your own armor. Just paint these over furrows till they fill. When you're done patching the hole, you'll want to put a layer of this stuff from the green canister on. It's called *flare*. I'll show you why . . ."

She pulled the telescoping barrel out on my little laser rifle and fired across my leg. A brilliant green flame shot up wherever the laser touched.

"In back you paint with the blue canister." She shot the back of my leg; a piercing whistle erupted momentarily. Her intonations were forceful like those of a samurai. "It's called *scream*. If you ever see a flash of light come off you or hear that whistle, it means a sniper has hit you. You block immediately. Understand?"

"Yes, I understand."

"Good. Later on, we'll try to teach what you need to know to stay alive." She sounded concerned. She folded up the laser rifle and put it in a compartment at my knee. Along my right leg was a sheath containing a thin but

sharp machete. She removed it and considered putting
my crystal dagger in its place, but decided it wouldn't fit.
She checked a couple of compartments at my waist and
found no place for the dagger. I took it from her and
began strapping the old wrist sheath to her arm. She
smiled, pleased at the gift.

I said, "I saw some men fighting in the simulator—
three against many. How much can you teach me of what
they know, of the mental states? *Munen*. Instantaneity.
Whatever else you've learned?"

She glanced at my feet. "You were watching our
chimera samurai fighting humans. I can't teach what
they know. You're too . . . human. Do you understand?"

"You mean I don't have the genetic potential. But the
samurai who taught you are no better genetic specimens
than I. They must have taught you something. None of
you could fight so well two years ago. I could learn what
they know!"

"In time, perhaps. But we don't have access to the
biofeedback monitors necessary to teach you a high
degree of precision or Perfect Control. We took a drug
that helps to induce Instantaneity, something from the
Eridani system. I'll get you some. In a couple of weeks
you might build up to where the state comes naturally
when faced with danger. You won't be able to train
yourself to initiate it in that time."

I smiled wistfully. All that time García had wasted
trying to prove to Zavala the superior genetics and
training of the samurai. And now it all came clear: their
battle drugs were superior to ours. I wondered if Zavala
had ever felt inclined to repay García.

The chanters kept up their shout of "Let's go home!
Let's go home!"

I looked into Abriara's eyes. "What are my chances if
I go through with this? Without training. What does the
computer say?"

"Not good."

"How good?"

Abriara shrugged, not eager to speak. "One in a
hundred—but you'll do much better if you stick with us.

Think positive. Was it not you who once said, 'The future looks bleak only to those who refuse to dream in color'?"

"It was not me who said that." I nodded toward the old barn where my compadres were building toward another riot. "I think I should be with them. I do not think I'll fight the Yabajin with you. I'm sorry."

"If Motoki Corporation gets its way, you won't have a choice," Perfecto said from behind me. I turned. I hadn't heard him coming. He was twenty meters away, beside the building. Miguel was with him. They ambled over and hugged me, patted me on the back, smiling. "Ah, it is good to see you, my amigo. It has been a long time."

"Too long," I said.

Abriara picked up my cigars, my kimono. "I'll go find you a place to sleep." She walked back toward the hut and I was painfully conscious of the way her hips rolled beneath her silk kimono.

Perfecto kept his arm around me till after she rounded the corner and gave me a strange look, almost angry, that quickly turned to a smile. And Miguel held back a laugh. "Did you see the soft eyes she was making at you?" Miguel asked.

"Ah, and the don here looks as mournful as a cat in heat! I think both of them have raised the temperature in this valley by a good two degrees. It must be the don's new youth. He looks very aristocratic, very handsome, don't you think, Miguel?"

"Ah, yes. If I were a woman, my heart would be fluttering like a caged bird!"

"It's a good thing we came when we did. I'd hate to have found them love-wrestling on the ground," Perfecto said. They both chuckled and I hung my head in embarrassment. When the air had cleared, Perfecto said, "As I was saying before, don Angelo, I don't think those men will be able to stay here in Kimai no Ji. Despite your incredible new handsomeness, most of the Japanese think we are ugly. They don't want to look at us, and they call us *tengu*, demons."

"That's right," Miguel added. "The people don't like us. They put this camp way outside town so they won't have to look at us—so we can't pollute their culture."

"Yes," Perfecto added. "They wanted to leave you all asleep up in the cryotanks till the war is over, but the owners of the ship made them take you.

"But the officials at Motoki don't want you down here, and they especially don't want to leave you while we're making the assault—so I think you'll all end up having to come. Garzón will probably just have you hang back behind the samurai."

"That does not sound so bad," I said. I nodded toward the building where the men kept up their chant. "You'd think they'd be willing to go along for the ride."

"Oh, they're not upset about that," Perfecto said. "Motoki Corporation docked them for pay while they were in the cryotanks—twenty-two years of lost pay." His voice was bitter, very emotional. "Many of those men had families like mine that depended on that pay!"

I was shocked by the enormity of the injustice those men had suffered. The poorest had agreed to fight only because they knew it meant their families—brothers, sisters, widowed mothers, and even their own children—would no longer endure the incredible hardships brought on by the war in South America. For some, leaving their families was an ultimate sacrifice, an act of love. And now they found that only two weeks after they'd left Earth their families had been cut off from the boon their sacrifice had represented. For some of those men it meant family members had died in poverty. Young sisters may have been forced into prostitution while invalid mothers starved.

"All of us sympathize with them," Perfecto said. "All of us are angry. We didn't learn of this injustice until just a few days ago. I think the ship never would have made it to Baker if people had known. Can you feel the wrath in the air, the electricity?"

I nodded. I'd felt it when I first entered the room with the gamblers.

"I have not felt such tension since the riot!" Perfecto said. "I have not felt such tension in many months!"

"It's true!" Miguel said. "Things quieted down till a few days ago. After the riot things changed. The samurai treated us like amigos—especially when they saw how well we fight. Most of us advanced to the rank of samurai. But the locals here treat us like dirt. General Tsugio, the head man, laughs at the idea of non-Japanese samurai, and he's threatened to reduce our pay if we don't get our compadres to act complacent. Now you look into the eyes of our men and you can see what they think. They think they should never have come. They think they should not fight. But what can we do? We can't go back, because we can't pay the Greeks for the ship. We can't find jobs elsewhere. We must either fight the Yabajin or starve!"

"Can't you go over General Tsugio's head?" I asked. "Can't you talk to Regional Company President Motoki? This is not such a big town, he can't be very busy."

Perfecto shook his head. "On Baker everyone has his place. They believe in what they call the natural hierarchy: man is better than woman. A corporate executive officer is better than a corporate warrior, who is better than a corporate farmer, who is better than a noncorporate farmer. All Japanese are better than Chinese who are better than Koreans. And somewhere in the dust among all the species of worms are Latin Americans. Mother of God! We are both non-Japanese and noncorporate workers—we don't have a permanent contract with the corporation. We are so far down their list even Garzón can't talk to a company executive. He's only allowed to speak to General Tsugio and his aides."

"I don't understand," I said. "What would they do to you if you tried to talk to a company executive?"

"Ignore you," said Miguel, "or beat you. It depends on how badly you offend them with your attempt."

Perfecto nodded, and rushed on to explain. "It's their vertical society structure. Their vertical society structure caused this war. You see, when both parties settled here their social engineers believed they were each taking slightly different paths to the same goal. They hoped to teach their people basic ethics of work, cooperation, subservience to society, an ideal of austerity. Motoki's engineers taught the doctrine of *Isshin*, restoration, saying they were simply reverting back to a "natural order" of things, relearning ancient ideals that still lived in their hearts. But the Nationalist engineers believed subservience to society stifled individual creativity, so they modified that aspect of their society. They taught revolution—telling their people they were creating a new tradition, that they were discovering their own strength and beauty as a race. And so the nations diverged.

"But though they have much in common, both Motoki and the Yabajin each has a vertical society. Each believes it's at the pinnacle of the human hierarchy. Each believes its own members are the finest representatives of humanity in the universe. And the only way they can prove it is to kick out the teeth of their rivals."

Perfecto seemed quite upset, and I laughed at the idea of the inhabitants of Motoki being the supreme race in the universe. "And what do they think of you chimeras?"

"The samurai have grudgingly become convinced," Miguel said, "that we chimeras are better fighters than samurai, but we still don't measure up. We've never learned 'corporate spirit,' and that proves our weakness."

"And if they are so perfect and we are so useless, why do they need us?"

"Cannon fodder," Perfecto said. "They need us to fight automated defenses at Hotoke no Za. They do not believe they can win such a battle, so they hire someone to die for them. Someone who doesn't matter. They want us to clear a path, just to open a door so the samurai can get into Hotoke no Za and prove who's superior."

I remembered the holo of President Motoki thanking us for coming to fight the machines of the Yabajin. "But that's not so hard—not from what I've heard."

"Not hard for us, because we're not technophobes. The defense networks unnerve the samurai on a very deep level. These settlements were founded because the Japanese saw themselves losing technological supremacy to the Chinese. To this society, the machine symbolizes their one great failure, reminds them of their defeat."

"Ah! Have you noticed how they shun cybernetic upgrades?" I asked.

Perfecto nodded vigorously. "They shun a thousand

other technological advances, too. The Alliance has placed some strict offensive weapons restrictions upon us, but we could easily design legal weapons to defeat the Yabajin defenses—rifles that fire corrosive liquids rather than solid projectiles, multiple-layer ceramic-based armor. But Motoki is obstinate: if they won because of a technological advantage, they believe it would negate the whole reason for fighting the war— they must win because they are superior people, not because they have superior weaponry."

"These people are crazy!" I said.

"I agree," Perfecto said. "Still, they pay good money." He shuffled his feet. "Besides, every foreign culture seems a little crazy if you view it from outside. General Tsugio's aides have requested that we come to a special meeting in the morning. I think General Tsugio will want to address us about the morale problem. Tsugio-san is a great believer in singing company songs and offering impassioned speeches." He looked back at the house. "Do you want to go in and listen to some music, watch the fights?"

There was nothing better to do. We went inside and chatted about inconsequential things and watched simulated battles most of the evening. Zavala fought in one battle. He and some others vanquished four combat teams and entered Hotoke no Za, and I was surprised to see how skilled he'd become. Much had changed.

Yet in a world where I had to study constantly to keep up with the advances in my own small field of medicine I'd become adept at change. I could handle change, even bad changes. My friends had taken my body and made it young again; I could accept that. It was a common procedure. The samurai had kept me in cryogenic suspension for two years, and that was harder to accept. They'd cheated me of training that would help me stay alive on Baker—and as I watched the simulations, seeing our men battle the patrols, weasels, ANCs, and cyber-tanks while trying to negotiate mine fields—I began to realize just how dangerous my ignorance was. I had never beat the samurai in the simulators, and could not do it now. Also, my *compañeros* had changed; I could almost accept that. But I was terrified by what I'd seen in Abriara's eyes: she was happy, serene.

I searched my mind and tried to discover why this disconcerted me, and I remembered when I was young I once went to a strange church with my mother. In this church people pretended to receive great spiritual manifestations. They spoke in tongues, babbling nonsense, and rolled on the floors and praised God while they frothed at the mouth—all to impress one another with their feigned holiness.

And because I was young they terrified me with the same unnameable fear I felt now, and I thought they were under the influence of the devil. I believed Satan was in that church. But as I grew older I realized it wasn't the devil that had terrified me—it was the strangeness, the unknown, the face of the alien.

And now when I watched Abriara singing with the crowd or looked upon her as she studied the battles I beheld the face of the alien once again. She was alive inside and I was dead. She'd witnessed great horrors and lived a life of desperation. Like the countless refugiados I'd met she'd been emotionally dead inside. She'd been brutalized and broken beyond repair, and it was *right* for her to be dead inside. But here she was suddenly brought back to life, and the flame inside her seemed to burn like some magic tallow candle in the wind, obstinately refusing to extinguish no matter how fierce the storm. No one should have the power to change that much.

I tried to imagine what influences could have changed her: she was a chimera. She wasn't human, not in the way I'm human. Could her engineers have created a new being with an emotional resiliency rivaling anything believed possible? I doubted it. Not by design anyway. No one understands the biochemical mechanisms that control emotional resiliency that well. I'd read precious few articles on the subject, and those had been written a hundred years before when sociologists were studying those who best coped with the nuking of Europe.

Another thought came to mind: Zavala's speech patterns had shifted toward those of the samurai. Given his respect for their doctrines it seemed only natural that he'd ape them. In a way it signaled something I hadn't anticipated—a sociocultural shift that might have affected our entire crew. Perhaps by coming into contact with the samurai we were becoming like them. Certainly the way Zavala asserted that "Battle steadies the mind" indicated he was falling into their way of thinking. I'm sure Motoki's social engineers would have been proud of the fine job they'd done of twisting Zavala's brain.

But it didn't seem probable that Abriara's contact with the samurai could have initiated her internal change. The samurai tried to veil their emotions, but I'd noticed on several occasions how they overcompensated in expressing emotions. It seemed to me they feigned passion poorly because they, like the refugiados, were emotionally emasculated. Dead inside. So the answer had to lie elsewhere.

I went back inside and watched the holos, met Mavro. He'd found someone to tattoo a new tear on his cheek and he'd shaved his mustache; otherwise he was the same. The simulators went off early and I wasn't tired, but everyone else found spots on the floor and began to sleep, a hundred people to a small building. There was barely room to turn over.

I went outside to look at the stars and Perfecto followed me. The opal kites in the atmosphere baffled my eyes. Their platinum sheen was like gauze or cobwebs reflecting sunlight. The men in the barn continued chanting, but it somehow seemed muted, deadened by the night air. I could barely distinguish the samurai in black armor circling the barn beneath the trees. Perfecto dropped his codpiece and let his penis hang out. I thought he'd urinate but for several minutes nothing happened.

"What are you doing?" I asked, nodding toward his penis.

Perfecto looked down at his member and said, "I thought I'd let my penis out for a breath of fresh air, but now that it's out, all it wants to do is play." He waited a moment more, then began urinating on a sapling. "Aaah, it comes—finally."

I hadn't peed on a bush since I was a child in Guatemala. Somehow it made me feel nostalgic, so I joined him.

When I finished I said, "Perfecto, was Abriara really making soft eyes for me?"

He laughed. "Yes. She makes soft eyes whenever talking about you—ever since you saved her from getting raped by Lucío."

I was shocked. "I didn't save her from getting raped! I got there too late. There was nothing I could do!"

Perfecto frowned and looked thoughtful. There was a long silence. He finally hissed through his teeth. "I thought not. She told an improbable story, saying you'd wrestled a rifle away from someone in the nick of time and saved her."

"Why would she say such a thing? How does she think she'll get away with it? Didn't Lucío and his compadres spread the truth?"

Perfecto frowned harder. "Two of Lucío's compadres died under the crush of bodies when the ship was spinning. The rest were put in the cryotanks as punishment for breaking into the ship's armory, so they haven't told the truth. But I think she tells this lie because she believes it. All one must do is look into her eyes when she speaks. She believes she was not raped. Perhaps Abriara was not strong enough to handle what happened to her. Maybe her mind snapped. I've spoken with her about unpleasant incidents from her childhood and she claims that they too never happened."

"The rape by the mestizos?"

"For one. She says she got the scar above her ear from an accident while playing baseball. She doesn't seem to remember her three years in prison."

I felt like vomiting. I couldn't believe what Perfecto was telling me. All that health, all the joy I'd seen in her eyes was just the sign of greater sickness. "What have you done about it?" I demanded. "How can we help her?"

"Just leave her alone. Angelo, since that day, Abriara has changed. She seems to be at peace for the first time in her life. Perhaps . . . perhaps her only chance for happiness lies in her ignorance. Her deeper mind knows this."

"We must confront her with the truth!" I said. "We must help her to face it!"

"Maybe someday she'll come to the truth on her own. I've tried to confront her many times, to hint at the truth, but she just blocks it out."

I put my hands on my hips and looked up at the sky. I felt as impotent as when I'd witnessed Abriara's rape. A sudden violent resolve filled me. "Perfecto, I'm going to kill Lucío. I'm going to rip off his testicles."

He was silent for a moment. "I agree. We can't risk going into battle with him. We should do it soon." He sighed.

That night as I lay shivering on the floor in my armor I dreamed of Tamara in her wheelchair. Garzón had pulled her microspeaker from the jack at the base of her skull so she couldn't speak. Garzón stood over her, stroking her hair and watching her intently. His hands slowly petted her neck, her shoulders, crept down to press firmly on the nipples of her breasts. I could tell he was going to rape her. I could see the excitement in his eyes, the tenseness in his arms. Tamara's eyes were wide with hysteria.

I woke to the sound of nearby thunder that shook the room as if it would split the building. Rain drummed on the roof. I was shivering with cold and Abriara was spreading a white kimono over the top of me, though I don't think it did much good. The room was cramped with sprawling, snoring bodies. I turned over to look up at her.

"Go back to sleep," she whispered. "This will keep you warm."

"Why doesn't someone turn up the heat?" I asked.

"There isn't any."

She began to move away, gingerly picking her way through sleeping bodies, her battle armor clacking softly. Never had I seen her do something unselfish before. *She is alive inside,* I marveled. I wanted to thank her, but thanks did not seem enough. "Abriara," I whispered. She turned to look at me. "I want only good for you!"

She grinned and found herself a place to lie down a few meters away.

I wondered if I was crazy. A few weeks ago I'd imagined I was falling in love with Tamara. My feelings for her were still strong. Now I found my affection for Abriara growing and it doesn't take a great mind to realize both women were horribly damaged. I wondered if what I felt was love, or was it simply the pity one feels for an injured animal? And if it was simply pity, should I pursue a relationship with either woman? One wouldn't be particularly inclined to buy damaged merchandise in the market. Certainly I'd never consider buying a shirt that had one sleeve longer than the other. Yet I found myself drawn to Abriara in spite of the horrible scars on her body and on her heart. I told myself nothing but trouble could come from such affection. I told myself, *Robles was seeking to create a perfect breeder when he created Abriara. Combined with this, nothing is so grasping as a Chilean woman (except perhaps a Bolivian), so if Robles has given her a stronger desire to breed, she'll cling to you forever. You'd become her prisoner. You wouldn't be able to step from the house without her demanding where you're going. You won't look across the street without her worrying if you're admiring another woman! Besides, as emotionally scarred as she is, she'll probably ax-murder you someday!*

Ah, but if I could just once gaze into her silver eyes and stroke her chocolate hair! I'd be lost forever! If I could but once taste those honeyed lips and run my hand beneath the curve of her breasts!

One doesn't successfully remain a bachelor for thirty years without developing a great capacity to fall out of love. I dreamed of living with her in a small house, a few chickens in the yard. If Robles truly had created a breeder, Abriara wouldn't be satisfied with less than a dozen children. *Ai ya yi*, I imagined the headaches their screeching and fighting would cause. Then I weighed all this against the potential for happiness and finally decided it was better not to get involved with a probable ax-murderess.

The next day I hoped for an opportunity to get Lucío. The morning sun burned the clouds away and I found Fernando Chin, the xenobiologist, in the front yard collecting bodies of *oparu no tako* that had been electrocuted during the thunderstorm. He had perhaps fifty different species, ranging through many different sizes and shapes, and he was freezing samples of genetic tissues. I stood beside him and watched the barn where Lucío was kept. The men had quieted during the night, but with morning they began chanting anew, "Let's go home! Let's go home!" I counted sixteen samurai guards around the barn, and I couldn't see how to get to Lucío.

Fernando Chin kept looking up at me, and he began to explain how he was going to determine the ages of the species through means developed by genetic paleontologists.

I didn't really listen to him. The task of getting to Lucío occupied me. I pretended to help Fernando and watched the barn. There was no way to sneak in. I casually sauntered toward the barn to see how the samurai reacted. Two detached themselves from the shadows under a tree and walked toward me. I stooped as if to examine a shiny rock and picked it up—an irregular white crystal sprouted a small cauliflower head of brilliant red. One samurai studied the crystal a moment.

"Ruby," he said. "Very common in hills. Look for them there. Stay away from here!"

I put the ruby in a pocket, then exercised most of the day, practicing various spins and crab walks that would be useful when hit by laser and plasma fire. I felt strong, and with my nerve bypass and young muscles I was quicker than ever. But it didn't seem enough. Abriara introduced me to a medic who gave me several doses of Motoki battle drugs. I asked him for the chemical formula but the patent was still the sole property of Motoki Corporation. He described how to take them and warned me of dangers. "You won't have time to train yourself to reach Instantaneity, but you may find that if you become excited then Instantaneity will find you. You may recall a moment in your life when time has slowed, and you may have even noticed this effect when using our old battle drugs. The effect will become much more pronounced with this. You must use great care when the moment of Instantaneity comes: time will stop and you'll be tempted to do many things at once. However, your metabolic rate will not increase enough for you to do much, understand? If you try to run forward a few steps, you'll use all the oxygen in your system and you'll stop. You'll feel as if you hit a wall, and you could even die if you overexert yourself. You must take care during Instantaneity to use economic motions, to move as little as possible to achieve your desired goals, understand?"

I understood perfectly.

"One more thing," the medic added. "Once you take this drug, the effects will be with you for life. Once you begin to achieve Instantaneity, you must learn to control it for your own sake, understand?"

I nodded and took the drug.

Twice that day a truck came from town and dropped off food—tubs of cold rice and seaweed, barrels of pickled eggs and vegetables, fresh raw fish. Sickening things. Worst of all the coffee tasted weak and musty, as if it had grown in a swamp. The inhabitants of Motoki had a saying, "Luxury is our greatest enemy." What they considered self-denial, however, I considered self-torture.

Toward evening the men in the barn began shouting and screaming in a frenzied pitch. Their guards sent emissaries to town and soon General Tsugio, a small frowning bald man, showed up and demanded that Garzón quiet the men. Tsugio announced that everyone would be docked wages if the demonstrators didn't calm down. Being raised in a culture where each individual is a slave to the whims of his society, he couldn't understand that we had no control over the demonstrators, that they wouldn't be quiet simply because we were being punished with them. He believed we secretly sympathized with them, that we were spurring them on. Perhaps he was right.

No truck came with dinner and Garzón quoted one of Tsugio's aides as saying we'd have to go without food till we "learn that we live by the beneficence of Motoki." Some men grumbled a bit. Some hunted in the fields by the city's defensive perimeter but brought back only a few rabbits and quail. Garzón called a meeting with his leaders at sunset, ostensibly to discuss the morale problem, and they closeted themselves away for hours.

When they returned a captain came to our barracks and said, "Things were worse than we'd hoped. A shipload of mercenaries hired by the Yabajin is due to arrive from Earth within five days. Most are homeless Colombians who left Earth three months after us."

"But they couldn't get here so soon!" One of our company exclaimed.

"Not if they kept their ship's acceleration rate down to the legal limits," the captain objected. "But of course they elected to pay a stiff fine rather than lose the war. Nearly all of them are refugiados who hired on after kicking the socialists out of their homeland. The chimeras wouldn't come, not with the war in South America going so well. The Colombians didn't have samurai to train them, so it's impossible to tell what they know, but it's safe to bet they know what they're up against. And since they outnumber us two to one they'll make good reinforcements for Hotoke no Za.

"Our employers at Motoki demand we move our attack ahead of schedule. We're to leave in three days so we can assault the Yabajin before the Colombians shuttle down. Also, they demand that *all* our men take places at the front lines—even those who missed training. They say it is not their job to fight the machines."

The news didn't settle well. Men who were sitting beside the holograph, gambling on the outcomes of simulated battles, abruptly quit. Grumbling conversations rose around the room, but there was no argument—only a consensus of opinion. We'd been snubbed, poorly fed, and treated without respect. Motoki Corporation was in violation of its contract since computer simulations revealed that we'd still have a sixty-two percent death rate if we attacked Hotoke no Za. Beyond this, no one was willing to force the demonstrators into battle, nor did they desire to battle the Colombians—men they'd fought beside only months before. Within an hour we'd made up our minds, and our captain went back to General Garzón with our response: "Tell Motoki Corporation to go to hell."

Garzón relayed our message to General Tsugio, and he apparently received it with great equanimity. No samurai surrounded our camp, no reprisals were made. At dawn a truck delivered food, and we practiced and exercised as usual. Tsugio and his aides drove into camp shortly after breakfast. They were smiling and quite pleased, but after conferring with Garzón, Tsugio left in distress, frowning and scratching his bald head.

Garzón announced over a loudspeaker that we should quit practicing, since "We want them to realize we're not willing to fight for them." Apparently the concept of "going on strike" didn't translate into Japanese. They'd believed we planned to fight but that we'd refuse the aid and advice offered by their military. On Motoki when a man strikes he continues to work, redoubling his effort so more is accomplished. This causes upper management to lose place, since the worker proves he doesn't need the manager.

Motoki had never met with passive resistance. I whiled away the afternoon by disposing of outdated medicines from my bags while corporate minds determined their next move. We expected retaliation, more threats and abuse.

At dusk, Kimai no Ji emptied. We watched in surprise as everyone in the entire city marched up the road, raising dust. I imagined them bringing clubs to beat us, but 44,000 Japanese dressed in their finest attire walked up the road and stood on the low hills encircling our valley—grandmothers, fathers, infants. The young men carried giant Motoki corporate flags, a crane flying past a yellow sun on a green field, and they waved them back and forth furiously, swaying their entire bodies. General Tsugio led the city in singing "Motoki Sha Ka" ten times, while children accompanied the singers on flutes and drums.

It was perhaps the single strangest moment of my life, a life that sometimes seems an endless succession of strange moments. It was an obvious appeal for help. When the singers were done, individuals and families descended into the valley and took us by the hand and began to lead us to town. I saw Master Kaigo walking beside an old woman, and our whole combat team went up to meet him.

He shook our hands, bowing repeatedly. "This is Sumako, my wife," he indicated the ancient woman. She had blue-gray hair, wide-set eyes, and a flat face. Her wrinkles showed she'd lived a life of hardship. She couldn't have been over seventy, but didn't hold it well. She wore a kimono of peach silk that had the quality of beauty the Japanese call *hade*, the beauty of bright colors. It was the kind of thing a young woman would wear.

"She is very beautiful," Abriara said.

"Oh, she is just a stupid woman," Kaigo said, trying to be polite by demeaning his family in public. I hadn't really considered till then what his trip to Earth had cost him. He'd returned to Baker to find his wife decrepit with age and his other family members apparently dead. He continued, "We would be thoroughly filled with gratitude if you would consent to partake of dinner with us."

We agreed and he led us to town, pointing out the beauty of the plum and cherry trees, the Buddhist temple on the hill. Sumako hurried home while Kaigo delayed our arrival by showing us the National Terrarium, a giant dome that enclosed a portion of land that had never been terraformed. Thousands of ultraviolet trees like reeds of seaweed lived there, along with rare mosses and Baker's own equivalent of fungi. Native insects and giant land crabs crept beneath the bushes. All the while Kaigo kept up a continuous monologue describing the natural beauty, the wonders, of Baker, telling how the Yabajin sought to destroy everything they'd dreamed of building, the greatest society in the

universe, a Japan restored to the era of light. He showed
us the corporate executive headquarters, a small five-
story building of steel and concrete that seemed impos-
ing to him because it was the only building in town that
stood more than two stories. Then he took us down to
the river, to Old Town—the giant industrial park beneath a second glass dome where they manufactured
everything they needed from ceramic teacups to cloned
children to biomining equipment and detergent. Kaigo
told how his great-grandfathers had built the dome at
great personal cost, suffering ecoshock due to prolonged
exposure to an alien environment.

I understood what Kaigo was trying to do. We
wouldn't fight for enemies, but he hoped we'd fight for
friends. He was showing us his national treasures, trying
to instill in us a love for his little home, trying to sell
us a dream. Yet a whining undertone to his words
indicated he wanted something even more—he desperately wanted us to admire all Motoki had done, to
admire him and his people. It was all rather shabby and
pitiful.

He took us home. We went into a little foyer and took
off our shoes, donned silk slippers. Kaigo called for his
wife, and Sumako opened the door leading to the main
house, kneeling on the black lacquered floor and bowing
as she slid the door back to let us in. The house was large
and open with a roof of large planks. Lines of dark tile on
white floors executed peaceful rectangles. To another it
would have been beautiful. But nature abhors a rectan-
gle and I disliked the sense of order imposed upon the
house. Kaigo demeaned the timbers his house was built
from, spoke of nothing but the dilapidated state it was in,
apologized for all his failings and lack of graciousness,
then showed us his *tokonama*, an alcove in one room
decorated with plants and stones. At first I thrilled to see
his tiny thousand-year pine—a natural curve of gray
trunk, a sprawl of green needles falling into entropy. But
it was not real nature, not real entropy—only a pains-
takingly manipulated counterfeit. Kaigo's people had no
real love for nature. They only loved to imitate nature. I
listened to him recite his failings. In his own eyes he was

being a humble man, a fine host. But after a time I wondered if it was not his own way of fishing for compliments.

We were forced by convention to deny his shortcomings. "Ah, what a beautiful garden, Kaigo-san! Nothing of its exquisite symmetry and perfection existed in my village in Colombia!" Zavala would say, taking the lead, and we'd parrot variations of his remark.

Kaigo had a beautiful home and we ate an excellent dinner. Kaigo belittled Sumako's talents as a cook, and she happily agreed with all his pronouncements while we rebutted their appraisals of her taste and talent. Then Sumako continued to deny she had any culinary skills at all. Though all her self-deprecation sickened me, I thought Sumako was quite charming, almost comical in the way she accepted her humiliation. I felt sorry for her. I kept finding myself thinking it was her that should have been rejuvenated instead of me.

After dinner Kaigo took Mavro, Perfecto, and Zavala to the *sento*, the public baths, while Abriara and I walked among the cherry trees by the river. Many other Latin Americans strolled along smelling blossoms and gazing at the lights shining through the paper walls of the houses, getting their first look at Kimai no Ji.

"So, what do you think will happen?" I asked.

"About tonight?" Abriara said. "Nice place. Maybe they'd even be nice people if we ever really got to know them. I'm not sure I want to die for them."

"I agree. But I can't understand why they've decided to like *us* all of a sudden."

"They don't. Not most of them. I'm not sure they ever will. Did you see the terror on the faces of the children when they came to sing to us?" I'd been so stunned I hadn't seen it. "I think we've got them confused. They see it as being only right that we should want to continue to fight for Motoki. The way they see it, our contractual obligations and fear of death should only be minor considerations in deciding whether to continue this war. We should continue to fight because, from their point of view, it is the only way for us to save face. Angelo, after the first riot, things really calmed down for a long time.

The Japanese put all those they held responsible into the cryotanks and never mentioned the riot again. They imagined it was an individual act of cowardice on the part of a few people, and that most of us would be humiliated if we were reminded of the deed.

"But now the cowards are all locked up and Motoki still can't figure out why we won't fight. So they're grasping at straws. Maybe they invited us to their homes because they think they've offended us—they treat us as if we're as low as the *eta*, the lowest of their people. Now, I think, maybe they've decided foreign samurai should be given a slightly higher status—that of a low-level corporate worker. That's the only reason I can imagine that they'd invite us to their homes—unless they just want to burden us with another debt of *on*."

She continued, "And if that's what they're after, it just might work."

I looked at her in surprise. "What do you mean? Who'd care about that?"

"Zavala, for one. Didn't you see his eyes glow? Dinner and a bath with the samurai! He was in heaven. It's something he's wanted for two years. Mavro and Perfecto wanted it, too. That's why they're at the baths now. Hell, even I wanted it."

"I don't understand? What did you want?"

Abriara sighed and looked at the ground. "I wanted . . . respect. I want them to respect me, to make me feel like I belong. You know, all the time we were on the ship the samurai avoided us. They're arrogant. Even when some of us began to acquire the rank of samurai, they still didn't fraternize: it's part of the cultural engineering program, you understand. For their social engineering program to work they must isolate themselves from any society that would contaminate them. It's the first law of social engineering. I'm surprised they let us into their homes tonight. It means they're desperate, they're willing to risk all they've accomplished in the hope that we'll help them."

"So you think some of us will join them just because we want respect?" I asked. "I was afraid you'd say something worse. I was afraid you'd say some of us would join them because we're becoming like them."

"Cultural pollution works both ways," Abriara said, "and you've got a point. For a long time the samurai have been training us to 'live as one already dead.' It's a mystic phrase, and they apply the philosophy to more than just battle. It doesn't mean simply to be willing to give up one's life for a cause, it means that one should be dead to one's own will, to one's own desires. In some ways, the inhabitants of Motoki have learned to be like sheep, to act without thought simply because it is the will of their leaders. Angelo, I've seen that type of passivity growing in some of our compadres. You may be right. Some of our men may fight simply because they don't give a damn about their own welfare."

We were walking back to camp, past a house with an immaculate lawn decorated with large, odd-shaped rocks.

Three men were walking toward us—all Latin Americans wearing white kimonos, laughing about some private joke. I stepped off the walk to let them pass, and I suddenly realized the rioters had been released from their barn. The man closest to me was Daniel Sosa, one of the men who'd raped Abriara.

The recognition of Daniel and his death seemed instantaneous. My body knew where to find the hilt of my machete even if my mind did not. I ripped the machete from its scabbard and swung down into his neck and through his rib cage. Such was the quality of the steel that it sliced cleanly through his vertebrae. Daniel was human and didn't have infravision. I think in the darkness he didn't recognize me, never saw it coming.

I grabbed a man he'd been speaking to, a short man with the wide nostrils of an Indian, and held the machete to his throat. "Where is Lucío?" I shouted.

He'd died so many times in the simulator he didn't fear my blade. He regarded me coolly. "Daniel's sergeant? I haven't seen him for half an hour, not since dinner. He was going to go to the bathhouse with the others." Abriara drew her machete and stood by me.

The city was full of public bathhouses. I asked, "Which one?"

He shrugged.

"Where did you dine?"

"At Master Tanaka's, up the street, third house on the left."

I shoved him away, and he didn't seem inclined to fight. He was no one I'd ever seen before. I jacked in a call to Perfecto and warned him Lucío was free and was heading for a bathhouse. He thanked me and promised to join the hunt immediately.

I looked at Daniel lying in a bloody heap on the ground. I felt nothing for him. I was ecstatic he was dead. I charged up the street toward the business district—a cluster of simple wood buildings with no garish signs denoting the nature of business inside. Kimai no Ji was small enough that one could learn the nature of a business by word of mouth. One could discern the bathhouses by the loud laughter that came from within, by the steam that fogged the windows and boiled out when a door opened.

I rushed toward the first bathhouse I saw and Abriara shouted, "Wait! Wait for the others!" I ran in. My teeth began chattering. Lucío wasn't there.

Four doors down the street was a larger, more ornate establishment. I lunged through the brightly lit *genkan*, the entrance where clothes and shoes were stored. Several white kimonos hung on pegs along with the fine silk kimonos of the samurai.

Voices and the smells of warm water and cedar issued from a darkened doorway. I stepped through and looked into the bathhouse. The only light came from a series of large aquariums that circled the room, where giant white carp drifted among lilies. Perhaps forty naked men sat in a huge, brimful tub of cut stone and cedar. Hot water from an artificial spring in one wall poured down over igneous rocks to land in the tub. I didn't see Lucío at first. His hair had been cut and was no longer arranged in the snake-dance style. The scar on his face had nearly disappeared.

And he didn't see me, standing in the lighted doorway, my white hair shining brightly. He had never seen me backlighted before, and so he saw only a silhouette, an icon. He saw only the dim, genetically remembered form of General Torres.

Lucío's face collapsed into an expressionless putty, and his mouth dropped open. His pupils dilated as wide as coins. He didn't move. And I stood waiting for the bonding to complete. Abriara rushed into the *genkan* behind me.

A samurai looked at my dripping machete and said in flawless Spanish, "Take your fight into the street. Don't bloody our bathwater."

Lucío's arms began to twitch and he began to shake. His pupils constricted and he became cognizant of where he was. Even then he still did not recognize me.

"Get out of the tub!" I commanded him.

He gasped in horror, "Angelo!"

"Get out of the tub!"

He stood up and climbed over the lip of the tub. "Angelo, what do you want with me? What will you do with me?" he asked in confusion. He was completely naked, skin dark as an Indian. His penis and testicles hung loose after the scalding heat of the tub. He tensed as if to strike, then looked at my feet; his face filled with sorrow, as if he couldn't bear the guilt of his own thoughts. "You plan to kill me," he said, more statement than question. He reluctantly raised his fists and cocked his knees, taking a defensive stance.

I stepped forward carefully, searching for an opening. "Angelo, no!" Abriara shouted. She lurched through the doorway and grabbed at my elbow, holding me back. All the Japanese modestly covered their privates and ducked down into the tub. Heads floating on the water. "Don't you see? He's not Lucío anymore! He doesn't have a personality of his own. He's like Perfecto and Miguel and all the rest. He becomes what he thinks you want him to be!"

"I know! I don't want him. He's hurt you too much. I want him dead!"

Lucío's mouth became a little O of grief, the grief of a

would-be saint rejected by God. "I can never please you?" he asked.

I watched him closely. I didn't answer. He leapt forward, grabbed my machete by the blade, ripped it from my hand and turned it on me. "Look," he said, nostrils flaring, "Look! We don't have to fight! I don't have to kill you, and you don't have to kill me! They've already done it to us—" He nodded toward the samurai in the tub. "We go fight their battle, and we don't have a chance!" Lucío licked his lips and watched me nervously, trembling.

He pressed the machete forward so its tip pressed my throat. His hand shook uncontrollably. He could have hacked me to pieces in that moment.

I reached up and pushed the blade aside, and he didn't resist. He just stood there trembling. I wanted to kill him. I wanted to rip him apart with my bare hands. I looked down at his privates, hanging loosely in the warm air. "You may leave," I said. "But your testicles will stay!" Then I drove my knee up into his groin with all the force I could muster. The lip of the teflex knee pad on my armor caught the flesh of his scrotum, ripping it as if I'd struck with a clam shell. He plummeted backward without a sound and slammed into the floor on his back. His groin was covered with blood. I'd planned to let him go at that, but I looked at him and my anger did not subside. The punishment was not enough.

"*Indio! Mamón!*" I screamed, and kicked him in the ribs several times, and he was in too much pain to resist. I kicked his face, then dropped to my knees and slugged him in the ribs, trying to break bones that felt as hard as rock. I found myself screaming at the top of my voice and I ran to the corner and grabbed my machete and yelled, "Get up, you pimp! Defend yourself so I can kill you!" I wanted to kill him, yet I also wanted to drop my machete as I'd done when I first decided not to kill Arish. Yet the machete felt as if it were glued to my hand. There was a commotion in the *genkan* as Perfecto ran into the room.

Lucío lay on the floor and sobbed. I wanted to kill him, I wanted to leave him. Instead I pulled his left hand out and stepped on it, swung my blade down on his closed fist, chopping off his fingers, hoping that would satisfy me.

It was not enough. I could not set my machete down. "Come on, *Indio!*" I yelled, and he just kept sobbing.

I raised my hand to ram the machete into his belly.

"No!" Perfecto shouted, and I looked up. He leapt across the room and in one swift move grabbed my arm and kicked, striking Lucío's face with his foot, snapping his neck.

Lucío began twitching. Perfecto's face was a mask of pain. "I will do it," he said softly.

He slowly pulled his own machete and hacked off Lucío's head.

Perfecto stood staring at the corpse, his shoulders hunched.

His expression gradually changed from a wistful sadness to surprise. "He was not fighting! He was one of us!" he shouted in horror, and stumbled back from the corpse. Grief was written on his face, in his eyes.

He howled in pain and fell to his knees, as if he'd just killed his best friend, and then he sat on his knees and just shrieked. Tears streamed from his eyes and he held up his hands and stared at them.

I'd seen him kill once before and I'd believed it had cost him nothing. But this time it cost him much.

I could not bear to hear Perfecto scream. I staggered back into the *genkan*, shaken. My hands were trembling and my breathing ragged. Pinpoints of white flicked before my eyes. I cleaned the blood off my knees and hands with a white kimono I took at random, then walked back to camp alone.

Baker's larger moon lit the way, an orb of dull blue. There were still many mercenaries out, laughing from behind the walls of houses as if they were celebrating.

My fight with Lucío hadn't been half as gratifying as I'd hoped. All those nights of my youth in Guatemala when I'd wandered the streets looking for Quintanilla's soldiers after they'd killed my mother, I'd dreamed of fulfillment. I'd imagined a steady peace, a gentle and lasting elation would follow the vengeance. And I'd hoped to gain such peace by killing Lucío.

But I kept feeling I'd sinned. Once again I'd gone too far, and knew there'd be a price to pay. When I killed Arish it had cost me my home, my country. And once again I'd acted rashly, and as a result Perfecto might well be sitting on the floor of the bathhouse screaming his grief for hours. I might lose him as a friend, I thought. If Perfecto hadn't bonded to me, he wouldn't have killed Lucío. He did it because he believed I wanted it, the way he'd killed Bruto because I'd stamped the act with my approval. I couldn't imagine such mindless devotion. Yet I might well have just strayed so far from what was right that even this society of mercenaries and bonded chimeras would not forgive me.

I reached camp thinking these gloomy thoughts and Abriara soon came in behind me. "What do you think you're doing here?" she shouted, and her silver eyes blazed with anger in the moonlight. Her anger showed I'd been right, I thought. I'd lost her as a friend. "Perfecto needs you! He's sick with guilt! Go to him! Now!"

I turned and went back toward town and met Mavro and Perfecto halfway. Perfecto was hunched and walking slowly and Mavro held him by the arm, guiding him. Perfecto was sobbing loudly. I reached them and took Perfecto's arm and just by touching him I felt almost as if his guilt was physically transferred to me.

Perfecto looked up at me. "Why? Why were you going to kill him?" he asked. "You had nothing to fear from him." Perfecto's mouth was twisted in dismay. His perfectly even teeth gleamed in the moonlight.

"I don't know," I said honestly. "I was so angry at him I could not put down my machete. I tried to stop. I couldn't."

Perfecto nodded and looked down at the ground, as if such a flimsy answer were sufficient. "He was one of *us*," he mumbled. "Lucío was one of us."

I wanted to explain how it was, so I rushed on, "I've been killing people ever since the day we met, and I don't know why! I killed Arish and Juan Carlos, and I would have killed Lucío, too!"

Perfecto nodded and kept walking. "You killed them

because they violated your territory. You humans do not
understand this. They violated your territory, so you
killed them. Think about it and you'll see I am right."

The thought was so strange, so out of place, I was
stunned. Perfecto was a territorial creature, and I could
understand why he'd kill if another person violated his
territory, but I was surprised he'd attribute his own
motives to me.

Then a realization struck. I'd killed Arish in my own
house, on my own floor. When I'd chased him outside
I'd thrown down my knife, unwilling to kill him. But
when he'd violated my territory I'd shown no mercy!
And Juan Carlos—I'd strangled him because he was
entering module B of the spaceship! And Lucío—had
never violated my territory. I had no reason to kill him.
Perfecto's theory seemed to collapse.

"But Lucío did not violate my territory!" I said loudly.
"I had no reason to kill him!"

Perfecto continued hobbling toward camp. "Then he
violated the territory of a friend. It is the same. We
protect our friends as we do ourselves. He raped Abriara
and removed some of her fingers. Those are horrible
violations. So you killed him for violating the territory of
a friend. It is the male thing to do. Still—the danger was
past. You should have been able to let him live. If you
ever need my help dealing with such matters, I am here,
amigo." Perfecto continued hobbling back to camp and I
stopped.

I didn't speak. When I'd looked at Abriara's genetic
program I'd been impressed at how different she was
from a human. I'd told myself never to make the mistake of viewing her as a person like myself. Perfecto's
thoughts underscored the importance of remembering
the differences. It clarified something for me: I'd been
surprised by Abriara's overreaction to the riot, by the
consuming terror that had been aroused when she feared
her own rape. As Perfecto had said, rape is a terrible
form of territorial violation. And because Abriara was a
highly territorial creature, the fear of rape affected her
more severely than it did humans. And I wondered if
perhaps that was why her mind had snapped after the

rape, after her fingers had been cut away. And in the same flash of illumination, I finally understood the deeper meaning of the chimera slang word *Quest*: when one goes on a Quest it is not enough to kill, one must also humiliate the victim by violating his territory.

And when I'd killed Lucío I'd lived up to the code of the Quest. My subconscious mind wouldn't allow me to simply kill him. I'd been systematically mutilating him—trying to castrate him, remove his hand, violate his most intimate territory—his body.

Yet even as I violated him, Lucío—a creature of heightened territorialism—had refused to fight. He'd let me violate him because he'd bonded to me. The genetic bonding was so immutable that even as I'd killed him he'd given himself to me. He'd not only let himself be killed, he'd given his life to me willingly, to be thrown away however I chose. If I'd continued chopping him apart piece by piece, he'd have given each piece to me. With each hack of my machete Lucío had forgiven me.

And finally I understood why Perfecto had howled in grief.

I slept little that night, reliving each small moment of what I'd done over and over. In the morning I felt numbed with more than morning cold. Tsugio's advisers flew into camp on a hovercraft, excited and aggravated, and met with Garzón. Minutes later Garzón met with his highest officers. Abriara received a call and said we were to march to town in full combat gear. She ordered us to set our helmet mikes to channel A, subchannel 0. On that setting we'd receive orders from officers in our direct chain of command without being able to respond or talk among ourselves. It's a channel selection one would only use in combat. Abriara seemed to avoid my gaze as I looked at her. Our relationship had changed; I realized that she'd lost respect for me.

Abriara had been right, I concluded. Garzón had agreed to fight the Yabajin, and this was our muster. We'd get our supplies and vehicles and leave. It didn't seem to matter. Many men had brought favorite weapons or armor from Earth—Halifax plasma rifles, Bertonelli heavy combat lasers, YCB flechettes. They armed themselves and we prepared to march. Perfecto sat in our barracks with a dozen others playing cards while the rest took formation outside. I wondered at this. As I took a last look around the room I told him to hurry and he just sat on the floor looking dejected. "I'll catch up," he said.

We marched to town in columns of four hundred men each, down past the business district in the center of town to the airstrip by the industrial park. Everyone was tense, silent. It was sunny and windy and the ocean waves breaking against the sand a kilometer off sounded like rushing wind. Two large yellow zeppelins sat on the airfield. General Tsugio and a few hundred Japanese men and women were there, surrounding three Japanese girls dressed in white, sitting *seiza* on white blankets and staring off toward the sea. A holo crew had set up cameras and they were taping the proceedings.

General Tsugio pinned a microphone to his chest. His mouth was drawn into a scowl. He gazed at the cameras, then looked at the microphone on his lapel as if it were some newly discovered insect. He was preparing to put on a show.

When we'd formed our columns and stood at attention, General Tsugio suddenly glanced up as if noticing us for the first time. He straightened his back and glared with great authority like some barbarian king. He began yelling in Japanese and the speakers in our helmets spat strings of Spanish. "Last night we brought you to our homes in friendship! And what do you do? You use the opportunity to seduce our daughters!"

The men in our company chuckled. "What arrogance!" Tsugio shouted. "You think it humorous? You think it humorous to pollute our bloodlines? We have discussed this at the highest levels! It has come down from Regional President Motoki himself: it is Motoki's position that you were hired to fight the Yabajin—not fornicate with our women.

"These three women have dishonored their nation, their families, and their corporation. They shall redeem their honor!" At that moment it was as if an invisible glass fell in front of me, and for the rest of the day I walked as if in a waking dream, viewing things as if they had no bearing on me.

Three of Tsugio's aides each approached one of the girls dressed in white and stood directly before her, facing her. A family member of each girl took position at the edge of the blanket to the girl's right. Three samurai dressed in green armor each took a place to the left of a girl, drew a long sword and placed it at the back of a girl's neck. The aides then handed each girl a short sword, a *wakizashi*, and the girls wiped the blades clean with tissue and pressed them to their abdomens.

The aides spoke quietly to the young women a moment, then nodded. Two girls disemboweled themselves quietly, and the samurai swung their longswords and decapitated them before they had time to embarrass themselves by crying out.

The third girl just sat with her blade pointing at her belly. She looked at the corpse of the girl to her left, and her stoic countenance dissolved into panic. She dropped her sword and started to rise, and the aide in front of her grasped her hands and forced her back to her knees. All the Japanese were visibly angered and shaken by her cowardice. The girl's mother rushed forward and began speaking to her insistently, trying to calm her. She put the sword back in her daughter's hand and made motions with it, raking it toward her daughter's belly, indicating where she should insert the blade.

The aide spoke to the girl for a moment longer and she broke into tears. He stood at attention again, and the Japanese watched expectantly, eagerly. He nodded to the girl and she inserted the sword into her belly perhaps the length of a finger, as if to test the pain. The samurai above her lopped off her head. Like good soldiers, my *compañeros* and I remained at attention.

General Tsugio began babbling about the courage these women had demonstrated. "Even our women have more courage than some of you! See how they face the inevitable with equanimity. Their courage should be a great example to us all. Some people begin to wonder at your courage. Some people even laugh at you! When will you make up your minds to fight? Must you starve?" and he went on and on. Our men shifted on the balls of their feet, and I could feel their unease. Someone behind me shouted, "We are afraid of nothing!" Others grunted their assent. The holo tapes caught it all. The people of Motoki having failed at bribery had decided to try to embarrass us into fighting.

When Tsugio finished his harangue Garzón stepped forward. He was nervous; he licked his lips and brushed back his hair with one hand and surveyed us intently. I could tell he intended to try to charm us into fighting immediately. "*Muchachos*, General Tsugio, and people of Motoki," he addressed us. Someone whispered over his helmet mike, "Get ready," and people fidgeted up and down the line. Garzón continued, "Our men have worn their armor to this meeting today to show that they are indeed ready and willing to fight! They are men of war, not cowards to be laughed at!

"Not since the days of Cortés has an army of so many Spaniards met on such a distant shore with so great things before them." I found it humorous that Garzón had elevated Indians, chimeras, and persons of every nationality to the status of Spaniards. He looked at us worriedly and there was tension in his voice, genuine fear. "But though we are small in numbers, I would remind you of the great things accomplished by *Pizzaro*!"—he emphasized the name *Pizzaro*—"and his little band of a hundred eighty men!"

With a shock I suddenly understood what he planned. He conjured the name *Pizzaro* as if it were a secret code, and indeed it was, for the inhabitants of Motoki had never studied the exploits of the *conquistadores*, had no knowledge of their treachery. I could feel the tension in Abriara standing beside me, and I suddenly knew why she was nervous, why some men had stayed behind in camp. I looked toward the industrial park where the armory was located. We'd have to take that first, and I knew by instinct it had already been attacked. Indeed, a man in full battle armor was standing on the roof of one low building waving a green signal flag.

"And like Pizzaro," Garzón continued, "we find ourselves in a beautiful new world. And like Cortés, our ships are burned behind us! We have no choice but to go forward and fight! The choices thrust upon us are hard. No one wants to make hard choices. None of us wants to send our untrained *compañeros* against the Yabajin and watch them die! But what else can we do?"

Garzón paused just to make sure everyone figured out what else we could do. "In accordance with the laws of the Alliance of Earth Nations, I hereby publicly announce our intent to revolt and form a new sovereign state."

A man in the crowd shouted, "Garzón for president!"

And as one, five thousand men shouted, "*Viva Garzón!*" and drew their weapons.

There was no skirmish. The Japanese dropped their mouths in surprise and looked around frantically. A half-dozen Bertonelli lasers blew into General Tsugio and his aides.

Captain Esteves shouted, "Follow me!" and began running toward the small hill where the corporate offices were located. The rest of our columns split, most heading for the industrial park where the inhabitants of Motoki worked. Yet our men were running in confusion. Only a few of our leaders seemed to know what to do. We left a stunned crowd of Japanese standing on the tarmac behind us. Abriara shouted over her helmet mike, "*Muchachos,* exercise restraint! Kill only when necessary!"

Running up that hill I felt strong and quick and powerful. I was used to heavier gravity and the short run failed to wind me. We ran past a row of houses and several chimeras simply leapt, grabbing the eaves and pulling themselves onto the roofs in a single graceful movement; then they charged over the rooftops and thus gained surprise as they shot at the feet of civilians who'd come out to learn why guns were sounding.

Battle armor lends its own brand of anonymity. I ran as part of a crowd, cut off from the rest of the world. I couldn't smell the singed blood and hair of our victims as we shot anyone who showed signs of resistance. Even the booming of the flechettes or *zwoosh zwoosh* of the plasma rifles came to my ears distantly. Only the surprise and fear and rage on the faces of our victims came through to me, as if I were simply watching holographs of the Japanese we passed. In some spots, real scuffles broke out. In spite of the confusion, our men fought magnificently. I pulled my little chemical laser from its compartment, but didn't shoot anyone. We waved our weapons and frightened most people into inactivity. Fear seemed enough. Motoki only had a hundred armed samurai on duty, and I caught glimpses of some of them up on the hills, shooting at our armored men with their weak lasers. A couple of men came out of houses and tried to wrestle weapons from some of us. They got tossed aside like bean bags, then we fired into them.

I realized Garzón must have planned this overthrow— at least his officers seemed to have known about it. Though our attack was confused, our leaders were not surprised at the idea of attacking. Though he'd never gained control of the ship to force it back to Earth, Garzón had outwitted the samurai. I admired Garzón's audacity.

We shot out the glass panes to the corporate headquarters and ran into the building, I was happy to hear the distant horrified shrieks and watch the expressions of terror on the faces of the secretaries just inside the door. I ran up the elegant marble stairs behind a crowd of men who either shot or sliced open any corporate executive who tried to slow us down, so that at times the corridors were choked with bodies.

The other combat teams split off at lower levels, but Abriara, Mavro, Zavala, and I continued to the top, to the communications rooms where Motoki's only radio and holo station were located. A radio announcer was standing over a chair, yelling excitedly into his microphone. Mavro swung him by the arm and tossed him against a wall.

I ran into the holo studios and found four cameramen leaning out a window to shoot scenes in the streets below. Their faces were contorted in such masks of horror I couldn't help but look at a monitor on the floor that carried a 3-D image of their broadcast.

Outside some mercenaries dragged President Motoki from the offices and led him into the street. Garzón was there in a hovercraft, floating in the middle of the boulevard. Motoki waved his hands and shouted in Japanese. A microspeaker pinned to Garzón's lapel translated, "Wait! Wait! Perhaps I've handled this affair poorly!"

Garzón put a revolver to President Motoki's head,

pulled the trigger. Motoki's head exploded. Motoki fell gracefully to the street.

I looked at the faces of the men in the camera crew and knew they were already destroyed. The symbol of all their dreams was just a heap of quivering flesh. The shock of what they'd witnessed staggered them like a physical blow. There was rage in their eyes and hope- lessness and determination.

And I realized Zavala had been right all along. We'd been fighting a war of spirit and didn't even know how to win.

The death of President Motoki had immediate effects. Our coup had been relatively bloodless, but the four cameramen suddenly spun and saw me.

There was death in their eyes. I opened fire and fried them where they stood, then rushed to the window. For the next half hour I stood at the window, shocked by what I saw: all across the city the Japanese were running from their houses shouting and pointing toward the armory. It seemed every samurai in town quickly dressed in battle armor. They attacked without benefit of battle plan or weapons. Several thousand samurai along with many women and old people joined in suicidal charges on the armory. They were no match for a thousand of our heavily armed soldiers. The Bertonelli lasers boiled through their armor as if it were made of paper, and YCB flechettes cut them to ribbons. In some places the charred bodies of the Japanese became stacked in piles two meters high.

In twenty minutes thousands of the Japanese died. Those women most distressed by the initial failure to dislodge us set their homes aflame with themselves and children inside, and the flames swept through the south end of town. Whole families committed seppuku. Most citizens were content to simply throw themselves to the ground and weep in shame and ineffectual rage.

It seemed incredible Motoki hadn't seen it coming, hadn't set up internal defenses, but in over 2000 years the Japanese had never had a revolution. In a society that catered to every whim of its corporate leaders, people couldn't conceive of a man disobeying an order from above. They couldn't imagine us striking down superiors.

Our men barricaded streets and dug in, while squads of them searched homes for weapons and armor. Those of us still fresh from the cryotanks were given menial tasks. I was called over my helmet mike, and spent the day with two others heaving corpses onto a lifter so they could be taken to the airfield, identified, and left for next of kin. There seemed to be an endless line of corpses, gray-headed men with twisted legs and grimaces of pain, toddlers with faces blown off, housewives with pinpoint burns in the backs of their heads. I lost count of the dead at two thousand. Three times within the first hour I came upon corpses so hideously brutalized I was forced to remove my helmet to vomit. I soon became weak and dizzy from the task. We cleaned the streets in front of the armory first, then began working through town. But every time we got a street cleaned, some old woman would run from a house with a knife and throw herself at our mercenaries. I witnessed it a dozen times. And each time, the mercenaries would begin to chatter over their helmet mikes, saying, "Here she comes! Here she comes! Watch out for her knife!" and let the old woman get within two meters before they fried her. It became a sadistic game.

I kept remembering the suicides of the young girls dressed in white. The ceremony itself had been beautiful, like a wedding. I'd seen the eagerness, the anticipation in the eyes of the crowd as they watched the seppuku. They had a vicarious love of suicide. At first it seemed proof of their moral sickness, but as I thought about it, I began to see the beauty of it: in a land where everyone is subservient to the whims of society, to kill one's self in an effort to secure a good name in that society becomes an act of ultimate selflessness. It's a supreme example of the individual giving up his own identity in an effort to fit into society. Yet, at the same time, he escapes his society and its oppressive dictates: for while the suicide is guaranteeing himself a place of honor with his peers, he simultaneously cuts himself off from them forever, ultimately asserting his own individuality.

I could understand the actions of the people of Motoki. But though they acted according to the dictates of their own culture, it seemed to me that the dictates of their culture were oppressive, unnatural, and morally repugnant. I felt it was their duty to step outside their society and act on their own, to forget the stupid whims of society. But then, I remembered don José Mirada teaching me that a man who does that will lose the rewards his society offers. I'd done exactly that, and I was suffering the consequences of my recklessness. If I hadn't killed Arish, I'd still be on Earth. I wasn't sure I'd be willing to take such a risk again. And I realized if I were an old woman of Motoki, I'd have thrown my life away by running into the guns of the mercenaries.

By noon the city was quiet except for the sounds of weeping; the streets were empty except for an occasional Japanese who furtively scurried from work to home or the wisps of smoke that curled along the sidewalks and over the corpses like snakes. Garzón announced over our helmet mikes that our revolution had been accomplished within the bounds of Interstellar Alliance law. He applied to the Alliance ambassador aboard the orbiting Marine base Orion Four and received admission to the Allied Nations. This cleared the way for our seizure of all Motoki's financial assets on Baker so we could buy passage back home. All we had to do was hold Kimai no Ji for twenty-three days, till the *Chaeron* could be reoutfitted for the trip, and we could return home.

I had no time to think about his promise. I was too busy stacking corpses onto the lifter.

At sunset five thousand men, many of Motoki's best samurai, charged from their homes and overtook seventeen outposts on the north end of town. They captured eighty rifles and lost two-thirds of their force. By then they weren't strong enough to secure a defensive front, so they retreated to their houses. Garzón let them play their game, but after midnight he sent several hundred chimeras to the north end of town with electronic sniffers. They recaptured all the weapons.

Thirty-four hundred men, all in prime fighting condition, were then dragged from their homes in ones and twos and executed in reprisal for our own losses. It seemed a sound military decision—depleting the fighting forces of the enemy at no cost to ourselves—making the Japanese victims of our reptile logic.

We on burial detail followed like scavengers and threw bodies onto trucks. At many homes wives and mothers and children of the men to be executed put up a struggle and were liquidated. Family members clung to the dead, and we forced them away before disposing of the corpses. One old man attacked us with a knife and we chopped him up with our machetes. Thereafter, we kept one man on guard while the others worked. Long after midnight we came upon a heap of bodies. One woman was so warm she still glowed silver in the dark. Her hand flopped as we neared and I had a sudden unreasonable hope she was still alive, that I could save her. I ran to her and laid her on her back, began checking her wounds. She'd been shot through the belly with a pulse laser. Her face and hands had the mottled glow I attribute to dead people—the lack of hotpoints where blood surfaces near the skin. But I'd seen her move! I knew she was alive!

I yelled to my compadres to get me some bandages, to help me save her. I began pushing on her chest, trying to force air into her lungs. A compadre pointed out that she was dead and pulled me away. I looked at her a long time, and slowly realized they were right. They told me to get some sleep, and I stumbled away.

It had been an incredibly long day, and visions of horror swam before my eyes—images of charred bodies, broken bones, mashed faces. I bumped into a wall and realized I'd fallen asleep on my feet. I knew I wouldn't be able to take any real rest.

I felt I needed relief, and I remembered Tamara's promise to build a dreamworld for me, a place to retreat. Several times during the day I'd seen her in her wheelchair, buzzing around outside corporate headquarters.

I wandered through the dark streets past row after row

of mercenaries who hid behind piles of dirt, down to a retail electronics outlet by the industrial complex. I broke the front window to the building, climbed in, and helped myself to a power pack and a dream monitor—an industrial model like those used to run teaching programs for schools, then returned to corporate headquarters and climbed the marble stairs. The halls were no longer choked with bodies and an army of small maintenance robots was buffing the blood and broken glass off the floor.

I found Tamara and three others in the communications room playing old tapes of corporate officials at work, then subtly altering the images. Tamara was jacked into a computer outlet at a table full of equipment, interfacing with the holographic cameras alongside a man at an instrument panel. Another woman at a sound board was translating phrases into Japanese, then feeding them into the computer so it could synthesize new voiceprints to dub over the voices of the speakers. An Indian was hurriedly viewing boxes of old wire tapes, looking for things to alter.

I came in behind Tamara and touched her on the shoulder, moved around so she could see me.

"Hello, Señor Osic," the little speaker pinned to her kimono said. She sounded busy, harassed. She remained slumped in her chair, incapable of voluntary physical action. Her eyes didn't even blink.

"What are you doing?" I asked.

"Making propaganda tapes."

I looked at the holo they were running. President Motoki was sitting at a table with several men, General Tsugio and some high-level corporate types. A tiny crystal screen on the table down by Tamara's hand flashed a written message:

ANGELO, WHAT ARE YOU DOING HERE? LEAVE! I'M BEING MONITORED. YOU CAN'T HELP ME!

I nodded to let her know I'd received the message. I wanted to promise her help, to warn her of what Garzón was planning—a cymech prison little better than a brain bag. I wanted to apologize for her current predicament. Instead I sat heavily in a chair. The holo showed the

corporate officials conversing for two minutes then the
gentlemen got up, bowed to one another, and everyone
but Motoki left the room.

When it was done, the girl with the voice equipment
shouted, "Voice over!" and played a new soundtrack, one
where Motoki told a few jokes that, by tone of voice,
sounded bawdy, then the gentlemen at the table responded with guffaws of laughter.

"Rewind and take," the girl called. A tone sounded
from the holo, and the tape played again. But as
the Japanese spoke, Tamara and her friends changed the
scene. President Motoki grinned halfway through
the conversation and related a bawdy joke. The austere
countenances of the corporate officials gave way to
chiseled smiles, encouraging Motoki to tell jokes that
eventually brought snorts and guffaws. Then the corporate officers got up and left the room in good spirits,
leaving Motoki alone in his chair. Motoki swiveled away
from the table, and for a moment faced the camera. The
scene cut with an image of Motoki rising from the chair,
his face a devilish leer.

Tamara and the man beside her reviewed the tape
repeatedly, smoothing over rough spots, glossing it till
one could never prove it had been altered. I'd heard of
people altering tapes using computers to generate
graphics; I'd never seen it done this way, with a dreamer
creating entire images from her head. It vastly quickened the process.

When Tamara was done I nodded toward the holo. My
brains felt scrambled. I closed my eyes and leaned back
in my chair. "What was that all about?"

Tamara said, "We're trying to invent a plausible
excuse for Garzón to have shot Motoki."

Tamara's compadre spoke without raising his head
from the console, "We've been monitoring communications around town and found that most Japanese are
outraged. When reduced to its basic elements the
babble comes down to, 'Motoki gives us food. Motoki
gives us clothing. Now the *tengu* general shoots him as if
he were a common *eta*!'"

"So what's our excuse?" I asked.

The man snorted a laugh, "Motoki told bad jokes about Garzón, criticizing his character, and Garzón heard about it and in a fit of rage decided to avenge his honor."

"Why don't you just tell the truth, let them know we don't think their precious corporate deities are worth guano? Let them know we killed him to prevent an uprising after the takeover."

The gentleman working at the computer said, "If you want to know the secret of life, don't ask Military Intelligence."

Tamara's microspeaker said, "We have to give them a story they can understand. We can't tell them we don't believe Motoki was a superhuman. They've seen indications of class superiority all their lives. If someone is born a little awkward, it only proves he's a throwback to some *eta*, an inferior class. If someone excels, it's because he carries the superior genes of corporate executives. All the predictions become self-fulfilling.

"So, we tell them what they want to hear. We tell them we respect them, we admire them, we even love them—but we are a great and proud people, their cultural equals, and thought it only just to kill Motoki when he offended Garzón."

I asked, "Do you think they'll swallow such a tale."

"We don't know. All the men you saw in Motoki's office are dead, so there won't be any nay-sayers to rebut us. Our real problem is that Garzón is only a military leader, so the Japanese don't see him as having equal status with a corporate official. But we're building Garzón's image—giving him royal ancestry, making him a direct descendent of Cortés; on his mother's side he comes from a family of industrial barons. We're also boosting the image of pre-industrial Spain—giving it steel swords that rivaled those of the Japanese, making the Italian artists honorary Spaniards."

I snorted at the idea.

"I know, it sounds stupid," Tamara said, "and the whole idea disgusts me. But these people have absolutely no idea what's happened on Earth over the last two thousand years, so they're ripe for just about anything we want to tell them. We'll start airing these tapes in the morning. It may not work, but I'll bet it smothers a few fires."

Tamara's coworker rose and crossed the room, leaving Tamara alone. She said, "What can I do for you?"

"You told me once that you'd build a dreamworld for me. I've been stacking dead bodies into piles all day. I want to sleep in peace. I want—" I suddenly realized I had no idea exactly what I wanted. Escape? Peace of mind? No—release.

I'd been sickened by stacking dead bodies all day. I felt soiled after the dirty business with Lucío. I needed the internal fortitude to look upon such ugliness dispassionately.

I held my breath and resolved to take a step into the darkness. "Once you stimulated my emotions directly. I know such technology exists. You can do it again; you can program what you want into the computer on my monitor. I want you to record an emotional state, a deadness, that will let me learn to kill without remorse."

The next tape came on, another meeting of Motoki with his officials. Tamara didn't move for several seconds.

"The streets are full of people who can do that already," she said sadly. "Why do you want to be like them?"

"Until I gain their power, I am at their mercy!"

Tamara considered my answer. "I won't."

It was late and I was tired. I didn't have the will to argue. I raised my laser rifle level to her nose. She looked down the barrel. "You'd be surprised at how close I've come to feeling such callousness already," I whispered. "Perhaps I don't need your help. Perhaps all I must do is wait. Perhaps even now I could pull the trigger on you and I'd feel nothing. Shall we see if I can?"

Sweat broke out on her forehead. She stared into my eyes, afraid. She feared her own powerlessness. She said, "You've been practicing violence. I told you to practice compassion."

"When? When did you tell me that?"

"In the simulator," she said. "When I told you to

become fluent in the language of the heart. Yet you continue to practice violence."

I hadn't understood her words—had barely had time to think upon them. Perhaps because of my training in medicine I'm predisposed to view the human animal as a complex set of biochemical reactions. I tend to think of people as reacting toward situations only on the basis of genetic programming. Yet I saw that Tamara had told me to practice compassion as one would practice kicking a soccer ball, and I hadn't understood. I was predisposed to be deaf to such advice. And I saw that she was afraid because she saw that practicing violence and compassion were mutually exclusive. As you enhance your capacity for one, you diminish the capacity for the other. She was afraid I really would pull the trigger. I confirmed her fears with my words. "That's right. I am past feeling," I said. "I think I will pull this trigger."

Tamara laughed a calm steady laugh. It sounded strange coming from the microspeaker. "You lie. If you were past feeling, you wouldn't ask for dreams to make you evil. I know better. When I first came to you I told you I'd die if you balled me over. I threatened you with guilt. I tell you again, old man, if you hurt me: guilt!"

She stared at the gun.

I wanted to pull the trigger. I wanted to slap her. I held the gun against her nose and did nothing.

"I'll build you a world of my choosing, old man. Jack me in," she said. I unplugged the computer cord from her cranial jack, then shoved the plug from my monitor into her socket. It took her thirty seconds to build a world.

"Thank you," I said when she was done, wondering just what she'd chosen to build. I left, went down to the street where some forty compadres, including Captain Esteves and my own combat team, camped behind a barricade of dirt. There I jacked in the dream monitor, and at first was lulled by waves lapping the hull of a tiny sailboat that rode through an endless sea. It seemed a relaxing place, a fine place. I set the little dream monitor on automatic so that it would immediately flip on when it registered the REM associated with the beginning of a

dream. I wanted to be lulled by this dream, to live in the
dream only. But as I slept, Tamara's dreamworld
changed. I remained on the boat, but I entered a
nightmare world where I was filled with a love for all
men. I was on a tiny boat still, but I knew that in the
ocean on the horizon many were drowning.

Two hours later I was wakened by screams and
flechette fire. I listened to reports of samurai raids in
diverse parts of town. I was so bone-weary I wanted to
sleep again. But I looked around at my compadres and
saw everyone awake, tense, talking softly without helmet mikes. I couldn't sleep. I couldn't betray my friends
by sleeping while they were in danger. I erased the
program Tamara had given me for the monitor.

After several moments, Captain Esteves said, "We
just lost another forty amigos up by the temple. Samurai
with laser rifles came out of a false wall and surprised a
whole bunker. We've got men up there now, checking
the situation out. Apparently a tunnel catacombs the
city. It's impossible to tell how many people may have
taken refuge there, and some of them are armed. So
keep your eyes open. How many casualties does that
make now?"

"About six hundred altogether," someone said.

Esteves sighed. "*Huy!* We can't continue to sustain
these losses. We can't allow even a ten-to-one casualty
ratio. This city is too spread out; we need four thousand
of us to occupy it for any amount of time. Garzón should
have penned them all up on the north end of town. And
those Japanese know it. If we get below our critical
numbers, they'll start tearing holes through us fast.
What if the southern samurai come from the farming
towns to brave our defenses? We can't fight them off and
control our citizens at the same time."

Someone beside me spoke without engaging his helmet mike. His voice sounded distant. "I don't understand. Why don't they give up? You'd think after this
many casualties, they'd just lie down for a few weeks and
be glad when we leave."

A man beside him said wistfully, "They're all crazy. Do

you know, it has become the custom that when samurai patrols meet in the desert, their leaders strip off their armor and duel with swords for the right to continue their missions. The winner continues toward his destination, and the losing team returns home. I heard a friend say they videotape these battles and show them on the evening news. Their warriors have become incredibly quick and graceful, like dancers. They call it 'the beautiful style' of war. That is how crazy they are. They think war is beautiful."

"No, that's not the reason they refuse to surrender," I said. I wanted to understand, so I grasped at straws. "It's President Motoki. If Garzón hadn't killed Motoki, everything would have worked out all right. They'd have let us live. I saw it in their faces when they watched the murder. They went crazy when Garzón killed Motoki. I don't know why."

Zavala broke in. "Because we all owe Motoki a debt of honor, everyone on this planet—you, me, them. He was our employer. The debt of servant to master. And now the only way to repay that debt is to kill Garzón and the rest of us."

I knew his guess was right. He'd given an answer I'd never have been able to fathom. Zavala with his cultural shift. "Do you believe we owe a debt of honor?" I asked.

Zavala's helmet swiveled. "I don't know. If I was certain, I'd kill Garzón and the rest of you and repay the debt."

"I think Garzón believed he was only killing a political rival," I said, hoping to placate Zavala. "I have a friend in Intelligence who practically admitted as much. They're trying to come up with an explanation that will satisfy the Japanese. It was an accident."

"It was no accident," Perfecto said. "Garzón knows his enemies."

"There was a general in Guatemala once, who said all wars are an accident," Abriara mused. "He said humans were not built for war, that their territorialism was only meant to be expressed in the way of herd animals, through ritual nondeadly combat."

"You mean the way sheep or cattle do, by butting heads?" Mavro laughed.

"Exactly," Abriara said. "Throughout history, most human combat has been ceremonial—among the ancient Greeks one or two champions fought while armies watched. Among African tribes the victors of wars were elected on the basis of spear-throwing contests. It's the human equivalent of head-butting. Someone wins yet no one gets hurt. It sounds as if the Japanese, with their 'beautiful style of war,' are returning to this method, pitting champions against each other instead of fighting it out to the death. However, this general didn't use historical evidence as a basis for his argument. He stated emphatically that the best proof was that humans are not emotionally equipped to kill one another. If they were, genocide would be the most natural solution to territorial disputes."

I found myself listening with interest. I thought it strange that a military general should come to such a humane conclusion.

"I think this general was stupid," Mavro said. "I don't mind killing people."

I suddenly realized I should know this Guatemalan general, this caballero. But I'd never heard his philosophy. "Who was this general you speak of?" I asked.

"A man of your own country—" Perfecto said, "General Gonzalvo Quintanilla."

I gasped and my head reeled. "You liar!" I shouted. "Gonzalvo Quintanilla was a murdering despot! He could not have said such things—not a man who tried to overthrow his own country!"

"You are mistaken, Osic," Abriara said, her voice barely civil. They were the first words she'd spoken to me that day. "You confuse General Gonzalvo Quintanilla with General Gonzalvo "El Puerco" Quinot. Quinot tried to overthrow Guatemala."

"I know my own history!" I yelled. "Quintanilla's men raped and murdered my mother! I hunted the *putos* for months! Don't tell me about Quintanilla!"

Perfecto touched Abriara's arm as a sign for her to humor me, which enraged me even more. Abriara said in mocking tones, "Ah, forgive me, don Angelo, I didn't mean to anger you. I must be confused. I had no idea you were old enough to have lived in Quintanilla's day."

This seemed a very strange thing for her to say. When we'd first met, I'd looked as if I'd lived my sixty years. Abriara was being barely civil to me, and I was angry. I moved away from the group and watched the street leading down to the river. I felt confused and frightened that everyone had contradicted my tale of Quintanilla— so frightened I dared not speak of it, dared not think of it. Eventually my eyes became heavy, and I slept.

The sound of gunfire shook me after a few minutes. Baker's smaller moon, Shinju, the pearl, had just risen in a ball of purple. The fires still sputtered along the hillside as low-lying timbers continued burning in houses where people had roasted themselves. Fifty samurai were just finishing an attack.

They were rushing so quietly from a tunnel concealed in a hedge it could have been a dream. They carried white ceramic tiles, armor plates from hovercraft parts, as shields. For weapons they had clubs and knives. We responded by shooting the samurais' legs from under them.

It was a suicide attack. Deaths just waiting to happen. A few samurai made it to our lines, and there was a brief scuffle.

Afterward a dozen of our own men lay in crumpled heaps, their teflex shattered. We rushed forward, dug into the bodies, and found four men dead, another six with broken bones, bruises and stab wounds. Esteves secured the tunnel, called in a report.

We were all sobered by the incident. The samurai had only been upon us for a second, yet they did much damage.

As the medics left, another forty troops walked down the hill, dispersed among the nearest houses, and began firing into homes with plasma rifles and lasers, setting the dwellings ablaze.

Esteves ordered us to burn ten houses for each man we'd lost, to force the Japanese to submit, but I knew it would do no good. We could not force the inhabitants of Motoki to surrender. In our society, we admire the strong man. We revere our petty dictators, and we make it easy for them to gain control. But the Japanese would not accept us—would not surrender to Garzón. Master Kaigo had said it long ago: "On Baker, there is no surrender."

We left our bunker and carried out the order. At nearly every house, someone tried to bolt through a door or dive through some translucent paper wall. We let the women and children leave, but any male more than twelve years old we fried. My mind became numb and my hands became numb. I flipped off my external mike, sealing myself from the world. I watched what we did from a distance. I couldn't smell or touch or feel anything in my armor. Only the sound of distant shrieking Japanese came through, and everyone appeared to move in slow motion. After the first few, the killing became almost automatic. It was as if the armor moved of its own volition, empty inside. I was willing to fry them all. I imagined that we'd just continue the job, finish the whole town. Tarmara's propaganda would never be able to placate the Japanese. We were locked in a death grip and neither party could escape, neither could allow the other to live.

We were still burning houses, flames roaring and licking the sky, when the sun rose. I was on a hillside with the south end of town spread below me and the ocean to the west. We'd come to a house and begun shooting when a young man, perhaps fourteen, long in the legs but still a child in the face, came running out. I fired into him with my little laser, painting a line of platinum across his groin, and he staggered forward with a cry and sprawled to the grass, when an explosion rocked my feet. A kilometer away, down in Old Town, a whole wing of the industrial complex collapsed, the roof caving in as if the building had imploded. The great crystal dome over Old Town broke. Huge sheets of blue-tinted crystal dropped like cascades of rainwater, followed almost immediately by an explosion that tore the top three stories off Motoki's proud corporate headquarters. Though the explosion occurred half a kilometer away, I had to duck to avoid falling debris.

At first I thought it was our work, perhaps part of some plot to further demoralize the Japanese, extinguish their corporate spirit. But almost immediately someone pointed toward the industrial complex and shouted, "That's where they housed the company AI! All our external defenses are down!"

I looked back at the corporate headquarters, remembering that only a few hours before, Tamara had been on the top floor. Down in the valley below people began to shout and gunfire erupted: from a dozen places in town, several hundred samurai in green bug suits came boiling out of concealed tunnels—from beneath a large movable stone in the park, from behind a fake wall at the back of a garment shop, from an abandoned warehouse. Our mercenaries shot them with their lasers, forcing the samurai to slow and spin while flechettes cut through their armor. There were screams and flashes of silver as laser fire superheated the air. Someone fired a flechette nearby, and I searched frantically to see the target—an old woman armed with a club rushing from a house. And everywhere, everywhere, the Japanese were rushing from their houses. Amid all the commotion, I saw several men pointing to the south. Five huge yellow Mercer superfast zeppelins were zipping in low over the hills, coming in at 400 kph from the settlements in Shukaku and Tsumetai Oka. With the company artificial intelligence down, there'd be no response from our neutron cannons or cybertanks. And all other automatic defenses would only hit targets near ground. Roughly half Motoki's population lived in the southern settlements—those zeppelins would be loaded with samurai.

The whole world seemed to shrink down to one point. I was transfixed by the view of those zeppelins. I'd been trained in Guatemala to run a cybertank by remote, and I thought, *My God, if I knew the code so I could just jack into one of those tanks, I could fry those zeppelins.*

The sight of the zeppelins filled me with dread, and I stood motionless, waiting for Garzón's voice to ring through my helmet, waiting for him to issue orders for us

to form a defensive front. He didn't speak, and I
wondered if he'd been killed in the explosions. I saw that
all we'd done by taking over Kimai no Ji was to build a
castle of cards, and with the invasion from the south and
revolt in the town the cards were folding in upon each
other. It was as if the ground were slipping from beneath
me, and I felt myself dropping.

And then the zeppelins flew over a low hill near the
south edge of town and one lone cybertank on the hill
suddenly flickered to life. A beam of pure energy split
the sky and touched on each zeppelin in turn, and one
by one the zeppelins burst into fireballs. Multiple
concussions rocked the ground seconds afterward, and
houses shook with deep roaring booms that hit the hills,
then echoed and echoed.

Portions of each zeppelin continued to hang in the air
even after the explosions, and huge pieces of flaming
material flaked off the burning structures. I tried to see
if I could recognize any of the smaller cinders that fell
from the zeppelins as humans, but they were only
shapeless charred forms.

I looked around me and saw that everyone, Japanese
and mercenary alike, had stopped to watch the explosions. At the doorstep of every Japanese home the
people stood and stared at the sky with horror, mouths
agape and teary-eyed, gazing at portions of zeppelin still
clinging to the air.

The Japanese seemed to wither. They didn't scream.
They didn't cry. They didn't throw themselves on
our warriors. Guns were still booming, sounding like
the pop of firecrackers after the deep explosions of the
zeppelins. The mercenaries cleaned up the last of
the armored samurai. As quickly as the revolt had begun
it was over.

One by one the Japanese at the doorsteps bowed their
heads in apparent defeat and returned to their houses.
We went back to our bunker.

The rest of the morning was quiet. Garzón declared
martial law and ordered all Japanese to remain inside.
The Japanese obeyed as if it were a decree from their

own corporate deities. A dozen tunnels were found and destroyed under the city. One end of the theater collapsed after an explosion in a tunnel caused its foundation to crumble. In the early morning Tamara wheeled up the street in her chair, heading toward the Buddhist temple, and I was elated to find her still alive.

I waved and shouted to her but she just passed me by. Perfecto and several other men went downtown and returned with enough food and drink to make a fine lunch. We cooked a small pig in a fire pit in the street, then took turns sleeping in the afternoon.

But I couldn't sleep. All the things I'd seen replayed over and over in my mind—every person we'd killed, over and over.

In the late afternoon, a large mechanical silver spider with six legs walked up the street and stopped at the bunker below us and squatted near several men, who soon filed off one by one. The spider had a tiny laser turret on its back, and it took me several moments to recognize it as an ancient message carrier, the kind used by military personnel when they don't want to risk interception of radio or laser transmissions. When the spider reached our bunker it went over to a compadre, and a computer jack extended from a cable. The man plugged the jack into the socket at the back of his helmet. A few seconds later he unplugged from the terminal, got up, and trudged down the road.

A moment later comlink tones sounded in my head. I engaged the comlink and a mechanical voice said, "Prepare to receive recorded instructions from the messenger, please." The spider approached and I jacked in. An image formed in my mind of Garzón standing in an empty room, back lights shining on his silver hair.

"*Muchacho*," Garzón said, "as you know, our external defenses are down. We've confirmed that it will be impossible to build a replacement artificial intelligence.

"The inhabitants of Motoki's southern settlements took a great risk this morning, and their invasion attempt failed miserably. We remain prepared for all contingencies.

"We now estimate Motoki has suffered some twelve

thousand casualties. These losses have not gone unnoticed by the Yabajin. Our vulnerability has not gone unnoticed." Garzón's image faded, replaced by an aerial photograph of Hotoke no Za. "Two hours ago, some four thousand troops left Hotoke no Za." The picture expanded by degrees until one could make out the tiny images of hovercrafts flying low over a river, leaving an intricate weave of V-shaped wakes behind. "We can expect them to reach us in about six days. It will require all our energies to meet their challenge successfully. It will also require a moderate amount of cooperation by the inhabitants of Motoki. In the past hour I've negotiated with members of the Motoki family for a gradual withdrawal of troops from residential areas of the city so that we might prepare to fight the Yabajin. If you've been selected to receive this message, report immediately to Captain García for reassignment at the east wing of the industrial complex. Speak to no one."

I got up and looked around warily, then headed down into Old Town to the industrial complex. Spires of broken crystal still jutted up around the sides of Old Town like giant sections of broken eggshell.

By the time I reached my destination, three hundred mercenaries had gathered. García escorted us into a huge machine shop filled with drills, grinders, welding lasers, universal tooling robots, a hundred tables sparsely lighted by high windows. About twenty men were hard at work at one end of the shop, frantically constructing a small computer to drive some of the tooling robots, since the AI was down.

General Garzón was standing on a table, his helmet off, the sunlight shining on his hair. His eyes were glazed and bloodshot from lack of sleep and he hung his head as if in contemplation. He waited twenty minutes for everyone to arrive before speaking. "Compadres," he said with a sound of resignation, "Did you ever see such a sunrise as the one we saw this morning? A lavender sunrise? I do not think I ever saw any such thing on Earth. I was down near the beach when the bombs exploded, looking at some rocks that thrust out of the water. There was a great flock of cormorants nesting on the rocks, and when the bombs exploded they jumped into the air and flew as if scattered by a shout. It was very grand. I do not think I have seen its like on Earth."

Garzón looked up, held our eyes. He spoke softly: "I will not lie to you." He sighed. "We are in a bad time. As things stand, we cannot continue to hold an advantage over the inhabitants of Motoki for long. Our satellites show that many thousand Motoki samurai in the south are preparing to launch an attack to dislodge us. They are shuttling men into a camp some forty kilometers to the south. We estimate that they will attack within three to four days, and we don't have the power to stop them. Even if we could stop them, the Yabajin troops outnumber us ten to one. We cannot defeat them all and hope to quell rebellions in the city at the same time.

"We have considered our options: capitulation; retreat; unification with Motoki to fight a common enemy; genocide of the inhabitants of Kimai no Ji. For one reason or another all these roads lead to annihilation. If we follow any of these courses, we won't live more than a few weeks. I have a plan that gives us some hope, but I must tell you this: We'll never be able to return to Earth. We'll never be able to return. You must not hope to see your families or friends or homelands ever again. We can never return!"

The crowd groaned and everyone cast desperate glances around the room. I felt panic rising in my throat, and I felt something else—there is an umbilical cord, so to speak, that ties each of us to home and family. It isn't a physical thing, it's an emotional thing. Yet it's real none the less. And I felt that imaginary umbilical sever as if my emotional ties to Earth were being physically slashed.

"I can think of only one solution to our problem—" Garzón added, raising his fists in the air, and all eyes looked upon him. "And it is a plan born of desperation. We may sit here and fight the Yabajin, fight the samurai of Motoki. If we do that, we will surely win shallow graves!" He opened his left hand, and, in a melodramatic display, let dust sift to the floor, glittering in the sunlight. "But if we follow my plan and succeed, we will

win a world, a world where the sun rises lavender!" He
opened his right palm, and his glazed eyes glittered like
gems. He held in his palm a small red ball, a child's
globe of Baker.

Garzón's plan was audacious. He would let the Yabajin
cross the continent, so their hovercrafts would not have
enough fuel to return home, then we too would cross the
continent and attack their capital at Hotoke no Za and
claim the planet for ourselves. It was a desperate plan.
The grandiose scheme of a madman, and I wondered:
could this have been Garzón's idea from the beginning.
Did he see himself as a *conquistadore*? Did he so
desperately want to steal this planet?

That afternoon, Garzón took Motoki's only space
shuttle and placed ten squadrons aboard with three
cybertanks stripped of armor and sent them north of
the city. Then, while Motoki's southern samurai approached, I spent three sleepless days with several
hundred others tearing the plasma guns off four hundred
hovercrafts and replacing them with a quickly thrown-
together version of the Houser .50 caliber machine gun.
We used molds made from the YCB flechettes to create
two thousand copies of that rifle, then filled the rest of
our days loading bullets. Since we were no longer
officially headed by Motoki Corporation, we were no
long subject to the weapons limitations imposed against
the corporation. We replaced most of our energy weapons with simple projectiles. Dirty and deadly. Neither
the Yabajin nor the southern samurai had had time to
prepare for such a contingency. They couldn't have
upgraded their armor before leaving. They'd been fighting with energy weapons for so long they were locked
into tradition.

I'd have slept if I could, but I knew that to sleep was
to die. A strong wind blew from the sea, and the rain
beat heavy on the roof. At times I found myself asleep in
spite of my desire to stay awake. Standing, in a line,
loading bullets into clips still hot from the forges, lulled
by fingers of rain drumming on the roof, I'd find my head
snapping up only to realize I'd been loading clips in my

sleep. Sometimes I heard voices—mocking, derogatory snarls from imaginary throats, my mother shrieking at me like a demon when I was a child: "What's the matter with you? Don't hit your sister! *Pendejo!* Little goat fucker! What's the matter with you?" I felt reality collapsing around me. I didn't believe my sweet kindly mother had said such things, but I wasn't sure any more what she may or may not have said. I listened to those nearby, men bragging of those they'd killed in battle; their voices were no more comforting than my hallucinations.

We maintained complete radio silence from our compadres and worked away from the prying eyes of the Japanese. Garzón insisted this was imperative, for after the bombing of our AI, a Colonel Ishizu was caught sending messages by laser to an outpost twelve kilometers outside town. He confessed to spying for the Yabajin and it was he who'd organized the destruction of the city's defensive perimeter—not so the southern samurai could enter, but as a prelude to invasion by the Yabajin.

On the third morning we finished our weapons. We needed to outrun enemy hovercrafts, so we resorted to the old "Mexican hair" trick. In a null-g vacuum chamber one can pull superheated high-carbon steel into flakes so thin they float in the air like dandelion down. When this is thrown over the rear of a hovercraft, the next few hovercrafts to follow suck steel wool into their air intakes. The engines foul so quickly the damaged hovercrafts drop like stone. We found a great deal of steel fiber in a warehouse and packed it into sealed canisters that exploded on contact with the ground. A great many mercenaries gathered as we worked, and began loading all the valuable tooling equipment into the city's eight zeppelins, often simply unstrapping the gondolas and strapping on machines that couldn't otherwise be moved. Garzón did this as a last resort. If his plan didn't succeed, we'd need to be able to build our own defenses. But to do that, one needed tools.

We didn't finish our labors too soon, for we heard the distant sound of puff mines exploding on our southern border.

We went outside in the afternoon sunlight to load the hovercrafts with our new rifles and Mexican hair bombs. Each person got a bomb to hook to his utility belt. Our eyes were dazzled after three days in the dark. The zeppelins lifted above Old Town and streaked north. The sky was a blue gauze cut by a yellow lightning zag of opal kites. Someone behind me hummed a pleasant tune, like the drone of a bee. My eyes watered in the brilliant sunlight, and I felt fragile, ready to break. My hands shook.

Our men had already begun an orderly retreat from all parts of town, and we met at the hovercrafts at the airfield. Like many others, I got in my assigned hovercraft and removed my helmet, and my compadres soon found me. When everyone was more or less loaded, Garzón gave his signal and as one we headed north—away from Kimai no Ji, away from the southern samurai who cautiously advanced.

Garzón's plan was deceptively simple—wait north of the city till the Yabajin came to attack, then head for Hotoke no Za and take over their capital. Alliance law favored any government strong enough to establish global consolidation. If we could defeat the Yabajin at their capital, we could count on the Alliance to back our claim as the sole legal government on Baker.

We drifted slowly through the ruined town, a jumble of hovercrafts. Whole sections of the city had been burned black. The work of genocide we'd begun our first night had progressed steadily—for every one of our dead, twenty houses had been burned. No more than twenty thousand Japanese were left alive. There were mounds of charred bodies left unburied, body piled upon broken body, horror mounted atop horror.

We were eating the dust stirred up by our compadres, so Abriara whipped our hovercraft out to the far edge of the procession. I got a good view of the atrocities we'd committed. No one chattered over the helmet mikes.

The last few inhabitants of Motoki left their houses and clapped and cheered as we departed. A city made up almost entirely of widows and orphans. We were bristling with weapons, yet the Japanese stood and clapped almost in our path. If I'd removed my helmet I'd have been able to smell the breath of their old women as we passed.

Perhaps five hundred remaining samurai had been prepared to fight. Some came dressed in full armor to watch us leave. They'd somehow concealed this armor in spite of our shakedown. Some samurai carried knives, clubs, swords.

As we traveled up the road Master Kaigo stepped in front of us, huge even among the largest men in the crowd. He was dressed in his green armor and carrying a long sword in one hand, his helmet in the other. My heart skipped a beat at the sight of him. He watched the procession intently, and I was glad to be invisible behind my armor, anonymous. Yet through long familiarity he discerned his old pupils and waved us down. Abriara stopped the hovercraft.

"I will come fight for you!" he shouted. "In Hotoke no Za, at Buddha's Throne!"

Abriara said, "Why would you fight for us? The Yabajin are coming here." Her voice was wary, hesitant, bored.

"I made an oath as a child, someday to fight at Buddha's Throne." He smiled a deadly smile. "Yabajin will be there, too. I've taken my tea. My mind is cleared. I am prepared for battle."

"What of your wife?"

His smile faltered. "She is dead."

Up the road I saw other hovercrafts stop as samurai talked to their pupils. Abriara simply shrugged. "What do you think, *muchachos*, do we have room for our old friend?"

I did not trust Kaigo. I was very weary, and in no mood to play games. I raised my laser rifle to his face, and Kaigo frowned as if my threat were a minor insult. "A man of honor would speak truth when asked his intent," I said. "Why do you wish to come? Would you kill us in our sleep?"

Kaigo shook his head. "I would not harm you. I swear it!"

Mavro said, "Then it is Garzón you samurai seek to

kill. You want to avenge Motoki. Swear on your honor that you would not harm General Garzón!"

Kaigo's frown deepened and his eyes blazed. "How could I swear such a thing? A samurai could not live under heaven without avenging his master! I would die first!"

"You won't avenge Motoki. You won't have the chance," I said. "Why don't you kill yourself now? People in your culture love suicide—I have seen it in your eyes!"

Kaigo spat on the ground. "And your people love murder! I've seen it in *your* eyes!"

Rage filled me, bowled me over like a wave. Mavro swung his turret and pulled the trigger; with a single *whuft* the plasma split Kaigo's forehead and for a moment his head filled with light as if his skull were a lightbulb. Kaigo dropped to his knees and pitched backward.

Abriara began to shift in her seat uneasily, preparing to drive forward.

"Wait!" Mavro said, and he leapt over the side of the hovercraft and retrieved Kaigo's sword. "A fine souvenir of our vacation in Kimai no Ji!" He laughed.

I just stared in surprise. We'd killed many people, but no one who'd showed us any kindness. No one who'd taken us into their homes and fed us. A strong breeze was blowing into our faces. Up ahead, a dozen old women began throwing stones at our men. Our mercenaries opened fire, cutting them down. I imagined the way our men would be talking among themselves, joking with one another, saying, "Here comes a mean one! Watch her! Watch her! Don't let her get too close!" before they opened fire.

Your people love murder, he'd said, and the words sang between my ears. *Your people love murder.* I'd once nearly concluded that I'd joined a society of murderers, but the idea had seemed so insane I'd considered the thought an aberration.

Like everyone else, Mavro was surveying the city, taking a last look. "Ah," he sighed. "Our job is at least half done." Behind us buildings began to explode as our demolition crew leveled everything that could possibly be of use to the Yabajin: the sprawling buildings and warehouses in the industrial sector, the shops in the business sector. They were small explosions, calculated to do minor damage, to topple the buildings. The Japanese stood by the roadway, a line of ragged scarecrow people. Even after three days, parts of the city still smoldered. Strong winds and rains had stripped the blossoms from the plum trees. Kimai no Ji looked liked a garbage dump. Garbage-dump buildings good for nothing, garbage-dump people. And, as Mavro had said, we were only half done with this planet. *Your people love murder.*

The explosions lasted several minutes and I was tired, lulled nearly to sleep, till I realized the explosions had stopped and I was listening to a pounding in my own ears. My head felt heavy, and my eyes were gritty. Almost indiscernibly the sound of distant explosions drilled itself into my consciousness, but this time the explosions were not behind us, they were ahead: Garzón had sent cybertanks ahead by remote to clear our path of puff mines. There'd be no tanks left to defend the city.

We headed north a kilometer away from town, past our old barracks. The air seemed tinted yellow as it sometimes does when one is tired, and every line was unnaturally distinct. In some bushes I saw a pile of twisted naked bodies, Japanese women who'd been brought here to be raped before they were killed. There were dozens upon dozens of them, bare legs wrapped around torsos of other victims, on their faces the stupid expression of surprise so common to those who've just died. My stomach tightened in anger and Mavro said "Look! Disposable people—use them once and throw them away!" His tone was more sober than his words implied.

The fuel depot exploded behind us, sending up a huge fireball that colored the world red. I didn't turn to look. I gazed forward for what could have been seconds or hours. In the orange light of the fireball I saw something move in the bushes on the hillside.

At first I thought it was a cat. But a small girl with slim

hips was running through the pines, scrambling through a thicket like a wild animal, struggling up the hill away from us. She turned her head to peer over her back, and I saw a pale European complexion, dark eyes, dark brown hair tinged with almond curving to cup her cheeks.

"Tatiana!" I called, for surely it was Tatiana.

Someone shoved me and Abriara shouted through her helmet mike, "Wake up, Angelo! Be sharp! Switch your helmet mike to subchannel 672."

I snapped to attention and found the world was nothing like it had appeared in my dream. We were zipping through a pine forest in a narrow valley behind a dozen other craft, and all around, detritus was dancing in the air, thrown in our wakes. I felt fevered from loss of sleep. The sunlight slanting through darkened trees took on a hard edge. I reached down to the controls at my chin and dialed in a subchannel to my compadres.

"Ah, I had a terrible dream!" I said. "I dreamed we passed a pile of women who'd been butchered by our amigos."

No one spoke for a long moment. Abriara said bitterly, "We did."

CHAPTER 15

The day grew gray and cold. We kept watch behind, making certain the southern samurai didn't follow. I felt numb and dirty and my head throbbed. I'd been wearing armor nearly a week and longed for a chance to bathe. My mind kept returning to the image of the dead women, a tangle of arms and legs and hair. I couldn't think. I couldn't imagine anyone doing such a thing. Yet I'd seen the corpses. *Your people love murder.*

I watched the anonymous people in hovercrafts beside me, men hidden beneath chitin. I'd felt hollow when I'd killed only a few days before, and with my thoughts numb and sluggish, I was still hollow. We were all just hollow suits of armor. Dragonflies. I'd seen a film once where a dragonfly hovered over a field and snapped up bluebottle flies, eating them while on the wing, tiny mandibles shoving fly meat down its gullet. *Death on the wing. We are death on the wing.* I knew who'd killed the women at Kimai no Ji, the hollow men who were just like me. *Your people love murder.*

I remembered how I'd spent my time in Miami in my youth sunning myself like a lizard on the rooftop of my apartment, dreaming of escape from the hollow people, seeking to learn to live a life of passion. I remembered my village in Guatemala as a child, where men occasionally peed by the roadside, and choked back tears when told a heartwarming tale, or laughed themselves to tears at nothing at all. There was passion. All these years of running and I'd never escaped the hollow people. I'd never found my passion. This war had diminished me.

All my life I'd sought passion, to experience the full
range of emotions. Now my focus had narrowed to one
emotion: I was on a quest to regain compassion. And I
was losing even that. *Your people love murder*.

Kaigo's last words were so obviously untrue. I didn't
love murder. I could have dismissed his words if there
hadn't been so much blood on my hands. His sentiments
overwhelmed me. If I considered them seriously, I'd go
insane. *But you are already insane*, a voice whispered
inside me. *You are already insane*. I shoved the evil
thoughts away and fought for control.

Our journey over Baker promised to be a journey
through strangeness. Only twenty kilometers from town
the native flora and fauna began to appear: a pair of light
blue lips perched in the seam of a tree, apparently some
parasitic plant. A great river wound among the hills like
a giant gray serpent. Here were many short native
grasses under the giant firs, sprouting buds like oily
black eggs. Opal birds skimmed over the water at great
speeds, dazzling entities of glass shooting above the gray
river. We halted to camp and Garzón released three spy
balloons to watch the hills nearby. No one had followed.
It gave us the opportunity to try to make up the sleep
we'd lost.

A frigid drizzle began and the cold water seeped
through our armor, chilling us. We fanned out to search
for shelter from the rain. Most combat teams took refuge
under windfallen pines, but we spent nearly an hour
searching for a camp, and wandered afield three kilometers from our compadres. Mavro insisted there must be
a nice warm cave somewhere. We came upon a large
pale-blue hollow log, big enough to hold us, and Zavala
badly wanted to camp inside, but Mavro fired his laser
into it and both ends of the log snapped closed tight. If
we'd been foolish enough to step inside, we'd have been
swallowed whole. We finally found just what we were
hunting: along a hillside in some dense brush beside a
creek the skull of a giant carnivore was lodged against a
tree. The huge skull was just large enough so the five of
us could sit in comfort beneath the upper palate, protected from the wind and rain. The skull was strangely

translucent in its thinner parts, so one could almost see through it, and the skull was not like the skull of any living creature I'd ever seen—it was very sleek and angular, and the teeth in the jaw were strange for a carnivore. Like the cartilage teeth of some kinds of fish, the teeth and jaw were all one bone—simple jagged ridges on the edge of the jaw.

We stuffed the crevices under the skull with dry grass and twigs, making our shelter air-tight, then got a large rock and gradually warmed it with short bursts from my little laser. We removed our helmets and the air was crisp and pure. We were all very cold by then, and we just sat and rested our eyes while the sun set, trying to get up enough energy to cook dinner. A day on Baker is only twenty hours long, so when the sun sets, it sets a bit more rapidly than on Earth, especially if one is in the mountains on a cloudy day. It almost seems that the world tilts away from the light instantaneously. That is the way the sun set.

After a long while, Zavala grunted and said somewhat nervously, "I wonder what kind of animal this was? I wonder what it ate?"

I thought it a strange question. We'd seen river dragons, the Kawa no Ryu, in simulation several times. They are large purple serpentine creatures, with limbs so small they cannot walk, but must slither. I knew this must be the skull of an extremely large specimen. The teeth were worn and broken with age. I pointed to the fangs behind Zavala's head and said, "Those teeth are obviously meant for catching and holding prey," then pointed to a tooth by my foot, "and this tooth has long ridges on it, for grinding meat. This animal was obviously a carnivore."

This frightened Zavala all the more. "Sí, but what does it eat?"

Mavro said, "It is obvious that it feeds on something slow and dumb and fat. It must have eaten Japanese!"

Everyone laughed in low guttural sounds. Mavro went to the hovercraft and got some foil packets of rice and vegetables, a couple bottles of sake. I felt suddenly relaxed, at ease, and was content to remain awake. We cooked dinner and while we ate Zavala said, "Do you know what this reminds me of? It's like sleeping in the bush with my friends as a youth! Does it not feel the same to you?"

I hadn't slept in the open for many years, and I had to agree—there is a feeling of excitement that comes with sleeping in the open.

Zavala said, "Let's tell scary stories! Have you heard of the vampire brain?" He told the old yarn about a man so wise he lacked companionship of his own mental caliber, so he built an artificial intelligence wise enough to carry a conversation at his own level. When the man died the AI became lonely and constructed a bio-intelligence, a brain that weighed twelve kilos and inhabited its own cymech. But in order to remain alive the brain needed a constant supply of blood, and Zavala related all the bizarre and ingenious ways the bio-intelligence found to feed itself. It was a silly tale that was old when I was young.

"I know a story," Mavro said when Zavala finished. "And it's true: when I was a youth in Cartagena, running with the Low-Tech Boys, I had a friend named Xavier Sosa, and he was born with the Gift. He scored a 991 on the psi tests. In all the galaxy there may not be three hundred men who had the Gift as strongly as he did, and the Alliance watched him closely, waiting for him to mature so they could put his powers to use.

"Xavier spent a great deal of time staring into space at worlds all around us that no one else could see. He said reality is like an onion, with an endless succession of layers beneath the one outer layer we can see. We perceive but one layer of reality in our state, but he'd use the Gift to unwrap reality layer by layer, to see what was beneath, to perceive a whole new level of the universe we cannot comprehend. There are beings and peoples on every level. Some of these beings take different forms in our world and some of them have no form at all. Humans inhabit several universes simultaneously, but most of us are only aware of circumstances on one level of reality. For instance if we were to become aware of the alternative universe the Gifted call sixteen, we'd perceive ourselves much like plants—balls of colored energy with tendrils of light, lacking all volition. Not creatures that act, merely creatures that are acted upon.

"Once, Xavier and I were listening to music and I became uncontrollably frightened of nothing at all. Xavier peered at me for a long time then waved his hand and the fear left me. He said a creature had attacked me on level sixteen, and had been feeding on part of me.

"In that universe we're nothing because we are far from the center of ourselves. But in that same universe the creature we perceive as a simple sea snail is revealed to be a being of rare and glorious intelligence.

"All of you know that in such a universe the Alliance is waging a war. They send all the psychics into battle. Only the Gifted understand the nature of this war, and only they can perceive the nature of the enemy. Only a handful know how to battle on this level."

Mavro paused. I'd heard such tales as this but didn't know if I believed them. Certainly I'd never heard this rumor stated with as much authority as Mavro's tone carried.

Mavro sniffed, fired his laser into a rock by his foot, and held his hands out to the warmth of the glowing rock. "Xavier could never explain what he sought to do, but he explained the stakes: he said that if we won the war, a time would come where in an instant all mankind would unite in their minds. They'd perceive the nature of the threat within the other universe, and at the same instant the threat would be abolished. With it, all selfishness and greed would be abolished. He believed that someday this will actually happen. Not in our lifetime, perhaps not in a hundred lifetimes, but it *will* happen.

"When he was fourteen, he told me he'd learned to perceive the place the Gifted call Ten-sell, and there he'd watched our warriors battle the enemy. His gift was not mature, and the Alliance did not plan to recruit him for many years, but he told me he'd gone to this place and challenged a creature to combat. He planned to engage this being. I asked him many questions about it, and he could only explain that it looked like a large black piece of twisted metal, and that it too was not at the center of itself in this place; it too was at the limit of its ability to perceive him.

"I asked him about the danger to himself, and he explained that to do battle he must leave his body and travel to Ten-sell, carry the center of himself to a place where time does not exist. If he lost the combat, he'd forfeit his lives in several universes. Parts of him would die. But his greatest fear was that if he became thus damaged, he'd not find his way back to his body. He'd have no way to guide himself home, and part of him would be forever lost.

"He asked me to watch his body while he was gone, to stand guard with the rest of the Low-Tech Boys. We were supposed to stand over him and call his name.

"So we went to his house and sat beside him on his bed. He closed his eyes and stopped breathing and we called to him and administered CPR. But he never returned to his body. We buried him.

"A week later I felt him nearby. I did not see or hear him, but I felt him. Whatever part of him was left, searching for the rest—for that lost body. I've felt it many times over the years. I tell you this story now because he is here, standing just down the hill."

Goose pimples rose on my arms. Mavro's tale struck a chord deep inside me, making me uneasy, perhaps because his description of Xavier so closely paralleled my feeling when I thought I'd encountered the ghost of Flaco. Perhaps because his story about a man who'd lost part of himself so closely paralleled my own feeling that I'd lost part of myself. I felt haunted once again and I got up. "Does anyone want a drink of water?" I asked.

No one did. "Don't use the bottled water," Abriara said. "Drink from the stream."

I went down to the stream. It was ten meters wide and perfectly bowl-shaped, as if it had been dredged—a look typical to streams that the river dragons inhabit. Apparently they widen and deepen the channel as they wriggle over it many times. However, this creek had many bushes along the bank. The dragon that lived here had been dead for several years.

I looked down into the water and considered drinking it. The thought was too revolting, and I decided I wasn't really thirsty. Besides, I'd only used my thirst as an excuse to get away from Mavro. As I recalled his tale, chills shook me.

I began wandering along the creek bank thinking of Xavier doomed to forever search for a part of himself. I was exhausted, physically, emotionally. After all my years of living I was still searching for a passion that should be strong and vital. What did I feel? A creeping sense of hollowness? It is not the mere presence of violence that makes one become hardened, I said to myself. I'd lived with violence all around in Panamá and never been hardened.

It is my battle armor, I thought. *It cuts off the senses, makes everything untouchable.* I was exhausted, nearly hallucinating. It seemed wise to trade a little sleep in the hope of feeling *something.* I decided a cold bath would help. My balance was off and I stumbled as I stripped my armor and left it by the shore, then waded into the cold stream. The water was deeper than it looked, and I found myself over my head after only two paces. I swam a bit, thinking of nothing, till some large creature as hard as stone brushed my leg. I hurried to shore and dressed in my pants. I drew my machete and leaned against a tree, closed my eyes, tried to rest.

The bath had done no good. The cold water had numbed me and I couldn't feel the machete handle in my hand. I'd sought to feel something, but all I felt was cold, an occasional pellet of rain dropping on me, the wind playing over my chest, tightening my nipples. It wasn't enough. I didn't crave physical sensation.

I craved the depth of passion I'd felt when Tamara shoved her tiny dog's heart in my chest. I'd felt more alive, more vital, than at any other single moment in my existence. *Become fluent in the gentle language of the heart.* Her words formed the core of an argument I couldn't agree with. One couldn't practice compassion the way one practices to kick a soccer ball. At least, the idea seemed absurd. But her sentiments were sound.

The feeling she'd given me, I craved as an addict craves drugs.

Without thinking, I set out for Tamara's camp, toward the hill where Garzón's surveillance balloons hovered. I took only my machete and wore only my pants and crept through the dark woods alone, guiding myself by my faint infravision. The ground was wet and thick with pine needles. I moved almost soundlessly. I walked to the base of a hill and found a small clearing thick with fern and Baker's own short grasses. Leaves rustled at the hilltop and I froze in position. A shaggy deer-like creature came running toward me over the hilltop, pursued by a larger creature—half dog, half bear. I'd seen that particular carnivore in the simulator, hunting in a snowfield. In the simulator my laser had only angered the beast.

They were running through the glen, and there was no cover. I gripped my machete. The shaggy herbivore rushed past, brushing my left arm. Its head and mouth were shaped something like that of a deer.

Now the carnivore will turn and attack you, I thought, and I prepared. But the carnivore was intently watching its prey, and didn't even roll its eyes toward me. At the last moment I decided not to attract its attention rather than risk a thrust with my machete. It thundered past, stinking of mud and garlic.

The beasts crashed into the water of the creek down the hill, then thundered through the brush on the other side. I waited a long moment. I didn't know how common these big carnivores were, didn't want to meet one farther up the hill. Such a creature wouldn't be able to digest me, couldn't process my protein and fat. Still, a creature of instinct wouldn't know that.

I decided it would be best to speak to Tamara in the morning, and sneaked back through the trees toward my armor. My eyes felt gritty and heavy. Half an hour later I neared the creek where I'd left my armor. The ground was brushy and I crept. Over the gurgling water I heard twigs snapping in the brush. I was so sleepy I couldn't be sure of the noise. I didn't want to go nearer, yet felt I must retrieve my armor.

I shouted, "Who's there?" thinking to frighten any creatures hiding in the dense brush, and immediately a soft feminine voice with a foreign accent shouted, "Who's there?" in return, and many women said, "Who's there? Who's there? Who's there?"

I thought crazily that somehow several Japanese women had followed us and were stealing my armor. I leapt through the brush and came face to face with a creature that could have been a giant spider or crab. It was black in the dim light and stood a meter tall at the shoulders, though its carapace was twice as wide. It had two immense claws as thick as my body. Each claw held a small bush which the creature waved as if to ward me away. The creature said, "Who's there? Who's there?" in its soft feminine voice. Holding branches between us, it backed toward the creek.

There were dozens of these giant crabs and they all held bushes in their claws and said, "Who's there?" as they slowly backed into the water.

I was so astonished I didn't move. Each crab had an organ like a collection of tubes at the base of its mandibles, and the voices issued from these. I shouted, "Angelo!" at the last few creatures. In return they parroted, "Angelo! Angelo! Angelo!" as they dropped over the bank into the creek.

My armor was strewn all over the place. The giant crabs had dragged pieces everywhere. I picked up the armor and went back to camp. Abriara was awake, sitting at the mouth of the skull. I told her of the giant crabs.

"The Japanese call them *manesuru onna*, the mimicking women," Abriara said. "They're very common near coastal waters." She looked at me for several seconds. I was still wet from my swim, dirty from my walk. She said, "Angelo, are you in pain?"

They were the first soft words she'd said since I'd mutilated Lucío. "No," I said. "I was just thinking."

"You were thinking painful thoughts. What were they?"

Only a few days before I'd told myself that I didn't want her affection, and after fighting Lucío I'd became afraid I'd lost it. I found myself revealing my deepest feelings. "When Master Kaigo died he accused us of loving murder. I wonder if his words are true. When I fought Lucío I wanted with all of my heart to put the machete down, to stop tormenting him—yet I could not. Do I love murder? And when I saw the dead women outside of town—I keep thinking such a sight should destroy a person. Such a sight should make it impossible to live. Yet I feel myself hardening to it. I feel myself becoming numb. And I wonder, do I love murder?

"When I was a child I used to access the dream networks. Always I admired it when the good man killed the bad man out of vengeance—and I realize now that I may indeed have been trained to love murder. And maybe that is why I could not stop killing Lucío. Because I love murder, because I've been trained to believe that good men can kill bad without consequence. But I feel the consequences inside me. I'm dying. And I think maybe it is this society that has done this to me. Maybe this society is evil. And if it is evil, I should remove myself from it. I feel a need to escape the way a man feels a need to escape prison."

Abriara looked at me a moment. "Every man must believe in his own innate goodness," she said. "No matter how loathsome a person is, he will hold up his good points to himself and look at them and say, 'I am a good person.' And because of this need to believe in one's own innate worth, all people obey nearly all the strictures placed upon them by their society. You do not paint your face with sunsets, eat popcorn for breakfast, or walk down the sidewalk backward simply because you know your society does not condone such behavior.

"Now you have committed murder and wish to blame your act on society so you can continue to believe in your own goodness. And certainly some would agree that your society is at fault. Our society does love murder. As you say, we were raised on violence in every form and we consider it worthy entertainment. But according to the social engineers, all societies seem evil and insane when viewed from the outside: a socialist looks at us and sees how we are brainwashed into believing we need

objects to make us happy. He sees our society riddled
with corruption due to commercialism. Yet we look at
the socialists and are shocked that their society does not
help them attain the labor-saving devices we worship.
The socialists live a hard life. Who is more evil, the
socialist or the capitalist? Both societies are equally evil
in the eyes of a social engineer, and from the outside we
can see the evil in all societies, yet each sees itself as
being correct. Yes, you do live in an evil society. Yet we
could look down through history and find a hundred
societies that loved murder more than ours does. Kaigo's
society loves murder as much as ours does. And as you
said, they love suicide, too. You say you feel a need to
escape your society. But don't you see that in order for
you to see the evil in your own society, to some degree
you must have escaped it already?"

Abriara watched me steadily. "You may find a society
that doesn't love violence. But even if you find such a
society, from the outside it will appear evil to you in
some way. You are too much of an individual to fit
comfortably into a society that was created by another."

I thought about it for a moment. I'd never heard
Abriara discuss such ideas, and it somehow seemed
incongruous. "Where did you learn about these philos-
ophies?" I asked.

"I studied social engineering in Chile. After all, one
must know the enemy," she said, referring to the Nicita
Idealist Socialists in Argentina. Everyone had known for
years that the Idealists would start a war. Their philosophy demanded it.

I dressed in my armor, went to our shelter, and lay
down. Perfecto was awake, watching me with half-closed
eyes. I said nothing. If Abriara was right, I considered,
I'd never find a better society to serve than the one I
already belonged to. Yet it seemed that somewhere
there should be a society I could serve without feeling
repugnance. I considered the anarchists of Tau Ceti, the
skeptics of Benitarius 4, the Justinians of Mars. And
Abriara was right—all the cults disturbed me at some
deep level.

I dreamed I strolled over a stone bridge where clear water poured through a narrow channel. By the banks of the stream were the great dark crabs, the mimicking women, gathering rushes. The grass on the hillsides was the color of jade, and everywhere was the sweet smell of Baker.

In the distance I glimpsed a man, an old white-haired man dressed in a fine gray suit, who carried himself with dignity and grace. He furtively glanced back at me over his shoulder, then stepped behind a hedge. My heart quickened. I felt I knew that man, but could not quite place him. I thought if only I could see his face, I'd be sure. I hungered for his presence.

And I, I was dressed in sweaty, muddied battle armor, for I'd been practicing in the fields. I chased after that man, ran to the hedge shouting, "Señor, señor! May I have a word with you!"

But when I reached the spot where he'd been, he was gone. I cast about, searching for him, and saw him farther on, speaking to a young lady, admiring a thicket of plums where boughs of pink blossoms cascaded from the trunks like water from a fountain. I called after him, and he stepped into the trees. The young lady looked about, searching for the cause of the gentleman's unease, and I gave chase.

Behind the thicket of plum was a trail bordered by lush grass. And the gentleman was upon that trail heading into a pine forest, too far away for me to hail. I followed, fearing to go into the dark forest after him. But I did press on into the forest, along an unused path overgrown with moss. I called to him and my voice fell dead among the pine needles. My feet crunched over twigs, breaking them as if they were small bones. The path was misty, and several times I thought I'd lost it. Yet I gave *chase, twice glimpsing his gray back in the distance.*

I came to a clearing where there was a small white house with papaya trees and orchids in the yard. It was my home in Panamá, and behind the house the whistle of a maglev sounded as it rushed over the tracks that crossed Lake Gatún. It was beautiful, and it felt so good to be home.

I walked up to my house, opened the door, and smelled the familiar scents of home. I looked on the floor where Arish had died, and there were no bloodstains, no sign of his existence. Yet a great disquiet filled me at the sight of the spot, a great emptiness. I heard voices— the young girl Tatiana laughing in amusement—and I saw Tamara at the top of the stairs sitting straight and beautiful at the table, gazing in rapture at the partially concealed form of the old man who had his back turned.

I shouted, "You there, señor! I beg your pardon!" Tamara gasped at me in horror as I bounded up the stairs, muddying the handrails with my dirty hands. Tatiana also sat at the table, and she lurched back in her chair to escape. The old Angelo turned to face me, and his eyes were alive and fierce. He was angered to see me.

"Get away, you vicious dog!" he shouted. "Why must you pursue me?"

I fell back, stunned by his wrath. I looked around at the shocked faces of my friends. I didn't know what to answer. I pulled a revolver from my pocket and fired into his face.

When I woke, the rain had stopped and the skies were clear as far as the eye could see. Garzón's spy balloons had climbed far into the sky. We took it easy. Garzón wanted us relaxed when we met the Yabajin, and just as important he didn't want us to get too far from Kimai no Ji. He wanted the Yabajin to believe we were like vul-

tures, simply waiting for the Yabajin to fight with
Motoki's samurai while we hoped to clean up the last of
them after the battle. He didn't want them to realize
we'd attack Hotoke no Za—not until they'd come so far
that they wouldn't have the fuel to return home.

Perfecto watched me most of the morning, giving me
evil glances. I kept expecting him to speak. Marvo went
to visit friends and Zavala and Abriara went to wash in
the stream, leaving Perfecto and me alone. "Angelo," he
said, "I saw you speaking with Abriara last night." His
face revealed a barely controlled rage, and I wondered
momentarily if he was angry because I'd spent time with
Abriara. I'd seen something of this in his eyes when he'd
found Abriara helping me dress. Did he have designs on
her himself? I wondered. He continued, "And several
nights ago you went for a walk with her instead of coming
to the baths with me. So I must ask you, Who is your
favorite person?"

He was jealous of Abriara. With his heightened territorialism I should have seen it coming. "You are my
favorite male friend," I said. "Abriara may be my favorite
female friend."

He stared at the ground in shame. He knew he could
never have the kind of relationship with me that Abriara
might have. I wondered if all bonded chimeras became
so jealous. Would they end up fighting for my attention?
And I also realized something else—Abriara and Perfecto had both been seeking my affection ever since I
woke from the cryotanks. Both had sought to advise me,
to counsel me, to meet my emotional and physical
needs. They were both struggling to become my confi-
dant, my best friend.

"Then, if you marry Abriara," Perfecto said, "may I
live next door to you? May I come help do your
gardening once in a while, or just come to talk and drink
beers?"

"You will always be welcome in my home," I said.
"You are my best friend."

Perfecto considered a moment. "Good, so long as you
know I am your best amigo!"

Abriara came walking up from the stream a few

minutes later and Perfecto hailed her by shouting, "Abriara! I am Angelo's best amigo and you are his best amiga!"

After my experiences with the strange animals the night before, I couldn't imagine staying on this planet for the rest of my life. Garzón had promised that even if we beat the Yabajin, we'd never return to Earth. I couldn't imagine this. I was afraid I'd forget what Earth was like. I remembered the ease I'd felt in my dream of Panamá, the way my mind was refreshed by the familiar comforts of home. Yet, I'd lost myself at home. I'd left my compassion there on the floor when I'd killed Arish. And I wondered if I returned to my home in Panamá, would I find myself there? I wanted more than anything to build a new world in my dream monitor, an illusion of Panamá as it had been when I left.

Late in the morning I took my monitor and walked to Garzón's camp. I didn't hear or see any dangerous animals, though many times I heard rustling in the brush as small creatures the size of guinea pigs foraged among rotting leaves. At Garzón's camp they'd built a roaring fire, and a good two hundred men sat around it and joked. The cold seemed to be dissipating, but the fire still felt good. Tamara sat near Garzón, the only person wearing battle armor while slumped in a wheelchair. Garzón never let her out of his sight. One could almost imagine an invisible leash five meters long attached to Tamara's neck with Garzón holding the end. I knew Garzón wouldn't like me to speak to her privately, but he seemed distracted.

Garzón was intently telling a funny story about a man who went to a restaurant in Mexico once a week after the bullfights so he could eat the *huevos fritos de güey*, the testicles, from the bull. This went on for several weeks, and the man was well satisfied, but one day the waiter brought his plate, and instead of the huge testicles he so much relished, the plate had only small testicles the size of walnuts. The man asked the waiter, "Every week after the bullfight you bring me large, fresh, delicious huevos the size of oranges! Why do you bring me these little things now?" And the waiter answered, "But señor, the bull, he does not always lose the fight!"

This joke was received with such applause Garzón immediately launched into a story about the secret police in Peru. People clung to every word. Seeing my chance I bent near Garzon's ear, held out my monitor, and asked, "General, I'd like to reconstruct a dream-world of my home in Panamá and wondered if I might get Tamara to help?"

Garzón nodded and waved me away, happy to be rid of the distraction.

I went to Tamara's wheelchair and pulled her back from the fire explaining, "I'd like you to build a world for me: my little home in Panamá," then switched the monitor to *interactive*, plugged a jack into the base of her helmet, and jacked myself in.

Tamara was already at work building Panama, riding the back of her giant bull as she stared at empty spaces, and entire buildings sprung into existence. I felt a thrill of hope and anticipation. This would work. This would work. This world would make me better. But it wasn't the Panamá I remembered. She'd started on Lake Gatún and had put the southern shore so near that the maglev rails crossing the lake were practically in my backyard. My house was correctly proportioned but the houses of my neighbors, though elaborate in detail, were not correct in design. They were the houses of strangers. Yet she did much good work and this gave me hope. She urged her bull forward and walked through my yard, putting sky, land, insects, and birds all in place, and made the air heavy and humid with a slight tang of sea breeze while billowy white clouds floated lazily over-head, casting shadows on the lake. Details that would have taken me weeks took her only minutes, and I let her build a world for me while I watched to see what I'd have to change.

When she was finished she said, "Is there anything else?"

I sauntered around the yard. She'd made it perfectly, the palms and irises in place, dark papaya seeds on the grass where the fruit bats had spilled them the night before. I walked in my house and found the carpet in the doorway worn just as I remembered, and my stereo in the kitchen was still tuned to the proper channel. There were minor problems, mostly tiny omissions, but I opened my refrigerator and found my favorite brand of beer inside, opened a can and it foamed out over my hand; it tasted wonderful.

I looked around the dreamworld, and I couldn't have asked for a better job. I could fix it all with just a little work. But something was wrong, something I couldn't fix. I still felt hollow, like a stranger who didn't belong in this house. The ache was in me. I remembered the man in my dream, accusing me with his words. The thing I searched for was the man I'd been. I walked back out onto the porch, where Tamara still sat, mounted on her bull.

"It isn't enough," I said.

"What more do you want?" Tamara asked.

"I have always dreamed of living life with passion. With zest. Somehow, I've lost that. You've sometimes made me feel things inside. You did a thing I've never seen done by a professional dreamer: you seemed to stimulate my hypothalamus, stimulate emotions, directly instead of relying on the context of the world to arouse emotions. You made me feel that passion."

Tamara nodded. "Normal dreamers aren't allowed to use such equipment. It's too dangerous. I sometimes need it for my job."

"I wanted you to make this little house so I'd feel the way I felt in Panamá. I want to feel—in love with the world."

"In love with life," she corrected.

"Yes. That is what I want." And the desire burned in me. I craved that feeling, had craved it since the day I'd left Earth.

Tamara shook her head, and her eyes were soft, thoughtful. "I'd help you if I could, but four days ago you wanted to die inside. You don't know what you want."

She was right. I felt I was balancing on a narrow rope, unsure which way to fall. "And even if I did what you ask, even if I commanded the monitor to stimulate your emotions directly, it wouldn't change you. You could remain hooked up to the monitor all night, but when you took it off you'd still feel empty and dead inside. I showed you that vision only to let you see what you were leaving behind. You . . . you'll have to find your own way."

I looked in her eyes and saw a wonderful thing: she was lying. When she said I'd have to find my own way, she'd lied. "You're lying to me! You know more than you say. You believe you can help me, but you are not willing to admit as much! What could you be thinking?"

Tamara stared at the ground and considered. "No. I cannot help you," she said. "Take your monitor and go help yourself."

That afternoon I took my monitor into the woods, sat with my back against a rock, and jacked into the world Tamara had created. Many minor details needed correcting.

I began with my house, a simple white house. I put in the plaster cracking from the walls at the foundation, a few chips in the red tiles on the roof. I began designing it exactly as I remembered, creating a perfect record so I'd never forget. The homes of my neighbors, the howling of the monkeys on the south side of the lake, the sights and smells and sounds of the feria, all these I'd create over the next few days. And when I finished, I'd have a world where I could spend a day in my booth in the feria peddling my medicines. Everything would be as it had been.

I was acutely aware that this could have still been mine if I hadn't killed Arish. Tamara could have spilled her secrets to the guerrillas; it was insane to kill Arish.

I was decorating the mantelpiece in my den, recreating the vases and lace doilies I'd inherited from my mother, when Perfecto jacked in beside me.

He watched me. "I was worried about you. You look so, so—preoccupied, pensive. I thought you might be afraid of our upcoming battle."

"Not really. The Yabajin don't have a chance in the open. We'll just cut them down. Hotoke no Za will be the hard one. I don't know how to beat their remote defenses."

Perfecto nodded. After a time he said, "This must be your house. A fine house."

I showed him the house and yard, explained my plans. I indicated where I'd make the feria. He nodded, smiled sadly, and said, "I suppose that's all right. I guess it's not too crazy."

"What do you mean?" I asked.

"It's just that—are you sure you're not planning to escape into the past the way all old people do? I can imagine you just sitting here every day sucking images from these crystals while your body wears down."

"No! I swear to you, that is not what I plan!" I shouted, stunned by the image he portrayed of me.

Perfecto licked his lips, put his hand on my shoulder, then jacked out.

I looked around the rooms, tried to remember it all, drink it all in. Then, I let the illusion collapse as I jacked out. I left the monitor there in the woods.

Early next morning Garzón's zeppelins full of tools sped north away from the coming battle; our space shuttle full of men and cybertanks left for Hotoke no Za; and we took the hovercrafts out on the river toward Hotoke no Za and the approaching Yabajin. The river made a fine road that could carry a hundred hovercrafts abreast. We left at full throttle and in an hour passed mountains that would have taken weeks to negotiate if we'd gone cross-country. The pine forests gave way to vast savannahs where robin-egg-blue grasses sprouted leaves of feather. River dragons thirty meters long sunned themselves on the sandy shoals of the river and flowed into the water like snakes when we approached.

A child may see an animal or plant yet not perceive its existence. Only after several years may he learn to distinguish between a daisy and dandelion. In the same way I was a child in my perception. When I say I saw a field of grass with feathers for leaves, I describe only what I perceived on the surface. I simplify in order to describe, yet the simple description is inaccurate. For there were other plants—strings of dark ultraviolet tape, grasses shaped like tiny pines, rope vines with incredibly thick bulbous roots. Yet the mind can't discover all these shapes at once. Just as one doesn't perceive the myriad variety of weeds in a wheat field and doesn't perceive the insects that play among the field, my mind couldn't individualize the things I saw. I couldn't individualize the opal birds or see how many species there were. My mind revolted at the task. My eyes ached and a splitting pain filled my head when I tried to catalog the diversity of animals and plants. Often I didn't know what I saw.

On the river we once came upon hairy round creatures like coconuts with tails and no sign of head nor feet. The tails spasmed insanely, pushing the creatures over the water like tadpoles. I imagined them to be like muskrats back on Earth, and jacked in a call to Fernando Chin; he said it wasn't an animal at all, only a seed pod with a tail to propel itself to a spot where the acidity level would allow it to grow. A few minutes later I saw creatures shaped like wheels with spines rolling along the river bottom. I asked Chin what type of plant or animal they were, and he said they were just sections of endoskeleton from some animal.

The sense of alienness was compounded by the many whistles and clicks that came from animals in the underbrush, and by the lavender cast to the sky, and by the bands of opal kites twisting like rivers across that sky, and by Baker's moons that shot over the horizon twice a day. Because of the pain these new perceptions gave me, my eyes automatically riveted on familiar things—the occasional grove of willow or oak along the riverbank, the back of Abriara's suit, the shape of the hovercraft before me.

In another three hours we passed a second set of mountains, very steep. Because of the high level of carbon dioxide in the atmosphere, the rains on Baker were more acid than those on Earth, and one could see the effect of this acidity engraved in the old rocks. The cliffs were marvelously chewed away. Nature had sculpted a thousand hideous faces—old men with sunken eyes and bulbous noses, twisted monstrous limbs. Many weathered stones were hundreds of meters high, like hunched giants. Twice we had to skirt waterfalls. The river narrowed considerably, and the spray raised by hovercrafts in front drenched us. The river had eroded a deep canyon, and when we made it past the mountains we came up out of the lip of a canyon to a desert plateau where alien ferns sprouted from cement trunks like barnacles. Many of Baker's plants have developed defenses to the high winds, and one common defense is the ability for leaves to withdraw into sheaths in the trunks. These ferns had this ability, and because the wind was gusting the plants were constantly withdrawing, then tentatively folding back out.

On the horizon was an endless desert of red dust. In the far distance great red clouds swirled in the air, and because of the heat dancing on the desert floor I saw a line of fire across the horizon. Our trip had been very quiet, since none of us spoke through our helmet mikes, but suddenly Garzón shouted through our helmets, "*Muchachos*, you see the enemy before you! Now you will fight the Yabajin! Now is your chance for great deeds! Set your helmet mikes to channels A, B, and C, and let your sergeant give you your subchannels. Fight bravely!"

Then the truth of it struck me—the line of fire on the horizon was heat warmed by engines from the Yabajin hovercrafts, and the dust drifting like firelit smoke was blown by their passage.

CHAPTER

16

I switched open the channels on my helmet mike and the voices of the hundred men in our squadron filled my helmet with shouts of "*Yiiii—hiiii*, they come! They come!" and our squadron leader ordered us to form a triangle at the north end of the group and assigned numbers to each sergeant so they'd know where to place themselves in formation. At the same time Abriara shouted for me to take my armor repair kit from my pocket and set it someplace convenient, and I began fumbling through the compartments of my armor looking for the things I needed, and set the repair kit in front of me, then checked my flechette to be sure it was loaded and the safety was off and I turned on the targeting laser on my rifle and I could see the air shimmer in front of the rifle and knew right where the center of my spread would hit and was convinced I could shoot from the hip. I opened a box filled with clips full of ammunition, then looked straight ahead and waited.

My head was reeling and I felt nauseated, and wanted only to close my eyes. Abriara increased our speed to maximum, and the hovercraft rattled as if it would break as we bounced over the desert. The air was so clear we'd spotted the Yabajin at thirty kilometers. With armies traveling at full speed we had six minutes till we collided. My nostrils flared and I was suddenly terrified: we'd already lost four thousand men to the Yabajin in space; they'd managed to have an agent blow our defenses in Kimai no Ji. I didn't know much about them, but I knew better than to believe we could surprise

413

them, better than to underrate them. Garzón had
wanted to bypass them altogether—yet they had managed to block our path.

And here we were flying toward them at 120 kph,
trusting our ancient projectile weapons would surprise
them. I couldn't believe we'd get away with it. I couldn't
believe the Yabajin would wear nothing better than the
thin armor meant to baffle heat weapons. My jaws
clenched, and I tried to remain calm.

Abriara veered far to the left and took her place in the
formation. Our thousand ships formed a great wedge
with the four hundred craft that had received the Houser
machine guns forming our front ranks. Those with
Housers were both blessed and cursed: their greater
firepower would let them blow away almost anyone who
got within range, yet they'd receive the brunt of the
attack. I was glad our hovercraft hadn't received such
weapons.

In a protected position at the center of our V, I could
see Garzón's craft. Tamara's wheelchair was there sitting
next to a turret manned by the general himself, but
Tamara was not visible. Someone must have laid her on
the floor of the craft.

Over the helmet mikes the compadres in my squadron
shouted bets—"Three to two that the de la Cuzco team
gets the most kills. Three to two!" de la Cuzco's team had
taken the outside corner of the whole triangle—the most
dangerous spot. In answer came, "Barzun down with a
million on de la Cuzco to win; Barzun for a million!"
Then a deep voice: "Mott here, I've got two million that
says de la Cuzco will get fried. Two million says de la
Cuzco gets fried!" Then de la Cuzco shouts over his
mike, "I'll take that bet!" and everyone laughed, since de
la Cuzco wouldn't have to worry about paying if he lost
the bet.

All the men were laughing and betting extravagant
fortunes that would have taken years to accumulate back
on Earth. The Yabajin formed three fronts, each 200
meters behind the other, and their hovercrafts were
bunched in pairs so we'd be forced into a crossfire when
we went between them. Garzón ordered all craft to veer

north, and we did so, then paired up hovercrafts so we
were floating side by side so we could counter with a
crossfire of our own. The Yabajin responded by shifting
north. I made some mental calculations to figure how
long we'd battle if we made our pass at top speed:
Figuring a 200-meter range, and considering that we
would be passing at 240 kph over a total distance of 800
meters, we'd be in range of their weapons for less than
twelve seconds; this whole battle would last less than
twelve seconds, even though we'd pass through three
fronts.

I couldn't imagine risking my life three times in
twelve seconds. Garzón ordered all craft back on course
toward the Yabajin, and I exercised the state of *munen*,
no mind.

The laughing and betting of my compadres continued,
but their voices seemed to fade into the distance. The
Yabajin craft, that was what mattered. I watched them as
a cat watches a mouse, ready to pounce. My jaw didn't
quiver, my teeth didn't rattle. I felt calm and in control,
and even though our own craft was twisting and bouncing as it encountered new slopes and angles in the desert
floor, I imagined I could see a path that would lead us to
the Yabajin. I imagined I could pick my target at will
and the enemy would fall under my guns. I felt invincible, the way all good soldiers feel just before they die in
battle.

We seemed to be rushing toward them slowly, too
slowly. I watched their men in the distance as they drew
close, in armor the color of the red sands behind them,
and saw the sun gleaming off their teflex battle armor.
Yet time did not stop for me. I did not achieve Instantaneity, that state of mind where eternity is found in a
moment. Abriara claimed she and others had learned to
attain that state at will, and with her elegant Eridani
chemicals that may have been true. I hoped to attain that
state of mind in this battle, believed my chemical patch
had been on long enough to produce the effect; yet it did
not happen for me.

I had no thoughts of life or death, victory or defeat. I
desired only to do my part well, to aim and fire perfectly.

I didn't experience the fear necessary to catalyze Abri-ara's drugs.

We floated toward the Yabajin as if sliding through a long dark tunnel. We came in upon their first line and simultaneously both armies began to fire. The beautiful and peaceful *whuft, whuft, whuft* issued from the Yaba-jin plasma turrets, like the sound a pigeon makes beating its wings while trying to hover. Our hovercraft rattled as it bounced over the ground and I bent my legs and balanced myself as I held my rifle poised. Superheated air sparkled silver as the Yabajin fired their lasers. And we thundered our answer with Housers and Flechettes and all before us the Yabajin hovercrafts seemed to rip apart in midair.

Splinters of armor flipped up like shingles tossed in a storm, and I saw the left arm of one Yabajin turret gunner rip away as if it were made of papier-mâché. A hovercraft before us became a fireball that engulfed two other Yabajin craft, and the drivers of the Yabajin zagged in confusion, trying in vain to retreat from our onslaught. I heard screaming that did not come over helmet mikes and realized the Yabajin were screaming in surprise and pain, and then we were into them—a hovercraft of startled men coming up on my right—a front turret gunner gone, flakes of red armor in the air as if he'd just exploded; a driver hunched over a burning control panel; a laser gunner staggering backward with a gaping bloodied wound in his shoulder as he fired off a burst; a plasma gunner clinging to a turret, shooting into the air over our heads—and then I fired into the laser gunner and the armor in his helmet splintered and exploded and a shell pumped into my Flechette and I fired and the plasma gunner broke in two at the waist. A white flare blossomed on my forehead and my right eye closed down. That momentary touch would have fried the retina of a real eye. I rubbed my hand in front of it, swatting away some Yabajin sniper's laser blast as if it were a mosquito.

The hovercraft of our compadres in front of us was taking heavy fire. The rear Houser gunner was spinning and the forward gunner had dropped. Perfecto went to his knees, plasma dripping from his chest plate—pinned to the floor for the duration of the battle. We were coming in on the second ranks and I didn't have time to think: the oncoming craft veered to ram us and I fired two shots before I took out the driver. He veered left and hit reverse as he died, and his companion craft to the left didn't have time to react to his maneuver: the companion craft slid in over the top of the wounded craft and rolled in the air like a badly thrown discus, crashing into the ground in front of us. It exploded into flames then we came in upon the last line of Yabajin.

They'd slowed and were turning to give chase some four hundred yards behind their compadres. We opened fire at long range and kept it up, but they seemed to part before us like dandelion seeds blown in the wind and we fired once as we came parallel, then there were no more targets for me. They split away from our position on both sides, and we burst through their lines. Mavro reached back and tossed a packet of Mexican hair into the air, and it exploded behind us; thin blue flakes of steel floated on the wind. I unclipped my bomb from my belt and tossed it in a mad rush, and everywhere, men went for their hair bombs. A wall of black steel fibers raised behind us.

In front and to our left a soldier tossed a Mexican hair bomb—but he was too close to us, too close, and I knew we'd hit that hair before the Yabajin did.

Abriara veered right and cut her engines so the hair wouldn't get sucked into our intakes; we soared and dropped. The bomb exploded almost beneath us, and the air crackled as with static electricity as wisps of steel spattered the skirt of our hovercraft.

Then we soared over the danger area and Abriara restarted the engines. Behind us some Yabajin pressed through the veil of Mexican hair and many of their engines burst into flames immediately. But some Yabajin soared over or circumvented our barrier and gave chase at a distance.

I quickly surveyed the damage to our troops. Behind us several craft floundered under the hands of dead drivers, and hordes of Yabajin were attacking and over-whelming these unfortunate men. I counted fourteen

combat teams going down in this manner. Even among
the main ranks our hovercrafts took damage—burning
bits of plasma ate through teflex plating like fiery
serpents. Everywhere our gunners were hunched and
sprawling as if dead. Yet almost to the man our gunners
began to rise to their feet as if returning from the dead.
They were only letting the plasma cool on their armor.
We'd taken surprisingly few casualties.

I removed the half-empty clip from my gun, and
inserted a full one. The desert stretched before us, an
open highway. We could have turned and slaughtered
the few Yabajin that followed. We had the firepower. But
they were only the first obstacle to our conquest of
Hotoke no Za and Garzón didn't order us to attack.

The few dozen Yabajin could follow if they wished. It
didn't matter. Halfway back to Hotoke no Za they'd
simply founder in the desert for lack of fuel.

I'd been holding my breath. My chest was tight and I
noticed something wrong—our compadres were pulling
away; the Yabajin behind us were gaining.

Oily smoke issued from under our hovercraft and the
turbines in two intakes whined as if in pain. The whole
hovercraft began turning left in a slow arc, meter by
meter, and we slid out of formation in front of our
rear-most gunners with their big Housers and across
their paths.

"I can't hold this speed!" Abriara shouted through her
helmet mike.

Zavala's helmet swiveled toward the dozen Yabajin
craft closing in behind. "Don't slow down!" he said.

We passed to the left of the last three gunners and
they began pulling ahead of us. The whining of our
damaged turbines grew to a whistle. *This isn't supposed
to happen*, I thought. *In practice this never happens.
Our crafts are invincible in battle. They never fall apart
on us.*

Perfecto shouted over his helmet mike, "We're going
to blow those two engines at this rate! I can repair the
damage if they don't blow! I'm going to disconnect their
fuel lines," and he got down from his turret, crawled on
the floor up by Abriara, lifted some panels, and stuck his

head down under the craft. I noticed puck marks in his burned armor on the back of his legs, and took out some resin and began filling the holes for him. We continued in our wide arc, heading more northeast than east. The two whining engines suddenly stopped, while the other sixteen engines hummed. "Got them!" Perfecto said.

He crawled to his knees.

Some men in the other crafts noticed our predicament and began to chatter. "Sifuentes's team has engine trouble. Give you six to one they don't make it! Six to one!"

"Don't waste your money, *cabrón*!" Mavro shouted. "Things aren't so bad!"

I laughed at his joke. We rumbled up a small hill. "Compadres," Abriara said, "we cannot go on like this. We cannot keep up. I think we should cut away, head north for a while and hope the Yabajin do not follow— but it is a risk. I will not do it unless we all agree."

"Do it!" Perfecto shouted, and Mavro said "*Sí*" and I whispered "Yes."

Zavala said, "Let me think! Let me think!" and Mavro growled, "We don't have time for you to think!"

We topped the hill. It dropped quickly into a wide but shallow gully. The hovercrafts before us were bouncing across it. The cement ferns grew tall here—six or seven meters high. The desert appeared flat and even, yet I'm sure it must have held many small gullies like this.

Abriara said, "Here's our chance," and she veered into the gully and headed almost straight north, following the contours of the land. At top speed our hovercraft barely cleared the cement stalks of the ferns and actually knocked the tops off some while the leaves of others sucked back into the stalks. The depression deepened just a little ahead, enough so we could almost hide in the fold of ground till the Yabajin passed if we could maneuver over the taller ferns.

Zavala shouted, "Are you crazy? We can't go in there!"

"Good," Abriara said, plowing into the ferns, "then the Yabajin can't follow!"

If the Yabajin had been a kilometer farther behind, they would not have seen us split away, but the trail of quivering leaves gave us away. We watched the hill to our rear, and as the Yabajin came over the hill one man pointed at us and five craft split away to give chase. My heart sank.

"This is not so bad!" Mavro said, "This is not so bad! This is not so bad!" and he turned his turret so it faced the Yabajin.

"We'll follow this gully for a few minutes, then we head back to the mountains, back toward Kimai no Ji," Abriara said as if speaking to herself. "We can beat them in the mountains. Everyone hunch down—help cut down the wind resistance!"

Perfecto squatted on the floor, then got out his resin pack and began patching his armor. Mavro hunched and pointed at my forehead. "You'd better paint that spot quickly," he said, "before we meet the Yabajin," and suddenly everyone was patching their armor with resins. Abriara kept her attention on driving. I listened to the comforting chatter of our compadres heading for Hotoke no Za, but our little head mikes were not meant to carry signals over a dozen kilometers. Sometime while we repaired our armor, the voices began to crackle and break up.

When Perfecto had his own furrows filled, he inched forward and began working on Abriara's armor. He suddenly shouted, "Abriara, you forgot to throw your hair bomb!" and he unsnapped it from her belt.

"I was more concerned with other things!" she said. "Keep it. Throw it when it will do us the most good."

We continued down the gully for several minutes and watched for a place, any place where we could throw the bomb and be sure we could take out some Yabajin. But there was no such place. We didn't have to turn back toward the mountains—the gully we followed wound back in that direction. We kept dropping lower and lower, and the sides of the gully became steeper, like those of a bowl, and the ferns disappeared altogether. The Yabajin were slowly gaining. In ten minutes they closed to within half a kilometer. In another ten minutes they'd be sitting in our laps.

Abriara raced past rock formations at top speed. Ahead, stony red pinnacles seemed to spring from the ground in vertical cliffs. To hit one would be like hitting a wall. We crossed a ridge and dropped toward a broad but shallow brown river that meandered along the feet of the mountains. Pale gray trees and Baker's native grasses grew along the riverbanks. The wind whistled across the folds of my helmet.

The Yabajin thundered out of the winding gully just three hundred meters behind us. A laser gunner hazarded a shot, and a silver beam split the sky overhead. Abriara bolted through the trees till we hit the river, then followed it north over the sluggish brown water.

The Yabajin drew close, and there was no place where the river channel narrowed enough so our bomb would do any good. If we tossed it, the Yabajin would just slip around the danger zone. I watched the samurai, picking my targets. One hovercraft had only one gunner aboard, a turret gunner whose armor was shattered at the shoulder, and he kept himself propped against his turret. The craft behind it had two gunners.

Abriara shouted, "Lay down grazing fire in the water!" and I remembered our race down the valley in the snow. I reached under my seat and grabbed a laser rifle and fired into the water. Mavro and Perfecto began firing with their plasma turrets, and the water boiled behind us. A fine mist raised, but not enough to provide a smoke screen. The trick had worked in the snow at night, but the sun overhead pierced our thin fog.

The Yabajin were nearly within firing range. The three forward plasma gunners shot into the air at a sixty-degree angle as if firing at incoming aircraft, hoping the plasma would rain down on us. We twisted over the meandering river and watched plasma spatter behind.

"I'm going to throw this bomb," Perfecto said. "It won't do any good, but I'm going to throw it!"

Mavro raised his own turret and opened fire at the sky.

"Continue with the grazing fire—all of you! Wait until we get around this next bend!" Abriara shouted.

I glanced ahead: the bend ahead was wide, with a

narrow rocky shoal. She cut into the inside corner of the bend like a racer, skirting a line of trees, plowing through a thicket of rushes, and the Yabajin followed.

"Now!" Abriara shouted.

Perfecto dropped the bomb into the thicket, then he and Mavro began firing into the air. I picked up the flechette. Perfecto's bomb exploded, and the Mexican hair spread out near the ground and began to drift up. I opened fire on the driver of the first Yabajin craft, even though my shot wouldn't penetrate his armor at that range; I only hoped to distract him.

The first two craft cut the corner and plowed into the Mexican hair and their craft seemed to dive nose first into the ground, splitting apart and bursting into fireballs. Two more craft came in behind, hugging the same corner, but they cut engines and dove while the last craft veered out over the water.

Mavro laughed and fired plasma into the air at them and shouted, "They will not be so quick to come in for the kill, now!"

And it was so. The Yabajin slowed dramatically and for the next ten minutes followed at a discreet distance. We sped north till the river sharply twisted up into the mountains. It became nothing more than a path for river dragons—the banks were pushed up as if the creek had been dredged, and every few hundred meters we'd find a pond. The banks were covered with tall, elastic trees with tiny blue leaves that fluttered nervously in the wind. The trees were so dense a hovercraft couldn't navigate between them, and the Yabajin were forced to follow us up the river in single file.

The trees in the canyon gave way to sheer cliffs of weathered stone where hideous ogres were sculpted in rock, pitted black eyes and granite brows, rocky chins where brown opal birds frightened by our approach dove with a screech and fluttered among the cliffs, seeking escape.

The canyon abruptly ended—a waterfall tumbled from a cliff a hundred meters high. Our hovercraft couldn't make it up the incline and our path was blocked.

Abriara slowed to a stop and we faced all guns to the

rear. The Yabajin in their dusty red hovercrafts floated in behind. I thumbed the chin button on my helmet for telescopic vision, and the helmet optics hummed in response. On the three remaining craft were ten battered warriors. One gunner had blood pumping out his helmet at the ear; another had been shot in the rib cage and was pressing scraps of armor against his wound seemingly to keep from bleeding to death. The hovercrafts pulled into line in the narrow canyon, creating a wall of steel. They kept just out of range at three hundred meters.

The gravel and boulders on the stream bank glistened from the spray of the falls. Perfecto jumped down from his turret and grabbed the old sword Mavro had taken off the corpse of Master Kaigo. He pulled it from its black lacquered sheath and flashed the steel blade over his head and shouted, "Come, let us fight as men of honor! The winner continues his mission. The loser returns home!" He reached up with one hand and unsnapped his helmet, dropped it to the ground.

"What are you doing?" Abriara whispered.

"I'm going to see if I can talk them into a fight, one on one," Perfecto said. "Remember? It is the 'beautiful style of war.' It is their custom."

The Yabajin looked at one another in confusion and held a hurried counsel. All of them wore the little *wakizashi* of the samurai thrust into scabbards in the armor at their hips, but only a few carried the large *tachi* swords for combat.

One flipped the external mike on his helmet and in halting Spanish shouted, "You do not know of our ways, *Nanbeijin*. What do you know of honor? You broke tradition and assaulted us with projectiles. You seek the right to continue your journey, yet plan to murder our wives and children. How can we allow this?"

Perfecto puzzled this through a moment. Then answered, "I do not wish to fight you with guns. If we match our superior weapons to your superior numbers, who can say what will happen? I wish to fight as a man, my sword with your sword. No matter what the outcome of our meaningless war, I wish to prove that I am superior."

The Yabajin were staggered with amazement. They consulted among themselves. At length, one big samurai who wore his *tachi* scabbard over his back dutifully pulled his sword, reached up with one hand and un-snapped his helmet, let it fall to the floor.

I gasped. The Yabajin was only barely recognizable as human. He had huge yellow eyes like those of a tiger, and the supraorbital ridges of bone over those eyes were so huge they gave a misshapen appearance, leaving a hump where his temples should have been. He was bald, and at first glance one would have thought his skin had been dyed in patterns by an artist—olive green in color, with swirling zebra stripes of yellow ochre. But one had only to look for a moment to realize the bizarre twisting pattern was not dye—the pigments somehow too closely approximated flesh tones. His skin color was obviously the work of genetic tampering. I'd known Hispanics in Miami who paid to have the skin tones of their offspring lightened so they'd better fit in with the anglos. I'd seen the blue skin proudly worn by the few self-righteous Hindus left in East Islamidad. But the Yabajin was different. He stripped off his armor piece by piece, and he was naked beneath the armor, so that he revealed his whole body. The olive pubic hairs at his crotch converged with tufts of yellow-orange hairs at his navel. He was supremely muscular, with abnormally long fingers and toes. Two large brass discs engraved with Japanese characters were somehow attached to his breasts. I couldn't conceive a purpose for these discs, either as a form of cybernetic upgrade or as a simple mechanical attachment. Then I suddenly realized they were merely decorative, and that he wore his skin as if it too were an ornament: he conceived of his entire body as a work of art. The overall effect of these changes terrified me. I'd never been terrified by chimeras, perhaps because all the ones I'd seen appeared to be nearly human. But this man terrified me on a primal level.

Perfecto stripped down to his shorts. With his barrel chest, his arms and legs appeared narrow, almost lanky,

in comparison with the Yabajin. But it was all illusion.
There was great strength in those limbs.

"Be careful with this one," Abriara whispered. "They'll
put their best against you first."

"Sí," Zavala added. "Even when he is dead and jerking
on the end of your sword, keep away from him."

"Of course," Perfecto said. He jumped from the
hovercraft to the rocky shore of the stream.

The Yabajin stepped from his craft and picked his way
toward Perfecto, hopping from boulder to boulder. They
met each other midway, then bowed deeply.

They extended their swords, holding them in front
with both hands, and stood a few paces apart, watching
each other's eyes. The Yabajin's yellow tiger eyes stared
unblinking. Without glancing at footholds they felt their
way near each other with infinite caution, the way a
mantis moves as it stalks.

Perfecto's hands shook and from moment to moment
his grip tightened. He snapped his sword forward, trying
to draw out the Yabajin with a feint. But the Yabajin
didn't take the feint.

Perfecto snapped the tip of his sword forward; the
Yabajin swung down in a vicious arc. Perfecto parried,
turning the Yabajin's blade, then stepped back.

Without warning, without a constriction of the eye or
a visible tightening of the muscles, the Yabajin sprang
forward and swung.

And Perfecto achieved Instantaneity. I didn't witness
his moves they were so swift, but in the next moment
Perfecto's sword plunged through the Yabajin's heart
and Perfecto reached into the air, grabbing the Yabajin's
hands so his sword wouldn't fall. Blood spurted from the
Yabajin's chest and ran down his belly, and I thought
he'd crumple, but the Yabajin grappled for the *tachi*.
The samurai was exercising Perfect Control—stopping
his heartbeat, stopping his breathing. By rights he'd be
dead in ten seconds, but by stopping his heart and
allowing his body to continue functioning till his oxygen
depleted he could continue fighting a moment longer.
Yet the more energy he wasted in his struggle the
quicker he'd lose consciousness. Perfecto sought to hold

the Yabajin, to force him to exhaust himself in a futile struggle.

The Yabajin broke away and his right hand blurred as he reached for his *wakizashi*. Perfecto smashed the samurai in the chest with a knee, pushing him back.

The Yabajin leapt for Perfecto, swinging his *wakizashi* in one hand and holding his *tachi* in the other. But Perfecto leapt from reach. The samurai stopped at arm's reach and tossed his short sword, missing badly, then sprawled face forward on the ground and lay motionless.

He didn't breathe or thrash. He lay so still it looked as if he might never have been alive.

Perfecto pulled his sword from the samurai's belly, then shoved the blade into the ground and stood with one hand on the pommel, watching the rest of the Yabajin. Perfecto said, "Was he your best? Are none of you better? Or are you willing to concede my superiority?"

The sight filled me with nervous energy. Only nine Yabajin were left, and the one with the wounded chest slumped to his seat and sat gasping as he watched Perfecto's performance.

A second Yabajin began to undress—a black man with cinnamon patterns in bands and circles and swirls like those on the wings of a moth. His right leg was a bioprosthetic—instead of toes he had three great talons and a spur on his right leg, yet the skin pattern was the same as on his left leg, as if a skin culture had been grafted over a metal prosthesis. He had a great bushy mustache and beard, and he shouted, *"Kuso kurae!"* as he pulled out his sword and jumped to the ground. He threw off his armor in a fit of passion, and I remembered how I'd felt after being defeated in the simulators, how I'd hoped in vain of winning and had always come up empty. That was the expression on this man's face.

Abriara whispered over her mike, "They're getting angry. They won't let this go any further: they have to keep their numbers up. Don't any of you twitch a muscle, but if I say the word, open fire. Angelo and Zavala, you take the gunners. Mavro, you get the drivers."

The Yabajin neglected to bow to Perfecto. Instead he charged, swinging his sword, and Perfecto concentrated on blocking his blows. The Yabajin was graceful and practiced, explosive and cunning. His rain of blows whistled through the air and with each stroke his blade twisted at the last moment, making it difficult for Perfecto to parry. This man didn't care for life or his own defense; he sought only to kill, and it was all Perfecto could do to parry—he had no time to safely execute a counterstrike.

On perhaps his sixth swing the Yabajin twisted his blade in midair and the blade rang against Perfecto's wrist guard. The guard snapped, and the samurai's blade sunk deep into Perfecto's right hand.

Perfecto kicked the Yabajin in the knee and tried in desperation to riposte the blow, to strike past the samurai's guard.

It was a stupid move. A suicidal move. Both of them were undefended. Both would die. Mavro saw this and as Perfecto stepped aside, striking at the Yabajin, Mavro fired his plasma turret into the samurai's chest.

Abriara hit the forward thrusters and our hovercraft whined and lurched back toward the Yabajin. Perfecto dropped to the ground behind a boulder and we whizzed over him. I opened fire on the samurai gunners and blew one man off a turret and wounded his companion in the face. Then a wall of fire opened up from the Yabajin turrets, pure white streams of molten ore streaming at us. Plasma washed over my chest and head and my armor flared in warning, but I blasted two more gunners.

Zavala fired at five times my rate, and four scurrying gunners virtually exploded while I took out the Yabajin who had the chest wound. Abriara jammed the thrusters in reverse as we crashed into a Yabajin craft, then Mavro shouted, "Get down!" and kicked me forward to the floor.

Zavala was still shooting three rounds per second. I didn't even hear a time lag as he slipped in a second clip. I thought, *My God, he's a dead man!* believing he'd

decided to go out in a blaze of glory, ignoring his plasma
hits.

Zavala's shells were blowing through the teflex armor
of the Yabajin. I could see the splinters churning in the
air over the lip of the hovercrafts, as if he'd fired into
dummies filled with sawdust. He shot all the samurai
three and four times—even those who'd been lying dead
aboard the hovercrafts for the last half hour.

I counted to fifteen while the plasma dripped off my
armor. There was a hot spot on my chest like a live coal.
Mavro had saved my life by kicking me forward. I'd have
tried to squeeze another two seconds of fighting into the
battle.

I looked up at Zavala. Pure white flames issued from
cracks in his armor at the knee. A puff of oily smoke
boiled out his foot. He dropped and I rushed to him,
pulled off his armor. The frames of his prosthetic legs
were fine, but the cords that served as muscles had
melted beyond repair.

"How in the name of God did you keep from getting
fried?" I shouted.

Zavala shrugged. "I ducked."

Mavro and Abriara were both down after taking
plasma hits. They waited for the plasma to burn off, then
sat up. Perfecto climbed over the back of the hovercraft
and reached in a compartment under the floorboards and
pulled out the emergency medkit and began putting a
tourniquet above his wrist. His left ankle had a round
black hole where plasma had burned through.

"You could have got me killed!" he shouted. He was
ecstatic. "You could have got me killed but you didn't!"

The cut on Perfecto's hand was deep, to the bone, and
I was forced to operate on him there, to splice the blood
vessels, staple the wound closed, and spray it with a
resin bandage. I gave him a large dose of painkillers. His
arm began to swell immediately, and I knew he would
not be using his right hand for a few weeks. Perfecto's
leg was a little easier to treat, since the wound was small
and didn't pierce any major blood vessels. All I had to do
was cut the charred flesh away and bandage it.

Afterward we removed our helmets and rested. The

air was filled with smells of smoke and burning flesh—a satisfying smell like roast pork. The alien scents of Baker's plants nearly dropped me. I'd smelled the sugary turpines before, but never so intensely, never at such close range.

For the next two hours Abriara and Mavro worked on the hovercraft. They pulled out the damaged props and replaced them with parts scavenged from the Yabajin crafts. They also took fuel rods, weapons, and food from the Yabajin. The Yabajin had beer in their hovercrafts in a cooler under the floorboards. We sat in the sun on the rocks and drank beer and ate.

It felt good to be alive and eating. Mavro and Perfecto talked about how well the battle had gone, how we'd all been surprised to find Zavala alive in the end. Often I laughed with pure relief and the others did too. Zavala drank a great deal, as if he'd won the war single-handedly. He felt generous and kept saying, "You did good, Angelo. You did good in the battle. I'm sorry if I ever doubted you. We'll turn you into a samurai yet, *ne?*" He'd pat my leg when I got near and say, "Such fine legs! So strong! I wish I had legs like that!" Then he'd wiggle his hip so his prosthetics would flop about pitifully, and laugh. He kept offering me drinks of beer as if his were the last beer left in the world.

We were only four hours behind the army, but Abriara wanted to hurry and regroup. We propped Zavala in a corner behind Abriara. Perfecto was in no condition to stand at his turret. We let him drink several beers and take a pee, then bundled him in his armor and set him in a chair next to Zavala with a flechette. Some of his armor had taken a hit from the Yabajin plasma guns, and a glove had holes melted into it the size of tangerines, so Zavala went to work with his little repair kit plugging the holes in Perfecto's glove. I took Perfecto's place at the turret.

We buzzed back down the stream, out of the mountains, through thickets of trees with nervous gray rattling leaves, out into the desert. Zavala said, "Let's not go this way. We will not be safe if we follow the army. It's too late to follow them."

The hair raised on my neck and I had a premonition he

was right. I didn't say anything to indicate my agreement. I wish now that I could have seen Zavala's eyes as he said it, seen that distant inward look as he consulted the source of spiritual knowledge. We thought it was only the liquor talking, and Abriara continued on. Zavala seemed to forget his own concerns immediately after voicing them. He and Perfecto sang an old song about a man who was drunk and searching for his bed in a hotel but accidentally kept crawling into bed with the strangest people. We hummed over hills and through an endless desert filled with tangled vines.

Just as twilight fell we came up a small incline in the desert—not a hill really, just a fold in the ground. Perfecto shouted, "Slow down! I think I'm going to throw up—the beer!"

Abriara stopped the hovercraft and said, "Get it over with!"

Perfecto stood up and leaned over the edge of the hovercraft and began fumbling with his helmet, unsnapping it, then straightened and scanned the horizon suspiciously. He snapped the helmet back on and his uneasiness touched us. We began watching the horizon. Perfecto sniffed and said, "Do you smell that scent? Do you smell it?"

We were all wearing our helmets, and were cut off from the sensation of smell

"It smells like flowers. Like orchids maybe. Not like the desert." He sniffed the air in his helmet and looked back at me, then began to swing his head toward the front of the craft.

Zavala shouted, "No!" and his legs wiggled as he began trying to push himself backward. Thirty meters uphill a creature burst from a hole in the ground and sand and twigs exploded away from it. It reared in the air five meters tall, like a giant red mantis—peaked head with bulging faceted eyes, thick body with six legs spread wide, enormous forelegs poised back in the air like stingers on a scorpion. Its forelegs snapped forward and by instinct I ducked. A ball hurtled toward my head at such tremendous velocity I couldn't escape.

The ball shattered my helmet, knocked me to the

floor. I looked up at the sky; Mavro screamed and fired his plasma turret, liquid comets burning overhead, and a rifle sounded three times. The shots splattered into the flesh of the beast, and it thudded to the ground with a grunt. My ears began ringing, and my eyes wouldn't focus. I smelled orchids, very strong, as if entire fields of them were within my grasp.

"A desert lord!" Perfecto shouted. "It got Angelo and Zavala!"

I felt someone tugging me, pulling at my arm, dragging me backward. Tough fingers began prying the pieces of broken helmet apart, cracking it like a lobster shell, removing it from my face. I tried to find my tongue, but the words came out sluggish. *"Eshtoy bien,"* I said. I'm fine.

"Angelo's alive!" Perfecto said, his face swimming above me.

Someone jumped off the hovercraft; battle armor rattled. "Zavala's not," Abriara said. "His skull is shattered."

I couldn't believe it. I struggled to my knees. Part of the back of my helmet was still attached to my suit, and I pulled it free. Abriara was on the ground, leaning over Zavala, obscuring my view. Zavala's armor was fine but his helmet was smashed to pieces and smeared with blood. The platinum shine was soft and muted on his chin, no hot points left. The blood was cooling in his veins. Abriara moved aside, revealing Zavala's face, forehead dented as if squashed by a cannonball. His vacant eyes stared up. The corpse of the desert lord smoldered up the hill.

I leaned against the rail of the hovercraft, clinging for support, and found myself blinded by tears. My ears were still ringing, playing a single low tone, almost a buzz or the sound of a horn. Everyone was silent for a long time, and just stood there looking, unmoving.

"We should bury him," Perfecto said.

Abriara and Perfecto stared at Zavala. Mavro hopped down from the hovercraft and searched the ground, then retrieved a ball and brought it to me—a round stone the size of a large orange, perfectly smooth, as if it had been worked by hand.

"You should keep this!" he said. "A desert lord's throwing stone. It must have been deflected by your helmet. You're lucky it didn't kill you."

Something rattled up the rise, the sound of battle armor, and the dead desert lord's abdomen started heaving upward. Another creature was struggling from the hole, pushing the desert lord aside.

"Look!" I said, as a second desert lord stuck its head from the ground.

"It's just one of the females, a desert lady," Abriara said without turning to look. The creature crawled from its burrow and stared at us. It had a thick abdomen serving as counterweight to an upright torso, a head on a thin stalk. But the female had no front legs to throw stones. The sockets at its upper shoulders were empty, as if the forearms had been pulled free. Our helmets were designed to look exactly like the face of this creature.

The desert lady watched us forlornly, glancing from us to the dead male and back again. A second female pulled herself from the burrow, and a third. Everyone but me ignored the creatures.

"We can't bury Zavala here," Abriara said. "The females will eat him. Let's load him on the hovercraft."

Abriara and Perfecto grunted and lifted Zavala up to the rail on the hovercraft, then heaved him over like a sack of stones. Mavro wandered around the hill, went up and inspected the big dead desert lord, then went and stared into its lair. The females barked and snorted and leapt back from Mavro as he approached, yet seemed more curious than afraid.

"These creatures know how to treat their women," Mavro said, eyeing the females. "Pull off their arms so they can't resist your advances!"

"The males don't do it," Abriara said. "Their mothers pull them off when they're born, making them dependent on the males." I wondered how she knew this, then remembered the first rule of battle: Know your enemy. Abriara knew we had more enemies on Baker than the Yabajin.

"Hah! You should see this hole!" Mavro shouted. "It's a perfect circle inside. It's got cement all around, like a swimming pool. And they've covered it so you can't see it from above." He kicked some dirt into the hole, then walked over and pulled himself back up on the hovercraft.

My limbs felt heavy and my head was numb, yet curiosity drove me to ask, "They make cement? Are they intelligent?"

Abriara shook her head. "Desert lords? No. They mix dung with gravel and vines for cement—it's an inherited memory. They're no smarter than monkeys—just more bloodthirsty."

I felt guilty for speaking, for asking inane questions when Zavala was lying dead. I was unaccountably angry at the samurai for not teaching me about these animals earlier, though even if I'd known of them it wouldn't have saved Zavala.

Everyone hopped aboard the hovercraft and Abriara fired up the engines. She said, "What shall we do with the females? They'll starve without the male."

"Leave them," Mavro said. "Maybe they'll find another mate."

We drove off. The desert ladies raised their heads and a trumpeting whistle issued over the prairie. They began chasing after our craft like dogs tailing the vehicle of their masters. Darkness fell behind us as the sun dropped beneath the horizon.

Abriara drove for an hour under the light of Shinju, the pearl, Baker's smaller moon, till we hit stony ground, then we got out to build a cairn for Zavala. My knees were weak and wobbly and I couldn't carry rocks for the cairn. I let the others perform the labor.

I felt so down and empty I wondered if the others felt the same. I kept expecting Abriara to break down and weep, or one of the others, but they just dutifully carried rocks to the pile. Abriara once promised she wouldn't mourn if one of us died. Now that Zavala was dead she seemed to be living up to her promise. And I wondered if I'd been right. Was she really alive inside? Or had she too died to emotion?

We buried Zavala under the stones and Abriara had us kneel as she said a prayer. She wept in spite of her promise.

We prepared to leave and Abriara stopped and looked off in the distance behind. "Those three females have followed us," she said. "They're running toward us, about five kilometers away." My infrared vision wasn't good enough to discern such details at that distance. "When a male desert lord kills another," she said, "the females mate the victor. Those females will want to come live with us. We'd better not leave them—they might dig up Zavala."

We loaded into the hovercraft and turned back. We met the females only a kilometer away, and Mavro sprayed them with plasma. The plasma burned through their exoskeletons and lighted them from inside, and the pale blue of veins and organs stood out perfectly. Their exoskeletons were remarkably clear, like yellowed plastic, and I marveled how much that clear exoskeleton reminded me of the flesh of other of Baker's animals.

After killing the desert ladies we turned the hovercraft back, and for the next several hours, intermixed with the sweet sugary turpines of desert plants, I could still smell orchids.

CHAPTER

17

Abriara drove zigzag through the desert all night, seeking the trail of our army. The ringing in my ears lessened, but my head ached and I couldn't focus my eyes long, so I took painkillers. The night sounds and smells on Baker were intriguing—the whirring wings of opal birds, the whistles and cries of unseen animals singing a strange chorus, the music of a universe where I didn't belong. The scents were even more amazing— many of Baker's animals communicate chemically, and residues of chemical markers along with turpines of plants became a constant barrage. Often scents were pleasant, like the orchid analog of the desert lords; often the odors were offensive, like the bitter musky tang where Baker's five-meter-long armadillos left their slime trails.

I could feel a madness coming on, the madness of ecoshock, of exposure to the alien. I remember reading in college about problems faced by those who gained eyesight in adulthood after having lived entire lives in darkness—a man fell from a four-story building as he leaned out his window to pick roses he imagined to be only a meter from his hand, men driven to fear when trying to negotiate crowds they could easily handle when blind. The burden of sight was often too much for such people. Those who couldn't cope often resorted to having their optic nerves severed so they could return to the comfortable world of the blind. Those who were impatient sometimes pulled their own eyes from their sockets. Such is the pain of ecoshock.

The night sounds and smells on Baker were intriguing. Yet only the afternoon before, I'd been buffeted by prolonged contact with an alien environment. I'd felt relieved to be insulated from the scents and sounds by my armor. But now that my helmet was shattered, I was naked, exposed. I'd thrown away my dream monitor and had no way of escaping the sensory overload to come. Darkness was my friend. In the dark I could close my eyes and not look upon an alien environment. The desert was my friend. The lifeless desert was nearly free of the scents and sounds that assaulted me. And so, as we traveled through the desert, I closed my eyes and tried to face the inevitable without mentioning my predicament to others. Surely, I reasoned, there'd have been fatalities from our battle, and someone in our army would have a helmet to fit to my suit.

Twice Baker's large blue moon, Rojin, the old man, and once the small white moon, Shinju, the pearl, shot overhead. I had difficulty focusing. My vision was blurred. At dawn Shinju rose with the sun and for a few minutes the sun was in partial eclipse. We'd still found no sign of the army and were getting desperate. My eyes hurt and I mostly kept them closed.

Abriara said to herself more than to us, "They must have driven through without camping. Perhaps they're afraid the Yabajin will turn back on us. Or maybe they learned something of importance and decided to push straight through the night."

If she was right, we'd be delayed in reaching our compadres by at least a day. Already the sun shining on the wings of multicolored bands of *oparu no tako* assaulted my sensibilities. I massaged my temples and stifled a moan. We had larger matters to worry about: without the help of Garzón we didn't know exactly what route to take to Hotoke no Za. We couldn't hope to find our compadres if they'd gone too far ahead—their hovercrafts wouldn't leave a discernible track on the hard desert. And with the zigzag pattern we'd resorted to in our search, we were getting farther behind all the time. The ground was covered with many white growths, a whole tiny forest only a meter tall, like hundreds of fungi that had baked and shriveled down to a hard cement. Our army could have raced over this unpromising terrain and still left no trace.

Our compasses were inadequate guides over a long distance. The continent Kani is shaped something like a crab, with its face pointing north. Hotoke no Za is situated by the sea on the southeast while Kimai no Ji is situated on the northwest edge of the continent. We could try making a straight line southeast, but there were endless jungles, great canyons, and mountains between us and Hotoke no Za. We could easily waste time trying to find passes over mountains or become hopelessly stranded in impenetrable jungles. However, to the northeast the maps showed a great plain and broad inland seas with only a few small hills and mountain ranges. It was a land that often froze during the winter, and not many plants had adapted to this harsh environment.

Perfecto believed we should go north till we reached the sea, then follow the coast down to Hotoke no Za. If we didn't camp, we might arrive in Hotoke no Za with our *compañeros*.

Mavro violently disagreed. "We must try to follow the route of our compadres," he said. "It would be cowardly to do otherwise." For once, I applauded Mavro's macho thinking. I hoped to find the army as soon as possible, but felt too exhausted to speak. Abriara reluctantly agreed with Mavro and began making a broad sweep to the south.

At noon we began to find occasional ribbons of dark ultraviolet grass protruding from the white cement, and in the distance we discerned entire fields of tangled orange vine, a vast savannah of native plants. The thought of traversing that area repulsed me.

The sun brightened, as if over seconds someone turned up a dimmer switch on the lights. I was watching the savannah at the time and thought only that a cloud had parted above our heads and the sun was finally shining full on us. I'd have thought nothing more of it except that Abriara said, "Ah, damn, did anyone else see that?" and there was such anxiety in her voice I immediately looked up. There were no clouds above.

"Yes, I saw it!" Mavro shouted nervously. "The sun just jumped in magnitude!"

Abriara said, "Sí, that's why Garzón traveled all night. He must have got word of this, a forecast from Motoki's communications satellite, and took the others to safety!"

My mind was sluggish. I couldn't think. "What will happen?" I wanted to ask, but my words just came out, "What? What?"

"The sun jumped in magnitude!" Abriara said. "Things are going to heat up! This whole planet will heat eight degrees over the next twenty-two hours! And we're in for storms like you've never seen—the wind will cut across this desert at 150 kph and the sand will rip you apart. The sky turns brown with dust blown up from the desert. The Japanese call the brown air the *chairo no sunaarashi*, the tea winds. We've got to get out of the desert!"

Abriara turned to see the reaction on my face and said, "My God, what's wrong with your eyes!"

"They hurt," I said, and everyone stared at me.

"They're crossed," Mavro said, kneeling before me. "Watch my finger! Concentrate." He held his finger up and tracked it back and forth. I couldn't follow it.

"They hold straighter a little bit when you concentrate," Mavro said, shaking his head.

"I guess you got hit harder than we thought," Abriara said. "I'm sorry, Angelo. We should have checked you over immediately. You're the doctor, what can we give you?"

The news must have put me in shock. I concentrated, trying to remember what to do for a concussion, and could think of nothing. Perfecto laid me down, gave me some water. He searched the medical kit and found an oral anticoagulant and an anti-inflammatory. It was better than nothing, and I didn't have the energy to direct him further.

Abriara desperately plowed east for an hour till we were well into the band of grasslands, then swept around straight north. The terror of my compadres surprised

me. The sky remained clear and no great winds arose.
The day was sunny and pleasant. The heat soon made me
ill and I began to vomit. If not for the heat and my head
it would have been a simple drive through the country.
I was tempted to believe that the anxiety of my friends
was exaggerated.

Yet as we crossed the savannah, I couldn't fail to
recognize my own danger. The light-orange creepers
with dusty red leaves like thin tongues assaulted me with
an acidic scent of orange; yellow seedpods on trees
begged to be eaten with a scent of taffy. A lizard the size
of a monitor with a single eye pointing forward and
another on the back of its head spit an oniony spray at
the approach of our craft, tiny eight-legged grubs the
size of mice skittered along branches and leaves and gave
off a powerful stench with no earthly analog. Ecoshock.

We followed a northerly course for an hour, then
found a broad expanse of grass churned and crushed by
the passage of a thousand hovercrafts. We were a day
behind them.

"Which way should we go?" Abriara asked. "Shall we
follow the others?"

"The smart thing to do would be to go back toward
Kimai no Ji," Mavro said. "We could make it to the city
in half a day."

He was speaking in vain. We couldn't go back. Not
after what we'd done. The thought of even heading that
direction filled me with guilt. I couldn't go back and
witness what we'd done to Motoki even to save my life.

"Northeast, I think," Abriara said. "There were some
mountains in that direction. Go northeast to the bottom
of the inland sea Aruku Umi, and from there we head
straight east to the ocean. Mavro, you drive. I need
rest."

I didn't speak of my rising sense of panic. Abriara was
right—it would be safest to search for shelter and my
fear of ecoshock should not have been a factor in her
decision. I was convinced I was being selfless and
gallant, and people who are selfless and gallant are
rewarded with miraculous abilities to stifle pain and

recuperate from illness. I wouldn't be destroyed by my strange environment so long as I was gallant.

Mavro drove the rest of the afternoon and I tried to sleep. I opened my eyes several times to bleak landscapes—rolling plains of red sand and rock with nothing more than the tiniest starflower plants. The sun was so bright that every shadow seemed perfectly defined—that which was in the light was revealed in every detail; that which was in shadow didn't exist, as if a shadow were a black hole that sucked all light into it. Mavro woke us once to show us a herd of small red land crabs stretching kilometers in all directions. They were marching north through a plain of cracked gravel that offered nothing to eat, apparently scurrying from nowhere to nowhere.

I thought upon Garzón's plans for conquering the Yabajin. All had gone well so far, but I couldn't believe our luck would continue. The plan depended on too many factors. We'd beat a path through the Yabajin and had cowed them from continuing battle. With luck they'd assault Kimai no Ji, and we weren't concerned about the outcome of that battle. We'd blown all the fuel in town along with the industrial parks and Motoki's zeppelins. They wouldn't capture any vehicles, and if they tried to shuttle men back to Hotoke no Za in zeppelins, Garzón was confident that his shuttle full of men and cybertanks could hold them off, keep the zeppelins from entering the city. But the key was the Colombians. Garzón counted on the Colombians to revolt from the Yabajin and form an alliance with us. He suspected they had no sense of honor. I suspected his plan would backfire.

We traveled all day over hills and through a forest of live *mizu hakobinin*, huge animals shaped like water barrels. We had seen their bones in the simulators on my first day, and had naively called them "coralwood trees," thinking the mere skeleton to be a live plant. I tried to cope with my environment by making associations, by comparing animals and plants to familiar things on Earth. The parasitic yellow vines that hung from the *mizu hakobinin* like guts dripping from the belly of a

wounded jackal were really not so different from epi-
phytes and parasitic vines in the jungles of South
America. Musky armadillos were everywhere, plodding
over foliage on tiny feet, leaving trails of stench and
half-eaten plants. A basic herbivore—a deer in function,
a giant potato bug in form. We passed bushes where
sweet kidney-shaped fruits rotted in the sun and thousands of opal birds and tiny rodents fed on the fruit. No
different than a field of mangoes being eaten by macaws
and opossums on Earth. We spent hours crossing the
great sea Aruku Umi, then came to forests of tall,
pepper-scented, spindly blue-gray trees with red blad-
ders full of gases attached to each branch of leaves so that
the branches waved in the air. No different than forests
of kelp living underwater on Earth. The forest was very
thin and we had no trouble navigating. But the associations didn't hold, didn't relieve the pain, and along the
way I found myself breaking up.

We passed a *mizu hakobinin* and Mavro said he
wanted a drink. We stopped and he shot into the
exoskeleton of the creature to open a hole. The exoskeleton cracked and thousands of liters of water poured out,
and in the water were hundreds of creatures—translucent frogs with no front feet, tiny mantas the color of
syrup, armored eels with vicious teeth, insects of every
description. The *mizu hakobinin* had within it an entire
sea with its own ecology.

As we watched the *mizu hakobinin*, large platelets of
chitin floated to the open hole and began blocking the
draining water, like shingles in a gutter, and suddenly
the flow stopped. The creature had repaired itself.

Yet the animals from its belly writhed on the hot
ground and died. The *mizu hakobinin* wasn't a simple
analog of a barrel cactus, and the difference seemed
profound.

Mavro didn't want to drink after seeing all the bugs in
the water. We drove away and I closed my eyes and shut
out the sights. I held my breath and cut out the scents.
I hummed to myself, and stifled all sound. It was not
enough.

From time to time some sound or scent intruded so

that I involuntarily opened my eyes. Everywhere was
life: eight red spiders the size of cats sitting in a crevasse
of a fragmented rock, whirring bits of chitin together like
locusts—*alley cats growling love songs in the dark*, I told
myself. An evil-smelling opal kite wrapping its plastic
green wings around a hanging red bladder like a chrys-
alis, presumably to gorge itself on some fruit—*bats in my
papaya tree back home*. A pond of stagnant brown water
where blue eels swam in circles near the surface, chasing
their tails and moaning—*the song of a catfish*. Near the
top of a clump of reeds clung the discarded exoskeleton
of some old giant nymph as long as my hand, with a face
as horrifying as that of a fly—*dragonflies sprouting
wings*. A gust of wind kicked up over a field of yellow
cotton, sending fluffballs to scatter in the air with the
scent of ether. The pollens made my sinuses swell shut.
And in that field a pack of creatures that could have been
tailless yellow wolves with hairless faces triumphantly
whistled their joy as they fed from the carcass of an
overturned armadillo. At sunset a gnarled gray tree
sprouted flowers so white the last sunlight reflected off
them like torches. All these things magnified the ache in
my head. I wanted to claw my eyes and puncture my
eardrums. Ribbons of yellow and green and purple and
blue *oparu no tako* filled the evening sky—like veins,
the veins of a womb enclosing an embryo. And I realized
this planet was a living thing, with an ecology, a bio-
sphere all its own. I felt a mystical sense of discovery.
What will grow in this womb? I wondered. The air was
itchy with electricity. Huge thunderheads loomed on the
horizon, like the residue of a dozen mushroom clouds
after a nuclear attack. All my instincts screamed for
me to hide. I wept and cursed and found myself digging
up the floorboards as I searched for a medkit with
painkillers.

And then my body must have closed off my senses, for
I lost all consciousness. My subconscious sent me terrible hallucinatory dreams, dreams where images of Baker
were superimposed with images of Earth. We were
bouncing over uneven rocks in our hovercraft in the
deserts of Baker in twilight. Voices were jabbering in my

ears, nonsensical conversations carried on by people long dead. "Did you see Señora Cardosa?" my mother was saying. "She's gotten so fat. Such a shame." My father shouted at her, "I don't care about that! How will we live if they raise our taxes again?" I listened to the babble as if it were of no more import than the drone of a bee. In the desert sky simple strands of ribbon floated high in the air where the opal kites should have been. And along the horizon I could make out something, something that ran upright like a person. I struggled to pick out details and my eyes turned to telescopes. I saw vividly two desert ladies stumbling over cracked red stones, their arms torn off, blood dripping from the stumps at their shoulders. I blinked and tried to block out the sight, and they pleaded, "Angelo, Angelo, come back and feed us!"

I knew those voices—the child Tatiana and Tamara. They were running toward me, their arms and breasts hacked off, pleading, "Angelo, Angelo! Please!"

I reeled away and everything went black. Zavala began speaking in calm, informative tones. There was much laughter in the background, as if he were at a party. I leaned forward to hear and arms restrained me, clasping my chest. I tried to speak but my lips were burned by wind and sun. I realized I was wearing my helmet and people were chattering over helmet mikes. I couldn't see. The arms around me were the arms of Zavala holding me as he whispered in my ear. Zavala said, "Of course every culture appears equally evil from the outside, but if you look inside, you'll see that most oranges are cancerous. This is what gives you such bad breath, listening to people who've been programmed by social engineers. But I've known some people who've been programmed on chromosome 117 at gene 21755394200001 and they're perfectly resistant to viruses and visitations. Stick the knife in his belly, you lucky *cabrón,* and watch his eyeballs shine!" I peered up through a haze. Zavala wasn't holding me. The grinning head of a purple river dragon stared at me with tiny black eyes among folds of fat.

I blacked out again. Two eyes shone at me from above, one blue, one white. It was Flaco, with a flash of lightning for a malicious idiotic grin. He spoke in a voice of thunder. "*Hola*, Angelo! Where have you been? We've all been waiting for you here in paradise and now the party is just about to begin. There's *duros* at the venders in the feria—banana-flavored or passion flower."

"I'm sorry," I said. I couldn't think where I'd been. "I got lost. The war. I've been busy killing people."

"Hah! Too bad! That's what happens when you serve an evil society," Flaco chortled.

The accusation cut me like a scalpel. "I don't! I don't serve evil." But unbidden I remembered my youthful commitments to don José Mirada, the many times I sincerely vowed I'd serve society and gain its rewards. And I remembered how I'd discerned for myself that I was entangled in a society of murderers. And his words rang true. I was a servant of an evil society.

"High priest to a congregation of demons," Flaco said. "Don't deny it. Inhuman *socialistas*. Good for nothing but fertilizing the garden. But, ah, we have all your favorite flavors of *duros*. Banana-flavored or passion flower, which will it be?"

He demanded an answer with his gaze. His eyes blazed. His eyes penetrated my very being. "Banana!" I shouted.

"Hah! Wrong answer!"

And I realized I was wrong—I should have opted for passion flower, passion flower to make me live a life of passion. Even Zavala would have known the answer. "I'm sorry!" I shouted.

I was staring up at dark clouds; Rojin and Shinju were just vanishing behind them. We were in the desert again, overlooking the lip of a canyon in the dark.

Abriara was sitting with me, leaning against the rail of the hovercraft with her arms around me, comforting me. "Be calm," she said. "Be calm." She'd removed her own helmet and placed it over my head. The neck rings didn't fit, and I could smell distant sugary turpines. The wind was gusting in wild fits, buffeting the hovercraft, and out over the canyon a large rock fifty meters in front of me pointed toward heaven like a solitary finger. From this rock issued a plume of ghostly blue and silver forms, like sheets of cloth or willow wisps, that silently climbed into the night.

Everyone was watching them. "Look at them!" Mavro said in awe, "Have you ever seen anything like it?" There was a whispering of sand blowing over stones.

Everyone just sat and watched for a long time, and I realized dully that it was a flock of bioluminescent *oparu no tako* riding the thermals up out of the canyon and higher into the air. Their underbellies shone with pale blue, and my eyes registered their body heat as platinum. A dull red bolt of lightning struck the distant rim of the canyon.

Mavro fired up the engine on the hovercraft. He skirted the edge of the desert.

The wind whistled over my helmet. The canyon we skirted was but a crack in the world, and I kept feeling we'd slide into it. I began breathing heavily. I closed my eyes, tried to block out sensation. *Think of other things,* I decided. *Occupy your mind.* I held my helmet and tried to imagine my home in Panamá, the good times in the feria. The pain was unbearable. I moaned.

"Are you awake?" Abriara asked. She leaned close to hear my answer. The microphone on my helmet was off, so she touched her forehead to my helmet so she could listen.

"*Sí.*"

"What's wrong? You've been passing out and shouting at us, laughing one moment and raging the next. I think the blow to the head made you crazy, but I don't understand why it took you so long to get this way?"

"Sensory overload," I said. "Ecoshock. There are too many strange scents and noises. I can't handle it."

"We had two years to get acclimated," Abriara said. "After six months the computer began dubbing in background noises and smells on us."

"Yes, that is the way it should be done. Get acquainted with the terrain slowly." I lay there and closed my eyes. I wanted to take off the helmet so I could rub my temples.

"What can we do for you?" Abriara asked.

"Wrap something around this helmet. Seal out the

smells and noise. That would help. Then just talk to me, help me keep my mind off things."

I heard the shredding of cloth and Abriara began wrapping my neck. "I could put a resin coat over this material and block you out totally, but I don't know what the fumes might do," she said as she worked. "What do you want to talk about?"

"I had a bad dream—" I said, "a dead friend accused me of serving an evil society."

Abriara chuckled, a lighthearted laugh. "I suppose so. If—as the social engineers contend—every society is equally evil, then anyone who serves a society would be serving an evil society."

She said it with such ease I don't believe she understood my concern.

"Ah! Ah! But if a society is evil, then one must ask, What is evil?" I thought I sensed a way out of this—if I clouded the issue and became hopelessly snarled in philosophical arguments, I wouldn't have to come to grips with the sense of guilt that threatened to overwhelm me.

Perfecto standing at his turret said, "Violation of another person's territory is the root of all evil. It is the sole definition of evil." His words surprised me, partly because my helmet mike wasn't on and I hadn't realized he could hear me, partly because his answer was so totally unexpected.

Perfecto continued. "When one person steals, he violates another's territory. When one person kills, he violates another's territory. When one person sleeps with the spouse of another, he violates another's territory. When someone lies about you, he violates the good name you have attained through your actions. With you humans, all your moral codes are ultimately based on your territorialistic natures. All that is evil can be seen as arising from violating another's territory."

Perfecto's answer was such a novel concept that I had to ask, "Then what is good?"

Perfecto said, "To allow others into your own territory; to deny your own territorialism: it is good to give your money to the poor. It is good to give your coat to the naked. It is good to give the homeless shelter in your own home. It is good to perform a labor for another so that you enlarge his domain while diminishing your own. You humans believe it is *good* to deny your own territorialism."

I couldn't accept such a simplistic philosophy. Perhaps Perfecto was just seeking to distract me with petty arguments, I wondered, and therefore he was baiting me. Yet he'd spoken along a similar vein when he said I'd always murdered to defend my own territory. I'd never considered the possibility that he'd have developed a whole moral philosophy based upon territorialism. I considered his words. "It seems to me that there must be goods and evils that have nothing to do with territorialism," I said, though I could not then and cannot now think of an act of good or evil that is not tied to the concept.

Perfecto thought for a moment. "No. Territorialism is the sole biological medium by which you humans define good and evil. Some moral codes have nothing to do with good and evil but simply designate a person as a member of a culture, and because of this you humans have sometimes imagined that good and evil are only relative, that they have no basis in a biological or spiritual reality. For example, a devout Jew may look at another Jew who denies the need for circumcision and think the man evil, but everyone outside the culture realizes that the act of denying or affirming circumcision is not a moral question. It is simply an act of affirming membership to a culture. You wear the clothes that you do and use the nonverbal expressions that you do simply to designate your membership in your culture. Yet if you were to suddenly dress in black and take long walks after midnight, other members of your culture would assert that you were evil and dangerous.

"You humans have always codified your rules for good and evil based entirely upon your territorial instincts. That is all good and evil is. I'm surprised you haven't noticed it in the past four thousand years. I—"

I cut him off. A thought struck me, a challenging thought. "Then, according to your moral theories, Perfecto, since your territorialistic nature has been genetically strengthened, would you not say that you chimeras are naturally more moral than we humans?" This question seemed very important, for some socialists claimed they'd strengthen morality by diminishing human territorialism. They believed true communism could only be achieved when we no longer thought of ourselves as individuals, but as part of a group. Other socialists claimed this would only lead them to design a slothful race who had no motivation to increase their productivity.

"Perhaps. On instinct we are more aware of what is socially acceptable among our own kind. We chimeras are less disposed to violate the territories of others, yet we are also less disposed to give up our own territories—to be good," Perfecto apologized. "But perhaps the degree of one's territorialism does not matter—what does matter is how one acts toward one's territories and the territories of others. When we sin against others we pay a higher price in guilt."

"Then why do you fight this war? Why do you not recognize and respect the territories of Motoki and the Yabajin? Why did you kill Lucío?"

Perfecto hung his head and did not answer. Abriara said softly, with anger, "We chimeras do not respect the territories of humans because you have never respected our territories. Always you have feared us—because we are strange, because we are stronger than you and smarter and more powerful. So your people took away our homes, kicked us out of our own countries, denied us equal pay, and tried to deny us our self-respect. Humans have lost the right to be treated as moral equals. You ask Perfecto why he killed Lucío. He did it for you! So you would not—"

"Enough!" Perfecto shouted.

Abriara continued, "—so you would not bear a burden of guilt for murdering Lucío! He saw how your guilt ravages you, and—"

"Silence!" Perfecto yelled. A growl came from his throat, and he began shuddering. I realized he was weeping. And I realized Abriara was right. Perfecto murdered Lucío so he could take my own burden of guilt upon himself, and he'd poured himself a cup he couldn't drink.

I slept again, a sleep not so encumbered by evil dreams. I woke briefly once and we were hurtling through a storm unlike anything I'd ever seen—dark red night was upon us and clouds thundered. Three tornadoes were touching down upon the desert floor just ahead, yet I felt a peculiar lack of concern. Perfecto was driving into the storm and Abriara was huddled on the floor ahead of me, her head wrapped in a rag to protect her from stinging sand. I considered Perfecto's philosophy of territorialism and looked at my own concepts of good and evil through his eyes. And though I found that I could see things exactly as he said, and though his philosophy has colored my thoughts ever since, I struggled to find holes in his logic. I could not believe that chimeras were genetically engineered to be more moral than humans. Yet I remembered the Nicita Idealist Socialists, the nonterritorial humans they had sought to engineer, and the tales I had heard of the inhuman murders committed by those creatures. And I thought long about those people whose territories we violate, and those to whom we give our own territories, and realized that most of my life I had done neither—given and taken nothing—and as a result, most people I had known were just strangers who passed me on the street.

I woke a second time in darkness, in a still cave while the wind raged outside. I was no longer wearing Abriara's helmet, and the cave smelled damp and full of dust.

My dream of Flaco disturbed me. He'd accused me of serving an evil society. And if my society was evil, I considered, then I was evil for seeking its rewards. It would be like accepting money from a criminal. I marveled that all through my elderly years men had called me a *caballero*, a gentleman, and I'd considered it a compliment. But when one looks at the word *caballero*, one sees that it stems from the same root as *chivalry*, and to call a man a *caballero* is to say that he is a gentleman, a man of fine breeding, bold and strong, powerful in war. Only in a society of murderers could such an epithet be considered a compliment.

The social engineers contend that all societies are equally evil. And this belief allows them to create any world they want, regardless of the suffering it will cause. I decided that their philosophy is a ruse, meant only to fool themselves. I could not live in an evil society.

I decided to leave my society, and I wondered if I could stay if society somehow changed. The only vehicle I'd ever seen for enacting a change in a society was that used by the Idealist Socialists—and their techniques had always sickened me on a gut level. The first creed of the Idealist Socialists begins: "We believe that in order to achieve a harmonious relationship among men, we must form a new society with nobler ideals that exalt mankind above the individual man." Those are fine-sounding words. They simply say that they believe the society is more important than the individual, and I've never been certain of the virtue of arguing the point.

However, they believe that for a program of social engineering to have the desired effect, the community to be engineered must exist in cultural isolation. Thus a very fundamental creed of the Idealist Socialists is that for their "noble experiment" to succeed they must destroy competing cultures either by infiltration or genocide. This may seem a fine solution for a person who believes in Nicita Idealist Socialism, but for those of us who are not so inclined the idea stinks.

And as I pondered it, I realized the Idealist Socialists pollute their own society as they create it. They pee in their own drinking water, so to speak, for they pretend that their *ideals can flourish in society while their individuals become corrupt*—pretend it's possible to set dedicated socialists to undermining the freedom of others and murdering innocent civilians without having their own people lose the love of humanity that Nicita Idealist Socialism purports to engender.

And this is why those of us who view Idealist Socialism from outside the culture are so easily persuaded the entire system is evil. We see the murders, the treachery, the destroyed lives and lack of respect for humanity the Idealist Socialist outlook engenders, and we are revolted by the whole system. As Abriara had said, every society appears evil to those outside it. I could easily see the evil in Idealist Socialism. But I'd taken longer to see evil in my own society.

I determined to never again serve an evil society. I'd never serve my society. I began to look into my heart, examine my beliefs and consider how to root them out. *But how can a man free himself from his subconscious beliefs?* I wondered. As Abriara had pointed out, we each have thousands of expectations thrust upon us by our culture. I expect people to wear shoes and comb their hair. I couldn't root out even such minor expectations, so how would I root out attitudes ingrained over a lifetime, attitudes I wasn't even aware of? It would be easier for a fish to exist outside water. I began to see that I'd have to leave my society. To stay would pollute me. Among all the petty utopias floating between the stars, I reasoned, there must be a place where I could find peace.

I slept again and woke in searing sunlight and the wind was whistling through pale trees that waved as if they'd break. Bright clouds raced across the sky and the ground was wet. A storm had just passed. I was lying by my side on dark ultraviolet grass that twisted in coral shapes, looking over a small pond with steep banks, almost round in shape. Abriara, Mavro, and Perfecto were drawing water from the pond in a pail and drinking. My lips felt parched and cracked.

A creature walked out of the trees on the far side of the pond—a dark oily green animal with a long segmented body and small claws. It walked close to the ground and may have been no taller than a cat, but it was as long as a man. I tried to discover what it reminded me of—a scorpion with no stinging tail, a crab that had been pulled out of shape. I tried to pin it down as herbivore, predator, or scavenger, but had no data. It skittered into the water. And I realized it was *itself*. Alone.

I didn't know if it had an analog on Earth and couldn't describe it as being "like" anything at all, for there was

nothing on Earth like this creature. To make simple
associations, to pretend Baker's life-forms were like
anything on Earth, would be unjust. It would leave me
confused as to their true nature and might ultimately
prove dangerous.

Abriara gave me a drink and I was very dizzy. "Are you
feeling much better?" she asked. She sat beside me and
laid my head in her lap.

"Some."

"What can I do to help?"

"Talk. Occupy my mind with pleasant things," I said.

"Then let's find something comforting. I'm curious,
what's it like to have a family? Your mother is dead—so
tell me about your father, brothers, and sisters?"

"My father?" I said. "My father is . . ." and I could
think of nothing. My father. I could remember my father
sitting in the chair crying over my mother's death while
Eva's children climbed over him. And I could remember
nothing after that. Nothing. Not only had I never seen or
heard from him again, I couldn't remember ever having
wondered where he was. The feeling was totally inex-
plicable, as if I'd entered a classroom to take an exam and
found a professor who insisted on testing me on a subject
I'd never even heard of. My father. I backtracked. I
could remember all about my father from before my
mother's death. "My father," I shouted, "was a weak and
cynical man. He was hopeless, frustrated. Quitting one
job after another. He used to say, 'The unexamined life
is not worth living, but the examined life is no better.'
After my mother died, he . . . he . . ."

And I was stunned. After my mother died he ceased to
exist for me. I stood up and a terrible fear took me. I
could think of only two explanations: either I'd suffered
brain damage or something so terrible had happened to
my father I'd blocked it out completely. I wanted to run,
but there was nowhere to run. I worried greatly and
ended up taking an overdose of painkillers to help me
sleep again.

We crossed over some great plains and came to a small
canyon of packed dirt. And in this canyon we passed
through a series of large worn stones that were sculpted

perfectly round, like globes. Each stone stood some eight meters high and they were arranged in the valley in a huge spiral like the paintings left on the caves of some Australian aborigines. The circular stones had sunk a bit into the ground over many hundreds or perhaps thousands of years. Yet the sight of them filled me with awe. They were very much like the tiny stones the desert lord had thrown at us, yet these were immense— and the fact that they were arranged in a spiral seemed to hint that they'd been created as part of an effort by an organized community. I kept expecting to see caves or stone doors leading into the hillside, paintings on rock walls. But I could see no hint of who or what had fashioned these stones.

We made the coast that afternoon. I tried to dredge up memories of my father, yet I could think of nothing, absolutely nothing. I wondered why I could have possibly blocked out my memories of him. Had I found that it was actually *he* who had killed my mother? Had he killed himself in a cowardly manner just after my mother's funeral? I thought that if I envisioned a scenario that was close to the truth, perhaps I'd suddenly remember him. And I became aware that there was another hole in my memory—the hole where Tatiana, the child in my dreams, would fit. Why had she been so important that I continued to remember only her face and her name? I couldn't say. The wind continued to rage. We camped that evening and my compadres propped me against a tree. My arms and legs refused to respond as they should. I had barely enough energy to feed myself, and my arms and legs felt weak like those of an infant. I wondered about my father long into the night.

I woke the next morning in the hovercraft, whizzing over the ground. I was lying on my back and could no longer hear the roaring surf. I felt dissociated from everything. From my past, from my friends, from my world. The sky was deep red as if at sunset and there were no clouds. And no bands of *oparu no tako* weaving across the sky. They'd been decimated by the storms. We passed under a tree, a battered palm with shredded leaves that rustled like paper, and the sight of something so intimately familiar struck me to the heart.

I am returning to Panamá, I thought with insane glee. *I am returning to Panamá.* The sun shining on battered leaves reminded me of an incident that had long lain dormant in my mind. I can't remember when it happened, or in what country, but it seemed like something from my childhood: I remember lying on a cot, looking out a window. There was a line of trees between two open fields, and a troop of monkeys was crossing through the trees from one forest into another. And the feeling I had at that time was that it was I that was traveling, and the monkeys were standing still.

I lay in the bottom of the hovercraft and the feeling I gained from seeing that one battered palm, the memories it brought back after the strange fauna of Baker, filled me with a sense of ease, of euphoria. And against all knowledge to the contrary, I felt that I was returning home, reentering the borders of my own lost country.

As the day progressed we passed many palms. By noon we reached a land that was totally terraformed and forested. White cockatoos chattered in the trees and feasted on fruit, and there was no doubt we'd reached the land of the Yabajin.

We camped at night and for the next two days followed the coastline south. Day and night the gales blew steadily, rushing from the cool seas into the hot interior, bringing occasional brief squalls. Yet the sea here was a narrow band and the storms dropped little rain. The dust thrown up into the atmosphere from winds in the desert colored the sky a dull yellow-brown during the day and made for spectacular red sunrises and sunsets. I began to feel a bit stronger, and that night I lay awake beside the campfire and listened to the others.

Abriara had been filled with anxiety that day, stressed and tired. Whenever anyone spoke to her, they had to address her two or three times before she would answer. After Mavro went to sleep, Perfecto said, "What is on your mind, little sister?"

"I am just . . . I don't know. I want it. I want this planet so bad!"

"Yes," Perfecto said eagerly. "I know. I feel it, too."

Abriara said, "When we were children, in Temuco, remember what it was like in the compound? We had nothing! Absolutely nothing that we could call our own! Captain Guerrera would give us our clothing or our toys, but nothing ever belonged to *me*—just me alone. If he gave us shoes, he would always say, 'Now remember to share.' I hated it."

"I know," Perfecto said. "I hated it, too. They created us to be territorial, then gave us nothing to own. Let us keep nothing."

Abriara laughed. "Remember how we used to hide things under our beds when we were children? And Guerrera would come and clean everything out from time to time. I found a doll in the gutter and hid it for months, moving it, wanting it not because it was beautiful or clean or even a decent toy, but just because it was *mine*."

Perfecto smiled, "*Sí*, Giron and his sticks. Remember how he used to find sticks and bring them home— nothing special about the stick—just plain sticks. If he is still alive back on Earth, I'll bet he has a mountain of sticks in his house."

"That is the way I feel now," Abriara said. "I want this planet the way Giron wanted his sticks. I want a home. I want it so bad I cannot think straight! If we win this war, I think I will die of joy."

"Ah," Perfecto said. "Would it not be good? To have a whole planet to ourselves. This longing, it is in our bones. I never thought I could want so much. Yet I do not want to kill the Yabajin. I pity them for what will happen when we reach Hotoke no Za."

On the afternoon of our third day of following the coastline we came to the first sign of civilization: we found an abutment that jutted into the sea, and on a gray stone cliff was painted a huge white Japanese character, a single word. I have no idea what the word was, but it seemed a warning. Above the character was painted a gleaming white samurai sword, and over the top of the sword in streaming red was a piece of graffiti—a single bloody eye.

We stopped the hovercraft, and stared at the symbols for a long time.

"Do you suppose it's a warning?" Perfecto asked.

"I'm not sure," Abriara said, "but I'll bet we're not far from Hotoke no Za. Perhaps not more than a few kilometers."

"No," Mavro said, "I don't think so. We can't be that close yet. I studied the maps for a long time, and I don't think we're within two hundred kilometers."

Abriara said, "Do you want to blunder forward and find out the hard way? We don't even know if the city will be visible from the coast. I don't want to hit a puff mine or come sliding in under some hidden neutron cannon mounted in the rocks."

"Maybe there won't be any defenses left to the city," I said hopefully. "Maybe our compadres have already reached the city and shut off all the automatic defenses." With all the Yabajin we'd met in the desert, the entire male population seemed to have left the city. It would be defended only by women, the very old, and the very young. And of course, the ten thousand Colombian mercenaries would have shuttled down.

"No, the defenses won't be down," Perfecto said. "Even if Garzón made it through the desert, he said we'd give battle at dawn on the ninth day after leaving Kimai no Ji. We still have till morning to find them. And even if for some reason he decided to fight the battle early and has already won the city, Garzón will get the defenses operating as soon as possible to make sure there are no reprisals from Motoki or the Yabajin."

The thought of trying to run the gauntlet of remote defenses unnerved me. It was a task I hadn't trained for, one I'd witnessed only in simulation, and that single episode of viewing the city's defenses had shown me my weakness. I did not want to go south.

Abriara said. "Let's head inland, see if we can find any sign of Garzón. If they've already headed into the city, they should have left a trail of blown puff mines and fried ANCs."

Abriara veered inland through the trees. It took two hours to navigate through ten kilometers of jungle, and from then on the jungle thinned into an arid grassland. I was fumbling around in my pockets with nothing better to do, and found the stone I'd picked up at Kimai no Ji. I sat and looked at the little cauliflower ear of ruby.

Mavro saw me and asked, "What is that?"

"A ruby," I said, and he turned all his attention to me. "I found it at Kimai no Ji. Apparently, they are very common here. All the metals in the planet. Rubies, emeralds—they're just quartz crystals with copper and iron in them. They're nothing here."

"Hah!" Mavro said, "A real ruby? It makes sense—all the metals. Perhaps there's gold in every river, rubies in every backyard lot, and we just don't know about it!"

And as we traveled on, I wondered if maybe he wasn't right.

That night we traveled three hundred kilometers in a great semicircle through bands of jungle, then came to a thick belt of forest that bordered a wide river. We were certain it had to be the river that flowed through Hotoke no Za—we'd seen the pictures of the Yabajin hovercrafts going up this river and it was the only one so large on the map, and we followed it south and east, feeling our way toward the city and its remote defenses. Abriara would often say as if to herself, "We're going to make it! We're going to make it!"

An hour before dawn we came round a wide bend and the river channel before us went straight. No trees impeded our southeast view along the channel and we saw a great light from a city set on a hill, but the lights were red and reflected off clouds of smoke.

The city was on fire.

Abriara watched the dull red billows of smoke above
the city. "What's going on?" she said. "Did he attack
early?"

"It must be the Colombians," Perfecto said. "Maybe
they accepted Garzón's offer and decided to burn the
city. Or maybe they're fighting the Yabajin in the city
now and the fire was an accident." The fire and smoke
looked very distant, perhaps eighty kilometers off.

We watched the hill several moments. Abriara murmured, "There's no fighting going on up there. If there
were, I'd see laser fire flashing in the clouds. There's no
battle raging out there."

Mavro said, "Then it is the Yabajin burning their
homes before the battle. They know we are coming.
They know what will happen. They want to leave us with
nothing."

His words struck me with the force of truth. They'd be
burning their city this night, just as the inhabitants of
Motoki had burned their homes while committing mass
suicide.

Abriara sighed and said, "If the Yabajin are burning
the city, then Garzón must not have persuaded the
Colombians to join us. Otherwise the city would be ours,
or there would be some sign of battle. If Garzón is still
waiting to get in, we should meet him downriver. They'll
have to camp downriver." She pulled back on the
throttle. The hovercraft raised in the air as she brought
our speed up to full. Mavro and Perfecto began firing
plasma into the air, and the entire river was bathed in

light. Abriara shouted, "Angelo, throw all the food and
water overboard—any excess weight. It is certain that
there will be some unexploded mines in the river and I
don't want to find them the hard way. Pull all the laser
rifles out and keep one handy. If we have to take a swim,
hold onto your rifles."

I began pulling up floor panels and dumping everything we didn't need—blankets, an extra turbo, water
and food. I handed out laser rifles, and we slung them
over our backs. It took all of five minutes, then I stuck
my head over the edge of the hovercraft and watched the
trees go by.

We followed the river, and the next half hour passed
quickly and silently. My heart was pounding in my chest
and my breathing became dry and ragged.

Perfecto tapped his helmet. "Do you hear that?" he
asked. "We must be getting close to the army! I can hear
chatter over the radio. We're right behind them. They're
going in!" Almost immediately I heard the sound of
gunfire, and lasers began flashing over the city, making
pinpricks against the clouds, against stone battlements
set on the hill. The sun hadn't yet risen, but daylight was
imminent. We were twenty kilometers north of the city
and Abriara pulled back on the throttle as hard as she
could, and we picked up speed. Everywhere the sound
of distant gunfire crackled in a steady barrage.

"Ten minutes till we hit their defensive perimeter,"
Abriara shouted. She began shouting a comlink code,
jacking in a call to someone I didn't know. She shouted
her name and asked for a status report.

Perfecto began yelling at me, "Little Brother, I think
we will be going in at the tail, so do not have many
worries. If you hear the metal squeal or the sound of
crackling paper, it means we're taking a hit from a
neutron cannon. You jump out of the hovercraft quick,
okay? The ANCs only hit things that move and take up a
space that covers .008 degrees on its horizon, so it will
choose the hovercraft for a target instead of one of us. If
we take a hit, you jump—then look for that cannon, and
burn off all its sensors. If you land in the water, get out
of your armor quick. The insulation on your laser rifle

will make your gun float. You swim to your rifle and carry it ashore with you. And if you hear a high whistling buzzing sound, it's weasel rockets. Shoot them from the air. The city's defenses are spread pretty thin, but when we present a front, all their mobile defenses—the weasels and cybertanks—will pull toward us."

Perfecto made it all sound so easy. But the truth was, nothing is ever so easy. The Yabajin had been beating us worse then we anticipated all the way. From the plague aboard the ship to the destruction of our defensive perimeters at Kimai no Ji. Only once had we surprised them with superior weapons, and they'd had five days to remedy that inequality. Even if they had only women fighting, those women would be armed with weapons equal to ours.

Abriara abruptly reversed all thrusters and the hovercraft floated slowly over the dark water. "*Muchachos*," she said. "I just got a status report: Garzón's plan has failed. The Yabajin saw what we did to Motoki, and they never shuttled the Colombians into Hotoke no Za. They didn't trust them. The Yabajin overthrew what was left of Motoki. Our defenders here shot down six Yabajin zeppelins, but three more were able to bypass our defenses and land yesterday morning. They may have as many as three thousand samurai defending the city, as well as thirty-five thousand civilians. They may have been able to upgrade their weapons. Perhaps even their armor."

"Then what are we to do?" Perfecto asked.

"We have no choice. Garzón chooses not to believe there are three thousand samurai in the city. We must go forward and fight to the last man. Take no prisoners."

She was right. We couldn't back away. If the Yabajin were given time to regroup as a nation, we'd never be able to hold out against them. The only hope was to attack with everything we had.

"Then let's do it," Mavro said.

Abriara jerked back on the throttle and we hummed in. Ten kilometers from the city we came in upon the first ANC—a smoldering pylon well-hidden behind some logs. A dozen of our craft were floating in the water and there was no sign of our compadres.

Abriara picked up speed. We came to a bend and for a moment could see the city once again: on the sides of the mountain the morning sun struck Hotoke no Za and the whole city gleamed golden. The city was set upon a stately granite hill and all along the hilltop were factories and homes. But these weren't the thin paper houses of Motoki, rather they were neat brick domes in earth tones of cinnamon, yellow ochre, and dull green; gracefully curved with palms and green grasses in the yards. Everywhere, smoke was still pouring from the large domes at the interior of the city, and even at ten kilometers we could see hundreds of our hovercrafts, tiny dots, racing to the hilltop to meet the Yabajin.

Our men were coming in upon the southeast side of the city, and I thought it odd. They should have been coming in from the northeast, from the river, and I wondered if perhaps the river turned south around the mountain.

Perfecto shouted, "Abriara!" and our hovercraft began to crackle and scream. Abriara vaulted into the air, and Perfecto grabbed my right arm and nearly ripped it from its socket as he leapt from the craft. I had time enough to realize we'd taken a hit from an automatic neutron cannon and to think to hold onto my Flechette rifle. We hit the warm water and our hovercraft forged ahead a hundred meters and exploded in a fireball.

I gasped and lay on top of the water and felt it filling my armor. I stripped off my leg pieces and unbuckled my chest plates with one hand, still holding my rifle. The others were doing the same. The chest plates dropped away and the laser rifle slipped from my back and popped to the surface like a cork. I grabbed the straps to the laser and the flechette and held them in one hand, kicked off the ankle pieces to my armor, and pulled off my left hip piece. My right hip piece still had three loaded clips in a pocket. I kept it on. I tried kicking toward the south bank of the river, but the armor dragged at the water.

Perfecto came holding a laser rifle in front of him like a life jacket and grabbed my arm and pulled.

"Hold onto my rifle a minute," I said, pushing the flechette into his hands, "I've got to get my ammunition." Perfecto took the weapon and I opened my leg pouch and pulled out my clips, wrapped them in my shirt.

Perfecto swam closer and grabbed my right arm again, twisting it. He looked in my eyes and whispered, "Tell the others you are injured! Tell them you can't go on! Don't risk assaulting the hill, Little Brother, or I will be forced to hurt you!"

Perfecto's eyes were dilated, spooky. He twisted my arm again and pain lanced through my shoulder. He was intent on protecting my life even if it meant wounding me.

He twisted my arm again and I gasped. "All right!" I said. I dropped the empty leg piece and kicked to shore slowly, conserving energy, protecting my injured arm. I was still very weak from my illness. The river flowed sluggishly and the water smelled brackish. Abriara got to shore first and sat for a long moment, watching the bushes along the riverbank ahead of us. Then she flipped on her targeting laser and aimed carefully. A moment later a thin ray of smoke boiled up as paint burned off a well-camouflaged ANC pylon.

We swam up beside her. She was breathing heavily.

"My fault," she said. "Garzón must have turned off into the brush. He knew this river would be riddled with ANCs and cybertanks up ahead."

"Sí," Perfecto said. "I saw the trail they left just before the ANC hit us, but you were looking up at the city. The trail is back here! But I think Angelo is hurt on his gun arm. I don't think he can go on!" Perfecto helped pull me from the river.

Abriara studied me with obvious concern.

I rubbed my shoulder. "I'm all right," I said.

Perfecto stared at me a moment with great sadness. His fists clenched and I thought he'd hit me, do anything to stop me from going forward. He took my flechette and said, "Follow me! I'll take point," and began walking upriver, limping from his wounded leg, beating his way through the thick brush. I did not like this. He was putting himself in danger for me, giving his life to me the way Lucío had given his life to me.

We soon found the trail the others had taken: plasma had rained through the forest as they forged ahead, knocking out puff mines. The ground was burned and scarred, and the foliage cut low. Just inside the brush line a dozen hovercrafts were down, blown to pieces by an ANC. The trail was littered with the broken bodies of our mercenaries, yet the ground cover was so amazingly thick that you almost never noticed a corpse until you had stumbled over it. Perfecto went fifty yards ahead of Mavro. Abriara and I followed at fifty–yard intervals behind Mavro. If one of us stepped on a mine, the rest wouldn't be blown apart. We scavenged the broken bodies of our compadres and began piecing together armor as we hurried forward, following the trail at a near run through the low brush. Neither Mavro nor I found helmets that would fit, and I quickly gave up. We were only five kilometers from the front. Every dozen meters we'd cross a pit where a puff mine had blown, and twenty times we came upon wrecked hovercrafts, empty of occupants. A dozen black cybertanks lay scattered by the wayside, and for every one I noticed I'm sure four or five must have lain decimated in the jungle, for I often noticed holes in the foliage burned by intense gunfire.

The sound of gunfire continued in the distance. Everyone was very quiet. They concentrated on their tasks—watching the ground before them, watching the brush for signs of movement.

Perfecto shouted for us to halt, and stood staring ahead. There'd been a long empty stretch with no sign of puff mines. The Yabajin had chosen to cover the ground thoroughly rather than to keep the mines sparse and surprise us, so when we'd gone ten meters without encountering a mine, we knew something was wrong. Perfecto reached down and scooped up some handfuls of dirt and tossed them ahead. Mines exploded under the impact of the falling dirt. Perfecto smiled and shouted, "It was nice of our compadres to leave this path so clean, no? No puff mines. No weasels."

I looked at Mavro. Sweat was streaming down his forehead and his eyes were blank. The sweat of *mugga*, of perfect concentration, was upon him. We came out at the edge of the jungle at the base of the hill. Rifles still crackled on the hillside and I could easily make out the small shapes of men in green bug suits climbing. Like ants they streamed over gaps blown through a high wall and into town. I was surprised they were so close. Five black cybertanks were putting up from the jungle. Men with lasers were sprawled before them, frying off sensors. One tank lurched up a steep incline, then flipped on its back. Another putted out of the jungle at the base of the hill and sprayed deadly laser fire over twenty men in less than a second.

And in this vast clearing lay hundreds of our dead. A great light exploded from town and streamers shot up into the air like fireworks, a thousand trails of orange fire. Perfecto shouted, "A tree of death!" pointing at the streamers, and as each streamer of fire neared the ground it exploded, sending shrapnel off in every direction. Men fell by the hundreds. The Yabajin had upgraded their defenses. And we had no Colombians inside town to fight for us.

We ran for our lives, hoping to cross the open space before another tree of death exploded. We were still a kilometer from the front when Perfecto looked to the side and he ducked. I heard a high piercing whine and five weasels—missiles as long as my arm—came whistling through the brush from the north. Perfecto fired several shots in rapid succession, blowing them from the sky. But he hit the last weasel only a few meters from his chest. Shrapnel plowed into him, shattering his armor in a shower of green.

He whined in surprise and stepped backward, his chest a ragged tatter of blood, and fell. I rushed up to him and he gasped and tiny air bubbles issued from holes in his chest. Mavro reached down and grabbed the flechette from Perfecto's hand, then stood guard over his body, watching the skyline for more weasels. "Did you notice," Perfecto said through his helmet, and the feedback in his microphone made his voice sound like the growling of a dog, "something strange? No mosquitoes. In this whole big jungle, there are no mosquitoes!" He reached up and pawed my face, as if in a caress, fell back and died.

Up the hill people were shrieking, the Yabajin shrieking and dying in the streets of Hotoke no Za, the explosions of our guns. I looked up and the sun was climbing bitter yellow in the sky. A terrible wrath filled me. The Yabajin had taken away my friend and I hated them for it. I wanted to rush up the hill and lay it bare, but I looked down at the mess in Perfecto's chest and knew I couldn't leave him, couldn't bear his nonexistence. He had given me his life. And I hoped to give it back.

I looked at my hands. They held only a gun. I should have had my medical bag. I looked at his wounds—a pulmonary bag to plug the hole in his lungs, a liter of artificial blood, a resin bandage over the wounds, a slave to keep his heart beating. That is all it would have taken to keep him alive. I could have saved him if I'd had my medical bag. I pulled out my machete and slit the foam insulation on the barrel of my laser around the frozen tubes that held the nitrogen coolant, then cut the pinky finger from Perfecto's left hand and shoved it near the nitrogen tubes. I slit off a shred of his bloody kimono and wrapped the barrel of the laser rifle, hoping it would insulate the specimen of Perfecto's flesh, keep it from spoiling.

"Ah, look at the doctor—" Mavro said, glancing back at me. The sweat of *mugga* was on his face and he watched the ground. "The old man is turning into a ghoul."

I made no comment. I'm sure he understood what I was doing, but in the ghettos of Cartagena no one took tissue samples of the dead for cloning. In a world teeming with people waiting to be born, each with something unique to add to the gene pool, cloning can only be justified for those whose genetic makeup can be classified as an "irreplaceable treasure." Few people are genetically worthy of the honor. Perfecto and the other chimeras were perhaps the only people I'd ever met whom I considered worthy to be cloned.

Abriara's voice was very husky. "You're going to make a copy of him, aren't you?" She said. "I think that's wonderful of you. I love you for that."

"Fine," I said, and looked up the hill. I remembered Perfecto's words from the first time we'd met: You and I will both die on Baker. His prophecy was becoming fulfilled. He was dead, and I could feel myself dying to compassion, dying to joy, dying to hope. And when all those things are gone, nothing of value is really left. I could feel myself becoming an empty shell. We were at the bottom of the rice paddies and above us on the plateaus were banana fields. A few hovercrafts had overturned there while trying to climb the steep slopes. I could see no sign of defenses. A few cybertanks were putting up the hill on our flanks, far away. There may have been more weasels, but most had been taken out by those who went before us. Half a dozen ANC turrets were smoking on the cliffs at the base of the city. There was nothing to stop us from entering Hotoke no Za. They wouldn't have mined the banana fields.

I jumped up and shouted and rushed toward the city. I slogged through the fields toward the city, and Abriara shouted, "Wait! It's still dangerous," and rushed to take a place in front of me, and Mavro rushed to be first. His eyes glinted dangerously. The sun shone brilliantly on the tattoos of his pale blue tears, making them look as if they were etched in light.

I pumped my legs and slogged through the rice paddies and tried to be the first of our trio to make it into the city. But Abriara was stronger and quicker than me, and she charged up the hill before me, and Mavro seemed to just dance through mounds of mud that held me fast.

I stripped off my armor as I ran, not willing any longer to be encumbered by it.

We got out of the paddies and it was an easy run through the fields, then a steep climb of half a kilometer as we mounted the hilltop. We rushed through a breach in the wall into the streets of Hotoke no Za, and there were dead bodies everywhere and the sound of flechette fire suddenly became very loud. Abriara directed us to run between two houses, giant igloos cut of pale yellow stone, and there were three Yabajin samurai in red bug suits lying dead on the ground between the houses. I did not want to ruin my tissue sample, so I slung my laser over my back and took the rifle from a dead Yabajin. Down below us the city stretched two kilometers in a narrow and orderly band, down to the sea, and the city was a wreck—a long black furrow had been raised through the center of town by the crash of an air vehicle, and whole buildings were leveled because of this terrible wreck. Only a shuttle crashing at high speeds could have wrought such devastation, I realized. A hundred of our hovercrafts wove through the streets, spraying death from plasma turrets, jagged knives of steel from the Flechettes. The view was obscured by great clouds of smoke.

We crossed a street, running for our front down by the ocean shore, and there were Yabajin everywhere—little old Yabajin men in white kimonos with skins of leopard spots gutted by flechettes, little old ladies with green tiger stripes scorched by lasers, a toddler with his head bashed in. I saw only one dead mercenary in the city streets. We rushed toward a wall of smoke, and the smoke dyed the whole landscape in shades of old-lace yellow. I felt the wind on my body, and the sun shined in my face, and heard the booming of our guns nearby, and I was wild with glee. *This is the way it should be*, I thought. *Fighting without armor. Fighting when every part of you feels alive. This is the way it should be.* Everywhere the houses and buildings were of the same dome design; now and then some large building would sprout buttresses like unwieldy arms. Smoke rose from many domes, and some Yabajin lay in the doorways, their charred remains attesting to the popularity of self-immolation as the preferred form of seppuku. *Make it painful, ladies*, I thought. *Make it painful.*

We scurried up the street where the sounds of battle were particularly fierce, but the strange acoustics of the city played tricks on us. Always the sounds of battle seemed just ahead, just ahead, just a few meters ahead.

A laser flashed platinum in the air before me and I dodged and rolled and shouted with glee. We were only a kilometer from the sea. I jumped up and looked at my attacker—a compadre in a green bug suit who shrugged in apology. Yet I knew I'd reached the outskirts of the battle. There were many large buildings here, domes in earth shades, and I knew I was in a business district.

I heard cries directly ahead, the mewling shriek of a woman in pain, and I rushed under a buttress and through a cloud of smoke. Ahead, Mavro was firing his flechette into a dome. I heard a startled cry to my right, checked the doorway into a dome. Smoke was pouring out the doorway, and I could see nothing. I fired once, lancing my beam through the doorway at waist height, and someone shrieked and fell.

I turned. Abriara was watching the street, her pulse laser at ready. Mavro dodged into his dome, still firing. Down the hill our men advanced and the dead Yabajin were stacked so thick that in places one would almost have to wade through the corpses. The Yabajin seemed to have no defenses, no three thousand samurai, seemed not to have been prepared for us at all, and I couldn't understand this. I saw three domes downhill explode and collapse as one. The Yabajin were blowing their city.

I was too far behind the others. I was too far behind. There were no living targets before me. I had to rush forward to find my targets. None of the Yabajin were wearing armor. I fumbled with the burst regulator on the laser, turning it off. I ran past Abriara and past the building Mavro had entered. Abriara shouted and gave chase.

I ran down the streets past a dozen compadres in green armor who were methodically assaulting two burnt-out businesses as if the Yabajin would be hiding in there, past a hovercraft full of mercenaries that were firing plasma in an arc so it would rain down on the city half a kilometer away.

I rushed two blocks through the business section, running over the pavement, scraping the skin off my bare feet. Three youths in yellow skinsuits rushed from a building and I strafed them across the back and turned to see where my compadres were. And suddenly I realized none of my compadres were before me—I'd reached our front lines alone with plasma raining in the streets before me. I could kill them all.

I shouted and looked up the hill and suddenly a Yabajin woman ran out the doorway of a dome. She wore a light-blue skinsuit, the color an executive might wear, and her skin was pale yellow with red flowering dots, deep blue under the eyes. Her epicanthic folds were greatly exaggerated and her dark hair was pulled back. She lowered her eyes and looked at a laser rifle. She was fumbling with a laser rifle, trying to get the safety off and point it at me.

I pulled up my laser and raked silver fire across her rib cage. She opened her mouth in surprise and stared up at me, and she knew she was dead. She fainted, kicking backward as if to get out of my way, sprawling on the street. And in that moment I felt a tinge of vertigo and my heart hammered and I achieved Instantaneity. She was falling—eyes rolling back for the last time, tossing her rifle in the air in fright. The smoke was blowing up the streets, twisting around the domes as it felt its way up the hill. The sky was nearly free of *oparu no tako*, washed clean by thunderstorms and buffeting wind. I could make out only a single yellow-green strand of them, flowing through the sky; and across the morning horizon were millions upon millions of individual *oparu no tako*, flashing golden and white in the sunlight, like bits of mica. And nothing else was alien. The orchids on the tiny lawns, the squat palms and giant ferns in the yards—I'd seen them all my life. The domes, like women's breasts jutting in the air, were simple houses. And the dying woman, falling to the ground with a grimace on her face and her pale yellow skin with rose-colored blotches, she was a simple woman, not unlike a million women I'd seen. And somehow she fit with the landscape. It was as if the smoke rolling up these streets, curling around the earth-tone huts, the sky glittering with golden mica, the dying woman with golden skin and rose highlights, were all part of a giant canvas, a perfectly conceived landscape painted by a master artist. And I felt what can only be described as a sense of *convergence*. This woman, this planet, was nothing like Earth. Yet I suddenly felt able to accept the differences. I felt as if I became part of Baker.

This Yabajin I'd just fried was a person who loved, who felt concern for people I knew nothing about. She was not Yabajin. She was human. And she was human not because of her similarities to me, but in spite of her differences from me. I looked around, startled by the realization, and saw that everything was strange, stranger than I had imagined. Yet everything belonged.

I wasn't in Panamá anymore. I looked up the streets, along the hills. My compadres were running among the Yabajin, firing into them. The Yabajin weren't putting up much resistance. There were not three thousand samurai as we'd been warned. Their zeppelins may never have landed more than a few hundred to defend the city. And all those appeared to be dead. Most buildings were burned and gutted. Only a few Yabajin had elected to live and fight. Like the inhabitants of Motoki, the Yabajin were suicides who believed they couldn't defeat us. Few fought at all, and none had weapons to pierce our armor. None were firing projectiles. They were doomed. Yet my *compañeros* didn't seem cognizant of this fact.

Up the hill a young girl dodged out of a building. Two mercenaries turned and fired automatically. She crumpled, skidded in a pool of her own blood. The same two mercenaries slowly advanced on the building she'd fled, as if it housed a dozen samurai. They were completely unaware that the battle was over, that the war had been won.

I did not find the internal strength to drop my weapon, as I'd tried so hard to do while killing Lucío. I simply lost the strength to carry it any farther. I ran to the woman I'd shot. She was lying on the ground, gasping for breath, but she was breathing. She was breathing! *I can save her*, I thought. *I can save her!* and a fleeting realization shot through my mind—from the moment I'd killed Arish, I'd been searching for someone to save, for some way to redeem myself. I'd dragged

Tamara's half-dead corpse to Sol Station. I'd tried my best during the plague to save at least one man. Even when Lucío killed Bruto, something in me cried out, "There is someone to save!" and at every turn my resolution had been defeated. And I thought: *If I can save one person for every one I've killed, somehow, the score will even out. Somehow I'll be free.*

I ripped part of her skinsuit off and covered her wound. Her skin was pale and she was in shock. I put my little laser rifle under her feet, raising them. I looked up, surveyed the streets. I needed a medical bag, some resin for a bandage, painkillers and vasoconstricters. I searched the streets as if the medicines would just be sitting there in a bag on the pavement. I wondered if there was a hospital, but each building was marked only by Japanese characters. I saw a hovercraft slowly descending the hill toward me. I raised my arms and shouted, ran up the hill toward my compadres.

"I need a medical bag!" I shouted as I approached.

A turret gunner spoke, and the speakers on his helmet growled, "What are you doing without armor on?"

"I don't need armor. The Yabajin aren't putting up a fight," I said, as if that explained everything. One gunner dug under the floorboards and pulled out the emergency kit, tossed it down to me.

"*Gracias*," I yelled as I grabbed it and ran.

I found the Yabajin woman exactly as I'd left her. I probed her wound and found a slow leak in one lung, damage to some blood vessels beneath her sternum. I plugged the small holes to the lung with a tube of pneumatic foam and simply spliced the blood vessel. I sprayed her over with a resin bandage, and injected her with DAP to bring her out of shock.

Abriara came up to my back while I was finishing.

"What are you doing?" she shouted.

"Saving people! These people aren't fighting back. Help me! Get another emergency kit," I yelled, and she threw down her gun and sprinted back up the hill. I ran up the street and found an old man whose eyes had glassed over, a girl of twelve who was past saving. I found a plump woman whose hips were so wide she looked as if she'd mothered many children. She huddled in the street with a leg filled with jagged knives from a flechette. Her left kneecap was blown away. Blood was pumping from the wound in a steady trail. She was panting like a wounded animal and clawing at the pavement in an attempt to escape me.

I held her down and applied a tourniquet to her leg, injected her with a painkiller. She looked at me in resignation and let me do the work. There was not much that could be repaired on her leg, not in a short amount of time. It would be better to stabilize her and keep the tourniquet on, I reasoned, even if it meant we'd later have to take off the leg. She could always grow a new limb.

Abriara came with a new medical bag, and shouted, "Down there! There's a whole crowd of people down there!" pointing toward the shore.

We ran down toward the beach and found thirty people in one knot on a street corner. Perhaps ten of them were still alive. I began working feverishly, and case ran into case—a boy child with his hips blown away, an old man with flechette wounds in his back, a teenage girl who took a plasma hit to the breasts and had the wits to dive forward and let the plasma drip off. I sat and worked quickly and guns exploded all around but no one fired on me. It seemed miraculous we could be engaged in medical work in the middle of the battle, but no Yabajin assailed us and none of our compadres hit us by mistake.

Time seemed to slow and a moment lasted forever. I worked and Abriara ran from hovercraft to hovercraft, bringing supplies. I once lifted my head and realized that not many people were shooting, I could have been working for minutes or an hour, I wasn't sure. I calculated that I'd administered to perhaps twenty people, at an average of two minutes per person. I couldn't imagine that I'd only been working for part of an hour. I was rocked by a large boom as a building exploded nearby.

And each time I raised my head to gasp for breath, Abriara pointed to someone else in need and I bundled my things and hurried on. We eventually found ourselves near some warehouses, and there were a dozen wounded in one little pile. I began working on a young girl and heard a scraping sound, looked up.

Someone in a green bug suit was dragging a wounded woman to the corner. The mercenary left the woman, ran off searching for more wounded. Another compadre came and threw off his helmet, a chimera with deformed ears, and dipped into my medical bags. His name was Faustino, and he explained quickly that he'd worked as a nurse in a field unit in Peru. He was very good. His hands were quick and clever.

Two more compadres, anonymous in battle armor, dragged in wounded. I was very surprised by this. I realized that suddenly we had the beginnings of a field station, and soon we'd have many wounded.

I heard a steady, insistent *boom-boom-boom* in a large dome just three doors up the road. It seemed to be the only sound of gunfire nearby. Abriara was up the street, carrying an old man on her shoulders. I realized that whoever was shooting was making a great deal of unnecessary work for us and this filled me with wrath.

I stalked up toward the building where the gunfire sounded. Abriara was walking under the arch of a large industrial building, and suddenly the whole building was shaken by an explosion. It lifted a decimeter in the air then the walls collapsed. Abriara looked up and an entire brick arch fell upon her in a jumble of stone and twisted steel girders.

I ran to her. There was no sign of Abriara beneath the stones. I stood in shock, looking at the mess, and began pulling off bricks. I figured that they covered her to the depth of a meter, and I heaved them away as quickly as I could. But I heard the continued sound of gunfire nearby.

When you uncover her, she will be crushed, I thought. *There are people to save. Everywhere a million people to save.* And I knew it was true. There'd be nothing left of Abriara beneath that rubble.

I ran to the great dome where I heard the gunshots, and even from the door I could hear the shrieks of women. I ran in. The dome was a theater. Light shone in from round windows that encircled the dome near the

top, and there was a stage down front. A hundred
women had taken refuge in the building, and one man in
armor stood at the entrance with a flechette and fired
upon the women who scurried between seats to escape
him. As I watched, one woman got up to run for a second
exit, and the man spun and fired on her. He was a
spectacle of precision and balance, grace and speed,
immersed in the state of *munen*, striking with the speed
of Instantaneity, moving with the practiced eloquence of
Perfect Control. He shot his victims as if they were
targets, taking perfect aim. He epitomized all that the
samurai had taught us to be. All the women screamed.

I shouted, *"Muchacho!"* and ran up behind the man.
He spun and saw I was Latin, then turned to fire upon
the Yabajin women again. I knocked his rifle from his
hands and yelled, "There is no need!" He looked at me,
then looked down at the rifle as if to pick it up.

I ripped at the latches of his helmet, shouting, "There
is no need!" and pulled it free to see if I recognized him.
He was a dark-eyed man of middle age. He was nameless
to me. His face could have belonged to any of a thousand
refugiados I knew. His eyes shone with an inner light,
and he had the sweat of *mugga* upon him.

He stared at me, stunned, not quite aware of why I
was yelling at him, like a dreamer being awakened from
his revelry. His face shone with rapture. Suddenly his
eyes focused and he became cognizant of me. *"Qué
glorioso!"* What glory! he said in amazement.

Outside, the sound of gunfire ceased. A muted cheer
was rising from the city as our men finally realized
victory was ours, finally realized the magnitude of what
they'd won. And even though I was sickened by the
petty creatures we'd become, I too felt a thrill as I
realized we'd won a planet. I went outside and watched
the other men. Happiness seemed to course down their
bodies like sweat. I saw a *compañero* with his helmet off,
and joy seemed to stream from his hair.

I turned and ran to help the wounded.

The day seemed endless as we pulled in the hundreds
of wounded and stabilized them and later moved them to

the hospital. It became a great labor, requiring the industry of over eighty people. The city was ours and the Yabajin were set up in a prison camp well before noon, and Garzón pronounced himself president of Baker. The Marine command floating in orbit gladly accepted our petition for membership in the Alliance of Nations as a consolidated planet, and the continuance of our occupation of the planet was confirmed. The Alliance preferred a stable world government over any other arrangement, regardless of the cost in human suffering, and by taking both capitals we gained recognition as the sole legal government under terms of law favoring any government that attained global consolidation. They were happy to have us clean up the mess on Baker. Happy to sanction our victory.

I learned that the Yabajin were unable to match us in projectile weapons that morning because their armory and industrial centers had been destroyed: several hours after the Yabajin zeppelins had made it into the city, a mercenary named Ovidio Cordosa had some amigos help him fill Motoki's shuttle with rocks and boulders. He then went out to sea and came in on Hotoke no Za at 1500 kph and crashed into the Ro Industrial Complex, killing himself and several hundred samurai who'd been feverishly upgrading weapons. The name of Ovidio was upon the lips of everyone, and many thought we should honor his heroism by renaming the city after him. *Ovidio* sounded like a good name for a city to me.

Garzón came and parked Tamara in the hospital in the afternoon and she silently watched while we put the broken Yabajin back together. I could feel her watching my back like a raven.

I filled her intravenous water bag once. She commended me on my work, but otherwise we didn't speak. In the afternoon I was working and suddenly realized I was still carrying my laser rifle strapped to my back. I took out the tissue sample from Perfecto and refrigerated it, then worked long into the night. At midnight Garzón came back and took Tamara, treating her once again as if she were a dog on his leash. He spoke with her softly, making plans for the immediate detention and deportation of all male Japanese. I worked till I was emotionally and physically exhausted, then walked out in the street to look for a place to sleep.

I wandered up by the theater where I'd last seen Abriara alive. The street was well lighted, and this surprised me, since so much of the city had been destroyed. No one had removed the stones from on top of Abriara, and I thought it was something that should be done by her amigo. I didn't know what had become of Mavro. My back ached and my eyes were tired, but I began lifting the green pumice stone myself.

Each stone was huge, weighing perhaps fifty kilos even in the light gravity. I was afraid to look upon Abriara, afraid she'd be mangled beyond recognition. But when I'd pulled most of the bricks off, I found the old Yabajin man she'd been carrying, crushed and broken, and Abriara's hand was poking from beneath his corpse. It glowed platinum with warmth and the veins stood out hot and clear.

I tossed several more bricks away and suddenly the whole pile moved and Abriara pushed aside the bricks and looked up at me. Her face was battered and bloody and there did not appear to be a place on her body that wasn't badly bruised. She tottered to her feet and I helped pull her from the wreckage. She staggered forward and fell to her knees.

"I . . . I thought you were dead!" I said.

Abriara looked back at the collapsed building with contempt, as if the stones were puny things, toys for children. Her voice held a note of surprise as she said, "I may be human, but I'm not *that* human!"

And I laughed in relief and took her to the hospital.

Abriara nursed her wounds in the hospital for the next two days. Miraculously she had only two cracked ribs. Apparently the upgrades in her collagens made her bones more than pliable. I'd have sworn only a jellyfish could have survived such a battering. I questioned her about it, and she said the Yabajin on her back took most of the beating, and the bricks just "looked heavier than they were."

Mavro and I met in the morning and retrieved Perfecto's body, and buried it in the cemetery. Afterward I worked in the hospital like a dog, welcoming the forgetfulness that came with work.

Garzón spent a great deal of time getting the defenses to the city back in order. A large contingent was sent to clear out the smaller settlements in Motoki, loading refugees aboard zeppelins to take to a remote island prison while we arranged their shipment back to Earth. Our men were still afraid of reprisals—sniper attacks, bombs in the buildings. Fifty hovercrafts full of Motoki and Yabajin samurai were caught on our borders within the first two days; all the samurai were out for Garzón's blood, and they'd crossed the desert in terrible storms to get it.

One could see the general fear in the way people tended to huddle in groups around the campfires at night and wear armor even when off duty. As fast as we stabilized our Japanese patients, Garzón transported them south. "Let the Yabajin care for their own," he said. "It will give them something constructive to do." He said this in spite of the fact that many Yabajin women treated us as if we were supermen, their biological and cultural superiors.

Our own losses were as bad as predicted. Garzón had lost several hundred men in terrible sandstorms while crossing the desert. Another forty percent of our men died in the final assault on Hotoke no Za. Twenty-five hundred were left. Not enough to hold the planet if the Japanese revolted.

Yet our men would never think of leaving this planet. I saw Abriara one morning outside the hospital: she was sitting on the ground, holding a handful of dirt from a garden, just gazing at it. I watched her for several minutes, and I knew she could never leave. One way or another, she would die on Baker.

Garzón struck a deal with the Colombians, offered them a share of the planet; very few were willing to lose the opportunity to become wealthy landowners. We began offloading them from their ship almost immediately—a task that would take well over a week.

And at night I still dreamed of Tamara struggling for her freedom. I still dreamed of the child Tatiana, a girl whose name I remembered and nothing else. And I wondered what had ever happened to my father, why I could remember precisely nothing about him, and I worried. I performed a brain scan upon myself to see if I had any dark holes where cells had died, and I could find nothing clinically wrong. I'd expected to find nothing. Memories do not each reside in one part of the brain as if sitting on the head of a pin. They are scattered and repeated all throughout the brain. Even minor brain damage should not have robbed me so totally of a memory. So I threw myself into my work all the harder, hoping that as I healed others I'd heal myself, and in moments of solitude I sat in a corner and chewed the skin from my knuckles.

I was working in the afternoon when Abriara decided to try to take a short walk. She had many deep bruises and was badly swollen, and though she wanted to help in the hospital, it appeared the work was too much for her. I put her arm over my shoulder, and helped her walk.

She breathed heavily, and her breath stirred my hair. The scent of her, the touch of her, were exhilarating.

She abruptly turned to me and said, "You look better now. I'm glad you're doing better."

"What do you mean?"

"Just better. You look better." Abriara considered for a long moment. "You once told me I'd shown you your dark face. You said you'd learned of your capacity for viciousness, and this disturbed you very much. I spoke with Perfecto about it often while you were asleep. Perfecto was afraid the vision would destroy you.

"Yet he said, 'It is too early to tell. If he is not destroyed, he will destroy his own capacity for viciousness, for now that he has unmasked the beast, he must slay it or be devoured.' He often wondered if you'd win this battle. When you fought Lucío, I thought you'd been destroyed. But now I look at you and see that you have won.

"Everything worked out all right. You were not destroyed because you remained true to your compassion."

I considered her words. I'd felt totally alone in my struggle. I'd felt that Abriara and Perfecto had been speaking to me of my problems only to gain my confidence. Yet others had been helping secretly all along. Abriara with her wise thoughts, Perfecto with his selflessness. Yet I felt Abriara was praising me unjustly. If I'd won a victory, where was my feeling of triumph? I didn't feel triumph. I looked at my past and all I felt was sorrow and emptiness. At night my nightmares still condemned me. "Nothing has worked out all right," I said. "For a time, I felt as if I lost myself. Now, I feel I've found myself again. I killed people, and the fact that I changed my mind and remained true to my compassion does not undo my wrongs. And sometimes I wonder if I didn't wait to remain true to compassion until it was convenient, until that very last moment when I was no longer in danger. Nothing has worked out all right." And I realized it didn't really matter to me anymore whether things worked out well or not—all that really mattered was that I remain true to that compassion.

An hour later a man wearing the battle armor of a mercenary came to the hospital, pushing his way through the crowded room. He saw me and raised a rifle to fire.

And in that moment I achieved Instantaneity and dodged to the right. The shot fired into the wall beside me.

I watched the barrel of the rifle, and it did not move toward me. The man seemed unbearably slow, like a sick and feeble man; I felt I could have dodged his shots all day. I had never fought while in this mental state before, and I marveled at the difference. An orderly who'd been standing around for the past two days came to life, jumped over a bed, and kicked the mercenary in the head. He crumpled to the floor. Several people pulled off the mercenary's helmet and revealed a dark-skinned man of obvious Arab ancestry. Another Alliance assassin. An orderly jacked in a call to Garzón, then they hauled the assassin away. I was surprised and saddened by the event.

Garzón's personal aide came into the hospital moments later and held a whispered conversation with Abriara. She frowned at him, then he looked at me and left. She appeared very disturbed, and for the next hour I watched her but didn't question her. Finally, she waved me over and said, "Angelo, let's go for a walk— outside," and she put her arm around me and slid off her bed.

She didn't speak as she guided me out the door. The sun was unbearably bright and the wind was warm and humid. The smell of ashes was everywhere and tiny white ashes were whipped along the street by the breeze. She guided me to a large beige dome, and outside the dome on a table lay a set of battle armor and a flechette rifle. Abriara nodded toward the armor and said, "Put it on," and I did. There was no helmet.

When I'd dressed she looked in my eyes and said, "Garzón's inside. He has a job for you. He says it's dangerous." She put her arms around me and embraced me.

I remembered Garzón's hint that I should take a job as an assassin. I didn't relish the idea of speaking with him. I picked up the flechette and walked into the dome, down a wide hallway of paneled wood. Garzón's aide was sitting outside a door.

"Garzón will see you inside," the aide said, nodding toward the door.

I opened the door and saw a room full of people, technicians working with holographic imaging equipment, a trio of cameras aimed at the door. I could not imagine what was going on. I thought they were making a movie of me entering the room. I swung the door wide, a little embarrassed to be on camera, stepped in, and saw a man standing ten paces away wearing the armor of a mercenary.

He raised a bolt pistol to chest height and I achieved Instantaneity. I shouted, "No!" and tried to dodge, thinking even as I rolled to the left that no one can dodge a bolt pistol.

Nothing happened. No blue ball of electricity shot across the room. A dozen people were seated behind the mercenary, including Tamara and Garzón. Tamara was hunched at a desk, a cranial jack rammed into the back of her skull. She said, "Santos, play back the tape." On the table before her, a tiny image of me staggered back in surprise, shouted, "No!"

"I'd say the reaction shot looks very nice, very convincing, wouldn't you?" Garzón asked her.

"Yes," Tamara agreed.

Garzón turned to me. "It seems we have a problem. Captain Farouki is dismantling the Allied Marine base, preparing to return to Earth, and he is loath to leave unfinished business." Garzón waved his hand: in the corner of the room, nearly obscured by machinery, the

Arab assassin slept in a chair. He wore a metal band around his head, like a thin crown of platinum, and the band was connected to a computer jack. He was obviously drugged. "And for once, *I* caught the assassin. The Idealist Socialist contingent in the Alliance blames you for their great failure in South America, and they do know how to hold a grudge. We thought it best here in Intelligence to simulate your death, throw them off your trail. *Tamara* asked that you be brought in to see how she accomplishes this, and we thought it might add to the realism if for only a moment you believed you were going to die. You'll have to assume a new identity for a while, you understand? At least until the Allied Marines leave." He turned to Tamara and nodded, indicating that she should speak.

Tamara didn't turn her wheelchair to look at me or acknowledge my presence. She simply said, "Give us a neural map on the assassin."

An image came on the holo in front of Tamara. It was a ghostly rendition of a human brain, and within it hundreds of pinpoints of red light curved like glowing worms through his parietal lobes, flashing across his cerebrum and dipping down into the limbic system, each light glowing, dying. He was a man who was concentrating on a plan. Garzón came over and brought me near the holograph so I could watch. "You're familiar with neural mapping," Garzón said. "We monitor the electromagnetic fluctuations in the brain and map the firing of individual synapses. We've played around a little for the last hour. We've got him on a dream monitor and through association we've been able to elicit his memories of his capture—sights, sounds, smells, thoughts, emotions. Here, let's put it on the holograph." He flipped a switch, and the memory played through. The assassin himself was a blank space, a vacuum in an otherwise inhabited world. He was creeping toward the hospital past mercenaries in green bug suits. He made no move to attack them. He walked into the hospital and saw me, fired his rifle, heard a noise, and turned to see a blurred foot landing in his face.

Garzón said, "The map you see here shows the

assassin's memory of his capture. Tamara will stimulate the memory to keep it repeating. Now, watch." Garzón nodded and a technician stepped forward with a syringe. He injected a small amount of opaque yellow fluid into the assassin's carotid artery. Over a period of two minutes all but a few red dots on the holo disappeared. The memory was gone.

"You no doubt know of omega-puromycin and a few other drugs used for mind wipes. Most are effective only for helping a person forget a recent memory, one registered within the past half hour, because they simply inhibit electrochemical activity in the brain. Yet the military has often found them advantageous in spite of their shortcomings. But some drugs can affect long-term memories—those that are already chemically stored—by dislodging neuronal pathways between axons and dendrites in the cerebral cortex, thus turning a man's mind into a tabula rasa, a clean slate. They too have been used from time to time. Yet their effects are too obvious, they are such a clumsy tool.

"But this drug is new. It's a selective drug for erasing long-term memory—and therein lies its power. I don't dare tell you its name, lest you as a pharmacologist go home and figure out how to produce a batch. But we can take any man, any mind, and wipe what we desire from it. And when we're done, Tamara can insert a new memory. We can make him remember, make him believe, whatever we desire. We can program the human mind."

The little holograph in front of the assassin went clean, and Tamara began inserting memories, simple dreams like one would watch for entertainment. But Tamara was a professional, an artist. Her worlds appeared perfect down to the smallest detail. One would remember the dreams she gave as truth. She began with the attack on me, showing me in a hospital room, alone, and a blue lightning ball shot from the belt pistol as I shouted and raised my palm to ward the blow. The assassin then approached my corpse and inserted a needle, taking a tissue sample, and withdrew from the room. As he did so, an aide came and took a tissue sample from my arm—obviously so that he could plant it on the assassin and thus create the physical evidence of my demise.

I suddenly felt warm and very uncomfortable. The technicians began to silently withdraw, pulled the assassin from the room on a stretcher, and I knew Garzón was not showing me this merely to intrigue me. He said, "And when he awakens, the patient of this operation will only be in a slight shock—disoriented, momentarily confused. But he will never know what happened." Garzón was watching me, and his eyes glittered with anticipation. There was an expression on his face that seemed incongruous—pity, sadness.

And suddenly in my mind I was back in my bedroom in Panamá, jacking out of the dream monitor, stumbling around the room, unable to recall the names of common household objects. A blank spot where recollections of my father should have been. I remembered my compadres speaking of the great philosopher general Quintanilla as if he were some hero and I were some fool who knew nothing of history. And I knew that something was wrong with me, terribly wrong. I'd left more than my compassion behind when I left my home in Panamá. *All I want is away.* "You fucking whore!" I shouted at Tamara, "What did you do to me? I never wanted to leave Panamá! Not once in my life had I thought of leaving Panamá! You put your wishes in my head! What did you do to me? What did you take from me?"

I glanced to my side; there was a table with a set of headphones and other equipment on it. I ripped off the headphones and threw them at Tamara, aiming for the back of her head, but my arm twisted at the last instant and the shot went wide. The very thought that I'd considered hitting her filled me with guilt, a terrifying sense of guilt. I reached for my machete and drew it out, took a step toward her, intending to stab her, and knew I couldn't kill her, knew that in a thousand years I couldn't bear the thought of harming her no matter how angry I became, no matter how justified the act. I threw the machete on the ground in rage. I began trembling, and my breathing came ragged. My teeth chattered, as they always do when I'm about to kill.

"I think Tamara wishes to be alone with you now," Garzón said softly, "to speak with you privately." He studied me a moment, keeping between me and Tamara, guarding her.

Tamara's wheelchair spun, and Tamara faced me. Her face was slack, empty. Her microspeaker clattered, "Angelo won't hurt a woman. He never could hurt a woman." Her voice issuing from the microspeaker was calculated to sound challenging, cold, "Could you?"

I suddenly saw that her words were true. She knew me better than I knew myself. I'd quit fighting in the battle to take Hotoke no Za not because I'd shot a person, but because I'd shot a woman. A generic woman. To kill men in battle, even innocent men, hadn't bothered me. And I'd been such a fool. I'd been so self-congratulatory when I pretended to myself that I'd regained my compassion.

There was no apology in her eyes. "His mother told him never to hit a girl." Her tone carried a smirk in it.

"That's right! That's right!" I shouted, remembering all the times my mother had said it, remembering how I'd found those very words on my tongue as I slashed Lucío's face. "You did that to me?" I cursed and wanted to draw near to strike, but found myself pacing back and forth like an angry dog in a cage, just out of reach.

Garzón watched me and Tamara, confused, and I knew what confused him: Tamara's challenging tone, her boastfulness. It wasn't like her at all. He said to Tamara, "Very impressive. Very impressive conditioning." He nodded to me and said, "Don't hurt her. She changed the deep structures of your mind, erased patterns of thought built up over a lifetime. But she can fix that. She can give you most of the memories back. She's been trying to recall what she took from you for the past two years. I'll leave you now." And he walked from the room, leaving it empty but for me and Tamara.

I shrugged and stood, furious and unable to act. I waited long for her to speak.

Tamara regarded me distantly and I couldn't understand the meaning of that empty gaze. "I did my best work on you," she said. "I never got to make many changes in others—minor reprogramming for intelligence work. But I wasn't at my best that afternoon and never got to complete the work I was doing on you. I left some blank spaces in your memory, and that should have warned you something was wrong. But you never caught on, did you?"

"I knew," I said. She sounded so sure of herself. "I found some blank spaces. I can't remember anything about my father except him weeping after my mother died."

"Fake. I faked that dead-mother thing." Tamara watched me. "Still, you ran according to my program."

"What do you mean?"

Tamara watched me distantly. "You figure it out!" Her eyes focused on the tray where a package of syringes sat next to the vial of yellow liquid. "Give yourself point two milliliters of that. I have some cutting to do. I've got to delete that radical program before I insert the new memories."

"You don't need to cut out any more," I said, suddenly wary. "What do you mean by radical program?"

Tamara said, "It's a term. A program is a set of memories we add to get you to act or behave differently than you otherwise would. For example, I'll program our assassin to tell his superiors he killed you when he'd otherwise have to report his failure. We call that a program. A radical program goes one step farther: we design a program that leads to a specific compulsive behavior—one learns to think in certain patterns, to behave in certain ways based on past assumptions. A child who learns to lie his way out of trouble quickly develops a tendency to lie. Any time he's faced with a dangerous situation he immediately tries to lie his way out of it. Over years this response can become so ingrained it becomes the equivalent of a radical program." She stared at me. "I placed such a program in you."

I felt terribly defensive. "What kind?"

She looked toward the holograph in the corner. A picture of a brain registered there and red worms of fire wriggled through it. "I call it a parietal-hypothalamic loop. When you view any woman being harmed, you immediately associate it to the torture of your mother and similar incidents I programmed into your memory. The strong sense of horror caused by that memory triggers you to recall the plans for vengeance you never carried out, and you immediately desire the peace of mind you believe vengeance will bring. You react with compulsive violence, regardless of the cost to yourself. I placed this pattern down hundreds of times across hundreds of thousands of neuronal pathways. You can't react in a manner contrary to your program."

I knew she spoke the truth. I'd responded with violence to Abriara's rape. And I'd seen Jafari's attempt to capture Tamara as a form of rape, a man abusing a woman. And so I reacted on the basis of her programming like a puppet dancing on the strings of its master. But I could see no need for her to remove the program, to risk letting her steal more from my mind. "Why should I let you into my mind?"

"Do you want to fly into a rage every time you hear about a woman getting beaten?" Tamara asked. "Look what it's already cost you. Inject yourself. Jack in," she said. Her eyes glanced to the corner, to a dream monitor on a table.

The whole situation was so bewildering I couldn't think straight. I didn't trust her, yet she seemed to be doing this for my own good. I walked to the table, filled a syringe, and injected it, plugged the computer jack into the socket at the base of my skull.

And found myself in a cold desert where wind swept over barren sands, and seagulls whirled overhead like confetti. The sky was gray. The scene made me nervous. Tamara appeared before me and she watched me a moment: I remembered General Quintanilla's attempt to overthrow Guatemala, my mother's blood spattered in droplets behind the china cabinet, my own rage, the rape of my sister Eva and the despair I'd felt at that time. And suddenly it was as if all these things had happened only in dreams, vivid dreams that I recalled clearly, but dreams nonetheless. I'd never haunted the alleys at night with a gun in my pocket, searching for Quintanilla's solders. I'd never felt that keen rage and despair. And dozens of other memories came to mind and dissipated in intensity in just the same way—a time in my youth when I'd fought a man in a bar for laughing as he told of how he'd beaten a girlfriend; an incident where I'd slapped a young boy in the feria for hitting his sister.

A great pain filled my head, and I could hear a noise like strands of rubber snapping, and I heard the sound of a great wind and fell unconscious.

I roused slowly and stared around, unsure where I was. A woman was sitting on a desert floor, staring up at seagulls. I walked over to her and just gazed at her silently. She paid no attention to me, and I wandered in circles till her name flashed in my mind, *Tamara*. I ambled back, recalling where I was.

She looked up at me and said, "Ready?"

"Yes," I said, not sure what I was confessing readiness for.

And a hundred memories came rushing into me. I lived through them in dreamtime where a few seconds felt like hours. Moments from fifty years of life spread out before me, and I walked through them as if living for days. Most were shadowy things—a smell, a touch, voices whispering in a darkened room. The mind doesn't really store everything as some claim; rather, our mind tricks us when we push it too hard, filling in details from the imagination. Rare were the memories that burst upon me in full clarity so that I understood all the implications. And the memories didn't come in single episodes, engraved in crisp detail. Rather, they were much in form like neurons within the brain—a cell reaching out, touching a cell, which reaches out to touch ten other cells. Each memory recalled ten other similar bits of memory, till the whole were woven inextricably together to form a story of a person or thing that had been important to my life.

I remembered my mother in the years after I went to Mexico to study morphogenic pharmacology. I knew now my mother hadn't been raped and murdered. She'd lived pleasantly with my father in a suburb for many years, and I recalled snatches of conversations we'd held over the phones, a bright recollection of nostalgic joy I'd felt once while visiting her for Christmas. I remembered riding north on a maglev through a jungle and seeing some young men by the tracks wrestling to pull an enormous anaconda out to its full length. The smell of cigar smoke was strong. I wondered as I lived the memory why this Christmas had been important, and I recalled that my mother had been Catholic most of her life, but when she was sixty-eight she'd suddenly converted to Baptist. She'd insisted on being rebaptized by immersion, and had sent money so I could take the maglev up to Guatemala for the ceremony. My sister Eva had snubbed her on the occasion and my mother was deeply hurt. I remember being on my mother's back terrace on a sunny day and seeing a stack of comic books by her hammock: the comics were all Christian comics about bad people going good, gangster kids in the ghettos finding Jesus—*Pablo Little Frog Meets Christ, The Stiletto and the Bible.* I remember my father sitting with me, drinking coffee for breakfast, and him laughing about my mother's conversion. "She lies in her hammock all day and reads those comics," my father had said, thinking it a good joke. "Noooo—" I countered. "Sure!" my father said, waving his hand, "she even sleeps with them out in that hammock all night, instead of sleeping with me!" And I worried for her health if she slept out at night, and remembered thinking that instead of growing old, my mother was growing strange. She began to phone me regularly, and at every call she'd tell me of some evangelist who would be speaking in Colón in the near future, urging me to go see them. Several times she broke down and cried as she told me of how she feared for my spiritual welfare. My mother died suddenly from an aneurysm two years later, and my father blamed the sudden death on her habit of sleeping out-of-doors.

And even though my wife and I had been separated for seven years, we went to my mother's funeral together, and thus the memory of my mother recalled my time with Elena. The Elena in the dreams looked nothing like the Elena of my memory. She had no facial resemblance to Tamara that I could see, and I realized Tamara had planted that memory so that I'd feel bound to her. Elena was plump and short with light brown hair, and she wasn't too bright. When I married her she seemed to have a strength of character, a drive about her, that made me love her. She would talk about her sex life as openly as she would offer her opinion on a local politician, and I confused this openness with basic honesty. I'd met her in college. Like me, she'd spent part of her youth in a village in Guatemala, and she lacked the social sense of one raised in the city. Our ineptitude at handling social affairs made us cling to one another. We married soon out of college, and she tried to drive me toward earning a fortune. She got pregnant on our honeymoon and, when we got home, she announced that I should go to Miami and set up a practice and earn lots of money selling rejuvenations for the *niña* (she was convinced the child would be a girl from the moment she learned she was pregnant). My wife had often seen holos chronicling the wealth and decadence of families in Miami, and in each show the wealthy seemed to have a morphogenic pharmacologist on hand, someone to make sure their youth never faded. I found more decadence than wealth in Miami. Elena gave birth to a son while I was in Miami, and when I returned to Guatemala I saw my son Victoriano for the first time. The joy and sense of mystery that washed over me upon seeing Victoriano that first time washed over me as I recalled the event. In that moment, it was as if my son had been born to me.

Elena clung to me for seven years, and I soon decided on a lark to set up practice in Panamá, but always she nagged about our dilapidated little home, the roaches under the sink, my general lack of ambition. I came home early from work in the feria one day and began shaping the fern beds behind the house, digging at the roots of the ferns so they wouldn't grow into the lawn. I sat in a chair in the shade and was drinking a beer when a young Rodrigo sporting a beer belly came running around the back of the house, shouting, "I think Elena is leaving you! She has Victoriano and she's taking everything!" I ran to the front of the house and found Elena toting all her things to the curb. She shrieked at me, an actual shriek, which seemed strange coming from a woman who so seldom showed strong emotion, and she cursed me for my laziness, for lying in the backyard to drink a beer while the "family rots from poverty!" She left me that day, and I remembered letters, simple statements of credits due to doctors and schools for services rendered to Victoriano. I sent letters and cards to Victoriano on special occasions but never heard from him. A lady who lived down the street came over one night with a bottle of wine and tried to seduce me. She claimed Elena had left me because she'd found a sex partner with some rather peculiar tastes, and this woman told me she much preferred my tame brand of straight sex. Some things she related she could have only known if she'd actually spoken to Elena about our private lives, and I became convinced Elena really had cheated on me.

And then I went to my mother's funeral, and not only Elena came, but she brought Victoriano. Victoriano was twelve at the time—a handsome young man with shoulders that were growing broad. His muscular build was much like his mother's, and he wore a white shirt open at the front to advertise his manly features. I thought he was charmingly funny, and after my mother's funeral we went on a walk and stopped at a vendor's for some *bole*. We spoke for a long time, and it was obvious he was in awe of me, that he thought it was a great thing to have a father who sold morphogens. I thought his whole attitude was very funny, but I liked him, and after the funeral he began to answer my letters. And when he was twenty-three he suddenly married a fine girl, a Spanish girl far above his station, moved to Gatún to a house just three blocks from me, and got a job repairing equipment on public transit systems.

The knowledge that I'd had a son who lived just down the street from me filled me with awe. I wondered where he was now, what he'd thought of the news reports that proclaimed his father to be a desperado. Victoriano had me over for dinner every Sunday, and we had many good times. And after three years his wife gave birth to a daughter named Tatiana, and I loved her as if she were my own child. Elena had robbed me of the enjoyment of seeing Victoriano grow up, so I took all the joy I could in helping to raise Tatiana. And the memories Tamara gave me of the girl were exact. The young child with the fine chiseled features and dark shining hair was the same child I still held in my fragments of memory, and I knew my memory was true. Tatiana was a child of quick intellect, as first children often are, and from the time she was three weeks old I held great hopes that she'd develop a fine mind. She was a very loving child, and her embraces when I left her home were always fierce and passionate and prolonged. Her hair always smelled clean, and often I envied the man who would someday marry such an intelligent, passionate woman with clean hair. It seemed to me to be the best combination of attributes a woman could attain.

Often Flaco would come and visit me at my booth in the feria. He was a friend of Victoriano as much as of me and he'd always bring a small gift of candy or a flower for Tatiana. Flaco always worried for her future and would speak about the encroachments of the socialists on our borders and murmur about bad things to come. And I remembered a neighborhood cat, a street cat with no name, a gray female that lived off canaries and garbage. The cat had given birth to kittens just a few weeks before I fled Earth, and Flaco and Tatiana and I had gone to great lengths to capture a kitten from a local drainage pipe. And I remembered the snatch of the dream, of Tatiana asking me to keep the kitten for a few days while we schemed on how to get her parents to let her keep it, and I understood why that kitten had bothered me so, why I had such a strong emotional attachment to it in my dreams. And I remembered coming home that day I first brought Tamara to my house; and as Flaco and I sat on the porch and drank beer waiting for the spider monkey to walk up our street, Flaco had spoken of the socialistas and their encroachments and wept bitterly at our prospects for the future.

And I understood what Tamara had done. She'd given

me memories of pain and hate to make me violent, to make me kill Arish. Then she'd cut me off from all my memories of my family, of my loved ones and close friends, because she wanted someone to take her off-planet. She couldn't afford to leave me with any emotional ties, any moral obligations that would lead me to stay. And so she'd severed all the memories of my family, and nearly all the memories of my friendship with Flaco, and had left me lying on the bedroom floor. I'd wondered how a bowl of milk had appeared on the back porch for the kitten, and I remembered placing it there myself. But Tamara couldn't even leave me that, couldn't even let me have an attachment to a dumb animal.

And then the memories twisted and I felt slightly uneasy. The memories that came next were not associated at all with people I felt close to, rather they were memories of small things I'd done, of moral choices made. I recalled an old woman I helped make young, a doña Yolanda, a woman who was something of a *bruja*, a reputed witch, down in Colombia. People from many villages came and offered me small sums of money to buy her a rejuvenation. At first I'd declined, for it sounded to me as if she were robbing the poor by claiming to have mysterious powers. But by chance I learned from a compadre something of her methods: she went from village to village and cared for the sick without price. She'd been trained as a nurse, but she often used local herbs to heal because her patients were too poor to buy medications. Because of her use of herbs, the locals proclaimed her a *bruja* even though she didn't claim magical powers. If the woman had been Catholic, she'd have been sainted. The more I learned of this woman, the more impressed I became, until finally I mixed the meager offerings of the peasants with my own savings and purchased a rejuvenation. I did it for *life*. I did it because she was a woman who knew how precious and fragile human life was.

And I remembered the times I wept and prayed and struggled in an effort to help my patients. A young couple from Costa Rica once came to me with a child that

had been born without arms. The parents couldn't afford
to keep buying prosthetics to fit the child as it grew, but
the young boy was unable to grow arms because of a
seemingly noncomplex reversal in one sequence of
genes. Usually one can simply take a cell sample, repair
the damaged cell, clone the child, and get the arm buds
from a developing embryo to graft into the damaged
child's flesh. It is no great matter after that to grow the
arms. However, this child had no tolerance for the
grafted buds, and we failed twice to heal him. I finally
had to resort to preparing a virus to repair the damage to
the specific gene, then I had to keep the child in a viral
isolation chamber in my home for two months while I
made sure the infection was complete. After that it was
no great thing to generate some arms. However, while
we had the child in the house, Elena and I let his mother
live with us. Elena gave me hell for it, nagging me night
and day, accusing me of lusting after the child's mother.
She remained convinced that my deed was motivated by
sexual attraction for the child's mother. I couldn't deter
her from thinking this, and since I felt that regaining the
child's health was more important than the anguish I
received from Elena's wagging tongue, I ignored my
wife. This incident seemed pivotal in leading to my
eventual divorce.

And the list of these acts of moral choices went on. I'd
done similar things many times, and the Angelo Osic
that Tamara showed me was not the man I felt myself to
be. He seemed too kind, too generous, too giving. I
could understand why Tamara had threatened me with
guilt, why she'd told me that "if you ball me over, I die."
The Angelo she showed me couldn't have resisted such
a threat. But I was not that man anymore.

And I remembered last of all my very first moral
choice of import—the incident that seemed to guide my
later career. It was the incident in my childhood, in
Guatemala, when I witnessed the slaying of the Batistas
Sangrientos, the vicious family that murdered people for
their organ parts. One of the boys that was executed was
my age, a young man named Salomón Batista. He was a
great jokester with a somewhat crude mind, yet among

the children he'd always been a leader. He was always
leading us into trouble with the old people in town.
Salomón was a young man with tremendous energy and
physical strength, and always he was the best among us
in sports and wrestling. I'd been terrified when the
captain made the young children form a line, terrified
when I watched Salomón plead for mercy and claw at his
father and beg to be killed with his father. I watched
Salomón pee his pants in terror, watched as the captain
told his men to lower their guns, to aim and fire. And
when the shooting was done, and the Batista family was
lying dead on the ground, I walked over to Salomón and
looked in his eyes. His face was bloody, as if someone
had just smeared it with a bloody rag, and it was
splotched with blood that had spattered from his brothers. And I looked into Salomón's eyes and saw them
staring out, already glassy. His hands were still twitching. He hadn't been dead for three minutes, yet his eyes
were as glassy as if he'd been dead for hours. The smell
of blood was strong in the air. I looked at him and
realized that as I'd watched a miracle had occurred: that
vigorous young man had been unmade. The spirit had
left his body while I watched. It seemed a miracle that
he had died. Yet I realized it was a greater miracle that
he had lived at all. I vowed at that moment, at the age of
twelve, that I'd spend my life fighting death.

The images quit coming. The smell of blood stayed
with me. Tamara watched me, sitting cross-legged in the
dust of the plain. The seagulls wheeled overhead. "Is the
tape done so soon?" she said.

Anger settled over me, hot and thick. I felt violated at
the deepest core of my being. I wanted to see my family,
to know the end of their stories, to see how their lives
turned out. She'd not shown me much. She'd said she
had a forty-percent memory loss, yet she'd not given me
back sixty percent of my life. She'd given just enough to
let me know how much I'd lost. I ached for the loss.
"What of my father, and my sister?" I asked. "You gave
me no memories of them. Only peripheral memories."

Tamara snorted. "Tough luck, old man. My brains were fried. I don't have any idea what I took. It didn't seem important."

I couldn't believe her reaction, couldn't conceive such callousness from her. I'd once observed that we always dehumanize those we are about to kill. I wondered if somehow in her mind she'd come to hate me, had learned to see me as less than human so she could continue hurting me. And I was filled with a sense of loss and dread. I wanted to return to Earth, to find my family. The ships were being prepared for the return trip, but they'd be filled with Japanese men angry for what we'd done. I'd never make it home alive on one of those ships. And even if I did, could I find my family? My father would no longer be alive. Victoriano would be an old man. Even Tatiana would be nearly sixty. If she remembered me at all she'd have no emotional attachment to me. And Panamá wouldn't be the same.

I could never go back. Never. And Tamara didn't even care. She'd used me like a rag and then thrown me away. "You whore!" I shouted. "You whore!" My teeth chattered and the world turned red. I saw her as if through a fog. I jacked out.

I got up from my chair and rushed toward her. I was free! I was free! She'd freed me from the compulsion that kept me from attacking. Never had I felt such hatred. Never had I felt such rage. I could kill her! I could kill her now!

And yet, I'd dedicated my life to fighting death. I stood and watched her. Struggled with my ache to kill her. Then I struck her on the face. Once. Twice. Three times. Knocking her back so her wheelchair spun around. Drops of blood spattered from her nose. Yet I wanted to kill her. Wanted to do more than just kill her. A Quest. I took her by the throat; it was soft and warm and slender in my hands. I could snap her neck, I realized, and I very slowly and purposefully squeezed.

It takes a long time to strangle a person.

Her head lolled up at me and her face turned red. She watched. I felt very cold, distant. A single tear welled up in the corner of one eye.

And I remembered another Tamara, the Tamara who had let me taste her undying compassion in the simulator, saying, "Listen, listen. Become fluent in the gentle language of the heart." And I recalled the look of her eyes in the simulator, the way she watched me as if I were some rag doll torn apart, full of pity and condescension. She knew I was destroyed because she was the one who'd destroyed me. She wanted to make me live again because she'd stolen life from me. She'd wept because she knew how she was destroying me aboard ship. And I saw that pain in her eyes again. Even now she was manipulating me, and she was weeping because she was destroying me again.

She *wanted* me to be her killer. And she knew what it would cost me.

I gasped and jerked away. She'd wanted to die in Panamá. She'd wanted to die rather than be placed in a brain bag, and she was unable to kill herself. She'd freed me because she wanted to die.

"Finish it!" Tamara spat from her microspeaker even as her lungs gasped for breath. "You hate me! How could you feel anything but contempt for me?"

She was right. I no longer felt attracted to her at all. I felt as if I were poised on the head of a pin. The old Angelo couldn't have killed her. But I couldn't escape the changes I'd gone through since meeting Tamara. I felt capable of killing her. I wasn't sure I'd suffer remorse. Yet, I was free to choose. I stepped away, resolved to throw down my weapons forever. "No," I said. "You know of Garzón's plans for you. You know of the prison he will make for you—"

"Finish it—now!" Tamara shouted.

"—and you know that we have no escape from Baker. So you want me to execute you. A mercy killing—"

"Kill me before it's too late! Garzón will make me hurt others—an endless parade of them!"

"But I am dedicated to life!" I shouted even though it felt untrue. "You will live!"

Tamara watched me and tears streamed down her cheeks. Then she began to laugh, a laugh of pain and self-derision. "You're with him. With Garzón, aren't

you? When we were in Panamá I needed someone to
save me. Someone big and strong. And you were the
only chunk of meat available. When you jacked in that
last time I really thought you were Arish trying to
manipulate me. So I attacked, knocked you out. Then I
got up and found you on the floor, found Arish alive." I
nodded, recalling how it had been. "I was sick. So sick
and weary. I wanted to escape. I wanted Arish dead. You
wouldn't have taken me away. You wouldn't have killed
for me." She choked back a sob. "I was sick. Feverish at
the time . . . so crazy. I gave you a deep program. I
programmed you to take me to the Garden of Eden. And
look where you brought me!" A noise came from her
microspeaker that could have only been a snort of
derision.

I looked at her in her wheelchair, imprisoned in a
wasted body, unable to move, totally destroyed. And in
a few days, I realized, Garzón would imprison her in a
cymech, bring about her greatest fear. All her scheming
had brought her to nothing. She said. "So. You don't
need to kill me. You have your vengeance."

All my good intentions had brought her to nothing. It
was true—she was living her worst nightmare. "I have
my vengeance." I nodded. "You are a sick, miserable
little woman. From the time I met you, you've always
believed that death was the answer to all life's problems.
How pitiful! How narrow-minded!"

"You don't know what Garzón can do to me! You don't
know what cyborging will do to me!" Tamara cried.

"I've known Body Purists before. Your fears are
unjustified. You will only be put in a cage where you can
harm no one," I said, and I turned to go.

"You're wrong!" Tamara said. "I didn't want to hurt
you. I was terrified and sick and I didn't know what else
to do. But I swear I never wanted to hurt you!"

I remembered our meeting in the simulator, when she
showed me what it felt like to live. She'd tried to atone,
I realized. I stopped.

She continued, "You've never sifted through another
person's memories. You've never been intimate with
their thoughts. You live under the delusion that everyone thinks like you. But I've been into many minds,

have witnessed thought patterns that would horrify you. Twice I've been within the minds of military cyborgs. The military surgeons cut out parts of the hypothalamus, chemically block certain hormonal secretions, cut them off from the world of emotion. And because they cannot feel, cannot empathize, they lose all semblance of a conscience."

I turned to her. I'd been living too close to sociopathy for too long not to be disturbed by what she told me. I suddenly understood why she was so horrified by the thought of imprisonment in a cymech, why she'd run so desperately from Jafari, why she'd made paranoid accusations about me being a cyborg.

"It's true," Tamara said. "The military prefers them that way. It makes it so much easier for them to get on with their jobs. When you delivered me to Garzón he promised me freedom. He promised to let me go if I'd help him for just a while. But you've seen the way he clings to me. He'll never let me go. And he's constantly complaining about my annoying tatters of morality. I've turned him down on too many jobs. If he puts me in a cymech, he'll make me a military model. And eventually I'll learn not to care. I'll see human minds and emotions only as something to manipulate. I'll become infinitely more evil and powerful than you believe me to be now."

I considered her words. Motoki's military training had struck at my own fragile morality. Two weeks of it and I'd felt as if I'd forever lost the ability to feel compassion. What would happen if that capacity were surgically removed? How long would Tamara or anyone last?

"Then," I said, "I must find a way to free you if I can."

"And if you can't," Tamara said, "I would rather die."

"I understand," I said, knowing that I would have to be the one to kill her. "How many people know of your role in Intelligence?" Tamara gave me six names, Garzón's closest advisers. I walked to the door. And a final thought struck me. I realized that someone else had fallen under her knife: "But in payment you must give Abriara Sifuentes back her memories!"

Tamara blinked in surprise but made no other sign

that she understood me. I thought she'd deny removing anything from Abriara. She asked, "Why?"

I shouted, "Who do you think you are to steal her past?"

"I took only painful memories, memories of rape," Tamara said in defense. "I took pain! If you had a patient with cancer, you'd cut out the cancer. Those memories were eating her like a cancer. No one should suffer what she's suffered!"

"You and Garzón—you are not so different! With a little power you set yourself up to be God!"

Tamara said softly, "If I set myself up to be a god, then let me be a considerate god. Think of what you ask! You want me to give back her pain? You want that to be the price of my freedom? Then free me! Go ahead! But you'll have to watch her die inside!"

I left the room and wandered the streets of Hotoke no Za. Was Tamara right? Should Abriara be forced to relive the memories that had killed her inside? I did not know. It would be a cruel thing, too cruel to imagine.

The sky was hazy, reddened by clouds of dust. I needed a plan to free Tamara and had to be certain it would work. The most direct solution would be to kill Garzón and the technicians who knew of Tamara's abilities. There was so much blood on my hands. And I was dedicated to life. It took hours for me to think of it, yet Garzón's own fear of Tamara suggested a more difficult—yet morally correct—approach. I had seen his fear of what Tamara could do, and I thought, *Why not immobilize Garzón and his advisors and let Tamara carve their memories of her from their skulls?* I would not have to kill; no one would be really hurt.

I checked a clock, and the quickness with which Tamara had operated on me suggested that such an operation would take her only a few hours. Perhaps less. And once she'd eluded them, Tamara would be free to live on Baker like anyone else.

I went back to the hospital and phoned the *Chaeron*, checked Tamara's medical records. As I'd thought, they'd somehow mysteriously appeared shortly before our arrival on Baker. Her verified genotype was listed in the records, an index to her cell structure. I went to the hospital's genetic engineering section and fed the records into a gene synthesizer and began creating a clone. I'd need to seed her brain with cells from a cloned embryonic cerebral cortex if I was ever going to get her to walk, and I'd need some neural growth stimulator. Repairing her neural system would take time, perhaps a few weeks.

I called up the medical records of those who knew of Tamara's position in Intelligence and familiarized myself with their faces. I made up a batch of a mild neurotoxin that paralyzed anyone who received it into his bloodstream. There were six of them, and I knew I'd need help. I began considering my resources. I needed someone who wouldn't ask questions. I needed someone powerful. I knew of four chimeras who'd bonded to me. Miguel was still alive; he'd come into the hospital with a leg wound and spent a day just watching me from the bed. I wasn't so sure about the others. Still at nights I'd seen men around the campfires on the hill. And I knew how to induce bonding among the chimeras. The thought revolted me, but I knew where to obtain help.

I spent the afternoon in the gene lab with a cell specimen from Perfecto, split the chromosomes, and created a dozen fertilized cells. I put them in a broth and let them begin replicating.

That night, I went up on the hill to the bonfires. A thousand mercenaries had gathered, as they seemed to gather every night, and they sat around the campfire and spoke of their battles and told jokes and sang songs. I met Mavro, sat beside him a bit. He was depressed and sad. He said, "I never made it to captain, and now the war is over. What will I do?" I had no answer for him.

Garzón put in his appearance, dragging Tamara along in her wheelchair. He too knew the value of sitting in the dark, the light playing upon his silver hair while he waited for a chimera to bond. He appeared very calm, very much at ease. I tried not to stare.

Abriara came up to the bonfire, brought some good beer she'd found and sat beside me, and she didn't say

much. I listened to the singing. She'd washed her hair,
and it smelled sweet.

"I didn't see you much today," she said.

"I was down in the gene lab, making clones of
Perfecto."

"All day? Are you going to build an army? How many
copies do you need?"

I laughed. "I just wanted to watch the zygotes grow,
be certain they formed properly. I think two. I think I'll
make twins."

"You know there's a whole wing of the hospital filled
with incubation chambers. It's been sealed off for eighty
years, but the equipment has been maintained."

"I know," I said.

"If you want any help raising the children, I'll be
available," she said. She was sitting very close, leaning
into my body space. I understood what that must mean
for a chimera to share something that personal. I reached
down and took her hand and she squeezed mine.

That night I met with Miguel and two of the chimeras
who'd bonded to me, and I didn't talk of my plans for
Garzón. Instead we talked about their pasts and made
friends.

I didn't feel good about what I was doing as I plotted
Tamara's escape. I was confused. I was unsure about why
I'd saved that Yabajin woman, why I'd tried to save them
all. If I'd done it because of Tamara's programming, then
my morality was indeed a sham. But I wasn't so certain
Tamara's programming had caused me to act as I did.
When I killed Arish I'd done it for Flaco. In my mind I
was avenging Flaco, not saving Tamara. And when I'd
killed Juan Carlos I'd done it only for myself. And when
I stopped trying to kill the Yabajin I believed I'd quit
because I felt kinship to her as a human, a factor outside
Tamara's programming. I'd only tried once to kill for a
woman, and that was when I tried to kill Lucío for
Abriara. And I saw that something more had affected my
basic decisions to kill: Tamara's radical programming
convinced me that to some extent we do program
ourselves. We do build up patterns of thought over a

lifetime. And I wondered if I didn't kill because I'd been practicing violence, just as she'd said. And I'd only stopped practicing violence when I realized how it was destroying me.

I vowed to exercise compassion, to create a deep program that would affect the entire way I related to others—just as a little fifty-kilogram weakling can exercise his muscles to become the strongest man in the world. I could see from Abriara's example, from the way she tried to nurture me in secret, that it didn't matter if one were not strong in that capacity by nature. It could still be trained. And I felt as if I were at the top of a hill staring down at a golden path, and upon the path, in my mind's eye, I could see the man I would someday become.

Our society in Panamá glorified the man of contradictions—men of steel and velvet. I've known men who try to be both. In my experience they always fail. And I saw that practicing violence in the simulators really had been causing me to lose my ability to feel compassion. I could feel myself dying. And I'll always believe that if I'd continued training with the samurai, I would have trained away my capacity for compassion. The way of the warrior is the way of death. I'd have become as empty as the refugiados, as Mavro, as the samurai themselves. And so if by myself I've attained any level of morality, then perhaps it is a matter of fortunate circumstance as much as of choice. I was fortunate to have been put in the cryotanks after the riot, fortunate to have friends who tried to help me become something better. Tamara believed I'd run according to her program, and to some degree it was true. But her view seemed too simple to explain everything.

I spent the day thinking upon these things and cataloging my memories of my family. I wrote them down as much as possible to make sure I'd never forget again. I checked with the ships in orbit and found that I could get passage back to Earth on the crew's quarters of the *Chaeron*, thus minimizing the risk of contact with the Japanese.

I decided to leave Baker forever.

I thought of Tatíana and Victoriano, of my sister and father and the possibility of other family members on Earth, and I was drawn to them. I could not bear the thought of staying on Baker—it was more than the evil memories of the place: it was the evil future of the place. The society my *compañeros* had formed was brutal and corrupt. We'd seized the planet because of greed and were murdering its inhabitants at every turn. I couldn't see a future for such a society. Indeed, after four days we had done nearly nothing. The city was in rubble and no one was cleaning it up. No one was rebuilding. The mercenaries strutted around and patted each other on the back and did nothing all day, then huddled around bonfires and sang and gambled and got drunk and told jokes all night.

All afternoon I thought depressing thoughts. I made my plans for Garzón. That night I went to the bonfire and drank and sang and acted like an idiot, the same as everyone else. And when Garzón left for the night, pushing Tamara along in her wheelchair, I got up and followed, hoping to learn something about his nightly habits, learn where I could waylay him. A good dozen chimeras followed him, the same way that my chimeras followed me. I saw that it would not be easy to subdue Garzón, for he was never alone. Everywhere he went, the eyes of his chimeras were upon him.

We were walking back through town toward a large home that Garzón had taken as his own, when a hovercraft came roaring over the hill from the jungles. It was obviously one of ours, since the automatic defenses let it into the city. I figured it was just one of our patrols. Four ragged mercenaries were on the hovercraft, and as they came into town one of them shouted anxiously, "Garzón!" and looked around. They were obviously frightened.

I wondered what had happened, if they had spotted a party of Yabajin in the jungle.

Garzón shouted, "Here!" and the hovercraft veered toward him and stopped just a few meters from his face. The chimeras that followed Garzón began jogging forward, eager to hear the news. A turret gunner on the hovercraft unsnapped his helmet and pulled it off: he was Japanese.

He shouted, "I am Motoki Hotayo!" and he and his men opened fire with plasma turrets and flechettes. Garzón was still pushing Tamara in the wheelchair, and the samurai fired right through her. Plasma seared through her, setting her afire like a blazing torch, and a shot from a flechette nearly took her head off.

I dropped to the ground, and around me the chimeras began unstrapping their rifles. The hovercraft engines whined, and the vehicle lifted and soared back toward the jungles and everywhere the chimeras were shouting in fury and the samurai kept firing even as they retreated, creating a rain of death. Someone managed to fire two shots at the samurai with a flechette, but the bullets bounced off the armor. Within seconds the samurai's hovercraft retreated beyond the city wall, and then it was gone.

I got up. A dozen of the chimeras that had been closest to Garzón were either dead or wounded. Someone was shouting, "They killed Garzón! It was Motoki Hotayo, the president's son!" and everywhere people were running from houses with their armor and weapons.

Several chimeras grabbed the remains of Garzón—a burnt corpse full of glowing worm holes where plasma had eaten through, shredded by metal bullets—and rushed it down to the infirmary. Others looked at him and saw that it would do no good. And those chimeras who were bonded to him, who loved him most, threw themselves on the ground and wept.

I walked over to Tamara, slowly.

There was practically nothing left of her. A charred body, without hair, wearing ashes for clothing, too horrible to describe. I stood by and waited till her body cooled, laid her on the grass.

Tamara's eyes were staring up into the night sky, as if watching the stars. The eyeballs were blackened. She had no eyelids left. People were shouting and carrying the wounded toward the infirmary, and I realized dimly that I should go down to help them. A mercenary in bedclothes ran up, carrying nothing but a rifle in his hands.

"Was she a friend of yours?" he asked. I did not answer for a long moment.

"No," I said. "She was my destroyer." He nodded, mystified, then took off his shirt and laid it over her endlessly staring eyes. He mouthed the words the refugiados always speak over their dead, "Free at last."

I ran down to the infirmary to help with the wounded.

That night I found Abriara and took her on a walk and told her how Tamara had reprogrammed us. I told her of her rape aboard the ship and what I remembered of it, and showed how it differed from her own memories. Abriara pulled my face toward her and looked in my eyes. "Is this some elaborate hoax?" She laughed nervously. "Are you trying to get rid of me? I'm not being too pushy, am I? We can take things slow if you want. I know you have not given yourself to a woman for a long time."

I was tempted to chuckle. I didn't think that her squeezing my hand had been forward. I didn't feel distressed. I felt only sad. "This is not some elaborate hoax," I said. "This is honesty. We can go back to the lab and I'll show you the equipment in her head with a sonogram, if you wish."

Her voice became very high, very threatened. "What? What are you talking about? I won't go there with you. You're lying to me! You're trying to trick me! Nothing bad happened aboard the *Chaeron*! Nothing bad happened!"

"I don't want to hurt you! I won't lie to you. To refrain from telling the ugly truth would only be a lie. Perhaps I'd never have told you of this, Abriara," I said, "because the knowledge can only hurt you. But I know that you begin to have some feelings for me—and you must understand that these feelings are based upon a false pretense. I tried to save you from Lucío—I'd have saved you if I could—but I did nothing. I am not the man you think I am. Your memories of that moment are fake—a program inserted by someone else—and much else of your past has been taken."

Abriara stared at me. In the darkness I don't know what her silver eyes could see. I could read little of her expression. "It's true that I feel something for you, Angelo," she said. "But even if your story is true, I have feelings for you because of a thousand little things you've done: the way you treated me as an equal, the way you suffered when you did wrong, the little kindnesses you committed."

I looked away from her. "You may tell yourself that now, but it will never change the truth."

She was silent for a long time, carrying on an internal argument. "Let's go," she said at last, and her tone betrayed her own fear.

When we got back to the hospital, one of Garzón's technicians was dissecting Tamara. Though I've seen many dissections, this one sickened me more than I could imagine. He'd removed the temporal and parietal regions of the skullcap and was pulling platinum wires from her head. Hundreds of tiny neurosynaptic adaptors were plugged to every center of her brain—aural, visual, tactile, emotive—they ran to a small processor just above her cranial jack.

"Pretty fancy equipment, no?" the technician said as casually as if he were carving lettuce for a salad instead of dissecting an acquaintance. "I've known professional dreamers—the kind that create settings and act for the dream networks. None of them had equipment like this. None of them!"

Abriara stood away from the operating table, horrified. I hadn't wanted her to see the truth in this ugly fashion. The look on her face pained me. Her expression betrayed the horror chimeras always feel when they've been brutally violated.

"What will you do with it?" I asked, trying to distract Abriara, to keep her mind off her problem.

"Sell it! Someone is going to want to start a dreamer's network around here sooner or later. I could make three good hookups out of this!"

Even though I was sickened by what was happening, I looked at the gray matter of Tamara's brain and part of me marveled at her mind. She had known us so intimately—had understood our thoughts and fears and desires so well. She was an unrivaled cartographer of thought. A dreamer of dreams. She'd been too talented for our puny world. I was disgusted to see her treated this way.

I took Abriara outside and she collapsed in my arms and wept, then suddenly staggered up and began running, as if to escape. I grabbed her arm and slowed her and we walked together for a while. Abriara wept for a long time, then said, "Perfecto used to question me about my past—just after the riots. He insinuated that bad things had happened to me. I did not believe him." Her chest began to heave and she breathed heavily, as if she'd vomit.

"People I'd known all my life told me I'd changed. That I'd become happy for the first time in my life!" She stopped and stared straight ahead for a time, as if viewing something I could not see in the darkness.

"I think perhaps they told the truth," I said.

"You say this woman destroyed you. But she tried to *save* me!"

"Do you not feel cheated," I asked, "that I couldn't save you from Lucío?"

"Yes, I feel cheated. Yes, I feel cheated—but not by you!" Abriara said. "All the things I remember you doing are things you'd have done if you could. At heart you are the man she imagined you to be."

And in my heart I knew that her words were true. And I saw that—as I'd hoped—my honesty had not driven Abriara away, though it caused her pain.

It rained heavily that night, and the next day Abriara came to the hospital at noon. She'd made a special lunch and she asked if I'd accompany her on a picnic. I agreed and she led me to a hovercraft. We flew south out of town, and we wore no armor. Abriara had found a dress with a bright pattern of flowers in many colors. I wore my white kimono. I was very uncomfortable, going outside the city without armor. My clothes were so thin even sunlight could pierce them. We spoke of inconsequential things and Abriara asked me to relate everything I could about my family. The concept of being a member of a family fascinated her. She took me to a long peninsula with several dunes on it forty kilometers south of the city, and we stopped at the north end of the peninsula and ate lunch.

When we finished eating, Abriara said, "Come with me over the dunes. I have a surprise to show you."

We began walking over the white dunes, taking it slow and easy. The sand was heavy and wet after the rain, and the walking was easy. The sea smelled crisp and clean, less of decay and dying than the oceans of Earth, and Abriara took my hand. I fantasized that she planned to throw me on the ground and make passionate love, and the thought saddened me.

"You're thinking painful thoughts again," Abriara said. "What are you thinking?"

"I've decided to leave Baker on the *Chaeron*," I said, "so that I can search for my family. The ship leaves in three weeks. I am thinking I will miss you."

Abriara clasped my hand fiercely. "You can't go back! There will be nothing for you on Earth! Don't you see? You don't know how much things will have changed. You have no future there. What can you be thinking?"

"I cannot see a future here," I said. "There are too many bad memories."

"We can make good memories," Abriara said, and she held my hand roughly. I remembered the night I'd had an intimation of what life would be like with a grasping Chilena who was a chimera to boot.

"It is more than the memories, more even than my family," I said. "I have always sought to serve society, but now I find that my society is not as good as I believed it to be. I do not think Baker will be a nice place to live. Once the Japanese men have been deported, our men will mate with their wives. It may not happen today, but in a few years. And when this happens, our two societies will become hopelessly mingled. Our love for murder, with their love of suicide. I do not think it will make a good mix. I do not think I can serve a society I so strongly disapprove of."

"But . . . but," Abriara gasped. "But you can change

society, make it better. In fact, it is your moral obligation! Remember San Miguel de Madrid?"

I said, "I am not familiar with the pantheon of Catholic saints."

"He lived in the twenty-first century. He was a survivor of the bombing of Madrid. After the nuclear bombs dropped, he crawled from the rubble and his hands were burned to a crisp. All around him people were giving up, people were dying because they were convinced it was the end of the world. But Saint Miguel believed it was his duty, his moral obligation, to make sure that he lived, to make sure he built a world where such a thing could never happen again. He only lived a few weeks, but his courage saved many people. He too saw an evil society, but he did not serve society, he served the future."

And the truth of her words struck home. If I followed don José Mirada's teachings I'd be serving society for the rewards it offered. All my morality would be a sham. But if I served a society that didn't yet exist, what rewards could I hope to gain? My only possible reward would be that possibly someday the society I hoped to create would spring into being. Her choice was the only right choice.

"Ah, now I see you are smiling. You like the idea?"

"Sí," I said.

"Then you will stay? We will need someone like you. We will need someone with silver hair for Perfecto's children to bond to. We will have our own home, a mansion, and you will be a great influence on people . . ." And she talked on and on, making her plans for me.

No, you are a morphogenic pharmacologist, I thought, and you can find the gene that controls the bonding in chimeras. In a week this land will be swept with a virus that will destroy that gene. And you can create a virus that will wipe out the chimera's sociopathic bent and give them a greater chance for peace. And you live on a world distant from other worlds, and you are free to create a society of your own choosing through social engineering. I do not know who I am—

the Angelo of Tamara's dreams, the Angelo who killed Arish. I do not know if I can ever become the man I desire to be. But I believed that whether the sources of evil were genetically linked to territorialism, or whether they were defects in the chemical thought processes, or whether they were perpetuated and flourished within our society because of deep programs built up as we learned to think, I had the tools to destroy them. And yet I had to wonder at the morality even of that. To use the tools of social engineering to twist the minds of others as the engineers of Baker had done—the idea repulsed me at a basic level. I wondered why, and connected it immediately to Perfecto's theories of the nature of evil: To try to twist the ideals of another is a violation of the territories of the mind. *Yet no one consulted you before they created your deformed world,* I thought. *And you cannot consult the unborn as to their desires. You must do what you feel is right.*

We came over the last sand dune and looked out over the jungle. There was a white mountain in the distance, as if it had been carved of salt, and behind it was a row of purple mountains. I realized I was looking at the white mountain I'd seen on the little holo while I was riding the shuttle up to Sol Station from Earth. I was standing in the exact spot where the photographer had been standing when he took the picture!

"Abriara, when I was leaving Earth, I saw a picture of that white mountain! I was so insane with fear and shock I was jabbering. I told Tamara I'd take her there, and I believed we were going to paradise!"

Abriara said, "All the travel posters show that mountain on their advertisements. It is the mountain Hotoke no Za takes its name from—Hotoke no Za, the Throne of Buddha. If you like it, we can go to the land office and stake a claim. You're entitled to much land, and it's still early enough that you can get whatever you want.

The sight of that mountain thrilled me. I felt that I really was standing at the gateway to paradise. And suddenly a voice inside me said, "Remember, remember: whatever good things have happened to you, the best is yet to come." My hair raised on end, and I felt an overwhelming excitement as I realized it might be true. My heart began to race and in that moment I achieved Instantaneity, that state of mind where one can live a lifetime in a moment, and I saw all my plans and all my dreams and the twisted path I would walk as I sought to become a man of compassion, to live a life of passion, and to change the world, and at the end of the path was the old Angelo, the man I could become again. Someday there would be peace. Someday I would forgive myself. Someday there would be passion.

We stood on the hilltop, and Abriara pointed down to the bottom of the dunes. A river entered the ocean there and the tide was out. There were many rocks, and on the rocks was thick blue moss, and among the moss were thousands of giant midnight blue crabs a meter across the back at the carapace. I recognized them as *manesuru onna*, mimicking women. Abriara laughed and said, "Let me speak the first word," and we ran down the sand dune toward the mimicking women, swooping upon them. They began clacking their carapaces as they picked up shreds of seaweed and held them in front of them as if to hide.

Abriara shouted, "Happy!" And a thousand mimicking women whispered, "Happy! Happy! Happy!" as they clacked and rattled and retreated into the sea.

About the Author:

Dave Wolverton is married and is the father of two beautiful daughters. He is currently employed as a technical writer for the computer industry and has worked as a prison guard, a missionary, and a business manager. He has a long-standing interest in paleontology, neurology, genetic engineering, and physics. He is seeking a degree in English, and has won several awards for his short stories. *On My Way to Paradise* is his first novel. A slightly altered version of the first two chapters of *On My Way to Paradise* won the grand prize in the L. Ron Hubbard Writers of the Future Contest for 1986, and was published in *Writers of the Future, Volume 3*.

About *On My Way to Paradise*

I began writing *On My Way to Paradise* in the spring of 1986 in response to a dream: I dreamed I was on a dusty market street and the sun was glaring; peasants in white were milling about, and a horribly emaciated woman was walking toward me, her dark eyes boring into me, and she held a bloody stump at the end of her right arm. I wanted desperately to help her, to give her something. When I woke, the dream haunted me, and I decided to write a story in which I'd give her a new hand.

I set the story in Panamá, though I've never been there. I've know Latin Americans all my life—as neighbors, roommates in college, girlfriends, inmates when I was a prison guard. I studied maps of the area around Panamá, looked at pictures, and tried to imagine what it would be like to live there. At one point, I was studying maps of the area around Lake Gatún, and noticed that no one lives on the south side of the lake. I imagined that monkeys would live there, and that when the train whistles blew the monkeys would begin howling. A few days later I met a man who'd just returned from a two-year stay in Panamá, and I asked if he'd ever been to Gatún. He'd passed by on a train from Panamá City to Colón, and remembered only that when he reached Gatún, the conductor blew the train whistle and on the south side of the lake thousands of monkeys began howling in fear. I knew I was ready to start writing.

During that same week, a friend told me of a nephew in Portugal who began first grade. He refused to wear a white uniform to school on his first day, and he was so castigated by other children that thereafter he wouldn't go outside without wearing his school uniform. I thought it interesting that children would display their territorialistic instincts so dramatically, so I decided to write about territorialism in the story. Since my narrator was Panamanian, I wanted to use stylistic tools available to him, and wrote the story in a combination of cyberpunk and Latin American realism, then sent it off to the Writers of the Future contest.

But while waiting to hear the contest results, I began having dreams about Angelo: mercenaries in battle armor huddled beneath an alien skull, telling jokes about their rivals. Giant dark crabs in a mist-shrouded forest, whispering with soft feminine voices. A Desert Lord, like a giant mantis, bursting from a hidden lair in the sand to throw its stones. I decided to turn the story into a novel.

In a national magazine I read an article called "Why I Hate the Japanese," and I wondered why the company would publish hate literature—unless America still hadn't resolved its feelings from World War II. I decided to put Japanese in my novel and make them sympathetic antagonists. Since I was fifteen I've studied ancient world literature, trying to see how ideals evolve in various cultures and subcultures. No one writes books on the subject, so I study on my own—survey the religious writings, poetry, folk tales, and laws of a society just to see what I can learn about their world view. I began studying the Japanese—interviewing people who'd lived in Japan, reading Japanese-English dictionaries—and also studied psychological portraits written for military and business reasons. I then developed the psychology for Motoki's corporate society, tested it by asking questions to some kindly Japanese professors (who don't want their names revealed because they taught me how to swear in Japanese), and began playing with ideas for conflicts. I wanted the struggle between the Latin Americans and the Japanese to be more than just a clash of personalities—I wanted to show entire civilizations in conflict, and with these two groups it wasn't hard to do.

I begin writing with goals in mind, and develop a story that allows me to play with the ideas and conflicts that interest me. I do this as an intellectual exercise—a way of making the requirements for the story more rigorous so that I must struggle to achieve my best as a writer. When I began to outline *Paradise* I had a list of forty things I wanted to accomplish. Here are a few:

- Since I know how well ideals evolve from age to age, from culture to culture, I wanted the novel to reflect the fact that our descendants will think differently than we do, that they will be alien. Therefore, I wanted to write a novel where moral codes were extrapolated based on current trends—something I've never seen done before.
- Since I'm convinced our bodies are poorly designed, I wanted to write about genetically engineered humans, but I wanted the engineering to be more than cosmetic—I wanted to show humans on the verge of losing their humanity.
- I wanted to write a novel that worked on various levels, so that even if you read it only as a simple adventure, you could still enjoy it—though I'd hope readers would see beyond that.
- Because I see science fiction diverging into entrenched subgenres, I wanted to combine some things I like in SF—social SF, cyberpunk, romantic SF, world creation. I also wanted to write what I call "Biofiction," in which the biological potentials and motivation of humans are thoroughly examined as we hypothesize changes to humanity. I see it as one way to discover what it truly means to be human.
- In 1985 I began developing something which I call the "Stress Induction/Reduction" theory of writing. It's based on the belief that we seek nonthreatening stress for entertainment so we can increase our capacity to handle real stress in our personal lives; I wanted to play with some of the techniques I developed for this kind of writing. For example, in one technique, called

"Audience Attack," the author induces stress in the audience by attacking the sensitivity or the preconceived notions of the audience. The technique proved very useful in writing this story.

- I wanted to write a novel about a warrior who learns that the best way to win a battle is by throwing down your weapons forever. I don't think the modern world can long endure if we continue to believe that wars are worthwhile.

- I wanted to write about problems common to men. Specifically, I wanted to write about the emotional death that comes to young men as they are taught to stifle their emotions, as they eventually forget how to feel anything at all.

- I wanted to write about my own struggle to retain sensitivity in a society where masculine sensitivity is seldom rewarded, where various incarnations of Conan the Barbarian are displayed as role models on Saturday morning cartoons.

By having goals in mind, I find it easier to begin outlining a story. But as I plot and rework the novel, things begin to firm until the story and characters take on a life of their own. I reach a point where I almost feel as if I could pack up my brain and move into this imaginary world—and as much as possible, that's just what I do. And that's when the writing becomes fun, because that's when I start discovering things. For example: I often wondered how heightened territorialism would affect the chimeras' moral codes, but I didn't know until Perfecto began telling Angelo that "territorialism is the medium by which we define good and evil." I sat back and thought, *interesting idea, but nutty*. I felt as if I could see the world from his point of view—where territories are not just physical things, not just land and body space, but also exist in our relationships as we possess families and friends, occupational goals, ideals, reputations, dreams. I could understand what Perfecto was saying, but I refused to write the words for several months as I pondered the implications. I eventually found that I could not successfully argue against Perfecto's view of the world—in fact he showed me things more clearly than I'd seen them before. This is where the fun of writing comes in, in making little discoveries by observing your world and characters closely.

So, people are asking "What's next? Do you plan a sequel?" Well, eventually. But poor Angelo has earned rest, if not a spot in paradise.

My next novel, *Serpent Catch*, deals heavily with world creation, biofiction, and the romantic tradition of SF. I'll be exploring some of the root causes of phobias and obsession. The novel is set on a world created by genetic paleontologists as a terrestrial zoo, with various continents populated by animals from the Pliocene, Mesozoic, and Jurassic eras. The story is set in the far future, when the word "extinct" simply means that living specimens of a creature are temporarily out of stock, when humans are not really quite human anymore.

Serpent Catch tells of a young man, half human and half Neanderthal, who undertakes a perilous quest to a far river in hopes of catching a sea serpent in a giant barrel, and at the same time must learn to capture a serpent that dwells within him—a hatred of his own father that threatens to destroy his chance for happiness. Even for those who are well traveled in the realms of the imagination, *Serpent Catch* will carry you to places you've never dreamed.

Special Offer
Buy a Bantam Book
for only 50¢.

Now you can have Bantam's catalog filled with hundreds of titles plus take advantage of our unique and exciting bonus book offer. A special offer which gives you the opportunity to purchase a Bantam book for only 50¢. Here's how!

By ordering any five books at the regular price per order, you can also choose any other single book listed (up to a $5.95 value) for just 50¢. Some restrictions do apply, but for further details why not send for Bantam's catalog of titles today!

Just send us your name and address and we will send you a catalog!